GATES OF HEAVEN

GATES OF HEAVEN

GLENN ARBERY

Wiseblood Books

This is a work of fiction. All characters and events portrayed in this novel are either fictitious or used fictitiously.

GATES OF HEAVEN
Copyright © 2025 Wiseblood Books, Glenn Arbery

Wiseblood Books
Post Office Box 870
Menomonee Falls, Wisconsin 53052

Cover images:
"Major General William Tecumseh Sherman Wearing Mourning Armband,"
        by Brady & Co., 1865, public domain
"Life and deeds of General Sherman including the story of his great march
        to the sea," by Henry Davenport Northrop, 1891, public domain
Cover design: Roseanna White
Typesetting by Roseanna White

ISBN: 978-1-951319-28-1

To Ginny, as always,
and to the memory of her beloved nephew
James Ramsay Hofmeister (October 25, 1965-July 19, 2024)

CONTENTS

PART III: HOMECOMING

But nothing unclean shall enter it, nor anyone who practices abomination or falsehood, but only those who are written in the Lamb's book of life.

~ Revelation 21:27

Sherman'll never go to hell. He'll flank the devil and make heaven despite the guards.

~ Confederate prisoner,
quoted in Burke Davis's *Sherman's March*

PROLOGUE

Mount Washburn, 1877

IT WAS HIGH SUMMER, BUT A HEAVY FROST HAD COVERED the camp the night before, and now a breeze chilled the men when the horses stepped into the shadows on the narrow mountain path.

"Wasn't no witnesses," said Dupont. "Who's to say he ain't made it all up?"

"No sir," Sherman insisted. "The Blackfeet killed his trapping partner and stripped Colter naked and gave him a head start."

"What do you mean, a head start?" Tom said. He rode a little ahead of Sherman, next to Orlando Poe. Fresh out of Georgetown, he was awkward among the men even after several weeks of camping.

"He was the prey," Sherman said.

"They meant to chase him down and kill him," Poe explained. "After they caught him, they would torture him to death. It was sport for the young Blackfoot warriors."

"That's barbarous!" Tom exclaimed.

"What I say is a squaw got his clothes off," said the sergeant from Massachusetts, a short, red-complexioned Irishman who had run into him drunk in the early morning the first time Sherman visited Vinnie Ream. "And her buck surprised them and he was the one chasing Colter. Yes, boys, such a thing happened to me back in Natick when I dove out the window into the snow in my lily-white altogether."

Tom looked down sharply as the men laughed.

"That's enough, Logan," Poe said. "You men mind your talk."

"Thank you, Col. Poe," the boy said.

Good God. William Tecumseh Sherman's son, prim as his mother.

As the trail narrowed between two pines, one of them with a bulbous canker, Tom's bay mare bumped against Poe's short-tempered paint and almost reared when the smaller horse tried to nip it.

"Those Blackfeet meant to skin him," Sherman said over his shoulder. "Colter saw it, so he dared them to give him a head start and then high-tailed it buck naked down to Yellowstone. Outran them all except the one he had to kill."

"Tell you what," said another soldier. "I seen a few church ladies would scare me off quicker than getting skinned."

"I'm still feeling the sorrow and the pity for that poor woman took the clothes off Logan," Dupont said. "She hoped to find a little something under all that blarney. But not that little."

"Jealousy, boys," said Logan, his brogue coming thick.

Tom urged his horse forward away from the laughter and pulled a rosary out of his pocket.

"Jesus, Mary, and Joseph!" Logan shouted. As his horse reared, he grabbed for the saddle-horn. Sherman saw the mottled coil of a rattlesnake but Dupont was quicker with his pistol and the snake's head disappeared. Cursing, Logan fired at its writhing body, and a bullet ricocheted and went whining into the pines toward Tom.

"Watch out, goddamn it," Sherman snapped.

Tom's mare had spooked. The boy was sawing the reins. Poe rode forward to help him steady the animal.

"I can handle her," the boy said hotly.

Sherman had seen many officers like Tom, not natively brave, but too proud to let themselves panic or flee in battle. Men holding themselves to a code. Willie would have had the unconscious courage that Sherman had found in himself at First Bull Run and showed the world at Shiloh-—the clarity of it, the fearlessness when other men in battle cringed and acted in confusion. Willie would have had it. Tom did not. It was not Tom's fault, he told himself. But whose? Ellen's?

Dupont met Sherman's eye and tilted his head at the peak of Mt. Washburn looming above them.

"We can ride most of the way."

"Let's walk up from here," Sherman called back to the others. "Dupont can keep the horses."

Poe quickly nodded and dismounted.

"I hate a rattler," Logan said to Sherman by way of apology as he handed the reins to the packer.

"You're more dangerous than it is."

"That ain't what that poor woman in Massachusetts said," Dupont grinned.

Sherman could see his own features in Tom, softer and more refined, slightly angelic. Nobody would ever say that the boy was the devil in the flesh, which a woman in South Carolina had said to Sherman's face when his men burned down her house. It had been his idea to bring the boy out West after his graduation from Yale to roughen some of his Eastern manners and wear down the prudishness that came from having his head full of Catholic notions from his mother and the priests at Georgetown. He had a fine intelligence. His comments on Lord Dunraven's book, *The Great Divide*, had interested the men the night before. He did not mind camp rations or fresh game or fish, but he was finicky about their trail latrines and uneasy about sleeping on the ground night after night with packers and tough soldiers whose talk ran to whores and liquor.

But this was the son he had now, this one, Thomas Ewing Sherman, who had borne the burden of being the oldest male child since Willie died in Memphis. He would never be what Willie would have been—a fine, bluff, fearless man, another McPherson—but Tom was well-suited for the legal training that would free his father from having to manage the family's finances. He would be better than Sherman himself, who had been honest and conscientious, but somehow sour with money, unlucky, wheezing with asthma and inhaling burned niter paper out in San Francisco during the days he had run the bank, back when Tom was born and two-year-old Willie was the little boss of the house.

"Father!" Tom said, breathing hard from the ascent as they reached the peak of Mount Washburn. He looked at Sherman and Poe with an exalted expression. "It's just as Lord Dunraven describes it, even the clouds. Do you remember his descriptions? Those 'little fragments of rainbow?'"

Sure enough, the colors of the spectrum shone through the edges of rain clouds far out over the mountain landscape. Sherman smiled and nodded.

"His meditation takes place exactly where we stand this very moment," Tom said. "Don't you think his book is a classic?"

"Some fine descriptions of Yellowstone," Sherman said.

"It reminds me of Jupiter looking down on the Scamander in the battle between the Greeks and the Trojans. Or contemplating the future of Rome on the Tiber."

Sherman shook his head. "The man's a joker. He says the English gave up the Oregon territory without a fight because the salmon in the Columbia River wouldn't take a fly. Besides, he's wrong about this mountain." Dunraven mistakenly thought that all the rivers ran from Washburn, north and south, east and west, and in a long excursus, he imagined the course of each river over the whole of America west of the Mississippi.

"But listen," Tom said, pulling the book from his pocket. "'The outlook from such a commanding point elevates the mind, and the soul is elated by the immensity of Nature.' Don't you feel that here?" He stepped up onto a boulder and turned to the east. "This way, the Missouri River, the Great Falls, the Dakotas, the convergence with the Mississippi, and downstream to St. Louis and all the way down through the South to New Orleans." He made the sign of the cross in the air as though he were already a priest. Like what De Smet would do. Nothing would please his mother more than for Tom to join the Jesuits. Ellen Ewing Sherman, celebrated by bishops and cardinals for her piety and her good works in the Church. But good God, the idea of Tom as a Jesuit sickened him. Gen. William Tecumseh Sherman's son—a Roman Catholic priest. A goddamn eunuch in a cassock.

"This way"—Tom said as he turned to the south and again made the sign of the cross—"the Green River joins the Colorado and descends through the Grand Canyon to—"

"Let's walk over this way," Sherman interrupted roughly. He led his son down from his pulpit and away from the other men, who were smoking and pointing down the way they had come and the way they would need to go the next day or two. "Let's be quiet and take it in."

Somewhere out there, one-armed Oliver Howard was chasing Chief Joseph of the Nez Perce, who had broken out of the reservation again.

Sherman had plunged into Yellowstone to stay out of the way of reporters while his old subordinate finished the job.

Tom stood looking southward, and Sherman stood silently watching his son. Last night's reading, it was true, had given rise to his own unvoiced meditations, and they came back now, as though he could see over the whole of his past from this height. His bitter years in San Francisco. His misery in the law office with Dan McCook. His happy year as a college president down in Baton Rouge. First blood at Bull Run. The humiliations and accusations of madness early in the war up in Kentucky. The redemption at Shiloh. Grant and the siege of Vicksburg, the long eastward progress over the year and a half through the heart of the Confederacy—Meridian, where he had first unloosed the cruelties that would become his signature in Georgia and South Carolina. Chattanooga. Resaca, where McPherson had failed him. The long supply lines that had been his constant worry with Bedford Forrest on the loose. Kennesaw Mountain, where he had sent men by the hundreds to their deaths at the Dead Angle—men from Oliver Howard's division. Atlanta, where McPherson had died. The fall of Atlanta and Lincoln's reelection. Then the greatest boldness—the decision to abandon supply lines that could not be defended and give his men license to plunder the property of rebels all the way to Savannah.

War is cruelty, they quoted him.

War is hell, they said he said, as though he had invented war. It was hell whether he said it or not. But from the gates of hell came his undying fame. Atlanta burning. The March to the Sea and the smoke of their passage. The immolation of Columbia. This Irish Lord Dunraven had earned nothing like the glory that generation after generation of men would give to William Tecumseh Sherman.

But his own wife could not see it. *What will it profit a man if he gain the whole world and suffer the loss of his soul*, she would say. His son could not see it. Vinnie saw it. Mary Audenreid. The consummation. Glory was the women he won.

"Thank you for bringing me, Father," Tom said, startling him again. "When I stand here, I feel what the Lord must feel as He looks down on the world of men. It is both exalting and humbling."

Sherman lifted his chin toward the eastern horizon.

"In the world of men, you're a Sherman, Tom."

"Proudly so."

"Your last name means something as far as you can see, east or west, and far beyond that. This name saved the Union. It helped kill off the buffalo to get the savages on reservations. It helped lay the rails from the Atlantic to the Pacific." He turned toward the west. "This is going to be a settled and proud America in your lifetime because of what was done in the name of Sherman."

Tom was silent for a moment. "And thank God for Fr. De Smet and the Jesuits," he said.

"The Jesuits?" Sherman said sharply.

"Like the priests in Mexico after Cortez," Tom added. "Bringing salvation to temper defeat."

De Smet. Good God. The Frenchman—or maybe Belgian, he could never remember—had visited them in St. Louis. A beggar like they all were, living on handouts instead of making honest money by building up the country. All these priests wanted money for the poor niggers or the poor savages. Sherman once wrote to Grant that they needed to exterminate the Sioux, "men, women and children." Conversion complicated matters. You had to pretend to be dealing with Christians, and it weakened the necessary resolve. Those Southerners were Christians, but he had been the one strong enough not to care. He had gutted their superiority and complacency, their hope in God's providence. He had the resolve to burn their houses and barns and suffer the rage and the curses and the scenes of misery. He was the dark angel of the wrath of God.

To hell with the Jesuits.

"Salvation, Father," Thomas repeated.

A quick, familiar shimmer came, infinitesimal separation from the inner watcher, the feeling of waking up not from dreaming but from being dreamed. Observation from within, not alien, but the presence that gives rise to who he is and observes him at the same time, *writes him*, like a diarist whose only work he is. It infuriated him that he could not turn quickly enough to see this watcher who had already written him and given rise to the very thought he was thinking. He was the tantalus who could never drink from the spring of consciousness where he arose because, being conscious, he was already flowing away from the source. If he gave in, he could be at peace with this presence that was his enemy and friend, his intimate and estranging enemy. But what would he be then? Who would be saying I Am?

"What could be more important," Thomas says, waving his hand, "than to bring these people to God?"

Despite the constant nagging, Sherman had resisted conversion his whole life. His foster mother, his wife, now Tom. He wanted to do what needed to be done without religious second-guessing. He thought of John Bell Hood absurdly telling him that the expulsion of families from Atlanta transcended "in studied and ingenious cruelty" everything that had happened before "in the dark history of war." Sherman had relished Hood's idiocy, because it gave him such range for ridicule. Hood was a convert—baptized back in the spring by Bishop Leonidas Polk, whom God had seen fit to promote to the heavenly choirs on Pine Mountain before Kennesaw with a cannon shot from Sherman's battery. Hood's words still made him laugh: "In the name of God and humanity I protest."

"Let's go, men," he called to the others. "Where's that damn packer taken our horses? We need to get off this mountain and make camp somewhere that won't freeze us to death. I'm getting hungry. Somebody shoot us a deer. Or Logan can fry a rattlesnake."

PART I

SHERMAN TAKES COMMAND

I believe God governs this world with all its life, animal, vegetable and human, by invariable laws, resulting in the greatest good, though sometime working seeming hardships. The idea of a vocation from God seems to me irreligious and I would look for the inspiration of a vocation in the opposite quarter (the Devil). When anybody assumes "vocation" their reason and all sense ceases and man becomes simply a blind animal. My idea of God is that he has given man reason, and he has no right to disregard it.

William Tecumseh Sherman,
Letter to Maj. Henry Turner, July 7, 1878,
concerning Thomas Sherman's announcement
that he would enter the Jesuits.
Quoted in *General Sherman's Son* by Joseph T. Durkin, S.J.

1

THE ASSIGNMENT

CLASSES AT BRIDGER COUNTY HIGH SCHOOL HAD BEEN canceled again when local Covid-19 cases started to spike in mid-September. Two high school freshmen from the reservation tested positive, and so did a town girl who volunteered at the nursing home, and that was it: back online, just like in the spring. Jacob Guizac bridled at the idea of sitting through Zoom classes his senior year with the same assortment of clowns and cowboys and nerds he had known since they moved to De Smet just before sixth grade in 2014. What exactly was the point of school, anyway? Last year, three girls had insisted that they were cats and needed a litter box, and the principal had to take them seriously. Now the cross-country season was canceled. He would have skipped senior year to go to Transfiguration College, where classes were going on in person, but they were three weeks into a semester already condensed because they were sending everyone home at Thanksgiving.

"Why don't I just homeschool?" he said to his parents.

His mother balked at the idea. She had recently taken up landscape drawing, and she liked her time alone. She loved the red cliffs to the east, the rock formations north of them, and the foothills sloping up into the Wind River Mountains to the south and west. She had been relieved—maybe a little more than relieved—when Jacob's intense five-year-old sister started preschool earlier that fall. Now little Marisa was back home, loud and full of unreasonable moods, changing clothes five or six times a day, and pretending, sort of, to keep up with preschool online. His mother balanced the prospect of organizing Jacob's instruction against the prospect of watching him fume in front of his laptop day after day, and she found a happy solution: turn him over to his father.

"And you call the school," she said. "They're not going to like it that the president of the student body drops out."

He made the call. The principal was clipped and formal. His guidance counselor sounded wounded, as though it were a judgment on her. Bridget Roberts, Jacob's student vice-president at BCHS, called him tearfully, pleading with him not to abandon her, but he told her that he would not do another whole day of his life online—and besides, most of the events they had planned were canceled.

Meanwhile, his father thought about it for a day.

"I'll do literature with you," he said. "Give me a list of everything you've read in the past two years. I'll see if Abel Johansson can tutor you in math and science. And if you want to learn mapping, I know a woman here in town who's mapped the Red Desert down below the Oregon Buttes. For history, how about you do a project on the Civil War with Braxton Forrest?"

"Sounds great," Jacob said, genuinely impressed.

"Let's do it in concentrated five or six-week blocks. That way, you can put all your attention on one thing at a time. How about you start with history? I'll get in touch with Cump."

Jacob had agreed without hesitation—even though, ironically, it meant conversations on Zoom. He loved Prof. Braxton Tecumseh Forrest, who owned the old Stonewall Hill mansion in Gallatin, Georgia, where the Guizac family had lived for four years back when their name was Peach.

"My dad says to do something about the Civil War," Jacob said in his first Zoom call with Prof. Forrest.

"Pick something hard," Forrest replied, "and call me back."

Jacob thought about it for a couple of days.

"How about why Lee fought for the Confederacy?" he said in their second call.

Forrest sighed and shook his head. "Come on, Buford."

Nobody called him Buford anymore. *Buford*. Buford Peach, that old name from Gallatin, from birth. That time before the devil came to get them. Before Alison Graves.

"What's the matter with that?" he asked.

"You can't do anything with Lee right now. They started taking down statues of him years ago. This young professor at Walcott—otherwise pretty conservative—calls Lee a traitor. Robert E. Lee! If you say something about Lee's piety toward Virginia, he gets stern and impatient and tells me that Lee swore an oath as a U.S. soldier to uphold the Constitution. Absolutely humorless, like there's nothing more to say, as though a primary loyalty to his state were unthinkable. Lee's a traitor—that's that. My woke son-in-law's worse. He gets high-toned about Lee having two runaway slaves whipped. I guarantee you there was more to the story, but don't get me started.

"Anyway, too soon for Lee. This year they're after Columbus himself again. They don't want America to exist at all. *The New York Times* has its 1619 Project to make sure we understand everything as racist. The left has attacked U.S. Grant. They'll get to Lincoln, you watch. But they won't touch Sherman. Why is that? He was as racist as any Southerner—look at Stanton's suspicions of him. And then after the war, he urged the extinction of the buffalo to starve the tribes of the West into submission and get the transcontinental railroad built. Why does he get a pass? My theory is that all is forgiven because he marched through Georgia burning down people's houses and making private property itself subject to Union loyalty. The left would hate to lose that precedent. He made Georgia howl so he gets a pass. I'd say do Sherman."

"Seriously?" Jacob exclaimed. "Sherman?"

When he told his father what Forrest wanted him to do, his father said that Faulkner had once described "a kind of entailed birthright father and son and father and son of never forgiving General Sherman." His paper—he might call it "The Birthright of Unforgiveness"—was due on November 2, the day before his eighteenth birthday, which was Election Day 2020. Five weeks away. Democrats and Republicans were so divided there was talk of civil war. That sounded ridiculous to Jacob, especially the more he read about the real one in the 1860s. Where were the regional divides, for example? Well, maybe Wyoming against Colorado. Still, his father said that Donald Trump vs. Joe Biden felt like the last days of the republic.

"Why are you doing Sherman?" his girlfriend asked.

He tried to explain. Why was he doing this project at all when nobody else was doing anything like it? Nobody his age who was homeschooling, nobody doing classes remotely at the high school, not even the seniors at Transfiguration College, who were writing theses this semester.

Over the weekend, Jacob read a little about the burning of Atlanta and the March to the Sea. Today was the 28th of September, a cool Monday morning, his third call with Prof. Forrest. He sat with his laptop in the shade of the lilacs and Russian olives. A black-billed magpie alighted near him on the old buck-and-rail fence at the edge of the lawn and hopped along looking at him and flew off. Far down below, hawthorns and chokecherries were beginning to color where Wolf Creek twisted through their property. The thickets of willow and currant that overcrowded the banks were already losing their summer denseness, and glimmers of water shone through the branches.

His laptop dinged.

"Good morning," he said when Forrest appeared on the screen, holding a mug of coffee.

"Morning, Buford. Folks okay?"

"Yes sir." Jacob could not read the titles on the bookshelves behind Forrest's desk, but by shape alone he recognized Shelby Foote's *The Civil War* and Douglas Southall Freeman's four-volume biography of Robert E. Lee. He had seen them in the study at Stonewall Hill.

"How's Mrs. Forrest?" he asked.

"She hasn't given up on me." The old man took a sip from his coffee mug. He was still larger than life at almost seventy, but his face was showing his age, and his hair was now white and thinning. "How are you getting along with Cump?" Forrest asked him. "What have you read?"

"Cump?"

Jacob was puzzled, because his father called Forrest Cump.

"Sherman's nickname, from his middle name, Tecumseh. Just like mine."

"Yes sir. Well, so far I've looked at Shelby Foote," he said, "and read some stuff about the March to the Sea."

Two fawns and a doe paused on a path halfway down the bluff and looked uphill at him.

"Some stuff," Forrest said. "What does that mean?"

"I poked around some on the internet."

"Poked around on the internet."

Jacob felt the heat rising into his face. He shifted in his lawn chair.

"Yes sir. Wikipedia. Some websites."

Forrest stared into the camera at him. "You've got five weeks from today to write a hundred-page paper and you're poking around on Wikipedia."

"A hundred pages!"

"I don't know how you're going to do anything worthwhile in less than that."

Jacob could not move.

"Buford? Are we breaking up?"

"No sir, but, you know, I run every day and I have—you know, I have a girlfriend."

"A girlfriend!"

"Yes sir."

"What's her name?"

"Emily."

"I hope Emily likes hearing about Sherman. I'd say read the *Memoirs* and a couple of good biographies to start with, maybe Marszalek and O'Connell to get some contrast. For historical context, probably Royster's *The Destructive War* and Shelby Foote's account of the Western theater of the war—starting with Shiloh. You also need to know what Sherman did to the Indians on the Great Plains after the war. You need to know about his marriage to Ellen Ewing and his affairs, especially the one with Vinnie Ream. You should be able to choose the moment in his life that you think best explains the man. Was it the bank failure in San Francisco? The death of McPherson? The death of Willie?"

Jacob had no idea what he was talking about.

"Make it good," Forrest said, taking a sip of his coffee. "Surprise me. But here's the main thing. You're what, eighteen?"

"Almost."

"How ambitious are you?"

"Ambitious? I mean, I don't know. What do you mean?"

"Do you think you'd be content just getting a job, getting married to Emily, going to church, helping out as a coach or whatever, not being perfect maybe but not doing harm, just playing out that ordinary life until you die?

Or do you want something more? Fame or prominent positions of leadership or great wealth, things like that?"

"I don't care that much about money, but I guess I want—you know, to do something I might be famous for."

"Sherman became world-famous. When you're reading about him, ask yourself if he wanted that enough to pursue it deliberately. Did he study the situation and play the game and take the steps needed to become famous? Are you willing to do that for the sake of fame?"

"I mean . . . I don't know. I got elected president of the student body, but it's not like that was a big dream or something. It just sort of happened."

"So do you feel like you have these gifts and you wait to see how God wants you to use them? Like you're called to do something?"

"More like that."

"My wife likes this thinker named Edith Stein and she read me a passage the other day. Give me a minute while I find it." When Forrest disappeared, Jacob sat in confusion, wondering what he was getting at. A minute or more passed before the old man reappeared with an apology. "Can't find it. But this is one of the most brilliant women of her time, and she's just become a nun, and she writes to her superior about how she lives each day, not by making plans, but by opening herself to what God wants her to do that day. In other words, it's the opposite of ambition. Do you understand what I'm saying?"

"Not really."

"Basically, it's whether you do what you want or what God wants."

"But how do you know what God wants?" Jacob asked.

"Because I'm your teacher and I'm giving you an assignment. I have you for five more weeks, that's all, and I expect you to spend every waking minute of the next five weeks writing—no, let's say every waking minute of the next three weeks *reading* everything you can by Sherman and about Sherman. And then you can spend every waking minute of the last two weeks *writing*. The deadline is midnight on Monday, November 2. Ask yourself about Sherman's ambition. Ask yourself about fortune and providence. You're a good writer. Make it ready to publish."

"*In five weeks?*"

"Five weeks. Make the commitment or I'm not going to do this. Download books you can listen to when you run. Is Emily smart?"

"Yes sir."

"Get her interested in what you're reading."

"I mean—"

"Or else call her up and tell her you can't see her until after the election."

"Maybe I can get her interested."

Forrest smiled at him.

"While you're reading, keep an eye on what's happening nationally right now. Does it really feel like something historic is about to happen? Is it like the 1860 election? Or is it all just a referendum on Trump?"

"Yes sir," Jacob said, his misery rising like a spring flood in the creek bottom.

"This should be fun!" Forrest said. "See you next Monday. Tell your father I'm about to call him."

"Yes sir."

2

SAGE GROUSE

FROM THE TABLE IN THE DINING ROOM, KARL GUIZAC watched his son through the open screen of the sliding glass door as he talked to Forrest. The morning was two hours older in New Hampshire, but here the acres of sagebrush to the south were still in shadow. Beyond the dirt road, sunlight hit the foothills that rose for miles into the distance. The boy sat leaning toward his laptop in a lawn chair beneath the Russian olives, as still as a setter on point. He smiled, wondering what Forrest was telling him. After sitting for a moment, the boy said something to the screen, nodded, gently closed his laptop, and clamped both hands on top of his head like the captain of the Titanic spotting the iceberg. A moment later, Guizac's cell phone on the kitchen counter vibrated hotly.

"Want me to answer it?" Teresa called.

"Please."

She shook a palmful of coffee beans into the grinder with her right hand and reached with her left.

"Hello? . . . Well, good morning to you, Braxton. How's Marisa? . . . No, I haven't seen him yet this morning . . . Oh, you just talked to him? Okay, there he is, I see him still outside. . . . Well, no, you'd better talk to Walter yourself. He's right here."

She raised her eyebrows and handed Guizac the phone and went back to the coffee.

—Walter? I just scared the hell out of your son, Forrest said.

"I saw that," Guizac said. "What did you tell him?"

—I told him he owed me a publishable hundred-page paper on William Tecumseh Sherman in five weeks.

Guizac waited for him to say it was a joke. He did not.

"You're serious? A hundred pages in five weeks?"

—Let's see how he does.

"Meaning?"

—Don't tell him it can't be done.

"There's a point to this, I guess?"

—Trust me.

"Oh man," Guizac said. "Well, you're the professor. Unlikely as that seems."

—Hey, you used to be a damned good one, Forrest said.

"I doubt that."

A dreary feeling of the classes he had allegedly "taught" at the technical school in Waycross, Georgia, rose upon him.

—What? Forrest said to someone on his end. Hold on, he said to Guizac. After a moment, Forrest was back. Ask Teresa to keep Cate in her prayers. Her husband's off the rails.

"You don't want my prayers?"

—Cut it out, Walter, Forrest snorted.

It hurt his feelings a little. Not much, though, considering.

"Okay, so what's her husband done?"

—Affair with a woman at his office. Open, no attempt to hide it. Meanwhile, every kind of verbal and psychological abuse aimed at Cate. Blaming her, blaming the church, blaming us.

"Blaming you for what?"

—The fact that he's tied down to a family. Of course, I don't have a great track record myself, and I feel that coming back at me from Cate.

"It sounds like we need a bottle of bourbon and a long afternoon in the study down at Stonewall Hill."

—Like we used to do. Speaking of which, how's the *Grouse* this week? No new movies to review, I guess, with Covid shutting everything down. How long can your boy Wyatt stick with Turner Classics?

"He's binge-watching *Chicago P.D.* while he gets over his Covid."

After Forrest got off the phone, Guizac watched Jacob pacing outside, a tall, lean, fine-looking high school senior, long past the strangeness he had exhibited in the momentous summer of 2014. A better runner than his father had been at his age, Jacob was also brilliant in his classes, not political by nature but nevertheless elected president of the student body almost by acclamation.

The boy disappeared from view through the glass door and reappeared in the east-facing windows, where Guizac watched him walk over between the lilacs and stare down at the creek bottom, his fingers still knotted on top of his head. He could see the boy's thoughts like one of those speech bubbles in a cartoon: *What about Emily?*

Guizac felt for him, but it might not hurt to cool down that romance a bit. Emily Turnbow, from all reports, was the best of an excellent freshman class at Transfiguration. Dan Kennedy, who taught her in Humanities, had joked about how the girl seemed a little distracted from her reading. Professors at Transfiguration could read signs of disengagement the way card sharks could read tells. Back when he was teaching, the slightest sign of any level of *engagement* would have called for marching bands and fireworks.

Was he ever a good professor, as Forrest said? Forrest himself was not. He had some academic fame because of his book *The Gameme*, but he was an indifferent performer in the classroom. Not as bad as Marvin Landford, that famous scholar of the South, a massive man who would open his mail and read through it during class with a few perfunctory remarks aimed in the direction of the assembled students—despite which Guizac learned a great deal. Unlike Landford, Forrest prepared for his classes, but he scorned the usual academic expectations. He said that the most memorable professors were paid for being *who they were*, which students should consider themselves privileged to experience.

Guizac himself had never wanted to teach, in the sense that he had never especially wanted to impart knowledge to others. Maybe he was just too selfish—too centered on his own art. He had never thought much about "pedagogy," had never considered teaching central to his identity, and he was surprised when the word *pedagogy* roused professors like gamecocks. They flashed and spurred at the very mention of it. In Socrates Johnson's dictionary, a regular feature in *Sage Grouse*, pedagogy was defined as 1) *a form of constipation associated with the unnatural consumption of paper;* 2) *the overstuffing of ornamental pillows with the feathers of flightless birds.* Too harsh, but his favorite professors had all strayed into teaching because it gave them the financial means to do what they really loved, which was not the art of the classroom, but real conversations about books and ideas with brilliant people.

If Guizac had once been any good as a professor, it was when he was still the poet Walter Peach working through the lyric tradition, or reading Melville, Dostoevsky, and Faulkner seriously, or learning Homer, Shakespeare, and Dante with students entranced by what he helped them see. No question, he had enjoyed talking about the best books with smart young people who were just discovering them. He had loved it when students showed flashes of the real thing and taught him something. That's what Forrest was seeing with Jacob—and why he was pushing him.

Forrest did not mind pushing. He had pushed Guizac into journalism back in Georgia and again in Wyoming. In August of 2014, just coming out of witness protection, the Guizac family (formerly the Peaches) arrived in De Smet, Wyoming, and Guizac did not know how he would support them. For the previous four years back in Georgia, he had edited Forrest's *Gallatin Tribune,* but that life had evaporated when Josiah Simms found him—more accurately, when Josiah Simms, Nora O'Hearn, and God Almighty discovered him at the same time. A long story. When they got to Wyoming, he had enough savings for a few months, but at the age of forty-seven, he owned nothing to speak of. Forrest was wealthy from a vast stock windfall a decade earlier, and he had offered Guizac the down payment for a house. Guizac's wife Teresa found a place in the foothills of the Wind River Mountains a few miles outside De Smet, and Guizac looked around for a job—anything but teaching. In late August, he had hired on with Wyoming Weed & Pest, and for several weeks he had worked with a witty young woman from the reservation named Kyra Whitewater. They would drive the official pickup through the gaps of fences into fields of sagebrush and proliferating invasive species—leafy spurge, spotted knapweed, houndstongue, various kinds of thistle—and tramp around through deer scat and cow patties and horseshit, spraying chemicals, disturbing the mule deer or antelope, startling up pheasants, sometimes walking among cows or horses the owners had left there even though the animals could get sick from the pesticides.

In mid-September of that year, his boot slipped from a log while he was climbing over some deadfall to get to a patch of leafy spurge. His right foot wedged down between two trunks as he was falling. He screamed as his ankle snapped and screamed again when he fell into a black hawthorn. *Oh my God, don't move! That thorn's so—wow.* Kyra had said. He felt the blood dripping from his mouth, but he could not move, suspended in agony. Kyra had to leave him to go back to the truck to radio for help to extricate him. While she was gone, pinned as he was, he could only look in one direction, and he saw a gate farther down the creek bottom. Upright posts and a crossbeam, and through it a sunlit vista of grasses and cottonwoods, towering red cliffs. A grazing pronghorn turned and looked at him. *Strange, down here with no road*, he remembered thinking before he passed out. Kyra had not noticed a gate, and afterwards, he could never find the place again. With his ankle in a cast and his face bandaged, he was out of commission for weeks. A three-inch thorn had missed his eye but punched through his cheek and into his upper gum above a molar, which required several trips to a dentist (without insurance) and still got infected. He had not worked for long enough to get much by way of worker's compensation, and Weed & Pest was winding down its fieldwork for the year anyway. In October, he was about to answer an ad for the produce section of the local Safeway when Forrest called him.

Guizac explained his dismal job prospects.

—Why don't you teach?

Always the teaching.

"Even if I wanted to, the semester's half over."

—How's the journalism out there? Forrest asked him.

"I checked to see if the *De Smet Weekly* needed anybody," Guizac told him. "The editor laughed at me. She can hardly afford to pay the electricity in the office. Everything's online."

Forrest wanted to help get something new going. After some back and forth for a week, they settled on an online journal with some daily news content, weekly reviews, and editorials like the ones he had written as Walter Peach for the *Gallatin Tribune*. Forrest said he would occasionally write a longer piece. Guizac liked the name *Sage Grouse*—an endangered species in

Wyoming—because it described the endangered conservative perspective and the tone of thoughtful grievance he wanted to strike about contemporary politics and culture. Satire and good sense, never mere rancor. Teresa told him *Sage Grouse* sounded like a high school literary magazine. "Or maybe a Western a cappella group," quipped his daughter Rose, who preferred her new name, Magdalena, until people started calling her "Mags." She had been finishing her last year of high school at Bridger County that first year in De Smet.

—I'll subsidize it for a year, Forrest said. Then we go for sponsorships instead of regular ads. Maybe several subscription levels. I'll see how it's done.

Guizac found a couple of students at Transfiguration to help him get started. The number of hits grew week by week. Wyoming liked the politics of *Sage Grouse* but showed no more interest in cultural sophistication than the citizens of Gallatin had. He started getting new responses from across the country when Transfiguration put up a link on the college website, then a well-connected board member at the college started linking it on his site, and after a year or two, he had tapped into an audience not limited by state boundaries and not easily defined. When he passed 100,000 unique visitors, the *Jackson Star-Bulletin*—conservatives across the state called it the *Red Star*—did a worried story on him. Guizac had just resurrected his "Ask Socrates" feature and invented Wyatt, a post-transgender rodeo cowboy, to offer down-home commentary on movies. In a recent dialogue with Socrates Johnson, Wyatt explained what it meant to be "post-trans."

SOCRATES: Welcome to the program, buddy. Heard you had the Covid. Hope you're wearing a mask, even though you're calling in. You just never know whether them Chinese figured out how to spread it through the phone. You still spending all day in front of the TV set?

WYATT: Well, it don't spread nothing worse than bullshit.

SOCRATES [coughs]: Watch your language there, my friend. Look here, Wyatt, before you get to movies, I got to ask you. Everybody in the Fox News All-Stars at Perk's Peak wants to know why you come out being post-transgender when you're the same hombre you was before that spell as Wynona. Bruss Box gets hot about it—he laps up all that gender stuff down in Cheyenne—and he says, "Wyatt Moore ain't a damned thing but cisgender." What do you say to that?

WYATT: Bruss Box don't know shit from shoe polish.

SOCRATES: I won't put up with no profanity.

WYATT: My bad. But that hurts. Bruss Box. Sweet Jesus. He can't tell the difference between being cisgender and being honest to God post-trans like me? Ain't you seen the YouTube?

SOCRATES: Well, I mean—

WYATT: Hell yes, you seen it. Everybody seen it. I went out Wyatt and come back Wynona. You can't tell where it was from the video, but it was up in Cody. I was in my clown suit trying to draw off Tornado from the boy he'd just throwed like a mad wife throws a wet dishrag and that bull whupped around on me. I lost my head and tried to jump over him. Bad mistake. His horn come up and caught me you-know-where and *ka-foosh!* turned everything inside out, which is what I mean is outside in. I was singing a high note like Madeline Kahn in *Young Frankenstein*, which it used to be my favorite scene. A one-punch total, they told me, didn't spill a drop of blood, even though it hurt like—listen, I can't talk about it, or I might get the PTSD right here on the air, which it would be worse than Hillary's PMS back in the day. You try spending a couple months in the hospital trying to figure out how to pee and getting poked at while everybody's watching you on YouTube.

SOCRATES: I hope you wasn't married.

WYATT: Naw, living with my mama.

SOCRATES: What did your mama say, you don't mind me asking?

WYATT: Mama always wanted a girl. But Good Lord, Socrates, I wasn't about to ask my mama how to be one! I had to find out online by myself.

SOCRATES: Bruss says you shaved your legs.

[Pause]

WYATT: I ain't going to dignify—I mean, Bruss Box wouldn't know a body razor from a cheese grater. It was a tough time, but I finally busted into a female bronc riding circuit. Them other girls thought I was cheating because I was really a man, which is, I mean, it's not how they acted when I was one. Anyhow, down in Cheyenne, I got throwed up so high off a bronc I did a double flip and come down on my feet with my legs stiff as fence posts like jumping off a roof without bending your knees and *Whoomp! Hot tamale!*

Damn if long-lost Wyatt ain't popped out! Welcome back but which it was embarrassing. All them girls saying *See? See?* like I been keeping a secret. So I am by god the only post-transgender cowboy in rodeo and Bruss Box can just twist his pantyhose.

One of the young reporters at the *Star-Bulletin* did an interview with Guizac that the paper elected not to run because it might backfire on them. They did quote bits of Socratic insensitivity in an editorial. They accused Guizac of belittling the deep psychological issues of gender dysphoria and the surgical and hormonal subtleties of gender transition. In the name of enlightened progress, the *Star-Bulletin* righteously advocated the side of any issue most destructive to nature, virtue, God, marriage, freedom of religion, and Wyoming.

After Donald Trump defeated Hillary Clinton in 2016, Guizac was featured in the *Wall Street Journal*'s weekend Review section. Socrates Johnson had predicted a Trump presidency months before the Republicans had even settled on him as their candidate—not that Guizac liked Trump, but he understood the widespread discontent with the policies of the Obama administration and the fear of what Clinton would do. His Socrates pieces were singled out by Ross Douthat in the *New York Times* as one of the most accurate gauges of populist sentiment in the Trump era. That attention reached all the way to Gallatin, Georgia, where people remembered Socrates Johnson, and Karl Guizac was soon outed as Walter Peach, who had disappeared two years earlier, and the *Times* did a story on the fact that he was the child of the 1960s radicals Alison Graves and Harris Akers. People in Wyoming might care about whether the hijacker D. B. Cooper—the one who parachuted from an airplane in 1971 with $200,000—was hiding out somewhere on the reservation, but not about neo-Rousseauean educational ideology. Nobody in De Smet ever mentioned the name Walter Peach and so he kept calling himself Karl Guizac and the rest of the family kept Guizac on official documents and reverted to their old names at home. Except for Jacob.

Meanwhile, Rose graduated from Bridger County High School with scholarship offers from across the country and chose the University of Dallas, where she turned back into Rose and double-majored in history and English with a senior thesis on Faulkner and the Western theater of the Civil War.

She won a nationally coveted internship at *Last Round*, a Catholic journal of literature and politics based in Manhattan, which brought more attention to *Sage Grouse*. Now she was off in rural France for a year, writing a book on the New Agrarianism.

"Coffee's ready," Teresa said. She set down the tray on the coffee table for their ritual of saying their prayers and talking over the coming day.

Just then, Jacob slid the screen door aside and came indoors with his laptop.

"A hundred pages in five weeks," he said grimly.

Guizac took a sip of his coffee and started to smile. It was hard to rattle Jacob, but Forrest might have done it. "Dostoevsky wrote *The Gambler* in three," he said. "Robert Louis Stevenson wrote *Dr. Jekyll and Mr. Hyde* in six days."

The boy met his eyes.

"All I know about Sherman is what you've told me—how he made war against the civilian population of the South, how the March to the Sea is the hinge in American history, how the forced reentry of the Southern states means that allegiance to the Union supersedes the consent of the governed. I don't know enough to say anything intelligent about Sherman. How much do I have to read to write a hundred pages about him?"

"I'd read Shelby Foote first, just to get the overview," Guizac said.

"It's three volumes! The shortest book is over 800 pages!"

"I'll be happy to talk as you get into it. You should get the shape of Sherman's career, his personality, the backdrop of American history, all that, and then you can concentrate on what in particular you want to say."

For Guizac, the very name of Sherman summoned up his foster mother, Lucinda Devereaux Lawton. Dying of cancer, she would tap the famous Matthew Brady photograph—the fierce, hawk-eyed, frowning general, nose tight with anger, scorn etched into the line of his cheek, mouth, and chin hard with hostility, right hand tucked napoleonically into his uniform.

This is what the devil looks like, she would rasp.

As a child, he had hated Lucinda for trying to turn him against the mother he knew as Rosemary, but he had agreed to hate Sherman, too.

Look at him, Walter. The demon Moloch in a human body. He burned homes by the hundreds. He stole the food and ruined the livelihood of free people, and for these depredations he received the adulation of the multitudes of the new Babel of the North with its great machines and towers of idolatry.

Remember that man, she said, jabbing the picture with her fingertip.

3

EMILY TURNBOW

EMILY WAS NOT CERTIFIABLY GORGEOUS LIKE JACOB'S classmate Grace Haversham, but she also did not go through the world as though she were watching herself in a mirror. She was not a budding supermodel like Eva Jacowski a year below him, whose face made him think of famine and billions of dollars. But he would rather look at Emily Turnbow than anything. He met her at Dunx to tell her about his assignment.

"I have to write a hundred pages about Sherman before Election Day," he said, taking a sip of scalding coffee.

"Who's Sherman?"

He liked watching her mouth when she said it, as though the name were something she might have to spit out in her napkin, like the pit in a date.

"Gen. William Tecumseh Sherman. The one who did the March to the Sea."

"A hundred pages?" The lovely lift of her eyebrows.

"I don't think I can go to the dance on Saturday."

"They canceled it," she said. "Dr. Weald keeps getting horrified emails from people in town about Transfiguration students not wearing masks. They think Covid's the worst thing ever and they don't believe we agree."

"Professor Forrest says I should get you to read about Sherman. Maybe his *Memoirs* or one of the biographies."

Her mouth dropped open.

"He wants to give me an assignment, too? Do you know how much I have to read?"

"It would help to be able to talk about a passage or two, just—"

"Jacob!" she cried. "We're just finishing the *Iliad* in Humanities and then we have the *Odyssey* starting on Wednesday. Then we're doing three tragedies and two of Plato's major dialogues. There's a quiz every time, and *this is just one class!*"

He had met her in mid-May when the first Covid shutdown had just started to relax in Wyoming. It was a sunny midweek afternoon, warm enough that his father had him painting the toolshed, and he was planning to run when he finished, maybe up into the sandstone hills on the state land to the north and then down the other side and back along the road. But suddenly, between one stroke of the brush and the next, he had an overpowering urge to start running right that second, as though the goddess Athene had appeared with the command *Run!*

So he had pounded the lid on the paint can with the side of his fist and laid the brush across it. He remembered glancing back at the house, almost hoping for intervention, but he already had his running shoes on as though to be prepared for this moment, and compulsion swept him like a riptide. He ran up the driveway and down Sacajawea Court to Washakie Road, where he headed toward town, running faster and faster, veering onto the grass or gravel and waving when he met cars.

In town, at the intersection with Tyler Street, he stayed on the road because the sidewalk was taken up by mothers and strollers and unleashed toddlers. He turned left onto Ninth, passing faculty houses and poor stretches of double-wide trailers and then the middle school. He burst across the intersection at Main Street just as the light turned green. A block later he turned right onto Sheridan and sprinted down the five-block-long stretch where there were no stop signs, dodging behind a car that drove through the intersection at Fourth without ever seeing him.

Sweaty and panting and splotched with red paint, he slowed to a walk outside Dunx, the college coffee shop on the corner of Third and Main, and stepped onto the sidewalk, hands on his hips, catching his breath after the fastest five miles he had ever run. He needed some water before the easier run back home. A girl sat at a table by herself. She had her right hand on her purse as if she were about to leave and was just starting to stand up when she looked and saw him and sat back down. She gave his condition a once-over and her light hazel eyes met his eyes.

"Nice shirt," she said, and he felt a jolt, hard and definite, and his knees gave a little.

"Thanks," he said, wiping his face on his sleeve and plucking the wet shirt from his stomach. "I'm Jacob Guizac."

"Oh, I know," she said, and unspoken knowledge somehow sang through her intelligent eyes and her mouth, her mouth especially. She pushed a glass of water toward him. "I was just leaving."

He took it and drank it all and set the glass down. Her eyes had not left his.

"So what's your name?" he said.

"I didn't have to ask you yours," she said, and her mouth adjusted a little, as comfortable as a wren on a branch.

He waited, but she did not tell him.

"I guess I can find out," he said.

"A little work won't kill you," she said, and her mouth did something else, a little pout almost. He felt the jolt again. Her complexion was olive, olive like sun and Greek islands with sea nymphs, beneath the thickest blonde hair he had ever seen.

When she smiled, something happened to his heart, which was already pumping hard from the run, and he touched her tabletop and backed off the curb onto Third, then turned and sprinted across Main Street against the light. An eastbound pickup swerved and blasted its horn irately all the way past Second. He hit an easy stride a block south on Third. He felt her eyes on him and just before he cut west on McKinley, he lifted his right hand over his head and waved without looking back, imagining the little tuck, irritated and flattered, at one side of that mouth.

What was it about her mouth? And who was she? If he had been any slower getting there, if that light at Ninth and Main had been red, if he had lost ten seconds somewhere, he would not have met her.

He would ask around to find out who was new in town. He'd heard about parents so sick of Covid regulations elsewhere that they had picked up and moved to Wyoming. Maybe his mother had heard something from her friends in the book group of Transfiguration wives.

He sped up on Tyler Street, and where Tyler split left to become Middle Fork Road just at the edge of town, he angled off right onto Washakie. The peaks of the Wind River Mountains rose white in the distance beyond the foothills.

He had felt things for girls before. A year ago, he walked in the hallway at school with Naomi from the reservation until her brother's friends surrounded her one day after school and threatened to cut her face if she kept hanging around with a white boy. She stopped coming to school. His Arapaho friend Joseph had told him about it later. He'd been smitten with Grace Haversham for a few minutes once after she smiled at him in English class. He sat with her at lunch that day, but she kept glancing around the lunchroom to check out what everybody thought.

And Gretchen Newsom. He thought about the time sophomore year when De Smet had just won State in cross-country. His record time in the 10K had put them on top, and he must have felt a little too good that night. There was a school dance at the old American Legion Hall, and he was holding her tight in a slow dance when she suddenly gasped and shoved him away right in the middle of the dance floor. *So outraged*, as his buddy Ray told him later, grinning. It got to be a joke. Gretchen Newsom. Pretty embarrassing—but that was just hormones, arguably. No wonder some of the stricter churches frowned on dancing.

This girl, though—the amused control, the flirting mockery in her composure. *Nice shirt*, she said, and those light hazel eyes looked at him straight on, and there was a jolt of recognition somewhere deeper than his whole body, sexual as all hallelujah but more than sexual, like something that happened at the exact place where *Jacob Guizac* officially attached to Life Itself, where a voice said *THIS ONE* and it felt as solid as the coupling of train cars, the docking of fates and destinies and immeasurable futures, but quiet, without clangor, soft as the seal of a kiss.

She saw it happen. And that mouth smiled a little.

An hour later, showered and changed, he knew her name. Emily Turnbow. Her father was the new music professor at Transfiguration College, where she would be a freshman in the fall. She was a cellist. Just hearing her name, he could see her left hand upturned on the outdoor table, the fingertips curling onto imagined frets.

His mother raised an eyebrow and found the new professor's phone number. When he called, he did not have to ask for her. She answered the phone herself.

"Emily Turnbow," he said.

—It's been an hour, she said. He pictured the way her mouth controlled her smile. Over an hour.

"Well, I had to run all the way back home. It's five miles."

—You could have hurried, she said.

All of June, he did not spend a moment away from her if he could help it.

By the Fourth of July, time had split in two: something you could measure with clocks versus the right now of Emily Turnbow. Her image impressed itself on everything he did or thought, and when he was with her, he could never get close enough to her. The only thing that could keep him from kissing that witty mouth was the impossibility of seeing her smile at the same time. He lived like a bird dog on point. He ached. He was a Mae West joke. He wanted her to yield herself up, pure blossom to unmannerly bee, but he also adamantly wanted her not to, and he liked it when she kept him from the famous deed by an infinite teasing reserve. Scenarios of desire brimmed over in his sleep, much to his embarrassment. Fr. Peterson said this was normal— well, unless he was thinking about somebody too much in a sinful way. Okay, so when was it sinful, exactly? He despaired of waiting for years until they could marry, but he knew that he needed to pass over some threshold into manhood before their love could finally stop being pure obsession and begin brimming over with babies, he guessed, and filling church pews and never stopping, good Lord, never stopping until they fell apart, old and spent and happy, and died with all their progeny standing around them in the ranks of their generations, and they rose up together through the gates of heaven, young again, and flowed through each other's transfigured bodies in the unending bliss of God Almighty.

Running sometimes helped burn off the excess of his love in pure exhaustion. That morning of the Fourth he ran all the way into town in the climbing heat and saw people gathering for the parade. The traffic on U.S. 287 had been rerouted through the back streets on the north side of town, so he turned from Ninth directly onto Main, pretending he was in the marathon at the Olympics and he had just burst into the stadium and everyone was cheering him on to the finish line. He sped up, dodging children, lifting a hand to families he knew, and he had just broken the imaginary ribbon across Fifth when he heard a distinctive booming voice.

"Jacob!"

Dr. Marcellus Turnbow loomed above the sidewalk. Jacob himself was taller than almost everybody—he had leveled out last year at four inches over six feet—but Dr. Turnbow was closer to seven feet. Emily and her mother and her younger brother Sibelius, who reputedly lived for *Call of Duty*, stood a few feet away under a big, sideless tent the Kiwanis had put up in the parking lot of True Value.

"We were just out for a walk," Dr. Turnbow said. Palms out, he gestured at the crowds two or three people deep stretched along the sidewalks all the way down Main past Third. "I thought the parade was canceled."

"It was," Jacob said, still catching his breath. Emily wore white shorts and white running shoes and a sleeveless blue shirt that swelled nicely under its Transfiguration logo. A pink broad-brimmed straw hat shaded her eyes. "My dad says Bruss Box pulled some strings to get the highway blocked for a couple of hours."

"Who's Bruss Box?"

"Brussels Box. The state senator. People call him Bruss. It was all kind of last minute. Dad says it's election year and Bruss needs help."

When Dr. Turnbow put his hands behind his back and turned to gaze down the street, he reminded Jacob of the giraffes at a safari park his family had visited once. He was so tall he might have been grazing the young leaves of the trees planted along the sidewalk. Smiling at the thought, Jacob glanced at Emily, whose mouth was in the daylight, a perfect sardonic tease playing at the corner of it. Transfixed for a moment with lust, he turned away and took a few steps as though he were still recovering from the run. On the other side of Main in the dirt parking lot of the Bronco Motel, a cluster of Shoshone men from the reservation smoked and gestured. Near them, graybeard bikers and their girlfriends were setting out trail stools and folding chairs and drinking from brown paper sacks, all their gleaming Harleys lined up in the shade of a cottonwood. Farther down the block toward the center of town were large families that Jacob did not recognize, maybe local Mormons. Scattered elderly couples sat under umbrellas, leaning their heads together, cupping their ears.

"Sup, Jacob?" someone called.

Coming down the sidewalk were Ray Schurg and Joseph Littlecloud and a few of their friends from his class in high school.

"Not much."

They shared a few fist bumps.

"Party over at Ethan's tonight," Ray said. "His uncle's got these awesome skyrockets."

"Thanks. Maybe I'll get over there."

Joseph glanced at the Turnbows, paused on Emily, and looked back at Jacob, who flicked his head sideways. Joseph did a subtle lift of his eyebrows and said, "Catch you later," and the group moved on.

"Friends of yours?" Mrs. Turnbow said with an air of provisional disapproval.

"Yes ma'am. I should have introduced you."

Faint, inept band music rode on the morning air, and the lead car rolled into sight from the curve beyond Ninth Street.

"So this is the famous parade," said Dr. Turnbow, wincing at the music. "The triumph of the local."

"Not really. Usually, it's a lot bigger deal."

"What do you mean?" asked Mrs. Turnbow.

He explained that long-time residents of De Smet usually roped folding chairs in place along Main Street a day or two before the parade to guarantee themselves a good seat. Every group in town came up with some kind of float, and anybody who had any reason at all to be looked at would walk along and wave and throw candy, which of course no one could do this year because of Covid. In the intersection next to Dunx, a platform was usually set up, and a local businessman named Harry Lagrange—the emcee of most public events, a man with "enormous resources of groundless enthusiasm," as Jacob's father described him—commandeered the microphone year after year and announced every single driver of a vintage Mustang or Model-T, every single knitting circle, every Shriner on a mini bike, or eight-year-old rodeo star. Not this year, though. There were no mini-bikes, the rodeo had been canceled, and this parade was a shadow of the usual one.

They watched the high school swim team go by. The sophomore girls at the front of the float were pretending to do the breaststroke, which ordinarily would have interested him.

"Dr. and Mrs. Turnbow," Jacob said on a sudden inspiration. "What if I take Emily up to the cemetery tonight to watch the fireworks? It's the best view in town."

"The fireworks were canceled," Dr. Turnbow said with certainty.

"Yes sir, the official ones at the rodeo grounds. But people in De Smet explode anything they can get their hands on. It looks like the town's being bombed."

Mrs. Turnbow put her hand on her heart.

"The cemetery up behind the church?" said Dr. Turnbow.

"Yes sir, I know the best spot. You should all come. We could have a picnic. We need to get there early, though."

Sibelius frowned and pushed his glasses up his nose. Mrs. Turnbow asked how many people usually went and where they parked and whether they respected the graves and how long they would be there if they went. She finally declined, to his great relief. She said it was up to Emily if she wanted to go.

"I love watching towns being bombed," Emily said.

They got there early with a picnic dinner and sat on a blanket on the downward slope, hugging their knees, leaning against each other. As soon as it was dark enough, the vast display began. It was a cool night and the whole valley below them crackled and boomed and erupted with fireworks all the way from the nearby neighborhoods across the U.S. highway to the far hills west of town beneath the Wind River Range.

She wanted them to tell secrets about themselves. She told him a funny story about wearing braces and not knowing she had spinach stuck in them. She told him about a sleepover when her best friend's older brother tried to get in bed with her and she screamed.

"You screamed? What did he do?"

"Ran!"

"Did everybody come in? What did you say?"

"That I dreamed a monster tried to get in bed with me. Everybody looked at Bo. Apparently, this wasn't the first time."

She told him about her music teacher in high school, a man named Ellsworth Clupper, who would stand behind her and pull her against him when he was showing her how to play the violin.

"What do you mean, pull you against him?" he said.

"You know," she said. "Like you do."

"Well, that's embarrassing," he said. "So you're comparing me to your creepy music teacher."

"Oh, there's no comparison," she said.

They were quiet for a long moment. "You're hiding something," he said.

"Always," she said. She leaned over and lightly bit his earlobe. "What about you?" she whispered.

"You think I'm hiding something?"

"Aren't you?" She shoved his shoulder. "I heard something happened to you."

He smiled and ran his hand over his head. He had already told her more than he had ever told anyone.

"I don't want you to think I'm crazy. This was when I was eleven."

"Oh my God," she said. "So it's true, isn't it?" She turned on the blanket to face him, her face serious with sorrow. "Somebody did something to you."

"It's more complicated than that. We used to live in a big mansion called Stonewall Hill before this man named Josiah Simms—" He compulsively sucked in a deep breath, almost a spasm, as it all came welling back up. "Whoa, I really don't want to talk about it."

"Who's Josiah Simms?"

"It's a long story. But the thing is, in the summer of 2014, I started knowing things I had no way to know."

"Like what?" Emily asked.

"My father owned an old house out in the country overgrown with kudzu, and I knew—"

"What's kudzu?"

"You know what, let's talk about it another time. It's too complicated. It's just I would have these moments when I could see into somebody's life.

Not like empathy—I mean, not like I observed them and imagined what they were like. It was *being* them, feeling and thinking the way they would, wherever they were. I was that person, in that body."

"Like who, for instance?"

"Somebody I would just glimpse, like a little girl going into the school building from recess or a flagman on the highway. Or I could be reading a book. I would be there one second and the next I would vanish into this other person's life. It's hard to explain. My parents took me to a child psychiatrist in Jackson Hole."

When his voice tapered off, Emily was staring out over the valley.

"Does it ever happen now?"

"No."

"So you don't turn into me?"

"That would be—"

"Stop. Don't even say anything. And I wouldn't want you turning into Sibelius all of a sudden. But knowing you're a nutcase answers a few questions I had."

"Thanks."

"So it hasn't happened since when?"

"Since I was twelve or thirteen. I would sometimes have flickers of it. But not since then. Not since my hormones kicked in and I became a talent scout for my DNA."

"Good luck with that."

"You could be the answer."

"Tell your DNA to calm down." She turned and kissed him, which did not help. "I have to ask you. What did the psychiatrist say? Seriously, Jacob."

"She told my mother that her psychiatry practice presumed that mental experiences had a materialistic and evolutionary basis. She said she had never had a case like mine. She said I might have some issues with trauma, but not normal ones. She could not help me. I did not fall 'within the parameters of her profession.'"

"Aren't you special?"

They fell silent, leaning together, holding hands, looking out over De Smet Valley. It was after ten o'clock, and the fireworks were dying down except in one spot out on the Loop Road far in the distance. Ethan Roberts' party, maybe. The uncle's awesome skyrockets. There was a series of them, climbing in intensity, a pause, another series, a longer pause, and then a rocket went up higher than any of the ones before. It burst into even higher symmetrical arcs whose burning tips began to drop and then burst upward again—*again*—multiplying, higher each time, until explosions red, white, blue, hung there, fading, then bursting into a glitter of stars and then dropping liquidly, fading to nothing as he kissed her and a faint roar of acclamation rose from all the distances.

4

FORREST IN SITU

THIRD DOWN AND THREE ON THE KANSAS CITY 18-YARD line. Swelling crowd noise.

Denver, down by four touchdowns in the second quarter, breaks from the huddle. John Bell Hudson coolly situates himself behind the center for the snap and does a quick read of the KC defense. He starts the snap count, stops, barks out an audible, and Pearson, the running back, shifts to his left. The wide receiver moves to the top of the screen. John Bell backpedals for a shotgun snap, resumes the count, hut *HUT HUT*. Kansas City does not take the bait and jump offside. At the snap, the tight end Gecowsky slants across, open—but he's open because Kansas City's linebackers blitz. John Bell's fake to Pearson is crushed backwards so fast John Bell doesn't have time to get out of the way, and Eli Jones, the huge Kansas City defensive end, sheds his blocker and hits John Bell at full speed, just as he's lifting his arm to pass. The ball rises, fluttering—

"Can you turn that off?" Marisa stood in the doorway, waiting, tense with grievance.

Forrest raised the remote, muted it, and changed the channel to the Cowboys game.

Her purse was clutched tight against her side. "I'm going out to clear my head. Would you please please please call Cate?"

"What did she say?"

"You know that girl Jason is sleeping with? Melina something? The editor at the magazine? Her parents flew into Atlanta just to meet Jason, Cate told me. I mean, my God, Braxton. *To meet him*—as though he weren't already married! What kind of people would fly in to meet their daughter's adulterous lover? Better people than we are, apparently, because Jason told Cate she roped him into getting married and then coerced him into having kids because *we* wanted her to. He told her he never wanted children."

"Sweet God, what a—"

"Do you know what else? Jason told her . . . I can't even say it." Marisa burst into tears. "He told her he wished Jimmy, Clare, and Avila were dead."

"I'll kill him!" he shouted. Rage surged up in Forrest so violently that he drove to his feet and almost blacked out. Blood sang in his head and he staggered, throwing out an arm for balance and hitting the lamp. He fell back into the chair as the lamp crashed and shattered, trying to heave himself back up. "I'll fly down there right now and kill him!"

"Stop it! Just call Cate. She's devastated, Braxton. She's in the darkest place she's ever been."

"I'm going down there. I'll kill that slimy bastard."

"Your specialty. Good God."

Her bitterness stung him.

"What's the matter with you?" he said. "Why are you going off on me?"

"How about you don't go to jail for killing Jason Zitek?"

"I actually walked Cate down the aisle and gave her to that piece of shit."

When his daughter had first cast her name into Zitek's ugly cactus of consonants, he had grumbled at the insult to aesthetics, but now that the man had turned out to be such a piece of shit, everything about him was infuriating.

"You liked him, Braxton! You got him his job at the magazine."

It was true—the man's wit, his observations on culture and politics, even his cooking. Forrest had loved Jason. He had loved their marriage.

Forrest was no saint, but by God, he had never treated Marisa like—

"That thing is so huge it's obscene," Marisa said.

She glared at the TV and back at him. He was still holding the remote. He pushed the off button.

"I got it for the election," he said.

"No, you didn't." She opened the purse and dug inside for the car keys. "You got it to watch your son. I thought you were writing a book."

She tilted her head and raised her eyebrows and let the comment strike home—at least a hundred blank-pages' worth—before she walked away. When she opened the back door, late fall in Portsmouth broke through the opening before she slammed it shut.

He sat there. *Your son.* Decades of silent reproach broken from her by their daughter's misery. Her unspoken accusation: his sins were being visited upon the children. And meanwhile he was a paragon of idleness.

He sighed and turned on the television and changed the channel back to the Broncos game. Still 28-0, and Kansas City was inside the Denver red zone, about to score again. Mahomes, sweet Lord. As good as John Bell, no question. Better, maybe. There was always somebody better, whatever you did, whoever you were. Better commentators on America, even if he did finish his book.

Mahomes took the snap but the tackle on the left side of the line had started up too early. Five-yard penalty, repeat the down. Commercial break.

John Bell carried the sins of the fathers as much as Forrest did. *Sins.* Hell yes, they were *sins*, and they were passed down to him by his adulterous father and to his father by his adulterous grandfather. Now Forrest passed them on to his children in turn, his daughters with Marisa and his daughter with Marilyn Harkins—even, it might be, the son he never saw or knew at all, the one with—God, what was her name? A sick feeling came over him. He couldn't even remember her name? Something Honeycutt when they were teenagers. She had his son that he never knew about. Patricia?

Sins, hell yes. A tether of sin, hooked hard into his soul, held him in the church and kept him going to confession and Mass—well, if the church was open. His soul might be saved, Covid-19 permitting, *if* there were confessions. *If* there was Mass.

Another commercial. He stirred with irritation. The Church had sold away its moral authority in the sexual scandals of the past three decades, and now it kowtowed to the state, abandoning even the faintest hint that the sacraments were more important than the disease. Religious liberties were under outright attack from the whole Democratic Party. To them, the very idea of sin was just another conservative microaggression. Governors like

Whitmer and Cuomo would never get pushback from the rotten cardinals and archbishops and bishops and priests who had corrupted the Church, all of them afraid of being exposed in court, even if all of them weren't creepy perverts like McCarrick. And then there was the Pope himself, who appointed worldly temporizers like Cupich or Farrell or Gregory to higher positions and passed over real men of faith like Chaput and Gomez. Look at the Vatican's willingness to sell out the real church in China to Xi Jinping with his imperial ambitions—what was that if not a harbinger of what was to come?

Still, where else would he go? Protestant mainline churches were selling out faster than Rome. He was a sinner. Somehow, in the great karmic economy of retribution, he was responsible for what Jason Zitek did, as though his own story granted that piece of shit permission to screw his editor and condemn his own children and consider Stonewall Hill—the old plantation in Gallatin where Hermia Watson had her ministry with pregnant women—the world's central symbol of patriarchal whiteness.

But he wasn't responsible for that asshole, not like that. He had never hated his family. He was never cruel to Marisa. Before the downhill moral slide that began with Hermia, he had been faithful to his wife.

His son.

Cate's misery had revived Marisa's own, and she was rehearsing his sins: his son, John Bell Hudson, with Hermia Watson; the same Hermia Watson, his daughter, not with Marisa, but with Marilyn Harkins, his own half-sister.

Only once in a bout of 3:00 a.m. wakefulness had the full horror of the incest overwhelmed him, but many times he had been transfixed with metaphysical terror by these apparent coincidences that added up to an *intention* manifestly not his own. But whose? God's? If not God's, whose? Hermia Watson lovely at twenty-two, and Braxton Forrest at forty: their blind convergence in Chicago over a weekend after he gave a lecture on his almost-famous book, *The Gameme.* Too much to drink afterward. Hermia had been a graduate student, emotionally frail, susceptible, full of admiration, altogether willing, deliberate even.

Never had he intended the worse sin.

It had all been brought to accomplishment in a darkness denser than the shadow over Oedipus, whose way was inked from beginning to end with Delphic warnings. Where was the oracle for him that said, *You will couple in love with your unknown black half-sister and have a child with her?* or the one that said, *You will beget upon your own child, whose existence you never suspected?* or the one that said, *Your own child will have a son with you, whose name she will not know until his fame goes up to the heavens?*

John Bell Hudson, Heisman finalist and now starting NFL quarterback, was the mirror image of his father Braxton Forrest at that age. Only better.

Not to mention his *grandfather* Braxton Forrest.

The same man.

Who was also John Bell's uncle. No, great-uncle. Somebody should do a chart.

Finally, the game appeared again. He unmuted the TV and focused. Kansas City was on the Denver eight-yard line, second down. Mahomes faked a draw and then fired over the left side into the end zone—and the Denver safety intercepted!

Forrest sat up. The safety wisely took a knee. Mahomes called out something to his tight end, Travis Kelce, who was coming back toward him, palms raised, and they walked together toward the sidelines, Mahomes gesturing, as the Denver offense trotted onto the field. In the middle of the linemen, taller than any, came John Bell Hudson. On the first play, he faked to the running back and stood up, like a lion rearing up among oxen. He looked left for a quick slant, but then, sensing something, threw right, and the football, rising and rising and gently falling in its arc of sixty yards, settled soft and light, with one last securing turn of its perfect spiral, into the outstretched hands of the wide receiver, who never broke stride as he streaked down the sideline behind the defenders.

"*Touchdown!*" yelled the commentator.

John Bell was on fire. By halftime, Denver had forced two fumbles and scored twice more. Kansas City still led, but the momentum had shifted.

God, the boy was good. Forrest could not sit still. Muting the halftime banter of the hulking commentators—he didn't recognize any of them anymore—he found his phone and took his coffee mug into the kitchen and rinsed it and stood for a minute looking out over Prescott Park at Memorial Bridge, replaced a few years back, and Badger's Island beyond it and farther still across the water at the houses of Kittery in the slanting light of the cool, late-October Sunday afternoon. He thought about calling Cate. *Hey, Catnip.*

One little drink couldn't hurt. He opened the liquor cabinet and clinked through bottles until he found the Woodford Reserve and poured himself a couple of shots. Just as he took a big sip, his phone buzzed—*Marisa*—and he choked on the bourbon. He set the glass down, coughing up the burn of it, not answering. He drank a glass of water.

Her text came: *Call Cate.*

Okay, he texted back.

But it would not go well. Everything Cate said would be full of bitterness and recrimination, and he would have to hold the phone to his head during her long, tearful pauses. Implicit in every comment would be the disgrace he ought to feel at his own lack of judgment about Jason. It would all be *his* fault.

Shit, maybe it *was* all his fault.

He opened the laptop on the kitchen table and emailed Cate a quick message of support and told her that he would call her in a couple of hours. She would see right through his cowardice and selfishness—she knew the Denver game was on—but she also knew nobody hated the telephone more than he did. Better to have Marisa in the house to take over the conversation, even if all they did was criticize him.

Just as he was closing the laptop, an email popped up. **Sherman tomorrow?**

Jacob Guizac. He had no idea why Walter Peach and his family kept using the names he had made up and assigned to them when they were supposedly in witness protection—how long ago? 2014. Six years. The name had been a joke, but maybe Walter didn't want to go back to "Walter Peach," which his radical mother—Alison Graves, 1960's radical—had similarly made up. Forrest wondered if continuing to use Guizac was a variety of reproach to him—or maybe some kind of homage to the ruse that had given them a new life.

Buford was whip smart, but he used a font size so tiny Forrest had to enlarge it to read it:

> Prof. Forrest, can we Zoom tomorrow morning at 7:00 MDT? I found out that Sherman stayed in a tavern in Marietta from mid-February to late March of 1844. I have a feeling something happened there. The Army sent

him to find out whether volunteers from Georgia had falsely claimed that their horses were killed in the Second Seminole War. What's cool is that he says in his *Memoirs*: "We remained in Marietta about six weeks, during which time I repeatedly rode to Kennesaw Mountain, and over the very ground where afterward, in 1864, we had some hard battles." He kept diaries back in 1844—they're online in the archives at Notre Dame—and he wrote about going to the top of Kennesaw on Mar. 3. He wrote Thomas Ewing to ask for Ellen's hand the very next day, Mar. 4, 1844.

Thanks, Jacob

What the hell? Forrest shook his head, but he set up a Zoom meeting for the next morning. He closed the laptop and sat down just in time for the second-half kickoff.

Denver came back to win 48-28, and John Bell Hudson passed for four more touchdowns in the second half, tying Sid Luckman's record for seven touchdown passes in a game and finishing with 533 passing yards, second all-time to Norm Van Brocklin's 554 yards in 1951, the year Forrest was born.

Hell *yes*, his son! Marisa was still not home, so he stalked around the house whooping. He opened the front door and yelled *Yes!* before he saw Judith Brockman ten feet away on the sidewalk. She stepped back in horror at his outburst. Her Shih Tzu convulsed into a fit of barking. White hair freshly buzzed short, Judith was wearing one of the three-ply masks she sold in her bookstore—blue today, which meant that she must have run out of rainbows. She glared at him, hand on her heart, and pulled on the leash and sternly said, "*Gaga! Gaga!*" to the little animal. Judith lived two houses down on Marcy Street, and Forrest had often fondly imagined the punt that would send her dog yapping and pinwheeling high into the air, all the way across the street and into Prescott Park.

From the stoop, Forrest smiled down at Judith and Gaga. Just for fun, he feinted at Gaga, and the pitch rose higher as the tiny beast cowered behind Judith and then charged from the other side and cowered again, looping Judith's calves with the leash.

"You asshole!" cried Judith, trying awkwardly to balance and extricate herself.

"Need some help?" He stepped toward her, whereupon Gaga lost her mind entirely, advancing and retreating until poor Judith's ankles were bound tight. Helplessly, she teetered, eyes stabbing him, and then toppled. He caught her in his arms, and Gaga followed, suspended from the leash, hung by the collar, throttled and gagging.

Judith glared up at him, her face just inches away.

"Put me down!"

Forrest squeezed her against him. "Think Trump has a chance?" he whispered.

"Braxton! My God! Put her down!" Marisa cried from the doorway behind him. "That poor dog!"

He put her down. But Judith's ankles were still bound tight, and she tipped against him again as Gaga, chastened, made strange hacking noises. Marisa rushed down to help, and Gaga strained at her, barking hoarsely.

"*Gaga!*" Judith cried fiercely.

Gaga cowered. When Marisa gingerly unsnapped the leash from her collar, Gaga bolted down the sidewalk toward home until another cry from Judith stopped her and the poor animal crumpled in the fallen leaves beside the sidewalk and flipped cravenly onto her back, paws in the air.

"*Come here!*" Judith said as Marisa unbound her ankles. Gaga slunk back, and Judith, stepping free of her bonds, gave Marisa a curt nod and re-leashed the poor dog, whose true plight had lifted her in Forrest's regard. Judith walked furiously away without a look at him.

"I have to say," Marisa whispered, "that was quite a scene."

"You caught us at our most intimate."

She laughed and gave him a little sideways hug and started back inside. "So were you able to help Cate?" she asked, turning toward him.

Uh-oh.

"I was just about to call her."

5

THE MONDAY MEETING

A WEEK BEFORE THE ELECTION, HE HAD WRITTEN ONLY twenty pages of the hundred he owed Prof. Forrest on Gen. William Tecumseh Sherman. Bridger County reopened its schools, but Jacob did not return. It meant missing the cross-country meets, but he was glad not to be back in the classroom, even though he would have had a shot at a cross-country scholarship. His mother, who had more time now with Marisa back in pre-K, had been urging Jacob to get back on the team. Some of the Transfiguration faculty's homeschooling teenagers played baseball and basketball for Bridger County High School, so it might have worked, but right now, he hated to think of meets, because they would mean time away from his Sherman project, which engaged him more than anything since his map obsession when he was a fifth grader back in Gallatin.

He had read five biographies, and strange things were happening that he hesitated to bring up to Emily, much less to Prof. Forrest. The visions were back, if they were visions. He would be reading Charles Royster or John Marzalek or Sherman himself, and suddenly the present moment would collapse and he would plunge into the kinds of episodes he had tried to explain to Emily over the summer. Reading diary entries, he would find himself within Sherman's existence and begin to fill in details—the mosquito in a piece of amber on a side table, for example. The look of a pen's nib and an ink well and a faded purplish splotch in the wood of a desk. A leather folder with loose papers of different sizes in it. A calico cat. He would see the hair of one of Sherman's men, hacked unevenly—a patch of bare neck and some stray hairs longer than the others that stuck out from under the cap.

He had no idea what Prof. Forrest would think when he read it. He worried that his mother would read some of these things, and he hoped that Forrest would refrain from mentioning his racier passages about Sherman. This kind of lustiness just seemed right for Sherman, who was like Stanley Fields in his class, redheaded and always talking, almost manic, obsessed with girls.

Jacob's writing voice, as one teacher called it, had already been "mature" in eighth grade—maybe because he had read so much and reading came so easily to him. His father had been a poet before the accident with his brother, and the house was full of books. He had skipped the usual children's series, except for the *Chronicles of Narnia* and *Lord of the Rings*, and by the time he was ten, he had read Cervantes, Fielding, and Dickens. In his earlier teens, he had read Dostoyevsky and Flaubert and Nabokov and Garcia Marquez.

He dreaded this meeting. He knew already what Forrest would say: *why are you wasting your time on this minor episode?* A month ago, he would have done the call outside, but a cold front had blustered in and stripped the Russian olives on the south side of the house. This morning, a herd of mule deer had wandered into the yard to eat the olives on the prickly branches. Among them, a buck stood in the middle of the yard, his eyes closed, his muzzle straining straight upward as though he were testing the air for some sign, or sensing Jacob's thoughts. Jacob watched until the deer's head dropped. The thermometer on the refrigerator said it was -7 outside. How could the animals stand it? He had spent an hour on Friday getting firewood for the wood stove into the garage, but when it was this cold, the house's furnace burned propane all day and all night.

He made himself a piece of toast and poured a cup of coffee to take back to his room. He still had fifteen minutes, so he sat on the bed with his laptop and checked his email and opened some news sites. Not a word from Emily in two days. She had said she would be swamped with papers and reading. But her silence hurt him.

When the hour neared, he got off the bed and set his laptop on the desk in front of the window and sat down in the chair. He stared out, looking west over the outbuildings at the first light on the butte slanting upward in the distance, the last red outcropping before the Winds.

At 7:00 sharp, he clicked on the Zoom meeting link in Forrest's email from the night before.

Forrest was already there, waiting for him.

"You watch that Denver game yesterday?"

He forgot that people cared about football. Especially Forrest.

"No sir, we don't have TV."

"John Bell Hudson threw seven touchdown passes."

Jacob recognized the name and nodded pleasantly. Forrest sighed.

"How are your folks?"

Jacob glanced out the door of his room. His father had just sat down at the dining room table, fiddling with his car keys and muttering at something he was reading while Marisa danced around him in a tutu saying, "Look, Daddy! *Daddy!* Look at me!" His father looked up distractedly while his mother poured some Cheerios and granola in a bowl.

"They're fine. Well, Mom is. Dad—I don't know. Listen, is this a bad time? Do you want to do this later?"

"No, I'm here. What's this about Marietta?" Forrest asked.

"I mean, it's like something happened there," Jacob said. "I got this—"

He hesitated to say.

"This what?" Forrest said, impatient with him. "Tell me about Marietta. This is when? 1864?"

"No sir. 1844."

"Right, right, you told me that."

"So Sherman's there on Army business settling claims. He's staying in a tavern in Marietta with a Col. Churchill and his family, and one Sunday—"

"Before you start, listen to me a second."

Jacob sat back in his chair, dreading what was coming.

"This essay," Forrest said, "is due a week from tomorrow. You're in 1844 when he's still a few years out of West Point. He hasn't even gone to California. You're *twenty years* from his greatest achievement, which was the March, and before that you have Shiloh—"

"Yes sir, but—"

"Then Vicksburg. My God, Buford, and then Meridian. And in 1864, you have the whole Atlanta campaign. Kennesaw Mountain, the death of McPherson, the burning of Atlanta, the March to the Sea, the destruction of Columbia early the next year. After that comes the end of the war, national adulation, then the Indian Wars, and then his affair with Vinnie Ream, his son breaking his heart by becoming a priest. And it looks like you're stuck on something that happened in Marietta in 1844."

Jacob nodded, maybe a little too vigorously.

"Well, I mean, I know I need to do all of that. I've read five biographies and the Royster book, but I get these—kind of flashes, I guess you'd call them."

"Flashes?" Forrest asked.

"Yes sir. I mean, details. And like I'm—like I'm him."

"Him?"

"Sherman."

"Like you're Sherman? Sweet Jesus."

"Yes sir."

Forrest suddenly looked up and moved aside as Mrs. Forrest leaned into view.

"Buford!" she smiled, and his heart lifted a little. "Are you doing okay working with this old curmudgeon?"

"Yes, ma'am."

"How's the family? How's my sweet Little M?"

"She'd be okay if Dad would say something about her tutu." He glanced out the door again. "He looks like he just got staked down over a bed of fire ants."

She laughed. "Say hello to your mom for me."

"Yes ma'am."

After Mrs. Forrest was gone, Forrest stared at Jacob, pursing his mouth.

"How about you give me an example," Forrest said, "of one of these"—he made little quotation marks in the air—"*flashes*."

"So I've been reading Sherman's diary from 1843 and 1844. It's online at Notre Dame. His entries start out pretty detailed in mid-November of 1843 right when he left Lancaster to go back south after seeing the Ewings. At first, he's writing several pages a day. He meets a friend of his named Charles Anderson in Cincinnati. This would be a Saturday."

"I'm having a hard time here, buddy."

"Wait, so Sherman says he and Anderson weren't 'scrupulous as to religious matters,' so they made other plans for Sunday—not church, in other words. They have breakfast, they listen to a lecture, but then Anderson takes him to meet an artist, Miss Martin, of French descent, from the hills around Marietta."

"Georgia?" Forrest said.

"No sir. There's a Marietta in Ohio. This girl has just recently come to Cincinnati to learn art, and Sherman obviously likes her. Can I just read you this?"

"Go ahead," Forrest sighed.

"'*A more vivacious quick enthusiastic being I never beheld, rather pretty, about twenty-one, yet courage or impudence enough to attempt anything.*' I can't make out every word," Jacob said, "but I know he says '*No false modesty concealed in her efforts the finest parts of the female form. Breast arms and legs were little encumbered except by the lightest drapery that showed the symmetry and form.*' He spends three or four pages just describing her paintings."

"Okay," Forrest said, interested at last. "So you're thinking this is his code. She's a different kind of artist. A *fille de joie.*"

"Sir?" Jacob said. He had been thinking of a code, too.

"Look at the adjectives he uses," Forrest said. "Read it again."

"'A more vivacious, quick, enthusiastic being I never beheld.'"

"Right. And saying that she has *impudence* enough to try anything—literally, that's shamelessness. And no false modesty. He's talking about her and not about her art, right? That part about being 'little encumbered' with concealments."

Jacob paused and then shook his head.

"No sir, I mean. I think she's really an artist. Sherman was pretty good himself—first in his class at West Point in drawing. Marszalek includes one of his drawings in his biography. So he'd be interested in her talent, like Vinnie Ream's later. I don't think he would care about her if she weren't an artist. And I think the same thing about the woman in Georgia."

"What woman?" Forrest frowned.

"This was the—I don't know what to call it. I just *saw* it. Another artist he meets, a French woman."

"He mentions her?"

"No, that's the thing, he doesn't. I just saw it. This was the flash. He's staying in this tavern in Marietta working on claims against the Army with Col. Churchill, who's the inspector general for the Army and has his whole family there. Sherman must be busy during the week, because he doesn't write much in his diaries except on Sundays. On Sunday, March 3, 1844, he writes about riding up to Kennesaw Mountain, and he has an entry two days later on Tuesday, March 5, when he's apparently just written to Mr. Ewing—"

"Ewing? This is the senator, his foster father?"

"Right, Sen. Thomas Ewing, who raised Sherman in his house after Sherman's father died."

"I know that."

"Sorry, but Sherman wants to marry Ellen Ewing. His foster sister."

"Okay," sighed Forrest. "Tell me."

"Well, it's March 3, 1844, early Sunday morning in Marietta. He's downstairs having breakfast in the tavern."

Jacob paused, embarrassed now, but also confident. How could he explain it? He could just send it, he guessed.

"That's the flash?" Forrest asked.

"Do you mind if I just send you what I wrote?"

"You can't just tell me?"

"No, sir."

"How long is it?"

"Not that long. Like four thousand words or so."

Forrest thought it over.

"Go on and send it. Are you around this morning? I'll read it and get back to you."

"Yes sir."

When Forrest closed the meeting, Jacob checked his email to see whether Emily had written back. Nothing. Not since Friday. Bleak misery blew through him. Even in late August when she came back from the three-week backpacking trip in the Winds, she was subtly different, attuned now to the girls in her group and the days he had not shared. Her courses, her classmates, the boys she was meeting. More than boys—some of the upperclassmen were already men with their own authority. And who wouldn't love Emily?

She had been funny back in September when he first explained his assignment about Sherman, which was more demanding than anything she had to do at Transfiguration—not that the college wasn't tough enough. But as his obsession with Sherman grew, so did her irony. He could hardly talk about anything else with the deadline so close. Friday night at the Granite Gill, she had had to interrupt him in line to remind him to order, and he accidentally ordered a pizza with meat and then didn't notice until he was halfway through. At the table, he explained to her how paradoxical it was that Sherman was the great destroyer of the South, because he had spent a long time there early in his career and he loved the Southern people. In fact, just before the Civil War, he was the founding headmaster of what later became LSU. He wasn't an abolitionist. In fact, he hated abolitionists and admired plantation life.

"Seriously?" Emily said.

"He thought slavery the best thing for black people."

Her mouth did a dubious twist, and she glanced around the restaurant. She waved at some other Transfiguration students a few tables away, including a black girl in the junior class. Had she overheard him?

"I'm too loud," he said quietly.

"You are a little bonkers on this topic," Emily told him. She cut a piece of fried fish with the side of her fork and looked at him as she put it into her mouth.

He leaned forward and whispered intensely, "He burned and pillaged the system he admired! That's crucial to who he was. He became the most admired Union general besides Grant because the people of the South he loved all hated him. My dad's foster mother used to call him *the demon Moloch incarnate.*"

Again, she glanced at the other table. He wondered—not for the first time—if she was embarrassed to be seen with him.

"I'll stop," he said. "Sorry."

"I've got a big paper to finish for tomorrow," she said. "I mean, five to seven pages, not a hundred. But a big part of the grade."

"Humanities?"

"The *Odyssey*. I've got some ideas, but they're not coming together."

"Write about pigs," he said.

"Pigs, right."

"So if Circe went into the cafeteria tapping people with her wand, how many of your classmates would turn into pigs?"

"Louis Grimwald, for sure." She covered her mouth as her imagination ranged over the circular cafeteria tables. "Oh my God. We've got a whole herd!"

"So you need a good swineherd," Jacob said.

"Dr. Weald talked about that in class," she sighed. "Odysseus as a swineherd. Eumaios as a better one. No, I want to do something surprising."

"Surprising to Dr. Weald?"

She nodded and her mouth twisted again.

"Yeah, Anya surprised him with something she said about Eumaios, and he stopped class and said that in all the years he had been teaching, he had never thought of that. I love Anya—I mean, she was in my group on the twenty-one-day trip—but I was just burning up with jealousy. Like why couldn't *I* be the one to surprise him?"

"You care that much what he thinks?"

"Dr. Weald? Yeah. I do. I don't know why, but I do. There's something about him, like he already knows more about you than he would ever say, even under torture, if he thought it would hurt you to know it. I can't explain it. I just want to write something nobody has ever written and surprise him."

Jacob felt his own pang of jealousy.

"Okay," he said. "Here's something nobody has ever written. Sherman was in Marietta, Georgia, for two months in 1844, and he used to ride up to Kennesaw Mountain, which was the site of one of his biggest battles twenty years later, and something happened up there."

Emily speared a waffle fry. "Sounds riveting."

"Really, nobody has written about this, and there's no proof, but I could *see* it."

He thought how the scenes had come into his mind.

And then somebody threw ice water in his face.

"What the hell!" He bolted angrily up from his chair.

Four or five people stood around him, including the restaurant manager, a tattooed woman in her thirties. "Has this happened before?" she said. "Should we take you to the emergency room?"

Everybody in the restaurant was looking at him.

Jacob had no idea what they were talking about. Emily was sitting with her chair pushed back from the table as though she were ready to bolt.

"I'm fine," he said, raising his palms. "So you want to tell me why you threw water in my face?" he asked the long-haired boy, glass in hand, who was obviously the guilty party—one of the Transfiguration students, much shorter than he was.

"Just trying to help."

"Help with what?"

The others looked at Jacob, then at Emily. They shook their heads, dispersed, returned to their seats.

Jacob sat back down, still fuming.

"Do you know that guy?" he asked Emily.

"Jacob, are you serious? You don't know what just happened?"

"I know that jackass threw water in my face."

"Listen to me," she said quietly, leaning toward him. "You were talking about Sherman and suddenly you just switched off."

A dark qualm went through him.

"What do you mean?"

"You just sat there staring. You didn't hear anything I said. I must have said *Jacob* like ten times, and I shook your arm, and it didn't make any difference. I thought you had had a stroke or something. I started panicking. My friends came over to help, and the waiter went to get the manager, but you didn't respond to anything. People started coming in from the bar to look at you. It lasted for—I don't know—five minutes, maybe, but it seemed like an hour. Finally, Jerome tried the ice water and you came out of it. You don't remember any of this?"

"No," Jacob said. "No, I was somewhere else." He felt a rising panic.

"You scared me to death," she said. "What do you mean you were somewhere else?"

"Like what I told you about this summer."

Half an hour later when they said goodnight, Emily gazed at him with an unreadable expression. She kissed him quickly and drew away.

For weeks, he had known that what they had felt in the summer would not return, but he could not stand the idea of losing her. He could not stop thinking about her. He would even pray for help but then he would imagine her seeing him and smiling and suddenly he would be pulling her against him and kissing the soft lips that kept him awake and then governed his dreams, where he had rivals. Kings and conquerors vied for her however they could, whenever she would let them. Her face, her mouth, and when she turned away, her hair, which was a magical lure that heroes would seek—hardened men, scarred from many battles, riding their gaunt horses out of the steppes for a chance at the prize.

He stood up, ready to go for a run to clear his head, but as soon as he did, he remembered that he needed to send the Sherman piece to Prof. Forrest, so he sat back down, wrote "Here it is" in the subject line, attached the document he had written over the weekend, and sent it.

A second later, the reply came back.

I'll get back to you in an hour.

An hour. He could run ten miles in an hour.

6

SUNDAY ON KENNESAW

March 3, 1844

A ROOSTER WAS CROWING IN THE NEXT BLOCK WHEN
Cump tiptoed down the tavern stairs in the half-light. Somebody was in the
kitchen—the low clink of plates, a glimmer of shadow and light off the glasses
on the bar, a low humming that sometimes broke into words. Mattie, one of
the Parkinsons' slaves. She had not lit the oil lamps, so he found a box of lucifers on a shelf behind the counter and lit the one nearest his table, adjusting
the flame and resettling the chimney.

It was Sunday, too early for the family of Col. Sylvester Churchill. Every
morning at eight o'clock, solemn Sylvester carefully descended the tavern
stairs and commanded the room from his table in the corner, ordering his
dependents to their seats. Cump would have to give Mrs. Churchill a formal
bow and pay his respects to their daughter Mary, who would someday squeeze
a higher register of rectitude into some preacher or professor. He would shake
the hand of nervous Charles, who always avoided his eyes, while the Colonel
expounded on the hypocrisy of supposedly Christian men who bilked the
government. Cump had an hour before the Churchills would begin gathering
to process to the Episcopal Church. He planned to be up on the mountain
before the church bells began to ring.

Mattie, still humming softly, bumped open the swinging door with her
hip and set a stack of clean plates on the counter. She was a slender woman

but sweetly ample when she came into full profile. When she noticed the light and turned and saw Cump, he already had his finger on his lips to silence her. He gave a quick upward nod to the Churchill rooms, and she shook one hand as though she were throwing off water. *Col. Churchill,* she would mutter whenever Sylvester was not in earshot, *like to drove her crazy. Picked over his eggs like he was looking for maggots. Couldn't nothing satisfy him and she had to act like she ain't never seen a piece of toast done right before he come to teach her.*

Her face shone in the lamplight as she came close. His age or not much older.

"You up early. What you want this morning, Capm?" She put a hand down on the table next to him, her fingers flat on the wood, the palm perpendicular to it. His own hand would not bend that way. She raised an eyebrow at the ceiling. "They ain't up, praise Jesus. I'm bout to go strangle that rooster."

Cump smiled at her and ran both hands into his hair and left them there, looking up at her. "How about some of that good ham you served me yesterday and three or four eggs and two pieces of toast? Unless you're making your pancakes."

"Unh-unh, baby, ain't no pancakes yet. I got coffee brewing."

"I bet you're going to bring me some nice and hot."

Her big smile flashed up and she touched his shoulder.

"Now that Miss Mary, she bring you what you want. I ain't talking coffee. She love her all that red hair sticking up every which way."

He drew his head back in mock alarm, tightening his lips to imitate Mary Churchill.

She covered her mouth to catch her laugh and flapped the other hand at him and went back to the kitchen, where he heard the humming start back up.

As Mattie cleared away the dishes, she said, "How them eggs suit you?"

"Just right," he said.

"What you drawing?"

He turned over his pad to hide it. "You. Not good enough yet to show you."

"Me?" Her voice was light and wondering. She set down his plate and stared at him.

"The way you came through the door and set down the plates."

"How come you draw that?"

"I just liked the way you looked."

"Show me."

She stood next to his chair and he turned over the pad. She gazed down at it, and a hum started up deep in her body.

"You ain't going to church, Capm? You ain't been since you come."

"Too much church back home."

"Can't get too much of Jesus. Unh-unh. What you need"—she nudged a hip lightly against his shoulder—"is to let me sing for you sometime." He could smell the kitchen on her clothes and another undersmell. Without thinking, he ran his hand over the curve of her bottom. "You better watch out," she said a little hoarsely. "Miss Bernice catch you, I ain't gone hear the end of it."

"*You* better watch out," he said, pushing his chair back and pulling her onto his lap. She shied back up, smoothing her apron, glancing out the front window at the street in the first light. After a carriage went by, she met his eyes. Directly upstairs, as if someone had been watching them, a board creaked, and Cump cocked an ear at the ceiling. They waited, listening.

"They ain't up," she said, throaty now. She took his hand to pull him up. "Come on. You ain't got to hurry nowhere, Capm."

He pushed his chair back, but just then came the sound of the door in the kitchen.

"Mattie?" Mrs. Parkinson called with a querulous tone. "*Mattie!* Where are you?"

"Here I am, Miss Bernice."

When Mrs. Parkinson pushed through the swinging door a moment later, Cump was bent, pencil in hand, over his sketch pad on the cleared table, pulse hammering in his temple. "You need some more coffee, Capm?" Mattie called as she strolled back toward the kitchen with his plate and utensils.

"No, thank you," he said formally.

At the swinging door, she stood aside for Mrs. Parkinson, who stared at him, perplexed, still wearing her night cap.

"Lt. Sherman!" Mrs. Parkinson cried, clutching her robe together at her throat. "I didn't recognize you out of uniform. And up so early! I'm not even dressed."

"I have an appointment this morning, Mrs. Parkinson," Cump said, putting his supplies back into the knapsack. "Have you met Ned Barbour?" He stood and put on his jacket and hat, hooking his arm through the strap of his knapsack. "He's an artist from Charleston visiting his sister, and I told him I would take him up to Kennesaw."

"Well, it looks like a beautiful day," she said. "We have a new preacher I'm dying to hear again. Before you go up, you and Mr. Barbour ought to—"

"Maybe next week," Cump said.

Behind Mrs. Parkinson, Mattie's humming suddenly broke into a thrilling alto.

"*Went down to the river Jordan,*
Where John baptized three
Well I walked to the devil in hell
Sayin John ain't baptise me."

He stood transfixed. By God she was good.

"Mattie!" Mrs. Parkinson cried. "You're going to wake up the Churchills!"

"Oh Lord! Hush my mouth!" Mattie said.

Cump nodded his goodbye to Mrs. Parkinson and left the front door unlocked when he went out.

It was a cool morning. He stood for a moment and watched a slave girl sweeping off the stoop of a house across the square, the rhythmic twist and swing of her body. He thought of the Martin girl in Cincinnati and her instinct for capturing motion with a few quick pencil lines, and he wondered whether Lucette Barbier of New Orleans had the same lively talent.

Lively she was, he smiled to himself. He took a deep breath. Gracious sakes, as Mrs. Ewing might say, Mattie had roused him. How was he going to behave himself now? He walked north on Church Street, his knapsack over his shoulder, his body thrumming like a hummingbird beaking a blossom.

Ned Barbour, he would call Lucette in his diary, in case anyone ever read it. Suppose Ellen Ewing found it—or the ponderous Thomas.

He had an hour before the rendezvous. He wondered why Lucette's aunt in New Orleans had arranged for this pretty niece from France to spend a month with an elderly relative in Marietta. Lucette had quickly established her own regime, as he saw when he first met her in Marietta Square attended by two slave girls who seemed genuinely terrified of her. She was drawing a girl sitting on the grass near the central fountain. She had welcomed his interest, then and afterward, without a shadow of reserve.

As he turned northwest onto the street toward Kennesaw Mountain, thick hedges of azalea bloomed around a stately home set back from the road. Magnolias and oaks shaded the groomed lawn, traversed by walkways of brick or flat stones. Dogwood flared snow-white in the sunlight that angled into the shadowy recesses. Redbuds stood thick along the brick sidewalk.

Misnamed. Not red at all. Magenta.

Not that red hair was red. Sticking up every which way.

He heard the muffled clop of hooves coming up behind him and turned politely to greet whoever it might be.

"Arrêtez!" cried the woman in the passenger's seat of the phaeton.

Lucette already! Her white-haired slave, sour-faced, reined in the bay, not looking directly at Cump, who stepped into the road and smoothed his hand down the horse's twitching flank as he approached Lucette. A broad-brimmed straw hat shadowed her face.

"Miss Barbier," he said, touching his forehead. "Aren't you ashamed? You're an hour early."

"Je ne pouvais pas attendre," she said. "I went by your—*comment ça s'appelle?* Hotel?"

The old man grunted and shook his head.

"Something wrong?" Cump said to him.

"Ain't no business of mine."

Lucette moved to let him onto the seat beside her, but she did not move much. When Cump sat down, his thigh pressed against hers, and she met his eyes, taking his hand. She wore a dark skirt and a painter's smock over a blue blouse that showed a soft shadow he would love to pencil in his rendering of her—*décolleté* as Mrs. Ewing would say with disapproval.

In front of them, the old man stretched his head sideways, flexing his narrow shoulders.

"Samson," Lucette said, *"à la montagne."*

Samson sighed and clucked his tongue and started the horse clopping forward.

"Samson?" whispered Cump.

She turned and kissed him with a heat that embarrassed him, exposed as they were in the public road. An early carriage was coming toward them a block away.

"Lucette," he said, pushing her gently away. "I don't want gossip getting back to Col. Churchill."

"Moralité conventionnelle!" Lucette hissed as the brougham drew close opposite them, and an elderly couple peered at them from inside. "We are free. What do we care?"

Conventional or not, kissing pretty women on the public street on Sunday morning would get back to his superior, and he had to keep the approval of men like Sylvester Churchill to advance his career. However it happened, rumors also always got back to Thomas Ewing, who suspected that Cump's desire for his daughter Ellen was easily distractible. Ewing's suspicion disinclined him to entrust her to this redheaded foster son, intelligent but unruly, who had grown up in the same household.

Cump needed Ellen with him now, pious as she was, to help him channel his robust *énergies*, as Lucette called them, in more acceptable ways, which in turn would help him impress those who could promote him. A vicious circle—if he were married to Ellen, he could behave himself in the way he needed to behave to be allowed to marry her. But in any case, he needed promotion. Military distinction would change Ewing's mind.

Lucette pulled his head to her and kissed him hotly again after the carriage passed.

"You brought drawings to show me?" Cump asked, his body thrumming again. Sundays always made him ardent, but this one in particular would go in his diary.

"Oui, Monsieur Sherman."

"Say Cump."

"Oui, Coomp. Un dessin de toi."

She slid a drawing out of her satchel, and there he was on his back, asleep, in the Adamic state.

"Good Lord."

He pushed it back in her satchel, and she laughed out loud.

At the base of Kennesaw Mountain, Lucette gave Cump her satchel to carry and left Samson with the carriage. They started up the trail to the top, but Lucette soon pulled him into a thicket of flowering rhododendron still wet with dew where his *énergies* were focused and allayed. Gathering herself afterward, brushing off the leaves, Lucette smiled at him. "You will draw me?" she said, offering herself.

He had never met a woman so frank, not even in the taverns near West Point. Not even Clemence Martin in Cincinnati.

"Mary Churchill would find it," he said.

"She is your true love, *n'est-ce pas?*" she said. He smiled, stretching like a cat. "You think I would like to be your true love, *non?* But I do not believe in this idea, this true love."

"You did a minute ago."

"*Non,* Coomp. I am free, and I give you—*comment le dis tu? Plaisir, jouissance, délice.* My gift, *une offre.* This true love, it is a way to own, *oui?*"

"What about Samson? Don't you own him?"

She exploded with contempt. "*Ce n'est qu'un nègre!* He is not—" She made a gesture toward her head, her heart, and threw her hands wide as if to show the scope of her freedom.

"Lucretia!" The sharp cry of rebuke startled them. Barely visible through the leaves and flowers, a stern middle-aged matron stood just twenty feet away, dressed in black and bonneted as if for church, holding a long slender stick, flexible as a switch. She had to have heard them. Twenty or more dispirited children in Sunday clothes, boys and girls together, were being driven like sheep up the path to the top of the mountain, but the woman was looking back down the path at two huge, wheezing slave women, Lucretia apparently being one of them.

"Hurry up!" the matron said. "Or I will leave you here!"

The slave stood, gasping dangerously for breath. "I trying. I ain't used to it, Miss Clarice."

"Useless!" Miss Clarice cried, raising her stick and approaching Lucretia. The children had stopped, watching, and when the matron struck Lucretia across the back of her legs, making her cry out, one of the boys laughed, and

Miss Clarice turned fiercely toward the group. "Get up the mountain!" she cried. "The Lord God might care about orphans, but I am sick to death of you! Do what I tell you, or you will go hungry this day, do you hear me?"

"Yes, Miss Clarice," several voices said.

"Dr. Holmes thinks it will 'do you good' to see the view from the top. But where is Dr. Holmes? Do you see him here, Caleb Whitman, on this 'mission of enlightenment'? Do you see Dr. Holmes?"

"No, ma'am."

"No, neither do I. It has all been left to me. It is my bitter lot. Bitter as ashes in the mouth."

The children cowered back as Miss Clarice approached them with her stick. They turned and hurried before her up the path. Heaving and weeping, the slave women followed.

"Mon dieu," Lucette whispered.

After a moment, Cump and Lucette stood and brushed themselves off. He pulled her against him and kissed her and picked a petal from a blonde side-curl and traced with his fingertip the lips so full of scorn and play. She opened her mouth to it and he kissed her again. He held her face in his hands. He kissed her forehead, her eyes, her mouth, as her intelligent green eyes gazed up into his, not shy of desire, but open to it.

Asking him.

He shook his head.

"Miss Clarice might see us."

She made a pout and stepped before him into the gap in the rhododendrons. The springing branches asperged them with dew. A hundred yards up the trail, she remembered her satchel, and she waited while he went back and found it tipped over in their bower, spilling out sketches of him that he browsed quickly. The nude. Landscapes he did not recognize, a young slave girl washing clothes. Talent, but not like Miss Martin's in Cincinnati. When he caught up with her, they made their way up the trail, pausing whenever there was a break in the trees and a vista.

On the mountaintop in the lucid spring air, they spotted Miss Clarice and her band of miserable captives and veered off the trail to avoid them. Rarely was there a height where you could see flat countryside rather than other mountains in every direction. This was a god's-eye-view. He was Jupiter on Olympus, and here was Lucette beside him, his latest mortal conquest, the skin of her waist smooth and quick when his hand moved up beneath her blouse. By God, she was free with herself, not corseted by moral prohibitions like Mary Churchill—or Ellen, for that matter, much as he loved her wise counsel.

Lucette pressed his hand against her skin, and a deep thrill went through him. The Churchills evaporated from his concern, the strict Ewing household, his sense of anxiety about his career, the gnawing ambition to do something great, the irritable awareness of restrictions that had harried him at West Point and ever since. Happy in his presence, glad and open and imperious in her affections, Lucette did what she wanted, and so did he.

After they gazed out for a minute or so in the light breeze, she wanted to sketch the bare hump of Stone Mountain rising to the southeast out of the flat land around it. A monadnock, a dome-shaped intrusion of magma that Charles Lyell would have loved to describe in his geology books. Cump helped her settle herself on a broad granite ledge and strolled off, looking west at Little Kennesaw, a smaller peak, and beyond it to a line of diminishing hills. A presentiment came upon him, a brush from the wing of some coming thing. He should memorize this landscape. He should know it so well that he could draw it from memory. He turned, hands on his hips, and looked northwest at Pine Mountain and the hills to the north.

Down in Marietta, the church bells had started up, summoning the Churchills and the other Christians in their other denominations to their Sunday duty. He turned and walked over to look down on the town from a high ledge. His refusal to worship had been a concern of long standing for Mrs. Ewing and a grief for Ellen, but he could not feel what they felt about their consoling stories. He respected them too much to feign obedience to a God whose worship faded the more men knew about the laws of nature.

Competing peals came clearly through the morning air, and Cump could distinguish the two, now three, steeples issuing them, like the distinctive voices of hounds on the hunt. He had played Theseus once on the school stage. "We will, fair queen, up to the mountain's top / And mark the musical confusion / Of hounds and echo in conjunction." He felt another surge of elation, happy not to be straitened in Sunday clothes and herded into a pew. A decade of suffocation—the Latin intoning of the priest, the hypnotically swinging censer, the clouds of incense, the dreary homily teasing out dispiriting lessons from long-exhausted texts. How could Ellen love it?

On her rock, Lucette lifted her arms, lacing her fingers above her head, the smock's sleeves falling from her hands and wrists as she stretched luxuriously, nymph of the mountain. She turned to look for her lover. Her eyes again held their question, and he smiled back at her, tilting his head.

Twice more that day, the second time standing. Her back pressed against a tree far off the path, after they shared the cheese and bread and wine she had brought from her ancient relative's home early that morning. She did not pretend weakness or submission but met him with forthright avidity, her body young and strong, strength matching strength, her head thrown back, mouth open, thick blonde hair speckled with bits of leaf and curls of bark. His dryad.

When he returned to the tavern that afternoon, exhausted and happy, he went up to his room without being seen and wrote in his diary for the first time in a week.

> *Sunday Mar. 3. Still at Marietta. Walked out in company with a Charleston gentleman named Barbour to visit the Kennesaw Mountain which is a solitary peak about 800 feet above the surrounding country affording a very extended view. The Stony Mountain of DeKalb by name Etowa 27 miles off distinctly visible and the village of Marietta 3 miles off lies as it were at its base. The day was beautiful, in fact the whole spring has been in advance, the peach trees in full bloom and all the other vegetation budding but a late frost may destroy all.*

When the bell rang for dinner, it was almost dark. Mrs. Parkinson was serving supper to the Churchills in the otherwise empty dining room when he came down the stairs. She glanced up at Cump, her mouth tight, but avoided his eyes as she set down a baked chicken for Col. Churchill to carve as Mattie placed the other dishes of vegetables and bread. Neither Mary nor Mrs. Churchill would look at him. Mrs. Parkinson gestured him to the table where he had sat that morning.

"Lt. Sherman," said Col. Churchill, giving him one stern look and then fixing the chicken in place with his fork. "You've rejoined us."

"Yes, sir. I spent the day on the mountain."

"Not Zion, I understand."

The same old theme.

"No, sir," he said, taking up his napkin.

Col. Churchill applied his knife to the chicken, deftly removing a leg to give to young Charles before he started on the breast.

"A respect for the Lord's Day," he said, "might be expected of the officers of the United States Army, especially with the delicate mission entrusted to us." He gave a slice of breast to Mary, holding it on the fork with the knife as she lifted her plate. "Moreover, we expect honesty of those we investigate, and they expect it of us."

"Honesty?" Cump said.

"I believe you told Mrs. Parkinson you had an appointment with a gentleman from Charleston."

"Ah."

"That young French woman was not this gentleman, I believe."

Good God, had they been seen on the mountain? Impossible. No, but now he remembered that Lucette had stopped by the tavern that morning.

"No sir, she was not."

"Your behavior gives scandal to the citizens of the town."

"Scandal, sir? How so?"

"An assignation. On a Sunday. And a lie about it to clear your way? How conspicuously you choose not to attend church means little to me—"

"Oh, Papa!" cried Mary, unwilling to be indifferent about Cump's soul and pained—if Mattie was right—to hear of his affections elsewhere. Mattie paused at the back of the dining room, watching, and when he caught her eye, she pursed her lips and went out through the swinging doors to the kitchen.

"A French woman," said Mrs. Parkinson with infinite reproach. "At seven in the morning," she whispered. "Asking for you."

"It means little to me!" Churchill insisted righteously. "But it will mean something to the people of Marietta who watch us. It might very well mean something," he said, turning to look Cump in the eye, "for the progress of your career. And it might mean something to the good family of Sen. Thomas

Ewing that this—"

"Sir," said Cump, standing and dropping his napkin on the table. He would forgo the meal if it was to be an inquisition. He gave a quick bow and left the room as they all watched him, utensils in midair.

There was no point denying his acquaintance with Lucette or his transparent lie. God damn it, he had *told* her to be more prudent. The glories of his day with her faded, and as he mounted the stairs, he burned with resentment, embarrassed by his exposure, raging at the Churchills and the small-souled moral order they inhabited, but also at Lucette, whose contempt for ordinary caution now imperiled his future.

In his room, he lit the lamp, pacing. He had to marry Ellen. He would have married her already if goddamned Thomas Ewing had not kept getting in the way. He would write to Ewing tomorrow asking him to settle his fate as a bachelor one way or the other. Lucette was a passing pleasure. Mediocre as an artist. If she had seen who he was, her drawings of him would be better. Wrong around the eyes and mouth.

There was a soft knock on his door. He sighed, collected himself, and opened it, expecting Col. Churchill, but Mattie stood there with a plate of food.

"Ain't you bad?" she said. She brushed against him in the small quarters as she came in to set the plate on his desk.

"Thank you," he said formally.

"I don't see why you put up with them folks. If I run off, they be after me. Send the dogs. But ain't nobody say you can't do no better." She turned to face him. Her dark eyes looked into his, full of hurt, unreadable. "I ain't free," she said, "mostly. But you let me know what you need, honey. The Lord Jesus ain't give up on you."

"I'm more worried about Col. Churchill than the Lord Jesus."

"Aw, baby, come here." She put her arms around him, pulling him against her, and at first he bridled at the effrontery of it. A slave woman. *Ce n'est qu'un nègre!* But Mattie did not let him go. "Who you fighting?"

Later, she started singing as she went back down the stairs. "*Well I walked to the devil in hell / Sayin John ain't baptise me.*"

"Hush, Mattie!" came furiously up from below.

7

FIRST QUESTIONS

A BOY OF SEVENTEEN SHOULD NEVER HAVE BEEN ABLE TO write this piece. Lucifers, oil lamps, slaves. Forrest sat in his armchair thumbing the pages he had printed out. A liberated French woman. It triggered the instinct that teachers developed toward plagiarism—but how could this be plagiarized? Walter had certainly not written it.

He remembered Buford from years before at Stonewall Hill. During the time when Josiah Simms had besieged his family, he had shown a strange, fearless authority. He was the one courageous enough to go into the old house covered with kudzu and find the body of Walter's mother, Alison Graves. Later, Walter and Teresa had worried that the terrors of that time had caused psychological damage. Buford would have episodes when he went blank and unreachable for five or ten minutes. Later, he could vividly recount where he was, and the experiences seemed to be prompted by someone he had seen or something he had read. Walter thought they might be the phenomenon that Keats described in one of his letters as the poet having "no self" but taking on the identity of others. Teresa sought out professional help for him, but the specialist they found in Jackson said Buford had none of the usual markers of trauma. She had no idea how to diagnose him. In every other way, the boy was normal—present to those around him, excellent in schoolwork, a good athlete.

It was almost ten according to his iPhone, but still before eight in Wyoming. Maybe he could catch Walter at home. He wanted to talk to him about the boy's troubling version of Sherman—troubling mainly because of what it said about Buford and his girlfriend. He was surprised at himself for worrying about the boy's chastity, a concept anathema to his Boomer generation and even more so to the generation under forty as varieties of "gender" proliferated.

What was her name? Emma? *Emily*. Forrest would need to talk to the boy before showing the piece to Walter.

The boy's Sherman reminded him of Jason Zitek, his philandering son-in-law, and at the thought, his soul cramped with fury. The conversation with Cate had been excruciating. She was deep into a misery he could not enter. Forrest's offer to come to Atlanta and kill Zitek had met with a dry bark of laughter. *Dad, you're going to murder your grandchildren's father?*

Forrest found Walter's cell number in his contacts.

—Guizac, Walter answered drily after a couple of rings.

"You're still a Peach in my heart," Forrest said.

—What's up?

"Did Buford show you what he wrote?"

—Sweet Lord, I don't have time for Buford's homework. I'm just trying to keep up with the election. It's no contest out here, of course. People love this bastard."

"You want Biden?"

—God, no. I'm just sick to death of Trump.

"All the federal judges, Gorsuch, Kavanagh, and Barrett on the Supreme Court, the most pro-life president ever, the—"

—Imagine having a conversation with Donald Trump. Everybody decent leaves him or gets fired. He's pure infantile ego. He's going to lose the election, and everything he did will get reversed. I don't want every good thing I care about to be associated with Donald Goddamn Trump.

"Let's save this for later. Let me speak to Buford. I want to talk to you about what he wrote if he'll let you read it."

—I don't have time to read his history assignment. Listen, I'm headed to the office.

"I'll give you a call later. Tell him I'm opening a Zoom meeting in a few minutes."

—He went for a run. I'll tell Teresa.

Forrest stood up and stretched and took his cold coffee to the kitchen. Through the window over the sink, he could see the drawbridge between New Hampshire and Maine rising over the Piscataqua River. It had been years since he and Marisa drove up the Maine coast to Ogunquit or Damariscotta, where they had once spent Marisa's birthday weekend at a bed and breakfast. Or farther north to Camden, where they had taken Cate and Bernadette on vacation when they were little. He had made them climb Mt. Megunticook for the view out over Penobscot Bay and the islands—you could see Mt. Desert—and the distant Atlantic in the dark heave and swell he always associated with Robert Lowell's poem about Nantucket. Ten years ago on their anniversary, he and Marisa had left the girls with Marisa's mother, and they had taken the CAT ferry from Bar Harbor over to Yarmouth in Nova Scotia to spend two weeks touring, most of it in fog so dense they could hardly see past the windshield.

Ten years ago already—the first summer after he had come into the family wealth. After the first stirrings of his conversion.

A wave of melancholy came over him. He had been given this beautiful, wise wife, these lovely children, and he could see everywhere the strains and sorrows he had brought upon them by being who he was. He had even done it to Zitek. The man was too much like him. Cate's dark, grieved voice came back to him, low and tired. She was fighting for stoical acceptance, not turning to her faith since she had conceded to Zitek's scornful rejection of it in her attempts to keep the marriage alive, as though Catholicism itself were the problem. Or maybe it wasn't Zitek, but her own rejection of those of her Catholic former classmates who had a moralistic sense of art or poetry or struck her as mean or pietistic and pharisaical. Meanwhile, Zitek became a standard-issue leftist just in time to adopt the self-righteousness of the new Puritanism.

Forrest used the toilet and went back to the kitchen. He poured a fresh cup of coffee and fiddled with the foil on one of the half-and-half thingies that Marisa ordered from Costco. It was supposed to separate neatly, but it refused, so he stabbed savagely through the top with a kitchen knife and poured it in and sipped his coffee. Not hot enough. Never hot enough. He put the mug in the microwave and pushed the thirty-second button. Across the street in the parking lot of Prospect Park, people with Biden-Harris signs were surrounding two or three bikers with Trump flags projecting from their handlebars on each side. A young Biden woman, not getting too close, stretched out her neck to say something to them, but then three more—four, five—motorcycles came rumbling into the lot, big men, and the Biden people melted away.

Dread came over him. The election would not solve anything. Trump would lose and not accept the results. He would have endless reasons. He might use the military to keep himself in office.

Back at his desk, he started the Zoom meeting. The boy was already waiting, so he clicked to admit him. He stood there drying his face and head with a towel.

"So you took a run?"

"Yes sir. Into town and back."

"Just now? How far is that?"

"About ten miles. I just came in. Mom said you wanted to talk about what I wrote."

Forrest wondered if he could have ever run ten miles in an hour—six-minute miles or better. He might have run a couple of miles at that speed, but he wasn't built for distance. Different bones. The boy had Peach's leanness.

"Let me get right to it," Forrest said. "Marszalek makes Sherman sound almost prudish. O'Connell thinks he had affairs, later at least, but the Cump you're giving us is randy from the get-go. Can you explain that?"

"Yes sir."

The boy sat down.

"Do you need some water or something?" Forrest asked.

"Yes sir."

He disappeared and came back half a minute later with a water bottle, and Forrest heard the door close as he came into the room. He took a big swallow and set the bottle down.

"So what I saw was that it's connected to his way of ignoring rules at West Point, not going to church since he left Ohio at sixteen. What he says about Sundays in his diary, the way he writes about the Martin girl who's the artist."

"So you don't think he loves Ellen Ewing?"

"He does, but it's complicated. She's obsessive about chastity. She's also the daughter of the Ewings who took him in after his father died, and she's the most mothering part of the family. Mrs. Ewing never approved of him, and he felt that. She thought he was unclean. Maybe it was the red hair. Dad says people used to associate it with sensuality."

"Botticelli's Venus," Forrest said. "Good point. All those paintings of Mary Magdalene."

"Yes sir, so Mrs. Ewing made him get baptized before she would even let him stay in their home. But Ellen grew up with him. She loves him, and he loves her. What he hates is the horror of sex she gets from her mother."

"Jansenist," Forrest speculated.

"But he also counts on her. He knows she'll be faithful to him. Meanwhile, he has all this sensuality fueled by rage and restrained by ambition."

"Nice antithesis," Forrest said. He looked at the boy and took a sip of his coffee. "Go on."

"He owes too much to the Ewings. Thomas Ewing enjoys having power over him, I suspect—not that he thinks about it. Cump wants independence. I mean, it's like he almost has a private sacrament of rage and frustration that liberates him from them without affecting what they can do for him."

"A private sacrament?"

"Maybe a secret sacrament is a better way to say it."

"Why call it a sacrament? It's just a sin."

"Okay, but his defining sin. His real religion. The sex is like the sacrament of transgression."

"You sound like Foucault," said Forrest, taken aback.

"Who's that?"

"Never mind. Go on."

"It would horrify Mrs. Ewing if she knew. He has to make sure she never actually knows. He likes saying all the right things and portraying himself as sternly moral when he's actually covering up things like his affair with Lucette. He treats Ellen the same way he treats her mother. I think there's a revenge on the Ewings in the fact that he even wants to marry his foster sister."

"Maybe it's just safe. Maybe he's terrified of other women."

"No sir. He loves women. I guess he feels enough difference from Ellen that it isn't incest. He really does want to be married to her and be respectable to the Ewings. And he's not exactly a hypocrite. It's like he has his own code."

"Okay," said Forrest. "So you're going to use this scene to set up later things? I'm guessing the attack on Kennesaw Mountain."

"Yes sir, that's what I'm seeing."

"My other question was about Mattie. Sherman's racist as hell, which is pretty obvious in everything he writes. It seems like you're ignoring that."

"That's what I saw," the boy said. "Did you ever read what Mary Chesnutt writes about plantation owners? They were all racist, too, but their houses were full of mulatto children."

He couldn't argue with that.

"So what's next?"

"I'm not sure. San Francisco, maybe. Or Shiloh or Memphis. Or maybe back at Kennesaw since there's not much time."

Forrest considered whether he ought to say anything more.

"Listen, Buford," he said. "I'll just be straight with you. I'm in a little of a quandary here. I want to ask your father to read it."

"He doesn't have time."

"What about your mom? What if I gave it to her?"

"I wouldn't want her to read it."

"Right. And that's because she would make surmises—"

"Yes sir."

"About you and Emily."

"Yes sir."

"Listen, Buford, God knows I'm not one to judge, but what you've written seems like evidence of the bitten apple. I wish I had taken a different path when I was your age." Forrest gazed at him, trying to read his expression. "How do you know how to write it? Would you let Emily read it?"

"She's got too much to read already."

"But what would she think?"

"Emily hates this whole project," the boy said bitterly. He sounded as miserable as Cate had the night before, and his eyes met Forrest's. "It's not about Emily and me. It's what comes to me about Sherman."

"See what comes to you next. And hurry up. You've got a long way to go to get back to Gallatin."

"You want me to write about Sherman in Gallatin? I don't think he—"

"I'm kidding. But get to work."

8

YOU LOSE

CHICK LEE, SOLE OWNER AND PROPRIETOR OF THE LEE Ford dealership he had inherited from his father and his grandfather before him, had a small, dark-green ornamental dish his daughter Alison had given him, a shallow scoop carved like a horse's head, and he used it to keep up with his pills—the blood pressure pill, the diabetes pill, the cholesterol pill. At night he would sometimes need a zolpidem, and in the morning he always took his omeprazole to keep his acid reflux in check. In his mid-sixties, he had started paying more attention to the ads with ex-NFL players talking about ED; he had experienced enough trouble to mention it to his doctor, who prescribed sildenafil (the famous Viagra) to see if it helped, which it did, given what it had to work with. He tried to walk a couple of miles every day, and he got to the gym when he could—mostly weights so he wouldn't lose muscle mass.

He was okay, wasn't he? Basically pretty healthy? But he was having a hard time not thinking about having to die. He wasn't *old* old, but old enough not to kid anybody. He could see it on the faces of people who had not seen him for a few years—he called it that little *Chick-click* of recognition, like *Oh, that's right, you're old now.* Middle-aged men would defer to him in line and say *Excuse me, sir* in a way he didn't quite like, though he did it himself to old old people. Having to die sometime in the next ten or twenty years—maybe thirty, you didn't know—helped focus the questions though. *Are you ready? Can you die in peace?*

He wasn't ready. He couldn't die in peace.

He read the Bible every day, and he taught a Sunday school class at the First Baptist Church. *Long, long ago in a country far away, a man who was God in disguise died for you.* Not *disguised*, though, *really* God.

Really really? Sometimes none of it made any sense to him. But then other times he was convicted of the truth of it deep in his heart.

Six days a week, he still went to work. His office at the dealership had a window that looked out over the showroom, and for months now the bleak truth of the Covid economy had kept it empty. He laid off most of his salesmen and mechanics. Most days, he came to his office and sat there reading the news online—lately all Trump and Biden and the nomination of Amy Coney Barrett and debates and Covid maps and how important Georgia's Senate races were. Everything was about race, nothing was about cars, and so when sun glare flashed from the front door of the dealership that Saturday morning, he sat up as if it were a revelation.

The door opened. *Customers!*

In came two girls in the black-and-white uniform of Eula's House at Stonewall Hill, both of them pregnant, one of them otherwise redheaded and narrow, the other one heavy and black. And behind them—Lord God—came Hermia Watson.

She saw him before he could hide.

"Chick!" she called, waving. The two girls also saw him standing there, hands on the back of his chair. He waved back and slipped on his loafers and walked through the outer office.

His secretary had been coming in two days a week to keep up with bills, but unopened mail had stacked up since she left with Covid two weeks earlier. At least she wasn't here to see Hermia, who looked amazing, not overripe and biological, all milk and fat like the two girls, but cool and constructed, crafted and fit and beautiful even in jeans and a white turtleneck and a short jacket that showed off her perfect cream-colored oval face, the feline eyes, the generous mouth.

"Chick Lee," she said as she walked out onto the showroom floor like a model, smiling like she had a home in Beulah Land instead of Stonewall Hill.

"Hermia Watson," he said, "beautiful as ever."

"Woo hoo," said the redheaded girl.

"Hush, Siobhan."

Chick's wife Patricia thought uniforms for the girls at Eula's House were a bad idea. *Everybody already knows who they are*, she would say. *I mean, look at them. It's like wearing some kind of prison uniform, the poor things. Why doesn't that woman just let them blend in?* Chick thought it might be difficult for crowds of four or five young, pregnant girls to blend in anywhere. He thought the uniforms helped protect them, like the habits of nuns. The uniform said, *Watch out, we're organized, so hands off.* It must have been Hermia's idea. Or maybe it was Marisa Forrest's idea.

What was embarrassing right this moment (and he felt the blush rising from his neck) was that he and Hermia Watson had slept together once. The summer of 2009 had been a strange time, and he had not set out to do it, but there it was, and this little zone of bashfulness surrounded them and pulled them together. The two girls, keyed in to anything about sex, stood watching as Hermia approached Chick and gave him a small kiss on the cheek.

"Woo-hoo!" The two girls did a fist bump and strolled off to look at one of the new hybrid pickup trucks in the showroom.

"How you been, baby?" Hermia asked in a whisper, pressing just a little too close, maybe unconsciously, but maybe to remind him. God, she smelled wonderful. She was supposed to be holy now.

"You ought to give a man some warning," Chick whispered back. "I'm not as young as I used to be. My heart could blow out like a bad tire." He stood back and looked her in the eye. "What brings you to Lee Ford after all these years?"

"Looking for a car, sweetheart," Hermia said, raising an eyebrow at him. "I need something to take these girls around in."

"You can get them all in the same one?"

"Depends," she said. "It's twelve now, and I'm expecting a few more. I've had as many as twenty-two."

"You'd need a school bus. And what would it say on the side? Hermia's Honeys?" He tipped his head at the girls, who had opened both doors of the pickup and were looking inside.

"That's just mean." She gave him a soft swat on the shoulder.

"I don't know what kind of money you have," he said.

"Baby," she said with a droll mouth, "I've got the Forrest Foundation."

"Good old Braxton," Chick said, smiling. His old friend Braxton Forrest—her father. And also her son's father, according to the legend. He wondered if John Bell Hudson ever sent money to his mother.

"You know what I really need, Chick? Some understanding from Gallatin."

Chick nodded and sighed. "What can I do to help you?"

Hermia touched his arm and nodded to his office. "Can we go in for a second? I need to say a few things I don't want the girls to hear."

He opened a hand toward the office door and she started toward it. Even where he lived on the other side of town, he heard people complaining about Stonewall Hill. The idea of Eula's House was to give the girls an alternative to having an abortion, but having a concentration of vividly pregnant unmarried girls in one place got people riled up, especially when these were women from bigger cities, all of them already displaying the evidence of—well, what exactly? Not exactly sex, because some girls in Gallatin did the deed enthusiastically in junior high—or even earlier, as he remembered from being a teenager in the 1960s. Jonquil Hayes discovered her calling in fifth grade.

It wasn't sex the town objected to, in other words, but the public display of the consequences. These girls were scandals because they violated decorum in a way that mere lust never did if you managed it shrewdly. Obviously, they had not used contraceptives (which were available everywhere), and they had not had abortions, also available, and here they were in Gallatin, burdening the decent population with their squirming little welfare babies who were cute at first and then grew up to become gang members and criminals. Priscilla Newton, one of the stalwarts of the Board of Education, had just written an op-ed piece in the *Gallatin Tribune* giving faint praise to the good intentions of Eula's House and then complaining about the bad example she thought its clientele set for the young people of the community. A household of pregnant girls trying to respect life and do the right thing was a good example, in his estimation. But he had heard a woman in Mary Jane Ryburn's Left Bank restaurant say that it was *a travesty, that fine old mansion occupied by colored girls who don't know how to keep from having babies*. Patricia got her nose up thinking about it. Men he knew called it Hermia's Cathouse.

Hermia stepped in front of him and opened the door. Chick glanced at her bottom despite himself.

"Y'all be good," called the black girl from the driver's seat of the pickup. The redhead leaned across her and wagged her finger.

When Chick closed the door behind them, Hermia turned and embraced him, pushing her face softly into his neck, and he felt his heart heave with confusion. Not once in more than ten years had they admitted their night together. Something bad must have made her turn to him now. He held her against him and then gave her a quick hug and stepped back so he could see her face.

"What's the matter? What happened?"

"I got a call. A bomb threat. A voice message. Kind of fuzzy. My aide Deirdre heard it first and got me to listen to it. A male voice. 'You better get those bitches out of there because that whole place is going to blow up.' It scared me, Chick. I got all the girls out."

"Sweet Lord. Did you tell the police?"

"I called. An Officer Smiley, very sarcastic. LaCourvette Todd is in Atlanta now."

"I heard that," Chick said. LaCourvette's competence and sound judgment had taken her to bigger things.

"Well I called her, and she told me to call the FBI."

Chick sat her down in the chair across from his desk.

"You don't have any idea who it might be?"

"Oh," she said weakly, lifting a hand and dropping it.

"Nobody has threatened you?" he asked.

"Sometimes I sit on the porch and feel the ill will all around me. I wouldn't know how to pick out a threat. Not until now."

"What do you mean?"

"The article in *Phoe*."

"What's *Phoe*?"

"The Atlanta magazine. It just came out today." She pulled a copy from her bag and laid it carefully in front of Chick. **The Best NEW BITES in Hot 'Lanta** said the cover. Pictures of chicken tenders and waffles. He glanced up at her, and she reached over to flip it open where a subscription postcard served as a bookmark.

The words "You Lose Plantation" were superimposed in black on a photograph of the front gate of Stonewall Hill in the springtime. Banks of azaleas, dogwoods, redbuds, the white columns of the house in the background. Standing at one side of the gate were two very pregnant black girls in the Eula's House uniform. "Locked in the big house," said the subtitle. Then the byline: Melina Lykaios. Chick started to read.

> Eula's House in Gallatin, Georgia—a town with a statue of a Confederate soldier on the courthouse square—bills itself as a "home for women," but it occupies the main building of a plantation that dates back to the days of chattel bondage, and for some women, those days have come again. "Referred" by agencies in Atlanta, Macon, and elsewhere, pregnant women find themselves in a regimented environment, forced to recite prayers, kept from using their cell phones or laptops, and subjected on a daily basis to the propaganda of the radical right. "Pro-life" is the owners' word for it, but the older term *slavery* suits the situation better—slavery to the master's religion, slavery to the idea that they are "sinners," slavery to political causes that never crossed their minds, slavery to the lifelong demands that unwanted children make on unwilling mothers.

Chick shook his head in disbelief.

"Has Cump seen this?"

"I don't know. It's on the website."

"And you got the bomb threat today, right after this came out? I'm calling him," he said.

Hermia's hand went to her throat. "What are you going to say?"

"That somebody's threatening to blow up Stonewall Hill!"

"I don't know if I'm ready to talk to him," Hermia said. She looked deflated and weak. Meanwhile the girls in the showroom had gotten out of the pickup truck and were smoothing their pregnant bellies down opposite sides in sync with each other; they came around the front and bumped into each other lightly, laughing, dumb as bunnies.

Chick found Forrest in the contacts on his cell phone and touched the number. Forrest answered on the first ring.

—Cate? he demanded. Whose phone is this?

Confused, Chick did not answer.

—Or is that you, Zitek, you piece of shit?

"Cump, Cump. Slow down, buddy. This is Chick Lee."

A long pause.

—It's a Georgia area code so I thought it was that—never mind. What's up?

"Listen, Hermia's here at the dealership. Somebody called in a bomb threat to Stonewall Hill."

—Was it Zitek? Forrest shouted. I wouldn't put it past that piece of shit.

"Who's Zitek?" Chick said.

He heard someone talking to Forrest.

—Chick, a woman said. This is Marisa.

"Marisa, it's good to hear your voice."

—Instead of Braxton's, you mean? Cate's been having some trouble with her marriage and he thought it was our son-in-law calling. He's been drinking heavily, according to our daughter. How's Patricia?

"She's okay. Listen, I'm sorry to hear about Cate."

—Somebody called in a bomb threat?

"That's right. Hermia's here with me. She got the call earlier today after the article came out in the Atlanta magazine."

—What article?

"It's in a magazine called *Phoe*. It's about how women are forced into slavery at 'You Lose Plantation.' Just a lot of lies, but—

—Who wrote it? Marisa asked, her voice climbing with emotion.

"Somebody named Melina Lykaios."

—Melina Lykaios? That's the woman Jason's—

Chick heard Forrest in the background. *Do you see this shit? I'll kill him!* Then he was back on the phone, his voice clotted with rage.

—Let me talk to Hermia.

Chick held out the phone to Hermia as if it were radioactive. She opened her hands at him to ask who it was. He widened his eyes. Hermia let out a breath and took the phone from him. She waved Chick away.

When was it he slept with her? The year Forrest came back from Rome and all hell broke loose. All those years ago, over a decade already. The year Marilyn Harkins died. And her NFL husband, Dutrelle Jones. The nurse at the hospital. That madness was the only way Chick would ever have slept with Hermia Watson. She had been shaken—broken—and he was there. Afterwards, he wondered whether she was trying to make up for judging her own mother harshly. She had gone away for years, writing books, teaching somewhere up north. She visited during the summer of 2014 when Walter Peach and all his family went on the run. Then three or four years ago she had some kind of conversion and quit her teaching job and Braxton Forrest gave her Stonewall Hill to start Eula's House. He would ask her about it sometime. Exactly what happened. What her conversion was like.

He walked over to his desk, distractedly fiddling with some of the Post-it notes he had left on the screen of his computer. *Call about restocking Pirellis. Pick up walnuts.* Hermia went into the corner by his file cabinets next to the window that overlooked the showroom. Her two girls were talking to the salesman who had wandered out onto the floor. Joe Ashburn. Chick let him work on Saturdays. Pale, a little smarmy, the man was not so much dishonest-looking as oblivious. People either called him Hashbrown because it sounded right or Hashburn or Heehaw because of the pork chop sideburns he wore like Roy Clark on the old show. He was showing the girls the features of the new hybrid Escape. Watching them nudge each other and roll their eyes, Chick almost didn't know why he employed the man. But pity was why. Look at him. And at least he had a salesman just in case somebody wanted to buy a car, even though nobody had all year. The PPP loan back in May had gotten the dealership over the hump so Chick could pay Hashbrown a pittance and keep Rufus in Parts and bring in his other guys now and then.

Hermia was deep into her conversation, murmuring. When she felt him looking, she held up a finger to let him know it would be a minute or two, so he walked out into the hallway and glanced at the service area. Buster Simpson had an old pickup on the lift. Nothing much else going on. Even six or seven months after the first big Covid outbreak in March, Gallatin was still pretty empty. People were just confused—the quarantines, the rigamarole of masks and nasal swabs while you waited in your car in the clinic parking lot. For most people, getting the virus was a joke, no worse than a cold, but he knew at least five people not much older than he was who had died of it.

And what if he got it?

What if he was one of those people whose lungs filled with fluid?

"Chick?"

Hermia stood in the doorway of his office so wonderfully poised that his heart turned over again. Did she know what she was doing to him?

"Braxton's going to sue the magazine. His son-in-law is having an affair with this woman who wrote the story. I remember meeting him, Cate's husband, a year or two ago—a smart man, edgy, and educated. He seemed skeptical about what we were doing, but Cate told me he'd had some bad experiences with the Legionaries of Christ when he was a teenager. I had two women a while back who hated it here, and they're the ones who talked to Melina Lykaios and made all those allegations. Nobody interviewed me or any of the other women, so I think even the threat of a lawsuit will make them retract the story. Marisa had a great idea. We'll hold an open house. We'll invite everybody in to see what we're actually doing. We'll stay out of the way and the girls themselves can talk. It should help, don't you think?"

He pursed his lips, thinking of what Patricia would say.

"When does she want to do it?"

"She thinks either the weekend before Thanksgiving or the one right after. She thinks I should announce it now to show we have nothing to hide."

Chick thought about who would come. A lot of people would be curious, he supposed. Just knowing more would help ease the general disapproval that had now spread to Atlanta and maybe the whole state.

"Look at those girls," said Hermia. He turned and saw the two of them backing Hashbrown against the car with their baby bellies. The man looked more panicked by the second. "I better get them out of here. Girls! Time to go!" she called, and the two of them spun away in opposite directions, laughing.

"Let me know what I can do to help you," Chick said. "Meanwhile, you should get up a notice in the *Tribune*, posters—whatever you can do to drum up a little publicity, right?"

Hermia gave him a hug on her way past him.

"Pray for me," she whispered. "Sometimes I don't know where to turn. Can you come by Stonewall Hill tomorrow morning? Just so *you* can see what's going on?"

As soon as he read the story, Forrest called his lawyer at Hayward, Hayward, and Lawton, the old, highly respectable Atlanta firm he had used in helping Hermia get Eula's House established. He outlined the obvious libel, pointing out that the presence of the women at Eula's House was entirely voluntary. The women who went there understood and accepted the rules of the house. They knew that they were giving up their phones and laptops in order to participate in the communal life of prayer and the educational opportunities Hermia was giving them—classes in English grammar, literature, and American history as well as instruction in household management. The pro-life position was not right-wing politics, but the reason for the very existence of the place as an alternative to abortion. Forrest emphasized that the mission statement of Eula's House had been promulgated publicly, and he offered to provide all the information necessary to show that Jason Zitek, a staff writer for *Phoe* with a close connection to Melina Lykaios, had a personal animus against Forrest himself.

The firm contacted the publisher, Winton Ludwick, with the evidence. The story had been retracted by mid-afternoon the next day. Forrest thought that Melina Lykaios would be fired, but instead, apparently with Ludwick's approval, she issued an apology, saying that her sources had misled her about certain details but asserting the continuing problem of perception, given the plantation setting. *Imagine the young Black woman, pregnant—obviously not by her choosing—who finds herself confused and overwhelmed by the condescension of others and billeted like her enslaved ancestors in the big house of a white owner. We at* Phoe *had some facts wrong, we admit, but we object to Eula's House nevertheless.* Forrest called his lawyer again and told him to press the libel suit unless Lykaios's supposed apology was removed. It disappeared within the hour.

Chick made excuses to Patricia for not making breakfast and got to Stonewall Hill early. He and Hermia sat at a table near the big eastern window in the dining room, enjoying the morning light, as the women finished their scrambled eggs or fruit bowls, glancing over, murmuring, speculating about who he was. All of them pregnant, like a distinct species at the zoo. Well, not a zoo. He saw the two friends who had toyed with Hashbrown the day before.

They waved and gave him looks as they left the dining room and waddled out into the great entrance foyer.

When the women were busy taking their dishes to the kitchen and cleaning the wooden tables, Hermia's two aides came over, ready to go over the plans for the day. Chick stood up to meet them as Hermia introduced them. Deirdre Kelly was a small, redheaded girl from Austin, Texas. Cute. Big dimples. "Can you imagine this little thing in the rodeo?" Hermia said, touching Deirdre's elbow.

"Barrel racing," grinned Deirdre. "I was state champion in my age group."

"I don't even know what that is," Chick admitted. She dimpled at his ignorance.

Jordan Alcarez was a tall, stocky girl with Hispanic coloring, not pretty but intensely present, with large eyes that took in Chick and the situation.

"Deirdre and Jordan both came down right after they graduated from Transfiguration College out in Wyoming. Teresa Peach told them about my work. You remember Teresa?"

"I didn't know her well."

"Deirdre's the oldest of eleven kids—lots of experience with her mother's pregnancies. Jordan's an only child, but she calms everybody down just by coming in the room."

Both the girls smiled and shook Chick's hand as they left for their duties. Hermia sat back and spread her arms at the extent of what she was dealing with on a daily basis when the culture itself felt so hostile to her, if *Phoe* was any indication.

"I know it's a good work. God's work. But I just—sometimes I wonder what it's all for, you know? What difference will it make in the long run?"

"You know it makes a difference. You just get depressed sometimes."

He felt odd being put in the position of a counselor, especially in the presence of a woman as beautiful and educated as Hermia was. What did they really have in common except that one night? That sin he had repented, though he thought of it sometimes.

"No," she said, smiling and touching his hand, just for a moment, but with a distinct impact—straight to his soul. "No, I call it melancholy, and I can't do anything to avoid it. I have to deal with it on a daily basis. I see these girls—these vivid creatures, this swarm of life that you find in them, hormones and flirtations and evasions and weird little rituals of cutting themselves and feeling feeling feeling. I went through all that. I was pregnant at fourteen, and my mother made me have an abortion. I had two more abortions on my own, God forgive me. I also had a baby when I was in graduate school. I know what the girls feel like, but this melancholy isn't just feelings. It's deeper, more about the meaning of everything."

"More like a God thing," he said. *A God thing.* Good Lord. He was flattered to be in her confidence, but she did not answer. "You need somebody you can talk to," he added lamely.

"You're who I need to talk to. You know me."

"I knew you briefly," he said. "Very briefly."

She laughed with such a pure delight that it stunned him.

"That ship has sailed! So long ago now." She looked into his eyes. "It's been confessed and forgiven. But that's the mystery of it, isn't it? I feel bound to you. When I'm in trouble, I feel myself turn to you." She let out a long breath. "It's like you're this little island of sanity and common sense. What's going on around us in the culture feels like a plague a lot worse than Covid."

He must have looked perplexed.

"I mean once these ideas get into your system, they make *your own body* a matter of discernment. *Oh my gosh, was I born the right sex?* I'm sick to death of discernment. All the good young Catholics I know—even Deirdre and Jordan. Always *discerning* whether they should take this job or that, or see this boyfriend or wait for some other guy, or go in a convent. Taking themselves so seriously, you know? At least they want to do God's will. But these girls who decide they're really men or vice versa? Why would you even raise the question? *Are you really a girl?* I can't imagine. With my body?" She gestured with both hands. "Or my mama? Good Lord. The whole emphasis seems like a made-up problem, but now it's everywhere, which says more about the power of suggestion than it does about the psychology of gender. Where do they get the idea that happiness has to originate in what they want? Where do they—well, anyway, Chick, it's like St. Paul says, all creation groans in the pangs of childbirth—something these girls will find out about sooner rather than later."

Chick stared at his hands resolutely. "I guess so," he said.

"Excuse me for a minute, Chick. I need to do my rounds and check on everybody. I'll be back."

He watched her walk away. No, the question of whether she was really a girl would never come up.

He had never told Patricia about that night with Hermia, though she intuited how much she attracted him. He was a little nervous even to be seen with her, even here, even by her own women. To his knowledge, there had been no rumors about what had happened years before—how would anybody know?—but on the other hand, Hermia Watson was lovely, a word he didn't use much, and the town's suspicion was—speaking of viruses—always viral. What puzzled him was the deep change he felt in her, simply being in her presence. Even a few years ago, there had been something unpredictable about her. She did not really know who she was, and she was liable to do anything by way of experiment, such as that time she had slept in the house out at Missy's Garden and claimed to have seen Miss Z herself, Zilpha Graves, in some kind of guided dream. Strange stuff, disquieting, that struck him as dangerous, like something you'd find in shady neighborhoods of Atlanta or the purple house outside of Macon advertising a fortuneteller.

But there was nothing of that feeling about her now. Just being around her, he felt understood, as though she could see directly into his anxieties and uncertainties and somehow bring him into the live presence of Jesus, who could heal what was wrong with his soul.

His soul. Sometimes he would lie in bed at night with his eyes closed and try to understand what people meant by the word "soul." When he was a boy, he had imagined it as something like the black box on an airplane that God would pluck out of the corpse to read the record of how you had done on the Ten Commandments checklist. Now, he thought of his soul as where he was, in this floating and flowing he couldn't pin down physically, a live unstopping inner tangle of feelings and moods and comments (*whoa nice butt look at this dork stop judging judge not lest are my pants zipped up my god she saw me*). Other people could talk to "Chick Lee" every day, but he never got to see the whole Chick Lee they saw, the one spilling a Slurpee on a stack of invoices, or brushing sweet roll crumbs into the trashcan from the front of his shirt while he muttered *dumbass* to himself, or hitching up his pants because he didn't have enough butt left to hold them up.

Everybody else could see him, but nobody else had Chick Lee's soul. His soul.

Did people think he was smart? Not really. Sharp? Nah. But he could think well enough—do a quick click-click-click about whether to fire Joe Ashburn or think about options at a meeting (should Lee Ford invest in electric cars?) and look at numbers and do calculations and bet on consequences. Some of the guys who worked for him got there quicker. He should study math again. Do math problems. The brain was like a muscle, they said. Do algebra: x = something something.

A headache started up just above his ear.

"Are you okay?" Hermia asked, touching his arm.

"I was thinking about my soul."

Hermia looked at him seriously and steadily. "Oh, Chick."

"Is that stupid?"

"Not at all. It's not exactly something you can catch in a net and hold up for everybody to see, is it?"

"Hermia," he said, "what did—I mean how did you—"

He fell silent.

"How did I change?" Hermia said. "I knew I couldn't get a prescription for what was the matter with me. I asked myself some questions, and then I tried to be quiet enough to hear the answers. I knocked and waited for the door to be opened."

"Like what questions?"

"Like what it might mean for my soul to be *saved*. What in the world might that mean?"

Driving back to the dealership, he kept thinking about it. *There's a difference between a soul and an immortal soul,* a visiting preacher from Atlanta once told him. *The word for soul in Latin is the root of the word animal. If something's animated, it can move by itself, which means it has a soul.*

A mosquito? Chick asked him. A spider?

You've been slapping souls on your neck your whole life. The soul is the form that animates the body.

So some really fat woman in stretch pants? You're looking at her soul?

In a way, of course you are. That's why you judge her, isn't it? Because she lets herself look like that? Her soul is what she is. If her soul were healthy, wouldn't her looks change? She could shine. When she dies, her soul leaves the body it formed and what used to be alive starts to decay.

I thought DNA gave you the form of your body, Chick said.

You shed DNA all the time, Mr. Lee. The police could get it from the fork you used at breakfast. You know those ancestry tests? They get DNA from a sample of your spit.

Chick thought about Roof's coffee can swarming with tobacco-smelling DNA.

DNA is just a polymer that follows the soul's instructions, like a blueprint you get from the architect. After you die and your soul is long gone, you're still full of DNA. They got it from the Romanovs a hundred years after they died.

What would it mean to save his soul? God help him.

9

BEAN BELAY

GUIZAC SAT DRUMMING HIS FINGERS ON HIS DESK. HE HAD thousands of words to write for the next edition of *Sage Grouse*, and he could not get a sentence out. Sometimes he would kickstart a column or a dialogue by talking into his digital recorder. Not today. What was the matter with him? He stared out at the parking lot at the back of the Grove Building and over the nearby houses to the Winds in the distance. A depression as dark as anything he remembered was gaining inside him, as though he had come downstairs one morning to find black flood water rising through his house. No way to get out except by wading into the flood itself.

Maybe the depression wasn't so mysterious. Maybe it came from his sense of national unmooring, the complete absence of common understanding between believers in traditional institutions and people who scorned the natural sexes and promoted queerness and transgenderism and redefined marriage and insured the murderous dismemberment of unborn babies as a fundamental right. Or was he depressed because the one standing up to these radicals and their destruction of the family was the nation's greatest vulgarian, the P. T. Barnum of politics, Donald Trump, the sight and sound of whom instantly repelled him? Right, maybe it was Trump and the election. If not the endless circus of Trump, then Joe Biden, who had conceded to every extreme of idiocy to get the nomination but whose real platform found its footing entirely in one thing: not being Donald Trump. Biden would be elected and undo what Trump had done and then die in office. Or he would succumb to dementia.

Then came Kamala Harris.

The noble American experiment in liberty was over. Its lingering death might take some decades longer, until the Chinese came and Americans betrayed each other and became as dead-eyed as the Hungarians after 1956 when the Soviets tanks rolled in. So was that what depressed him? Coming world calamity? Or was it personal grievance at the shape of his life? He would be an old man at the end of a long corridor, fumbling with the key at the lock of a room of ghosts, all of them seated like patients in a waiting room. Was it the idea that death would come before he had accomplished some fine, true thing? He had never written anything worthy of his talents, but he had long ago begun to feel that it made no difference *what* he did. He would die and be forgotten, and no one would remember him. Why was that? Because he had never risked himself enough to love without selfishness and share the whole of what he had been given. His heart was always pinched with the fear of hurt, the terror of love. He thought suddenly about his mother, who had abandoned him. He thought about his foolishness with Nora O'Hearn years ago, or worse, worse, with Lydia Downs. The death of his son Walter. His heart ached with a regret too complex to fathom. Now there was nothing ahead. Day after day, month after month, the long path to the grave with time ever diminishing, no freshness any way he looked, no happiness, no consolation from God, nothing but dull dread.

He knew he should see someone. He felt a momentary dislocation at the thought—trying to explain himself to some jargony stranger like the woman in Jackson they had taken Jacob to see. Or suppose there actually was someone who could help, someone whose wise and sympathetic eyes could look into his and find the field of affect that made him Karl Guizac or Walter Peach and reveal—just suppose—that this morose, hopeless Guizac was not who he really was at all. Even at the thought, something shifted again. Suppose the tension in his back went away and he could be grateful, even for one unclouded hour, for the life he had been granted, for his wonderful wife and his children and his near-fame. Suppose he could step out of his deadening habits into the exact same life he was already living, as if emerging from the shell of an inner chrysalis. Maybe he would taste the omelet Teresa made instead of just ingesting protein. Be present to her and to Jacob and Marisa. Maybe time itself would open.

Outside, a horn blasted so loudly it startled Guizac up from his desk: a jacked-up red pickup rumbled in the lane that took bank customers into the drive-through canopy. Ahead of the pickup was a battered car, and Guizac saw an old, broad-faced woman, maybe Shoshone, hold her left hand out the window and shake it up and down, as if the irate man behind her had been saying hello. She must have been there for a while. She placidly pushed the button and leaned out to talk to the teller inside. The red pickup—it had one of those freeway blaster horns—shook the glass in the office window with three extended blasts. No effect. The driver, a huge, red-bearded, red-faced, red-capped man (all different shades), opened his door and shouted something, but the old woman did not budge. Guizac laughed out loud. Red slammed his door, peeled backward out of the lane, squealed through a tight turnaround, and careened out into the street, nearly hitting a parked car, and gave the whole of Monday morning a big red finger as he roared onto Third.

Excellent.

His laptop was charged. Guizac put it under his arm, locked his office, and walked through the hallway to the front stairs in the glassed foyer and down to Main Street. Years ago when he ran the *Gallatin Tribune*, he had discovered that he could concentrate best when he had more distractions to tune out—noisy anonymous conversations, background music, constant motion, interesting places for his eye to alight without commitment. Dunx was full of Transfiguration students and professors he might know, so he would work in the coffee shop a block down the street. Waiting at the light to cross Third, he saw the old Shoshone woman's car coming slowly out of the bank at last and turning south. Across the intersection on the other side of Main, a student on a skateboard hopped deftly up onto the curb and with a quick foot flipped his board up into his hand, all one smooth motion. The day was brightening. It was cold as rip. He could feel Socrates Johnson beginning to stir at last.

Bells jingled when he pushed open the door of Bean Belay—wood floors, brick walls, a ceiling of pressed tin. The place was almost empty, the tables spaced farther apart than usual. One of the masked employees looked up at him from the counter.

"Sir, please wear a mask," she called, so he dug his black thing out of his pocket. As he was hooking it over his ear, he saw a glorious mass of thick blonde hair—Emily Turnbow, unmasked, with a coffee mug and the ruins of a muffin in front of her, talking earnestly to another girl at the only other occupied table. Glancing up, Emily saw him and her face changed. She held up a hand to pause whatever the other girl was saying and stood from her chair.

"Mr. Guizac!" she called, sounding amazed and sarcastic at the same time.

"You caught me," he smiled. He finished putting on his mask as he found an empty table and set his laptop down. Emily followed him.

"I've been worried about Jacob. Is he okay?"

"I just saw him running."

"Isabel and I were wondering about him," she said with a nod back at her friend, a pretty girl with Asian features who gave Guizac a quick wave.

"He's neck-deep in the Sherman project," Guizac said. "Can I buy you some coffee? Or a scone?"

"Thanks, I'm okay," she said, staying with him as he walked over to order. He felt a little flattered to be the object of her interest.

"Yes sir?" said the masked woman behind the plexiglass shield.

"A large drip, dark roast, with cream." They had to put in the cream these days. "And a strawberry scone," he said, tapping on the display. As she rang him up, he turned to Emily. "No, Jacob's fine. He was writing all weekend. I know he sent Forrest something."

Her quick hazel eyes met his forthrightly.

"He didn't say anything about the other night?"

"Not to me."

"He blanked out," she said, lowering her voice. "I don't mean fainted, I mean just zoned out for like five minutes."

He had just been thinking about the psychologist in Jackson. When the woman behind the counter set his scone on the counter, he turned with it and nodded to his table.

"Can you sit down a minute?"

She nodded and went with him and sat down.

"Sir?" called the girl at the counter. "You forgot your coffee."

Smiling, Emily went to retrieve it for him, setting it down and tucking her legs under her on the chair across from him.

"So we were at the Granite Gill Friday night," she said, "and Jacob was talking about Sherman being in Georgia twenty years before the war and, right in the middle of a sentence, he went blank. Like somebody pulled the plug. Like I wasn't there. He told me something like this used to happen?" Emily said.

"You couldn't get his attention?"

"I waved my hand in front of his eyes like you do for a joke if somebody starts daydreaming, but he didn't see me at all. He didn't hear anything I said. I started to panic, and some of my friends came over and it scared them, too, so they got the manager and we were about to call 911 when one of my friends tried dipping his fingers in some ice water and throwing it in his face. That woke him up mad. He had no idea any time had passed."

Guizac lifted his head and looked at the ceiling, letting out a long sigh. Everything had seemed so easy with the boy for so long. So uncomplicated.

"I thought I should tell you," she said.

He met her earnest gaze. She was so present—the thick blonde hair, the Mediterranean complexion, the expressive mouth, the absorbing eyes. He saw what his son loved. There was a kind of knowingness about her that did not make her seem bad or insinuating but just older than she was, as though she could see clearly into unstated motives and the ironies of situations, including her own youth and his age. She seemed like a witty rejoinder to the culture, a comic heroine from one of those comedies from the 1930s, a Rosalind Russell or Claudia Colbert. And something about her, something golden, reminded him of Nora O'Hearn. A small, forlorn longing guttered in his heart.

"Call him if you're worried about him."

"No phones in the Civil War," she said drolly.

She went back to her table. A moment later, she and her friend gathered their things and waved to him as they left.

He and Teresa thought the boy's strangeness years ago owed to what happened at Stonewall Hill when the mad Josiah Simms tracked them down. But this project seemed to be causing a relapse—the pressure of total immersion in the topic, the effort to get so much done so quickly because of Forrest's deadline.

His phone buzzed and danced on the tabletop. Speak of the devil.

"Guizac," he said laconically.

—Did the boy give you the Sherman chapter?

"My God, Braxton, it's already Monday, and I'm spinning my wheels this morning trying to get something written for the next issue. But look, I just found out from his girlfriend—"

—Emily? That's the girlfriend? What are you doing with her?

"She was in the coffee shop where I'm trying to work. She said Jacob had an episode—blanked out, like after we left Gallatin and moved to De Smet. I think this project is too much, Braxton."

—Sed contra, I think we're seeing something extraordinary. Buford told me he had *flashes* where he saw things. Not like he imagined them, but *saw* them. He even got defensive about it. I almost believe him. You need to read what he wrote.

"I'll read it tonight," he said. "I'll talk to you later. Let me get some writing done."

—Call me when you've read it. Oh, speaking of Sherman, you might want to check out what Zitek's trying to foist on Atlanta now. It's on the *Phoe* website.

"This is the magazine you sued?"

—Threatened to sue.

Alone for the moment, Guizac opened his laptop and checked *Phoe*. Zitek was arguing that Atlanta had rightly removed the slaveowner Lee, and now it should complete the symbolism by commissioning and erecting a new statue of Sherman in front of City Hall on the site of the house where he stayed in Atlanta. He should be honored for liberating the city and baptizing it by fire. The comments—most of them centering on what Sherman had liberated (silver, hams, chickens)—were amusing, but Guizac didn't have time—unless he could throw in a quip about Zitek's proposal on *Sage Grouse*. He had nothing for the next issue.

The website of the *Star-Bulletin* sometimes sparked a sardonic thought or two. One of the headlines caught his eye: Central Montana Catholic College CFO Accused of Fraud. Lyle Post, a man with an MBA from the University of Southern California, had a private side business, a fledgling distillery that he converted to the manufacture of hand sanitizer at the urging of the government. The Paycheck Protection Program was pouring money into businesses claiming to be having trouble meeting payroll because of Covid-19. With one or two people putzing around in a rented space with a little equipment, this enterprising fellow had represented himself to the Montana Business Council, which administered the funds, as a rapidly growing business with over 100 employees, and they had given him just short of a million dollars before they found out the truth from a local man astonished at Post's brazenness. The MBC obviously wanted the money back.

Meanwhile, the man had disappeared, much to the embarrassment of the college, which had also received major funds legitimately (they hoped) through Post's application for the PPP. The Board of Directors had unanimously approved Post's application for the money because of the unexpected shortfall, and the infusion from the PPP was a lifesaver, because the students had been sent home in mid-March, which meant that two months' of housing revenue had to be refunded. The same thing had happened at Transfiguration, Guizac understood; Post's fraud was undoubtedly the tip of the iceberg nationwide.

How could he write about it? Covid had not just interrupted the normal flow of things, it had somehow derailed people's common sense, as though reality itself had been suspended. People like Post quietly went mad with greed. For others, radicals of various sorts, it seemed like the revolutionary moment. When else would the unfortunate George Floyd episode have exploded into the apocalyptic condemnation of "whiteness" as the cause of all evil? Most unreal of all was the passion of an election between two irascible old men, neither of whom seemed to be entirely sane, much less competent.

By the time the bells on the door jingled again—several wiry Planetary Outreach instructors in masks—he was already in a zone.

BUCKY: GOOOOD morning, all you folks listening in your cars and cozy kitchens, this is the Bucky Whittlebone Morning Show and we're tickled to have as our guest the one and only Socrates Johnson, the Sage Grouse his own self. Welcome back, Socrates.

SOCRATES: Always good to wake up in the morning, Bucky.

BUCKY: Amen to that. Let's get down to business. Here we are a week out from the big vote. The liberal media's gushing over Basement Biden and Multi-Kamala and they don't give the Donald a snowball's chance in a banana republic. Good day to be a snowball in Wyoming, though, you ask me. I'm reading a clean -5 on my outdoor thermometer this October Monday morning.

SOCRATES: It's a bit nippy, now that you mention it. Probably should have worn a jacket. But look, it ain't no question Trump wins in the Cowboy State, but it gets better: all them pollsters are about to look like the last roundup of dodos, just like in the days of Hillary.

BUCKY: Trump wins!

SOCRATES: Whoa, whoa, whoa. Sit down now, Bucky. That's embarrassing.

BUCKY: My heart's doing a bronco.

SOCRATES: Sorry to say it, but it ain't no way. No way he wins. Not this time. It's going to yank down their britches how many votes he gets, but big media and big tech ain't letting him win.

BUCKY: They can't stop him if he gets the votes! How 'bout the Electoral College?

SOCRATES: I know you're just messing with me. Look at the Democrats and COVID-19. They got all them absentee ballots stockpiled to prevent the spread of Donald. And more to come if they need more in the swing states. They're just waiting to see how many it might be. And listen, this here's just a sidenote, but they can make up voters on demand. You don't have to prove who you are and whether you voted already, which it's racist to ask for.

BUCKY: What are you saying, Socrates? Just spell it out for the folks out there hanging on your every word.

SOCRATES: I'm saying get used to the idea of Joe Biden—but not too used to him. Kamala's in the dressing room.

Guizac looked up from his laptop as the bells jingled again. This time one of the new Transfiguration professors, a small, ironic-looking man in his thirties, came in with several older students. They masked on command and queued up to place their orders, spacing themselves on the Xs on the floor with exacting impiety.

He smiled at them and read back over the dialogue. Not his best. He had wanted to say something about the PPP loans but hadn't figured out how to work it in. It would play well enough in Wyoming. The true gauge was whether it would infuriate the Outreach table across the room. He imagined one of them reading it aloud. *Multi-Kamala! What's that supposed to mean?*

The problem was, Guizac loathed Donald Trump almost as much as they did. The idea of another four years of TrumpTrumpTrump made him want to walk into the creek below his house and descend to the secret caves of ice he had invented in his stories for Little M. But the Democrats just made his stomach clench. Biden and crew opposed everything Guizac believed in, which meant that he had to vote—again—for the Clown Prince of American history. Or not vote at all. Or write in a third-party candidate. Or ignore the presidential part and fill out only the bottom of the ballot, like friends of his had done for the last four elections.

The depression came back, heavy and wasting. It wasn't just Trump and Biden. Or *those people*, as Lee used to call the Yankees—the table of Outreachers, their blithe righteousness, their earnest willingness to chastise the incorrectness of others. Hatred boiled up in him. He closed his eyes, listening to the clatter of mugs and the hum of voices and laughter in the room. He breathed in slowly. He was in a bad way. He needed to talk to somebody. Maybe a priest. Maybe the chaplain at Transfiguration, a short, canny man on loan from a diocese in the Midwest. Would Fr. Isaias Peterson actually be able to order the mess that was Karl Guizac? Fr. Peterson was used to negotiating endlessly between the mostly legitimate claims of tradition in the college liturgies and the edicts of the local bishop, a coldly bureaucratic Pope Francis man. But how would he deal with a middle-aged anomaly who did not think Jesus worried much about how many candlesticks were on the altar? What would he do with this late, lukewarm convert, the melancholy scion of righteous 1970s educational radicals, inadvertent murderers, who had shaped him to be the poster child of the new age of liberation and then abandoned him?

Was it a matter of talking something out? Mostly, he was just a sinner. Confession would be good, taking God's side against himself and doing it from the heart and receiving absolution. But if he had to make special arrangements to see Fr. Peterson, he would lose his anonymity, even if he kneeled on the other side of a screen.

His phone juddered again on the tabletop. A Georgia number he did not recognize.

"Hello?" he said roughly.

—Walter? a woman said.

"I used to be," he sighed. "Who's this?"

—I'm not in the address book on your phone? It's Hermia.

Hermia Watson! Good God, why in the world would she be calling him? Possibilities raced through his mind—something had happened to the house or she had heard something about Rose or someone had turned up from the cartel that the Moccasin had run or she had found something his family had left behind—

"Hermia," he said.

—Walter, have you heard what's going on here at Stonewall Hill?

"You're running some kind of home for girls?" Walter said. "There's even a rumor you got religion."

—Got religion! she laughed, and it was a beautiful, clear, clean laugh, without irony or resentment in it. I had forgotten people said that! It's so wonderfully dismissive.

He listened to her merriment and glanced around the coffee shop. The Outreachers were just getting up to leave. One of them saw Peach and tilted his head and started walking over, a short, thick, broad-shouldered, blond-bearded man with a big earring in his left ear and a little Viking hatchet supplanting his right eyebrow.

"Just a minute, Hermia," Peach said. He muted the phone and looked up at the approaching man.

"Aren't you Karl Guizac? The man who writes *Sage Grouse*?"

"I am," he said.

The man extended his hand—but then withdrew it.

"Whoops, forgot about Covid," he said. "Listen, I'm on the other team, and I might have to shoot you when the war comes, but I have to tell you, I'm a fan of Socrates Johnson."

"Thanks," Peach nodded, holding the phone near his ear to show the man that he was in a conversation.

"I mean, Bucky Whittlebone!" said the Viking. "And Wyatt the post-transgender cowboy. Love it, man. And *The Evolution of Elitist Equality*. Man, you got me. I tried to order it on Amazon before I realized you made it up. The book and the girl who reviewed it."

He bumped his fist lightly on the table and pointed his forefinger before walking back to his friends. Several of them looked back at Guizac, shaking their heads at the Viking as they exited into the cold.

"Hermia," he said. "Sorry."

—No, that's okay, she said. I'm interrupting you. He could hear someone singing behind her. Listen, Walter, I just wanted to let you know what's going on. Has Braxton told you anything?

"Not much," he said. His laptop screen went to sleep, and when he tapped the touchpad to bring it back, it wanted him to reenter his password. "Hold on a second," he said and put down the phone and did it. "Okay, sorry again."

—It's just Gallatin, she said. People don't like that we're here. They think it's going to ruin the town to have us taking care of girls who got themselves pregnant.

Guizac sighed. De Smet and Gallatin were alike, good and bad, and a pregnancy center was just the kind of thing that would put some people off.

"What do you need me to do?"

—I'm not sure exactly. I don't know—we're all tied up with the fate of this place, all of us. This plantation house that somehow survived Sherman's March and outlasted the Forrest family. I think of all the things that happened here, you know? I've written books about people who lived in this very place.

Peach did not know what to say. What was she getting at?

—We had a bomb threat, she said.

He sat up in his chair, remembering the moment years ago when a gunman hiding in the old barn at Stonewall Hill had tried to kill him.

"My God, take it seriously!" he said.

—I do. I don't know whether to try to take all the girls somewhere else. I told Braxton about it, and I'm sorry to burden you, but I thought I should let you know. You and your family are part of our daily prayers.

"Thank you."

—Could you give my love to Buford? she said. He is such a prince. She laughed. I almost said 'such a peach.'

"He's Jacob now," Peach said.

—A wrestler?

"He runs cross-country."

—No, I meant his name. Jacob wrestling the angel? I got religion, remember? She laughed again with that joyful merriment he had heard earlier, a sound he would never have associated with Hermia Watson. But then she sighed. God help us, Walter.

"Amen."

—Don't forget about us down here in Gallatin. Pray for us.

She ended the call.

The coffee shop was almost empty, and a masked employee was clearing the tables, disinfecting them, dropping trash into the receptacles. Peach stared at what he had written so far. Socrates Johnson. But what about an editorial? A satire about fraud when the government was throwing out money like beads at Mardi Gras. Or another piece—maybe a satire of Planetary Outreach?

The ideas refused to get any traction. The Viking's compliments confused him.

No use. He closed his laptop.

He might as well read Jacob's manuscript.

10

SINNER

HE HIT HIS STRIDE HALF A MILE OR SO INTO THE RUN. THE cold bit into any exposed skin and burned in his lungs, harsh and good. He settled into the rhythm. At first his mind was clear, and he meant to go all the way to the Transfiguration campus to try to catch Emily before her first class, but as he topped the hill just before town, mistrust came over him. What if he got there and surprised her leaning toward some senior boy across a table at Dunx? What if somebody pointed and she looked out the window and saw Jacob Guizac standing there in the street staring at her stupidly? What if her mouth did a little pitying sideways pinch and she shook her head at him? *Seriously, Jacob?* He was already fading into a nuisance, an embarrassment. He was that boy she had liked in the summer. The one still in high school who had developed a weird obsession with the Civil War and Willam Tecumseh Sherman. The one who had gone into some kind of trance at the Granite Gill and embarrassed her in front of her friends.

He turned around when he got a few blocks down Tyler Street, not even stopping to walk, and then pushed himself on the way back, trying to burn off a hurt that had not even happened. His face was numb, and his hands ached even with mittens on, but the layers wicked the sweat away from his body. Thank God the wind wasn't blowing. He started praying the prayer his mother always said, timing it to his steps and his breath. *Lord Jesus Christ, Son of God, have mercy on me, a sinner.*

He had been so sure of Emily. Now he felt cast out. Wailing and gnashing his teeth in the outer darkness, hitting the sounds in his stride—*sin-ner, sin-ner.*

Sinner is all you are. You do the wrong thing. You *are* the wrong thing, always in the wrong, always turned away from the goodness you never reach. Never worthy of the beauty poured out on you, the love given so freely, the encouragement. That's why you needed the hope of salvation. Faith in God gave you inner joy. He would sometimes feel it so powerfully his whole body was on fire with it.

But not now. Not doubting Emily.

Just this morning he had read about Fr. Thomas Sherman, the great general's Jesuit son, who had been committed to an insane asylum when he was the age of Jacob's father. "Repeated confessions but no peace," he wrote at one point. "No hope whatever of eternal salvation."

His father sometimes had felt the joy of salvation, but not very often, he thought. But suppose you were William Tecumseh Sherman and couldn't feel it at all, not ever? And didn't want it. Sherman would never say *Lord Jesus Christ, Son of God, have mercy on me, a sinner.* Mercy felt to him like an inner concession that would erase his dignity. Ellen Ewing was always urging Sherman to reach out to God, but he wouldn't. He refused to think of himself as a sinner. He hated being urged to pray. He was always trying to get rid of the sense of sin. Sherman's real sin was not being born a Ewing and a Catholic, and even though he had been adopted into that house, he could never *convert* into what he had already been denied by birth. He could never be saved from being born a Sherman and not a Ewing, so he did not want to be saved.

Was that it? Or was it that he hated the obligation for gratitude that came with being saved, as he was saved as a child by the Ewings when his father died? He wanted to eradicate *the obligation to be saved.* He wanted to make desolation righteous.

Sin-ner. Sin-ner.

Snow was heavy on the peaks of the Winds beyond the foothills.

He sprinted the last hundred yards and stopped just short of the garage, panting hard, walking a few feet back up the gravel drive as he caught his breath. Immediately, the cold bore in upon him. He turned and opened the door into the garage. His mom's Honda was there, but his dad had taken the Subaru. He walked back and forth in the slightly warmer air in the semi-darkness of the empty bay. His breath plumed even indoors. After a minute or two of stretching, he caught up an armload of firewood from the stack he had made earlier and opened the inner door into the hallway that led to the living room and the wood stove. Warmth encompassed him.

"Jacob?" his mother called as soon as she heard him.

"Yes, ma'am?"

"You survived."

"Yes ma'am."

The phone vibrated in his hip pocket. He dropped the logs into the firewood box next to the stove, glanced at his phone—a local number—and went to his bedroom. His mother had her drawing pencils out on the kitchen table. She watched him all the way until he finally met her eyes. She mouthed *Emily?* He shrugged and shut the door.

"Jacob?"

Emily.

He envisioned her mouth the instant she said his name. She must be at her parents' house.

—Why are you breathing so hard? Emily said. You must be really nervous.

He smiled.

"What if I just got back from a run?"

—In this cold?

"You sound like my mother. Sorry about the other night. I embarrassed you."

—Are you okay? I've been so worried about you I could hardly write my paper. I just saw your dad.

"My dad! Where?"

—At Bean Belay.

"What was he doing there?"

—Writing, I think. I told him I was worried about you.

"Look, I'm okay."

—You scared me, Jacob. And the way you went after Daniel.

"I know, I'm sorry. I was kind of Sherman. I'll apologize to him. I wrote it out over the weekend and sent it to Professor Forrest this morning." She did not answer. "Look, I know you're sick of Sherman," he said. "Sick of me talking about him."

—I'm worried about you. Will you send me what you wrote? I need to understand what you're thinking about.

"You don't have time to—"

—Send it to me. I want to read it.

"Okay, I'll send it right now," he said. He put the phone on speaker and sat down at his laptop, attached the file to an email, and sent it, with a tremor of foreboding. "You should see it now."

A pause, the faint click of keys.

—I see it. I'll read it right now. Maybe we can go for a ride this afternoon. Can you get the car? I need to see you.

At three o'clock, he picked her up outside Dunx. The Subaru his father had bought a few years ago had a good heater to recommend it. When Emily got in, hooded and shivering in her winter coat, she said hello formally, without smiling, and dropped her backpack onto the floorboard between her feet.

"You read it," he said.

She nodded and looked ahead through the windshield, not at him. He dreaded what she would say. He drove up the hill, through the traffic lights, past the church. As they passed the city limits on the way south out of town, he glanced over at her profile.

"You're killing me," he said.

They drove past ramshackle homesteads of scattered trailers on one side and neat ranch houses on the other. Sagebrush prairies stretched east to the limestone ridges, herds of cattle to the west. They passed a frozen pond, an RV park. Emily gazed out, still saying nothing. They passed the intersection where the U.S. highway branched off toward Muddy Gap. They climbed gradually toward South Pass where the Wind River Mountains angled down and tapered out into the Red Desert of south-central Wyoming. Ridges blocked their view to the west as they went up the grades and around the long curves, but then the road took a long swing eastward, the ridges dropped away, and Red Canyon opened out to their right. Beside the road, the windsock had stiffened to an animated horizontal. Sudden gusts shouldered the car sideways as they climbed around the bend.

At the top was an overlook where they could see all the way back north up the canyon. Jacob pulled the front of the car all the way against the barrier, and they sat gazing at the miles of exposed red rock on the eastern side, the river glimmering under a new glaze of ice along the bottom, bordered by trees. Beyond the vast upward slope of the foothills to the west, far to the north, rose a range of mountains—not the Winds, maybe the Owl Creek range north of Shoshoni.

It was too cold to get out, too cold to turn off the engine, so they sat leaning forward a little, as the wind howled and shook them. Emily sat against the far door like a hostage.

"Why did you write that?" she said at last. "What does that have to do with being a general in the Civil War?"

"A lot. This is just the first part that sets up what's coming," Jacob said. She shook her head, but at least she turned to look at him. "I'm trying to get into his character. And that's what happened Friday night, like this is what I *saw*, not like I made it up, but—"

"I feel like I need to go to confession! You don't *know* Sherman was like that. I don't care what you say, you *are* making him up, so it must be because he's what *you'd* like to be. And you're making up Lucette. Do you want to tell me why Lucette is blonde? I don't know what to think. I know I'm not *Lucette*," she said with biting scorn.

"No, Emily, look, please." How could he explain it to her? Why *was* Lucette blonde?

"How about I read you something, okay?" She gave him a hot glance and bent down to unzip her backpack. Out of it she took the printout of his chapter. She flipped through it. "Here's Lucette for their *third time*, if I'm keeping up, this time against a tree: 'She did not pretend weakness or submission but met him with forthright avidity, her body young and strong, strength matching strength, her head thrown back, mouth open, thick blonde hair speckled with bits of leaf and curls of bark. His dryad.' Wow, what about that, Jacob? Remember how you brushed stuff out of my thick blonde hair after we were lying there watching the stars on the Fourth of July. Remember that? How about you show this to your mother? What would she think of me? What does *Professor Forrest* think of me?"

"It's just—I don't know, it's just what I—"

"Is that what you want from me? You want me to be Lucette?"

"No. God, no. Just Emily. Just Emily Turnbow."

"But you imagine Lucette. You have to imagine her. You're Sherman with Lucette, aren't you? You have to be."

"But this is separate from us. It's my assignment. It's about someone who's not me and not you."

"But it *is* me and it *is* you." Suddenly she was across the seat, her arms around him, sobbing into his neck. "Do you know what I felt like when I read it?"

She wiped her tears with her thumb and then wiped his and licked the salt of them. He held the wealth of her hair in his hands, the incredible harvest of her, pushing the fall of it aside to reveal her face, her wet lashes, kissing the softness of her skin just below her ear, taking in the smell of her, her self, her soul, stirred by the closeness of her body almost beyond bearing.

She mumbled something.

"What?" he said, pulling away a little.

"I said you're a lunatic. I think I should be locked up just for kissing you. You're not even eighteen."

"Almost," he said. "Next week."

She kissed him.

After a moment, she started laughing and he started laughing and they had to get out of the car into the cold to stop. He backed her against the door and she hugged him tightly against her and whispered, "God knows I love you."

"My DNA has found a 100% match," he whispered back.

"Where's Lucette when you need her?"

They started laughing again.

"I could die from this," he said.

She held his face in her hands and kissed him and kissed him again.

On the way back into town, Jacob told her that he had a week left, and then he would be done with Sherman.

"I've read enough," he said. "I just need to write all day and get to a hundred pages."

"Do you have a safe space?"

"What do you mean?"

"For your wacko trances?"

"Maybe my parents can chain me in my room."

"You know what you need to write, though?"

"The Battle of Kennesaw Mountain, the death of McPherson, and the beginning of the March to the Sea. Something about Willie."

"Who's Willie?"

"Sherman's first son, his favorite child. He died of yellow fever when Sherman's family came down to Mississippi after the Yankees won at Vicksburg. Sherman blamed himself for bringing them down there. Some people think he went insane afterward and that he burned the South as revenge for losing Willie."

"Do you think that's true?"

"Not the way they mean it. But it's not untrue."

He fell silent.

"Jacob!" she said loudly, nudging him.

"What?" he said, tapping the brakes, alarmed that she had seen something ahead in the road.

"Don't start thinking about Willie right now, okay?"

He glanced at her. Her mouth tucked at the corner.

"Right," he said.

"And let me know if Lucette turns up. I need to talk to her."

"I'm not in charge."

"Okay, Jacob, who is?"

He met her eyes, stung by the seriousness of the question. "Somebody else. Not Professor Forrest."

"Sherman maybe? Like he's been summoned back from the dead?"

He shivered.

"I hope not. I don't know."

11

ELECTION EVE

From: Emily Turnbow
Mon, Nov. 2, 2020, 8:37 PM (3 minutes ago)
To: me

Dr. Weald gave me a B on my *Odyssey* paper. I just couldn't get into it. Things are weird here. The first case of Covid on campus showed up yesterday. Everybody heard about it right after Mass. Now two of the guys who work in the kitchen have it, which means if it spreads, which it will, we might have classes canceled or go remote or whatever. I hate this. It's been a week since I saw you.

A guy in my section says the Democrats made up Covid to get rid of Trump. Is that insane or what? He says they figured out how to steal the election with mail-in ballots. Here's the problem: my dad says the same thing. What does your dad think?

You hope I'm going to say I think about you all the time, but maybe it's William Tecumseh Sherman I miss the most. I'd love to see Jacob in person just to check. How does tomorrow look? Election Day! Tell me you finished this thing.

Emily

From: Jacob Guizac
Nov. 2, 2020, 8:41 PM (0 minutes ago)
To: Emily Turnbow

I didn't finish. It's not over. I'm going crazy. I'm going to write all night but even if I write 200 pages I don't see how to finish. I might never finish. What if I get trapped in Sherman and it never ends?

   Jacob

From: Emily Turnbow
Mon, Nov. 2, 2020, 8:41 PM (0 minutes ago)
To: me

   I hate Sherman.

From: Jacob Guizac
Nov. 2, 2020, 8:42 PM (0 minutes ago)
To: Emily Turnbow

   Just don't hate me.

12

PREDAWN, ELECTION DAY

GUIZAC DID NOT SLEEP WELL, AND HE WAS ALREADY HALF-awake at four-thirty a.m. when his iPhone started its wake-up music. He rolled sideways and felt for it on the bedside table and touched the button. He might as well get up. He would get his coffee and sketch in some thoughts for *Sage Grouse*. Teresa was snoring lightly and he did not want to wake her. He quietly put his sleeping shorts in the dresser drawer in the dark and stepped over to feel for the pile of clothes he left every night outside the closet door: jeans on top, pullover sweater beneath it, slippers on the bottom. He dressed noiselessly and felt his way to the bathroom door.

When he came out, an unfamiliar angle of light fell on the dark living room from Jacob's open door. The boy must have fallen asleep finishing his paper—or novel, whatever it was—on Sherman. Thank God it was over and Jacob could move on to something entirely different—math, probably. Sherman had consumed the boy's life. He got into everything, including Guizac himself. Snatches of his dream returned: Braxton Forrest complaining loudly about the burning of Atlanta to a group of sullen people with Biden signs in the school gym at Bridger County High School, which was set up for voting. (He had to go vote, he remembered.) Someone behind Forrest was trying to control an elephant that was lurching around, knocking over tables and whole rows of booths. Men in jackets with Lion's Club patches were patiently following it, scooping up its massive poop with grain shovels and filling wheelbarrows with it and scattering sawdust across the linoleum floor.

He stepped in to turn off Jacob's lamp and stopped, surprised to find Jacob hunched over his laptop, surrounded by the books that Guizac had found himself pushing aside or picking up from the floor for weeks—biographies by Marszalek, O'Connell, Feldman, and McDonough, thick histories of the Atlanta campaign and the March to the Sea, Shelby Foote's massive trilogy, a book about Sherman's Indian wars in the West.

"Jacob," he said, and the boy started violently and whirled to look over his shoulder. His eyes were exhausted. "So you never even went to bed. I thought it was due yesterday."

The boy looked at him with an expression of such distance that a chill went up Guizac's back. The spells again, full force, brought on by this assignment.

"McPherson," the boy said.

McPherson? That would be Gen. James McPherson, the favorite of Sherman, killed in the Battle of Atlanta. Guizac remembered the story vaguely from many years before. Something about Sherman directing the battle, weeping, with the dead body of his friend laid out on a door across two sawhorses.

"You're just at McPherson?"

"I haven't written it yet."

What did that mean? Guizac sighed and shook his head. "Go to sleep, son," he said. "Oh—and happy birthday. Eighteen's a big one. We'll do something tonight."

He closed the door and felt his way toward the kitchen in the sudden dark, not used to the angle. When his thigh collided hard with the back edge of the sofa, he cursed softly. In the kitchen the blue light of the coffeemaker guided him as the coffee sputtered and hissed and trickled into the pot. He always set the timer the night before, much to the scorn of Rose, his Manhattan sophisticate of a daughter. Every morning when she was home, she performed coffee rituals more elaborate than Teresa's daily Yirgacheffe. *You don't want it just to be a habit*, Rose would say officiously. *Habit kills experience.* But Guizac was all about habit. He remembered a woman from Atlanta, some kind of designer or therapist or both who had come to Stonewall Hill. A friend of Hermia's before her conversion.

When you inhabit, *Walter, habits fold you* in. *To have habits makes a place your own. You in-habit it, you* habituate *yourself into it, so it becomes a* nest *of praxis as much your nature as your breath or your heartbeat.*

The way she said *fold* and *habit* and *nest* with her hands. *Praxis?* So earnest, so inhuman.

Guizac poured his first cup and sipped it, then opened the drawer beneath the coffeemaker, shook out an omeprazole and swallowed it with another sip of coffee, then put back the bottles and closed the drawer.

Trump was going to lose. He could do another Socrates Johnson dialogue, but he needed some hard news that made sense of things people worried about—the effects of the pandemic on the election, maybe. The Wind River Reservation had been hit hardest by Covid, so what about the vote out there? He suspected it usually went Democratic. He should check the history and then see how Trump did this time. Maybe drive out to Fort Washakie or Ethete, find one of the elders and—

"Dad?"

The coffee mug leapt and splashed scalding coffee over his hand.

"God—*dammit!*" he cried. The boy stood there barefooted, bleary. Guizac set the mug down and turned on the cold water to hold his hand under the tap. "Give me a little warning, okay?"

"Sorry."

"Sorry for cussing."

Guizac sopped up the spill with a paper towel. He fished a crescent of ice from the ice maker in the freezer and held it to the burn between his thumb and forefinger.

"I'm printing out what I finished so far," the boy said. "Can you read it?"

"Maybe tonight."

"Not now?"

"*Now?* I've got to figure out my Election Day stories."

"It won't take you long. Twenty minutes maybe. It's printing out in your office. If you read it, that can be my birthday present."

"What's so urgent?"

"I feel like—I don't know, like I need a year, a thousand pages. Like I can't say what I need to."

"Which would be what?"

"Like Sherman is the harbinger of Auschwitz and Hiroshima and the Gulag."

"Oh, come on. You sound like Lucinda Devereux."

"I need to know what you think."

"Do you want me to talk to Forrest about giving you an extension?"

"I don't know whether it's even for him anymore. It's like its own thing now."

"I have Abel Johannsen set up to start math with you next week."

"Dad, I can't!" The boy's hands clasped over his head. "Maybe after Christmas."

Guizac touched the boy's forehead with his forefinger.

"Don't lose it, okay? Get some sleep."

. . . .

He took a fresh cup of coffee into his home office. The boy's paper lay in the tray of the printer. "Big Shanty." Eight single-spaced pages. He sighed, already regretting the time it would take to read it. From a glance at the first paragraph, it looked like the earlier piece on Sherman in Marietta, which he had finally read at Forrest's insistence. That one had worried him. This was what his son thought Sherman was like? Gamboling on Kennesaw with a French girl? Jacob claimed these images were not made up, but given to him, more or less. It seemed to Guizac a way of thinking about Emily Turnbow, but Jacob claimed that it was Sherman. It was true that Sherman was consuming him.

At least it wasn't Trump. Suppose he gave his heart and soul over to the Donald? Millions of people loved the man. What was going to happen when Trump lost?

This was the day.

He had a vague notion of what to write. Bad things were afoot. A foot. Biden was an empty sock. He imagined a cartoon of an empty sock labeled JOE BIDEN with all these feet trying to slide him on. A rainbow of feet.

The country's leftward turn felt bogus to him, an illusion generated by the media. The insistence on gender issues, the hardening of racial divisions. Defunding the police? Seriously? All playacting until the murders started piling up. People were sick of Trump, but Guizac did not believe the American people would give pure insanity a mandate. Reality would out, but how long would it take?

He glanced at the clock. 4:53. Did he really need to be up so early? The voting at the high school didn't start for more than two hours. He picked up Jacob's Sherman. He could read it quickly before he started his morning prayers.

13

SHERMAN AT BIG SHANTY

IT RAINED FOR THE FIRST HALF OF JUNE, A STEADY, DRENCH-ing rain that turned every road to red mud and made the soldiers curse the war and the South and especially Joe Johnston's Confederates. The Rebs had retreated steadily through the woods and gullies, never on the run. Johnston had prepared defensive positions all the way back to Atlanta. His men could dig a trench and get inside it like those little clams at the beach that could disappear under the sand while you looked at them.

Whenever Sherman found a dry spot to stand, sometimes on a porch, sometimes in a depot, he gathered his officers to plan their next movement. His maps and papers clung together, moldy as grave clothes. On and on it rained. The men hunkered down miserably, the disconsolate horses hung their heads, the cooking fires sputtered on wet wood, the mess tents filled with smoke, the muddy red creeks and rivers rose.

Sherman felt his melancholy returning. It was the worst since Memphis. During the days, he rode as the rain pounded down, water streaming from his hat and his greatcoat as he checked the lines, urging on the soldiers. Johnston's sixty thousand men, spread thin across a ten-mile front, occupied fortified lines on the last ridges between the Union Army and the Chattahoochee River. Sherman remembered the terrain from his weekend explorations twenty years before. From the heights of Kennesaw and Pine Mountain, the Rebs could see every Union movement and anticipate the flanking maneuvers that had kept them moving backward all the way down from Chattanooga without a decisive battle.

He was so exhausted, he knew he would soon begin to make mistakes that he could not afford. His temper flared up easily. Another sleepless night in the tent would turn him into a tyrant. As the long Monday waned, he told his men to find a dry house for him to use that night, and they led him to a white two-story off a road near the rail stop at Big Shanty. It might have been in Ohio, except for the shabbiness. The small barn was already crowded with men. A weedy vegetable garden had a few bean stalks, a few scrawny squash plants. A cow stood morosely under the downpour near an empty chicken run. The oak tree in the yard—a schoolroom chair was tipped back against the trunk—would be good for shade if the sun ever came out again. Beyond the back fence, a field of laden cotton stalks slumped under the rain. Several of his soldiers had already spotted a gin house with a tin roof a hundred yards or so away, another dry place out of the rain.

Sherman gave his horse to his orderly and stepped up onto the porch while the sergeant pounded on the door. An old house slave in a collarless white shirt answered the knock, and behind him came a short, square white man loosening his bib. The negro stepped aside when he saw the uniforms, but the white man blocked the threshold like Horatius at the bridge.

"How can I help you, sir?" he demanded of the sergeant.

"Hard to say for sure unless you get out of the way."

"What do you people want?"

Sherman came up the steps and pushed past the owner and stood inside, dripping onto the hardwood floor as his men followed him in. The man's nose wrinkled, and even the slave put a hand to his face. Sherman supposed they all stank. They were a sorry-looking lot, no question. Their boots tracked up the floor with red clay as they crowded in.

"What do you want, sir?" the man demanded again, standing in front of Sherman, irate as a terrier.

"Your house," Sherman said. He wiped his feet on a rug in the foyer, scraping the side of his boot against the leg of a tea table, and flung the water from his hat.

"My house?" the man sputtered. Two more slaves—a boy about Willie's age and a huge woman—hovered with the old one on the far side of the parlor, watching Sherman and his men.

"Get out of the way," Sherman said, pushing past him, already pacing nervously, a hand in his hair, as he thought about the ragged disposition of his army and what they would do when the rain ended. He glimpsed his own lined and weary sharp-nosed face in a mirror and spun irritably back toward the owner. "Maybe we won't burn it down when we leave. How about that? Maybe this rain will save you. Who's got a dry cigar?" He frowned at the orderly who had showed up a day or two earlier, sent down from Chattanooga. Harvard boy, couldn't be more than eighteen. "You find any cigars? What's your name again?"

"Private Hayes, sir," he said, stiffening into a salute. "No, sir."

"Who these people, Massa?" the old slave interrupted. "What they wants?"

"These," said Massa, "are the goddamn Yankees."

The slave's face lightened.

"Naw, now. These is?"

"Show *Massa* out, Private Hayes," Sherman said. "Shoot him if he gives you any trouble."

"Yes, sir." Hayes opened a hand to show the master into the kitchen, but the man spat on the floor, and the Irish sergeant—Kelly or Sullivan or Logan—slammed "Massa's" head with the heel of his hand and shoved him staggering into the kitchen.

"The country needs your house, sir," called Sherman.

"It's not my goddamned country!" the man said.

The sergeant yanked open the back door and pushed the man down the back stoop into the downpour, where he got his footing and spun back around and scrambled into the threshold. He glared back at Sherman and his men.

"Damn you! You have no right!" He tented his eyes with his hands as rain from the roof battered his head. "I'm glad my wife is not alive to see her home treated this way."

The sergeant raised his rifle to hit him, but Sherman barked, "Let him in!"

He stood in the kitchen as the man came up out of the rain, dripping, water pooling on the floor in the lantern light.

"You want rights?" Sherman said irritably. "All you people have to do is acknowledge the Union, and you'll have all the rights you want. You ought to be glad we don't hang every goddamn one of you rebels."

"Unalienable rights, given by God!"

"Where's He been? Looks like He'd give you a little help," said Sherman.

"Blasphemer!"

"What the hell you stay here for, Reb?" said one of the soldiers, prodding him back toward the door. "You known we was coming."

"To protect my property!" the man said, looking around for the slaves who hung back in the parlor. "You niggers goddamn better be here when I get back!" he called. "You hear me, Leah?"

The sergeant shoved the man backwards, and this time he lost his footing, missed the stoop, and fell pinwheeling onto his back in the mud as the door slammed. The sergeant turned to the others. "You hear me, Leah?" he mocked.

Laughter broke out.

"All in all," Sherman said, "a sour exit."

"How come y'all run off Massa?" the old slave asked plaintively when Sherman went back to the parlor. One of the men had come up with a cigar for him, and he lit it from the lamp.

"Cause they's come to set us free," the boy said.

"Hear that, Uncle Billy?" one of his men said to Sherman. "You see this man right here?" he said to the boy, pointing to Sherman. "This man right here is General Sherman."

The slaves stepped back as if a lightning bolt had struck the ground in front of them.

"Thy Kingdom come!" the woman cried. "Lemme die, Lord! I done seen thy salvation." Her body trembled with the fervor of it. Her arms out toward Sherman, she fell suddenly to her knees and the glasses and plates rattled in a china cabinet across the room. A fine old vase on top of a bookcase tottered dangerously before a soldier caught it, grinned, and dropped it himself. It shattered across the hardwood as the woman swayed and moaned.

"What do you want me to do with these people, General Sherman?" Hayes asked.

Sherman put the cigar in his teeth and took off his wet greatcoat to hand it to him, shaking out his shirt sleeves.

"Hush now!" he said sharply to the slaves. "You, what's your name? Leah? You hush."

The woman's voice dropped away, but she still knelt, swaying, humming.

"Here I am, Jesus," she said, reaching forward to touch his muddy feet. The Irish sergeant crossed himself like one of his own timid little Catholics. Pious Tommy.

"Stand up," snapped Sherman. "Get me some hot supper and show me a dry bed."

"Come now, Uncle Billy, have a bit of joy with us," said the sergeant, wagging a bottle he had pulled from his jacket.

"Boys, there's a lot of fighting ahead of us, and I need a night's sleep. Take your liquor and your noise somewhere else. I mean it. I'll shoot anybody who wakes me up. And take this goddamn cigar—who gave me this thing? It tastes like hay with shit in it."

The men grumbled and shuffled out onto the porch, where he heard them hooting at the owner, who must have been lurking about.

Sherman ate the supper intended for the man they had thrown out in the rain—chicken, black-eyed peas, collard greens, and cornbread. Leah was a good cook. After dinner, she called the boy, who must have been her son, and told him to take the General upstairs to the owner's bedroom. The boy made a production of getting Sherman upstairs and showing him all the amenities of the room.

"Where y'all keep the freed folks at?" he asked Sherman shyly. "Y'all gone take us to the city with the streets of gold?"

Sherman looked at the boy and shook his head.

"What's your name?"

"Name Zeblun."

"Zebulun?"

"Yes sir."

"Where do you get these notions about a city of gold, Zebulun?" he asked roughly.

"Mama tell me," said the boy.

All across Mississippi and Alabama and Tennessee, the questions had been the same. Every goddamn one of them thought Sherman was the Messiah.

What did people expect after filling the niggers' heads with biblical fantasies instead of solid counsel?

"Is that old man your daddy?"

"Naw." The boy grinned and shook his head.

"How about you leave me that candle?" said Sherman. "I need to get my sleep."

Reluctantly, the boy left the candle. When Sherman did not hear footsteps going down the stairs, he flung open the door. "Scat!" The boy stood there stricken. "I walked to the devil in hell, you hear me? You can smell the smoke on my clothes."

The boy ran this time.

And all these abolitionists in the North kept pressing him to make them soldiers! They were good for digging trenches, but the more of them he gathered, the more they clogged the efforts of his army. The War was about the Union, and Lincoln had confused the issue with the Emancipation Proclamation. To the abolitionists, Sherman's victories were about Glory Hallelujah instead of forcing the rebel states back into the Union. That goddamn starry-eyed song. What he saw was death and dispirited men and threatened supply lines and endless rain and mud.

Alone for the first time in days, he sat down in a worn armchair to pull off his boots and socks, then he took off his wet uniform and draped it on a hat rack in the inward corner of the room. He dried himself with the towel that Leah had sent up and opened the netting over the bed and lay down naked, pulling the net as tight as he could at the corners. Two or three mosquitoes were already inside it with him. He lay still, sweating, drawing their fire. When they alighted, he flattened them against his skin, one on his stomach, another on the meat of his thigh. Was that all of them? He lay still. After a moment, another one buzzed around his head and he waited until it sat down on his forehead and then slapped himself and examined the bloody splay of its body in his palm.

God, he needed to sleep. The great, steady purpose that kept him riding the lines, checking his men, turning every effort toward the one end of military victory—that had not deserted him, but seeing the nigger boy brought back an old, familiar melancholy. Melancholy and responsibility and solitude. So much depended on him alone. 100,000 men, rail lines stretching back through perilous territory all the way to the bountiful supplies of the North. Nathan Bedford Forrest out there somewhere, a ghost, a demon.

Goddamn that stupid Sturgis. Brice's Crossing was an immortal victory for Forrest. He could not have warned Sturgis any more explicitly about the danger that Forrest posed. He remembered what he had seen after Shiloh, when he was following the Confederates supposedly retreating toward Corinth, and he had spotted Forrest's horsemen across some fallen timber. Seeing the Union advance, Forrest had not stopped to calculate the odds but had charged with his men, surprising Sherman's infantry and scattering the cowardly bastards in every direction. Far outstripping the other horsemen, Forrest had plunged among the Union soldiers alone, slashing in every direction with his sword like Coriolanus in the city of Corioles: "from face to foot / He was a thing of blood, whose every motion / Was timed with dying cries." Sherman was within a few feet of him. If Forrest had recognized him, he could have killed Sherman on the spot, but neither man knew at the time who the other was. He supposed he ought to thank God that he had survived. Ellen would say so but believing in God was what lulled you into complacency, tricked you into thinking that all was well, that you were protected, as he had in his camp along the Big Black River with his family all around him. Just then, this God of Ellen's had struck him down with Willie's disease and death.

God was like Forrest, retreating, disappearing, never being where you expected him, never reliably containable as the churches made you believe he was supposed to be. Forrest was the bold spirit that moved where it willed. Abolitionists said he was an evil slave trader and that God would curb him because his cause was evil. But suppose he was God's inscrutable will. He could fight like a demon and devils, too, took orders from God. That day after Shiloh, Sherman had seen a soldier hold up his rifle to Forrest's body and shoot the man point-blank, and the bullet had not even unhorsed him. Like Sherman, Forrest did not care about political causes. Real soldiers did not worry about slavery or states' rights one way or the other. They cared about winning. It was simple, as Sherman had written to Halleck: to have any claim over the Confederate states, the Union had to win the war, and to win the war, the Union had to do whatever winning required. That meant inflicting greater and greater suffering upon the whole population of the South until the war became unbearable. That meant he had to become a demon himself. Or the angel of death.

But it was not simple, was it? Not with somebody as bold as Forrest somewhere in his rear or on his flank. Even when he could sleep, he woke up thinking about Forrest suddenly appearing, harassing him, threatening his supplies. Sherman had no one like Forrest. True, he had that randy blowhard Kilpatrick and he would use him to his advantage, but the South had these young bloods, the most dangerous set of men that this war had turned loose upon the world. Splendid riders, first-rate shots, and utterly reckless. And Forrest was loose in his rear, thanks to Sturgis, who had asked to be relieved of duty. Granted, sir. Granted. Go home and tend your cucumbers.

The shadows of the bedposts angled sharply across the ceiling and the walls. The rain had picked back up in intensity. The air was heavy and hot. Maybe he could open the window just a crack and not get wet. He parted the net and pulled up the sash half an inch and lay back down. There was no movement, not even enough to make the candle flicker, though the flame had already drawn a moth that flung its darkness wildly around the room. The corners of the vanity across the room shone in the candlelight, the hand mirror and brushes abandoned there by the owner's late wife.

If he had been a praying man, he would have begged for some kind of breeze. He could smell the owner's sour-salty stink on the pillow—but what was the man's name? There was a Bible on the bedside table. He rolled over and reached through the net for it and found the family register inside and held it up to the candlelight. *Josiah Winston McPhee* was carefully inscribed next to the date March 4, 1844, when he had married *Henrietta Patience Sides*. Under "Children's Names" were listed seven, the four born between 1846 and 1854 all with "dec'd" next to them within the same two weeks of October of 1855 when their mother also died. Some disease that took them all. A pang of unaccustomed pity went through him. *What, all my pretty chickens and their dam / At one fell swoop?* He thought of Lincoln repeating the lines to him when they met—when was that? Early in the war, shortly after the disaster at Bull Run. He did not remember how Shakespeare had come up. It was before Lincoln's own Willie died, before either of them knew what it was to lose a child. Ellen would say it gave them both something in common with God, but he denied it. He stood with Lear over the body of Cordelia: "Thou'lt come no more, / Never, never, never, never, never."

He closed the book and blew out the candle and lay back down, thinking of McPhee's face in the doorway before the sergeant kicked him into the rain. The man had lost everything and now he was cast into the outer darkness Sherman had heard so much about from Mrs. Ewing. Even now, Sherman could hear McPhee out there. Here he was in the man's dry bed, while the man himself was out in the soaking rain, wailing and gnashing his teeth, as the Bible had it. But this was war, and war was hell, and hell was what the Old Governor must be saving up for Sherman, too, when the General got through playing God Almighty to the slaves he freed in Dixieland.

The boy had grinned when Sherman asked him if the old man was his father. *Naw.* Sherman saw it now. The old nigger was his grandfather. The boy got his light complexion from McPhee himself. From McPhee *owning* Leah in those lonely days after his wife died. All that big warm nigger body. Sherman knew he might have done the same thing. Leah bowing to him, *prostrating* herself. He could own her right now. If he called downstairs for Leah, she would come up and do his bidding and think she was the bride of Jesus. He would disappear into her like a blueberry into pancake batter.

Not Leah. But by God, a woman would be sweet. He knew his men were having their way with the slave women they freed, so why shouldn't he?

Maybe one a little more comely than Leah.

Outside, the rain fell as though some rip had opened in the old biblical firmament. He thought of his wet army, sodden and morose under the dripping trees, the heavy red clay sucking at their boots, discoloring leather and cloth and skin. Johnston had pulled back steadily, first from Dalton, then from Allatoona, and now to the triangle of Kennesaw Mountain, Pine Mountain, and Lost Mountain around Marietta. It was the missed chance at Resaca that still enraged him. McPherson had flanked Johnston at Dalton, swinging farther to the west than the Confederates anticipated, and he had been within a mile of the railroad at Resaca when he ran into a few thousand Rebs and thought that Johnston would come down from Dalton and cut him off. He'd followed the textbook, but if he had just pressed forward when he had the strength of surprise, he could have prevented Johnston's retreat by straddling the railroad in his rear as the rest of the Army pressed forward to annihilate the Confederate army. It would have been a superb victory.

Well, Mac, he had told McPherson, *you have missed the great opportunity of your life.*

He twisted in the hot bed. The goddamn waste of it since, the lost men. The delay was endangering Lincoln's presidency and the whole war effort. Mac was a spirited man and the soldier Sherman most loved of all his men, and he had defended himself, explaining his vulnerability, reminding Sherman of the discretionary orders, but he was *wrong*, goddamn it, he was *wrong* and he would know it eventually. Already he was ashamed for disappointing Sherman. Behind that shame lay the shadow of being the one hosting Willie in Mississippi when the boy fell ill. Willie had loved the man, but Ellen would never forget that the fever first struck the boy at McPherson's headquarters. Willie had been his true son. If there was a heaven, Willie would see McPherson there, General Mr. Mac, as he called him, who had always been his favorite among the officers. Up in paradise, where the waves move slowly through the silvery grasses in the sigh of the wind, Mac would spot Willie in the shade of the trees across the high mountain meadows. *Capt. Willie Sherman, is it?* Mac would call out, and Willie would wave and smile, and Mac would ride up with that erect posture that always thrilled the boy, his horse parting the grasses, and he would give Willie a sharp salute as though he were a full-fledged soldier.

McPherson had been on the Union right all the way down from Chattanooga, and now his orders were to cross behind Schofield and Thomas to take the Union left in front of Kennesaw Mountain. Give him a chance for redemption. Get some speed back into this great army with all its equipment and men, this huge and momentous thing stuck at the plodding pace of George Thomas. What was it he had written Grant? That Thomas would stop and dig in if he encountered a furrow? He smiled at the image. But he needed to get this army moving like a cat, make it give a good convincing feint. Sherman had trained the railroad teams like crack regiments. They could restore bridges and rails before the men had time to miss a meal. And by God, he was in charge of it all. It was what he had always longed for, a great decisive action that would carry him out of the shadow of the Ewings and into his own fame after years of failure. Stalled in California during the Mexican

War—and worse than that, playing the banker in San Francisco, weakened by asthma, harried by Ellen's endless longing for home, her exasperating piety and prudishness. The bank failures, the vigilantes. Those nights of gasping for breath, falling into hideous nightmares. Now he had the chance to do something on a scale not one of his old West Point classmates could have imagined. All his intelligence and experience, all his will and ambition, coming to focus on one thing.

Outdoors, the downpour made another long and slow crescendo. God Almighty was at it again, pouring upon him this weather he could do nothing about. Mired down wheel and foot and hoof, unable to move. If there were men shouting and singing in the barn, he would never hear them.

He remembered how he had listened for the children those days in San Francisco when Willie was a year old. 1855, the year McPhee's family died. When Ellen left him with the children. He had let her go home, not sorry to see her leave. It had maddened him how peevish she was, so chary of herself. He got mortally sick of it. He had his appetites, and by God, her priests could be eunuchs, but he would do what nature asked of him. If Ellen wouldn't accommodate him, there were plenty of women in San Francisco who would. An image came back to him from decades before, that girl on Kennesaw Mountain—what was her name? Lucy? Some French amateur artist visiting a relative in Marietta. Some kind of female sans culotte. *Lucette*. He would never take seriously a woman so easy with herself, but why couldn't Ellen be a little gamesome instead of whispering prayers in Latin when he inflicted himself on her? A little hint of relish, a little sweetness? The pleasure of it bothered her to distraction. She was always thinking of being safely back with her father in Lancaster. The God she prayed to was Thomas Ewing on High, whose claims on her were mighty and triumphant. That summer of 1855 she just left him, left him with all the small children and went back home while he was running a bank in a hard time. Just left him with the children and the asthma that almost killed him in those smoky rooms, that foggy city.

But William Tecumseh Sherman, not Thomas Ewing, was forging his immortality from the smoke and ruins of the Confederacy. Thomas Ewing had never led a great army deep into enemy territory. Thomas Ewing and all his bluster would be forgotten. Or there would be a picture of his stolid frown in Sherman's biography. The stern father forbidding the young lovers to marry.

Not that Ellen was such a prize.

Sherman smiled and stirred beneath the netting. Why not send down for Leah?

That huge mound of flesh sweating and slippery and crying out *Jesus* in this heat.

Maybe not.

He remembered the woman Ellen had hired to help him in San Francisco. He had stopped in the doorway of the laundry room to watch the sway of her slender body as she ironed. She felt him there and looked over her shoulder, and he told her not to stop and she held the iron in her left hand for a moment and smoothed the linens—strongly, surely—over the board with her right before applying the heat again, aware of him now, and there was a dark flash of knowledge in her eyes when she looked at him again.

What was her name? Gloria something. Not from Mexico. From Cuba.

Gloria Torres. He would whisper *in excelsis* in her ear when he wanted her to come upstairs to him.

Not like Ellen. Not ashamed of herself. Not trying to turn him into Jesus every goddamn minute.

Men's shouts woke him. It was already daylight, and by God, the rain had stopped. He sat up and cleared himself from the netting.

Twenty minutes later, he finished his coffee and Leah's fried eggs with toast and stepped outside onto the porch with the boy Zebulun trailing him, trying to hold his hand. He shooed the boy off.

"Go help your mama."

Near the barn, the Irish sergeant was snapping orders at five or six men surly with the aftermath of their liquor. He called for a horse, and an orderly led over a black mare.

"Better than that one yesterday, I hope," Sherman said.

"Dolly?"

"Give her to some Reb and she'll break his neck for us. Why can't I have a good goddamn horse? What's this one?"

"Don't know. Captured her last night." The boy threw on the blanket and settled the saddle in place, cinching it quickly, then slipped on the bridle as Sherman mounted and handed him the reins. Sherman stood up in the stirrups, looking around the yard and the cotton field for evidence of McPhee. He felt for the man somehow, and he wanted to tip his hat at least. Leah loomed on the porch behind him.

"Amen, hallelujah, Mr. Jesus!" she called.

"He ain't but Uncle Billy," one of the soldiers called back at her, but her humming broke into the balm in Gilead, a fine high soprano that brought back the memory of a slave woman at the tavern in Marietta where he stayed with the Churchills. He listened for a moment and nodded to Leah. The old black man and Zebulun stood in the threshold behind her. All of them waiting for Cump Sherman's Kingdom Come. The army behind him was full of farm boys from the Midwest. They would leave white women alone, mostly, but who knew what lust and meanness might rise up in them when they saw who they were liberating?

"Uncle Billy!" a lieutenant called. "You wanted to see Gen. Howard's lines."

Sherman turned and rode away with him, passing the pickets, finding the soldiers in better spirits just from the fact of not being rained on. Howard joined them. Pine Mountain and Kennesaw were clearly visible where the clouds had lifted away. The position on Pine Mountain could easily be taken if he moved forward and cut it off from the long line of Johnston's troops across the top of Kennesaw.

"They're looking right at you," his lieutenant said. "Some of the Reb brass."

"Bring me those field glasses."

The lieutenant stepped his horse over and leaned from the saddle to hand them to Sherman, who focused on the group gathered in a clearing not half a mile away. The gamecock posture, the insignia. Joe Johnston himself. Maybe the other one peering down at him through his binoculars was Hardee.

"That's pretty goddamn saucy," he said to Howard. "Let's throw a few shots at them."

Howard shouted an order to his battery commanders as Sherman handed off the glasses and rode on down the line into pine woods. A moment later— almost before the men could have heard the order—he heard a Parrott gun and saw the men up in the clearing scatter. He stopped in a spot where he could see through the trees. One of the generals moved off more slowly than the others—that would be the Fighting Bishop, Gen. Leonidas Polk. The man's gait reminded Sherman of Thomas Ewing. Polk had apparently baptized the other generals just last month, if the intelligence was right. Johnston, Hardee, and John Bell Hood. Holy boys of the Rebellion. How the hell they had all escaped getting their sins washed away until now baffled him. Mrs. Ewing had made sure a priest baptized him before she would let him into the house at nine years old.

A second shot came from Howard's battery. A third. Quickly done. He wondered if Leatherbreeches Dilger was doing the shooting, that white-shirted dandy of a Prussian artillerist. Up on Pine Mountain, Polk had disappeared. Crouching men ran toward where Sherman had last seen him.

Wait. He held his horse still and stared out through the opening in the pines, hardly breathing, as the lieutenant went on ahead of him. A cool breeze was blowing, a light rain had started back up, drops gathered and swelled with light on the tips of the pine needles that framed a stretch of corn and cotton, ragged woods, and the rise of Pine Mountain half a mile away, where men were acting out a scene of terrible dismay.

His heart surged with a strange and dizzying elation. They had killed the Bishop! Goddamn it, that had to be what it was. The clouds drifted into tatters as Polk's old God retreated, mortally wounded, giving over the promised land of cotton to the swarms from the North who would bring a terrible affliction.

Sherman's bones burned like coals poured down a cliff face in the cool night air. He lifted his face to feel the fine stinging rain, but it did not cool him. He could smell the fire to come.

He turned his horse roughly. He had strayed off the path. He pushed through a thicket of undergrowth, twisting to avoid the limbs, and came out sideways into a small clearing. He bent over to clear some torn brush from his stirrup as his horse stepped forward, and when he sat back up, he recoiled in horror. *Good God.* Just in front of him, a foot away, a bloated face stuck out a thickened tongue. Dead eyes bulged at him. Josiah McPhee, whose bed he had taken, hung, rotating slowly, from a limb overhead.

Had his men done this? No. McPhee must have ridden an animal and then kicked it away. His hands and feet were free.

14

THE RESERVATION

GUIZAC READ THROUGH "BIG SHANTY" IN TWENTY MINUTES. How did the boy know Sherman so well? Better than he knew his own father. Better than his own father knew him.

It was only 5:15. He should say his prayers and have coffee with Teresa and get his shower and then make himself something good for breakfast, maybe scrambled eggs and sausage and toast. Or maybe it made more sense to get breakfast at the Golden Bridle and take the political temperature of the farmers and ranchers. He imagined round-faced Everett Hames with his afflicted complexion and his suspenders and his huge stomach and his way of panting before he could start pushing his finger into Guizac's sternum. *Them crossover—Democrats—are gonna*—long wheeze—*STEAL the*—pant—*goddamn election.*

A long wheeze of his own caught in his chest and turned into violent coughing. He had to stand up and walk it off, leaning against the doorjamb, before he got his breath back. Maybe he should get tested when he went into town. He should collect his thoughts first. He pulled up the scriptures for the day from the USCCB website. Philippians. "Rather, he emptied himself, taking the form of a slave." He thought of Leah in Jacob's story. Not the form St. Paul meant.

Emptied himself. That was the hardest thing for Guizac. He said a few short prayers distractedly, thinking of the election. Pulled his mind back. No, just rote. Not getting any purchase.

Too much else on his mind.

And it was getting hard to breathe.

He decided what he could do for his election coverage. He'd go in and vote as soon as the booths opened at seven. Maybe go by the clinic and get tested if there wasn't too much of a line, and then he could visit the other polling places in the county. Drive out to the reservation to see how things were going there. Get Socrates Johnson to interview one of the old guys sitting out in the front yard of one of those tract houses on the reservation.

SOCRATES: So Mr. Whitefeather, how's Trump going to do on the Rez?

WHITEFEATHER: Who?

SOCRATES: Donald Trump. The president.

Whitefeather leans and spits next to his shoe and then raises his face with a complete absence of expression. Socrates wonders how somebody can do that.

WHITEFEATHER: I thought he got the Covid or something.

SOCRATES: Well, he bounced right back. Says he took medicine his own government won't let you take. Ivanamectin or some such. I tell you what, the buzzards were circling.

WHITEFEATHER: You ain't got the Covid, do you? How come you coughing?

SOCRATES [*changing the subject*]: Did you know the Sand Creek Massacre was the same month as Sherman's March to the Sea?

As he drove into town, he pulled off once in a fit of coughing that racked his lungs and left him feeling weak. When it finally ended, the ridges of the sand hills north of town were just reddening in the early light. It was a clear day after the hard freeze of the week before. For most of October, smoke had drifted eastward from the whole drought-afflicted West—rivers shrinking, lakes drying up, flames gorging on deadfall, uncontained wildfires in California and Idaho and Nevada and Montana. The pall had hidden the Winds and the Tetons.

But now it had blown away. Clear Wyoming air.

People would get out to vote, he suspected, because everyone saw this day as a continental divide in American history. Trump more or less intolerably stood for some of the right things whereas soggy old Joe Biden would promote

GLENN ARBERY

any insane and inhuman agenda of the Democrats if his people told him it would get him elected. He didn't need to court AOC and the other radicals. A toadstool couldn't help getting elected if somebody ran it against Donald Trump. Or a monogrammed sock. He wished he could draw that cartoon.

Why was it—he could feel a column coming—you could immediately picture analogues of Trump throughout the animal kingdom? Chimp Trump, Blowfish Trump, Frigatebird Trump, Rooster Trump—and yet if he didn't win, what righteous idiocy worse than Trump's would these Democrats let loose upon the nation's schools and hospitals and corporations? He gripped the wheel so hard it hurt his hands.

In the blocks adjacent to the high school, he passed thickets of signs. People were out early. On the sidewalk were outdoor canopies for local candidates. Della Richardson, a plump squarish woman running for County Commissioner, waved at him as if she were homecoming queen, and he waved back smiling. He turned into the crowded parking lot and stood in the line snaking into the gym, not recognizing anybody in the immediate vicinity. A few mothers pushing strollers, comparing their sufferings. Two or three lean and weathered older men in cowboy hats talking quietly. Two blustery younger men with forearms like hams and the bellies of Hawaiian kings. He recognized furious Red from the line at the bank, but it was strange to him that in a small town he had never seen so many of these people.

The line moved quickly into the lobby of the gymnasium where tables were set up with alphabetical signs so voters knew where to sign in. Caroline Stubbs, one of the ladies he knew from his brief membership in Rotary, recognized him and waved him over. She had on a bright pink mask, and she nudged a box of blue paper ones toward him, tilting her head at the sign on the wall behind her. **Please wear a mask.** Guizac picked one up and dutifully hooked the elastic over his ears and adjusted it as she checked the list to find the table for his precinct. She handed him a ballot.

"You can't get Jacob to go back to school?" she said. "Everybody misses him."

"He's doing a project. A hundred-page paper. I just read some of it."

"A hundred pages! On what?"

"Gen. William Tecumseh Sherman."

"I couldn't write a hundred pages to save my life! I bet he wishes he was back in school."

"Hasn't said so."

"Well, this Covid has everything messed up. God knows what's going to happen to us. You haven't had it?"

"Nope, but I'm about ready to get it over with."

He bent over in a fit of coughing that turned all the heads in the vicinity.

"You go get tested!" she said.

He raised his eyebrows, and she waved him uncertainly into the gym.

All over the building, people had on masks—people not so much careful as cowed and fearful before an endlessly hyped disease that ninety-nine per cent of them would live through just fine even if they got it. Numbers were climbing fast in the county, but seriously, he knew people trying so hard to avoid getting it that they ordered food delivered and then had all the packaging disinfected. Six feet distancing, hell—they wouldn't get within twenty feet of you. It made sense if you had Ebola or the Black Plague.

His temples began to throb as he looked across the space. People's heads were bent purposefully as they filled in their ballots at the chest-high upright booths. At the table for his precinct, the owner of a store that sold scopes and binoculars stood with studied offhandedness, as though he were a little ashamed to be caught performing a civic duty.

"Precinct five?" he asked as Guizac approached, lifting his eyebrows slightly and tilting his head.

"Karl Guizac."

He found Guizac's name and checked it off.

"That's right. You do the news thing. The website."

"That's me."

"Always sticking it to somebody. Good job. Too bad we can't vote for mayor out where we live," he said. "Or in the state senate race with Bruss Box against that Outreach nutcase."

"Tweedledum and Tweedledee," Guizac said.

The man eyed him.

"Never mind," Guizac said, and he took his ballot over to a booth and bent his head and disgustedly filled in the empty oblong next to Trump's name with the golf pencil. He recognized a few other names and filled in their little oblongs and then helped elect other Republicans whose mortal existence he had never suspected. He took his ballot back to—what was his name? Cody? No, *Colt*. Colt Stevens. Everybody called him .45.

"Not too much trouble, is it?" said Stevens, who fed Guizac's ballot into his machine. "And people think they have to mail in their votes."

"Seriously? In Bridger County?"

"Nah, out East. Big cities. People claiming they got Covid."

"I hear you."

In the car, he had a coughing fit that left him a little shaken. When it ended, he pulled out of the parking lot and gave Della a big thumbs up that visibly thrilled her. He turned left on 287 and headed north out of town toward Fort Washakie, thinking he would find the reservation's polling place and get a few exit interviews. Maybe they voted at the school out there, too. He secured his iPhone in the holder in the air vent, pressed the button, and asked Siri for directions to the Fort Washakie School. He was still waiting for her to master this difficult assignment when the phone buzzed and he saw Forrest's name.

"Guizac," he said as always.

—What do you make of it?

"Make of what? The moral decline of America?"

—Your son. He emailed me that you were reading the Big Shanty piece he wrote. Seventeen years old.

"Eighteen. It's his birthday today."

—Seriously? I'll have to get him something. But listen, how does he get this point of view? Is it just from reading a stack of biographies and letters in online archives? He gets Sherman's huge ambition playing off this tone of weariness—how the hell does an eighteen-year-old do that? And the nagging resentment against the father-in-law, this Thomas Ewing? The contempt for his wife that he veils from himself a little?

"You should see all the books he's got sitting around here. I trip over a new one every day. You're killing him with this thing, Braxton. Time's up. Call it off."

—Oh, bullshit. I'm not killing him. It's like he's broken open Sherman's identity.

"It's just his imagination."

—It feels true, like he's getting at what it was actually like to be Sherman in those circumstances. The way he thinks about Leah and the boy? The way he kills Polk?

"It's just talent."

—Give him some credit. There's something about it that spooks me a little, to tell you the truth. Like it really is Sherman and not just a guess. I don't think I could write it.

Guizac wanted to change the subject. The piece had shaken him, too, with its sophistication, but he had nothing to say yet about Sherman's thrust into the psyche of the Guizac family.

"Listen, I'm getting close to my turn out here. Before I go, Teresa told me Cate's having trouble?"

—Zitek. What a shithead. I want to go down there and beat him to death with my old Louisville Slugger. It might be worth spending the rest of my life in jail.

Guizac did not answer, remembering that Forrest had killed a man with his bare hands.

—In solitary, Forrest said. I'd get more written.

"Are you writing something?"

—Thinking about America and what it might mean. The heritage of freedom we've forgotten. The emphasis on our differences has made it hard to experience the common good—much less the gameme.

"The good old gameme. I'd forgotten all about that."

—Forgotten the gameme? What kind of friend are you?

"Something about Aeneas and genetics, right?"

—Right. You break the old cultural intactness. You become an undetermined half, like the gamete, ready for a new combination. Where do we see that right now? Instead, we've got two mean old men carping at each other.

"So what's the book going to be?"

—Unsentimental praise for the land and the people. Satirical but also sort of lyrical. Maybe a kind of travel book like *Dead Souls* or *Lolita*.

Lolita was a travel book?

"Don't you need some kind of project like buying and selling dead serfs or hiding the fact that you're Humbert Humbert?"

—A Silicon Valley billionaire's search for a roadside Cinderella of a waitress to marry, a real American girl, something like that. But let's talk business. What are you doing for the election?

"How about I interview a conservative in a blue state about the election—you, for example? What do you think Trump does when he loses?"

Forrest laughed.

—You're the guy with his thumb on the pulse of America.

The guy with his thumb on the pulse of America. How about *the guy with an oximeter on America's bird finger?* How much oxygen still twinkles through the bloodstream of the wheezing republic?

Speaking of wheezing, it was getting harder to breathe. He refused to think the thought that he was supposed to think. The unthinkable thought. No way he would think it. The car in front of him slowed and turned off toward Ethete. He slowed behind it. His head hurt. He stretched his eyes wide open and shook his head. Where did he get a headache at this time of day? He had given up drinking altogether after various failed gestures at moderation. He'd get a headache if he missed his morning coffee.

Think anything but the obvious unthinkable thought.

Glare lanced painfully off the windshields of traffic coming south toward De Smet. He needed some aspirin or ibuprofen. He could stop at the general store on the edge of Fort Washakie to pick up something. Another cup of coffee, a couple of donuts.

Or a couple of *boxes* of donuts so he could offer them to people willing to talk to him after they voted.

A few minutes later, he pulled into the store parking lot. WEAR A MASK OR DON'T COME IN said a hand-lettered sign on the door, so he pulled out the blue paper mask he had worn to vote.

It was busy inside. Glum men in work clothes and various kinds of masks queued up six feet apart at the row of coffee dispensers or grunted at the hot breakfast offerings behind glass near the cashier. Maybe he should get an egg sandwich instead of a donut. His head pounded and his chest hurt. First coffee, which would address most of what was the matter with him, then the aspirin that would cure the rest, then the sandwich. He found the right aisle for coffee and waited his turn behind a massive, round-shouldered man in a dirty gray sweatshirt whose greasy black hair was gathered into a braid as thick and patterned as a rattlesnake.

"I used to have a ponytail," Guizac said, and it sent him into a fit of coughing.

The man finished putting the lid on his coffee before he turned. His round coffee-brown face had a whitish scar that ran from beside his left eye down to his jawline. His black eyes, set close together, took in Guizac.

"You think I have a *ponytail?*" he said in a voice from the River Styx.

Guizac hesitated. "Looks like it to me," he said. "Me, I never had enough to braid."

He stepped past the man to get a medium cup and a paper sleeve.

"Maybe *you* had a ponytail," the man said. He was at least a head taller than Guizac. "My hair is sacred to the Great Spirit of my people."

"Okay," Guizac said, filling his cup, adding cream, stirring it, carefully fitting the plastic lid onto it.

"You show disrespect to my ancestors," the man said loudly, "when you call my hair a ponytail."

He felt the other men in the store turning to look. Guizac's head pounded.

"Listen," he said, not looking up, "speaking of your ancestors, you think they would vote for Joe Biden and Kamala Harris instead of Trump and Pence?" He looked up into the big man's eyes. "Who are you voting for?"

"None of your fucking business."

"What's it like to vote on the reservation? You think it actually counts or is it just a gesture? I mean, everybody's on the government dole, so you have to make sure nobody cuts your pay, right? You're automatically Democratic? But everybody else in Wyoming votes Republican, so what's the point?"

The man stared down at him.

Guizac tried to step around him with his coffee. No luck. He could see the donuts and sandwiches right over there. His head pounded. He was wheezing. No migraine aura, so something else not to be thought. Everything felt a little surreal.

"Where's the aspirin?" he called to the big woman at the cash register.

"Next aisle." Her hand rabbit-hopped in the air. Guizac turned away from Ponytail, but the man crowded him against the coffee counter. His hoodie smelled of sweat and marijuana.

"Leave the man alone, Black Bear!" the woman snapped from behind her mask. A pink mask, he noticed with peculiar focus. A black tribal eagle design on a pink mask. "I don't want no trouble first thing in the morning."

"He disrespected my hair."

"Leave him alone!" she said, slamming the register drawer shut and hurrying down the counter behind the glass cases of food to come out into the store. The other men waiting to pay turned irritably toward the big man.

"Come on, BB, we gotta get to work," one of them complained.

"You hear what he said?" Black Bear rumbled.

"Man, they all think we on the dole."

"And your own mama don't believe in your hair," an older man said. "She told me it ain't helped you get a woman."

The other men whooped, and suddenly the pressure of Black Bear's body was gone.

"Shit, she don't know what my hair gets me," Black Bear said. "I'm just messing with you," he told Guizac, putting a huge hand on his shoulder and giving him a little shake. "We don't get many white men insulting us this early in the morning. So what happened to your ponytail? Man, you don't look so good."

The other men turned back to their own business and the clerk glared over at Black Bear as she rang them up. A strange feverish ambiance grew around Guizac. His head pounded. The whole scene felt dreamlike.

"Hey, buddy, I'm asking what happened to your ponytail?" repeated Black Bear.

"A sniper shot it off."

Black Bear stared down at him and then shook his head and laughed.

"Good one, man. I deserve it." He held out his fist and Guizac bumped it with his.

Black Bear shambled up to the cash register, where he received a stern commentary from the clerk, delivered sotto voce. Meanwhile, Guizac went around to the next aisle and found the medicine. What would be better? Tylenol? Motrin? Bayer? Somehow aspirin seemed like the best option. Twelve aspirin cost five bucks? If you needed them bad enough, you would pay five bucks, you would, and the master elites of convenience-store theory knew it. Just like in airports.

He took the aspirin and coffee up to the counter.

"Sir, I'm sorry about BB," the woman said. She lowered her voice as she added, "He thinks he got magic hair, and he gets sensitive. Is this everything?"

"Could I have one of those sausage and egg sandwiches?"

"Yes sir. This one?" She pointed to one being kept warm inside the glass, and Guizac nodded. She wrapped it and set it next to the coffee and rang him up.

"And a box of donuts?"

"They ain't nothing but powdered. They ain't fresh."

"It's all right." As he handed her his credit card, he added, "Listen." He felt a cough about to start and fought it down. "Listen, I have a website called *Sage Grouse.*"

"You write that? I read it!" she said. "You do the Socrates Johnson thing."

"That's right."

"You must be Mr. Goozac."

"Gweezac," he said.

"Mr. Gweezac. I'm Amy Whiteplume. Pleased to meet you." She exposed her face for a second—a big warm smile—and held out her hand and he shook it. A chill went through him. "Your hand's kind of hot," she said warily. She reached under the counter and brought out a big plastic bottle of sanitizer and squirted her hands, offering it to him. He shook his head. "I hope you ain't getting the Covid. We had lots of folks die out here."

"Seriously?"

"You don't think dying is serious?"

"Sorry," Guizac said. "I hope I'm not getting it. I can't get it because— well, listen, I'm looking for the polling place here in town to do a few—" The cough overcame him and he looked at her as though he had fallen overboard and she were leaning over the side of the boat watching him sink. He bent double before he could stand back up. She stared at him.

"A few interviews," he said at last. "If you could point me in the right direction."

"I'm telling you, you sound like them people who died. You better not be doing interviews this morning." But she pointed out the window. "So people vote over at the school on Ethete Road. You see the turn right over there. You see that?"

"I see it."

"It's about a mile." She handed him the bag and her dark eyes took him in seriously.

"It's Election Day," he said. "I'm a journalist."

"Hold on." She reached under the counter again and came up with a forehead thermometer that she beeped at him. "You're almost 103!" she exclaimed. Before he could move his hand from the counter, she clamped an oximeter on his middle finger. "Stay put a minute."

"Come on, Amy, you ain't a damn nurse," said the next man in line. She ignored him.

"And this says 87! Jesus, Mr. Guizac, you need to get tested and get some medicine. It ain't safe for you to be running around."

"I don't feel that bad."

No way no way no way could he get Covid, not on Election Day. He'd work through it. His head pounded. Another chill shook him.

"You see that?" said the cashier, showing him a second reading. 103.8. "You got somebody I could call? How about Mrs. Guizac? You shouldn't be talking to nobody. You could be spreading it, you hear what I'm saying?"

"I hear you."

"You stay away from those people at the school."

"Yes, ma'am."

Guizac wobbled across the parking lot to his car, feeling her eyes on him. Inside the Outback, he washed down three aspirin with his coffee. He could at least drive past the school to see what kind of turnout there was. When he glanced back at the store, Amy Whiteplume shook her finger at him. She knew what he was thinking. Why did he care what she thought he thought, anyway? People felt entitled to give you advice.

He turned the key and put the car in reverse. His head was spinning a little, the wheeze was worsening, the pounding above his temples continued unabated, and the surreal feeling that had begun with BB spread to the nearby houses across the road—shabby government boxes, all alike, that could have come from a cheap kit.

A shimmer of ominous expectation came from the Winds on the western horizon.

He backed up carefully, watching the display from the rear camera, and when the warning signal beeped urgently, he slammed hard on the brakes. What was it? He could not see anything, but then there was a sharp tap on his window.

Amy Whiteplume. She stood back and took her mask off, pointing at him as he lowered the window.

"You're going to drive over there."

He twisted his mouth noncommittally.

"Give me those keys. What's your wife's number?"

"No ma'am," he said. He pulled the gearshift into drive and headed out of the parking lot. She was standing back there watching him. He glanced left and right and then swerved onto 287 and then turned toward Ethete.

The asphalt twisted up like a Möbius strip as he accelerated. By God, she might be right. Maybe he should not be—a cough yanked his right hand down and the gravel rushed and he was flying and

    he was

    screaming with pain

was being

a different time

carried

Some kind of bed. Strapped. Large shapes. Everything was moving.

    Sirens.

    Where's your mask?

    Why do I need a mask?

    Covid, stupid. We need to get him in isolation.

    What are you going to do about his arm, it's —

    Put him in the —

Mr. Guizac? Mr. Guizac?

    Tell him not to try to talk.

    Don't try to talk.

    His chest felt crushed.

    A sound like the rushing of waters.

    The smell of a woman's perfume.

When he opened his eyes, there were people in surgical masks and gloves leaning over him with their hair covered. He could see their eyes. One of them, a man, said:

Mr. Goozac?

Gweezac, Walter said. He was struggling to breathe.

Mr. Guizac, do you know where you are?

The reservation, he wheezed.

Did any sound come out?

Mr. Guizac, you are in Salt Lake City.

Salt Lake City? He tried to explain that he was on the way to the voting sites on the reservation, but all he heard was a faint wheeze. He could not breathe.

This is an intensive care unit. You have a severe case of Covid-19, and we need to keep you on a ventilator. Do you understand?

Walter wheezed.

Your lungs are some of the worst we've seen. We need to keep you on the ventilator, and that means we need to sedate you. Do you understand?

Where's my wife?

We have to keep you isolated, the man said. Sometimes when we put people under, on the ventilator, they don't come back. Do you understand? We lose about half the people we help this way.

Jesus Christ, Hartwell. Watch your mouth, somebody snapped.

Do you want to make any calls before we sedate you?

Another voice, softer.

Calls?

Or texts, maybe?

You mean—you mean in case I don't—

Well just to say hello, she said.

You mean goodbye? Where's my phone?

Someone handed it to him. Was it charged?

Walter needed to tell Teresa he loved her. Say goodbye to Jacob and to Rose. Jacob? Jacob was his son Buford. And Rose was Magdalena. With a groan of misery, he held the phone up. He always used his voice and then edited the text, but he could hardly breathe, much less dictate anything, and he did not want to try in front of these people leaning over him in their masks.

Privacy?

I'm sorry, Mr. Guizac. We're trying to help you here.

He wrote I love you in a text to Teresa. He did the same with the name that came up as Jacob Guizac, and then the one that was his daughter. This little electric message sent out into somewhere, carried to someone living by someone who might already be dead.

It's time, sir, said another voice, a deeper male one, a man, some kind of assistant.

Who?

I'm your nurse, Amos Littlewalker.

Nurse?

Nurses were women. Women nursed. Teresa nursing their baby was so vivid to him, her full sweet breast and her wet brown nipple and the hungry little mouth of their first son, the boy he—

I'm going to give you something to make you comfortable and help you go to sleep, do you understand?

Understand?

We need to put a tube in your

A tube in your

The man counting five four three two
Into your hands I commend my—

He fought for a long time. They had put a pumpjack out in the north pasture just across the rail fence from his lawn, and he was whacking at the horse, head pumping up and down when his stick got caught in it, and it started yanking him up and down and he was fighting back as hard as he could for a

Mr. Guizac?

Yes.

It was a woman's voice.

You keep fighting the ventilator. We're going to have to give you something to help you stay still. Do you understand?

Stay still?

You're fighting the ventilator. That's why we have to do it. Do you understand, Mr. Guizac?

Five four three two

into your hands

15

OUT OF JUICE

AS SHE SET HER COFFEE CUP IN THE SINK, TERESA GLANCED out through the window at the field of sagebrush past the Russian olives, thinking the movement in the corner of her eye was the usual herd of mule deer. But oh my. A pronghorn so close to the house. He stood profiled in the early sunlight, tan and white against the backdrop of the nearby gravel road and the distant foothills rising a mile or more away, their smooth gray-green inclines broken by oblique ridges and dark stands of juniper. She had drawn them a hundred times, but this animal gathered the landscape. He turned to look directly at her, and she leaned forward, admiring his lovely lines, wondering if she would ever be able to capture that kind of hair-trigger poise.

"Come on, Mommy!" Marisa said impatiently from the hallway to the garage.

The antelope bolted away. Irritated, Teresa glanced at the clock. 8:09. Plenty of time. Preschool was back in session, thank God—half a day, at least. The children had to wear masks and douse their hands with sanitizer coming and going, but it was good to have a few quiet hours. Sometimes the drive back and forth to the church hall on the far side of town was hardly worth the trouble, though, and this felt like one of those days. She needed to vote, which meant dropping off Marisa and driving all the way back across town to the high school. When she got there, she would run into people she knew and have to chat. Getting inside, taking a ballot, standing in the voting booth—all that would take twenty minutes at least, maybe a half hour.

After that, she had to pick up eggs and something for dinner at Safeway. And Jacob's birthday—a cake at least. By the time she drove back home and put everything in the refrigerator, she would have just an hour to get her paper and pencils set up and make a few lines on the paper before she had to drive back in and pick up Marisa.

"Do you have your mask?"

Marisa ran back upstairs.

Walter had been gone when she got up an hour ago. He wanted to write something for *Sage Grouse* about the election, and it seemed to her he was too nervous about it. Last night he had even complained about a headache. Now that people across the country paid attention to what he wrote, he felt a responsibility that probably wasn't good for him. The last thing Socrates Johnson needed was a sense of moral obligation to the American public.

Jacob worried her more than Walter. He waded deeper and deeper into his obsession with Sherman. The project had been due yesterday, but he seemed months away from finishing it. What a way to turn eighteen. She started across the living room toward his door to check on him when Marisa thumped back downstairs waving her mask, a pink thing with a Cheshire cat grin.

"I found it! Let's go!" she said.

"I need to see about Jacob."

"No, Mommy!" Marisa whined desperately, grabbing at Teresa's hand with both of hers and almost yanking her off balance. Teresa turned on her angrily.

"Stop it! What is the matter with you?"

"It's a party day! We get to wear different masks. I want to be Ivanka, and so does Betty Holmes, and there's only one of those. I have to get there first. I don't want to be Melania Trump or Jill Biden or Liz Cheney or that other one, the camel one."

"*Ivanka?* What kind of party is it?"

"A pretend party. Come on, Mommy!"

"Just a second, Marisa Belen!" Teresa snapped. "School doesn't start for another twenty minutes. We have plenty of time."

"Betty's going to get to be Ivanka!"

"I need to check on your brother."

Teresa knocked lightly on Jacob's door and opened it a crack. The boy was sprawled facedown across his bed, sound asleep in his clothes. She eased the door shut and turned to her daughter.

"Okay, let's go," she said, taking the keys from the table in the hallway and jingling them, pretending she was in a big hurry.

A year ago, they had traded in the big Sequoia that Braxton Forrest had bought them when they left Gallatin and they were supposedly in the witness protection program. Walter had a new Outback, and she enjoyed her all-wheel-drive Honda, which they had bought used but in good shape. Good pickup. Sometimes, just to thrill Marisa, she accelerated to seventy on the straight half-mile of Washakie Road before it resumed its curves around the hillsides on the way into town. She did it now. Maybe she could vote and do the shopping after picking up Marisa, but that would mean having her daughter with her in the store—

"Mommy, hurry!" her daughter urged her.

They were just turning onto Tyler from the stop sign at the edge of town. The speed limit was an absurd twenty-five, universally neglected, but lurking down the block was a De Smet police car.

"There's a policeman. Do you see him? When he pulls me over to give me a ticket, you'll be so late, you'll have to be Nancy Pelosi. Or Hillary Clinton!"

"No, Mommy!" She burst into tears.

They made it through town unticketed. As they pulled to a stop beside the entrance to the church hall, Teresa's cell phone rang. She did not recognize the number, but she answered it, waving goodbye to her daughter. The child opened the door, slammed it behind her, bolted toward the school steps, and disappeared inside the building.

"Hello?"

—Mrs. Guizac?

A woman's voice.

"Yes?" Teresa said.

—You're married to Mr. Guizac who does the website, the *Sage Grouse*?

A disgruntled reader. That's why Walter was nervous.

"Yes. Who's this please?" she said coolly.

—Thank God. I'm glad this is the right number. I had to call around a lot, but somebody had it at the college. Ma'am, my name is Amy Whiteplume. I work at the store in Fort Washakie, and I need to tell you Mr. Guizac's been in an accident.

"Oh God!"

Her hand went to her throat.

—He was out here trying to talk to people about the election and he was sick, he had a fever and bad oxygen. I think it was the Covid and I told him to get somebody to drive him home, but . . . Yes ma'am. I told him he was sick, but he wanted to go out to the school and BB was coming up behind him and he says Mr. Guizac just run right off the road and flipped over in the ditch.

"Is he—?"

—He hurt his head and he might have broke his arm but. He was upside down, hanging there unconscious, but the airbag and the belt held him up okay. The car was still on, BB says, you know? BB turned it off and got him stretched out on the ground and the EMT people hollered at him later because Mr. Guizac might have injuries inside but BB said what if the car blew up or something. Mr. Guizac's still unconscious. They took him to the ER in De Smet.

"Oh my God," Teresa said, squeezing her forehead. "How long ago?"

—Half an hour maybe.

"And nobody called me?"

—They said they called a number they had and nobody answered. So I tracked down your cell phone.

"God bless you," Teresa said. "Thank you."

—Yes, ma'am. You know when I saw how hot he was—he was almost 104—I told him to call his wife to come get him but.

"Thank you."

—It's okay. You're welcome. I hope he's good.

Trembling, she sat for a moment. She had to get to the hospital. Someone tapped on the window beside her, and she started violently. One of the preschool teachers. Teresa put the window down, expecting even worse news.

"Mrs. Guizac, would you mind pulling forward so the other cars can—"

"Oh! I'm so sorry!" Teresa said, glancing in the mirror at the backup and putting the Honda in gear. She moved forward slowly, aware of the other cars and the children running around her into the building. She eased forward out of the parking lot and then when the way was clear, she sped behind the church and out the drive to the main road. At the light, just turning green, she veered in front of the oncoming cars onto the street to the hospital and accelerated up the long hill past half a dozen side streets and into the drive to the emergency room, where the only parking place was a long way off. She parked and ran toward the entrance.

A red sign on the door forbade her to enter without a mask. She had left hers in the car, so she had to go back and get it, weeping and cursing the whole way. She ran back again, through the electric door, into the waiting area. A stern-eyed, masked nurse stopped her.

"Where's my husband?" Teresa cried. "Karl Guizac? Where is he?"

"Ma'am, you need to wait in your car. I will have a doctor call you."

"I need to see my husband!"

"Please turn around right now! We have protocols in place."

Down the hall, two doctors, an Asian man and a slender black woman, both in green scrubs, were talking in front of the doors to the interior of the hospital.

"I need to know how he is! He was in an accident!"

The nurse lifted her eyebrows. "Please wait outside the door."

Teresa stood outside the glass and watched as the woman walked briskly down the hall and spoke to the male doctor, who said something to the nurse, glancing up at Teresa, and then added something else, as did the woman doctor. The nurse nodded and walked back, pushing a red button to open the doors and join Teresa.

"Your husband is stable, Mrs. Guizac."

"*Stable.* What does that mean?"

"His vitals—blood pressure, heart rate. He came in with a fever that we've been able to bring down a few degrees. His blood oxygen has dropped into the 80s, so we have him on an oxygen mask. The x-ray shows a fracture in the left humerus, his upper arm. He has a bad contusion on his forehead and possibly a concussion, but it's hard to tell because he's still unconscious." Her eyes rose to meet Teresa's. "Please wait outside in your car. A doctor will call you if—"

"You don't even have my number!" she cried.

She must have sounded especially plaintive, because the nurse twisted her head aside and then looked back up, her eyes reddening.

"I'm sorry," she said.

Teresa's heart softened.

"I'm sorry to be so rude," she said, wiping her eyes. "I just want to see Walter."

"Walter?" The woman looked down at her pad, and Teresa realized her mistake.

"Walter is a family name."

"I was going to say, Mrs. Guizac, a doctor will call you. Please print your name and cell phone number on the pad at the check-in booth," said the nurse, tilting her head to her right. "And a description of your car, in case anyone needs to come out to find you."

A few minutes later, she walked unsteadily out onto the sidewalk from the ER. It seemed like days ago when she had driven from the school like a madwoman and burst into the building, but her phone said it was still only a few minutes after nine. What would Walter want her to do? He had gotten in the wreck because of *Sage Grouse*. It was Election Day. She needed to call Braxton Forrest! Election Day, and no one was writing for *Sage Grouse*.

She stood in the parking lot to call Forrest. Hardly any signal.

She had only 16% of battery charge left. There must be a charger in the car, maybe in the armrest box, but she could not remember where she had parked. The lot looked unfamiliar. A view unfolded out to the west across the southern edge of De Smet and past the ridges that rose like breaking waves toward the Wind River Range. She stared for a moment. Peaks showed jagged and white at the horizon. Had she come out the wrong side of the building? A bleakness of spirit came over her. Fresh tears came to her eyes. Where had she parked? She pressed the unlock button on her key fob, looking left and seeing nothing, then back to the right. She pressed again and saw lights blink far, far down at the end of the lot on the right. Seriously, that far? She hurried across the lot toward the Honda, leaden with what had happened. As she finally reached the car, a mule deer buck on the grass twenty feet away stopped and turned his head to regard her with mild interest. It had hardly been an hour since she had seen the pronghorn and dreamed of drawing him.

Hardly an hour.

She got in and turned on the car and started backing up.

Where was she going? The idea was to stay here. A doctor would call her. She sat for a moment in confusion and then pulled back into the parking place. Her phone had 14% left. In the armrest box she found extra McDonald's napkins, a caseless CD of Bob Dylan's *Blood on the Tracks*, a cleaning wipe for glasses, and a charging cord for Walter's iPhone, not her Samsung. There was no cord in the glove compartment either. The longer she waited for a call, the more her battery level would drop. In the meantime, she needed to let Jacob know. And the school! Who was going to pick up Marisa? They had one car now and she was in it and she had to stay here.

She dictated the same text message to Rose and Jacob. No need to complicate things by mentioning the accident:

> Your father has Covid. He's in the hospital and they won't let me see him. More later.

She pressed Send. An inspiration struck her—the reading group of faculty wives. She already had the whole list on her messages thread, and she found it quickly. She pressed the voice option and said:

> Friends, please help me. Walter had a wreck and he's in the hospital. He might have Covid and I have to stay in the car because they won't let me inside. Can somebody please bring me a charger for a phone that isn't an iPhone? I don't know what they're called. Hurry, please. I'm running out of juice, and the doctor has to call me. I'm in the Emergency Room lot down at the end to the left as you come in. Please!

She pressed Send.

11%.

She reread her message. Oh, Lord, it said he might have cold feet—and they didn't know who Walter was! She had to explain that. None of it made any sense. This time she used the keyboard:

> Covid not cold feet. Walter is our family name for Karl. Help!

Send.

9%.

There was a signal, but if she called Forrest, she might miss the doctor. *Lord Jesus Christ, Son of God, have mercy on me, a sinner.* She thought about the first time Walter kissed her at Duquesne. What year? The poem on a piece of yellow legal pad. She still had it in her billfold. She saw herself almost burning it. Lydia Downs. Holding it an inch from the candle while she stood there over Rose thinking *burn it kill her kill myself.* A minute as long as this one.

8%.

Nobody called. Nobody texted. *Remember O Most Gracious Virgin Mary that anyone who*

7%.

Off to her right, a big passenger van barreled up the road and swerved into the parking lot, honking the horn. Some ER emergency. No, it kept going past the Emergency room right toward her. Anna Johansson! Teresa flashed the lights.

Anna had the window open and she was holding something out of it. A charging cord!

Her phone buzzed—Harley Bauer, M.D.—and a text flashed up from Rose. Thank God. Rose. 4%. Another text—Amelia McDermott, Marisa's teacher. She froze with indecision, then touched the green button to accept the call from Dr. Bauer.

—Mrs. Guizac? someone said.

"Yes, this is she."

—Your husband has been admitted to the hospital.

Anna was gesturing for Teresa to unlock the passenger door, and Teresa held up a finger to ask her to wait.

"Well, I know, I was just in there."

She unlocked the door.

—He was being examined, the doctor said. Anna did a quick, scrambling search for the USB port and found it behind the cupholders. She plugged it in, inserted the other end into the phone as Teresa angled it out from her face, and whispered for her to turn on the car so it would charge.

—Now he is being admitted, Dr. Bauer continued, which means we don't think he should be released. His vitals are stable, and his fever is down, but his oxygen level is very low.

A chill went through her.

"When can I see him?" she asked.

Anna mimed turning on the car. Teresa switched hands with the phone and turned the key.

—Not for some time. He has to be kept isolated.

As the car came on, the phone did a little hiccup to say it was charging. Teresa puffed her cheeks in relief at Anna. *Thank you*, she mouthed. Anna feigned wiping sweat from her brow, waved goodbye, and got back into her van, whose deep interior stirred with bright Johansson children like a koi pond.

—Are you still there? the doctor said.

"Yes, sorry. Can I talk to him by phone?"

—Mrs. Guizac, he's sleeping right now.

"But I mean, *after*. I mean, do you think—"

Her voice broke.

—It's too soon to say, Mrs. Guizac. But it's a very serious case. We might need to fly him to Salt Lake City.

"Oh my God."

—We'll call you if there's any change.

"Should I stay here in the parking lot?"

There was a pause.

—I'm sorry, why would—did someone tell you to?

"I was told to wait in the parking lot."

—No, you—I mean, you don't need to stay here. Unless you have symptoms yourself?

The question took her aback. "Not that I know of."

—You've been exposed. You should be in quarantine for the next two weeks. If you start getting symptoms, go to the clinic and get tested. Is anyone else in the household with you?

"My teenage son and my five-year-old daughter."

—Get someone to buy what you need for the next two weeks and bring it to you. You should go home and stay there unless we call you to pick up your husband.

When he signed off, she wrote a text to Marisa's teacher.

Marisa's dad has Covid. She's been exposed. Can someone
bring her out to me when I come to the school?

How could she do it all? Jacob and Marisa restricted to the house. No
help. And she still needed to call Braxton Forrest. At least she could get
groceries before anyone knew she had been exposed.

16

FINISH IT

HE SAT ON HORSEBACK LOOKING DOWN FROM MT. IDA TO-
ward Kennesaw and Atlanta, and the landscape was beautiful in the clearing
day. McPherson had ridden up briskly beside him, boots and trousers spat-
tered with mud. His quick gaze was always somehow cheering, even in his
anger, as though any offense were a joke whose point he saw through before
the joke even started. A man of air. And melancholy. George Thomas came
up, too, his horse stepping as deliberately as Thomas did, staid and serious
and lumbering, a creature of earth. And what was he himself?

A flame, a shape of fire.

As he pointed south, he explained the shape of the mountain and the
obstacle of Johnston's forces in their way. Gen. Polk was dead. Would that
affect them? Very little. An ineffectual general, if a good bishop—whatever
that might mean. He speculated with them about what Johnston might do.
Defenses bristled on the mountain, cannons on the heights, trenches dug,
trees cut into a long abattis. He would not tell them his plan, not yet. He
wanted the battle, and he wanted it there, directly against those defenses. It
would be smarter to swing out wider to the right if the ground had dried. Was
it the dare of it that compelled him?

"Gentlemen, we have danced all the way down from Chattanooga, but
when these mutualities so marshal the way, hard at hand comes the master
and main exercise, th'incorporate conclusion."

"Sir?" said Thomas.

"Shakespeare, Gen. Thomas. Iago, to be precise. No more flanking. Frontal assault. The master and main exercise."

"Against those defenses?"

McPherson's face turned toward him. Maybe it was because he needed to relieve himself, but Sherman did not care to discuss the matter. Mac's quick, probing eyes were like a woman's. Emily Turnbow's, actually. There was a slight crust of dried mucus at the edge of one of McPherson's nostrils, a droplet of water on his mustache as his mouth opened to speak—but their horses startled, interrupting him, stepping nervously in place at a strange intermittent buzzing.

Sherman glanced behind him at the ragged lines of pine trees and the men at their cook fires. He heard a train coming down from Big Shanty through the valley of the Yellowstone, but he saw nothing that would make the sound, and then, close beside him, as he glanced back, McPherson's chest filled and filled and his mouth formed a great operatic O. So huge was his chest that the buttons burst from the front of his jacket and his shirt busted apart from within, cloth shredding. The exposed skin of his chest tore like wet newspaper and then the lurid ribcage and lungs beneath, suddenly exposed, broke open into clean halves, exposing the gleam of McPherson's beating heart before it disappeared beneath a swarm of bees.

Millions of bees. Hot and angry. They pulsed out from the cavities of McPherson's body in long buzzing bursts, swarming around the three generals' heads. McPherson looked down into himself and watched the bees with a peculiar embarrassment, like a man who

Phone.

Jacob sat up and felt around on the comforter. Where was it? Who was he? Walls and windows. Identity flooded back into him. *Buford Peach*—no, Jacob Guizac. The phone had stopped buzzing. He saw it on the desk where he had worked for most of the night. He still had on his clothes from the day before. It was broad daylight. 9:47 said the clock. Election day. His father had read "Big Shanty" that morning, but Jacob had fallen asleep before he could find out what he thought.

But right now, bathroom bathroom über alles.

As he stood there, listening to the music of his relief, he guessed that the phone would be Professor Forrest demanding another fifty or sixty pages.

Sherman was overdue, and Jacob still had a long way to go. He could still feel the dangerous profile of Kennesaw Mountain from his dream, the generals looking down on it, weirdly, the higher ridge on the left and the second, lower one to the right of it, tapering out toward Cheatham Hill. He had Kennesaw to go, the Dead Angle, the Chattahoochee, Atlanta, the death of McPherson, the March to the Sea.

He was supposed to be past the Sherman project by now. He and Emily were supposed to have time together as they did in the summer. He could just tell Forrest to give him an F. Or maybe he could write the scene from his dream, at least, and send it to Forrest before he asked for more time. Or he could finish Sherman in another year, maybe, if he put off going to college. Or in two years if he worked on it steadily but part-time.

He flushed the toilet. As soon as he got to the door of his bedroom, he heard the phone buzzing again.

He rushed in to pick it up, dreading the confession he had to make.

Not Forrest. His angry mother instead.

—Why didn't you answer my text messages!

He saw the number 5 in a red circle over the message icon on his phone. One of them was from his father. I love you. What was that about?

"Why are you shouting? The phone woke me up. What's the matter?"

—Your father had an accident and totaled the Subaru and broke his arm, but that's not even important. He has the worst case of Covid they've seen, and he's being life-flighted to Salt Lake City!

"Dad? I just saw him a few hours ago!"

He couldn't take it in. Life-flighted? That was serious, that meant—

—Well, a lot happened in a few hours. We can't see him. We all have to be in quarantine.

As she told him about his father and his fear rose, he tried to absorb the reality of it. If the family was in quarantine, he would not be able to see Emily for the whole two weeks before Thanksgiving. He hated himself for thinking it. With the phone at his ear, he went and stood at the back door and looked out past the Russian olives at the rise of the foothills of the Winds. He missed Emily's face across from him, that mobile and ironic mouth, those eyes that did not look away but gazed straight into him with a hot and merry challenge.

—Jacob? his mother was saying. I'm going to need your help. We're probably all going to get sick. Thank God, you're past this stupid project and you can —

"Mom," he said, "I'm not past it. It's not done. I've still got to—"

—Your father might be dying! My God, don't you understand? Who cares about Braxton Forrest's assignment? Give it up, Jacob! I need you.

He suddenly resented his father, who had recruited Forrest, who had imposed this impossible project he could not clear from his soul, not yet, maybe not ever.

Especially if he had to stay home and babysit his little sister.

But what if his father was dying? What if Sherman had died in San Francisco, full of bitterness and failure?

Idiot! Come on!

—Jacob!

"Okay, Mom!" he shouted into the phone.

She ended the call. He hated himself.

He stared out blindly through the sliding glass door. He hated Sherman. He hated the very existence of the man. If not San Francisco, why hadn't he died at Vicksburg—a question he himself had asked? Why hadn't he been picked off by a sharpshooter's bullet before Kennesaw as he had fully expected? He wrote about it to his wife and his daughter Minnie. But he hadn't died, and no one else in the Union could have done what Sherman did. This particular man, brilliant and irascible and full of hell. You looked at his picture, and you saw why Lucinda Devereux Lawton called him Moloch. You saw in the face of William Tecumseh Sherman what it looked like when God unleashed His absence on the world.

That's what Jacob had wanted to capture—this fundamental confidence in godlessness as the way and the truth and the life. Why couldn't he have finished writing it? He could have gotten closer to his dad. He had wanted to ask him to explain what he had said about Machiavelli and the effectual truth. He had wanted to ask him what he thought about Sherman's decision to attack Kennesaw Mountain. Frontal assaults had repeatedly been a disaster in the Civil War: Burnside's attack on Lee at Fredericksburg, Pickett's charge at Gettysburg. Sherman's brilliance had been in forcing Johnston backward with flanking moves that threatened to cut him off. Why Kennesaw?

But even if he had been here, his father would have been too busy to pay attention to him. The election, Trump vs. Biden, *Sage Grouse*, Socrates Johnson, the fate of the republic. And now Karl Guizac—or was he really Walter Peach?—was in Salt Lake City, unconscious, dying in obscurity while Sherman lived on in fame, and here was his only living son thinking more about Sherman than about his own father.

Outside, a mule deer felt Jacob's presence at the glass of the sliding door and turned to look at him, a mute, unexpectant animal gaze.

Jacob stared back, bewildered.

Had he already forgotten about Emily? Sherman had just taken over. He should try to call her. But how? The technology policy at Transfiguration forbade cell phones. He could call her home, but she would not be there. He could call the front desk, but what would he say? The Guizac family's quarantine wasn't anyone else's emergency.

He went to his laptop and answered her last email again, the one about Covid on campus.

I just got a text from my mother that

He struck that out.

Emily, my father has been life-flighted to Salt Lake City with severe Covid. He had an accident this morning, and so far he is still unconscious. They say that we have to be on two-week quarantine. How will I see you? I miss you. I love you. Jacob

When would she read it? It might be hours, even that night. He found the number of the college online.

—Transfiguration College, someone said cheerily.

"Good morning, I need to get in touch with Emily Turnbow, please."

There was a pause.

—Did you try her email?

"This is urgent. My father has been hospitalized—"

—If this is a family emergency, I can give you the number for her dorm room.

"Thank you."

She gave him a number that he already had and had already tried, as he told her.

—So you already have that number?

"Right."

—I see. Well, I'm sure Emily is in classes right now.

"Do you know when she'll be out of her next class?"

—Let's see . . . It should be pretty soon.

"And where is it?"

There was a pause, and the woman said, less cheerily,

—My goodness, I don't seem to have her schedule right in front of me.

He hung up and put his hands on top of his head. Email was probably the best he was going to do, so he would just have to wait to hear from her.

He went back to his email, not hoping for anything.

But there it was.

> From: Emily Turnbow
> Tue, Nov. 3, 2020, 9:52 AM (0 minutes ago)
> To: me
> Subject line: Your Dad
>
> I'm so sorry about your dad.
> I have to see you. I don't care if I get Covid. Write me back as soon as you get this and tell me where to meet you if you can come. I love you.
> Emily

Meet her? How was he going to meet her? His mother wouldn't be home with the groceries for at least an hour, and she would never let him take the Honda now that they were quarantined and she had to worry about what to do with Marisa, too.

But he had to see Emily. He could run. He would leave a note for his mother. In the meantime, he emailed Emily that he would meet her at Dunx. He waited for her reply. It was taking too long. He waited another minute, and then finally her message came. Classes had just been canceled and the college was going online. She wanted to meet at Subway, where nobody would see them. He put on his sweatpants and his running shoes and found a light pullover jacket. He left a note for his mother on a legal pad on the kitchen table, then started out the side door before he realized he didn't have any water—would he need any? maybe not—and started at a trot down Sacajawea Drive toward Washakie Road. He felt a little lightheaded from all the confusion of the day. His father's illness weighed on him. The Sherman paper, an obsession now, unshakable. He could not imagine how he would be able to finish it.

He began to pick up his stride around the first curve and into the long flat stretch. He and Emily would have to wait to get married. But how could he wait? His head hammered with desire. He wanted to be with her every day, and even the distance of a few miles of quarantine would be too much. What if they just ran off and got married? He could imagine Mrs. Turnbow's expression as he explained. *Everybody will think we're crazy, Mrs. Turnbow,* he would say, *but St. Paul writes in 1 Corinthians 7, 'It is better to marry than to burn,' and Emily and I are burning, or at least I am, and I can show you the scorch marks.* She would ask him how old he was. *Well, I'm eighteen.*

He was, wasn't he? It was his eighteenth birthday, and it was the last thing on anybody's mind, including his. He was old enough to vote. Not drink but vote. He should go vote while there was still time! But he hadn't registered.

She's too young! Mrs. Turnbow would say. *But soon someone else will love her or at least want her, though not the way I do, and then won't it be too late? Juliet is only* thirteen *in Shakespeare. Besides, Sherman could not have wanted Ellen Ewing the same way I want Emily. If you think about how long he waited to marry Ellen Ewing—I mean, years and years—you realize it wasn't because he could never find anybody besides the plain foster sister he grew up with. He never wanted her as much as he wanted to do something to the Ewing family—get back at them for being his benefactors, take possession of their treasure, get his seed into the Ewing line. And yet he never meant to be faithful. I'm not like that, Mrs. Turnbow. I don't want to cheat on anyone, much less Emily because I love her so much I could explode and take out half the county.*

Already in the middle of the run, he was going faster than he ought to, and he felt himself almost rise above his body as though he were somehow different from the legs or the pumping arms. As he topped the last hill, De Smet spread out before him. He was gasping now as he turned left, almost sprinting down the empty neighborhood street toward Emily. Signs for candidates on all the lawns.

He had never run into town this fast. As he turned the corner onto the sidewalk at Main Street, he stopped running, hands on his hips, then over his head, panting as he walked toward Subway, getting his breath under control. He did not see her. If she was not there, he would die right there on the sidewalk. His heart would stop. People would find his body and call his mother.

Gleam of gold through the dirty Subway window. He dodged across the street ahead of the oncoming cars and leapt into the parking lot. A team of workers in yellow helmets and high visibility jackets, all of them with masks dangling around their necks, bumped out the door, five of them— six, seven—already jawing their footlong sandwiches and slurping their huge drinks.

When they finally cleared the doorway, he stepped inside, and the older worker behind the counter, a Shoshone woman, looked at him with alarm, pushing her glasses up her face. He was streaming with sweat. Emily sat at a fixed metal table, tapping one foot and gazing north, as though he would come from that direction.

"Emily," he called.

She turned and her serious gaze took him in. The feel of her mouth against his was worth everything.

"Drink my tea. I got too much."

He flipped off the plastic lid and took three long swallows and set it back down, fumbling to get the lid back on. His legs felt shaky, and his head reeled a little.

"Are you okay?"

"I want to marry you."

"Eat something." She pushed her sandwich toward him, and he took a bite. Her eyes, her serious mouth. "Sit down, okay?"

He sat down, still breathing hard. She was going to tell him there was someone else. A wild desperation rose in him. He closed his eyes and saw blackened fields, gutted barns, chimneys and ashes where houses had been. Women stood bitter and forlorn with their arms clutched across their chests. Ragged, hungry children. The bodies of the dead, low crawl spaces full of spiders, strange shrines and flickering candles.

"Jacob?"

He focused on her.

"You went away," she said.

"I'm okay."

"What would happen if I stopped seeing you for a while?"

There it was. It had come. His heart seized, released, seized again. He was quiet for a long time. His heart might have stopped.

"I couldn't stand that," he said. "I love you, Emily." Forlornly, pathetically, he added "It's my birthday."

She pushed a flat package toward him. "I got you something."

He picked it up. Not a book, as he had first thought. Heavier.

"Open it," she said.

He tore off the plain paper. It was the size of a tablet computer or an e-reader. When he opened the leather cover, light wobbled and flashed into his face. Emily took it from him, folded the leather cover, and set it in front of him. And there he was: Jacob Guizac, eighteen years old, wild-haired and sweaty, puzzling over the puzzlement looking back at him. Was that a pimple forming over his eyebrow?

What was she telling him?

"Jacob," she said, "I love you, but half the time, you're not here even when I'm with you. You're off being somebody else. So promise me something. Once a day get this out and look at it and remember to be you instead of somebody else."

"Every time I look at it, I'll think about you."

"And finish the Sherman. Finish it."

17

THE WAY WEST

FORREST SCROLLED AGAIN THROUGH JACOB GUIZAC'S chapter on Big Shanty. He knew the boy's Sherman: a man with huge ambitions fueled by lifelong resentments. Jacob must have read hundreds of pages, maybe thousands, to get all this detail. The *Memoirs*, the histories and biographies, even the letters between Sherman and his wife—but nothing would have mentioned Josiah McPhee or a slave woman named Leah. Or what it was like to lie under mosquito netting on a hot Georgia night without even a fan to cool him.

He thought of football camp in Waycross the summer before his senior year, the exhausted players lying in the barracks trying to sleep before the first whistles roused them for predawn wind sprints. God help him, he had loved all of it—the sprints, the collisions, his mastery on the field and off. When a bully from some other school had goaded him in the mess hall, Forrest had picked up an apple from the bowl on the table and crushed it in his right hand. The whole place had gone quiet. He smiled remembering it. A legend in Gallatin, Chick Lee had told him years ago.

"Braxton?" Marisa called from the kitchen. "Are you going to vote? Our ward is at Little Harbor School."

Vote? What was the point? New Hampshire had swung far left in the past thirty years, and his lonely Republican vote wouldn't count for diddly-squat. Besides, he would have to vote for Donald Trump. He didn't hate him as much as Walter Peach did. He should vote. His duty as a citizen. His ticket to an opinion.

"You think there'll be lines?" he called.

"I doubt it. Not with everybody mailing in ballots."

"Give me a few minutes. I need to finish this email," Forrest said.

Good stuff, he started—and just then his iPhone began to buzz. Where the hell was it? He pushed aside papers on his desk and then stood and looked behind him and saw it on the seat of his armchair across the room. It had given up by the time he got to it, but he found the number in Recents. A Georgia number.

Something had happened to Cate. Zitek had done something to her or the children. The blood in his temples was pounding when he called back.

"Who is this?" he demanded.

—Braxton? A woman's voice, tremulous but formal. I want you to know there's not going to be a *Sage Grouse* today.

"*Sage Grouse*? What do you mean? Who is this?"

—Teresa Peach.

Instantly ashamed of how he sounded, he also felt a wash of relief that it wasn't about Zitek.

"Teresa! Sorry. I thought it was about Cate and her husband. The Georgia number confused me." Marisa came in making a face, already gesturing for him to give her the phone. "What's going on out there? Is the Wyoming landslide for Trump a little too—"

—Walter has been life-flighted to Salt Lake City.

He stopped in the middle of the room.

"What happened?"

—He was out at the Reservation and he blacked out and wrecked the car. He was hardly getting any oxygen in his lungs. It's Covid and they took him by helicopter to Salt Lake. I don't want to keep you, I just wanted to tell you there wouldn't be an edition of *Sage Grouse* on Election Day, and it's important, so—

Marisa took the phone from him.

"Teresa? What's going on?" She listened for a moment. "Okay, honey, now listen. No, hush now. Listen to me! Braxton and I will come out there."

Forrest opened his hands in astonishment.

When Marisa put the phone on speaker, Teresa sounded confused and tentative.

—That would be—you're all the way across the country! But if Walter—I have little Marisa, I mean, and Jacob's been working on Sherman all the time for Braxton anyway so if—and Braxton needs to do something with *Sage Grouse*. But what would you—I mean your obligations—"

"There's nothing holding us in Portsmouth," Marisa said.

—You'd have to—I mean you could have the whole upstairs except we might have Covid, so—

When she got off the phone, Forrest and Marisa stared at each other.

"You told her we'd go to Wyoming," he said incredulously.

"Poor Walter!" Marisa said.

"Right, but that's not why she called."

"Of course it is. What do you mean?"

"She wanted me to know about *Sage Grouse*. That there won't be anything about Election Day on the website."

"So what? Her husband might be dying, Braxton. What does she care about *Sage Grouse*?"

"No, she wasn't just telling me about Walter, she was telling me what Walter's absence means for the importance of the website. For his job, for their livelihood. That's why she called. I have to take over *Sage Grouse*."

"You don't think she would have called otherwise? I mean, you subsidize it, don't you?"

"Not the way I did at first. Walter's built up a network of donors and advertisers. He's earned their support, and he'll lose them if the site just goes dead."

"Well, post something about his illness."

"I can do that right now. But I can't do the website remotely. The local flavor is half of the appeal. So you're right, I need to be in Wyoming. Can you book a flight to Denver?"

Marisa shook her head.

"Let's just close up the house and drive out there."

"Drive to Wyoming," he said dismissively.

"Why not? Maybe it's providential. You've been talking for months about writing a travel book about America."

Forrest stared at her.

"You'll see a lot on the way," she said. "Lots of waitresses. And if you have to post something every day to keep the website alive, you'll get back into writing. The trip can be the backbone of your book, and in the meantime, you'll be helping Walter. You two are peas in a pod anyway."

By God, she could irritate the hell out of him, but when serious trouble came, her spirit floated clear, and he loved that about her. A few minutes later, he showed her a wavering blue line that ran west along the southern shore of Lake Ontario to Buffalo and along Lake Erie to Cleveland and Toledo, then on past Chicago and out through the Great Plains to Des Moines and Omaha and due west to Cheyenne and Laramie and northwest up to De Smet.

"2252 miles. Thirty-three hours."

"We can be there by Friday," she said. "Do you still want to vote?"

"I need to post something."

First he had to track down the code to access the website. Then came Braxton Forrest as Alter-Walter.

Folks, welcome to the Bucky Whittlebone Show on this beautiful Election Day. I'm joining you from Dunx Coffee in downtown De Smet, Wyoming, where I have as my guest the distinguished housefly—which I meant to say gadfly—Mr. Socrates Johnson. Well, Socrates, how you think it's going out there in America? What's going to happen if they get rid of the Donald? I bet you every damn absentee Covideer vote goes for old Joe just like dead Mexicans went for Lyndon in that Texas border county back in the day.

SOCRATES [*can't speak for coughing*].

BUCKY: Come again, buddy? You ain't looking too perky this fine morning.

SOCRATES [*wheezes and coughs, trying to talk*].

BUCKY: Huh? Hey! . . . Who are you guys? Where you taking—wait a minute!

A few moments of dead air.

BUCKY [*solemnly*]: Folks, the federals come in and took Socrates. That man is sick, and it ain't hemlock. If you was praying people, you might say a word for—wait, hold on, somebody is calling in . . . Say your name again?. . . No way, folks. I can't believe it, I can't believe it. We have here on the line this morning the publisher of *Sage Grouse*, Mr. Cump Forrest. Welcome, Mr. Cump.

CUMP: I hate to break the happy mood, Bucky.

BUCKY: You just come back from casting your ballot, I bet.

CUMP: Not this time, Bucky, but I'll vote again someday, maybe when one vote could mean something. Buddy, I need to give your listeners some news.

BUCKY [*sadly*]: It's Socrates, ain't it?

CUMP: It is, Bucky. But it's really about the man behind Socrates, Mr. Karl Guizac. He was on the way to find out how the folks on the Reservation were voting when he had an accident because he passed out from—

BUCKY: Don't say it. I can't stand to hear it.

CUMP: Not drinking, Bucky.

BUCKY: Not—you know.

CUMP: I hate to say it. Covid-19.

BUCKY: Cut it out. Not Socrates. I got it and it come down to one bad headache, one bad chill, a few days of lying around watching *Ozark*. I mean the Donald got it and—

CUMP: It's a shame to admit it can be worth the hype, but my buddy Karl has a case so bad they had to send him in a helicopter to Salt Lake City and put him in a coma so they can keep him on a ventilator. Say a prayer for Karl Guizac, folks.

BUCKY: Will do, Mr. Cump.

CUMP: While he's getting better, which we hope to God he is, we're going to make do at *Sage Grouse*. We've got a special thing going here, and we're going to keep it going while Karl's away. I'm driving to Wyoming and I'm going to be checking in from the road every day. We'll know early next week how things are shaping up. Meanwhile, who are you thinking of having on your show, Bucky?

BUCKY: I got a couple of rodeo girls who rode with Wyatt the Post-Transgender Cowboy after he was trans and before he was post. And I'm thinking I might can line up Joe Biden's hairdresser.

CUMP: You're pulling my leg.

BUCKY: Naw, same girl does my mama's. Mama's about bald, too.

CUMP: Listen, Bucky, these are hard times, but I've got your back, my man.

BUCKY: [*voice breaking*] I appreciate it [*sniffling*], dog if I don't, but don't get me sentimental. We got a cowboy tone here on the Bucky Whittlebone Show, and sentimental ain't it. And listen, if Socrates was here, he'd tell you a piece of his mind which if it's one thing Socrates ain't, it's sentimental. [*Squeak of a bottle being uncorked.*] Want a little something to perk up your java?

CUMP: Please. [*Glug of liquid*]

BUCKY: To Karl Guizac [*Mugs clink*]. Let's pray it's a quick recovery.

CUMP: To Karl Guizac [*Mugs clink again*].

The ending might confuse people (Cump was supposed to be on the phone), but Forrest posted it. Within a few minutes, comments were coming in. Sympathy for Guizac, comments about Covid, and so on. He closed his laptop and joined Marisa in packing what they needed for the trip. They set the thermostat at fifty-five, locked the house, and started south in the used BMW X3 Marisa had fallen in love with that summer—a dimension of her character he should have suspected when she started reading aloud Dan O'Neill's car reviews in the *Wall Street Journal.* They had given their Subaru Forester to Bernadette, who had flown up and driven it back to Dallas.

They made their way through Massachusetts to the Mass Pike south of Worcester, where Forrest set the cruise control on the BMW at eighty-five to blend in with the traffic, and they talked about what they should do on the trip and how he could keep *Sage Grouse* interesting over the next few days of highways, farmland, filling stations, rest stops, restaurants, and motels. He would be driving for eleven or twelve hours a day, so writing anything at all—before or after—would be a chore. Marisa said it would be easier if he could just comment on the country they saw and the people they met. Or he could turn their experiences into comic scenarios, maybe invent a character who remarks on things, something like Walter's Socrates. He could speculate about who had lived in the abandoned houses they saw from the Interstate. He could write about crossing the Mississippi the next day.

For several hours, they amused themselves by switching intermittently between Fox News and NPR. Marisa fell asleep just west of Albany, and

Forrest found himself thinking about Sherman. William Tecumseh Sherman. Forrest and Sherman both bore the name of Tecumseh, the great Shawnee chief who foresaw the destruction of traditions that Sherman would help orchestrate, the harsh agent of technological modernity and Machiavelli's "effectual truth." Was Jacob right about Sherman's erotic predilections, that use of sex as his assertion of freedom? Or did a kind of class-based Victorianism of manners keep him outwardly proper, as Forrest suspected? Or both? He had never finished his email to Jacob about the Big Shanty piece.

They stopped for the night about thirty miles east of Buffalo. It had been a long day, and as they dragged their bags to the door, a sign on the door of Buffalo Suites commanded them not to enter unless they were wearing masks. Forrest fished in his pocket, cursed, and went back to the car to get his while Marisa waited. Other notices assured them that unprecedented disinfecting measures were in force. When they stepped up to the counter, Kumar Patel, Manager, and Keesha Roberts, Clerk, looked up at them expectantly.

"Do you have a reservation?" asked Patel.

"Nope," Forrest said.

"Let me check to see if we have a vacancy."

Forrest lifted his eyebrows. There was no one else in the lobby, only one other car in the parking lot. Patel frowned into his screen as Forrest gazed down at his balding head.

"Where y'all coming from today?" asked Keesha pleasantly.

"Portsmouth, New Hampshire," Marisa said.

"Whoo, a long way! I bet y'all are tired."

"Excellent!" said Patel. "We have a room with a king bed! No extra charge! Would you like first-floor?"

"Wonderful," said Marisa.

Patel went through his spiel about when breakfast started (6:00 AM), Wi-Fi passwords, and safety precautions to protect their visitors such as distancing on the elevators. Forrest glanced at the clock behind the counter. Already 8:30.

"Any news about the election?"

Keesha pinched in her mouth and shrugged. Patel described the use of the sanitized remote and the available channels.

If he jotted some descriptions before they went to bed, he could post them the next morning and still be on the road before rush hour in Buffalo.

"Teresa just texted me that it's Jacob's birthday." Marisa exclaimed from behind him. "What a terrible birthday!"

Forrest took his card back from Patel and accepted the key cards and nodded to Keesha as they turned toward the hallway to their room. He had forgotten to get the boy something on Amazon. The image came upon him: Jacob obsessed with Sherman while his frantic mother grieved and the country careened into the dark without headlights and his father lay unconscious far away, in a distant city, hooked to a machine that breathed for him.

18

PRELIMINARIES

MR. PEACH.

Guizac, he said.

The judge sat above him to his right.

What we're about today, he said, is a provisional inquiry. We're looking at your qualifications for your upcoming death, should it occur. As I say, it's provisional, and you might need to repeat the procedure should you survive and fall back into your habitual pattern of life. Do you understand?

Not at all.

You'll be dealing today with Ms. Rodham-Cortez. Do you have an advocate?

I mean—I didn't—

You didn't make any provision for an advocate. Complacency, Mr. Peach. Never thought this day would come? So you're on your own. Let's get started. Prosecutor?

A sharp-faced woman in her late twenties, she wore her black hair pulled back and elaborately braided. Was it right to call it a ponytail? Her tight man's shirt and tie distorted distractingly over her breasts, and the twitch of her short black skirt, somehow both silken and leathery, contradicted the hard professional demeanor she adopted. Most disconcerting, though, was the cobalt-blue tail that came through a slit in the back of her skirt and dropped onto the dusty wooden floor, where it curled and shimmered as she walked, elaborately scaled, flicking up its barbed tip as if it were spearing dragonflies.

Its metallic sheen reminded him of the carefully painted fingernails of a woman who used to work at the post office back in Gallatin, Georgia.

He was watching the tail so intently that the next question startled him.

So you're how old now, Mr. Guizac? Mid-fifties?

That's right.

And you were in good health before this? She glanced down at the pad she held. Well, passable, looks like. Cholesterol levels pushing 240. And uh-oh, glucose. Your A1C shows you've crossed the border into Type 2 diabetes. Family history? Hard to know much about it, I bet, with parents like yours, she said, tilting her head at him.

Diet and exercise are keeping my numbers in line.

Really? If you say so. What kind of exercise?

I sometimes ride my bike to work in warm weather, use the elliptical trainer at the gym otherwise. Do weights occasionally. And there's always plenty of yard work.

Diet?

I like Michael Pollan's prescription: Eat food, mostly vegetables, not too much.

Trying to get rid of that little stomach, huh? She eyed him openly. How's your sex life?

There was a ripple of laughter in the audience, which he noticed for the first time, row upon row dimly visible past the lights. Was this a courtroom or a broadcast studio?

None of your business.

Really? I doubt that.

The barb at the end of her tail roused itself and rose behind her and came lightly to rest on her shoulder, pointing at Guizac as she reached up to groom the tip of it. Her whole body seemed to open to him as she drew close to the gate of his square wooden enclosure, pressing her breasts against the railing. He could smell mandarin, strawberries, patchouli, vanilla, pale flowers opening their mouths in the dark with soft exhalations.

He had no idea where these words came from. Patchouli?

Hmm? Nothing to say? Well, that is just so sad. The tail slumped back to the floor and she used both hands to pretend to drag it along. Loud laughter. I'm sorry for your loss.

Did I say anything about loss?

Oh, honey. She sighed and shrugged and glanced down at the pad. Three children. Magdalena, Jacob, and Marisa.

Four. We lost Walter, our oldest.

I don't see him listed.

He should be there.

Well, he's not, and this is the list.

I don't know why he's not there.

What difference does it make?

He was my son, he said hotly and then paused. I ran over him. I killed him.

Maybe you didn't just kill him, she said harshly, turning on him suddenly, tail rising like a cobra. Maybe you canceled him. Maybe what you did means he never existed.

He heard gasps from the audience. A few low boos.

That's ridiculous. Of course he existed. He was my son. He *is* my son.

So you believe in eternal life?

More gasps.

What do you mean?

You say he *is* your son. You mean he's still alive? Where would that be? Up there? She glanced archly up at the ceiling. Among the cobwebs. No? But isn't eternal life the whole point with you people? she asked. It's a fair question. Am I right?

With this question, she appealed to the audience, flexing her tail back and forth as she walked, like a cat rubbing itself against someone's leg. There was a murmur of agreement.

Yes, but the question is personal. I know Walter is my son. I don't really know what eternal life means.

Really? But you tag along to Mass every Sunday like a good boy? What do you do when you pray? I know you pray, even if it's only for show to yourself. Some weak kind of insurance, right? I *thought*—she shrugged for the audience—the deal was that if you believed in Jesus, worked through a checklist of good works, and passed the final exam, you got your ticket to eternal life.

That's a belittling way to—

Oh, wait, she said, eternal life is the English translation of, let's see—she peered at her pad again—*zōēn aiōnion* in the original Greek. *Vitam aeternam* in the Latin Vulgate. The Greek feels richer, doesn't it, because of the *bios*/*zōē* difference—personal biography versus life per se—and also because there's the distinction between either kind of life and *psyche*, which is the life of *sarx*, the flesh. You know about *sarx*, I think. So just to clarify, you believe this little *alter Walter*—who isn't on the list, I repeat—is nevertheless participating in unending *zōē,* even though he was too young to believe anything except the advantages of a dry diaper? So this is the whole infant baptism bit?

I don't know, he said. I mean—

Well, Mr. Guizac, said the prosecutor, the fact is, you don't know if he was baptized, because you didn't care, and you wouldn't go near a church in those days. You were an atheist and an adulterer to boot. Sounds like you're counting on your wife to get little Walter over the line.

Her tail snaked languidly across the floor. A cold terror seized him.

You look confused, Mr. Peach, she said.

I mean, don't you get eternal life either way?

Either way?

I mean, Heaven or Hell.

The studio audience was restless. He could hear a darker murmuring.

Hell, Mr. Peach? Is that where you think your son is? Or some kind of Limbo, which was officially disavowed by Rome in, let's see—she checked her notes—2007? Well, except he died before that, right? She smiled at the audience, which stirred appreciatively. I mean, maybe Limbo didn't know it had been disavowed.

My name is Guizac now, not Peach. Maybe that's why Walter's not on the list—because we changed our name. All of us except little Walter became Guizacs. So whoever made the list messed up.

Whoever made the list! She lifted an ironic hand to the audience, and scatters of nervous laughter broke out. Seriously? she said, turning to him. Should we let you proceed? Again she opened her hands to the audience. It would be entertaining, I suspect. What do you think? Does he qualify for Round One?

Yes? For the fun of it? Is that a yes?

19

FORREST IN TRANSITU

WHEN THEY ROLLED THEIR SUITCASES OUT TO THE BREAK-
fast room just after 6:00 a.m., a new man at the desk greeted them.

"Early start, I see!"

Forrest fixed him with an appraising gaze.

"Never early enough," said Forrest.

As Josh puzzled over the comment, he nervously touched the gold ring
piercing his left eyebrow. His purple fingernail polish shone in a sunbeam.
Vine tattoos climbed up from his collar onto the lobe of his left ear.

No one was in the breakfast area except a dour uniformed attendant
stocking a clear plastic display case with muffins. She seemed startled to see
them. Would she qualify as a waitress? The TV was on—pundits talking
about the inconclusive election, results still coming in from the mail-in
ballots, states too close to call. Trump had done surprisingly well, despite the
pollsters. But he was going to lose. One way or another, he had to lose, and
it was just a matter of how it happened and when they got to call it. No way
it was 2016 again.

Taking a tray and a plastic plate, Forrest lifted the lid off the first warming
pan. Fake scrambled eggs. He mounded them on his plate and from the
next pan added five rubbery link sausages the size of his pinky. In a small
refrigerator, he found a strawberry-flavored yogurt in a plastic container
about the size of a Keurig pod and a petite tub of Philadelphia cream cheese.

The muffin display case offered a plastic-sealed bagel, small and pre-split, that he unwrapped and pulled apart unequally and dropped into the toaster.

After it popped up, he sat down across from Marisa. She had one hard-boiled egg, a Styrofoam bowl of Raisin Bran, an orange, and a piece of wheat toast with butter and jam. As he accepted the tribulation of putting cream cheese on his bagel with a tiny plastic knife, she watched him without mercy. Once it was properly loaded, he tried to open a little packet of hot sauce and ended up using his teeth, then doused his eggs with the stuff. He stabbed a little sausage and put it in his mouth.

"How can you eat that?" she said.

"Just think of the industrious scientists who designed this nourishment for the human body *in transitu*."

"Mmm," she said over a spoon of Raisin Bran.

Up on the TV, George Stephanopoulos looked haggard and sincere, as though he had been awake since Trump took office. The other commentators were a telegenic new crop Forrest had never seen. He could remember Chet Huntley and David Brinkley, Walter Cronkite, Eric Sevareid. But these creatures were something else. Choreographed diversity, smooth good looks, crafted attitudes. Some of them seemed a little rattled, as though they were dangerously off script, but they artfully displayed human mannerisms. He watched them intermittently as he finished the last tiny spoonful of yogurt and then pushed the plate aside.

For the *Sage Grouse* website, he posted a piece called "Travels with Tecumseh" in which he exposed the time-traveling Shawnee chieftain to the experience of Buffalo Suites, including Kumar, Keesha, and Josh (all renamed), and described Tecumseh's bafflement at the breakfast Forrest had just eaten. Halfway through, he knew it didn't work. Socrates was a cultural trope, a persona whose perspective could be understood as cultural irony, but for most people Tecumseh was just a name from American history textbooks. But it was something to keep the website active, at least. He also started an Instagram-like comment section on election coverage. He wrote a quick opinion about cosmetically correct reporters and the dumbing-down of the news.

Marisa started clearing the table.

"How far can we get today?"

"Des Moines is about halfway," he said.

"How long a drive?"

"Thirteen hours."

Out of the hotel by 7:30, they skirted Buffalo, heading west along Lake Erie. It was a gray, cold day, and the traffic was so light that a strange mood came on him, as though he were as alien in this America as Tecumseh was.

Marisa paged slowly through her breviary, absorbed.

"St. Charles Borromeo," she said when he asked.

Vague images came to mind. Baroque architecture? Or was that Borromini?

"I give up."

"Council of Trent."

"I thought that was Bellarmine."

"Both of them. Borromeo is invoked in Manzoni's novel about the plague in Milan. *The Betrothed*. I've seen it mentioned several times since Covid broke out."

"Never read it."

As he topped a slight rise, brake lights began to blossom in long parallel lines ahead of him. On the iPhone map, the highway was colored red for several miles ahead. No alternate routes. At least they were still rolling slowly forward, he thought, and just as he thought it, everything came to a dead stop. Traffic on the eastbound side had disappeared, so something major had happened.

Ahead of him, a dirty white van advertised Picconi's Pipes on its back door—a small, comically manic cartoon plumber holding a handful of pipes like drooping spaghetti. As the dead stop settled in, the driver got out, zipping up his jacket, and walked over to the highway shoulder where he stood with his hands on his hips, looking westward. Other drivers and passengers opened their doors and got out, stretching, swapping seats or standing with their hands behind them or laced overhead as they stretched; some made calls, some adjusted hanging clothes or calmed children in the backseat or got things from the trunk. Great trucks rumbled in place, monstrous, atavistic, their transcontinental stride interrupted. They never inhabited the same reality as the cars beneath them. The drivers in their cabs high above the concrete lived in the stratum above ordinary traffic, committed to relentless motion between loading docks and distant cities, loads and timetables, showers in truck stops, wives and whores, rituals and pieties and sins, some bargain of livable habits, he supposed. Experts on waitresses. Maybe his imaginary billionaire could ride shotgun.

Forrest's phone still offered no information, no alternatives. Here they were, wherever the hell it was.

"Just be patient," Marisa said. "We're not going to make it to Des Moines. Do you want to listen to something?"

"Not yet," he said.

"I'm going to close my eyes. I didn't sleep well."

"Go ahead. I need to think anyway."

Yesterday, when he heard of Walter's illness, he had thought he could step in and take over *Sage Grouse,* but after the last two mornings, he was already straining. He couldn't do it for more than a few days. He had never been engaged in anything like day-to-day commentary on contemporary events, and he was always puzzled by the idiom of references and memes that everyone kept up with online and on their phones. Every day at *Sage Grouse* something had to be new—opinions, satirical pieces, cartoons, profiles of ordinary Wyoming citizens who hadn't done anything to warrant celebrity. Peach was good at it. He was used to the pressure of deadlines from his years at the *Gallatin Tribune.* But Forrest couldn't just jump in without any context. He had been spending his days underlining passages in the Webster-Hayne debates or thinking about Sherman and rereading Shelby Foote or the essays of Emerson or nineteenth-century poetry for this book on America that had been germinating for decades now. Or would he go with the billionaire idea, which sounded more like a novel. Or a movie. *Sullivan's Travels.*

He had to find somebody else who had something to say about Wyoming and national politics.

He sighed and looked around. The warehouses along the highway were huge, prefabricated things. Nature had been trounced except for the weeds that grew wherever there was a bare spot between buildings and parking lots and loading docks.

Is this America? asked his inner editorial.

What did anybody mean by *America,* anyway?

Nothing substantive came to mind, just phrases, as though some interference were jamming the inner attempt. *From sea to shining sea. The consent of the governed.* Did people still say that during Covid? *E pluribus unum.* What bullshit—everything nowadays was about enforced diversity. Were Judith Brockman in Portsmouth and Chick Lee in Gallatin citizens of the same republic? Donald Trump and Elizabeth Warren? Ted Cruz and Alexandra Ocasio-Cortez?

Socrates Johnson was good on the ironies, but Socrates Johnson was in a coma. Forrest imagined a man with blue light in his eyes like Stonewall Jackson or John Brown, tall and lean as Gary Cooper in his jeans and Patagonia jacket. He could be a radical organic farmer in the Wendell Berry vein or an ecoterrorist dreamed up by Edward Abbey or a prophet from Palo Alto who got a text from God on his iPhone. Or all of the above. He had his billionaire!

He walks between the stopped cars and trucks treating the massive shutdown as a pause in ordinary American life, an opportunity, like Covid itself, to reconsider reality. Daniel Webster Calhoun. "D. W." to some. "Dub" to his online constituents. He steps onto the roof of a car and raises his arms.

DUB: Honk your horn for the U.S.A!

A couple of mild, puzzled toots. A tractor trailer uses its air horn.

DUB: The United States of America! The Startup Nation!

WOMAN IN PRIUS LEANING OUT DOOR [*Judith Brockman*]: Why don't you shut up? [*Gaga contorts herself barking at Dub.*]

DUB: I am the voice of America!

JUDITH: Not my voice.

DUB: I'll tell you what we did and who we are. We *demolished* the class structures of the old world. When we were still getting our growth and proving ourselves, we won world wars. We built skyscrapers and bridges and huge dams, tanks and bombers and submarines, not to mention Little Boy and Fat Man. We took out Hitler and Hirohito at the same time! We were brash and happy in the wide world. Look at this highway, friends! *Just look at this amazing thing!* Eisenhower built the interstates after he won World War II in Europe with the Red Ball Express. It's all about supply lines. Wherever you need to go, you can get there faster, and the supplies will be there just as fast to support you. And wherever you are, this is the same America, from sea to shining sea. Take any exit, and it's always America.

Judith Brockman presses her horn to drown out Dub. He lowers his head and opens both hands toward the offending hybrid as though he were directing the crescendo of curses and airhorn blasts that answers her. A massive truck driver swings down from his truck behind the hybrid and snatches Judith's door open.

TRUCK DRIVER: You want me to rip out that steering wheel?

Judith shrinks away. In the back seat, Gaga goes mad with yapping. The truck driver, red-faced and side-burned in his red MAGA cap, nods to Dub to proceed.

DUB: You can cancel me, sister, but you can't silence hope and enterprise! She can have her say if she lets me have mine. [*A sudden darkness comes over Dub.*] But look around you, brothers and sisters. Is this America? Look at these warehouses full of things made by machines and stacked with their barcodes showing like the sign of the beast and delivered to homes where people move among Cartesian abstractions of—

TRUCK DRIVER: Hey!

DUB: What? Yes sir.

The truck driver's head tilts as he approaches Dub.

TRUCK DRIVER: The hell are you talking about, buddy?

DUB: I'm talking about what happened to America.

T.D.: I get my living moving stuff from these warehouses. And what happened yesterday is they rigged the election to get rid of Trump. I thought you was going to tell these folks the truth.

DUB: My friend, the election is the symptom of our national disease— not who wins but how our great nation has come to a choice between Joe Biden and Donald Trump.

T.D.: What, you're saying it's all about Covid? I'm with you there.

DUB: Did I mention Covid?

The truck driver leans close to Dub's ear.

T.D.: If this ain't about the Donald, then shut the eff up.

Red lights flashed, engines started. The jam was breaking up. Picconi's Pipes edged forward and soon they were all back up to highway speeds, the big trucks around him jockeying for position. From the other direction, eastbound traffic flowed smoothly. Forrest could not see the least sign of what had caused the delay.

His mind went back to the Donald.

How did Donald Trump get to stand for America? A man cobbled from self-celebrating hucksters and William Randolph Hearst and P.T. Barnum. A circus figure, a gigantic inflated Big Boy held down by ropes and bouncing between skyscrapers in the Macy's parade, now somehow occupying the White House. But the anti-Trump culture was all 1619 and rainbow parades and Black Lives Matter and defunding the police, as though America had always been a white cop's knee on the neck of a black man, all just an expression of white money and power and privilege. As though the whole of its history pointed to its apotheosis in Donald Trump.

"You keep sighing," Marisa said.

"Do I? Sorry."

"What are you thinking about?"

"Donald Trump."

"Well stop."

Late in the day, they had just crossed the Mississippi at Davenport, Iowa, when a call from Teresa came through the BMW's sound system.

—Walter might die. I should go to Salt Lake City.

"Oh my God," Marisa said. "Can Jacob stay with Little M until we—"

—But they won't let me see him even if I go.

She told them that Walter had regained consciousness briefly the day before.

—Half the people they put under don't survive. They asked him if he wanted to get in touch with anybody. He texted me to say goodbye! Oh my God, to say goodbye! I can't be with him even if he's dying. If he dies I can't be there.

Forrest and Marisa looked at each other.

"We'll say the rosary right now," Marisa said.

—Thank you so much, she said distractedly.

"We'll be there late tomorrow," Forrest said.

—You, too. *Okay*, Marisa!

"I'm sorry?" Marisa said.

—*Okay!* I said, you little brat. *Stop it!* No, ask Jacob, I'm busy, can't you see the—

Forrest pressed the phone button on the steering wheel to end the eavesdropping.

. . . .

After the night at a Marriott in West Des Moines, they slept too late and did not leave until nine the next morning after Forrest posted a quick update on Guizac and a comment on the election coverage. He did not try Dub Calhoun. *Sage Grouse* readers had not responded—at all, not even one—to his Tecumseh post, and there were no comments on election coverage, which disappointed him.

Stubble fields spread out for many miles on either side of the highway. Canadian geese flew over the Nebraska landscape in great raveling and reforming wedges. Flocks of starlings shifted and flowed in their complex improvisations. Lonely farmhouses. Complexes with huge grain bins. Great circles of center-pivot irrigation. At Kearney, they passed under the Archway across I-80, and when they passed North Platte ninety minutes later, the sun was already sinking behind a line of slate clouds. They listened to a C. J. Box novel that made the drive go faster. Game warden Joe Pickett and his smart wife Marybeth and their daughters and Joe's stone-cold, falcon-loving buddy Nate Romanowski. They gained an hour when they entered Mountain Time east of Ogallala, but they would not make it to De Smet that night. They bought hamburgers at a Wendy's drive-through in Sidney and kept going. It had been dark for over two hours when they checked into Little America in Cheyenne. Marisa called Teresa as soon as they got into the room.

—It's wonderful to hear from you. My husband Walter is in a coma in Salt Lake City, Teresa explained.

When Marisa reminded her that, yes, they were on the way to help, she seemed confused.

—Really?

Marisa was exhausted, and she went right to sleep, but Forrest was keyed up from so much driving. He took the headphones from his briefcase and watched an episode of *Fargo* on his laptop. He saw an email from Hermia Watson that he was tempted to snooze until the next morning, but he opened it.

A little warning

From: Hermia Watson
Wed, Nov. 4, 2020, 7:47 PM
(2 hours ago)
To: me

Braxton,

 I thought I should tell you about one of our girls who's causing some trouble at Eula's House. She's clearly underage, probably fourteen or fifteen. Her name is Miriam McPhee (or so she says—I have no documentation), but sometimes she claims to be *Josiah* McPhee. It would be funny if there weren't such a caustic knowingness about "Josiah" and if he didn't exercise such power over some of the more vulnerable girls. I'm sure it's a dissociative disorder, but the worry is that she/he seems completely aware that claims of gender identity have so much purchase legally these days. She might pose real problems for us, and I wanted you to know at least something about the situation.

 Ironically, Miriam is very close to term whether Josiah is or not. Please pray for her—and for me. I'm not sure how this one turns out. I will try to call in a day or two.

 Love to Marisa.

 Hermia

20

JOSIAH MCPHEE

HERMIA SENT THE EMAIL AND CLOSED HER LAPTOP, LISTEN-ing. A strange murmuring came from upstairs. Were they praying? She went out into the foyer and up the carpeted front stairs. Most of the rooms upstairs were dark, but she saw the light spilling into the hallway down at the far end from the old room where she had spent several nights years ago when Cousin Sally Dot Hayes had bronchitis. She heard the murmuring more clearly as she approached—they were praying the rosary—and when she stepped into the room, the women were clustered around someone. They parted to let her see. The girl had come just a few days ago from Atlanta, a small, very young, very strange, very pregnant girl named Miriam who sometimes said she was a man and wanted to be called Josiah. She lay drawn back against the wall like the stricken Virgin in Rosetti's *Annunciation*, panting like a shot doe, her huge belly toward them.

"What's going on?" Hermia asked.

The girl closest to her, Bella Amorosa—the girls called her Bammo—swung around, startled, her left hand on her stomach. She lifted the fingers clutching her beads and solemnly touched a knuckle to her lips.

Hermia knitted her brows. Seriously? Bella was telling Hermia to be quiet? But they were on the Fifth Sorrowful Mystery, so she fought down her anger and joined them. Bella led them in singing the *Salve Regina* and reciting the St. Michael prayer, and when they were done, the girl on the bed looked around wildly.

Hermia began to sit down on the edge of the bed, when suddenly the girl let out a high soul-scouring ululation. The girls backed away, their hands over their ears. Only once before had Hermia heard anything like it—an Ethiopian funeral when the mother of the dead daughter threw her head back and made the sound just before falling against her husband and other daughters in a faint. High and long and incredibly loud.

"Are you having the baby?" Bella asked. "Should we call the ambulance?"

Just as suddenly, Miriam fell silent and closed her eyes. She slid down into the bed and pulled the covers over herself and turned her face to the wall.

When she first opened the home, Hermia had put the girls upstairs in the old bedrooms originally occupied by the Forrest family when the patriarch built the additions to the house in the 1920s. In her two years as old Mrs. Hayes's helper, Hermia had lived in a small servant's bedroom beneath the back stairway, never in one of the larger rooms upstairs, and now she had resumed her old place because it suited her. After that summer of the troubles in 2009 when her father Braxton Forrest came into his rightful inheritance, she had not been in the house for years. Braxton had renovated Stonewall Hill and housed the family of his friend Walter Peach free of charge, while also convincing Walter to leave his miserable teaching job in Waycross and edit the *Gallatin Tribune*, which Braxton had purchased. The Peaches and their children, Rose and Buford, had occupied three of the large bedrooms upstairs, leaving one empty and converting the fourth that overlooked the side yard into a library and study room.

When Hermia convinced Braxton to let her open Eula's House, he allowed her to hire an interior designer from Atlanta to make arrangements for as many as five girls per room without using bunkbeds (for obvious reasons). The woman had suggested a starburst pattern of dividers and single beds radiating from a circle at the center of the room. These would give each girl a modicum of privacy and also a common space with bean bag chairs and pillows.

Maybe the designer's prep-school nieces would have liked it. Not Hermia's girls. When the first women arrived in vans, she had shown them the rooms and they nodded amiably. But then a natural sorting had begun, establishing the herd hierarchies, she supposed, with leaders and rivals for leadership and all kinds of bonding and enmities. Within two days, a group of teenaged girls had swapped their assigned spaces in other rooms with older women and congregated in a room where they removed the dividers and stacked them in the hallway. Hermia let them do it. Why not? They pushed beds together so they could sprawl. They dressed and undressed in front of each other without shame. They wept moodily and fought and laughed and curled up against each other while they slept. They would do each other's hair and endlessly compare their swelling bellies and breasts and feel each other's babies kicking.

Other rooms worked out their own arrangements. One even kept the starburst. Most of the women got along well enough. She tried to deal with whomever the Catholic agencies in Macon and Atlanta sent to her, and she never knew what she would get. Two of the women from Atlanta— the ones who had talked to Melina Lykaios at *Phoe*, both ex-addicts and prostitutes in their mid-twenties—were so vicious they could make the other girls cry with a word or two of comment, so Hermia put them in this room at the far end of the hall.

Thank God they were gone before Miriam came.

The girl had arrived two weeks before the election. When the van let her out, the only passenger, at the front of the house, she stood on the driveway, small and trembling, hardly more than a child, looking up at the other girls on the porch as the driver in a hoodie pulled away. She had a green wool Army blanket pulled over her head and shoulders. From her features and coloring, she might have been Mediterranean, maybe partly black. Her dark eyes had a mad, piercing quality to them. Each time her gaze alighted on one of the girls, she would nod slightly or wince or shake her head faintly and murmur something as though she were coming to a judgment—all of this in a few seconds—until her eyes came to rest on Hermia herself, and her head drew back and she whispered as if she were speaking to someone beside her.

Hermia had descended the steps and offered her hand. "Welcome to Eula's House."

The girl did not take her hand.

"Eula's dead," she said flatly with a hardbitten country accent. She pointed through the latticework level with where she stood on the driveway. "Died in the dark like a dog and her baby with her. Right yonder."

"Eula was a slave. I want to honor her suffering," Hermia explained, taken aback. "That's why I named it Eula's House."

"Ain't you a angel," the girl said.

Hermia controlled herself. Beneath the house, just where the girl had pointed, the women had made a shrine to honor Eula. Dierdre and Jordan had found an icon of the Blessed Mother and arranged it on an easel. Beneath it on the ground where Eula had been chained, they had arranged a tray of votive candles. The women came down, sometimes alone, sometimes in groups, and knelt in the soft dirt under the floor beams of the house to pray. They brought pictures of their families or their boyfriends, old letters, newspaper clippings, pictures ripped from magazines, keys, charms, high school rings, all manner of things that Hermia found disquieting and almost pagan. But it was worth it. Sometimes the whole body of women would gather there, climbing down the low steps and ducking through the low door and navigating the crawlspace to Eula's shrine, and there they would say the rosary and sing the *Salve Regina*.

"I tell her story to our new residents, but I don't know where you heard it—unless you read my book. I wrote about Eula in *Tell Old Pharaoh*."

"I ain't read no goddamn book. I see her ghost yonder chained down and wailing in the dark."

She saw a ripple of fear go through the girls on the porch.

"Is that right?" Hermia said mildly. "Well, this house has quite a history."

"You lucky Sherman ain't burned it. He might yet. Burned mine." The girl turned and looked across the grounds as if she were gauging the possibility of escape. "Both hands up. High noon," she said. "Like the day was under arrest."

Hermia followed the girl's gaze to the courthouse clock on the hill at the center of Gallatin half a mile away. Both hands straight up, as she said. During the two years she had lived here tending old Mrs. Hayes, she had never suspected that she could see the clock, because in those days, the grounds had been wildly overgrown and unkempt. Fallen limbs from the pecan trees and elms had crushed the dogwoods and redbuds that once defined the circular drive from the gate, and the pavement itself was hidden under many seasons of fallen leaves. When Braxton Forrest took ownership, he began the years-long process of clearing the yard and cutting back the hedges that bordered the street. The work crews had discovered flagstone patios, stone benches, masses of azaleas with old paths between them, beds of lovely irises. Now the beautiful downward slope of the front yard was once again gracefully punctuated by the meander of the low stone walls that gave the estate its name, and the courthouse clock showed clearly in the distance.

The girl turned toward Hermia again, meeting her eyes as though she were downloading her soul's hidden contents. But then the uncanny light and presence vanished.

"What do I do?" she mumbled.

"I'm sorry?" It took a second for Hermia to recover.

"What do I do here?"

"Okay, we need to get you registered and show you where you'll be staying. Come on up and I'll ask you the questions I ask all our new residents."

The girl slumped with sandbag heaviness against Hermia, who staggered back, feeling the girl's great pregnancy shifting from within as she held her. Hermia's aides Jordan and Deirdre hurried down the steps and got the girl back upright with effort. Close up, looking into the new girl's face, Hermia saw clearly that she must be underage. Officially, no one younger than eighteen could be admitted, but the unborn had not read that memo. Who had sent her?

The girl let herself be led up the steps. She stumbled and sagged with obvious fatigue.

"Jordan, let her lie down for a bit," she called. "When she's rested, can y'all bring her to my office, please?"

An hour later, the girl stood in front of her desk, her head still hooded by the blanket, and looked out at Hermia from the shadow of it.

"I didn't get any paperwork from the driver, so you're going to need to tell me your name."

"Form says Miriam McPhee. But my name's Josiah. Miriam's a girl's name."

Hermia tilted her head. "I'm sorry?"

"I ain't a girl."

"Is that right?" she smiled.

"The hell you smiling at? You making fun of me? I say I'm a man, what do you have to say about it?"

"Men don't have babies, and you're about to have one. Feel that?"

"Don't you touch me."

"Why do you think your breasts are getting bigger? Girl, you are about to experience the exclusive natural privilege of the female sex."

"Privilege, hell. And who says what's natural? Ain't you kept up? Who says men don't have babies? I can get this place shut down just for you saying I ain't a man, and you know it's the goddamn truth."

The girl locked eyes with her. After a moment, Hermia looked down, her face burning. It might be more effective than a bomb threat, because, absurd as it was, it was true.

She drew her breath in slowly through her nose, imagining the publicity. *Head of Crisis Pregnancy Center Refuses to Respect Birthing Person's Gender Identity.*

Of course, when she was shamed by the woke constituency, conservatives would rally to her. Donald Trump would defend her!

The ironies of it.

Why not humor the girl? It could be some kind of dissociative identity disorder instead of a setup.

But wait.

She smiled.

"What?" said the girl.

"So you're Josiah?"

"Mighty goddamn right. Josiah McPhee, named after my great-great-granddaddy."

"Well, I'm sorry, Josiah. We don't allow men in Eula's House. I'm going to have to ask you to get your things and leave."

The eyes burned with surprise and contempt, but then Josiah died away in a confused flutter of lashes.

The girl nodded, "Yes, ma'am," and smiled with embarrassment.

"Miriam?" Hermia asked.

As she did with all her women, Hermia asked her about why she chose to come to Eula's House. The girl gave flat, listless answers. The boy who got her pregnant had died in a motorcycle accident. Her parents were going to force her to have an abortion, but she found out from a friend about Eula's House. Keeping the baby was her way to keep Billy alive.

It sounded like a lie, but Hermia wrote it all down and had the girl sign her statement. She explained the customs of the residents—the strictly ordered day, beginning with morning prayer in the chapel before breakfast. She asked Miriam if she sang and told her about the choir that Nora Sharpe led. The girl nodded vacantly. Hermia explained the meals together in the Dining Commons, the free time, the library and the study sessions with her aides, who were recent graduates of Transfiguration College in Wyoming. The movie nights, the prohibition against smartphones and laptops.

"Can I answer any questions for you?" Hermia asked at the end of their interview.

"Just one."

Josiah's eyes burned into her.

"How did it feel to make a baby with your own daddy?"

Before she could stop it, the memory blazed up. She remembered that weekend in Evanston with Braxton Forrest in every part of her soul. *Your soul is not your body*, she always told her women and so the soul of Hermia Watson was not the body of Hermia Watson. *No no no no no* Hermia Watson's body was not her soul.

Only the exact and most intimate and inmost shape of it.

Carefully, she composed herself. How could she ever have suspected that he was her father?

"Let me show you to your room," she said.

21

COWBOY STATE

FOR BREAKFAST IN CHEYENNE, THEY FOUND A RESTAURANT called The Missile Stop. Forrest had not slept well, and he pulled into the parking lot irritated by his responsibility to keep *Sage Grouse* going. After the initial expressions of sympathy for Karl Guizac's illness and the laments for the disappearance of Socrates Johnson, no one had responded to his posts. That obviously meant one of two things: either they had already lost the usual readership—he needed to check the statistics on hits—or the usual readers considered his contributions mere filler. He should have claimed his own authority. He should have explained that they were additions to the mosaic of America he was piecing together as his fourth book. Or they might be part of the satirical billionaire-Cinderella novel germinating in his imagination, the one about finding a wife among America's roadside waitresses.

The Missile Stop had a bevy to choose from, but beauties they were not. Still, instead of trying to invent something for *Sage Grouse,* he decided to record the experience of breakfast as it happened.

The waitress, a round-faced girl in her twenties with HADLEY on her nametag, is a little chubby. She hitches her hip to one side and pushes up her glasses while she takes Mrs. Cump's order of coffee and poached eggs, fruit instead of hash browns.

HADLEY: Ma'am we're out of coffee mugs so it has to be them paper travel cups is that alright? We been awful busy this morning and the mugs just run out and listen I can get you fruit but tell you the truth it's out of them cans so it was me I'd just go with the hash browns.

MRS. CUMP: If a real coffee mug shows up, could you bring it to me? I don't like drinking out of paper.

HADLEY: Yes ma'am [*touching the tabletop with her fingertips, genuinely sympathetic, as though she suffered deeply with Mrs. Cump*]. How bout you, big old mister? You already at work on your computer, I see. Can't get away from it.

CUMP: I'm just writing about you.

HADLEY [*flattered*]: Nice try, sugar. But right in front of this lovely lady, you ought to be ashamed.

CUMP: I'll have the Missile Omelet with sausage and cheddar and jalapeños. Pancakes on the side.

HADLEY: How many pancakes, sugar?

CUMP: Three sounds good.

HADLEY: Lots of syrup like a big old sweet-talker?

CUMP: Lots of syrup.

MRS. CUMP: Are you from the South, Hadley?

HADLEY [*frowning with frustration*]: Yes'm. Tennessee. I try to get rid of sounding that way, but.

MRS. CUMP: Don't be ashamed of it. It's who you are.

The waitress makes a wry face and moves to her other customers. A minute or two later, she returns with two ceramic mugs of coffee.

HADLEY: Just look a-here [*she sets them down triumphantly*]. Y'all must be living right. I tell you what, we just can't keep enough of them and can't nobody figure out why. They just disappear. First thing this morning the manager sent me over to Walmart to get some more mugs but I swear to business you need training in karate, I mean people in there *fight you* for things. You go to pick something up and somebody'll push in front of you and yank it away from you. Crackheads, people on meth. Sort of like them zombie shows. [*She opens her mouth and makes her face go blank.*] I mean, not all the time. Just once or twice, but it was bad this morning.

MRS. CUMP: That's terrible.

The girl's face darkens with concern, as though Marisa has just caught her impugning Walmart.

HADLEY: But you know they's another Walmart across town and that's where I go now if I need to except this morning we was in a hurry and I forgot.

She is off to another table. A few minutes later she comes out with their food.

HADLEY: Sugar, I got them to cut you up some real strawberries and there was a little plastic doojiggy of blueberries in the fridge so I hope that's okay and I brought you the hash browns just in case. [*She sets down Mrs. Cump's plate and the fruit in a small bowl.*]

MRS. CUMP: You're a doll.

HADLEY: And here's your omelet and pancakes big old Mr. Sweetie.

When she leaves, they eat in silence for a moment. The pancakes are the best Forrest has tasted in years.

MRS. CUMP: What are you thinking? You're thinking something.

CUMP: The tritest of all thoughts.

MRS. CUMP: About the pancakes? Oh, wait. About *Hadley.*

CUMP: Oh, come on.

MRS. CUMP: What, then?

CUMP: About America.

MRS. CUMP: Oh no.

CUMP: We used to congratulate ourselves. We were the best. We saved the world from Adolf Hitler and Nikita Khrushchev. We assimilated every tribe and nation. We overcame our divisions. Southerners went off to fight for the Union in World War I, and Yankees were magnanimous enough to admire Robert E. Lee.

MRS. CUMP: Why are you thinking this way? [*She pierces a blueberry with one tine of her fork.*] Are you talking about America or about "white" America?

CUMP [*raising his hands*]: Et tu? I don't think it's racial. I think a lot of people feel like something they deserve has been taken away. Something their grandparents had—the vision of a generous America that used to be the hope of the world.

Marisa begins to smile, not looking at him.

CUMP: What?

MRS. CUMP [*as she meets his eyes*]: Cowboy hat, scuffed leather jacket, bolo tie, jeans. We get the noble Forrest profile, and then you turn to the camera, take off your Stetson, run a hand through your hair, and then you say—say that again.

CUMP [*solemnly*]: I think a lot of people feel like something they deserve has been taken away, something their grandparents had—the vision of a generous America that used to be the hope of the world.

MRS. CUMP: Now put your hat back on. Square it off like John Wayne.

CUMP: You'd vote for me and you know it.

MRS. CUMP: Want some pie?

When they finish their apple pie, Mrs. Cump asks Hadley for a pecan pie she had seen on the way into the restaurant—she'll take it to her friend—and the waitress happily brings it over and adds it to the tab. On their way out, Cump goes up to the counter to pay and stands there trying to figure out how to tip the girl for the meal but not the pie, but then he thinks about her trouble at Walmart. He adds a 20% tip for the whole amount.

He posted it verbatim.

Could Hadley be the girl for Dub Calhoun? Not a chance. Dub wasn't man enough for a real Cinderella. Forrest needed more of a cowboy.

Thirty minutes later, they squeezed among the big trucks that labored upward to Lincoln Pass on I-80. America. Abe Lincoln's monumental head bent pensively over the highway. Down the other side with its great long curves and trucks gearing back not to overspeed, the BMW bobbed along like a whaleboat in a great pod of whales and then shot free from the slackening rush in the vast valley where Laramie lay. West of Laramie, electronic messages warned of high crosswinds. Gusts would buffet the side of the BMW, and sometimes the tractor-trailer in front of him veered to the right and then rocked a little too far left. Closer to Rawlins, Elk Mountain rose out of the flat land, majestic and rocky. Clouds hovered upon its holy upper reaches.

At Rawlins they stopped for gas and the restroom and coffee. Forrest checked the *Sage Grouse* website for comments on his Hadley post. There were two. One said "WTF???" and the other said "This guy thinks he's Foster Friess." It stung a little.

Up 287 toward Muddy Gap, they climbed gradually to the continental divide where they could see ahead for forty or fifty miles to another range of mountains, and then the road dropped off into another vast valley floor. Forrest drove as fast as the sparse traffic would allow, and they reached Muddy

Gap a little more than half an hour later. He turned left and they climbed onto another plateau, sublimely barren, spotted with sagebrush, bordered by ancient mountains to the north. Signs pointed to Split Rock, a notch in the mountains like the V in a gunsight. They were crossing the floor of a salty ocean that had been receding for millions of years, landscapes entirely different from the East Coast. The mountains looming due west were the youngest on the continent.

As they dropped off the plateau toward the Sweetwater River, Forrest saw a house and a barn a mile or two north of the road—a pickup truck, a scattering of small trees. What would it have been like to settle here on the frontier, beyond the reach of civilization, without hope of rescue? Those were men and women unfamiliar with the comforts and pleasures he took for granted. But they were realer, maybe more joyful, maybe meaner and more selfish. Sparse water, communities of blood and tough friendship.

A UPS truck pulled out of the drive.

Melancholy swept over him. He sighed.

"Now what?" Marisa asked him.

He shook his head.

The road came to a T eight or nine miles south of De Smet, and when they turned north, small homesteads and barns appeared, ragged settlements. A great herd of black cattle stood in a field still bare of snow, not a cow moving, all of them facing northwest as though magnetized by something in the Wind River Range. After a few miles, Forrest topped the hill on the south of town and drove past various outlying businesses and RV parks, across the intersection, and into the heart of De Smet.

Traffic was light. The town looked deserted. A scatter of customers sat at the tables inside Dunx, the college's coffee shop at the corner of Third and Main. Outside, a professor stood talking to students. Across the street to the left was the building where Walter had his office.

The retail district was only a block deep on either side of Main. He turned left through the residential neighborhood that stretched for half a mile south to Tyler St. where he turned right at the fork to take Washakie Road. Its winding rise and fall twisted through the red-rock cliffs along Wolf Creek and then opened to the smooth rise of the foothills of the Winds several thousand feet from the valley floor, cut by cursive bands of snow and creeks descending from heights shaded by dark evergreens. A downhill curve took them across the creek. Forrest turned onto Sacajawea Court and drove up past a bare field and turned in past the outbuildings. Both doors to the two-bay garage were closed, but a Honda SUV was angled randomly onto the grass near the right side of the house with the driver's door open, as if its hurried driver had just dashed inside the house, fleeing some terror.

"I hope Teresa's okay," Marisa said.

Forrest got out stiffly, looking around. To the north were rounded domes shaped by the wind, backed by ragged, layered ridges of red sandstone spotted with junipers. A great, upward-slanting butte several miles west was profiled against the Wind River Mountains. Off to the south, the foothills rose mile after mile.

Marisa closed the Honda's door on their way to the sliding glass door off the deck. When she knocked, little Marisa came running up and flattened her face comically against the glass. Teresa followed her daughter, eyes wide. Her hair was wild, no makeup. She clutched a white terrycloth robe at the neck. She slid the door open but not the screen.

"My God, Marisa? Braxton? What are y'all doing here?"

Little Marisa kept pulling at her hand asking who they were until Teresa turned on her and snapped, "Stop it!"

"We've been worried," Marisa said. "We haven't heard from you all day. Let me give you a hug," she said, trying to open the screen.

Teresa shrank back. "I just got out of the shower. What are you doing? Don't come in! We're sick." She looked back over her shoulder and called, "Jacob! People are here!"

Marisa met Forrest's eyes. Inside, Jacob—who had grown to be as tall as Forrest since they had last seen him—came out of his bedroom in a t-shirt and jeans, raising a hand to them as he made his way around the wood stove and toward the door, where he stood behind his mother with his hands on her shoulders.

"How's Walter?" Marisa asked Teresa quietly.

"*Walter?*" Teresa said suspiciously. "How do you know Walter?"

"Teresa, honey, don't you know we're—"

"My husband is in the hospital in Salt Lake City."

"I know, sweetheart. Remember, we came out to help you."

"Oh, I don't know about that," she said vaguely.

"Dad's not great," Jacob said, shaking his mother gently.

"Don't talk about your father that way!" Teresa snapped.

"Mom," Jacob said. He held up a pause forefinger to the Forrests and steered his mother toward her room. Marisa pulled Forrest to the other side of the deck.

"My God, Braxton, she didn't even remember we were coming."

Before he could answer, the screen door squealed as it opened behind them, and the boy came out, pulling on a jacket. He pulled the glass door shut and glanced back inside before he turned to them.

"I bet you didn't expect that," he said, smiling. They had not seen him in several years, and Forrest might not have recognized him, now that his adult face was showing through—the strong nose and mouth, something Southern in the cheekbones. He had the same dark hair Forrest remembered—brown, not black—the light eyebrows, the clear eyes, greener than blue, that met yours straight on, without guilty evasion. There was a fine lucidity about him.

"She's been a little bizarre. She won't get checked for Covid, but I know I had a touch of it. Mine's better."

"Bless her heart. Your dad's not doing well?" Marisa asked.

"They're keeping him on the ventilator," he said.

They nodded, thinking about Walter. After a silence, the boy glanced at Forrest and held his hands wide. "I know you're being nice not to mention it. I'm working on it. I'm almost finished. All the stuff with Dad…."

It took Forrest a moment to realize that the boy meant the Sherman project.

"You've done enough, Jacob. Seriously, I didn't really expect you to write a hundred pages. And now with all this—"

He lifted a hand toward the interior of the house and the boy's mother, toward Covid-19 and the boy's father on a ventilator in Salt Lake City and Hadley and zombies at Walmart and an America painfully unraveling before the world.

"Will you read it?"

"Well, if I can get to it, but I don't expect you to—" The boy looked so stricken that he stopped. "Sure, Jacob. I'll read it."

"I'd better check on Mom."

Forrest stepped off the deck onto the dead grass and went past the leafless lilacs to the sagging buck-and-rail fence at the edge of the yard.

"Think they need us?" Marisa said, joining him.

He snorted but did not answer, and a moment later, Jacob came back outside.

"She's asleep."

"Listen," Marisa said to him. "We'll check into our room and touch base later. Do you have a phone?"

"Professor Forrest has my number."

"I'll call you when we get settled," Marisa said. "We'll bring something over for dinner. You take care of your mom."

It was already getting dark when he unloaded the suitcases from the BMW onto the luggage cart at the Holiday Inn Express. Their better clothes, which they kept on hangers, had been sliding around over their suitcases in dry-cleaner plastic since New Hampshire, and now he hung them on the cart's bar, balanced his laptop case and Marisa's various tote bags (books, makeup, gifts) wherever there was room, and pushed the unwieldy jumble through the automatic glass doors.

PLEASE WEAR A MASK.

He stopped to put on his paper mask, left the cart in the lobby while Marisa checked them in, and went back out to park the car.

"Third floor okay?" Marisa said over her shoulder as he came back inside. "View of the mountains."

He shrugged. The clerk, a plump, cheerful-looking woman in a floral mask, gave Marisa a paper sleeve with two keys for the room. Forrest wrestled the cart to the elevator. On the third floor he backed the thing out and steered it behind Marisa to the end of the hall. She looked tired walking ahead of him, her white hair a little mussed, her shoulders slanted, her upper back rounded from the scoliosis she had inherited from her mother. But when she unlocked the room, she gave him the smile that always brightened his mood. The pain she endured on a daily basis humbled him. He put down his briefcase to keep the door from swinging shut and hung the clothes in the closet just inside. To the right past the bathroom, a kind of kitchen—a microwave, a sink, and a Keurig—was open to a sitting area separated by a half-wall from the bedroom. A huge TV chattered in front of the king-size bed. Forrest found the remote and turned it off.

"Poor Teresa," Marisa said. She lay back flat on the bed and pushed off her shoes with opposite feet and pulled the blanket at the bottom of the bed over her. "Why don't you lie down?"

"I have to take the cart back."

She was already snoring lightly.

The elevator rumbled and dinged and opened. He rode down to the first floor and steered the cart into the foyer and left it next to the other two, stationary wheels out. No one was checking in. The clerk did not tell him to wear a mask—he had forgotten it in the room—but she shuffled something on her desk so she could pretend not to see him. He took the elevator back up and opened the door to the room as quietly as he could not to wake Marisa. But she was standing at the window with her back to him. She turned, her arms across her chest, her face full of dismay.

"Cate just called. Oh God, Braxton."

22

BUMMERS

MIDTOWN ATLANTA. FRIDAY, THE 6TH OF NOVEMBER, THE evening hour before the children's bedtime. A tricycle lies tipped into the untrimmed bushes bordering the clapboard beneath curtained windows. From the sidewalk rise steps to the front walkway of a modest house and a small porch surrounded by a wooden railing. A plain black mailbox hangs beside the door.

Inside, Cate Forrest Zitek has spent the day teaching three American history classes remotely for her community college students, competing for bandwidth with her children, who have spent the week complaining about their teachers and trying to keep up with their classwork online. But now they all have the weekend ahead of them. Cate is in the kitchen loading the dishwasher after a dinner of shrimp marinara with fettuccine, ciabatta from the neighborhood bakery, and a salad of mixed greens with bleu cheese crumbles. She rinses a plate into the disposal and takes a sip of Pinot Noir from the glass beside the sink.

CATE: Jimmy! Can you and Clare PLEASE bring me the rest of the dishes?

Jimmy, nine, loves to read. He amasses complicated details from the narratives of Tolkien or Greek and Norse myths, and he's already back on the edge of the couch in the front room absorbed in his fourth reading of Tolkien's Lord of the Rings. *Clare, seven, who takes after her Aunt Bernadette, cartwheels neatly into the kitchen but almost knocks the glass from Cate's hand.*

CATE: Do that outside!

CLARE: Sorry, Mom.

Jimmy pushes past Clare into the kitchen with two empty water glasses.

CATE: Where's Avila? *She softens her voice.* Avila, bring me your bowl, sweetie.

She hears the child slide off her chair in the next room. The booster seat tips off and thumps onto the floor, and three-year-old Avila, black-haired, with the huge eyes and tiny mouth of a nineteenth-century actress, comes in with her bowl in both hands, her bib plastered with sauce and bits of pasta.

A heavy pounding at the front door. They all go still. More pounding, angry and insistent. The children shrink to the back of the kitchen. They hear cursing. A key in the lock. The door opens so violently it rebounds from the wall and hits Jason Zitek in the head as he lurches into the threshold.

ZITEK: GOD DAMN IT! Why don't you open the door when I knock?

He stands there swaying.

CATE: What do you want, Jason? Can't you just knock politely instead of slamming your fist on the door?

ZITEK: I need my winter clothes. Get out of my way.

CATE: I'm not in your way. My God, you just barge in here and scare everybody to death?

ZITEK: I need my sweaters. Where's my goddamn overcoat?

The children watch him from behind their mother, terrified of his temper but ready to go to him if he shows any affection. He fumbles at the door of the bedroom and plunges in, cursing as he trips over a child's shoe, which he picks up and hurls into the dining room, knocking over a glass on the table. Cate follows him into the room. He goes to the closet, pushes aside her clothes, finds his overcoat, and throws it on the bed while she stands watching him. He goes to the dresser and yanks open the bottom drawer.

ZITEK: What did you do with my sweaters?

CATE: They're in a box in the laundry room. You haven't been here in a month, and they were taking up too much room. Besides, I didn't think you would want them since I bought most of them for you. You don't want to look like somebody's husband.

He curses and starts flinging her things from the drawer.

In the living room, Clare screams. Cate goes out to see why, and there, leaning forward through the doorway, is a woman, Melina Lykaios, who holds onto the doorjamb and recoils when she sees the children.

LYKAIOS: Jason!

CATE (*instantly furious*): Do you have the audacity to—get out of here! Jason, get this woman out of my house!

ZITEK [*from the bedroom doorway, seeing the terror on his children's faces*]: I got my stuff. Let's go, Melina.

LYKAIOS: You're the one who said we had to get your clothes.

CATE: Get out! Get out of my house!

She snatches up a heavy brass armadillo paperweight and holds it up, threatening Lykaios and driving her backward through the door. Terrified, Lykaios loses her footing as she scrambles backward and bumps into the railing of the front stoop. Her momentum carries her over it and she falls, screaming as her arm twists beneath her as she hits the ground.

Forrest stood looking out the window. Was that how it was? Worse? His rage rose steadily, hot and solid in his chest.

"Say something, Braxton."

"I'll kill him."

"That's always your—"

Marisa's phone chimed.

"Cate? . . . Oh, Teresa. I'm sorry, we just got a very disturbing call from Cate and were trying to think what to do . . . No, it's okay. I understand. Are you feeling better? We'll bring over something to eat, okay?… We'll just hand it through the door, then, but we'll be there soon."

23

SAVING THE SAGE

ON SATURDAY MORNING, THE NETWORKS RACED EACH
other to announce that Joe Biden had won. First across the line was Wolf
Blitzer at CNN, excited and humbled to announce the defeat of Donald
Trump. The results from Pennsylvania had come in, and the absentee ballots
proved to be decisive for that state's electoral votes, which put Biden over the
number that he needed.

Forrest had known for months that Trump could not win. It was too
bad that Walter Peach was unconscious in the hospital. Socrates Johnson had
been predicting this situation for months, and his comments now would have
had a special piquancy. So what would Forrest do instead? The question ate
at him.

After breakfast, they went by Safeway so Marisa could pick up more
groceries. Forrest sat in the car thinking about alternatives for sustaining *Sage
Grouse*, until she came back out and he helped her get the groceries from
the basket into the trunk. At the Peach house, she insisted on taking the
groceries inside. Forrest hovered near the threshold while Teresa described
the Covid protocols that had been recommended to her. Marisa exhaled
impatiently through her nose like a Sicilian matriarch listening to the excuses
of a teenaged daughter who turned up pregnant.

"Listen to me, Teresa," she said. "This isn't the black plague."

"Don't be flippant! Walter might die of it!"

"If we're going to get it, we're going to get it—"

"That's so fatalistic!"

"You said yourself that Little M was probably exposed to it at her school and brought it home and gave it to Walter, who for whatever reason got very sick. You might have it, but why aren't you sicker? It's unpredictable, and I'm telling you, I am *not* going to spend my week trying to avoid anybody who might have it. Especially you. Most of all you. Who I'm here to help." She turned and began putting down bags of groceries on the counter. "We're all going to get it at some point or another," she continued. "Do you want me to wear a mask? I'll wear a mask, even though I'll feel like a fool doing it. Do you know I saw somebody driving down the street all alone wearing a mask? In De Smet, Wyoming! I'll wash my hands every few minutes *if you insist*, but I *am* going to be here every day helping you. We drove here from New Hampshire to help you, and you're not going to stop us."

Teresa began to smile.

"I love you, Marisa. Do you know that?"

Marisa stopped putting the groceries away and looked at her.

Forrest left them and drove into town, where he went inside the college coffee shop and set up his laptop at a table in the back corner. For more than two days, from very early on Tuesday, Election Day, when Guizac had announced his plans to visit the Wind River Reservation, *Sage Grouse* had been dropping precipitously in daily hits, despite Forrest's efforts. They had been looking forward to Socrates Johnson's commentary on the election, and there was nothing but Tecumseh—where did that even come from?—and breakfast in Cheyenne. Thank God he hadn't tried Dub Calhoun. Readers were openly skeptical. Had somebody hacked the website and Forrest didn't want to admit it? Guizac had Covid, seriously? Everybody knew Covid wasn't a big deal.

He needed to put something online to keep the readership. But after an hour, he closed his laptop without writing a word.

They had a light breakfast the next morning and took Jacob with them to the ten o'clock Mass at Immaculate Conception. Teresa stayed home, afraid that Little M might be contagious. The priest was a burly former wrestler steeped in history who startled his congregation several times during a homily about the wise and foolish virgins by pounding on the pulpit to illustrate the Lord's point about being wakeful.

The air outside after Mass was cold enough to wake up anybody. The church was on high ground, and coming out of the sanctuary parishioners had a splendid view of the Wind River Mountains to the west. On the way out, Forrest shook the priest's hand—his grip was impressive—and thanked him. Within a minute, they were discussing lamp oil and the reasons kerosene had supplanted whale oil in the nineteenth century when Jacob interrupted to invite them to meet Emily Turnbow and her parents. Marisa whispered, "Ask Dr. Turnbow about finding substitutes for Walter."

As they approached, Jacob proudly presented Emily, who had a thick mane of blonde hair and a Sicilian complexion with lively, forthright hazel eyes and an expressive mouth.

"So you're the great oppressor," she said to Forrest, as Marisa met her parents.

He liked her immediately.

"I'm the one."

"Marcellus Turnbow," said her father from above. A voice on the sepulchral spectrum. The man towered over him—a rare thing in his life. The man had to be seven feet tall.

"Jacob tells me you teach music at Transfiguration."

"I do indeed, and your lovely wife has just explained your problem with *Sage Grouse*. You should talk to Ethan Weald."

Turnbow was surprised he did not know Weald, who had become president of Transfiguration when his predecessor, Dr. Gina Presson, had been hired away the previous winter to chair the Department of Political Philosophy at Notre Dame, where they had offered her triple the salary she was receiving at Transfiguration.

"Ethan never wanted the presidency, but he accepted it at the board's urging. And he likes *Sage Grouse*. He and Karl have coffee at Dunx on occasion."

"Good to know," said Forrest.

The next morning, Weald invited Forrest to his office, a book-lined space with a big meeting table and large windows overlooking Main Street. He was a white-haired, genial Southerner who had been in and out of academia. A decade or so before, he had been a theater and film critic in Houston, so he was well-acquainted with contemporary culture. He thought Karl Guizac was touched with genius.

"You know he had to be life-flighted to Salt Lake City?" Forrest asked.

"I heard that."

"This leaves *Sage Grouse* in a quandary. He's worked hard to build it up, and he was virtually the whole website. Its localism is something of a trope but it works. I'm wondering whether you know faculty who could help me. I think you know the tone of the website. Maybe you even know students who'd like to try their hand."

Weald's email went out that afternoon.

Dear Transfiguration Community:

You have surely heard that Karl Guizac, the brilliant editor of *Sage Grouse*, has been hospitalized in Salt Lake City with a severe case of Covid-19. Please keep him in your prayers. In his absence, the publisher, Dr. Braxton Forrest, is looking for talented people who can continue Mr. Guizac's work in this very interesting season. He hopes to hire writers and editors to divide the work that Mr. Guizac was doing single-handedly. As Dr. Forrest described *Sage Grouse*, it is local but national, theatrical but sardonic, factual but opinionated, irascible but wise.

Because of his own obligations, Dr. Forrest will need someone to handle editing, subscriptions, and contributions. This position will be well paid (subject to negotiation). Professors, this would be a good forum for opinion pieces about the election and its aftermath or the culture as it now appears. You might offer commentaries on contemporary books and films. As you know, *Sage Grouse* has a national audience; it has garnered attention from such people as Ross Douthat at the *New York Times*. Yet its focus on Wyoming remains crucial, because the Cowboy State remains a powerful symbol in today's culture.

Please email Dr. Forrest with your interest (braxton.t.forrest@walcott.edu or cump.forrest@gmail.com). He will respond promptly to set up an interview.

Sincerely,

Ethan Weald, President

The response was immediate and gratifying. Eight students expressed interest, and Forrest chose the three with the most experience, including a cartoonist Weald had mentioned and a tall, gangling satirist named Joe Brown, who for years had run a satirical online newsletter skewering the foibles of the college and the excesses of the day. Of the two Humanities professors who contacted him, Dr. Bitford Carbury had deep roots in the political philosophy of Leo Strauss, and Dr. Samuel Warner was a scholar of the Fugitive-Agrarians at Vanderbilt a century before. Forrest would retain a veto over editorial content, Dr. Carbury would solicit and edit columns on political topics, gratis, and the daily organization and general stewardship would fall to Prof. Warner, who had attended journalism school at Southern Methodist University as an undergraduate. With a stint at a city magazine in Atlanta years earlier (before he attended graduate school) and current work with his own blog, he had the background *Sage Grouse* needed. Unlike Carbury, he wanted a thousand dollars a week.

"That's pretty steep," Forrest said.

"Not for the work involved and the quality you want. If I didn't do this, I'd be doing online courses to supplement my income. I have six kids to feed. Transfiguration's not exactly rolling in money."

"Fair enough."

The next morning, a week after the election, he dropped Marisa off at the Guizac house. She wanted to entertain Little M and help Teresa fix breakfast. Snow was coming. On his way to the office in town, he passed Jacob, who had gotten up at four-thirty or five that morning to work on his Sherman project for a few hours before going on his daily run. Coming up behind him in the BMW on the last rise before De Smet, Forrest admired the long, tireless stride, the concentration. He gave a thumbs-up as he passed, but the boy did not notice him.

He stopped by Dunx to order coffee and scones for his new team. As he was waiting, Emily Turnbow gave him a wave from a back table. Just then the boy came in, breathing hard, and went straight to her without seeing Forrest until she said something and the boy turned around and waved.

Forrest walked over to the table.

"I passed you while you were running but you didn't see me."

"I was thinking about Emily," the boy grinned.

"Well I hope so," she said.

"I finished Kennesaw! I'll send it to you when I get back to the house."

"I can't read it until I get *Sage Grouse* taken care of. Then I might have to go to Georgia."

"Georgia? Seriously?"

At the counter, he picked up the coffee and scones and headed outside. It smelled like snow was coming. He crossed the street and took the stairs up to Guizac's office to meet with the new team. Readers missed Socrates Johnson, but they liked the Bub Cross cartoon of Biden trying to ride a Wyoming bronco, and gangling Joe Brown had introduced a character named Everette Polinski (who had a twin brother named Everett) moderating a short and very catty *just-us-girls* dialogue about Melania Trump between Hillary Clinton and Kamala Harris. Warner had a piece about a farmer in Hudson, and Dr. Carbury wanted to write about bureaucracy and especially overreach by the Bureau of Land Management. Forrest was feeling good about it. They worked out a schedule, aiming for a website redesign the Monday after Thanksgiving.

. . . .

Rinsing the dishes to put in the dishwasher, Teresa worried. Rose once told her that worrying was her vocation. Maybe so. It was different from prayer. She stared out at the snow and worried about neglecting Little M, who had to stay home on quarantine. She worried about being a good hostess to Braxton and Marisa, especially after the disaster of their arrival, when she had forgotten they were coming. She worried about Jacob's obsession with Sherman. It was over a week after the election and Jacob's miserable birthday, and the project was supposed to be over, but it wasn't. Most of all, though, she worried about Walter. For hours every day, caught up in small tasks, she forgot about him—forgot he was her husband, forgot he existed at all—and it made her worry that she was losing her mind as well as her husband, who was lying unconscious three hundred miles away.

She was almost grateful when her phone started up, even though the ringtone she had chosen—it reminded her of Philip Glass—now drove her crazy. She kept forgetting to change it. She pushed aside a pile of appeals from nonprofits and a day-old *Wall Street Journal* and found the phone between Orvis and Crate & Barrel.

UoUHSP, which confused her, then alarmed her.

"Hello?" she said, touching her sternum with her fingertips.

—May I speak to Mrs. Guizac?

"This is she."

—Mrs. Guizac, we need to confirm some insurance information.

Teresa fought down her irritation.

"Just a minute. I need to find the card."

The little way, St. Therese always said. In every moment, the little movements of the soul, the small acts of kindness, could be offered to Jesus. As she went into the living room to look for her purse, she prayed half-heartedly for the officious woman in Utah, probably a Mormon who thought Teresa was an infidel. She found her purse in the corner of the couch and felt into it to retrieve the wallet bulging with cards that Walter was always telling her to organize. *If you always keep the cards you use most in the same place, you'll know where they are.* She took the thing back to the kitchen counter and sorted through the sliding plastic spillage to find the insurance card. Walter wasn't exactly Marie Kondo himself. Who was he to—

Suddenly the image of Walter unconscious in a hospital bed weakened her knees. The ventilator, inflating and deflating her unconscious husband.

"I have it," she said into the phone.

—Seek and ye shall find, the woman said patiently.

Teresa sighed and read the information to her, and the woman read it back and asked if there were secondary insurances the hospital should be aware of.

—Because there's a substantial deductible.

"Yes, I know. We were okay until now. We've been pretty healthy. I'm sure you've encountered this situation often," she said, feeling her voice turn, "and I'm sure the hospital would be okay even if we didn't pay you a penny."

—Thank you for the information, Mrs. Guizac, said the woman less pleasantly.

"From what I hear, the government is pumping money into hospitals for anything you can claim is Covid-related, whether it's actually Covid or not," Teresa said.

—Have a blessed day, the woman said, ending the call.

A blessed day. It didn't sound Mormon. Evangelical?

Yes, I will have a blessed day, she thought. A blessed day on the little way.

Hungry, she opened the refrigerator and moved containers of leftovers—
an old peanut butter sandwich in a Ziploc bag (one of Little M's rejects
from her lunch box), a bitten apple, an empty box of almond milk (who put
that back?)—until she finally found the Greek yogurt and a few remaining
blueberries in a plastic clamshell.

She heard Jacob's door open. A moment later, the boy came into the
kitchen. Oh, he was a handsome thing, taller than his father, lean and
angular, and her heart surged with affection when she saw his thick brown
hair sticking out every which way. She'd like to draw it. Just the hair. *Remnants
of a Haystack Attacked by a Pitchfork.*

"Who was on the phone?" he yawned.

"The hospital. Not about your dad, just about insurance. Come here."

She set down the yogurt and took the oximeter from the basket next to
the mail on the counter and attached it to his finger. Then she beeped his
forehead with the temperature gauge. 98 on both.

"Can I borrow the Honda? I can't run until there's no ice on the road. I
need to tell Emily I'm leaving with Professor Forrest."

She stared up at him in disbelief.

"What can you possibly mean?"

"Whoops. Mom, may I go with Professor Forrest to Georgia to finish my
work on Sherman?"

"You're joking."

"No, really."

"Of course not, Jacob!" she exploded. "We have so many things up in the
air. Think about your poor father lying there in that bed in Utah."

"They won't let us see Dad. You said so yourself."

"What if, God forbid, we need to get to Salt Lake City quickly?"

"I can fly from wherever we are on the road."

"Oh, you can? It's not like there are major airports every few miles. I
cannot believe you would put this Sherman project ahead of your own family.
Seriously, Jacob, this feels a little sick."

"Sherman *is* my family," he said, putting both hands in his hair. "I don't
know how to explain it."

"It's an obsession."

"There are reasons for obsessions. This is *about* Dad," Jacob said. "Sherman *is* Dad."

She found a cereal bowl in the cabinet and set it on the counter, scooped yogurt into her bowl, and shook the rinsed blueberries into it. She sat down at the kitchen table and looked up at him and sighed.

"So now your father is Gen. Sherman."

Jacob laced his fingers and turned his wrists out and stretched up to touch the ceiling of the kitchen and then bent over to touch his toes. He rotated his shoulders and shook his arms to loosen himself and then sat down across from her. He was suddenly grinning.

"You have a cousin," he said, "who thinks he's the son of Sacajawea."

She smiled despite herself.

"Dear Cousin Jeffrey."

"A lot of things about Sherman remind me of Dad," Jacob said. "The foster parents, the two mothers. His wife who's more pious than he is. His resentment of the church."

"Your father doesn't resent the church," she said.

"Seriously? All those bishops? The McCarrick scandal? Pope Francis?"

Walter resented many things, Teresa knew, and he could be prickly about them in *Sage Grouse*. Patience, patience, Teresa. *The little way,* she reminded herself. Help me, St. Therese.

St. Therese, who did not have a dying husband or a teenage son. An image suddenly rose before her: not St. Therese the young nun suffering from consumption, but St. Therese as a plump French housewife, thirty-eight years old, yelling over her shoulder at her teenaged son and rocking a baby on her hip while preparing the cassoulet.

A tap on the glass door startled her. It slid open and Marisa Forrest bumped inside with several bags of groceries dangling from her hands. Jacob got up and helped her set them on the counter near the refrigerator while Teresa sat frozen at the table with her spoon suspended in the air.

"You caught me," she said, "imagining St. Therese of Lisieux as a middle-aged housewife."

Her friend had let her hair go white—the truth was, Teresa had actually not recognized her when they arrived the previous Friday—but her face had a lovely, live clarity that warmed the room when she tilted her head and smiled.

"As a woman in my reading group always asks, *very* compassionately, is there a story you need to share?"

"I was thinking about the little way, and I had this feeling I get sometimes—you know, that I'm out of luck spiritually because I'm not in a convent suffering joyfully with a wasting disease. Sometimes I feel like there's some baroque Catholic gene I didn't get that lets you savor the painful early deaths of young nuns. Like I'm supposed to pity them and revere them at the same time. I mean, you're Sicilian, and you've got the gene, right?" As Marisa gazed at her, Teresa felt herself blush. "I'm an ex-Methodist from Alabama. For me, it's like being expected to admire bad art. All that horrible *poshlost* on the holy cards."

To her embarrassment, Marisa did not answer.

"I'm just a bad person," Teresa admitted.

"I don't know if you're bad, but you sound like my husband, and he's bad."

"Sometimes I just—I mean, I love the little way, but."

"You should talk to Hermia Watson."

"Hermia Watson!" Teresa exclaimed.

"You didn't know she's a saint now?" Marisa said. "I'll show you the article."

It was hard to read her tone. Teresa remembered Hermia's visit to Stonewall Hill at Christmas years before. The woman had pretended that her father was the old undertaker in Macon her mother had married, when everybody knew that Forrest was not only her father but also the father of her son, the football star John Bell Hudson. It had been unnerving to listen to her lie so glibly.

For that matter, why wasn't Forrest himself stumbling around under the burden of the curse like blind old Oedipus, instead of tooling around the country healthy as a stud horse as he approached seventy?

"You knew she was at Stonewall Hill, didn't you?" Marisa said.

"Walter told me she was running some kind of home."

"Yes, for pregnant women who need help. There's one in Chicago she's modeled this one on. They serve pregnant teenagers, or sometimes women whose husbands or boyfriends abuse them and try to force them into having abortions."

"Mom," Jacob interjected. "Mrs. Forrest's here, so can I take the car?"

"Right now?"

"I need to tell Emily I'm leaving."

"You *cannot* be serious!" she cried, beginning to panic. "Marisa, please tell this boy that your husband has no intention of driving to Georgia with him."

"Driving to Georgia?"

"You see?"

"Well," Marisa said. "He might. Cate's situation, and now this business at Stonewall Hill."

"What business?"

"Threats. People in Gallatin don't like having the girls there. And now one of her women sounds like a serious mental case. I just got a text from Hermia, and I need to call her."

"Use Walter's office. That's where the signal is strongest."

When Marisa excused herself, Teresa kept Jacob standing there while she finished the yogurt. The boy shifted from foot to foot. She loved making him nervous.

"Whether I go to Georgia or not, I still want to see Emily," he said. "She couldn't come to Dunx this morning, and I missed her when I ran into town."

Teresa sighed.

"Well go on, then," she said to Jacob. "I mean go see Emily."

"Where are the keys?"

"Where they're supposed to be," she said.

Walter always put the car keys in the same place on the small hallway table.

"No, they're not, Mom. I've already looked."

"You've already looked. Presumptuous. They must be in my purse."

"So where's your purse?"

He was a handsome thing.

When Jacob set off the little bell on the door of Bean Belay, the masked woman at the counter did not even look up. "Mask please," she said automatically, and Jacob hooked his blue paper mask over his right ear and smiled at Emily—she had turned in her chair—before he covered his face with the thing. Already from outside, he had seen her hair.

"Suppose I go on a trip," he said, pulling out the metal chair to join her. "Would you forget about me? Would you fall in love with somebody else?"

Emily gazed at him. Her mouth registered various ironies as she waited for him to say what he was going to say.

"Professor Forrest needs to go to Georgia, and I'm thinking about going with him."

"Because of Sherman," she said flatly.

"I have to finish. You told me to."

Emily sighed. "What, you're going to write the rest of it in the car?"

"I mean, maybe some of it, but mainly it's seeing Kennesaw. And the path of the March. Seeing the landscape. I used to live there, but that was before this project on Sherman. Just being there will help me finish."

"How long will you be gone?"

"A couple of weeks. Maybe less. It's a lot of time in the car."

"Can you promise me that you will be through with Sherman when you come back?"

"I solemnly swear it to you."

"Classes end the day before Thanksgiving, two weeks from now. I've got papers to write and finals to study for, so it's not like I have a lot of time anyway. You know I want you to finish it. It's changing you. I think it's deepening you, but what if it's just making you more like Sherman?"

Jacob stared through the window at the sparse traffic. Mrs. Forrest was right: people drove alone in their cars, wearing masks. It was insane. Or they wore masks outdoors, walking on the sidewalk with no one within a block of them. It was a sad, numb, stupid, paralyzing time.

"What if my father dies?" he said aloud.

"Don't say that." Emily hushed him, putting her hand on his.

"Even if I go to Salt Lake City, they won't let me in. They won't let anybody see him. Think about that, Emily—suppose he's dying?"

Tears started to her eyes. "When would you leave if you go with Professor Forrest?"

"Tomorrow."

"*Tomorrow?*" The word threw a panic into them both.

Tomorrow.

"What are you going to talk about all that time ?" she asked him.

Half an hour later, when Marisa emerged from Walter's office where she had gone to make the call, she retrieved her laptop from her bag and sat down at the kitchen table and summoned Teresa.

"I told her to have an open house so people in town could see what she's actually doing. It will help squelch the rumors. Chick Lee's going to help."

"Why Chick?"

"Not sure. Maybe through his dealership."

"Not to be rude, but do you believe she's actually Catholic?" Teresa added.

"I do, actually."

She opened her laptop, typed a little, and then swung her screen toward Teresa, who leaned forward. She was startled to see the face of Hermia Watson—that oval face, the eyes—beside an interview in an online journal called *Prie-Dieu* edited by Deacon Leif Asquith from a parish north of Atlanta. After a brief description of Stonewall Hill as "an antebellum mansion" in Gallatin and an overview of the mission of Eula's House, the deacon treated Hermia as though she were a well-known spiritual guide. There was no mention of "You Lose Plantation."

NOTES FROM A LIFE OF PRAYER

What is your daily schedule of prayer?

I try to observe the hours. The Psalms have been part of liturgical practice since the very early centuries. It's not just a matter of reciting them, of course, but of trying to come close to God through these hymns of thanksgiving and praise and pleading. But that's not the only way to pray, of course.

What are the other ways that you have found fruitful?

Well, I learned from a friend of mine to say the Jesus prayer.

Teresa's heart heaved strangely. She had taught Hermia that prayer.

Can you remind us what that is?

When you breathe in, you say *Lord Jesus Christ, son of God,* and then when you breathe out you say, *Have mercy on me, a sinner.* You try to do it with every breath, so you pray without ceasing.

Doesn't it just become rote? Is it really prayer if you are just saying words?

That's always a good question with verbal prayer. Are you letting your mind drift elsewhere? Or is there some real engagement that you achieve simply through the intention and the repetition of the words? I think you can try to concentrate on the meaning of the words, or you can use them as a kind of underlying rhythm, a way of staying open to the presence of God. It's like saying the rosary. If you rise into real meditation, it can be fruitful even if you're not concentrating on the words themselves. But on the other hand, if you're thinking about needing to get gas for your car or picking up prescriptions at the pharmacy or plotting how to get even with a co-worker—is that really prayer? We want to say no, but maybe it is. Maybe God's work in us is simply hidden from our conscious minds, as Sr. Ruth Burrows says. Maybe what counts is making the effort.

What counts, you said. Do you mean it adds up somehow? Do you really think God keeps track of every little thing?

I think we need to feel that the unseen good we do participates in God. And it's not even our merit. The recognition of our own lousiness counts, in the sense that it acknowledges God. The effort to pray is good, even if you're distracted and mean and petty. It's like you've invited God to look at you, and that can't damage you, even if it hurts to see yourself as you really are.

How do you know that you've achieved an authentic relationship with God?

That's hard to talk about. Maybe the hardest thing for me. Sometimes I feel like if I can achieve a kind of listening silence, that's the closest I can be. Almost as though I'm not there but at the same time fully present. It's God moving in me.

Moving in you?

That may be the wrong way to say it. But there's a warming of the heart, a clarifying, a strengthening.

Do you bring your mode of prayer to the girls in Gallatin?

Oh, I don't know if you can ever give it to anyone else. I try to give them some of the practices, anyway. It's hard to know how seriously they take the routine or how effective it is. The best thing they do is sing. Some of them say the rosary. I pray for them all the time. I ask others to pray for them, too. These are young women the culture treats as failures because they bear a new life inside them. The rational thing, they're told, would be to abort their babies, but that would be a deep violation of the truth they feel within them. They wouldn't be at Eula's House if they didn't feel that truth. Our mission is to encourage them to remain open to life, and we help them in every way we can. Every one of them is unique, every single woman. It's never easy.

Thank you, Miss Watson, for the work you do, and thank you for taking time to talk.

God bless you for the opportunity.

Teresa sighed and looked up at Marisa when she finished reading.

"I remember when Lydia Downs convinced Hermia to try some kind of dream divination. It all sounded creepy and syncretistic. But not this," she said, tapping the laptop screen.

"Lydia Downs?" said Marisa.

"Don't get me started. Sweet Hudson Bennett. I still can't believe he fell for her and moved to Arizona. She got that project started out at Missy's Garden, remember? And then got bored with it?"

"I remember her now. Sorry. But Hermia had a real conversion. She stayed with the Nashville Dominicans for a month."

"Not as long as the beautiful Nora O'Hearn," Teresa said. "I should have said the Litany of Humility this morning."

Marisa laughed. "Help me think through how she would organize an open house."

Teresa remembered the gate to the circular drive. The pillared front of the house. A shudder went through her. She could not imagine going back.

"My goodness," Marisa said. "Hermia Watson."

An image rose before them both, and they gazed at it for a moment, met each other's gaze, smiled, and shook their heads.

"Hermia Watson."

"What have you heard about Walter?" Forrest asked that night as Teresa, Jacob, and Little M were finishing their dinner of roast chicken, sweet potatoes, and broccoli.

"Not a thing. I heard from the business office, though."

"Those places want their money."

Marisa's phone rang in her purse on the couch.

"It might be Cate," she said. She fetched the phone and nodded at them—it was Cate—and stepped past the table and slid open the glass door to step onto the deck, hugging herself against the cold. Teresa watched the outrage hit her. When the door slid back open a minute or so later, Marisa held out the phone as if it had bitten her.

"That woman wants to press charges against her."

Teresa put her hand on her mouth.

"For what?" Forrest exclaimed.

"Assault."

"My God, it was a home invasion. Cate was just defending her house. Cate could've shot her, and she would have been completely within her rights. Her neighbor saw the whole thing—"

"That woman says it's Jason's house and he invited her in."

"It's my house, not Zitek's," Forrest said, standing up. "My name's on the deed."

The same was true of this house, Teresa thought with a pang.

"My God, Braxton, to think we loved him," Marisa said.

"I'm going down there," Forrest said.

"You'll kill him."

Little Marisa had slid from her chair, and she was standing beside Teresa with her forefinger in her mouth, staring up at the huge, furious man. Forrest tried to smile at her, but his smile looked ghastly, coming as it did out of the dark rage that shook him. The child started tugging at Teresa to be picked up. Forrest shook his head and walked over to the glass and stared out over the Russian olives and the neighboring pasture with its brown grasses and sagebrush.

"I just want her out of Atlanta," he said, turning back to face Marisa. "I can take Cate and her kids down to Gallatin for a while. I need to check on Hermia, anyway."

"When people are threatening to blow up Stonewall Hill?" Marisa exclaimed. "That doesn't make *any* sense, Braxton."

"Okay! Okay!" he shouted. Little M burst into tears, clutching Teresa, who walked with her to the other side of the room, rocking her lightly. Teresa met Forrest's eyes, lifted her eyebrows, tilted her head.

"Marisa is a big help to me," she said.

"Right," Forrest said to Marisa. "You don't scare anybody. You can use Teresa's car and I'll take ours. I can be down there in two or three days and I can figure out what to do once I see how things are. Maybe I'll bring her here."

Teresa watched it fall into place. Marisa would bring her things from the motel, Forrest would go to Georgia. She surprised herself with a twist of resentment. She prized her quiet. At least Jacob would be here.

"You have to promise not to do anything to Jason," Marisa insisted.

"I'm not going to hurt him."

"I'll make sure," said Jacob Guizac.

Teresa's whole soul seized up.

"Oh my God! Don't even think about it," Teresa said. "No, no, no, no. I need you here."

"You really don't, Mom."

Her anger rose, but so did her recognition that it was true.

"You're just obsessed with Sherman. What would Professor Forrest do with you once he got there? They have all these family crises. And what about Emily?"

She was grasping at straws: she knew it herself.

The boy wanted to go with Forrest, and Jacob's earnestness was frightening, given the circumstances. Forrest had wanted a hundred pages to sound absurdly long, but he also wanted the boy to realize how difficult it was to deal with the whole reality of a man in so short a space. The more you tried to re-create historical situations, the more you discovered you were dealing with more than that one man, though he was a kind of infinity in himself. Wasn't that what he wanted the boy to understand?

It had just been a practical joke for Walter's benefit, like renaming the family Guizac, but if he had to ascribe intention to his instinct, it would be that history overwhelms you—all these souls caught up in the same moment that was unquestionably as real as this one, but that very moment was ungraspable by a single person living it, even one person looking to his own motives. All the sufferings and small pleasures and acts of lust or greed or cowardice or mercy, all the decisions, all the desire and pain and *consciousness* barreling along like the trucks on the interstate: and *there you were* sensing it, feeling it happen with a kind of despair and madness gaining on you. Suppose you entered the consciousness of someone like Sherman, aware that what he did affected millions of people.

The sky had clouded over, and light snow had begun to fall again. He would have to check the forecast to see whether he would be able to drive south in the morning. He felt the urgency of getting to Georgia, but he had foreseen the drive as an extended solitude when he could begin to think through his achievements, if any of them made any difference, and what he was going to do in his seventies. What was there left to do before he died, however his death would come? Could he find some opportunity to make Marisa and his daughter and grandchildren better off? They were okay for money, that wasn't what he meant, but what about something he might show them, share with them, teach them?

Marisa was used to his silences, but if the boy went with him, he would have to make conversation, day after day. Maybe he could turn the drive into the completion of the boy's tutorial. The old man shares the truths about life?

What did he know that Jacob Guizac needed to understand? He knew something about eros. They could talk about Sherman. The truth of literature, the burden of history, the necessity of memory. What had been gained, what had been lost, what had been forgotten. He might end up being important to the boy.

Suddenly, the whole thing seemed brilliant. Marisa could take care of Teresa and the little girl. He would drive to Georgia with Jacob Guizac.

24

ABANDONED

MR. GUIZAC?

The sound was coming from somewhere far above him, perhaps from between the two clouds drifting high over the Georgia landscape north of Atlanta. He felt a sharp prodding in his shoulder—here it was, the sharpshooter's bullet he had expected every day. Now his shirt would blossom with blood and then he would fall sideways from his horse thinking of—of—

A face appeared in the heavens, the nose and mouth covered by a white, oddly beaked mask. Two eyes peered down at him from behind a pair of owlish black-rimmed glasses.

Mr. Guizac?

It was the voice of a woman who had torn open the blue skies of 1864 like a tissuey curtain and conjured a room with fluorescent lights alternating with white ceiling tiles.

Other heads, other masks appeared in a circle around him, looking down. Were these the gods?

Surely not.

Mr. Guizac? We're bringing you out. Can you hear me?

He heard an odd, rusty squawk from the area of his throat. *Aaaack-haaryuuu.*

Mr. Guizac? Do you know where you are?

It did not seem right to ask. No, this must be the next phase of his examination. He had no idea where he was, actually, so he shook his head. He wanted to make a self-deprecating gesture, but he found he could not lift his hands, and as he realized that he was bound, he panicked, trying to shake free. They lifted something that had covered his nose and mouth, and he could see tubes coming into it.

It was hard to breathe. Where was he? Hands were pressing against him.

Mr. Guizac! Mr. Guizac!

He closed his eyes. A thought came to him like the first dove returning to Noah's Ark, the one with nothing in its mouth. He saw himself leaving the store on the reservation, driving toward Ethete to check on the vote.

Mr. Guizac!

He opened his eyes for a second and then closed them again. Now the second dove came back, and he took from the dove's beak a small strip of paper like the one in a fortune cookie, and he opened it. It was a note from Teresa.

Where are you?

Mr. Guizac!

He opened his eyes and focused on the owl-woman.

Do you know where you are?

Nawk, he answered sensibly.

You are still in the intensive care unit of the hospital at the University of Utah in Salt Lake City. Your wife has been keeping in close touch the whole time you have been here under sedation. You have Covid pneumonia. The air sacs keep filling with fluid leaking from the capillaries in the lung tissue, and it's difficult to get enough oxygen into you. We are going to have to induce a coma again to keep you on the ventilator, but now might be a good time to talk to your wife.

How long. Here.

About ten days.

He tried to speak but gave up.

You were life-flighted to Salt Lake City—when was it? she asked one of the others. Election Day, the first Tuesday in November, correct? What was the date? November 3. Today is Thursday, November 12. Sir! Sir! Please don't exert yourself.

Is my. Wife. Here?

Breathing was very painful. More than anything, he wanted to see Teresa and Jacob. He wondered if Rose had flown home.

No sir. Visitors are not allowed into ICU for any reason. But if you would like to talk to her on the telephone —

Is she. Here.

No sir.

She's not. In Salt. Lake City?

No sir.

The morning his mother Rosemary had left him alone at the house in the country outside Gallatin, Georgia, there had been bacon in the pan on the stovetop. She had just left in the car, and he had called for her. He had called for Rosemary. *Rosemary! Mama!* And looking up and down the dirt road, he had seen nothing but the mean woman from next door slowly coming closer. Not Rosemary. Not ever again.

Not alive.

We have your phone, someone said.

He shook his head.

You should call. I don't want to alarm you but sometimes—I mean it's difficult to say how long you might be under again this next time, so you might—

The hell. With it. Put me. Under.

Mr. Guizac, you can't blame your wife for the policies we are required to follow.

He shook his head again and felt the restless and uncertain stirring of the doctors and nurses above him.

Mr. Guizac.

Just. Fucking. Put me. Under.

PART II

THE NAME OF UNION

While the Union lasts, we have high, exciting, gratifying prospects spread out before us, for us and our children . . . everywhere, spread all over in characters of living light, blazing on all its ample folds, as they float over the sea and over the land, and in every wind under the whole heavens, that other sentiment, dear to every true American heart—Liberty and *Union, now and forever, one and inseparable!*

Sen. Daniel Webster, *Second Reply to Hayne,*
January 27, 1830

I would banish all minor questions, assert the broad doctrine that as a nation the United States has the right, and also the physical power, to penetrate to every part of our national domain, and that we will do it . . . that we will remove and destroy every obstacle, if need be, take every life, every acre of land, every particle of property, everything that to us seems proper.

— Gen. William Tecumseh Sherman
HEADQUARTERS, FIFTEENTH ARMY CORPS,
CAMP ON BIG BLACK, MISSISSIPPI,
September 17, 1863
TO H. W. HALLECK, Commander-in-Chief,
Washington, D. C.

1

GOING SOUTH

AN HOUR BEFORE DAYLIGHT, FORREST TAPPED LIGHTLY ON the sliding glass door. Teresa answered the knock and stood hugging her robe together, a little disheveled. Walter's early poems had described her as opulent—a word choice that suggested money (which she did not have) and hinted that she might run to fat as she aged. But she was slim and fit and the word still strangely applied. Her clear skin, the easy smile, the comfortable elegance of her motions.

"Don't you want some coffee, Braxton?" She still had the native Alabama in her voice. "I just made a new pot."

"Let me get my Yeti. I'll be right back." He had been planning to stop somewhere in town to buy coffee, but he brought his travel mug back indoors, enjoying the heat of the wood stove. Teresa tied the belt of her robe to free her hands and filled his mug for him with the Yirgacheffe he remembered from her rituals at Stonewall Hill. He preferred other beans, but it was the way she honored the friend who had meant so much to her.

"Braxton, listen to me," she said, putting a hand on his arm and meeting his eyes. "Walter got hit hard. You're not as young as you used to be, believe it or not. If you start getting sick out on the road, don't fiddle around. Get tested. Do you hear me?"

"Yes ma'am," Forrest said.

"You, too," she said to the boy, who had come out with his bag and knelt in the middle of the kitchen floor to tie his boot laces. "Do you have everything?" she asked him.

"Yes'm."

He stood and towered over her, smiling down. She hugged him fondly. Hugged him tighter.

"Oh, I'll miss you. Listen to me."

"Yes ma'am."

"The *only* reason I'm letting you go is so you get Sherman out of your system. Do you hear me?"

"Yes ma'am."

"Do you hear me, Braxton?"

"Yes ma'am," he said.

"I need help here, but you're useless anyway until you finish that . . . damn thing. Where did you put the credit card?"

He showed it to her in his wallet.

"What are you going to do about running?"

"I have my stuff."

"Well, get this damn Yankee out of your system. Call me every day. Text me where you are, okay?"

"Okay, Mom."

She hugged her son again tearfully and then hugged Forrest hard, not shyly, gripping him for a beat longer when he started to break the embrace.

"Be careful," she whispered, releasing him, and put her palm to his face. "God bless you." She stood watching them as they closed the sliding door.

It was Friday the 13th of November. The morning was clear and cold, the red concrete sidewalk half-hidden by the last leaves of the locust tree and the light snow he had tracked through. When Forrest popped the trunk of the BMW, the boy wedged his duffel bag next to Forrest's suitcase and then got into the passenger seat.

"Nice car."

"Marisa's," Forrest said. They sat for a moment looking at the first rose of dawn in the clouds above the red rock cliffs to the east. The light snow of the previous day had left a dusting of white across the hills to the north. Forrest started the car. Teresa stood on the sidewalk, clutching herself in her robe, her face full of worry. Behind her along the fence, several mule deer stood staring at her in mute apprehension. She waved goodbye from the sidewalk and then, as he backed up, Forrest saw her turn on the herd of deer, rushing at them for a step or two and waving her arms, which sent them bounding panicked over the barbed wire fence and off in every direction through the neighbor's field.

An hour into the drive, almost to Muddy Gap, the sun was rising over the Ferris Mountains. Forrest reached over to lower the visor to keep it out of the boy's eyes, and just then Jacob started up from his sleep.

"It was too much," Forrest said, wondering how to open the conversation that would take them through the days of the drive.

"What was?" Jacob asked, shading his eyes.

"Asking you to write a hundred pages on Sherman in a month."

"I could have finished if I had just done a research paper."

"No, it was too much."

"I got into imagining it. Did you read what I gave you?"

"Not the new part."

They were silent all the way down the long hill to the intersection at Muddy Gap with its one store. Forrest turned south toward Rawlins. A line of upthrust rocks rose into the early light like the plates of a stegosaurus.

"There's more I need to write," the boy said at last. "McPherson's death. Something from the March to the Sea."

A broad, desolate valley opened up toward the mountains far to the south. The landscape was apocalyptic. Shallow, evaporated lakes whose beds looked like broken terra cotta, strange islands of vegetation rimmed with white alkali. Near an abandoned cafe and gas station, a sign pointed west toward a scatter of buildings and refinery tanks in the distance.

Forrest mused about how to talk to the boy. The grandfatherly tone did not suit him. Back in college, Forrest had a professor named Martin Kilgore, a tall, stooped South Carolinian who taught Shakespeare and Milton and who would shed his professorial authority in his office to talk about growing up in Spartanburg. He would confess everything—his cowardice with a bully in his elementary school, the humiliation of trading his beach date to a football star for a six-pack of beer. He would sit in his office smoking cigarettes and reliving old injuries to his honor, as though he were trying to find the exact narrative voice for the novel he could never write. But he was always full of humor and irony, and he treated Forrest like a protegé, even though Forrest had never been like Kilgore, never humiliated by other boys. He had been the star athlete. He had drunk glory blossom by blossom like a hummingbird. He was the student Kilgore had always hoped for, and even though Kilgore was not a model of any kind, the man's candor about his life had given Forrest a realism about his past and a grounding he needed.

"Tell me about Emily," Forrest said.

"I thought we were going to talk about Sherman."

"I saw at Mass that Emily wasn't one of those girls who covers her hair in church."

"A lot of them at Transfiguration do. Some lacy thing like old ladies would put on an armrest."

"A mantilla," Forrest said. "These girls with their heads covered and their little round bottoms in tight jeans."

Jacob turned his head in surprise.

"You notice that?"

"Did you ever read Thomas Hardy on being old? 'Time, to make me grieve, / Part steals, lets part abide; / And shakes this fragile frame at eve / With throbbings of noontide.'"

"Does Mrs. Forrest know about your throbbings?"

"Cut it out. Let's talk about Sherman," Forrest said. "Tell me about Lucette in Marietta. That's playing pretty loose with biography."

"That's what I see about him," Jacob said. "We talked about this already on Zoom. He keeps up appearances, but he rebels against the piety always being forced on him."

"Let me just explain my question," Forrest said. "When I was your age, I was the town hero. I ran down onto the football field on Friday night and the whole town shouted my name. After a game, girls were ripe for the taking. Half the time I didn't even know their names. Sin was not a word that would ever have crossed my mind at the time. I was smart, I had read a lot, I had a lot of sexual experience by the time I was eighteen, but there is no way in the world I could have written about somebody else—especially somebody older—the way you've written about Sherman. I don't know if I could do it now. I'm trying to understand how you can do that. The writing seems too sophisticated for an eighteen-year-old. Is it about Sherman or about you?"

"It's about Sherman."

"Do you want to talk it out? I think we need to understand each other."

"I don't want to talk about Emily."

"Okay, Jacob. Never mind," he said with an asperity he could not conceal.

A tractor-trailer followed by a long line of cars came toward them—a slam of air pressure when the truck roared past, then smaller bumps and winces with each car.

"Sorry, Professor Forrest," Jacob said. "I just don't want to talk about Emily. What I'm writing about Sherman has nothing to do with Emily."

"Nothing?"

"She's none of your business and none of my parents' business."

"Okay, Jacob."

"I don't know why you think the subject matter would be out of bounds just because I haven't experienced it all. That's the whole point of imagination, isn't it?"

"Fair enough," Forrest said. "But there's something else—some kind of tone of maturity or experience that seems out of keeping with being your age. How do you manage that?"

Jacob stared out the window at the passing landscape spotted with sagebrush all the way to the mountains on the horizon.

"I've read enough of his letters and *Memoirs* to get the tone of Sherman. When I'm imagining a scene, I try to enter into the situation—the setting and the people who might be there and the way I might react if I were Sherman, and then I try to write that until it seems right. The space has to feel real, for example. It's the details that make it convincing. It doesn't seem that complicated or mysterious to me."

Forrest chewed his upper lip.

"Most people couldn't do it."

"Okay, but it can't be that different from acting, can it? Some people can become other people imaginatively, some people can't. It doesn't strike me as all that unusual. As for the sex, I've read *Madame Bovary* and *Lolita* and Joyce's *Ulysses*. Every show on TV has sexual situations, not to mention the movies and the internet. It just doesn't seem out of reach for me to imagine Sherman that way. Or to imagine being older. Observation counts for a lot—

just watching older people, for example. I suspect that writing things like this wasn't what concerned you at my age."

"Okay."

"Besides, guys are always talking about it. Bragging. Which girls did what. Things you don't want to hear about girls you respect."

"Locker room stuff? But you don't talk, I guess."

"They think I'm just being religious. Maybe so, but bodies are mysteries. There ought to be a kind of holiness about them."

"You mean about your private parts?" Forrest was starting to grin.

"There you go. You're just like those guys. I'm just saying it's—I don't know, private. Secret. I don't just mean the parts. Not exactly. It's the personal truth we cover up when we first realize we're naked. It's like my body has a wound that's shameful, but at the same time, it's—I don't know. It's the thing that's most personal because I can't help it. It's also how I participate in creation." He paused and stared out the window. "This sounds stupid."

Forrest grinned even more broadly.

"There has to be a better word than *secret*. It's hard to talk about sex. You know that line from Yeats's "Crazy Jane" talking to the bishop? 'Love has pitched his mansion in / The place of excrement.'"

Jacob shook his head. "Okay, never mind. You're the one who brought it up."

"I brought it up because I need to understand you. Come on, finish what you were saying."

Jacob gazed straight ahead for half a mile before he spoke again.

"I think the Bible is talking about this kind of mystery when it describes Adam 'knowing' Eve after the fall. It's deeply personal in a way you can't really help, as I said. I mean, everybody can hear you talk and see your face and your actions and your demeanor. But they can't see this mystery. I'm talking about sex but not just about sex. When somebody gets close to you, it ought to be somebody who loves you and protects who you are and has already committed their life to you. I don't get why people want to treat it with disdain."

Forrest sighed. "My God, Jacob, how can you think this way and write what you did about Sherman?"

"Because I'm not Sherman."

They passed a bare wooden hut far out in the sagebrush, a rusty tank half a mile from anything, a dry lake. Far away to the southeast rose a line of mountains, and on either side stretched the Great Divide Basin.

"Listen, call me Cump," Forrest said at last.

"That's what my dad calls you. Why that?"

"Nobody except my wife and your mom calls me Braxton. Cump was my nickname growing up. It's what your dad calls me. It's also what his wife and most of his friends called Sherman."

"What does it help if I call you Cump?"

"I suspend our fifty-year age difference so we can talk as equals."

"About college girls and their sweet little bottoms?"

Forrest sighed.

"I'm trying to understand you, Jacob. It might help you to understand yourself. When you're young, you have a vague notion about what you might do, and it seems like everything is up for grabs until you're in your mid-twenties when you discover you've already made your essential decisions. Your life has already taken on a direction and a tone, and it's not going to vary much from then on, regardless of what you actually end up doing."

"How is this talking as equals? You're just looking back on fifty years that I haven't lived through yet. I'm open to what happens. I'm not worried about what I end up doing."

"You think you're not, but that's really always at the back of your mind. You have to find out what it's really going to be like to be sexual. Who you're going to marry, what the shape of your daily life is going to be. The bed and the kitchen. What's your work going to be?"

"I'm going to marry Emily Turnbow."

"Do you want to be able to buy her things and live like the billionaires in Jackson Hole? Or do you not care about making money? Or do you care about it, but you're scared to put yourself out there and play the game and compete? Do you want to plan every child, or just accept whatever children come? Can you laugh together and talk about serious things for the next fifty years? Do you want a TV six feet across? Does getting drunk on a regular basis seem like it's going to be a major need? Do you covet solitude? Some guys your age feel a religious vocation, a real sense of God. Other ones just want to find some hot girl to hump in the bedroom of the trailer."

"Watch it."

Forrest glanced over, thinking he had crossed a line, but the boy's nod revealed a pronghorn antelope a few feet off the road a hundred yards ahead of them. Forrest slowed until the animal saw them and trotted gracefully away.

"Your whole life's ahead of you. But it isn't much time. And what you do at your age sticks. It's impossible to make you feel it enough."

"That's your fifty years talking again."

There was silence for a mile. Ahead of them, the road ran flat and straight before bending, far away, in a long curve up into a gap in the mountains.

"You were kind of a seer when you were younger back in Gallatin," Forrest said.

"My parents sent me to a psychiatrist."

"It would have messed me up to find the body of my grandmother in an abandoned house."

"You know. I've had some nightmares, but killing Josiah Simms must have been worse than finding my grandmother."

"You would think so," Forrest said.

"What do you mean? It didn't bother you?"

"Officially."

"Meaning what?"

"Meaning that I performed the emotions expected of me by my own moral sense."

"I'm not sure what that means. Performing emotions."

"Like you tell yourself what you ought to feel, but you don't feel it. I couldn't feel bad about Josiah Simms. The man was a monster. He tried to kill you and your whole family."

"But the way you killed him. I mean, crushing his skull. The intimacy of that must stick with you."

"What if I loved it? I've been able to crack walnuts between my finger and thumb since I was twelve. My friends in graduate school used to call me Beowulf. And Simms's skull was fragile, like a paper-shell pecan."

The boy mused for the next mile.

"You never felt any remorse?"

"Formally, as I say. And eventually it went deeper, but not for months."

"Did you go to confession?"

Forrest smiled again. "You sound like Marisa. Yes, I went to confession. Again and again."

"For killing him."

"For loving it."

The boy turned and stared at him across the car.

"I'm telling you more than I should," Forrest said. "It was almost out-of-body. Homer saw gods in moments like that. You're more than yourself, there's some greater presence. It happens sometimes—a few times in your life—when lust is too bloodless a word for the absoluteness of desire you feel. Rage isn't the word for what I felt with Simms. I felt transported. It's what heroes feel. Men you can't reform into conventional goodness, men who can save your city but who can't live a decent life because they always crave danger so they can feel that absolute thing again."

He was coming up too quickly on a tractor-trailer that he could not pass because of the new line of traffic coming toward him. 110 miles an hour and he had not even felt the speed. He hit the brakes and watched the needle drop.

"I'm telling you more than I should," he said again. "But that's the experiment. Can a man of nearly seventy talk candidly with someone fifty years younger?"

Jacob did not answer. Forrest passed the truck as soon as the traffic let him, smoothly hitting a hundred and then easing back down to eighty-five, where he set the cruise control.

"People are afraid of you," the boy said. Forrest glanced at him.

"Seriously?"

"My dad says they don't know what you might do. You'll humor the social contract to get by and be left alone, but your soul scorns it. Dad says you don't really believe the law applies to you."

Forrest was stung. "That sounds like the description of a sociopath. Your dad said that? When was this?"

"Maybe after you assigned me a hundred pages in five weeks. No, I don't remember. But that's what he still says. He says you're like him. You've converted, but you're Nietzschean at heart."

"Do you even know what that means?"

The boy smiled. "I'm telling you more than I should, Cump."

Forrest had no reply.

They stopped to use the bathroom at McDonald's in Rawlins and ordered breakfast to go. Sausage burritos were the easiest thing to eat while he was driving. When they turned onto I-80 and headed east toward Laramie and Cheyenne, electronic signs above the highway warned of sixty-plus-mile-per-hour winds and extreme blowover risks. Four eighteen-wheelers in a row labored up the hill ahead of them, swaying as the gusts hit them.

Forrest was just setting the cruise control at eighty-five to pass them when the hindmost truck pulled into the left lane a few yards in front of him and he had to slam on the brakes.

"Damn it!" He could not see the truck's mirrors, which meant the driver could not see him, so he pulled out onto the gravel of the shoulder and flashed his lights to let the bastard know how he felt the injury. As though it would make a difference. The truck edged past the next one in line incrementally, inch by inch, going maybe half-a-mile an hour faster, barely over sixty.

Forrest sighed and asked the boy to unwrap a burrito for him. Jacob doctored it with hot sauce and handed it to him carefully. A mile or so past the refinery at Sinclair, the truck in the left lane edged past his rival, opened a gap, put on his blinker, and finally pulled into the right lane, having gained what, exactly?

Forrest accelerated savagely. The road ahead was his.

"Asshole," he muttered.

"You want the other one?" Jacob asked.

"Sure."

While he ate the second burrito, swabbing his mouth with the napkin and conscious of not getting food on the seats of Marisa's car, the boy consumed a sausage biscuit with egg plus a hash brown patty and then he pried open his large coffee and emptied two packets of sugar into it. *Sugar!* Forrest had not put sugar in anything since the days of metabolism.

"My dad says the way you drive reveals your soul," the boy said.

"Oh brother."

"Like whether you obey speed limits, which means whether you're faithful in small things."

"This is St. Walter Peach talking?"

"If you don't take speed limits seriously except in the actual presence of police cars, you're all about the will to power."

"Cut it out."

"I'm just quoting my dad."

"You're just trying to hurt my feelings."

The boy smiled and took a sip of coffee.

"I'll talk about Sherman if you let me drive."

"I'm doing the driving."

"What about *my* will to power?"

"Maybe later. Talk to me. I wanted to give you an assignment that would make you dig into history, but I never thought you would go nuts. Your mother is seriously worried about you."

The boy nodded. A mile passed as he ate an Egg McMuffin and another hash brown. Astonishing.

"It's hard to explain," the boy said. "Sherman is like my dad."

"Bullshit."

"Unlucky—cursed, somehow. Wounded."

"Okay."

"Sherman loved art, he loved opera, and he knew Shakespeare as well as Lincoln did. But he felt shunted aside and dishonored the way my dad does. He resented having foster parents, even though Thomas Ewing was nationally prominent and gave him all kinds of advantages the way Judge Lawton did for my dad. Sherman missed the Mexican War, so he eventually left the military, which he loved and Ellen hated, and then there were all these banking failures that weren't really his fault. Ellen never wanted to be separated from her parents. She would write all these intimate details about their children—little Lizzie eating bread and butter even though she didn't have any teeth yet—but she would never commit herself to leaving Lancaster and living with him, probably because he didn't care about the Church. I think sex always worried her. I think Sherman always took his private revenge with other women."

"Revenge."

"I think he seizes a thrill of transgression. I know guys like that. It's almost religious for them."

"There's no record of his philandering."

"Burke Davis mentions a lady in Georgia who wrote to Ellen about Sherman's mulatto mistress. That's where I got Miriam."

"Who's Miriam?"

"That's right, you haven't read it yet. Anyway, it's obvious with Vinnie Ream when he's already prominent. Mary Audenreid told him when she was a young married woman that she liked him better than her husband."

"Vinnie Ream," Forrest sighed.

"Almost thirty years younger."

Forrest drove for a moment before asking the delicate question.

"You're not saying your dad is like that."

"I don't mean any disrespect. But I am saying it."

Forrest did not press him. As they got closer, Elk Mountain rose majestically from the flat pastureland around it. A cloud hovered over the peak of it as it had the week before. God over Sinai.

"Sherman never despaired, but he came close," Jacob said. "He didn't become a drunk like Dad did for a while. I think he always felt like there was something coming. Some huge thing. It makes sense that it would be destruction."

"Do you think your father feels something coming?"

"Right now he's just hanging on to his life. But I think he's always felt like he was reserved for something."

"What? Something he'd write?"

"I don't know. But with Sherman, it's like there was a moment in 1864 when America hung in the balance. Did the country have the will to push on to the finish of the war? There was some kind of miserable necessity at work, more or less like the decision to drop the atomic bomb on Japan. There was no way for there to be a good end. Suppose McClellan gets elected out of the weariness of the north? What then? As it is, Lincoln is pushing toward this permanent dark divide that he calls Union. You take all the states that have tried to secede and you force them back, you tell them they gave up the right to decide their own political destiny when they ratified the Constitution and then lost the war. One act of free will in the past canceled the possibility of ever reconsidering that act."

"Call it a covenant, like an indissoluble marriage vow."

"Somebody else's marriage vow several generations back," the boy said. "I understand what you're saying, but here's what I think happens. Sherman and Grant and Lincoln decide to gut the South. Part of it is just military—cutting the supply lines within the Confederacy—but the other part is psychological. You treat every Southern civilian as a traitor to the Union you're trying to force him back into. If you're fighting *against* the Union, you don't have any rights. You don't own the property that you've worked and given your life for and hope to bestow on your children. So the decision is to violate the South, spoil its beauty, rob it of its heirlooms and memories, push it to the very heart of insult and injury so this new so-called Union it's being forced back into is going to be stained with humiliation and defeat. It's like your wife wants to divorce you because you're so critical of her, and you tell her she can't divorce you because she took a vow. You beat her for even thinking of it. When she tries to separate from you legally, you rape her. She's humiliated and full of hatred but you beat her and rape her until she says she'll stay with you. You call it preserving the marriage."

"That's too extreme."

"Maybe not extreme enough."

Ahead of Forrest, trucks again began to form a blockade.

"What about freeing the slaves? Isn't that the only thing that would justify the destruction of the whole Southern way of life?"

"I understand that argument. But Lincoln had to wait until the semi-victory at Antietam before he could start to make Emancipation the reason for the war and announce the coming of the Lord. Slavery was constitutional. It was legal in 1861. The Southern people of that generation didn't invent the institution or establish the legality of it. It's arguable that their desire to secede was different from their desire to perpetuate slavery. A lot of them hated slavery. Slavery wasn't the real issue."

"Oh bullshit, Jacob. Of course it was. I have deep Confederate roots in my family, but you know as well as I do that slavery was the whole goddamn point. Everything was predicated on the supposed racial superiority of white men. We've got all kinds of documents. Look at Robert Toombs. Look at Alexander Stephens's Cornerstone Speech where he says the problem with the old Constitution is that it considered African slavery an injustice that violated the laws of nature, whereas the new Southern constitution would rest, and

I quote, 'upon the great truth that the negro is not equal to the white man.' *That's* the cornerstone."

"What about Sherman? Sherman didn't care about slavery. He agreed with Stephens. He was as racist as anybody in the South."

"So if he doesn't buy into the holy war, what do you see him doing?"

"For him it's personal. He blames the South for the misery of the war and the death of his son Willie. He had a civilized sympathy with Southerners when he was running the college in Louisiana, but now he just wants to violate the South. To justify what he's doing, he comes up with an ideological, unhistorical, maybe totalitarian, understanding of the Union as an entity prior to the states and prior to the very possibility of private property. He hardens his heart. He means to penetrate it, as he writes to Halleck, which means to rape it. To soil its honor."

"Literally?"

"I think so," the boy said.

"You always hear that white women were left alone. Not black women, who were supposedly willing since the Yankees were their liberators, though maybe that's just a pretext; I don't think they felt ownership of their bodies yet. Or maybe the Union men just didn't think they counted."

"Would Southern white women make official complaints about being raped?" Jacob asked. "Wouldn't they hide the shame if it happened? It would taint them in others' eyes, back then, to admit it."

"Maybe, but it's hard to believe the brutality of the Yankees wouldn't have been broadcast to the world. Oh Jesus, what's this?"

As he came around a long curve at the top of a rise, red and blue lights flashed at the roadside a mile or so ahead. A massive rig lay on its side in the median like an animal with a broken neck, the cab twisted the opposite direction from the split and spilling trailer. Broken boxes littered the grass. Every truck in the long line curving down toward the scene had its emergency lights flashing in homage or solidarity.

They sat at a dead stop for five minutes, saying nothing, both of them thinking about fierce Southern women. Then came a hiss of release and a great lurch by the rig ahead of them and they rolled forward at a walker's pace for a few feet and stopped again for another five minutes. An ambulance roared past them on the shoulder, siren blaring. Another one came right behind it.

When they finally got close, a state patrolman waved traffic into the right lane. Forrest could see both ambulances backed down onto the grass of the median near a huddle of paramedics. The passenger side of the truck cab was embedded in the mud where it had come to a stop. On the driver's side, high in the air, men in emergency gear knelt on the door and reached down through the window, straining to pull out a heavy body that other men inside the cab must have been lifting toward them. The men on top lowered it to others he could not see. A moment later, a stretcher came around the front of the truck and the paramedics slid it into the open back door of the first ambulance. It closed from inside, the lights went on, and the vehicle worked carefully up the slope and onto the shoulder and then raced away, siren dopplering. Up on the cab, the men were reaching down inside to lift out someone else. A woman, bloody, her head slumped to the side. One of her arms fell from their grip and hung. They were reaching down again. A boy, maybe four or five years old. Forrest did not breathe. Another smaller child, a girl. He saw them both stir and resist as the men handed them down.

"Thank God," he said, riveted by the sight.

A deafening airhorn sounded behind him and Forrest cursed. The truck ahead of him was already fifty yards away and the grille of a Kenworth filled the rearview mirror. Furiously, he accelerated past the long line of trucks working themselves back up to highway speed, all of them with emergency lights still flashing.

Jacob let out a long breath. "The whole family must have lived in there."

"Terrible."

"The woman was dead, wasn't she?"

Forrest nodded and crossed himself. He had just set the BMW's cruise control at eighty-five when his phone buzzed.

Cate Zitek.

He wished the last name could be surgically detached.

—Dad? Cate's voice startled him by coming through the car's speaker system. She sounded harried, and his anxiety spiked.

"Is he back? What's he doing?"

—I just had to get out of there. Everything in the neighborhood felt creepy, like people were looking at me funny because I pushed that woman off my porch and she broke her arm. I wish she had broken her fucking neck.

He had never heard her so unmoored.

"Are the kids with you?" he asked, lowering his voice. "Don't talk that way in front of them."

—*What?* No! She did not calm down. She wrecked my life. I can't sleep—I mean I drove fourteen hours straight with Avila screaming in her car seat—

"Drove fourteen hours where? Listen, you're on speaker in your mom's car and I don't know how to change it. Jacob is with me."

—Oh God, sorry, sorry, Jacob—I don't know who you are.

"Jacob Guizac," Forrest said.

—Dad, she said hotly, as though he were trying to burden her with a whole new problem, I don't know Jacob Guizac.

"Buford Peach. Remember, Guizac is the name the—"

—Right, shit, sorry, she said, lowering her voice.

"Watch your language, Cate," Forrest said.

—I'm sorry, Buford, she said, but I don't know why you're—look, Dad, I'm exhausted, Bernadette has the kids, she took them somewhere, the zoo or the museum or—

"*Bernadette?* You're in Dallas? I thought you'd go to Gallatin."

—With Hermia Watson? Don't you know the scrutiny she's under after that bitch Lykaios wrote that article? Did you read it? My God, Dad. I had to get out of Atlanta, so—. Now she was sobbing.

"Look," he said, "call your mom and she can call me to tell me what's—"

—just called her, she said a little too acidly. She said to call you. The point is, I left Atlanta, I'm in Dallas, I'm staying at Bernadette's with the kids, and Jason doesn't know where we are and that's how I want it.

Forrest sighed. Half his reason for the trip to Georgia was rapidly evaporating.

"Okay, we're already on the way. We'll see you in Dallas."

There was a long pause.

—Seriously? Like when?

The clock on the display said 9:53. Almost to Laramie. Going east from Denver, they would lose an hour going into Central Time. He raised a hand from the wheel.

"Midnight, maybe. I'm guessing."

—Tonight! she exclaimed.

"We've already been on the road for almost four hours. We were on the way to Georgia to see what we could do to help."

—You and Buford? she asked incredulously. Why are you roping him into this mess?

Forrest glanced over at the boy.

"He has a project."

—Okay, Cate said. Oh my god, the kids are coming in. *In here!* she yelled and then lowered her voice. I have to tell you some things about Bernadette before you get here.

"Like what?"

Her voice changed.

—Jimmy and Clare! Grandpa's coming! Hey, sweetheart, what's that on your face? Bern, did they—? He heard the children talking all at once. Dad? Cate said. It will be really good for the kids to see you. She lowered her voice again. But Jerome's kind of like he's never seen a diaper.

"Who's Jerome?"

—Listen, I'll talk to you later. But don't get here at midnight, everybody will be asleep, so.

"So we shoot for the morning? Maybe bring breakfast?"

—Okay, just—

The phone beeped. The call was lost. They drove in silence.

"So," Jacob said at last.

Forty-odd miles south of Laramie, they stopped at an old general store and gas station, used the bathrooms, and bought some coffee and snacks. In the parking lot, Forrest queued up Sherman's *Memoirs* on his iPhone and secured it in the phone holder attached to the vent of the BMW. Getting the audiobook to play through the sound system took some experimenting, but then they headed south again, using a shortcut to I-25.

Sherman's own writing had a lucid, military style, usually matter-of-fact. Sometimes the narrative captured a real excitement about the action he was describing. He was good on the attempt up Deer Creek off the Mississippi north of Vicksburg, where Adm. Porter had been stopped by felled trees. Scrappy Confederate attacks had pinned down Porter's men and almost made them abandon the boats. Sherman hurried up with his men, risking himself right along with them, and managed to counter the Confederate attack and save Porter, whose gratitude he describes wryly.

Sherman thought the Union victories at Gettysburg and Vicksburg in early July of 1863 signaled the inevitable doom of the South, which would be increasingly cut off from the rest of the world. Some in the North already saw the war as over. In August 1863, Gen. Halleck wrote to Sherman asking for suggestions about how to reconstruct the Southern states as they were conquered by Union forces. In response, Sherman argued against any attempt to constitute civil governments until the whole of the Confederacy had been defeated.

As Forrest took the exit onto the toll road that would take them to I-70, Jacob asked him to replay part of Sherman's long letter to Halleck. "I've read it before, and now I've heard it again, but there's something I'm not getting," he said.

"Play it then."

It took him a minute of jumping the recording backwards and forward in ten-second increments, but Jacob found the passage.

Another great and important natural truth is still in contest and can only be solved by war. Numerical majorities by vote have been our great arbiter heretofore. All men have cheerfully submitted to it in questions left open, but numerical majorities are not necessarily physical majorities.

Jacob asked Forrest to stop it.

"What do you think Sherman means by numerical and physical majorities?"

"If we're voting and there are five votes against one," Forrest said, "the five win. That's numerical. But if you're fighting and the one guy beats up the five other guys, that's physical."

"I don't see why he calls it a physical *majority*."

"I think it's just an obsolete sense of the word. Let me keep playing it."

The South, though numerically inferior, contend that they can whip the northern superiority of numbers, and therefore by natural law they contend that they are not bound to submit. This issue is the only real one, and in my judgment all else should be deferred to it. War alone can decide it, and it is the only question now left for us as a people to decide. Can we whip the South? If we can, our numerical majority has both the natural and constitutional right to govern them.

If we cannot whip them, they contend for the natural right to select their own government, and they have the argument. Our armies must prevail over theirs; our officers, marshals, and courts, must penetrate into the innermost recesses of their land, before we have the natural right to demand their submission. I would banish all minor questions, assert the broad doctrine that as a nation the United States has the right, and also the physical power, to penetrate to every part of our national domain, and that we will do it . . . that we will remove and destroy every obstacle, if need be, take every life, every acre of land, every particle of property, everything that to us seems proper.

For a moment, neither of them spoke.

"So," Jacob finally said, "'natural law' and 'natural right' mean superior force. If the North can whip the South, then the South has to do what the North says."

"Okay," Forrest said.

"But that's what I meant earlier," replied Jacob. "As a Confederate, you have no right to anything—your life, your home, any keepsake dear to you, your favorite chair, your volume of Byron—unless you submit to the Union. In other words, it's only the Union, not God, giving you any rights you have. It's a political ideology. There's nothing about a Creator or 'unalienable rights' to 'life, liberty, and the pursuit of happiness.' He means to force the South's submission to the federal government. Maybe he sees the implications, maybe he doesn't. It feels totalitarian."

"Maybe too strong a word, but I see what you mean," Forrest conceded. "It doesn't just apply to the conquered South. By this line of thought, there is no basis for any American's private happiness without a pledge of allegiance to the United States, which does not mean the plural states united, and it does not mean private rights partially conceded to the state or the state's rights as a state partially conceded to the Union. Instead, it means the one federal government, which exerts in advance from sea to shining sea a kind of eminent domain. Your life is just something it allows, and so is the property you think you own. Nothing you have is ever really yours, though you can keep it if you say the right things and pay your taxes. I think Sherman sees the implications well enough, maybe because he felt that way toward the Ewings. In other words, he had to concede to their conditions before he could get anything he wanted."

"That's okay if God sets the conditions. If being is a gift."

"But Sherman thinks it's not God but government and that government relies on force. He's a soldier, not a philosopher."

"He reminds me of Machiavelli," Forrest said.

For the next hour or more on their way down the bypass and then east on I-70, they listened to Sherman's account of the months after the fall of Vicksburg. Since he had to stay where he was on the Big Black River to guard against attacks from Johnston's Confederate army, his family had come down from Ohio to visit. His son and namesake Willie, nine years old, had a wonderful time with the men of the Thirteenth Infantry, who convinced him that he was a sergeant. Late in September, an urgent summons came ordering Sherman to Chattanooga with military aid and supplies after the devastating Union loss at Chickamauga. Giving orders and dividing his men, he and his family embarked at Vicksburg to go upriver to Memphis, from which he would make his way east with part of his army.

Willie already complained that he did not feel well when they left Vicksburg, and his condition worsened on their slow progress upriver. The doctor onboard said that it was typhoid fever. Despite all their attempts to save him, Willie died in the Gayoso Hotel in Memphis on October 3, 1863. With no time to mourn, Sherman sent his family north with the body of his son and pressed on with his preparations to hurry to the relief of the army trapped inside Chattanooga.

Forrest paused the audiobook as they came to the outskirts of Limon. They had not stopped since north of Fort Collins, and he needed gas for the car and a bathroom for himself. He cruised past the exits for Limon because US 287 looked like a major intersection on Google Maps, but it turned out to be well east of the city. No gas stations. The next town on their route was miles to the south.

"Well, damn," said Forrest.

Jacob pulled his laptop from his backpack. The road led through a landscape of extraordinarily bare flatness—stubble fields unbroken by sage or cattle, a surreal emptiness all the way to the shimmering horizon, east and west. The boy was silent, tapping at his keys or looking up things on his phone or staring out at the darkening land and the small, empty towns they passed—Wild Horse, Kit Carson. Sherman's prose and the live voice behind it had made Forrest muse about his own easy, self-congratulatory dismissal of this man whom Southerners of his generation grew up hating. In William Tecumseh Sherman was the great drama of the modern age. Here Forrest was, nearing seventy, and what had he ever done that would make anyone want to preserve his memory? Who would ever write a biography of him? Three books left behind, none of them immortal. Two perfectly legitimate daughters, three grandchildren. Also an illegitimate son he never met from a high school sweetheart. But it was really the two children from accidental incest, the second one born of the first and therefore both his child and his grandchild, that would have given him something to be known for if it hadn't been too shameful to reveal. And that left another dubious achievement: he had crushed a man's skull with his bare hands.

At the Loaf n' Jug in Hugo, Forrest addressed the toilet for a full two minutes. Relieved, he bought a large cup of coffee and a bag of cashews as the boy used the facilities, and they drove on.

Outside of Eads, with the sunset red against bare black branches far away to the west, the boy at last looked up. "I wish you'd already read what I wrote on the Battle of Kennesaw Mountain, but this actually comes before that chronologically. Can I read it to you?"

"Go ahead."

2

TYPHOID

WHEN THE GUNBOAT CARRYING THE SHERMANS FINALLY reached Memphis, it docked near the streets of downtown, and two of Sherman's men carried Willie up to the Gayoso Hotel on a litter as the rest of them surrounded the boy. Gentlemen with their cigars and newspapers looked up, startled, as this large party of men in uniform with a sick child in their midst burst through the front doors in the lobby. Some of them Sherman recognized from his earlier time in Memphis—businessmen he had known when he ran the city. Ellen, stout, devout Ellen, stayed close to the boy's head, cooling his hot brow with a wet cloth, unconcerned that he might be contagious, fingering her rosary in the other hand while Minnie and Lizzie and little Tom walked behind her and tearfully responded to her murmured Ave Marias. With Dr. Roler's consent, Sherman sent an orderly to fetch the best physician in Memphis and booked a room on the second floor with a view of the great river.

Willie lay in the bed, small and faded and moaning. The doctors tried cupping; they applied leeches to the boy's skin, the only time that Ellen looked away. They forced laudanum into his mouth and shocked him with whiskey. Hours passed slowly in an agony of slimming hope and growing gloom. Messengers interrupted frequently with a soft knock at the door. Sherman would step outside into the hallway, greet the men from his staff, look over the letters and telegrams—orders from Halleck, reports from his subordinates. A war was on despite his private grief. He had to dispose his troops and prepare to take his men toward Chattanooga.

Once, late in the day, with the sunset gleaming from the vast river with its gunboats and traffic, the child stirred from his sleep. Minnie sat up with excitement and went over to him.

"Stand back from him!" Ellen demanded, and the girl startled, but she could not contain her hope.

"Look out the window, Willie!" she said. "You can see the riverboats going upstream. We're going home on one as soon as you're better. We'll have a big one with a dining room and a band, and Mother will ask the captain to let you pull the chain for the steam whistle. People will hear you all the way up in St. Louis."

The boy lifted his head from the pillow, as if he heard her. But when the eyes opened, they were as dull as scuppernongs. He sank back and turned in the bed, small and burning, his fair small body stippled with rash, his breathing labored and irregular. Minnie burst into tears. Lizzie ran to embrace her sister, and Ellen rose, full of grief, to comfort her daughters before resuming her station, calling little Tom to her from the corner, where he had shrunk back from the confusion of suffering. Tom's despair spurred a fierce passion in Ellen, who turned suddenly to Sherman.

"Do something!" she cried, her eyes burning at him. "You called us down to that damned and infested country. Oh God, Cumpy, why don't you do something?" He stood stiffly at the foot of the sickbed. She had not called him Cumpy since he had forbidden it in San Francisco, where his childhood nickname had embarrassed him among his banking associates. Now she sank back into her chair, shaken by sobs.

"I will call Dr. Roler," he said.

"Oh, if only you would pray, God would hear *you*! Jesus heard the centurion. Call on Jesus! Show Him your faith. Our boy is dying."

He tightened his lips and closed his eyes. *Jesus,* he said. *Jesus.* Nothing. Those lines of communication had been cut. He met Ellen's beseeching gaze and shook his head.

"Oh," she said in a moan. "Oh, Cumpy, sit down at least. Why are you standing there? Sit down."

He refused. When the doctors returned, Willie's body was subjected to more experiments and afflictions, but Willie himself was increasingly distant, already entering that undiscovered country.

The children were on the floor asleep. He covered them with blankets. Once during the night, he sat down and slept. The light of the new day, October 3, woke him before the others. He roused himself and stood upright again at the foot of the bed. Asleep at her post, her head at a painful angle, Ellen started awake when Dr. Roler and the other doctor, Phipps, softly opened the door and entered the room. They stood at the bedside looking down at the boy for only a moment before asking Sherman outside into the hallway, where a passing chambermaid glanced up at Sherman's face and crossed herself.

"Mrs. Sherman will want a priest," Dr. Roler said.

His beloved Willie. A pang came, terrible and rending and utterly dark, like the spear thrust into the heart of the dead man to whom he could not pray. Was this pain itself the prayer Ellen had asked for? Was this agony his prayer to the God who was taking his son?

Or was this God's first touch of the hardness he had given Pharaoh's heart when He slew his first-born?

He went back into the room. The boy's breath came with great labor. He spoke to his wife.

"A priest!" Ellen replied. "Oh my God—quickly, then!"

St. Peter's Church was several blocks away. Sherman sent a young Irish soldier of the Thirteenth who had made friends with Willie. He went back inside to resume his place at the foot of the bed, still in uniform from the previous day. In twenty minutes, the priest came, breathing hard. When he saw the size and age of the boy, he hesitated to anoint him. Had he received his First Communion? No, but Ellen quarreled with him about the age of reason, about sacraments, about confirmation. Sherman could not contain his rage.

"Give me the goddamn oil then!"

They froze, but neither one's head moved. After a moment, the priest bowed in consent and anointed Willie and spoke over him in Latin. He stood, nodding quickly to Sherman without meeting his eyes, and left the room.

Minutes later, the boy's breath rattled loudly in his chest, rattled and stopped. They waited, nothing followed, and with a great cry, Ellen bent over their son's body, sobbing. The children ran to her, but Sherman, his eyes stinging, stood erect, his hands behind him, and gazed at the picture above the head of the bed.

A lithograph of Trumbull's *Surrender of Lord Cornwallis.* He had seen the original in the Capitol. A white horse dominated the center of the composition, its head bent toward the Americans on its left as the rider— not Cornwallis but an American officer, a Lincoln, he recalled, noting the irony of the name—reached down to his right, his gloved hand open toward the sword held by the redcoat beside him. George Washington came up modestly behind Lincoln between the ranks of French and American soldiers. Accepting the surrender.

His son was dead. That hope had been stripped from him. He had to arrange to send the family home with Willie's body. Willie had loved the life of action. He would honor Willie by living out his calling as a soldier more single-mindedly than ever before. He would not simply resume his duties, but he would preserve Willie's memory in his own fame. Mentally, he began composing a letter to Capt. Smith of the Thirteenth. *The child that bore my name, and in whose future I reposed with more confidence than I did in my own plan of life, now floats a mere corpse, seeking a grave in a distant land, with a weeping mother, brother, and sisters, clustered about him.* He would arrange to move out toward Corinth and on toward Chattanooga. Action would relieve this terrible darkness. He would send his family home and grieve when there was leisure.

The South that had killed his son lay eastward before him.

3

TRINITY

"YOU WROTE THIS BETWEEN LIMON AND EADS?" ASKED Forrest.

"It's just a draft."

"How did you think of the lithograph of the Trumbull painting?"

"I wondered what might be in a hotel room and looked up some things. What do you think?"

"It feels like a sketch. It doesn't get Sherman's point of view as fully as the Big Shanty chapter. What's his emotional attitude as he's coming into Memphis with the Chattanooga mission to organize and Willie's illness getting worse? You need something about the boat they came up on. Gunboat, you say. Is that right, or was it a regular steamboat? The river was low, so the pilot would have to rediscover the navigable channel of the river, which was always changing, and work around emerging snags. That could be a metaphor for you. Sherman seems a little inhuman standing there at the foot of the bed, but maybe that's what you want—an emotionally frozen stoicism, a soul divided between duty and love. You're vague on the doctors. No descriptions of them. But the main thing you're going for is the moment when Ellen turns on him and wants him to pray. That feels right. And so does Sherman's gratitude for the war. The action of it offsets some essential absence in him, and I think he loves the destruction it allows."

"His son's death twisted him."

"He wrote that letter to Halleck before Willie died, not after," Forrest said.

"I know. I still don't think I've got it. There's something deeply obsessive about him, something he doesn't understand about himself. It's like Willie was the self he wished he could have been if his own father had lived, if he could have had a clean, spirited, rational life without the Ewings and Catholicism. Sherman blamed himself for Willie's death, but he also blamed the South and most of all he blamed God. A few months after Willie's death, he started his war of destruction in the Meridian campaign. He bragged that Meridian no longer existed. He said, 'those who brought war into our country deserve all the curses and maledictions a people can pour out.' Willie's death sours any sympathy for the South he had left."

"Not by itself."

"Who's to blame for the war and Willie's death but these Southerners stubbornly maintaining their rebellion against the very country that gave them their life and prosperity? How can he help but hate them? By the time Grant is called East to fight against Lee, Sherman is ready. He's always seen the folly and hubris in the South's belief that it could defy the industrial North, but now he sees it in a new—"

The phone. *Cate Zitek.*

Forrest held up a hand to Jacob.

"Cate?"

—Where are you, Dad?

"Almost to Campo, Colorado."

—I'm in the ER with Jimmy.

He pulled over onto the shoulder. Her voice was low and tense, but she sounded more centered than she had earlier.

—I don't know if it was stress or the trip, but Jimmy couldn't breathe. Thank God I could leave Clare and Avila with Bernadette. When I brought him in, they thought it was Covid, so they made me stay outside, which terrified Jimmy. He tested negative, of course. They put him on a nebulizer and gave him a shot of steroids. When do you think you'll get here?

"It's almost five Mountain Time. We could still get there by midnight."

—No, like we said earlier, it will upset everybody if you get to Bernadette's in the middle of the night. Especially Jerome. Jimmy's stable, they've got him on oxygen and steroids. They'll probably send us home in an hour or so.

Jerome again.

"Did you talk to your mom?"

—I did. I'm so sorry to hear about Mr. Peach, is Buford still there? Buford? I mean life-flighted to Salt Lake City, the whole deal. Just when we were starting to think it was all—

The call broke up. They rode in silence for a few miles.

"I shouldn't have come," Jacob said.

"Maybe not," Forrest admitted. "But let's deal with the situation in Dallas."

Another mile of silence.

"My Dad is Willie right now," Jacob said.

Conversation failed, but without the pressure to speak. Silence suited them. They did not listen to the *Memoirs* or turn on the radio to hear election news. The drive from Amarillo to Fort Worth took five hours, five hours of the BMW's headlights probing into the West Texas darkness. They passed through many small towns, some with a traffic sign that said 45, some with signs that said 30 out of the self-importance of a row of street lights and a filling station or a small restaurant. Some towns, derelict, had no sign at all. Paralleling the railroad, they drove past enormous silos and vast featureless landscapes where a few lighted houses in the distance made Forrest wonder vaguely who those people were and what they did. He stopped in Childress to get a sandwich and some chips for each of them, refill the car, and use the restroom. They stopped again, even more briefly, in Wichita Falls, where Forrest bought the large coffee that he knew would keep him awake.

Jacob slept intermittently. Just before midnight, exhausted, Forrest found a Motel 6 on the northern outskirts of Fort Worth and checked them into a room with two double beds. He slept fitfully, pumped up by the caffeine, aware of the boy, embarrassed to be old and flatulent and having to get up to pee several times during the night. Late as it was, he set the alarm on his phone for six, because he wanted to get to Bernadette's apartment before she left for work.

The boy got up without complaining. Forrest dressed and used the bathroom.

"All yours," he told Jacob, who was looking into a small mirror. "What's that?"

"Emily gave it to me. She told me to look into it every day to remember I'm not Sherman, and I do it because it reminds me of her. It feels like she can see me."

Forrest smiled and shook his head. "I'm going to the lobby to see what they have to eat."

He went out into the dark parking lot and put his bag in the trunk of the BMW, still in the same night of their drive, the darkness continuous with the night before. A hint of coming day lightened the eastern horizon. The gas station adjoining the motel on the access road was crowded with customers now and the highway traffic on I-35 was picking up in intensity.

Breakfast in the lobby was nothing much. He grabbed muffins and coffee for both of them.

The road skirted the Dallas–Fort Worth Airport on the south before it merged with other rivers of traffic and then became I-35. The logjam thickened and slowed as they got close to downtown even though it was Saturday. Forrest worked his way over into the right lane to take the Calatrava bridge into Oak Cliff, crossing the river that flowed through a floodway between massive levees half a mile apart. Bernadette had told them on an earlier visit that fifteen inches of rain in three days back in 1908 completely changed the way the city fathers thought of the innocent-looking Trinity.

Jacob kept asking about Sherman, this time about why he felt obliged to pay back the military friends who invested in his failed bank in San Francisco.

"Jacob, let's put this on hold."

Forrest needed to pay attention. Bernadette lived in a neighborhood in North Oak Cliff near the Bishop Arts District. Had he missed the turn? No, still up ahead. Here. They pulled up in an open space along Childress Park, across the street from the house where Bernadette rented the upstairs. The neighborhood was old for Dallas, neatly kept. The house had a red front door, sculpted hedges, and a wooden bench under the maple tree. Bernadette had told them it was owned by an older gay couple—one a lawyer, the other an architect she met through her fitness work. A handsome minimalist metal staircase went up the right side of the house to the second floor. His daughters were sitting on the top step.

It looked like trouble.

He remembered the chopping fury of Cate's right hand from her arguments with Marisa when she was a teenager. Bernadette, compact and graceful, was dressed for work, bent forward, her hands on her knees and her head down. Her athleticism had always been the envy of her older sister, but her discipline had cool, rational underpinnings. She was less open to the mysteries, as Marisa put it, and more calculating about what she wanted in her life and how to get it. Cate was loose-boned and generally ampler in a becoming way, more intellectual, although she could flare into a passionate unreasonableness that drove her mother crazy—and probably drove Zitek to fury, as he might have admitted a year ago. Cate's intellect was gusted along by whatever moved her to love or hate, so her heights were higher, her depths more abysmal. Bernadette looked too patient, Forrest thought. A little too stoical.

"Why don't you stay in the car for a few minutes?" he said to Jacob.

The boy had assessed the situation, too.

"How about I take a run?"

"Be careful. Lot of traffic."

"I'll do laps around the park so I don't get lost."

"Have at it."

The boy got out of the car and started doing some stretches to warm up. Forrest checked his side mirror for oncoming cars and opened his door. As Cate gestured, Bernadette's eyes rose vacantly and alighted upon him, at first without recognition. Then a jolt went through her body. She spoke to Cate, who looked up and saw Forrest.

"Dad!" Cate cried. She started down the stairs toward him, almost tripping, and caught herself on the railing. She ran across the yard and between two cars and he was shouting for her to stop but she burst into the street without looking. A white van squealed to a halt a few feet from her, and she started back, one hand on her heart, the other over her mouth, while the driver lifted his hands in a show of outrage. He tilted his head ironically to see if she wanted to cross ahead of him. She waved him past, calling out that she was sorry, and as soon as he was past dashed across the street and threw herself against Forrest. He staggered back against the BMW. She sobbed into his neck.

"How's Jimmy?" he asked after a long moment of hugging her.

"Jimmy? Oh, much better, thank God. Still asleep."

"I'm so sorry all this has happened," he said.

"Oh, Dad, I had to get out of there. The neighbors were acting weird. The kids were terrified that the witch might come back."

"I have to say, I didn't expect to be in Dallas. What's going on with Zitek?"

"He's still in New York, I guess. I don't care where he goes. I hate him, Dad."

"Who's watching your house?"

"Laurie from next door. She's going to let me know if Jason comes back. I had the locks changed."

"Dad!" Bernadette called from the stairs across the street and lifted a hand in wary greeting. Starting down behind her came a long-haired man, medium height, strongly built, and fit. Early thirties, maybe late twenties. Jeans, sneakers, T-shirt, sports jacket, closely trimmed beard.

"Who's this?" Forrest said. Cate loosened her grip on him and stood back to wipe her eyes and nose with the sleeve of her t-shirt.

"Jerome," she said.

"He's living with her?"

"He's okay, Dad."

"Okay how? With my grandchildren here?"

"God, Dad, please don't say anything. What are you all of a sudden, Captain Puritan? Not right now. It's the least of our worries, don't you think?"

Up on the landing with its minimal railings, Cate's children Jimmy and Clare now came out, looking around for their mother, and after them toddled Avila, her youngest. He tensed, and Cate whirled around.

"Oh my God! Stay there, Avila!" she called. "Stay there, do you hear me? Stay right there!"

Bernadette saw the situation and bolted up the stairs two at a time to pick up the little girl and herd the other children inside as Cate recrossed the street and ran up after them.

Forrest looked at Jerome, who made no move to cross the street and meet him.

"You're Bern's dad," called Jerome indicatively.

Somehow the tone irritated Forrest and he felt his temper rising. *Bern?*

"Scared of Covid?" he called back.

"I mean—what do you mean?" said Jerome.

"You look like you're into social distancing."

"Yeah, no, I was just leaving."

"What's your name?"

"Jerome."

"Just Jerome? Like Prince or Beyoncé?"

Jerome looked puzzled, but the possibility of Forrest's sarcasm gradually worked its way in and he threw his hair back with a flick of his head.

"Jerome Fassbender."

As Forrest crossed the street, he heard someone running behind him and glanced back to see Jacob go past at an easy near-sprint, holding up two fingers. Jerome waited, cool and self-contained, but he drew back a little as Forrest stepped over the curb and his dimensions became more evident. Jerome offered his hand as if to show that he feared neither Forrest nor the infamous Covid-19 he was probably carrying. Forrest took it and began to crush it a little.

"So you're living with my daughter," Forrest said, lowering his voice.

"Jesus!" said Jerome, throwing his hair back again and trying to retrieve his hand. "You know. I mean, more or less."

"Which one? More? Less?"

Forrest thought of Zitek and held Jerome in place. After the first shock, Jerome squeezed back as hard as he could, but equality was elusive, and Forrest could feel the man's bones yielding in his grip. He toyed with breaking them. He pulled Jerome closer.

"Did you sleep with my daughter while my grandchildren were in the apartment?"

"Jesus. Come on, man," Jerome said, his face reddening, his voice rising. "Let go, okay? Sweet Jesus!"

"You're using Our Lord's name in vain, Jerome."

"Dad!" Cate called, a pleading alarm in her voice. His daughters were both clutching the slender railing as they watched from the stairs. "Dad! Come on up! The kids want to see you!"

Forrest doubted it, but he let go and Jerome backed away, hand dangling, as if Forrest might take a swing at him. When nothing happened, he turned and walked off quickly without looking back, waggling his wounded hand and muttering savagely. On the opposite sidewalk, Jacob raced by again. Three fingers.

A tidy little man in his sixties had come out across the threshold of the red front door, arms folded across his bathrobe.

"Everything okay?" he asked.

"Sure," Forrest said, stepping over and offering his hand. "I'm Bernadette's father, Braxton Forrest."

The man put his hands behind his back and shook his head.

"Covid," he mouthed silently with a wink.

"Of course," Forrest said with affected sincerity. "We must be so careful. I hope Bernadette's dear sister's visit isn't bothering you."

"Well, no, it's not me, not at all. But my husband is very sensitive to noise. It has been a little—how to put it?—*thunderous*, to tell you the truth."

"Thunderous," Forrest repeated. "It must have been Jerome, don't you think? In our family, we call him Jupiter."

"Oh, no. No, not poor Jerome. Maybe thunderous isn't the right word. It's all the little feet back and forth. Like having squirrels in the walls. Back and forth, back and forth. And the screaming in the middle of the night."

"Screaming? What could that be?" Forrest asked. "Was Jerome upset?"

The man glanced up at him now. Seeing Forrest's expression, he tightened his lips and backed across the threshold. Just before he closed the door, he said, "I know who you voted for."

Bernadette's door opened directly into the kitchen. Beyond it, the apartment sitting room was full of fabric hangings, books, simple furniture that somehow looked clever, and contemporary artwork by friends of hers. When Clare saw Forrest, she came rushing over and hugged him tightly.

"Sweetheart," he said. "You kids have been through a lot."

"Jimmy? Do you remember your grandpa?" Cate prompted.

The boy looked up from his book a little fearfully. "Hi, Boppy."

"How's the asthma?" Forrest asked him.

The boy's mouth twisted and he mumbled something and resumed his Tolkien. Convinced by now that Forrest was harmless, little Avila came over and clamped onto his right knee. A little sweetie. He bent down and picked her up, and she put her fingertip on his nose.

"Boppy," she said.

He felt his heart gearing down.

"Let's sit down and I'll tell you a story," he said. Jimmy looked up hopefully.

"One of the Greek myths?"

"I was thinking of a Gallatin story."

"Is Buford in it?"

"Absolutely. Katie and Beulah and Buford meet the ghost of old Mrs. Persons in the overgrown garden."

Just then, Cate's phone began to trill.

"Hello? ... Hi, Laurie...."

A long silence followed. Cate's free hand went to the tabletop, as if to steady her.

"What did the police do? . . . . Oh Lord. Okay. Okay. Thank you for calling."

She put the phone down. Forrest waited for her to speak. Bernadette hovered in the doorway, purse in hand, already late to work.

"Bern, can you take the kids to the park?" Cate asked.

"Cate, you know I would, but I have a presentation at ten downtown."

"Just for a few minutes. It's not even nine yet. Just so they know what's there? Show them the swings. Or the ducks in the pond."

Bernadette glanced at her buzzing cell phone and lifted it.

"Not right now," she said into it and pushed the button with her thumb. Jerome, Forrest guessed. "Okay, let's go, kiddos," she said.

"Boppy was going to tell us a story," Jimmy objected.

"Change of plans," she said, waving them toward her.

Clare let go of Forrest, glancing up at him in confusion. He put Avila down and did an offended comic shrug for their benefit as he urged them toward the door. Bernadette picked up Avila, and the other two children followed her.

"Ten minutes," she said over her shoulder.

She closed the door behind her.

"Jason came back," Cate said. "He's at the house and so is that bitch. I forgot to change the lock on the side door, so he got in, and he's been taking our things and throwing them out onto the street! All my clothes. All the kids' clothes. Their *toys*." Her face distorted. "Jimmy's books! Where people have to go around them or run over them. Jason told Laurie it was his house."

"That lying asshole. I bought that house. What did the police do?"

"He showed them his driver's license and it had the address on it. The officer told Jason to get the things out of the street."

"So they didn't do anything."

"I guess they see things like this a lot. I didn't have a restraining order or whatever—"

Forrest pictured Zitek full of righteousness. Jason Zitek, whom he and Marisa had loved—all the meals together, all their conversations. Talking over bourbon one night about Borges's "Library of Babel" and making up books that had to be in it, such as the 29th century parody of George Washington's film performance as Hamlet in the 24th century AI-generated novel about him.

His rage, still flickering from Jerome, turned dark and resolute. The baseball bat in the garage in Atlanta. He knew exactly where it was. A Louisville Slugger like the one his friend Lawton had owned when they were little back in Gallatin on those Saturday mornings in the summer in the backyard of Mr. Cater's house. Ash, like the strong ash spears in the *Iliad*. The slender, taped grip, his left hand tight against the knob. Hardwood barrel solid and alive, the pitch coming, the fine heft, and the sweet full swing and the god-almighty hedge-clearing wallop.

Zitek's hated head.

"I'm going," Forrest said.

Cate put her hand over her mouth. Her face dissolved.

"Dad, don't—don't."

"Make some excuse for me with the kids."

"Dad, please."

"I'll call you," he said.

"Dad, come on. Dad! *DAD!*"

But he was already thundering down the steps, speaking of thundering, and when he got back to the BMW, Jacob was passing again, holding seven fingers over his head.

"Stop!" Forrest shouted. The boy's steps faltered. Breathing hard, hands on his hips, he walked back and leaned in the passenger window that Forrest opened as he started the car.

"What's up, Cump?"

"I have to go," Forrest said, irritated now that he had given the boy his nickname to use.

"Sir?" The boy realized he was dripping sweat onto Marisa's car and swabbed it with the tail of his shirt and stepped back. "Go where? What do you mean?"

"Cate can book you a flight," Forrest said. "Take an Uber to the airport. I'll pay for all of it."

"Wait, we haven't even—I mean—"

"I have to go to Atlanta."

"That's always where we were going. I've changed my mind. I think I need to go."

Nearby in the Childress parking lot, a mother was unbuckling her children from their car seats. Beyond her, Forrest saw Bernadette beckoning the children. They were starting back from the swings and slides. Oh, sweet Jesus.

"Get in, goddamn it!" Forrest barked. "Hurry up, before the kids see me."

He would drive around the block and explain and then let Jacob back out.

"I thought you wanted me to catch a flight home."

"Dad! Dad!"

Cate was calling from across the street. The children saw their mother and the older two raced across the grass while Bernadette tagged along with Avila. Furious, Forrest turned off the BMW and stood outside it as though he were about to be arrested.

"You were going to leave?" Cate said accusingly as she crossed the street.

Jacob stood steaming in his running clothes as Clare and Jimmy ran across the grass with Bernadette close behind them. Clare clamped herself onto Forrest again, and he put his hand on her head. He knew what the matter was—the girl's father was performing his midlife crisis with a new pompadour haircut and a Greek girlfriend. Meanwhile, blasting hip-hop and rocking with the noise—*Say shake yo greasy bacon like a brudda from Macon*—a pickup eased by. Cate held the children back and put her hands over Jimmy's ears. Bernadette held up her keys and shook them at Cate, who waved her away.

"We're good. Thanks, Bern."

Jimmy crossed the street with his mother, but Clare would not let go of Forrest. Hundreds of miles of interstate rolled past in his soul. *Texas, Louisiana, Mississippi, Alabama, Georgia.* One long burning arrow aimed at the house where Zitek would be backing out the door with the couch he was stealing, and Forrest would say nothing before the first swing of the bat shattered the man's right elbow and Zitek screamed *what the fuck* as the useless forearm dangled away. But it was the next swing that mattered, the one after the surprise. The look of horror as Zitek saw who it was and lifted his other arm to protect himself and Forrest splintered that one too. The pause as he drew back the bat, Melina Lykaios screaming as the piece of shit tried to lift his broken arms in front of his head, tried to duck as Forrest aimed a base-clearing, World Series home run swing at—

"Grandpa!" Clare was saying, tugging at his hand.

He stared down at her.

"Can you take us to the zoo?"

"Dad," Cate said, pulling Clare off him. "You were just going to drive off to Georgia, weren't you?" She took his arm. "Come back inside. Let's get Mom on the phone."

Cate hefted up Avila and herded shy Clare and sullen Jimmy ahead of her. She kept exclaiming at how tall Jacob was. She herself had gone from being the pretty college girl Jacob remembered at Stonewall Hill to a young mother with a body softened toward the consolations of children—Avila pawing at her blouse, still wanting to be nursed, Clare clinging to her hand, and Jimmy, sweet Lord, whining about wanting to go home.

"How old is Jimmy?" he asked.

"He just turned two," she said, smiling down at Jacob as she climbed the stairs.

Jacob smiled when he heard the boy grumble.

"So you've been running?" Cate asked. "I ran some in high school and college—not competitively, just to stay in shape. But you run track, right?"

"He won state in cross country," Cump said behind him. *Cump*. The name wasn't working. Maybe just Forrest.

"That's so cool," Cate said. "And Wyoming, wow. What a state for cross-country. All those mountains. All that air."

"Lots of air," Jacob said. "Just not much oxygen in it."

They went through the door at the top of the stairs into a kitchen with a dining table to the right and cabinets along the inner wall. Plenty of natural light. But no wonder Bernadette had been eager to get to work. There were pieces of chewed bread and banana under a highchair, another mess of half-eaten things at the table. In the living room, Transformers littered the wooden floor. As soon as they got inside, Clare ran over and wadded herself into a corner of the sofa as though an explosion were coming.

"So Mom says you're writing about Sherman's march through Georgia?" Cate said, still interested in him, which was flattering.

"More about Sherman himself. Not just the March."

Just like that, he was imagining Sherman going home to Ohio and greeting the other children who only half-remembered him, missing Willie and finding Tom instead. A look of desolation shared with Ellen over the heads of their children. He would force a smile and act affectionate while inside he burned to leave and get back to the war and the clean rage of destruction.

"Want some coffee?" Cate asked him. "Dad, you need to call Mom."

"I'll go outside," Forrest said.

"Bern's bedroom," she said brusquely.

"I don't want to see evidence of Jerome," Forrest said.

"Well go back outside, then! But call her. And don't leave. Promise me."

"I won't leave."

"How about I go get us some doughnuts," Jacob said, and Cate turned to him with another big open smile.

"Would you? Dad, let him take your car. Mine's a mess after the trip."

"I'll do it," Forrest said. "I can talk to your mom on the way."

"No, listen," Jacob said, feeling a little edge of panic, "you need to see the grandkids, right? So I can walk or—"

"Dad," Cate interjected. "Give him the keys. Tell the kids a story."

"Jacob doesn't know where he's going."

"Neither do you."

When Forrest sighed and held out the keys, Jacob took them and Cate called directions after him as he ran down the stairs.

Despite riding in it for twelve or thirteen hours the day before, Jacob did not really know the BMW, so he sat for a moment in the driver's seat. The steering wheel had the cruise control on the left (unlike his father's Subaru)—not that he'd need it getting donuts. The right side of the wheel had various controls for phone and media that Forrest obviously didn't understand. The speedometer and the tachometer were equal circles on the dashboard with smaller displays for the fuel gauge and the engine temperature. The armrest between the front seats was a storage box, just like on the Subaru, but the cup holders were side-by-side under the display screen. He started the car and figured out how to put it in gear by pressing the button on top of the gearshift. Blinker, windshield wipers, washer. He knew he would get used to it—what it felt like to reach for his coffee, where to put his water in the left-hand door or keep his rosary in the hollow of the armrest.

How it accelerated. Whoa.

Davis Donuts was in a triangular building between one-way cross streets. Two people were ahead of him in line when he went in, and he waited while the one at the counter—a huge man with his head shaved up to a tuft of black hair erupting from the top like a volcano—kept adding to his order until he had three full boxes with a dozen donuts in each. The cashier, a small teenaged white girl named Britknee (name tag) kept saying *Yes sir, will that be all?* and then reaching for more donuts until the racks behind her were almost empty.

"You could leave some for the rest of us," said the middle-aged woman in front of Jacob, trying to sound funny about it. The fat man ignored her. When he finally finished and paid, he lumbered past them to the door, not excusing himself for taking up half the room in the place and making them have to back up.

Yes ma'am, how can I help you? recited the cashier without the slightest acknowledgment of exasperation at the previous customer. It was not kindness or professional courtesy, Jacob saw. Just numbness. Everything in her job, maybe everything in her life, was something else to endure. Her eyes were dead. Her soul was elsewhere, if she had a soul. She could have been a zombie or a robot. Circuit board in back.

The woman sighed and started choosing a few donuts from the remainders. Just then, a tall Hispanic man came up behind the cashier and started quickly refilling the racks with donuts fresh from the oven.

"Thank goodness," the woman murmured.

"I saw Javier coming," the man said, smiling over his shoulder. "I had to make more of the good stuff."

The woman bought a dozen and turned to leave, giving Jacob a quick, ironic widening of her eyes.

"Yes sir, how can I help you?" said Britknee.

Now that it was his turn to order, Jacob thought what to choose. His mother was always worried about giving too much sugar to little Marisa—or to his dad, who was always borderline Type 2 diabetes. Cate probably steered her kids away from sugar, too.

"Yes sir, how can I help you?" recited the girl for the second time.

He looked at her nametag and wondered about the k in her name. From kindergarten on, he would bet, everybody had tripped over it, trying to say Britk before they realized the k was silent. That it was *knee*. Brit-Knee. Had her parents done that to her for some unfathomable reason? Or was spelling it that way on the nametag a minor aggression on her part? Was the k a burr she had inserted just to roughen her name and distinguish herself?

"A dozen plain cake doughnuts."

She turned and filled a box and set it in front of him.

"Yes sir will that be all?"

He thought about being a kid offered a plain cake doughnut. *Nah.* Cate would rather just please her kids after all the trauma. He eyed the shelves and ordered four glazed doughnuts, four with chocolate frosting, and four pink ones with green sprinkles. He paid for the two boxes with the Visa card that his mom had given him.

"Have a nice day," the girl said.

Jacob leaned over toward her. "You too, Britknee," he said. Startled, she gazed up at him. "Deep down inside you there's a door. I say, knock on it."

It sounded stupid as soon as he said it, but her eyes changed and she gave him a small, tentative smile before her face flushed and her eyes dropped.

When he opened the door of the apartment a few minutes later, Cate smiled at the sight of two boxes of doughnuts but made a face that told him not to alert the kids. She pointed to the top of the refrigerator, where he quietly set them. She sat back down across the kitchen table from Forrest.

"Give us another minute or two."

Jacob nodded and went into the living room. He wished Cate and Forrest could go somewhere out of earshot. The children could hear the whole conversation from the kitchen, but Jimmy appeared to be absorbed with his Transformers and Avila had fallen asleep on the rug. Clare was reading. Or pretending to read. She glanced up from her book and watched him fold himself down on the floor with elaborate swami arm motions that made her giggle. He picked up a Transformer truck and fiddled with it as he watched Jimmy deftly manipulate a motorcycle into a robot warrior.

"Do this one," Jacob said.

Jimmy turned the truck into a dragon.

Seriously, Dad. What will you say to the police?

I don't know. Who's your lawyer?

I don't have a lawyer. I didn't plan any of this. It wasn't my idea to break up our family.

Jacob could feel the blood rising into his face. Jimmy worked the toys without looking up.

Well, you need a good lawyer.

Dad, she whispered. *The kids might hear us.*

Sorry. I'll find out who the best divorce lawyers are—don't worry about expense.

Divorce lawyer? Dad, I don't want—

Her sentence trailed off.

You don't want a divorce, Forrest said. *That's because you don't think this is real. But Zitek didn't do any of this out of a momentary temptation. This isn't a fling. He might even be using this woman as an excuse. I'm telling you, he doesn't think his real loyalties are to his marriage.*

Is that what you thought when you cheated on Mom?

Jacob could hear the coffee cup when Forrest set it down on the table. The silence.

I'm not the point here, Cate. I never deliberately wrecked my marriage. For all my real sins, at least I never did that. There's no going back from what he's said and done. You have to break this off. Seriously. Get an annulment. Get it started right now. Don't let this ruin your life.

Jacob looked up and saw little Clare's face. It reminded him of Britknee at the doughnut shop.

Mom thinks I should stick it out, Dad. I made a vow to Jason. Marriage is a sacrament. I'm starting to feel what that means. Mom's always talking about the graces of the sacrament, and God knows she's been through enough to find out.

Another pause.

Zitek's different.

Dad, I hate him right now, but I love him, too, he's the father of my children, he's—

"Mom's crying," Jimmy said, not looking up from his toys.

"Maybe not," Jacob said.

When the sobs broke through, Forrest's chair scraped on the floor.

"She cries a lot," Jimmy said.

"So do you," said Clare.

Jacob heard Forrest resume his seat.

Seriously, Dad, what did Mom tell you?

Just call her.

I want to know what she told you.

There was a pause.

She told me not to kill Zitek. She didn't think it would be in anybody's best interests.

Cate gave a bark of harsh laughter, and Jacob could not stand it anymore. He stood up from the floor and slapped himself on the forehead.

"Oh man," he exclaimed. "I just remembered where the doughnuts are."

"Doughnuts!" Jimmy said, brushing his Transformers away. Clare stood up, excited, and Avila started awake, immediately crying. Jacob stepped into the kitchen and got down the two boxes and opened them on the kitchen table.

"I hate to break this up," he said.

She dabbed at her face, looking up at him. Jimmy opened the doughnut box full of glazes and sprinkles.

"All that sugar!" Cate said.

"I mean—"

"It's okay," she said, smiling at him. "It's a holiday, right?"

"What holiday?" Clare said, crowding in.

"The day-after-we-got-to-Dallas holiday," Cate said.

"How about one of the chocolate glazed?" Jacob said to Jimmy.

A few minutes later, he sat with the children again as they finished their doughnuts, proliferating crumbs and sugary smears. Cate and Forrest were back at it.

Seriously, Dad. I thought of killing him too. But don't. What if you get there and you see him and you lose it like you did—you know that time—

I didn't "lose it" with Josiah Simms.

Dad—

Look, right now, the question is whether you're going to be okay here with Bernadette and this Jerome character. Your mom is right. There's no room. Bern is generous, but she has a job and a lot of complications. So go stay with your mom at the Peach place in Wyoming.

All of us crowding in there.

Teresa can go to Salt Lake City. Your kids can play with little Marisa, which will be great for her. It's cold out there, but it's beautiful. Lots of air. You should see all the air.

We just got here, Dad. That's two more days of driving.

It won't be the same. You're not running away, you're going somewhere. I've already checked the forecast, and it's clear until next week. You're already on break from teaching. You don't have a deadline. Just start driving and call me wherever you decide to stop and I'll pay for it.

What are you going to do?

Go to Atlanta and then down to Gallatin. The boy has a project and so do I.

What's your project? What do you mean?

It's still shaping up.

And Jacob's doing Sherman. Good luck with that.

4

SATURDAY MORNING

SHE WOKE UP COLD. SHE HAD TURNED OFF THE FURNACE overnight as Walter taught her to do, because otherwise its timed settings would kick on an hour or two early and wake them up. He loved heavy covers and cold air, and so did she, but he was always the one who got up early and turned the furnace back on and built a fire in the wood stove and when she got out of bed an hour after he did, she could go out to find the fire blazing. Her chair sat before the wood stove with a warm fleece covering it, like something out of Homer.

Now even Jacob was gone. Both of her men. Jacob rarely got up early, but he had an easy competence building fires that he had learned from his dad. Walter lying in the hospital, a ventilator clamped onto his dead body, his chest pumping up and down mechanically. She threw off the covers fiercely to make the image go away and clutched her robe around her. The indoor temperature on the thermostat read 57° when she switched on the furnace and heard it firing up on the other side of the house.

Marisa had moved in the day before, and she was upstairs near her little namesake. Maybe she would come down when the heat came on and she heard Teresa stirring. Maybe they could read a Psalm together. But Marisa had already said that she needed her time alone, which was also a kind of mercy toward Teresa's own privacy. She told Teresa about her silence— listening as acutely as she could, taking all of her petitions and leaving them at the threshold of her silence and stepping past them and going deeper for as long as she could stand it. It wasn't easy to be in that wordlessness before the Word. Teresa respected her prayer and tried to do the same thing, but she was always harrying God with petitions—for Walter, always Walter, for Jacob off to Georgia with Braxton Forrest, for little Marisa.

She tried to be quiet as she lifted a log from the rack next to the wood stove, careful of splinters, and opened the front glass door and set the log toward the back in the warm ashes. Walter had taught her to rest the forward-facing split side on three wadded sheets of newspaper tucked under the piece, then to angle three sticks of kindling across the paper onto the log. She lit the loose ends of the newspaper with a long lighter, and when it started to blaze up, she set another piece on the slanted kindling and shut the front door, immediately opening the side door to let in a strong draft of air. She made sure the bottom vent was open, and then added another piece of wood from the side as the fire began to crackle in that satisfying way she loved.

She had done it herself without her usual mistakes. It was a meanness in Walter to expect her to make mistakes. She thought about the anxiety he induced simply by sitting in the passenger's seat when she drove. But when she thought of him in a hospital bed in Salt Lake City, his mouth crusty like a sleeping child's, her mind refused the image, her knees went weak, she had to steady herself with her hand on the stovetop, the stone still cool to her fingertips. Why did she love him so?

Yesterday had brought no news except that he had woken up asking for her. They had told him no visitors were allowed, so now he knew that she was hundreds of miles away, safely back at home. She wondered if he blamed her. Did he expect her to lay siege to the building and try to get past the nurses and orderlies and the restrictions of masks? Little Marisa needed her. She could not just pick up and leave to go to him.

Once the fire was blazing up, she pulled her chair into place and went into the kitchen to make coffee. Teresa loved the exact heft of the beans in her palm. She filled the small grinder and started the filtered water heating in the electric kettle she had used for many years. The gray coating of her French press was flaking away, but there was good stainless steel underneath. *The Lord bless you and keep you.* She ground the coffee, watching through the clear plastic top of the grinder until it swirled smoothly, still a little coarse, then opened it and tapped it into the press. While the water was heating, she stood at the sink and gazed out the window to the south at the foothills of the Winds. *The Lord make his face to shine upon you and be gracious to you.* When she heard it boiling, she lifted the kettle and poured it over the grounds, filling the press to an inch below the top. *Belen, my friend, my holy one, pray for my Walter.* She stirred the brew and snugged down the filter screen with the top in place. *The Lord lift up his countenance upon you and give you peace.*

She heard Marisa coming down the stairs. Her friend paused at the fire and then stepped into the kitchen, hugging her robe around her.

"That smells so good."

Teresa quickly brushed the tears from her eyes.

"My little ritual."

A phone started up, not Teresa's. Marisa found her purse and out came her phone after a moment of scrambling.

"Cate?" She went into the living room. "Oh, no. Oh, honey." She held up a hand to Teresa to forestall questions and went upstairs, talking quietly. "Let me talk to him."

Teresa poured her coffee and took it to the dining room table. She gazed out at the red rock of the cliffs to the east, striations shaped by wind and water. Time without history terrified her. A thousand years were nothing, a million years, two hundred million. Animals and men and oceans were a drift of shadow across the slowly changing landscape. A vast, empty, unconscious play of elemental forces. Wind without spirit, light without understanding, ice and sun and rain but no soul in all the vastness to look upon it and wonder and give thanks for the glory of God, that incalculable expenditure of being.

And here she was, a little tangle of life in the immensities.

She prayed for Walter and his bitter soul. Why did she love him so much? she asked herself again. Walter, who had betrayed her and killed their son. Why did she love him at all? But she did, because he loved her and there was something about him that was unique and superb. She prayed that he would live. She prayed that he would be given some great, gracious gift always denied him, something that he would accept in peace. Grant him mercy and self-forgetfulness and peace.

"Well, you're not going to believe this," Marisa said as she came back down the stairs. "Cate is in Dallas—and so are Braxton and Jacob."

"In Dallas!"

"Cate drove her children there yesterday. Braxton and Jacob got all the way to Fort Worth and spent the night and got to Bernadette's place early this morning. They must all be exhausted. Cate thought Jason Zitek was in New York, but he's back in Atlanta, and he's throwing the children's things out on the street. Cate is trying to stop Braxton from going there to kill him."

"He would, wouldn't he?" Teresa said.

Marisa gave her a quick, hurt glance. The silence between them went a beat too long.

"Did Josiah Simms ever even exist?" Teresa asked.

"I know what you mean. He seems like a fable."

A phantom, a vaporous terror that had obsessed them all. But Walter had once seen Simms in the office of *The Gallatin Tribune*. Cottonmouth's men, as they called Simms, came after Rose and almost trapped her alone in the front foyer of Stonewall Hill that time years ago. She would never forget her daughter's terror, brave as the girl had been. An assassin hired by Simms had almost killed Walter and Buford. And Simms himself had captured Nora. Forrest had crushed the man's skull at Stonewall Hill. It would all seem unreal except for the tremor that would sometimes start up in her hand when she thought of it.

"I'd better get Braxton on the phone. I don't want to wake up Little M. May I go in Jacob's bedroom to talk?"

Thank God she had straightened it up and washed his pile of clothes.

"Of course."

"Something's coming, Teresa. I just feel it."

5

VICKSBURG

CUMP WAS ON THE PHONE WITH MRS. FORREST SEVERAL times that morning—he had still not figured out how to take it off the speaker system—as Jacob drove eastward across Texas and Louisiana. Cate was already on her way to Wyoming. Something bad was going on with one of the pregnant girls at the house in Gallatin. Something about Josiah. A pregnant girl named Josiah at Stonewall Hill? Just east of Monroe, when Forrest fell asleep in the passenger's seat, Jacob turned off Sherman's *Memoirs* and thought about Emily almost all the way to Mississippi.

After a particularly loud snort, Forrest came awake with a jolt.

"Pit stop," he said.

Jacob pulled over at the next exit. They filled the BMW's tank, used the restrooms, bought sandwiches and drinks, switched seats, and got back on I-20. As Forrest drove onto the bridge over the Mississippi, Jacob watched barges move slowly on the vast river, lines of flatboats joined like the double tractor-trailers he would see on the long stretches of highway in the West. Gazing north, he could not make the picture in his mind of the siege of Vicksburg work with what he saw. Forrest pulled off at the first exit in Mississippi and drove up the road closest to the river into the town of Vicksburg. Jacob wanted at least one detail that would give him a sense of the long siege, something that would make it real. He wanted to feel how dominating the Confederate guns were from the heights, but nothing cohered, everything about it confused him—the shifting river, the silting currents of intervening history between 1863 and 2020, the middling ordinariness of the town, the casino riverboats, the industry.

Driving back toward the interstate, Forrest parked at the welcome center overlooking the river, where they unwrapped their sandwiches. Jacob choked down a bite of pale ham and stiff cheese in gluey white bread with a swallow of Diet Coke.

"All this stuff happened, and we come here to look for it, and we find Vicksburg but not what happened. What happened isn't here. It's just gone."

"It's easier at Gettysburg and Antietam," Forrest said.

"It's more than just the place. It makes me wonder about history. When I read about it, I'm getting the story from a perspective no one ever had during the events themselves. All these connected things happened at the same time with all these causes, but at the time they're happening, there is no one person who can possibly see or understand them all. Grant might say, *Let's besiege Vicksburg* and execute this huge movement of troops, but where does the event itself even *exist*, you see what I mean? Say, the fall of Vicksburg. *How* does it exist?"

"It exists by happening," Forrest said, rolling his head on his neck and then fixing Jacob with a look. "We should hit the road. I've got Zitek on the brain. You're overthinking this."

"Am I? Where does history exist if not in the book or the photograph or the documentary?"

"It exists by having happened. By being crucial to a complex of causes. We understand things by their causes."

"But what does that mean? There's a compound of individual experiences, but where does the reality of history even exist before a historian, Shelby Foote, say, writes the history of the seven attempts to capture Vicksburg? What we call history makes you able to understand all kinds of actions and details collected into a context and a story—such and such choices, such and such accidents. But these things could not have appeared in that way to anyone during the time the things were actually happening. Time was going on in people's bodies and senses everywhere at once, and it's so complicated that you despair of trying to explain even some of the feelings and thoughts in one consciousness in one place in any minute—say, the minute or two of crossing this river on a cold Saturday in November of the year 2020, the car and the Mississippi and each other and our hunger and the reasons we're on the way to Georgia and Dad's Covid-19 and Cate's kids and Zitek and the Sherman project and all of it."

"Understanding itself is transcendence, you're saying? You're saying history is an invented consciousness that never existed in the lived world of the events themselves? But maybe there's an angel who stands above a place and time. Walter Benjamin talks about that somewhere. Maybe the whole meaning of history is comprehended in the attentive transcendence of the angel."

Jacob thought about it, moved and pleased.

"Nice, but isn't the angel just a trope? You're just personifying historical consciousness."

"No, I'm lifting events out of individual subjectivity into the being and presence of their intelligibility."

"So does the angel narrate them to the historian?"

Forrest smiled and shook his head.

They finished their sandwiches and disposed of their trash in one of the outdoor cans. Jacob gazed at the vast river, as world-famous as the Amazon or the Nile or the Rhine.

Forrest got back behind the wheel.

"So you're okay?" he said.

"I guess so. I read Shelby Foote's account of the seven different attempts that Grant made to capture Vicksburg—all these plans to go up rivers and down canals and inland and around and so on. Finally, the Union soldiers get past the guns at Vicksburg and come ashore down there somewhere, south of the city, and then they attack eastward toward Jackson to keep from being vulnerable to the rear when they besiege the city, and then they turn back westward and encompass Vicksburg with trenches and cut off its supplies. I see the reasons for all these movements. I understand them. I don't need an angel for that. I see that the whole Mississippi River will fall under Union control, and the Confederacy west of it will be cut off—the big picture, all of that. It's clear and manageable. But when I think about any one moment on one day, say on June 20, 1863, during the siege, it's too much. What it feels like to be even one person in one body in one moment. Say, a Union soldier from Iowa in a trench in the rain who just scared a rat from his knapsack—

or a ten-year-old girl inside the city, terrified and hungry and hiding in the basement as the Union gunships shell Vicksburg from the river. What does the grand strategy of the war in the West mean to her? Or the plans of Lincoln or Grant and Sherman?"

Forrest did not answer at first, but he smiled and was about to say something when his phone rang through the car's speaker system. Hermia Watson.

6

MIRIAM

NEW RUMORS WERE FLOATING AROUND ABOUT HERMIA
Watson and the girls at Stonewall Hill.

"Do you know that some of those girls were *prostitutes*, Chick?" Patricia said over breakfast. "You can't take Atlanta prostitutes and put them in the middle of a small town and think everything's going to be okay. Did you read that article?"

"She's trying to help pregnant women, Patricia."

"Help them find customers?"

Patricia was being unfair, as usual. Everyone in town was being unfair, and part of the problem was that younger guys, including some of the ones on the football team, kept cruising around Stonewall Hill to see if any good-looking, not-too-pregnant strays came out. Chick sympathized with Hermia's problems, but she had brought most of them on herself by not explaining well enough or consistently enough what she was doing. The open house was a good idea.

He was at the Ford dealership that morning when the topic came up again. Bill Sharpe wanted a new pickup, and he wanted Chick to help him, so Chick walked with him into the showroom to show him one of the new F-150s.

"How's your business been during Covid?"

"So good I feel bad about it," Sharpe said. "We'd developed platforms for virtual classroom meetings and shared screens before it hit, so we've been doing well in K–12 schools that have had to go online, colleges, anyplace where there's training involved. We've made a killing, even though we're competing against Zoom and Google Meet."

"Not so great here. It turns out people can't drive virtual cars."

Sharpe laughed. "Tell me about the new F-150s."

"Lots of new features, starting with these colors. This one's called Antimatter Blue. The interior would make an oil sheik happy. New co-pilot features for safety. Buy one for Nora. Buy a fleet of these for your team. How's Nora doing, by the way?"

"She has her hands full."

"How many now?"

"Three so far. All girls."

"Are you going to keep trying for a boy?"

"Is that what you call it? *Trying?*"

He laughed as Sharpe studied the sticker and frowned.

"Negotiable," Chick said. "Seriously, how's she doing?"

He remembered when Nora O'Hearn had been abducted by the monster Josiah Simms and left bound to a tree on the property out in the country that belonged to Walter Peach's family. 2014, six years ago now. She had not been raped—she said—but the experience had been so traumatic that she had gone into a Dominican convent in Nashville for over a year. Bill Sharpe had waited her out. Patient man. His trips up to see the nuns had gotten to be a joke in town. Protestants didn't understand nuns to start with—something about being brides of Jesus, which made you wonder why Catholics thought he needed so many wives (one was enough for Chick)—but Bill had understood he might lose her.

Chick couldn't claim any competence on the subject of nuns, but Nora O'Hearn was the most beautiful woman he had ever seen, and he worried about whether she was telling the truth about what had happened to her. His daughter Alison had been raped when she was a freshman in college. One of those stupid, drunken nights at a fraternity house. She didn't say a word about it until two years later when she started having emotional issues. When he found out, Chick wanted to kill whoever did it, but she did not remember who it was, which made him sick to think about. It crushed her to realize that she had put herself in the situation, and what crushed her had to pain him too. Now, years later, she had convinced herself that all men were evil and decided she was a lesbian. Last Christmas, she had brought home a plain, polite, chunky woman named Alice who was in charge of the accounts at a law firm in Atlanta. Alison said they were married. *I knew you wouldn't come to the wedding, so I didn't ask you*, she told them. What did that even mean if you both had the same parts? Alice and Alison. *Married*, for God's sake! It had almost killed Patricia. Alison was already in her late twenties, and the chances of her changing her mind, marrying a good man, and having children before they died had narrowed to a near vanishing point. It surprised him how much Patricia wanted grandchildren.

"You still with me, buddy?" Sharpe said.

"Sorry," Chick said. "Started thinking about my daughter."

"Nora's okay," Sharpe said. "She's strong. She has bad dreams, but one way she works through the trauma is by helping the women at Eula's House. Her year at the convent taught her a lot and drew out talents she didn't know she had. Have you heard those girls sing? I don't know what else Hermia is doing right, but she's nailed that."

"I told Hermia she should have an open house so everybody can see what she's doing at Eula's House. Maybe they should do a concert."

Sharpe shrugged. "That article in the Atlanta magazine was toxic. I don't know how you stop gossip. But Nora says the girls trust Hermia. They know she understands them. Those two who claimed they were imprisoned—that's all bullshit. Right now, though, she has this one bad case—this girl nine months pregnant who says her name is Josiah."

"Josiah? Seriously? That has to spook Nora."

"Ask Hermia about her. So can I take this thing for a drive?"

"There's one outside with the key in it. Come by the office when you get back."

He had barely stepped into his office when his cell phone sounded the theme music from *Bonanza*. **Braxton Forrest,** it said.

Uh-oh. He pressed Accept with a tremor of dread.

"Cump? What's up?"

—I'm coming to Georgia.

Chick's stomach clinched. He gazed out over the showroom and took a deep breath. Hashbrown was leaning over the hood of a dark blue Focus to breathe on a spot and polish it with his shirt sleeve and look at himself.

"Okay, so—"

—I need you to check on Stonewall Hill.

"Meaning what?"

—I mean go over there. Right now, if you can.

"I'm running a business here, Cump. Look, that bomb threat last month turned out to be nothing. Besides, the election's over. Even if it was rigged."

—Come on, Trump's just blowing smoke. But listen, Marisa was talking to Hermia about an open house idea. The problem is they can't show the place because of this girl that thinks she's a boy. She says her name is Josiah. Chick? Are you still there? Chick?

"I'm here. Bill Sharpe was just telling me about her."

—Chick? Chick? What's the matter with this goddamn—

He could hear Forrest, but apparently Forrest could not hear him. The call dropped and immediately *Bonanza* came galloping back. *Dun-ta-da-dun-ta-da-dun-ta-da-dun-ta-da DUN-tun.*

"Cump?" he said.

—Chick?

Not Forrest. Hermia Watson.

"Hermia. What's the matter?" he said.

Her voice was low, as if she were trying to keep from being heard.

—Can you come over? Right now? Please hurry.

Good God, why him? Why did they want him?

"Should I call the police?"

There was a pause. Meanwhile, Forrest was calling back, and several green and red circle options presented themselves on his display. Hold and Accept? End and Accept?

—Not yet, Hermia said. Please just come. I'll meet you at the back door.

"I'm coming." He tried End and Accept.

"Cump? I'm going over there. Hermia just called. What did she tell Marisa?"

—She said Josiah was asking for you.

"*For me!*"

But Forrest was gone.

Rattled, Chick opened the top drawer of his desk where he always kept his keys so he wouldn't lose them and his wallet so he didn't have to sit on it. His wallet was there, but not his keys. Where the holy hell were his keys? He scrambled the papers on his desk, patted around, looked on the chair seat, the floor beneath the desk. Where had he put the damn things? He tried to remember coming into the building.

Coffee. The Keurig between his office and Parts.

Hashbrown, humming, hovered.

"Are my keys there?" Chick asked. The man turned around, blank as unbuttered grits. "Next to the coffee," Chick said, pointing. "Do you see my keys?"

Instead of looking, Hashbrown tilted his head inquisitively. Chick pushed past him. Nothing on the small table. Nothing on the floor. He scanned the countertops, the showroom floor, and just then, the front door chimed and Bill Sharpe came through it. Thank God, Bill could give him a ride.

Chick held up his cell phone to Ashburn.

"I have to go. Can you hold the fort?"

"What, me?" Ashburn took a step backward and bumped the wall as though Chick were trying to mug him. "Me? How come you don't ask Roof?"

Chick glanced at Parts, where Rufus Olson leaned on the counter paging through the hot rod catalog he always brought to work. Feeling Chick's eyes on him, Roof stood back and tucked in his chin to let a long stream of tobacco juice drop into the coffee can between his feet.

If a woman customer ever saw him.

"You seen this pair of three-inch tailpipes you can get on a '93 Mustang?" Roof said. "Sweet Lord God Almighty."

Roof believed that women were helpless after a glimpse of truly manly tailpipes.

"Look here, Chick," Ashburn said, still mulling it over. "It ain't I don't want to help out, it's just I ain't being paid for that kind of responsibility. I mean, which we might could negotiate it, but I mean what if somebody was to—"

"What? Come in the dealership?"

"Shit, Hashbrown," Roof said. "Ain't nobody been in here on a Saturday since August."

"Right there. Look right there," Ashburn said, pointing at Bill Sharpe, who strolled up to them, tall and angular, dangling the keys to the F-150.

"I like it," Sharpe said, handing the keys to Chick. "Let's get started on the paperwork."

"Look at that," Ashburn said. "You see that?"

"Bill, can I ask a favor?" Chick said. Hermia's urgency burned in his gut.

"Just let me use the restroom," Sharpe said. "I'll see you in a minute."

"Which if it was at my pay grade," Ashburn said.

Chick went into his office just to get away from the man. *Joe Ashburn has an immortal soul,* he told himself, bending over again to look under his desk for the keys. But it was hard to imagine that God Almighty would want to tease out the existence of Hashbrown indefinitely, which would be like giving eternal life to a head of lettuce.

There was a tap at the doorjamb and Bill Sharpe came in.

"Listen," Chick said, steering him back out into the showroom, "I can't find my car keys. Can you run me over to Stonewall Hill? Hermia just called me."

"What's the matter?"

"Some emergency. Something about Josiah."

"Oh shit—Nora's over there with our girls."

As Sharpe roared into town in the Expedition he had bought from Chick two years before, Chick realized with a jolt of shame that he could have just taken a car from the lot, which would have simplified life for everybody. He glanced over at Sharpe, hoping he wouldn't think the same thought. They turned at the Confederate soldier and sped down Lee Street. Sharpe gunned it up the back driveway, scattering gravel.

Nora's blue Escape was not there. As they parked, Hermia swung open the back door at the top of the steps and gestured for them to hurry inside.

"Where's Nora?" Sharpe demanded.

"You should call her."

Sharpe stayed outside calling while Chick went in. There was wailing upstairs. Two of Hermia's wards—a small Hispanic girl and the redheaded one who had been in the dealership last month, now more hugely pregnant—stood in the kitchen hugging each other at every new wail.

"So what's going on?" he asked as kindly as he could.

"I think it's a demon. I think she's possessed." Hermia took a deep breath. "She knows about us," she said, meeting his eyes. "You know what I mean. And I never told a soul."

"Neither did I," Chick said, almost sure he meant it.

"She's been calling for you. Do you want me to go with you?"

"Maybe to introduce me."

"Don't worry. She knows you."

When they stepped into the hallway at the top of the back stairs, Chick heard a babble of voices from the room at the end of the hall. Hermia went ahead of him and paused at the door before beckoning him forward. His legs were shaky. When he stood in the threshold, he saw a very young, very pregnant girl sitting propped up against the headboard of an antique bed. The girl's legs were splayed out under the covers, and she had a hand cupped on the southern extremity of her belly. Three other pregnant girls—no, four—five—knelt on the floor at the foot around the bed as if they were paying homage to some Eastern potentate under a pagoda.

"Well, come on in, Sunday School!" called the girl on the bed in a harsh male voice. "Took your time, didn't you? Lost your keys."

How could she have known that?

"Who are you?" Chick asked.

"Sasha, tell Mr. Chick Lee who I am."

"She Josiah. She tell me things ain't nobody knows."

"Except me. I know what you did," said the girl on the bed.

"That's right," the girl said.

"And you better do what I say."

"Yes sir."

"You hear that, Sunday School? Sasha, tell Chick Lee why you do what I say."

The girl, sixteen or seventeen, round with fat, turned toward Chick. "Cause she own me," the girl explained. "She own my soul," she added, dropping her eyes.

"*She?*" snapped the girl on the bed.

"I mean *he*. Mr. Josiah, he own me."

"Get your pronouns right, you stupid cow."

The eyes of the girl on the bed burned at Sasha.

"Sasha!" Hermia exclaimed. The girl jumped as if she had been slapped.

"Yes, ma'am, Miss Hermia."

"Listen to me. Josiah does not *own your soul*," she said firmly. "Your soul belongs to Jesus Christ. What are you doing in here, anyway? You girls get up off the floor! Go downstairs. Tamara, have you dusted the furniture?"

"No, ma'am."

"Hurry up! We've got guests coming."

When the other girls left the room, the one on the bed closed her eyes. Chick stared at her—maybe ninth grade? Dark-haired, a pretty face, considerable breasts for one so young, full lips that pinched in when she was Josiah. They pinched in as he watched.

"Y'all need the bed?" said the male voice lazily, the girl's eyes still closed. "I can just move over. Been awhile, ain't it, Chick? You better take you one of them pills." The eyes opened and the strange light in them burned into Chick's. "But listen, I ain't got you here to pick on you. Ain't nothing good come of worrying with bygones. You had your little night, and you squeezed more sorry out of it than a whole box of Kleenex could hold."

"What do you want with me?" Chick said.

"I want you to keep him away from me."

"Who?"

The eyes rolled up until only the whites showed. "Zebulun! Fetch some water and help put out that fire! They didn't find my Miriam, did they? Tell my Miriam—"

"What do you want with me?" Chick asked. "What is she talking about?" he said, turning to Hermia.

"*What is* she *talking about?*" mocked Josiah. "*She she she.* Do I sound like a she? Plenty of *girls* here, but—AAAAH! AAAAH!"

A violent convulsion went through the body, and the girl's eyes rolled upward again. She gave another wail, whimpered, looked around vaguely, and locked on Hermia. Josiah was gone entirely, and seeing someone else—this small, scared, normal girl—made Chick's stomach clench.

"Oh God! Miss Watson!" Another convulsion. Her back arched, both hands grasped at the weight of her belly. "Oh my God!" A great gush of water flooded the bed. "Miss Watson, I'm scared, I'm scared. Something doesn't feel right!"

"I'm here, honey. Calm down, now. You're just having your baby, that's all. Let's get you to the hospital. While we drive we'll say a prayer together, how about that?"

"I'll call 911," Chick said.

"No, no, no," she said. "We do this a lot."

If he had ever felt more out of place, he could not remember when. She went past him out into the hallway and called for Deirdre. When she came, looking intense but not flustered—she was the aide who did barrel racing, he remembered—Hermia gave her instructions, and several women came into the room to help Miriam off the bed. Not Josiah, just a child about to have a baby.

"I'll be there in twenty minutes," Hermia called after them as they started down the stairs. She took Chick by the arm and led him over to the window that looked out over the small parking lot in back of the house. The women came out the back door walking the girl, who looked tiny and terrified. They got her in the back of a Toyota Highlander he had noticed on the way in—no idea whose it was. If Forrest funded cars for Eula's House, why didn't he buy them from Lee Ford?

"Josiah knew about us," Hermia said. "He knew about Nora, too."

"What Simms did to her?"

"No, he knew Nora had been in love with Walter Peach."

"*Walter Peach?*" he exploded.

"You don't understand Walter. They came pretty close to disaster, it sounds like. Josiah was saying she almost earned her scarlet letter, and her kids heard it. Nora was mortified. All the girls here saw Nora's reaction, just like they saw mine. It's exactly what can undercut us from inside. The devil at work."

"The devil? Really?" Chick said dismissively.

"I'm going out to the hospital."

Sunlight slanted across a patterned rug on the hardwood floor toward the front of the house. He could hear the murmur of the girls in their rooms, and he thought with a pang of Alison. As he stepped carefully down the first step in the gloom, he could feel the hollows in the treads on the back stairs. Halfway down was the landing and the door to old T. J. Forrest's office. Where Cump had killed Josiah Simms. Chick had been inside it once before the killing; Forrest had been renovating the house before the Peach family moved in, a year or so after the troubles that summer of 2009 when Marilyn Harkins and Dutrelle Jones died and he spent the night with Hermia Watson. He ran his hand down the banister and felt with his foot to make sure he had reached bottom and then found the door into the mud room and stepped to the back door, feeling his pockets. Where was his phone? Or his keys? He stopped and stood there staring at the empty lot. The idea of Joe Ashburn suddenly filled him with rage, as though it were Hashbrown's fault that he had lost his keys.

Just then, Hermia's Prius pulled into the lot.

"Come on!" she called. "I'll take you to the dealership." As he got in, smelling her perfume, and thanked her, she said, "Or maybe you want to go with me to the hospital."

"I'd better get back to work."

They did not speak again until she pulled up in front of the showroom. As he opened the door to get out, she touched his arm. "But can you check on me in a little while? I'd really appreciate it."

"I'll call you."

"Can you come by the hospital?"

When he got out, he closed the door and put both hands on the top of the car to speak back through the window. "You're worried the baby's going to have horns."

"A little," she said, smiling at him.

He must have been smiling too when he turned to go inside. As he opened the door to the showroom, Chick saw Joe Ashburn.

"Found your keys," said Hashbrown, lifting his eyebrows.

Chick's phone was on the desk under some papers. An iPhone message from Bill Sharpe fifteen minutes ago.

Sorry. Had to leave. Do you need a ride?

I'm good, he texted back.

He thought about calling Sharpe, but the idea of Nora O'Hearn in love with Walter Peach stopped him. He turned to his desk and stacked papers without looking at them. Bills, mostly, that he didn't want to face. Month after month of no sales. He stood up and looked out the window into the showroom. Ashburn was practicing approaches to the cars. Chick remembered demonstrating some of them to new employees, such as the subtle sweep of the right hand that revealed the lines of the car and then the steps like dance moves—a one and a two, and on the third, the left hand on the door handle, the opening door, the smooth welcome to the driver's seat. He remembered his father's best salesman, a tall man always smoking. *Like this*, he had said to Chick, and the trailing smoke of the man's cigarette seemed to outline the car front to back like a lifting bridal veil. That was when smoking was elegant and sales were seductions. What was his name? Charles? *Chandler*. Chandler Ellis. Somebody's husband had shot him. Chick remembered the funeral in the Baptist Church and his outrage that the killer had been sentenced to two weeks in the state mental hospital in Milledgeville.

What did he know at ten or eleven about small towns?

He should check on Hermia.

As if on cue, his phone buzzed.

"How are you holding up?" he asked, afraid of what else Josiah Simms might have said.

—Oh, Chick.

Fifteen minutes later, he stood in the waiting room of the Gallatin County Hospital, and Hermia locked him in an embrace he would have welcomed if the nurses had not been there to notice its length and inescapably intimate intensity. Embarrassed, he patted her back the way a high school wrestler would pat his opponent to concede a match. She squeezed him tighter.

"I've never lost one before," she said, and finally released him.

"Tell me what happened," he said.

"I don't think I can talk about it yet," she said. "It's just too horrible, Chick. You should've seen her. It wasn't Josiah, it was a scared little girl, a terrified child."

He was in over his head. How was he supposed to console her for something like this? He had the low, ugly feeling of being glad Josiah had been silenced.

"It was Miriam," Hermia said, as though she had read his mind. "This little girl Miriam, and I hardly knew her and here she was ripped open, hemorrhaging her life out, but she saw the baby, she saw the nurses hold her up, and before I could even say anything to help her make her way to Jesus, her eyes just went blank and there was that line on the monitor. That terrible flat line."

She hugged Chick against her again, even tighter. He gripped her self-consciously, aware of her breasts, her heartbeat, her heat. Tears soaked through his shirt collar. One of the younger nurses, a chubby woman, came and stood nearby with a clipboard, embarrassed to be intruding, looking down at the floor.

"Miss Watson," she said.

"It was so terrible, Chick!" Hermia whispered.

"Miss Watson," the nurse repeated, "I'm sorry to have to interrupt, but can you tell me the name of the—of the—can you tell me the name of the girl who—"

Hermia released Chick, and he heard her take a deep breath through her nostrils as she wiped her eyes and turned to the nurse, trembling as if with a chill.

"Miriam McPhee. I've never received proper paperwork for her, so that's all I know."

"So—Social, driver's license, nothing like that?"

"Nothing."

"So no insurance."

Hermia sighed. "I guess not. You'll have to bill it to Eula's House."

"Unless the state, maybe—"

"Right, maybe. We'll get it figured out. I'll come by the office, okay?"

"I'm very sorry for your loss, we just have to—"

"I know it's not you," Hermia said, touching the nurse on the shoulder. To Chick she said, "Can I see you outside?"

Chick went out to his car, the Lincoln Corsair he had been driving for the past few months, and he was just settling into it when his phone buzzed again.

Patricia Lee.

"Hello, honey."

—I hear you're out there at the hospital with Hermia Watson. What's going on?

"She asked me to help her with this girl who just had a baby. The girl died, and Hermia is pretty upset."

—Why did she call you? Why would *you* be the one she thought of?

"I guess she likes me, Patricia."

She hung up on him.

What day was it? Friday? Saturday. Saturday the what? Yesterday was Friday the Thirteenth, so today was the fourteenth. He closed his eyes. He was standing in a cornfield and men were laughing at him as his house burned. When he started awake, Hermia Watson was walking across the parking lot toward him. His heart did a complicated little flip. Well, he would say to Patricia, this was a mission of mercy. No use beating himself up over it. Hermia was a good-looking woman, and they had a history from long ago, and somehow it was all in God's plan, sin and all, he supposed.

He was about to hear something that he dreaded, he was pretty sure of that.

She opened the passenger door and got in, and he could smell her perfume again in the little gust that came toward him from the closing door. Somehow this news would get to Patricia also.

"We didn't know the half of it," she said. "It wasn't just Josiah."

"What do you mean?"

"One of the girls who brought her here told me that Miriam had lied to me about everything. Miriam told the other girls that there was no boyfriend killed on a motorcycle, which is what she told me. It was a preacher at a big church outside Griffin, a man who called himself Duke. Have you ever heard of him?"

"I don't know anybody up that way."

Hermia fell silent, and Chick looked over at her. She was trembling.

"He wanted her to have an abortion, and so did her mother, who finally relented and brought her to us," she said. "I wondered why there were no papers, but I thought it was an oversight."

"Statutory rape," Chick said. "They can put this man away."

"Oh, Chick," Hermia said softly. She bent forward in her seat, elbows on her knees, hands covering her face, and he put his hand on her back, her hot neck beneath her hair, until at last she straightened up and brushed her eyes with her fingers. She found a tissue in the box that Chick kept on the floorboard. "I'm just a mess." She reached over and put her fingers lightly to his cheek. "Can you imagine doing an open house after this?" As she opened the door, she said, "I don't really have anybody in Gallatin except you. You and Jesus."

Such a strange woman.

7

CONFESSION

"WE LOST HER."

—Lost who?

"The girl I told you about. The one who thought she was Josiah. She died, Braxton. She hemorrhaged." She heard her voice trembling. "She bled to death. I don't think she was more than fourteen."

—That's what you dread most.

"They were able to save the baby. A little girl."

—You'll take her home to Eula's House.

"I don't have the proper documentation. They might want to shut us down. I need you here."

—When?

"Soon. I don't know exactly. A few days."

—I'm already on my way to Georgia. You should call Marisa.

"I know. I know I should."

Of anyone she knew, Hermia Watson dreaded Marisa Forrest most. In the chapel, one of the new arrivals knelt on the floor in front of the image of Our Lady of Guadalupe. Hermia slipped in quietly and sat before the tabernacle. After an hour, she rose, aching a little, and went to her room beneath the stairway where she sat on the bed for a moment gazing out the back window at a squirrel scrambling up the limbs of a pecan. There was no use putting it off. Marisa was never impolite, never judgmental; it was just that she knew everything. Hermia hated the compromised feeling of financial dependency, and with Marisa there was no room for evasion. The Forrests funded Eula's House, and as the donors, they needed to understand the situation, and Marisa always sensed any lack of candor.

She took a deep breath. *Lord Jesus Christ, Son of God.* She released it slowly. *Have mercy on me, a sinner.* She pressed Call for Marisa's number.

After two rings, she answered.

—Hermia.

Hermia felt her heart ease, hearing the other woman's sympathy.

"Hello, Marisa."

—I heard there was trouble.

"So you've already heard?"

—One of the women claims to be a man named Josiah.

"She was a girl of fourteen. We lost her."

—Did she run away?

Why couldn't Forrest have told her himself? Why did he leave it for her to do?

"She died in childbirth."

—Oh my God! Oh no! Braxton didn't tell me that!

"He wanted me to tell you. It was—" She stopped, faltering between her desire to say something cogent and the horror of what it had really been like.

—I'm so, so sorry.

"This is just what we always dread, but it was—"

Her voice kept climbing uncontrollably, and she knew she sounded unhinged. She tried to collect herself.

—It was awful, Marisa said.

"She hemorrhaged during the delivery and they couldn't stop the bleeding. But they saved the baby. She's a beautiful little thing."

There was a long pause.

—The same girl who said she was Josiah.

For the next five minutes, Hermia described to Marisa the persona of Josiah McPhee, the clear-sighted, scathing presence, the capacity to uncover secrets, the insistence on being called by the male name rather than the female, his command over the other girls. Her real name was Miriam.

"At least we think so."

—And she's—excuse me a minute, Hermia, I'm getting a call from Cate. Please, just a minute. I'm trying to figure out how to—

The call went dead and a moment later Marisa came back on.

—Can I call you right back?

"Of course."

Hermia had not even told her the whole complexity of the situation. Miriam McPhee had come without any records, and inquiry by the State of Georgia would reveal Hermia's administrative deficiencies and the irresponsibility of Eula's House in taking in strays. You Lose Plantation. She could make excuses, of course, but when it came down to it, the State expected people to be accounted for, one way or another, especially if they ended up in the hospital and incurred expenses. She thought about all the undocumented immigrants in America and wondered how they were handled, but she also had the feeling that it wouldn't make any difference in this case. Her work was politically charged, subject to criticism from many in the community, benighted as it seemed, because of the various races of girls she took in, and vulnerable to the left because of its pro-life mission.

Her phone buzzed. "Marisa?"

—Oh, Hermia, what a mess. Cate drove all her children to Dallas yesterday to stay with her sister Bernadette. Braxton and Jacob Guizac were just there this morning. I convinced Cate to come to Wyoming where I'm helping Teresa—not that I've asked Teresa yet. But Bernadette doesn't have room for them all. Cate and her children can stay here in the Peach house, since Walter and Jacob are gone, and Cate's kids can play with little Marisa. This way, Teresa can go out to Salt Lake City to be with Walter.

"I'm sorry, I don't understand. Why is Walter in Salt Lake City?"

—Oh my God, you don't know? He had to be life-flighted to Salt Lake City last week with Covid—the worst case they've seen in De Smet. They've induced a coma to keep him on the ventilator, and they're not sure he'll make it. Please, please keep him in your prayers. Teresa needs to get out there to be with him, even though they won't let her into the hospital. She thinks just knowing she's there will help him not feel so abandoned.

Hermia pressed her free hand on the arm of the chair. "Oh my God," she said. "I just talked to him the other day."

—Braxton should be in Atlanta by tomorrow. I'll be praying for you.

8

TRUCK STOP

AT A TRUCK STOP IN MERIDIAN, THEY GOT A BOOTH TOWARD
the back of the restaurant. As soon as she saw them, the waitress approached
with tall glasses of ice water and menus tucked under her left arm. She looked
a little tired, but she was a pretty woman, dark-haired, maybe with some
Italian or Mexican in her genes, and startling green eyes that met Jacob's with
force and candor like Emily's. Early thirties, about Cate Zitek's age, Jacob
would guess. She wore tight black pants, and she left open the top two buttons of her white shirt. A paper mask was folded neatly into a front pocket
like a handkerchief. The yellow patch above her heart had the name Nelda
stitched in blue letters.

She set down the water in front of them and handed them menus, giving
Jacob a wink.

"How y'all doing?"

Cump's bottom lip came out as though he had been brought a problem
for consideration.

"Better," he said. "Because now I have Nelda in my life. I'm a billionaire
in disguise looking for a wife among the waitresses of America, and I think I
just found her."

"Oh, Lord," she said. "I already got one over yonder giving me fits."

She tilted her head subtly back over her right shoulder, where a thin
man in a blue jean jacket and a Kenmore baseball cap had his head turned,
staring openly at Nelda. Not a billionaire in disguise, though. "You see what I

mean?" she asked Jacob. "He lives right up the road. Colton Dozier, married to Anita, got three little girls, and he's been in here every sweet Jesus night this week, paying for a mess of cheeseburgers and chicken tenders just to look at me. I'm sick to death of him."

"Nelda," Forrest said, "love is a terrible thing. That fellow can reason with himself, but it won't make a bit of difference when he looks at you. I'm feeling the same thing myself."

Nelda made a face and sighed, putting her hand down flat on the linoleum tabletop which had a strip of metal around it. "I know how it feels. Happened to me one time. Ninth grade. A boy in senior year who looked just like this one"—she patted Jacob's cheek—"filled up every daydream I had like the goody in a cream puff. Cliff Butler. You ought to seen him run down the football field." She winked at Forrest. "What y'all want to eat?"

"Chicken fried steak," Forrest said. "Green beans, collard greens, and cornbread. What happened to Cliff?"

"He went off and got shot in Afghanistan. He never even knew my name."

"I bet he died saying it."

She shook her head and gave Forrest a look before asking Jacob what he'd like.

"Fried chicken," Jacob said, looking up at Nelda. "Green beans and fried okra. And cornbread."

"You boys ain't even looked at the menu," Nelda said.

"Just looking at you," Forrest said, "makes me think of everything on it."

Nelda shook her hand like she had burned it. Jacob watched her leave. She knew he was watching because she put her hand behind her bottom and did a little wave with her fingers, which embarrassed him.

"Cliff Butler paved the way for you," Forrest said.

Jacob shook his head and smiled.

"I've got Emily."

"Do you feel about Emily the way that fellow over there feels about Nelda?"

"I don't want to talk about Emily," Jacob said.

When Nelda brought their food, she had arranged two gleaming wedges of cornbread in a red woven-plastic basket with butter and two little tubs of honey. She checked to make sure they had everything they needed—salt and pepper shakers, a bottle of Heinz, Tabasco—and stayed to witness the first bite.

"Sweet Lord," Forrest sighed.

"Is that what you wanted, sweetheart?"

"When St. Peter meets me at the Pearly Gates, I'm going to ask him if their chicken fried steak is as good as Nelda's."

"They got rules up there, sugar. We reserve the right to refuse service—you remember those signs? All I'm saying." She tapped the table with a fingernail and walked off across the room. Jacob was starved; the food was excellent. He ate in a trance of satisfaction.

Halfway through the meal, they heard Nelda's voice. "Stop it, Colton!"

Jacob glanced up to see the man in the blue jean jacket trying to put his arm around her bottom. He could not hear what the man said, but Nelda backed away and slapped the hand reaching after her as the other diners, suppressing smiles, watched the show.

"Colton giving her trouble?" Forrest said, glancing up at Jacob but not turning to look.

"Looks like it."

"Just a minute."

Forrest slid over to stand up. He stretched and clasped his fingers over his head before turning toward Colton's table. Nelda glanced at him and disappeared into the kitchen. Colton was so intent on watching her that he did not see Forrest coming.

"Colton," Forrest said.

Startled, Colton looked up. He had a narrow face with prominent cheekbones and a recessive chin. He looked as though he had not slept in days.

"What you need?" he said roughly.

"You to behave," Forrest said, loud enough for everyone in the restaurant to hear him. "Most people don't know this, but if the gods get sick of you, they smite you with a bad love. Once it gets up in your blood and fries your circuits, I'll tell you what, Colton, it don't end well. Look at Phaedra and her stepson or Myrrha and her own daddy. I ain't talking about the one true God and I ain't talking about St. Paul, and don't ask me why the gods would hate you, Colton, though I can see why they might."

"The fuck are you?"

Forrest sat down opposite him, leaned forward, and whispered. He raised three fingers in turn: one, two, three. A few seconds into it, Colton sat back sharply and shook his head. Forrest shrugged as if to apologize, then held out his hand. Colton took it sullenly.

His scream froze every lifting fork, every chewing jaw, every sipped glass, and half-spoken word. Jacob sat with his own fork halfway to his mouth and watched Colton's body crumple while he screamed curses. Nelda rushed out of the kitchen to see what was happening and stopped cold. Colton's hand and forearm stayed still as stone in Forrest's grip while the man flailed with his free hand, knocking food and beer onto Forrest, whose expression was terrifying. Jacob heard the bones snap like pencils, chopsticks, icicles. Colton stood up in a voiceless scream, mouth wide open, and Forrest suddenly released him to stumble backward into an empty nearby table, scattering the condiments and place settings and chairs. The back of his head hit the floor hard.

Nelda and the other diners looked on in horror. After a few sickening moments of inertness, Colton stirred. He tried to get up, forgetting his ruined hand, screaming and falling back when he put pressure on it. Finally, leaning on the opposite elbow, he got halfway up and an old black man helped get him to his feet. Colton stumbled out of the restaurant.

Forrest brushed himself off as he walked back to take his place across from Jacob. His clothes were stained with ketchup and the refuse of Colton's dinner, his shirt and jeans wet with beer, but he sat down and took up his knife and fork to finish his dinner. Jacob felt shamed by his own cowardice in not intervening.

A moment later Nelda stood beside their table.

"Y'all go on. Just go on. Don't worry about the bill."

"I'm going to finish my dinner," Forrest said without looking up.

"Colton's brother's a deputy sheriff. He'll be here quick."

"I don't think so," Forrest said. "I said some things to Colton."

"Like what?"

"They don't bear repeating."

"I ain't gone thank you. I can take care of myself," Nelda said.

Forrest looked up at her now.

"He reminded me of somebody."

"You remind me of somebody," Nelda said. "Which is what I'm worried about. Y'all just go. Go on."

Forrest ignored her, cutting his steak, taking bites of his beans and collards, buttering his cornbread. Nelda sighed in exasperation and left them alone. Jacob saw furtive glances, shaking heads. No one came in. When he finished, Forrest stood up and left three twenties on the table.

"Keep the change," he said to Nelda on the way out. "Colton won't bother you again."

Somberly, she watched him leave, but she pulled Jacob aside as he passed her and held him by the elbow.

"That's a dangerous man to be traveling with."

Outside, he found the car already in front of the door, running. Forrest sat behind the wheel, head lowered. Jacob got into the passenger's seat. He could smell the food and beer on Forrest's clothes.

"Cump, don't you want to change your clothes? Are you okay to drive?"

"Stop calling me Cump. That experiment is over."

As they pulled out of the parking lot, Forrest brought up the map on the display screen. The route to Atlanta. Almost three hundred more miles, four hours at least. Forrest pulled out of the parking lot onto the road, then took the access ramp back onto I-20, where he accelerated to eighty-five. Jacob watched the mile markers flash by in the headlights as they passed a slow-moving pickup, then a line of tractor-trailers.

"Drop me off in Birmingham," Jacob said. "I can get a flight home."

"I thought you wanted to know about Sherman."

"Drop me off in Birmingham."

No response. For miles as they sped forward into the forested Alabama darkness, neither of them spoke.

"I promised you Sherman," Forrest finally said. "Play the goddamn Sherman."

"What are you planning to do?" Jacob said.

Forrest did not answer.

"I'll get directions to the airport."

Forrest leaned over and restarted the *Memoirs*.

Before the March to the Sea, Sherman stripped down the army to its essentials and sent everyone wounded, ailing, or otherwise unfit to the rear. The Union army left Atlanta exuberantly, and the first days of the March released the rollicking spirit of the bummers, who looted the countryside with impunity, burning houses and leaving women and children desolate—not that Sherman dwelled on their suffering in the *Memoirs*.

As they pressed southward, feinting toward Macon and Augusta, the mood darkened. A Union officer had his leg blown off when his horse stepped on a landmine, and Sherman forced captured Confederates to clear the road, mocking their finicky caution. He loosed the rage of his men on Millen, where prisoners of war had been kept in abysmal conditions, near starvation. He took Savannah before Christmas. His celebration in Savannah was interrupted by Edwin Stanton, the Secretary of War, who visited to grill him about treatment of the freed slaves and changed Sherman's arrangements for captured cotton and made accounting for it impossible.

"Are you following this? This tension with Stanton?" Jacob asked. Forrest stared ahead, not answering.

Okay, meanwhile, Sherman received orders from Grant to bring his troops by boat up the coast to help in the attack on Lee in Virginia. Sherman responded with a plan to continue their devastating march up through the Carolinas to approach Richmond from the south and threaten Lee that way. When Grant understood the circumstances, he fully supported Sherman's plans.

"Right?" Jacob said and paused the audio. "I mean, Grant was stalled at Petersburg and wanted help, but Sherman had spent six weeks showing what the despair of civilians could accomplish," Jacob said.

Forrest said nothing. He did not even nod. He stared wrathfully into the swath of interstate illumined by the headlights. The car smelled of beer and Colton.

More, then.

In winter conditions, overcoming floods and terrible roads and sporadic resistance from Confederate troops, the Union army made a feint against Charleston and then concentrated on Columbia, where the *Memoirs* became almost delicate in their evasions. Sherman pretended to complain that he could not restrain his soldiers once they got to South Carolina, the state they hated and blamed for the war. Jacob had read accounts of the burning of Columbia elsewhere, especially in Charles Royster's *The Destructive War.* When fires spread from cotton bales and flakes of burning cotton rose, borne on high winds, into the trees and shrubs and houses of the residential neighborhoods, the drunken soldiers made no attempt to save the buildings of the city. They punched holes in firehoses. They gloried in the destruction, sure that they would never be reprimanded. For his part, Sherman hardly mentioned the drunkenness of his soldiers, and he made considerable efforts to explain his personal interventions and his futile attempt to save the convent of some Catholic sisters. Ellen would need that reassurance, Jacob suspected. He stopped the audiobook.

"It was a holocaust," Jacob said. "It was like a preview of Curtis Lemay's fire-bombing of Tokyo."

Forrest did not seem to hear him.

"Maybe just let me out at the next rest stop. I can hitch a ride with somebody."

"Ride with somebody?" Forrest said sardonically. "That's what I'm going to tell your mother, that I let you out at a rest stop?"

"Something's the matter with you. I don't need to be—"

"Play the goddamn book. I'm just working through things."

After Columbia, still encountering terrible conditions, the Army of the West pressed on into North Carolina with various skirmishes and smaller battles until the columns converged in Goldsboro in early April. Gen. Robert E. Lee, recognizing that the end had come, surrendered to Grant at Appomattox on April 9. Shortly afterward, Gen. Joseph E. Johnston surrendered his army to Sherman in North Carolina. Stanton went to the newspapers with complaints and tried to have Sherman relieved of duty for giving such generous terms to the South.

When Jacob turned off the audiobook, Forrest did not even notice.

"So another bitter rebuke just when he becomes world famous," Jacob said.

Twenty miles west of Birmingham, Forrest let out a long sigh and shook his head. When Jacob glanced over, he still said nothing, but he had tears on his face. At the next rest stop, he did not drop Jacob off, and Jacob did not remind him as they approached the exit for the Birmingham-Shuttlesworth International Airport.

Jacob woke up an hour east of Birmingham when Forrest pulled off the Interstate at an exit for Oxford, Alabama. It was already eleven. When they stopped in front of the office of a Best Western and Forrest went in, still filthy, to book a room, Jacob nodded off again. Forrest startled him awake when he opened the door.

"Come on. Grab your bag. We'll get to Atlanta in the morning."

9

CLOVER

HERMIA WATSON HAD TWO PLACES AT STONEWALL HILL
that she considered her own, her bedroom and a tiny room off the pantry
where she liked to pray. Her office on the first floor at the front of the house
was accessible to anyone who wanted to see her, but her little closet was a
secret hideaway that old Thomas Jefferson Forrest must have built. She felt
strange taking it over, though she was in old Forrest's direct line in her round-
about way. How would it look on a genealogical chart? Her mother, Marilyn
Harkins, was the illegitimate daughter of Robert Forrest, old T. J.'s legitimate
son, with Pearl, a black servant whom Robert had loved more than his wife,
Braxton's mother. Hermia, unknowingly fathered by Braxton Forrest upon
his half-sister Marilyn, was doubly an heir, if such a thing were admissible in
any legitimate genealogy.

Fine word, *legitimate*.

Her little room was just big enough for an armchair, a side table, a lamp,
a small shelf of books, and a narrow window toward the side yard. Sometimes,
if she could not sleep, she would quietly leave her room and go to her secret
place. Here, in her most perfect silence, she read her favorite authors—St.
Teresa of Avila, St. Therese of Lisieux, Sr. Ruth Burrows—and she thought
about the ways that God had taken her tangled ancestry, her twisted story,
and made something of it. Sometimes she wept in gratitude, sometimes in
sorrow. Sometimes she sat in quiet exaltation.

Tonight, she thought about the child Miriam McPhee and the child of Miriam McPhee. What would happen to Miriam's baby? She had half-expected that the infant would have a palpable air of evil—horns, as Chick had joked—but the little girl was normal as could be. It was strange seeing her in the ward with the nurses, innocent of her mother and her father and the history of her begetting. But Hermia was sure she would hear from the authorities. Not the police, because there had been no crime—at least no crime that Hermia had committed. No, one of the state agencies would come after the child.

And she would have to say something when the hospital asked for payment.

Who is covering the expenses of this delivery?

Is someone going to claim the dead mother's body?

Who is responsible for the girl's burial?

Surely there was something she could do besides appeal to Braxton Forrest. He was already on his way, and she felt his approach in her soul. This big man, this beautiful man, whom age could not wither. He was more handsome the older he got, more seasoned and sure, and even at seventy, his leonine power was such that a look from him might stir up her sinful recollection. Her father. Her lover. Why would anyone ask for the spiritual advice of a woman like her?

How did it feel to make a baby with your own daddy?

She spread her hands, appealing without reserve to the mercy of Jesus. As Ruth Burrows taught, she was helpless, abandoned, empty of all good in herself, but open to His guidance, His presence. God's, not Braxton's. Admitting her smallness and emptiness, she also felt, deep in her soul, that conviction of trust that He knew her and would shape her and help her and save her. That demon Josiah had died with Miriam, maybe he was still loose, a parasite seeking a host. So many of her girls were ignorant and vulnerable.

Tomorrow was . . .

She was startled awake when Deirdre knocked quietly on the door to rouse her. Fr. Silber was here, she said. It was almost time for Mass.

It was Sunday morning. She had slept in the armchair all night, and she had a crick in her neck. Going through the kitchen and around by the back hall, she avoided the women coming downstairs and put on a fresh dress in her bedroom, splashed her face, brushed her teeth. She ran her fingers through the tangle of her hair and hurried to the chapel. She looked awful, but what could she do about it now? She was distracted all through Mass, and she hardly heard the homily. She was desperate to see Fr. Silber, but after Mass he left without even stopping in the sacristy, late to say Mass at St. Joseph's in Macon.

Still half-awake, she crossed from the chapel to her office and for a moment gazed out over the lawn and the elegant lines of the low stone walls, the dogwoods and redbuds, the tall oaks and elms that shadowed the grass. Turning to her desk, she tried to remember why she had come in. Deirdre had set the bills on the left side of the desk in a neat stack, and she poked at them listlessly—the last thing on her mind. Besides, it was Sunday. Forrest always covered the expenses, and he would pay for the new baby, who was healthy enough to bring home. She knew the women would cluster around the little thing, full of pity and interest. That was it: suppose some soulless agency insisted on claiming the child?

A knock at the door startled her.

"Come in."

It was Jordan, who stayed at the threshold.

"There's a visitor here to see you, Miss Watson." With a word to the visitor, she came in, closing the door behind her. "She says she's Miriam's mother," she whispered.

"Oh my God."

Hermia stood up and tried to collect herself as Jordan opened the door to reveal a woman in her thirties with short, thick brown hair cut like a man's. She was round-faced and pretty, taller than Miriam had been, with a no-nonsense air. She had on black slacks, a white blouse, and a black jacket with a Denny's logo.

Hermia stepped from behind her desk and offered her hand.

"I'm Hermia Watson."

"Clover McPhee. Thank you for seeing me."

"I'm so sorry for your loss."

The woman nodded but did not meet her eyes. Hermia offered her a chair as Jordan hovered uncertainly in the doorway.

"Jordan, could you brew us a pot of coffee?"

"Of course," Jordan said, closing the door behind her.

When Hermia sat down behind her desk, Mrs. McPhee lifted her eyes.

"Miriam . . . " she started to say, and then faltered to a stop. "I guess you knew her pretty well."

"She was a troubled soul," Hermia said, and Mrs. McPhee's eyes narrowed.

"She was okay until she met—listen, I want to know what's going to become of her baby."

"Mrs. McPhee—"

"Just call me Clover. I'm not married."

"We can take care of the baby, Clover."

"She's not yours," Clover said hotly. "What are you going to do with her?"

Hermia sat back in her chair.

"I don't want to make a legal issue of it, and the last thing I'd want is for some state agency to claim her. You're the grandmother."

"Grandmother!" Clover cried. "I'm just thirty-five years old, I just—" She started angrily tearing tissues from the box on Hermia's desk.

"Clover, one of the things we do really well is take care of new babies."

"It got so I didn't know who she was."

"Sometimes she told us she was a boy named Josiah," Hermia said.

Clover nodded. Hermia stood up and walked around her desk to sit closer to Clover.

"Tell me about the baby's father. You started to say Miriam was fine until she met somebody. Who did you mean?"

Clover's mouth tightened. "I knew you'd want to blame him."

"When Miriam came here, she told me the father of her baby was a boy killed in a motorcycle accident. But she told the women upstairs it was a preacher."

"It's Duke."

"Okay, so."

"It's hard to see it the right way if you don't know him," Clover said. "He saved me, and I obey him, and that's hard to understand for people who don't know him."

"Saved you."

A light came into Clover's eyes. "He told me people would want to blame him. Even arrest him. He has this saying. *To be great is to be misunderstood.*"

"Emerson," Hermia nodded.

"I'm sorry?"

"Never mind. You don't blame this Duke, then? Even though—"

"Blame Duke? I blame Miriam. Jealous is what she was," Clover said. "Jealous that he saved me. When he asked for her, I didn't want to at first because he wanted her. I guess I was jealous myself. But I had to think about what was good for her, and he could save her."

Hermia stared.

"Wait. Are you saying you *gave* her to him?"

10

SUNDAY MORNING

"I HOPE YOU CAN FORGIVE ME," MARISA SAID OVER COFFEE. "I asked Cate to come here with the children."

Teresa nodded, not sure what to say. She and Walter owed so much to the Forrests that she could hardly refuse, but the idea of having a displaced family descend upon her now was crushing.

Her face must have given her away.

"Oh, I'm so sorry, Teresa," Marisa said, standing up. "I should have asked, but I was thinking that this would let you go to Salt Lake City to be near Walter."

To be near Walter.

"I understand," she said.

To be near Walter, even though she could not see him. Even though he was in a coma.

"Jimmy wants to go home to Atlanta," Marisa said, pacing the kitchen tiles, "but that's impossible with Jason on a rampage. Cate told the kids I was in Wyoming, and Clare helped convince her brother. The children are rattled, and Cate dreads the drive, but if they take two days, it won't— Braxton reserved a room for them in Raton, New Mexico—and so the next day, tomorrow, they'll—if the weather's—do you know what the weather's going to do?"

Teresa began to smile despite herself.

Marisa sighed and sat down.

"We have a day to get ready," Teresa said.

"Don't you think Little M will like having other kids in the house?"

Everything was predicated on her own absence, Teresa realized. A small burn of resentment started up in her heart. She was being banished from her own house.

"I haven't said my prayers yet this morning," she said.

"I've upset you," Marisa said. "I'm so sorry, I'll just call Cate and—"

"Marisa!" The older woman looked up at her, stung by Teresa's tone of rebuke. "Just give me a few minutes to think, okay? I'm going to go outside."

She sat on the deck facing the sun. It was a clear, cold, windless Sunday, and since she was still in quarantine and should not go to church, she read the Mass readings in her *Magnificat* with particular care. The Thirty-third Sunday in Ordinary Time. The first reading was from Proverbs, and as she read it, she began to cry quietly. "When one finds a worthy wife, her value is far beyond pearls. Her husband, entrusting his heart to her, has an unfailing prize. She brings him good, and not evil, all the days of her life." Then the Psalm. "Your wife shall be like a fruitful vine / in the recesses of your home; / Your children like olive plants / around your table." Tears dropped onto the thin paper, right onto the Gospel and its parable about the talents. Did she fear the Lord enough? Had she done anything with all she was given? Had she ever really thanked God for their blessings? For Marisa? For this place they lived?

She gazed at the red cliff to the east, the irregular ridge line where mule deer would sometimes profile against the early light. The tough shrubs and junipers, the rubble of the scree. If she had her pencils, she would try to show how massively delicate it all was. She would need to outline the complex horizontals boldly, the layers of rock, sometimes continuous, sometimes broken into foot-thick projecting triangles. Near the top, a long slab of reddish sandstone angled down diagonally, held in place by a whim of friction. There were stretches of bare dirt along hundred-yard shelves of continuous tubular rock with cave-like spaces under them, where a single female goat—Walter called her Dolores—wandered alone, summer and winter, year after year. The cliff dropped through striations that looked like the rough-cut pages of stained and water-warped old books rescued from a flood. Layer upon layer.

That geological time she dreaded, that stony biding, ironized the living moment and belittled the duration of any life but God's. Maybe saving God from time was what nature was for—all the processes in motion that no living mind would need to witness and supervise, moment by moment. The imperceptibly slow settling of sea-stuff for millions upon millions of years of densifying and hardening at the bottom of the sea. And had God, moment by moment, patiently guided by hand its rise in the slow heave and shift of the ages of earth to its present six thousand feet above sea level? Or had He let nature's terrible relentless ongoing proceed without a superintending consciousness? Could God be surprised?

Down in the bottom, the trees were leafless now, and she could see the piles of brush that Jacob and Walter had cut from beside the creek in the summer and early fall. A strange, subdued melancholy came over her, then an even stranger shame.

Walter lying in his bed, hooked to a machine. Her Walter.

She would take Marisa's offer. Of course she would. Part of it was cowardice—simply to avoid Cate and her misery when she had her own worries. But part of it, too, was her obligation to be near Walter if she could be. Oh God, what would she do if Walter died? Would she and the children stay in De Smet? What would she do for money? Become a ward of the Forrests?

Even asking the questions chilled her. She hated having the thought—but Walter might very well die, and the life they had made would die with him.

She heard the door open behind her. Marisa came up beside her.

"You must feel like I'm running you out of your own home."

"I did at first, but no, sweetheart," Teresa said, touching Marisa's hand on her shoulder. "I'm just having to take it all in."

"I thought Cate's being here would free you go to Walter."

"It will. A Transfiguration student emailed me on Sunday that her parents live in Salt Lake City, and they have a small downstairs apartment that they will let me use if I need it. They built it for her grandparents before they died."

The girl's grandparents. Their anonymity pierced her, the anonymity they would all enter as soon as she and Walter, and then their children, and then their children's children all receded into the past, life upon life.

"I'm just scared."

Convulsive sobbing rose as irresistibly as nausea. Marisa held her. When she recovered, Teresa stood from the chair and embraced her friend and thanked her, wiping the tears from her cheeks.

"You've just got too much to deal with."

"What time tomorrow do you think Cate and the kids will get here?"

"Late afternoon."

Teresa nodded. "I'll get in touch with the couple in Salt Lake City. Have you heard anything from Braxton and Jacob?"

"They're almost to Atlanta."

11

FIRST MOTIONS

MR. PEACH, WE'RE STARTING. COULD I HAVE YOUR FULL AT-
tention, please?

The man sat across a steel desk from him. He had the blank, earnest look
of the true-believing Stasi agent in the movie.

Sorry? My name is Guizac, by the way. Where are we?

IFIB, the Interdum Fidelis Interrogation Board. Welcome.

Right. Thank you, I guess.

Let's get to it. A few preliminaries. I know you occasionally do something
nice when you go along with other people's ideas—usually your wife's—
but did you ever have an idea of your own just to do something good for
somebody else? When I look at the register, Mr. Peach—

Guizac.

When I look at the register, your FMS is—well, geez Louise, to tell you
the truth, it's over in the red zone. Over with the—you know—well, let me
turn the monitor around for you. There. You see what I mean?

FMS?

First motion of the soul. See this? This measures the current through
the soul's conduction nodes. The reading starts either below or above the
baseline and we can tell whether you're—well, look, you can see for yourself.
See this? Not good. I don't want to scare you, buddy, but what I see here is
self-absorption and that's about it.

What's it supposed to look like?

Mr. Peach—

Guizac.

You're going to stick with the name Forrest gave you as a joke? Okay, well, the problem here is that we aren't registering what's called "goodness" as the first motion of your soul in *anything*. It's always *me-first*, and then there's this pinched little wince of calculation about whether doing something nice for somebody else might be useful to you in the short run. Some agents call it a *flutter of conscience* but I don't think conscience applies to you. You don't seem to have a conscience.

I don't know what you're talking about.

Exactly.

There was a long silence. Finally, Guizac shook his head.

I really don't know what you're talking about, he asserted again. Is this about—I don't know, salvation and damnation? You said I was over in the red zone.

Let's not get too literal.

What do you mean literal? This is because I'm going to die, right? Or am I already dead? Is this about whether I'm damned or saved?

What does that even mean to you, Mr. Peach? The man sat back from the desk and put his hands behind his head. Do you have any idea what that means? What does it mean to be saved? Saved from what? From your life?

Look, I'm just trying to follow the script here. I'm thinking that being saved means not going to hell.

So you define it negatively. And going to hell is what?

I don't know—let's see, maybe being stuck with just yourself? Or stuck with you, maybe. No offense. Or maybe stuck with Jean-Paul Sartre.

Would it be hell to be stuck with just yourself forever?

God, yes. Cut it out. This is bullshit. Why don't you just tell me what's going on?

There was another long silence. The man put his hands on the desk and then touched his left ear, as if listening, and stood up and left without another word.

Moments later, a very pretty young woman came in. More than pretty. She artfully smoothed her tight skirt across her bottom and sat down across from him, knees together.

Artfully smoothed? she said.

I'm sorry?

You just thought that.

She wore a yellow blouse with the two top buttons open.

Where were these words coming from?

From you, the girl said. She smiled at him as she reached into her purse and drew out a pack of Marlboro Reds. She lit one up, and a large, heavy, glass ashtray appeared on the desk, a prop from the film noir classics of the 1940s and 1950s. She took a puff from her cigarette and laid it in the notched corner. Smoke trailed languidly upward. Very recherché.

Her brow wrinkled, and she touched her left ear. Instantly, cigarette, ashtray, smoke, and girl vanished.

A moment later, the same girl came in, this time wearing running shorts and a tight scoop-necked white tank top. Her face was flushed, and the plane of her chest shone with light perspiration. She glanced at her Fitbit watch and then up at Guizac. She was just getting her breath back. Her breasts juddered slightly with each heartbeat.

Juddered?

Quivered warmly? Trembled concentrically?

Stick with *juddered*, something said inside him.

Do you like me? she said as she sat down.

Now it was a dinner table. The tank top, crusted with black sequins, was part of her dress. A waiter (the Stasi agent) appeared from behind her and poured a glass of wine for her and one for Guizac. A dry white wine, very cold. A Pinot Gris from Willamette Valley, he noted.

Do I like you? Peach said.

Wasn't your very first thought that you'd like to go to bed with me?

Wow. Peach lifted his palms. Maybe we could have a glass of wine?

I felt it, she said, lifting her right hand and molding it around the wine glass. It was like a pressure, a kind of squeezing in the air, something that summarized me and gave me a grade. I felt, I don't know—assessed by the male gaze.

She met his eyes. Hers were a deep green, and there was something very deeply knowing in the sweet face.

He felt a jolt of desire.

See that? she said.

What?

I have the meter, remember? May I ask you a question? she said, leaning across the table toward him.

I'm all yours, he said.

What about your faith?

His heart sank.

My faith?

Of course. Your faith. So what does it do to your faith, feeling as you do about me?

I guess I don't know what you mean, Guizac said, acutely aware of how lame he sounded.

Faith? *Fides*, fidelity—remember faith?

What are you getting at?

Religious conviction. Loyalty to the promise you made to your wife. Both of those are faith, aren't they? Ways of being faithful? I don't know much about it myself, she said, wetting her finger in the wine and running it around the rim of her glass until it began to sing and then touching the fingertip to her lips. But aren't they pretty much the same thing? I mean, if you keep faith one way, you also keep faith the other way?

I mean—I guess.

I thought you were a convert. Did I get that wrong—let me check my—no, you're the one. It says right here you've had trouble before. Somebody named Lydia. I'm teasing. I know all about her. Not to mention *Nora*.

Come on, Guizac said, that was before.

Before me, you mean? Or before fidelity? Is that what you're saying? Help me out.

Well I mean—I, um—I'm not exactly. I mean—

You're pretty shaky on this faith business, Mr. Guizac. But *Guizac* is the name for the man after *Peach* was unfaithful, right? Your name after the move from Gallatin? The convert, the new man. No more problems. She smiled and adjusted herself in the seat, re-crossing her legs, and lightly touched herself just where he could not help but notice the soft inception of her cleavage.

No problems except for that really absurd little stir you feel? I'm flattered. I can see it right here on the register. Hmm. We aren't talking now about the first motion of the soul, by the way, Mr. Guizac. This is just the *ongoing you* of you. I'm just not picking up a lot of *faith* here, Mr. Guizac.

She was saying *Guizac* sardonically now.

This is unfair, he said.

Yes it is. She laughed quite merrily, a clear, guiltless, joyful sound.

You *are* funny, Walter, she said, quieting her voice to a murmur. May I call you Walter? Walter Peach? It's just—I've never met anyone quite like you. She said it so softly that he had to lean forward to hear her. Her hand closed over his. Someone so *stirring*. So bad at faith that—

He looked up and saw Teresa standing right behind her.

Good God. It couldn't really be Teresa because they wouldn't let her in the hospital.

He stood up and turned around.

There was nothing there. No diners, no blank wall. No floor. Nothing at all, as though someone had missed the assignment to fill it in. So this was the famous privation of existence. Where was everything, something, anything?

He felt behind him for the chair, not trusting that it would still be there, either. It *was* still there, thank goodness. He could have faith in it, was that the point? Cautiously, he turned back around. Now there was a bare wooden table from a school library and across from him sat a ferocious-looking man wearing the Roman collar. Why priests wore those collars, he did not know. He had never understood a lot of things about the Church, and he had a strong feeling that if he pried into them, he would be quickly disillusioned. Why he thought so, he did not know.

Goozac, said the priest. I can see what you're thinking, thought by thought. It's coming up right here on the register. You could easily Google priests and collars.

This is bullshit! Peach protested.

So now you're Peach? That's the way you self-identify?

Self-identify?

I thought you were still Goozac, and BOOM, here you are identifying as Peach all over the meter. I've got to tell you, by the way, you're right, don't pry into the Church stuff, because it's a mess from the local parish all the way up to Rome, where the cynical old sodomites in the hierarchy are trying to—OW! He slapped a hand on his ear. *Shit shit shit.* Okay, okay.

So, he said, clearing his expression and turning back to Peach. The collar was gone.

He wore a regular tie.

Better: he wore a light blue Oxford shirt and a dark blue silk tie with red diagonal stripes, tied in a full Windsor knot.

It appears that you have some issues with fidelity, do you, Mr. Goozac?

Peach tried not to think *I'm not the only one.* He tried not to have any thought at all. Simply to be. He concentrated on inhaling slowly and then letting the breath stream out steadily from his nose.

The "priest" made a frown and raised his eyebrows, amused.

Cut the crap. I'm looking at the register here, Goozac, and it's *sin, sin, sin* from the First Motion of the Soul all the way up to the soft inception of my cleavage.

The priest winked at him.

Peach stared.

It was the girl again.

I've never met anyone like you, she whispered. Did I say that before?

You did. You still don't mean it.

She laughed merrily.

No, sugar, I don't. But wouldn't it be pretty to think so? No, you're as common as—wait. She touched her ear. *Sherman?* she said. You can't be serious. Okay, I'll leave, but—no, I thought you said we could do whatever we—

She disappeared.

In her place was a man of modest bearing in the dark robe of a judge.

Mr. Peach, he said, the questions I'm about to ask you are optional in terms of *what* but not *whether* you answer. They are not addressed to you and yet they pertain to you in your proper person in terms of your salvation or damnation. Do you understand?

Not at all. Sounds pretty grim, though.

I am going to be asking you questions in your persona as William Tecumseh Sherman.

I do not have a persona as William Tecumseh Sherman. I am Walter Peach. Or Karl Guizac. My name has been kind of unstable, I guess, but my identity hasn't. I have never been and never will be William Tecumseh Sherman. My son's been writing about him, but.

There was a long pause.

Are you finished? the man asked.

That's all I wanted to say.

Then let's proceed. Mr. Guizac—or Mr. Peach, if you prefer—here's the first question to you in your persona as General Sherman. Do you understand?

Nope.

You will catch on quickly. Now here we go: do you feel a sense of fidelity to your wife, Ellen Ewing, who is also your foster sister? Or would you say that your marriage to her is less out of affection than out of a desire to affect the Ewing family in some strong way?

This is ridiculous, Peach said.

Please answer the question.

He felt a subtle shift inside him and Sherman came swarming into his mind.

She was cute as a child. She was the only one in the house who was always kind to me.

You didn't feel that it was a violation of your faith with the family to court your own foster sister? A violation of implicit trust? Perhaps you even felt that it was a mode of revenge for "The debt immense of endless gratitude, / So burdensome still paying, still to owe," as Milton puts it.

It wasn't like that. Nobody ever pretended that I was part of the family. Nobody ever said Ellen was my sister.

And yet you grew up in the intimacy of the same home. So what *was* it like? Did you share the family faith? Did you believe in God as Mrs. Ewing did and as Ellen certainly did?

No. Maybe there's a God, but as for the Catholic part, I went through the motions to get the benefit of being in a house of rich people who were also connected to other important people.

Did you ever feel that your courtship of Ellen was a way to loosen the bonds of her faith to God and to her family?

Sure, maybe—well, until the honeymoon. Not to be rude. I refuse to answer any more questions. You've already decided about me.

Really? Let me give you a glimpse of the alternative to answering the question, Gen. Sherman.

Table and interrogator disappear.

A child runs out the door of a burning house, her nightgown and hair gust upward with flame, she raises her hands in silent, agonized supplication. There are gunshots, horses rearing and bursting through shrubbery, women screaming, old men cursing.

Three men now, their faces downturned.

Do you understand what you're looking at?

That little girl was a deaf-mute. She didn't hear the warnings.

Tell us what you're looking at, Gen. Sherman.

The great house flames upward.

My glory. My salvation.

This is your salvation?

My everlasting fame. My revenge.

Do you believe in the Lord Jesus Christ, who took on humiliation and loss? Do you believe that he died to take away your sins?

Tell it to the niggers.

You have no faith in Christ?

None. Never.

You never believed in the resurrection of the dead?

Ridiculous fantasy.

Did you ever feel the obligation of marital fidelity to Ellen Ewing Sherman?

God, no. I needed her to make the Ewing stock into Shermans, to cross that pride and superiority with my redheaded get. To seed a prim Ewing womb with Shermans. I needed to dirty the favored daughter. Better still would have been to cuckold old Thomas Ewing outright.

The robed men stare down at the table for a moment before they lift their eyes again.

So you never felt the obligation of fidelity to Ellen Ewing?

Fidelity is for dogs. I like pretty girls, not dowdy matrons. Ellen was pliant when she was very young, but she turned dowdy and wincing, always having to pray that she could bear to complete her marital duty, as she called it. The only pleasure I got from her in bed was the thought that her father could not do to her what I was doing.

A silence falls.

I think we should take a short break, said one robed man.

Everything disappeared. Peach could not sense his own body or see his own hands, but he felt the stirring of a boundless misery, an anguish he could not escape, a burning desire with no object or end.

Now the three robed men appeared before him, seated at a high bench instead of the table.

Mr. Peach, a word of caution. You are speaking for William Tecumseh Sherman.

So you say.

So you are content with Hell?

Hell is my glory.

Another silence falls.

Are you speaking in your own voice when you say that, Mr. Peach?

What do you mean?

Are you speaking in your own person as Walter Peach, not as William Tecumseh Sherman?

Terror came over him. Behind the judges he could see a vast landscape of torment.

You told me to speak as Sherman.

But this is your own examination. You have been speaking as Gen. Sherman out of your own person, have you not? Speaking as you think he would have spoken in this circumstance?

Yes.

Do you understand anything from speaking as Gen. Sherman that you had not understood before?

He paused and thought before answering.

He's probably not as bad as I've made him. Maybe he was never conscious of the things I have had him say.

Then why did you say them?

It was what I saw from inside him when you asked me to.

Really? What else did you see?

Things about myself. That I love my wife Teresa despite all my failings. That I believe in God despite all my infidelities and weaknesses. That my soul is in mortal peril. That my salvation does not come through anything I can do to deserve it but through the mercy of Jesus Christ.

You say these things out of fear. Rote repetition of expected responses.

More than fear. Absolute terror—but I wouldn't be so terrified if they weren't true.

Do you make this profession of faith at the expense of Gen. William Tecumseh Sherman?

What do you mean?

Do you believe that he must go to hell in order for you to be saved? Do you need to be assured of the eternal torment of William Tecumseh Sherman in order to feel your own righteousness?

He paused for a long moment.

No, he said. He has his own soul. He makes his own choices.

Would you pray for the salvation of William Tecumseh Sherman?

Yes. Even though I'm not sure it would mean anything. He's been dead a long time. Hasn't he already been judged?

Why would you do it, then?

Because I hope somebody would pray for me, even if they thought I was a hopeless case.

The judges were silent. Then the one on the left spoke.

Pass.

12

PHOE

THE NEXT MORNING, FORREST STUFFED HIS DIRTY CLOTHES into the motel room's trashcan. Jacob emailed Emily about the scene with Nelda while the old man took a shower. Over breakfast, Forrest apologized to Jacob without explaining himself and laid out his plan. It was Sunday. They would drive from Oxford into Atlanta in time to go to the noon Mass at the Cathedral of Christ the King on Peachtree. They'd get lunch and then visit the offices of *Phoe* Magazine, where Jason Zitek worked.

"They work on Sunday?"

"Sticking it to Chick-Fil-A. The whole staff is slavishly woke. They work a four-day week, Sunday through Wednesday. Very radical."

Phoe should have been pronounced *fee* because it was a shortening of "phoenix," the symbol of Atlanta arising from the ashes of Sherman's destruction. But they pronounced it *foe*, which the publisher liked because it sounded edgy and anti-something, whereas *fee* sounded like you had overdrawn your bank account.

"*F-a-u-x*, more like it," Forrest said.

"What are we going to do when we get there?" Jacob asked, looking up from the third thick waffle he had made on Best Western's machine. Syrup dripped from his fork.

"You'll meet the famous Zitek."

Jacob stared at him, looking for clues.

"Why do you want me to go with you?"

"I have a responsibility to you," Forrest told him.

"Meaning?"

He did not explain.

"What are we going to do after that?"

"We're going to Cate's house. Lawful entry. I bought the house, and Cate gave me the new keys. I want to check it out. Pick up a few things. Wait for Zitek."

"After *Phoe*, can we go up to Kennesaw?"

Back in the room, Forrest told him to shower and put on his best clothes. Jacob had forgotten to bring ties, but he had a jacket and slacks for Mass and two Brooks Brothers shirts. At Forrest's insistence, he put on the lace-up shoes that pinched his feet. As he bent over his suitcase, he opened the mirror from Emily and made a face. Forrest groomed himself immaculately before putting on beige wool slacks, a light blue shirt, a blue-gray cable knit sweater, and beautiful, reddish-brown Italian loafers. He told Jacob that the shoes would have cost at least $500 in Boston, but he had happened on them in a thrift store in Durham, New Hampshire, where it was unlikely enough that he would find anything in a size 14. They had cost him $15.

They left by nine. Since they would approach Atlanta from the West on I-20 instead of on I-75, they did not follow the route of Sherman's army down from Chattanooga, which Jacob had hoped to do. When they crossed the Georgia line into Eastern time, they lost an hour, but they made it to the church a few minutes before Mass started.

Forrest followed the boy inside into a beautiful, vast, golden-feeling sanctuary and they found seats off the side aisle. The first reading was the famous one from the Book of Proverbs about a good wife. "She will render him good, and not evil, all the days of her life." He thought of Marisa. What could Forrest complain about with Marisa? She had her temper and her tendency to be exacting, but though she had been justly angry with Forrest she had not been like Ellen Ewing Sherman, who never wanted Sherman to be in the Army, never wanted to live in California when he left the military and became a banker, never considered being with him her real home. Jacob was probably right to imagine that Sherman's resentment took the shape of secret sexual transgressions. But Marisa had always been the wife Forrest needed.

For years he had been faithful, even though he had not been a believer; the ordinary temper of moral life ought to bind any man of honor to his word.

But then had come that weekend at Northwestern with Hermia Watson. And for years afterward, as if Hermia had broken some dam of his resolve, he had indulged his desire without the least hesitation, as though all law were suspended and he was living out some 1960s dream of free love, his own personal Woodstock. Students, women at conferences, babysitters. Had he done it because he despised Marisa's pious Catholicism as Sherman despised Ellen's? Not at all. It was more selfish than that, something that lurked in the dark, transgressive blood of the Forrests. It was never fueled by any resentment of Marisa's faults. Unlike Ellen Sherman, she had never demanded a life they could not afford. Even after they came into the Forrest fortune, she had not changed her habits—wanting the BMW was an anomaly—except to increase her charity. Despite his transgressions, Marisa had painfully but generously and genuinely forgiven him. She loved him. Like the woman in Proverbs, she aged with dignity and humor.

"Favor is deceitful, and beauty is vain: the woman that feareth the Lord, she shall be praised. Give her of the fruit of her hands: and let her works praise her in the gates." Forrest's eyes stung. *The gates.* The gates of Jerusalem, the gates of heaven, the gates of the city of God. If she truly loved him, maybe she would help welcome him inside, centuries from now, from her place of bliss, after his long, long purgatorial ordeal. If he made it there. If he could even be forgiven.

He thought about the feel of Colton's bones breaking and jolted back in the pew.

He thought about what he was about to do.

He stayed in the seat when Jacob went up for Communion.

After Mass, traffic was heavy but moving on I-75. They got lost for a few minutes when they exited into a thicket of one-way streets near Georgia Tech, but eventually they found Peachtree Center, parked, and walked a few blocks to the Atlantic States building. In the lobby, a middle-aged Asian receptionist directed them to the elevators and told them that the offices of *Phoe* occupied the twenty-fourth floor. As they rose with knee-loosening speed, Forrest brushed Jacob's shoulders and straightened his jacket.

The elevator doors opened onto a freestanding rectangle of wall with the name *PHOE* lettered into a bird on fire. *Burn it down* said one open wing. *Build it better* said the other. Beneath the logo, lounging far back in his chair behind the desk, was a man in his mid-twenties with one side of his head shaved; long black hair from the other side drooped over his face. He wore a light pink T-shirt with *Phoe* over his heart. He was so engaged with thumbing something into his smart phone that not even the bells of the elevator and the sound of the closing doors distracted him.

Forrest rapped sharply on the wood of the desk.

"Holy shit!" the man cried, his hair whipping. "Whoa, didn't see you coming."

"Now that," Forrest said to Jacob, "is fine hardwood."

The man behind the desk aimed his nameplate at them. Brantley Hupper. Forrest rapped on the wood again, shaking his head in admiration.

"Only the best at *Phoe*. You hear that?"

It sounded like particle board to Jacob.

"Not many people coming up, what with Covid," said Brantley.

"But you're the sentinel, just in case. Excellent," Forrest said. "*Phoe's* bench is so deep they can spare a man of your talents just to keep watch. You see," Forrest said with gravity to Jacob, "in an organization that positions itself from the outset on the farthest reaches of peripherality, even its own gateway figures embody cultural tropes. Like you, Mr. Hupper. Am I right? Outstanding."

"I mean . . . "

"I've been telling my young friend Jacob about the genius of your staff. He's particularly fond of—well, just ask him, Jacob," he said.

"Me?" Jacob said, as though he were Telemachos meeting Nestor on the beach near Pylos.

"You can do this," Forrest said.

"Mr. Hupper," Jacob said. "Does *Jason Zitek* work here?"

He said the name as though Zitek had just been awarded a Nobel Prize.

"Dude! Absolutely! Good friend of mine."

"Do you think my young friend could see where Mr. Zitek works?" asked Forrest.

Hupper's mouth was hanging a little open, as though he did not sufficiently understand his own importance. "I mean, like, you want me to see if he's here, or?"

Forrest held up a hand and shook his head.

"I mean," Brantley pressed on, "like, if he's here, should I like—tell him—you know, who's?"

Forrest shook his head. "Let's flank him."

"Sorry?"

"Just a metaphor of mine. In the revelation of character, I always tell Jacob, surprise is everything."

Brantley Hupper hiked up his jeans as they went around the *Phoe* wall into the open space of the twenty-fourth floor and its mazes of cubicles. Jacob could see maybe a dozen people, some of them with headsets, some with earbuds, some on the telephone or leaning forward to look at the screens of their computers or laptops. Half the cubicles were empty.

An Indian woman in a mask stood up when she noticed them, taken aback at the presence of visitors.

"Are you looking for someone?"

Brantley started to speak, but Forrest held up his hand to silence him.

"I know we're interrupting important work," Forrest said, "but I wanted my young friend Jacob to be able to see a major journalistic enterprise in action. Do you think someone could give us a quick tour of your offices? Or we'd be happy just to wander through."

Jade looked flattered. "I'm Jade," she said. "Welcome to *Phoe*. I'll take them from here, Brantley, if you don't mind."

"I mean, like, I could do it if—"

"I think they need someone familiar with all the aspects of our operation," Jade said.

Brantley started back toward his station, scratching behind one ear. Jade's eyes smiled up at them. She could not have been five feet tall.

"I feel like I used to around the basketball team," she said. "Are you grandfather and grandson?"

"Professor and student," Forrest said. "Mentor and mentee. We've just driven all the way from Wyoming."

"From Wyoming! Do you mind if I ask how you know about *Phoe*?" Jade asked.

"Are you kidding?"

"Sometimes I don't think anybody outside Atlanta has heard of us."

"That's hard to believe. I'm Dr. Braxton Forrest," he said, extending his hand, into which Jade almost put her own tiny one before she remembered the pandemic and withdrew it apologetically. "I'm professor emeritus at Walcott College in Portsmouth, New Hampshire. I'm a scholar of culture, and I concentrate on transitional moments when figures of symbolic importance rise to the public's attention. Some years back, I wrote a book called *The Gameme*, which predicted the Obama presidency according to some, and now that we're at another critical juncture, I'm especially interested to understand what goes into shaping the opinions and perspectives that we see coming out of *Phoe*. I'd like to enlighten my young friend—he's doing a special tutorial with me—about the thought behind your editorial policy. He's shown great promise in his own writing. I have to boast that he's something of a protégé."

Jade tilted her head with a friendly air at Jacob. "And what have you written, if I may ask?"

"I'm working on a novel about William Tecumseh Sherman," Jacob said.

"A novel, really? I'm surprised to—I mean, you seem awfully young for—"

"It's major," Forrest interrupted in an undertone.

Jade's eyes widened appreciatively.

"First let me show you our city," she said. Around the perimeter were floor-to-ceiling windows. Those facing south revealed downtown Atlanta, which seemed to Jacob miraculously full of trees. Rising from the cluster of buildings around Five Points was the golden dome of the Capitol. Gold from the mines at Dahlonega.

"When Sherman was in Georgia as a young soldier," Jacob told Jade, "he saw gold ore from Dahlonega. That's how he knew the gold ore at Sutter's Mill was the real thing. Most people don't know he was in Georgia twenty years before the Civil War. Or in California during the Gold Rush."

"Really?" murmured Jade, exquisitely noncommittal. "We have a writer who thinks Atlanta should erect a statue of Sherman."

She walked them down the first aisle and introduced them to a few journalists who dealt primarily with Atlanta politics or regional issues. One section of the floor was devoted to culture—music in Atlanta, theater, art museums. Another section did fashion, social trends, celebrities, weddings. She showed them the magazine's graphic artists and designers. In the back corner of the floor, facing north, was the office of the publisher, with his editors on either side. These had walls, regular doors, nameplates, and their own floor-to-ceiling windows. As they passed one door, Forrest caught Jacob's eye and tapped a nameplate with his fingernail.

Melina Lykaios, Managing Editor.

"And that's our space," Jade said, folding her hands. "Is there anything else I can help you with?"

"You ask her," Forrest said to Jacob supportively. Jacob cleared his throat.

"Is it true that Jason Zitek works here?"

"Well yes he does, as a matter of fact," Jade said, surprised. "He's the one I just mentioned."

"I just—I don't know, I mean, I'd like to meet him, you know, if—"

"I think he's in today," she said nervously. "I'll take you to his cubicle."

One of the journalists near them rolled his chair out into the aisle. "If you're looking for Zitek, he's in there." He tilted his head back toward the editorial corner. "With Lykaios." He lifted his eyebrows and rolled back inside his cubicle.

"Okay," Jade said uneasily.

"Better knock," the man called.

Jade walked them to the door where they had seen the nameplate. After a moment of hesitation, she tapped on it lightly with her knuckle.

"Melina?" she called brightly. "Melina, may we come in?"

A strangled exclamation shot through the cracks.

"Just a minute," a woman called irritably. "What do you need?"

"I have some visitors who'd like to meet Jason. Sam said he was in your office."

There were sounds of shuffling and mumbled curses, and a long half-minute later, the door opened, and a man with a pompadour haircut and a wolfish look flung open the door, his face flushed.

"Who wants to meet me?"

When he saw Forrest looming over him, Zitek froze.

"Jason," said Forrest. "It's been a long time," he said mildly, holding out his hand. "At least since Christmas past."

Zitek shrank back.

"No fucking way. I know that one. What the hell, Jade?"

"So you already know each other," said Jade, confused.

"I know Jason very well," Forrest said.

Behind Zitek, a dark-complexioned woman with straight black hair and close-set eyes stared like Kilroy over the edge of her desk before half-standing and grappling her chair up under her. Her left arm was in a cast.

"So who's this?" she said a little hoarsely, clearing her throat.

"Remember the guy who threatened to sue us?"

Her face changed. She began to straighten papers and fiddle with the mouse beside her laptop.

Forrest took another step toward Zitek, still extending his hand. Jade looked confused as Zitek backed away and bumped into Lykaios's desk, reaching back to steady himself and inadvertently tipping over a coffee tumbler, whose top popped loose and wobbled off as coffee glugged out and spread unchecked across Lykaios's messy desk.

"Fucking hell, Jason!" Lykaios scrambled to snatch things up—newspapers, bottles of makeup, pencils, stacks of copy, photographs, candy wrappers, an eyelash brush.

"What do you want?" Zitek demanded. When Forrest, smiling, did not reply, Zitek said, "I'm out of here," and made a move to leave, but Forrest blocked his path. "Let me through. You've made your point."

"I haven't made my point at all," said Forrest.

Jade gazed up, eyebrows contracting as she realized that she had been party to a ruse. A few people had left their cubicles to watch what was happening.

"Jacob," Forrest said, "that's Zitek. That's my son-in-law. The one who wants a statue of Sherman in the middle of Atlanta."

"Oh sweet Jesus," someone murmured behind them.

"Need a little more warning next time, Zitek?" somebody called from nearby. More journalists were coming out of the cubicles smiling, enjoying the show.

"Say hello to Jacob, Jason," Forrest said.

"Listen," Zitek said loudly, "this man is tight with Bannon. He's Trump to the bone. Talk about white supremacists, he killed a black man with his bare hands."

Forrest turned calmly to those gathering outside the office. Elegant and urbane, he looked anything but mad. Seeing their skepticism, Zitek cried, "He's the one who owns that plantation house Melina wrote about. Where they imprison women and refuse to let them have abortions."

"Jesus," someone muttered. There was a stir behind him. "Stop lying, Zitek. You put Lykaios up to that. You fed her all those lies and you let her take the heat when she had to do the retraction."

"These people might not know me," Forrest said, "but they know you. On the other hand, they might not know my lovely daughter, and I'm sure they don't know that you told her you wished your children were dead." There was a gasp. "Remember them?" Forrest pulled out his phone, swiped at it a few times, and held up a picture of Zitek with Cate, Clare, Jimmy, and Avila. He turned and showed it to the room, swiping from one photo to the next.

"Get him out of here!" Lykaios yelled, standing now from behind her desk. "Who let this man in? This is a workday. Everybody get back to work."

Nobody moved.

"I'm out of here," Zitek said again as he started toward the door.

Forrest blocked him again, staring into Zitek's eyes. Jacob saw, gaining on Forrest's face, the same murderousness he had seen with Colton. Behind them, the door of the corner office opened, and a tall, graying man with a bulbous nose stepped out angrily.

"What's the commotion?"

Blocking the threshold of Lykaios's office to keep Zitek from escaping, Forrest turned to meet the publisher of *Phoe*.

"Mr. Bullwinkle?" he said solemnly, offering his hand. There was a gasp and an outbreak of titters. "I'm Braxton Forrest."

The man's face reddened, but seeing Forrest's respectable appearance, he shook Forrest's hand.

"Winton Ludwick," he said.

"Ludwick? My apologies. Zitek always calls you Bullwinkle."

Ludwick reddened more as he glanced inside the office at Zitek and Lykaios. Zitek made another attempt to get past Forrest.

"Get out of the way!" Zitek was not a small man. He pushed at Forrest and then furiously struck at his face, but Forrest dodged the blow. When he tried a second time, Forrest trapped the fist in his right hand like an infielder snagging a line drive.

"Oh Jesus!" Zitek cried. His knees buckled. He sagged to the floor.

"So Mr. Ludwick," Forrest said, crushing the fist in his hand. "Are you married?"

"Someone call the police," Ludwick said. Little Jade quietly slipped away. "Let the man go, sir."

"I asked if you were married," Forrest said less genially. "Is there a Rocky to your Bullwinkle?"

Lykaios rushed over and started to slap at Forrest's arm and face.

"Don't!" Zitek said in his agony. "He'll kill you. The man's a killer. *Oh Jesus Jesus Jesus.*"

"Sir, let him go!" Ludwick insisted.

"Answer my question."

"My private affairs are none of your business."

There was a stir of muffled laughter among the employees, as though this were a matter of some irony.

"Let me ask you this, Bullwinkle," Forrest said, keeping up the pressure on Zitek's fist. He radiated a rage so intense it seemed inhuman, although he was outwardly calm and completely in control of himself, just as with Colton the night before. Jacob felt strangely displaced from himself. He could not get air into his lungs. It seemed entirely possible that Forrest would kill Zitek on the spot, and Jacob would see it happen without being able to stop it. "Would you marry somebody like Lykaios? She terrified my grandchildren and then accused my daughter of assault for defending them. That woman thinks Zitek is going to *marry* her. Her parents flew in from New York to meet him!"

"*Oh Jesus oh Jesus oh Jesus Jesus Jesus Jesus,*" Zitek prayed.

By now, more people than the ones who worked for *Phoe* pressed forward to see, apparently from other floors, and two security officers were pushing through them, a stout black woman and a short Hispanic man, both wearing black masks, neither carrying a weapon. They stood tensely near Jacob in the half-circle formed around Forrest and Zitek. He expected to hear the bones snap any second and then would come some other, worse thing, something that would—

"Cump, let him go!" he heard himself cry out, and Forrest looked up at him, surprised, as though he had forgotten Jacob altogether. Others turned to stare at him. Jade stood back at the edge, half-hidden behind a cubicle, arms wrapped around herself as though it were all her fault.

"Jacob says I should let Zitek go," Forrest said, holding up his left hand to keep back the security guards. "What do you say? Thumbs up, I release him. Thumbs down, we see what happens."

"Let him go, dude," somebody called.

"Is that you, Brantley?" Forrest said.

"Sir!" the Hispanic security man shouted. "Release your hold and step back."

"Let him go," others murmured, raising their thumbs. "Let the piece of shit go."

Forrest released Zitek, who sagged over for a moment cradling his hand before he got to his feet, staring at Forrest murderously.

"I'll kill you."

Forrest shoved him back into Lykaios's office and shut the door. "Let's go, Jacob."

Without hesitating, he strode past the guards and through the parting crowd toward the elevator.

"Sir!" the female guard called after him. Jacob followed Forrest, registering expressions as he passed—alarm, curiosity, admiration, fear, amusement, especially in the faces of two writers in their twenties who offered Forrest fist bumps. They cleared the aisle between cubicles and stood by the elevators across from Brantley's desk. Forrest calmly pushed the down button and they waited, watching the display above the doors as the elevator rose. 18, 19, 20.

"Sir!" said the two security guards, coming up behind them. "We need you to stay here and wait with us until the police arrive." Turning to face them, Forrest crossed his arms, looking down at them.

"No, we're going," Forrest said reasonably. "No harm done." His stare forestalled any attempt to stop them. The elevator dinged, the doors parted, Forrest and Jacob got inside. As the doors closed, they saw the confused guards gesturing.

Jacob did not speak to Forrest on the way down to the lobby. His phone buzzed in his pocket and he saw a text from Emily:

!!!!!!

He stared at it, confused, before he remembered that his last email to her had described Colton the night before. How would he explain Zitek?

When the doors opened, people had gathered, apparently waiting for them. The receptionist who had directed them to *Phoe* stood there, tense and guilty, as though she should have perceived the threat, but everyone stood back as Forrest excused himself politely, and no one tried to stop them as they left the building. Jacob and Forrest waited at a light, crossed the street, went up a block, climbed the stairs at the parking garage at Peachtree Center, and found the BMW, still without speaking a word.

He wanted to go home.

Forrest used his American Express card to get them a hotel room on the twenty-second floor of the Loews Atlanta Hotel in Midtown with a view of Piedmont Park to the east and Cate's Midtown neighborhood south of it. When Forrest looked at himself in the bathroom mirror, he saw the old man he was, nearly seventy. Zitek's fist had glanced off his right cheek, and there was a small contusion. His heart pounded as he thought about the afternoon. What was he doing, for God's sake? Why had he brought the boy? But thank God the boy had been there.

"Got you some ice," Jacob said, tapping on the bathroom door and handing in the overspilling bucket. Forrest thanked him and wet a washcloth and packed it with the small cubes. He lay down on the bed closer to the window, propping up two pillows for his head, and pressed the pack against his face, thinking back to Zitek's eyes. The onlookers' expressions. Sweet little Jade. Ludwick, who had these people's careers in his power.

Jacob came out of the bathroom wearing gym pants and a running jacket. He sat on his bed to pull on his running shoes.

"Can we go?"

The boy would run, Forrest would hike up the trail. Climbing Kennesaw would clear his head.

"Let me change."

He emptied the ice into the bathroom sink and put on jeans and an old flannel shirt and hiking boots while Jacob pulled up Google Maps on his laptop and sent directions to Kennesaw to his phone. The boy knew everything about the park because he had already written the account of the Battle of Kennesaw Mountain that Forrest had not had time to read.

On the way up Interstate 75, the boy was quiet and withdrawn.

"Do you want to talk about what happened?" Forrest finally asked as he turned onto the exit for Canton Road.

"I want to run the length of the battle lines," he said, "from the Confederate defenses on top of the Kennesaw Mountain across Little Kennesaw to Cheatham's Hill and the Dead Angle where Thomas attacked on the morning of June 27, 1864, on Sherman's orders. I want to see that. But when I come back down, I want to go home."

Forrest sighed and nodded. "We'll find a flight. I shouldn't have gotten you into this."

When they got to the parking lot of Kennesaw Mountain National Battlefield Park, they stood in front of the map in the Visitor's Center. It was 5.4 miles over both mountains and Cheatham Hill to the Illinois Monument.

"When should I pick you up?" he asked.

"I'll run back."

"Cut it out. That's almost eleven miles."

"I do it all the time." Jacob said. "It shouldn't take me much more than an hour, depending on the condition of the trail. But I want to spend some time getting a better feel for what happened that day. And what happened today. It's 3:30 now. I should be back here at about 5:30 or 6:00."

"Take your time," Forrest said. "I'll walk up and back. I'll be here."

The boy took off ahead of him up the trail to the top of Kennesaw Mountain. Sunday afternoon in mid-November. Days—weeks, almost—of sitting in the car had not helped Forrest's conditioning. A few other people were out, but he had the mountain largely to himself. It was not steep, but he was breathing hard halfway up. His knees were okay, thank God. They gave him trouble occasionally, but nothing like Marisa's: she had gone through a knee replacement several years back. Biking had been his exercise for years, long rides on the trails that replaced the abandoned railroad lines of New England.

If Jacob wanted to understand what happened here, he realized, he had to understand railroads—all the trains coming down from the North with supplies, all the Confederate rail lines destroyed by Sherman's men. Breathing hard, he stopped to read a sign about the Confederate position. Trees blocked the view and made it hard to get a feel for the battle.

Only at the very top of the mountain past the parking lot could he feel the lay of the land and see the vistas in either direction. He sat down on a granite ledge and gazed southeast toward the city and thought about Sherman's destruction of that city and the irony that it now housed Zitek and Lykaios. He felt again the utter hatred in Zitek's face when he pushed him into the office with that woman. He pictured Cate and her children on their exodus toward refuge in Wyoming. Thank God for the boy. What would have happened if Jacob had not said to let Zitek go? Or if Forrest had not listened?

He stood up and walked over to the other side of the ridge. He should take a few pictures to send to Marisa and Cate—the vista across Pine Mountain and north toward Rome and Dalton and Chattanooga. He framed shots on his phone and then used the arrow icon to text them to Marisa with a short note. On Kennesaw Mountain. He didn't need to tell her about Zitek yet.

He sighed and gazed down across the peaceful landscape. In this very place, in a frontal assault on Johnston's defenses at Kennesaw, Sherman had hurled the Union army at impregnable Confederate defenses. He had been completely defeated. But the defeat meant nothing. Within two days, Johnston had fallen back to the Chattahoochee. Then came Johnston's replacement by Hood, the Atlanta campaign, and the Fall of Atlanta that saved Lincoln's presidency. And then to crown it all, the March to the Sea. Sherman's fame would be everlasting. Sherman always argued that he had not changed the nature of war, but simply revealed it. He had invested his full talents in the immolation of a way of life that he admired—not quite the total war of the twentieth century, but its precursor, a war of devastation and demoralization. He had forged his name in destruction. Any time men thought of the Civil War, they would think of William Tecumseh Sherman, whose name and image had been anathema in the South of Forrest's youth a century after the March to the Sea.

And Zitek wanted his statue presiding over the city he destroyed. Particularly galling was the way he put it, which Forrest had quoted to Marisa. *The Christians say there are two baptisms, one by water and one by fire. Sherman saw that the South could never wash away its sins, and so he brought its baptism by fire: to destroy its plantations and ruin its pride and cast out its unrepentant denizens to wander forever in the outer darkness.*

He glanced at his phone. It was barely four o'clock. After everything he had put the boy through, the generous thing to do would be to go down and read what the boy had written about Kennesaw. He had the print-out in the BMW.

13

THE BATTLE OF KENNESAW MOUNTAIN

June 27, 1864

SHERMAN HAD JUST FALLEN ASLEEP ON TOP OF THE SHEET when Hayes called to wake him. He sat up confused, pushing off the mosquito netting. He had been dreaming about San Francisco again. Where was he? Headquarters, but where? He remembered lying down the night before, stripping down to his drawers in the heat. A cabin at the edge of some pine woods less than a mile from the front lines. Kennesaw Mountain loomed through the window. A tormented night. His mind had not settled until the last thought came: whatever would happen had already happened. It was already written in memoirs and histories, like the battles of Caesar and Napoleon. He was acting out what had to happen, and when he came back to this room at the end of the day, it would already be what it always had to be.

The mountain loomed, thick with rebels whose entrenchments had ruined the paths and groves where he and the French girl had spent a day defying the church bells. Lucette, he remembered as he pulled on his clothes and boots. Lucette with her drawings.

The bedroom door opened.

"Sir," Hayes said, handing Sherman a tin cup of coffee. "The generals are here."

The front room, the table spread with maps. Low voices. The word *abatis* mispronounced. That was Logan. And Howard explaining it was a French word so you didn't pronounce the terminal *s*.

"I need a few minutes," Sherman said.

"Yes sir."

He pushed open the back door and stepped down into the bare dirt yard. Predawn had given a slight reprieve to the heat, but it would end soon. Men were coming from their tents, stretching. A bugler played reveille somewhere up in the pines.

"Hot day coming, Uncle Billy," one of the men called.

"Taste of hell," he said.

"Yes sir."

Some of them would be dead before noon. In Hell itself, if there was one. Maybe that one with his Adam's apple and his beak of a nose. A year ago it would have cut him to the heart to think about getting men killed, but now his own callousness no longer surprised him. They were men on their own time but things to use on his.

When a mangy hound stirred itself and came shambling over, Sherman kneed the thing away. Inside the outhouse, a soldier was singing "Mine eyes have seen the glory," and Sherman rapped on the door. The soldier cursed and said to hold his goddamn horses. When he slammed open the door of the privy a minute later, pulling up his pants, he cringed to find the general waiting.

"Sorry, sir. General, sir."

"You have the whole goddamn woods, and you use my outhouse?"

"Sorry, sir!" He tried to salute as he buckled his trousers.

Sherman stepped into his stink and swung the door shut.

"The whole goddamn state to shit in!" he yelled.

Hayes had a fresh pot of coffee in the front room. Howard, McPherson, Logan, Thomas, all of them bending over the map Sherman had helped draw. Johnston's formidable rebel line bent westward in a great, eight-mile bow starting astride the Western and Atlantic railroad north and east of the mountain, ascending the spine of Kennesaw and down across Little Kennesaw and Pigeon Hill, and then crookedly following the rise and fall of the landscape above a creek all the way past the Burnt Hickory Road and the Dallas Road. On the left, McPherson would demonstrate at Kennesaw with Dodge's XVI Corps and attack in force at Little Kennesaw and Pigeon

Hill with Logan's XV Corps. Farther south, across the Dallas Road, George Thomas's massed XIV Corps under Palmer would force their way through the weakest part of the Confederate line and Schofield would attack at the far right.

All the way down from Chattanooga, Sherman had kept Johnston moving backward without once fighting a decisive battle, and if one came, he had wanted it to be on his own terms. *Had* wanted. *Had* wanted to catch Johnston in the open with the Chattahoochee in his rear. But the roads were still too muddy for the army to get around Johnston's left and threaten the railroad behind him. Schofield, feeling out the situation, had met the hothead John Bell Hood on June 22 at Culp's Farm, where the idiot Hooker claimed he was facing three corps—more men than Johnston had in his whole army.

For weeks, Sherman had been bogged down by the rain, and he had to regain his momentum before it became a stalemate. Three days ago he had decided on this day, June 27. The commanders had their orders. Artillery attacks would begin along the whole line at eight a.m.

"Hayes, where's my horse?" Sherman said.

The orderly ran out.

"Listen, Cump," McPherson said in a low voice as they stopped by the front door. "You couldn't get a mouse through those defenses we're facing on the mountain. And you want me to tell Dodge to 'demonstrate'?"

"Don't *tell* him it's a demonstration. Tell him to take the goddamn mountain. Tell him Johnston won't be expecting an assault."

"Men are going to die," McPherson said, and Sherman bridled at the humane reluctance that must have stopped McPherson at Resaca.

"Tell Dodge to take the goddamn mountain," he snapped. "And Gen. Logan, when you break through and get behind their trenches, roll them up to the left and clear off that mountaintop."

"Yes sir," he said gruffly, avoiding Sherman's eyes, dark and morose and unreadable.

Nothing happened as he had hoped. Dodge had demonstrated that his men's heads would be blown off if they popped up to look. Logan's troops had been stopped cold. But attacking the westward-facing salient in Johnston's southern line was the worst of all. Converging cannon shot and rifle fire slaughtered the men who tried it. All morning worse and worse news came. Young Gen. Harker was hit—and Dan McCook. Dan McCook. The heat was unbearable. The clamor was so enormous that men bled from their ears and noses.

Until almost noon, he thought the men could still break through—any good man would die for Uncle Billy, wouldn't he?—but then George Thomas sent word that he would lose his army if he kept trying it. Thousands of men lay dead or wounded. They had gained nothing. They had failed at every point.

And what was the reason?

He was.

The day waned, the losses mounted. At Howard's headquarters, Gen. Newton came up to him, furious about the attack on the Confederate salient. "Well, this is a damned appropriate culmination of one month's blundering."

Goddamn him, the impertinent bastard. There were reasons, but no explaining to a man who had just seen so many men die under his command because of Sherman's orders. Boys who grew up on farms in Ohio or Indiana or Illinois, learned to read and write and add and subtract as though it would mean something. Went to church, kissed girls. And all of it came to this moment when they started forward in the charge at an entrenched Confederate line hidden behind abatis. Rebs fired at them from head-logs when they came out into the open. They were like a fresh field of hay to a line of mowers with sharpened scythes. A Minie ball in the head or chest or groin was the fate their lives had been approaching when their mothers laid them down in their cradles and their tender lips blew bubbles of milk.

Lives were things he threw down like cards in euchre. This was power. This was being God, and being God was Hell.

A strange lightheadedness came over him.

The press already hated him because he drove them out whenever they came near his army. Now it would be like the time they had said he was crazy because he needed 200,000 troops to defeat the rebels in Kentucky. But it had been true, hadn't it? Nobody else had seen what it would take to defeat the Rebs. Now they would taunt him again.

Why had he made a frontal assault against entrenched lines?

Because it had to be done, it had to be done, it had to be done.

He had to bloody his army before it got soft. They were already soft, they wouldn't fight, that's what it was. Soft from not fighting enough. This would teach them again what war was. He had made it real for them because they had gotten lazy and sodden with inaction. A few thousand men dead, and the ones who survived had been humiliated—and now they would take it out on the Rebs.

Goddamn it, he was right about this. It was his decision and he had made it and he would stick to it and he would defend it to Grant and Halleck. To Ellen and to goddamn Thomas Ewing. But all those rebels were still up on the mountain. The little gamecock Johnston, all of them up there where he had spent the day with that French girl.

Lucette. The memory came back to him, a rush of feeling.

He had paid for that fine day. He had always known that one way or another, Col. Churchill had kept him sidelined in California, out of the war in Mexico. But Lucette had been splendid that day. And the slave girl, too. What was her name? Singing her way down the stairs afterward. *John ain't baptize me.* God, he missed women. He needed their charm, their beauty, their softness and smells.

A most inopportune stirring. Now came the wagons with the medics and the incontinent bodies of the dead. Now came living ones who had crawled like worms under the ceiling of live bullets, squirming back downhill through the gore of dead men, desperate to live, and those that made it rode the wagons back away from the fighting, their arms hanging, their faces sheathed with blood, limbs ruined, the lives that remained before them forever marked by the horror of this one day and the will of William Tecumseh Sherman.

Shouts and curses and screams from the pit of hell.

And all those righteous congregations up north safely singing glory hallelujah.

Freed slaves moved among the wagons, black women in their sack dresses raising their wails. There was Leah from the night he was in the house at Big Shanty. Huge Leah with her Massa McPhee and her Massa's little boy. Black men sang "I ain't got long to stay here" and put their shoulders to the groaning wagons to help move them through the mud, and hands reached out to touch the soldiers as if the spilled blood and open wounds were the flesh of Jesus Christ. The ignorance of them disgusted him. Where did these people always come from? He turned furiously in the saddle.

"Get them out of here!" he shouted to a group of soldiers, who looked at him stupidly. "Get those niggers out of here!" he yelled again, gesturing as he rose from the saddle. They started forward to herd the slaves away from the wagons. Leah's trembling soprano rose as the men moved toward them, and blacks spilled around them, refusing to be moved.

"Gen'l Sherman!" Leah shook with joy, and the negroes in their filthy clothes came crowding toward him, hats in hands, like dogs around their master or cows at a broken bale of hay. *God bless you, General Sherman. God bless you.* Hands came up to touch him. *God bless you.* And among them was a white girl looking up, more than pretty, her side pressed painfully against his right boot and stirrup by the crush of those behind her. What was she doing there?

"Stand back!" he shouted to those behind her. "You're hurting her!" and they stepped back, forming a semi-circle around him. The girl did not let go of his boot. She held on mutely like the raped girl in Shakespeare whose tongue had been cut out. Lavinia. Not white, though. Mixed. Her lips. Her green eyes startled him. In one motion, he pulled her up onto the horse behind him.

"Hayes!" he shouted.

"Yes sir!" The boy came running up, pushing his way through the slaves, confused to see the girl.

"I'm going to my headquarters," Sherman said. "Bring my messages there."

"General Schofield telegraphed that—"

"Do what I tell you, Corporal."

"Yes sir."

The boy hesitated and then pushed his way back through, waited for a wagon of dead and dying men to pass, and then hurried down through the milling men toward the cluster of officers on Signal Hill. Sherman sickened at the thought of them, all of them holding their cigars, leaning together to talk against the hideous noise.

The girl wrapped her arms around him. He felt her softness against his back.

"Better hold on to the saddle instead of me."

"I ain't never rid no horse," she said shakily.

"Hold on to me tight, then."

Another wagon of wounded men rumbled up on the muddy ground near them, pulled by a laboring mare. Sherman stepped his horse back out of the way. One of the men called out, "Too goddamn hot today, Uncle Billy." Sherman grimaced and touched his hat. When the near back wheel fell in a hole, men in the wagon screamed. As the wagon pulled past him, Sherman saw a boy on the back of it burbling as he tried to breathe, a pink bubble of blood growing from his lips and bursting, his eyes wild.

A new rage rose in him. He had to get out of this. He moved his horse roughly through the press of men, the girl clinging to him.

"How much for that filly?" somebody called derisively.

Sherman turned fiercely and other men looked at the one who had spoken. Filthy, narrow-faced, slouched over, the man watched Sherman come near him. He was about to say something else when he realized who it was and got sullenly to his feet. Sherman stared down at him.

"What are you fighting for, soldier?" he asked.

"I got drafted is all and I ain't had no three hundred to buy somebody to take my place. Ain't fighting for niggers," the man said, full of contempt.

"We're here to save the Union," Sherman said, "and you're deserting?"

"I ain't deserting. I'm standing right here."

"By God, it's a good thing I caught you. Get me some goddamn rope," he snarled at the other men. "Let's make an example of this coward."

"Uncle Billy, he ain't deserting. He was in McCook's brigade up there," a man said, tilting his head back over his shoulder at the continuing noise of the battle.

"Up where?" snapped Sherman.

"Up at that angle where the Rebs are. Men pinned down and screaming for water. Can't nobody move till it gets dark."

"How come this one ain't still fighting?"

"I fucking fought," the man said.

"And crawled back out of it and headed to the rear?"

The other men looked down.

"That's right," the man said, meeting Sherman's eyes. "Crawled through a pile of jelly guts and then saw they was what was left of my brother."

"Jesus Christ," said Sherman.

"What was *you* doing?" asked the man.

Sherman turned his horse savagely and stepped it through the backward surge of the wounded until he came to the road. Terrified of being so high up on the horse, the girl squeezed herself tighter against him.

It was a quarter mile to his headquarters at the edge of the pine woods. When he reined in the horse, he got off and reached up and swung her down and tied the reins to the railing. He had just stepped onto the porch when Hayes came galloping up.

"General!" he was shouting.

What worse news could it be? The day was lost.

"Sir! Gen. Schofield got a message from Gen. Cox," Hayes panted. "He says we can turn Johnston's left."

"*Now?* Good God. With what army?" The irony was too much. Why hadn't they scouted it out yesterday? "Tell Gen. Schofield to check it out *himself*, do you hear me? Go look for himself and then report back. It's too late in the day to make a movement now."

"Can you write down the orders, sir?"

"Give me the pad."

He scrawled the message and handed it to the boy.

"Keep everybody away until I come out," he told Hayes. The boy kept his eyes directly on Sherman.

"If other messages come, sir?"

"Goddammit, Hayes, keep everybody away."

"Yes sir." The boy was mortified for him, but he did not care. He waved him off, and as the bay clamored back up the road, he opened the door and pulled the terrified girl inside. She tried to twist free and he seized her so hard she cried out.

"Do you know who I am?" he asked her.

She would not look at him.

"A general."

"There are lots of generals."

"The one who tell everybody what to do."

"What's your name?"

"Miriam."

"Look at me, Miriam."

She still would not look at him.

"You niggers are the reason my men died today," he said.

He pulled his pistol and held it to her forehead, expecting her to tremble, but now the girl met his gaze.

"Pull the trigger," she said hotly. "Go on."

When he did not do it, she jerked the barrel of the gun down into her mouth and tried to force her thumb onto the trigger, but he pulled the pistol away.

"You ain't gone shoot me?" she cried. "What you want then?"

She hesitated, looking at him, then decided what he wanted. She took off her dress in one rough motion and stood before him, shining with sweat, defiant, and abject. She had bruises on her arms and thighs, a new abrasion on her side where the crush of negroes had pressed her against his stirrup, but her beauty moved him. The perfectly even teeth, skin like fresh cream in coffee, green eyes full of a mocking light. If there were time, he would have had her stand before him and he would have drawn the lines of her neck, her slight arms and full breasts, the double inward curve beneath her ribs and the soft furrow from her sternum down to her navel. To summon her with light and shading instead of flesh and blood.

"Put your dress back on."

She stared in confusion, but she did it, turning her back, and stood as if she were hurt that he was about to dismiss her. Through the window, he saw men gathering on horseback on the path back toward the front. The clamor of battle had at last begun to die away.

"Go in the bedroom."

The girl met his gaze, and now she was trembling as she obeyed. What did he mean to do? He did not know himself. He followed her and closed the door behind him and sat down on the bed.

"Please take off your dress for me, Miriam," he said.

She did it gracefully now and stood again before him, her hands swinging slightly, expressive and fearful and articulate. A lovely girl.

"Do you know who you killed today?" he said.

"I ain't kill nobody."

"Didn't you? Come here. Come stand right here."

She stood close before him between his opening knees. He breathed the musk of her, he smelled her fear. Her heartbeat shook the light skin of her breasts, beaded and running with sweat.

"You see this?" with his forefinger, he inscribed Johnston's line on the skin beneath her navel.

"Yes sir," she said with a shudder.

"I sent men against sharpened stakes and trenches where the Rebs could shoot downhill from behind head-logs. Rifle and cannon both. We couldn't break through and I knew it before I sent them. They mowed down our men. Men by the hundreds. Two fine young officers. I killed my own men. Why did I do that?"

Her hands came down on his shoulders, soft now.

"You ain't kill nobody."

"I had a law partner named Dan McCook when I was as low as I ever got in my life. I killed him today."

She pulled his head against her hot skin, and he could hear the heartbeat deep and fast. "Naw now," she said. "You ain't kill nobody."

His hands rode down the slick of her back.

"I had a boy named Willie," he told her.

"Naw, now. Hush, now," she said, and it was lovely, lovely the way she said the words and rocked his head against her breasts. His right hand rose to her and she fed herself to him.

"Hush, now," she said, quietly, solemnly. He lifted his face from her.

"Have you ever been up on the block? Has anybody ever put you up for sale?"

"No sir."

"You never had men bidding for you?"

"No sir. Can't nobody sell me now. You done set me free."

Horses outside. The orderly, speaking quietly to someone. They would not disturb him. He stood and freed himself and lifted the girl upon him.

"You home," she said with a small suck of breath. She put her lips to his ear and whispered, "You home now."

When they came out of the house, the men in the yard looked away, some amused, some disturbed. McPherson would not meet his eye, knowing Ellen as he did and angry about losing good men that morning. Howard was of course offended. George Thomas, stolid and humorless, nodded at Sherman, making no judgment, never surprised at the foibles of other men.

When he helped her up on the horse behind Hayes, she looked down at him soberly.

"How you gone keep them other men away from me?" she said.

His officers were listening, and she knew it. She was a lovely thing, but her presumption irritated him. He patted the flank of the horse and looked up at her.

"Tell them I set you free," he said too quietly for the other men to hear him.

Her face changed as his words sank home. Fear, hurt. What did she expect? He gave the horse a slap and she twisted to look at him after it turned and the boy spurred it into a canter.

"Damn pretty one," John Logan acknowledged from the side of his mouth.

"Sorry to keep you gentlemen waiting," Sherman said. "She wanted me to explain Emancipation."

A ripple of laughter went through the officers. Even Howard fought down a smile. Who was behind Howard? Orlando Poe.

His great rage was gone. In its place was a new equanimity. Willie was dead, and he had lost a great battle, which he would have to justify to Halleck but mainly to Stanton, that ambitious bastard. He had his reasons for attacking Kennesaw, and he would state them, but he already knew the loss would not sully his reputation. The Confederates had nowhere to go except backward. The roads were drying, the flanks opening up, the numbers beginning to tell more and more against Johnston. They kept collapsing toward Atlanta. He could smell the coming victory and the vindicating fame.

14

CATE'S HOUSE

ALL THE WAY BACK FROM KENNESAW, THE BOY HUNCHED over his phone texting his girlfriend, typing with his thumbs the way kids did. Sighing. Probably having to explain to Emily Turnbow why he was in Georgia with a madman.

"So now it's Miriam," Forrest said.

"Can we talk about it tomorrow, maybe? Maybe on the way to the airport."

They stopped by the hotel to shower and change. The boy was starving after his run, and Forrest told him they would eat at the famous OK Cafe on West Paces Ferry, but first they needed to stop by Cate's house to check it out.

It was five minutes away in a neighborhood of older homes from the 1930s and 1940s, most of them modest but refurbished, interspersed with new high-end apartments and condominiums. Cate and Zitek would never have been able to afford even their modest place—one-story, picture window—without his help.

He parked in front and got out.

"So what are we doing?" Jacob asked, opening his door and stepping onto the sidewalk.

Forrest held up a hand but did not answer. There was something in the tree in the front yard. A blue tricycle hanging upside down.

"Sweet Jesus," he murmured, thinking of the rage that must have hurled it there. He could not reach it and neither could Jacob by jumping.

The porch and the front door were under the gable on the right side. The porch railing had been broken and patched back together with duct tape. Plywood filled the square where the window in the front door ought to be. He crossed the lawn to the driveway and unlatched the gate. Children's toys and clothes had been flung everywhere. Picking his way through the clutter, he walked up the drive to the open garage, whose entrance was almost blocked by scattered tools—a rake, a hoe with a broken handle, a tire pump, a shovel, two bicycles.

Inside, against the inner wall, his baseball bat hung just where he had pictured it back in Dallas, the handle snugged between two sixteen-penny nails he had hammered there for Jimmy—*See that? This is how I used to hang it up.* The barrel of it was suspended from the knob straight as a plumb bob line. He took down the Louisville Slugger and smoothed the dust from it.

The sweet feel of it in his hands.

"What are you going to do with that?" Jacob asked uneasily, coming up behind him.

"Take it to Jimmy."

"I'll put it in the car," Jacob said, reaching for it.

"I'll hang onto it," Forrest said. A pulse beat in the side of his head above the temple. He fished a key from his pocket. "You go around and wait in front. I need to take a look inside and then we'll go eat."

Beside the back door, Cate's clothes lay in a sodden pile. Forrest opened the new deadbolt with the key Cate had given him. He smelled feces. What the hell had they done? He felt for the light switch, and he had just illuminated a show of destruction when his phone buzzed in his pocket.

Cate Zitek.

He stepped back outside into the better air.

"Did you make it to De Smet?" he asked without a greeting.

—That's tomorrow, Dad. We're in Trinidad, Colorado. The drive today wasn't bad. Avila slept most of the time, so.

"Are you okay about going there?"

—I mean, it's not our house. Clare and Jimmy are both crying because they miss home. Where are you, Dad?

He paused before answering.

"At the house."

She was waiting for him to say something else.

—Is it terrible? she finally said. Her voice was shaking.

He did not answer.

—Don't, Dad. Please don't. It's not worth it.

"I went to his office."

—Oh God.

"Jacob Guizac was with me. He's here now. Don't ever come back here. I can't believe I walked you down the aisle and gave you to Zitek."

—Oh God.

"Is there anything of yours I should look for? Books, maybe?"

—My God, I don't know, it's like that life ended, like—

"Don't burn your bridges professionally. How's your mom?"

—Fine. Always fine, Dad. Wherever she is, that's home. But I want *my* home. I want to be *home*, and I feel like everything that's happened makes it impossible ever to be home again.

"You'll get through this to something better."

Cate sighed and he heard how ridiculous his words sounded and his fury began to rise.

—Mom wanted you to call her.

"I will."

They ended the call. More and more raggedly, the pulse beat in the side of his head. Of course she wanted to be home. He should have had something wiser to say. When had he felt at home himself? Home didn't matter, though, did it, because it was all going to be lost anyway—to time, to death, to the idiocy of Zitek and people like Zitek. Every last thing he loved. What difference did it make what you—

—Braxton? Marisa said, startling him. He must have touched the number before he meant to. Did you talk to Cate?

He walked around the side of the house, clearing his lungs, trying to calm down. He held the phone in his left hand. The good weight of the bat hung from his right hand.

"I did. She sounds okay. Pretty blue."

—She's bound to be.

"Any news from Walter?"

—No change. Teresa's going to be staying with the parents of one of the students at Transfiguration and she'll visit the hospital every day, even though they won't let her in to see him. I'll tell you more later. Where are you?

"At Cate's house."

—Right now? You're at the house right now? How bad is it?

"I'll call you later. Let me get through this."

On the kitchen floor was one of the toys he had given Jimmy at Christmas, a model BMW Roadster with real rubber tires that would make a mad dash of twenty feet or more if you put it down and backed it up to wind it. Zitek—or maybe Lykaios—had stomped it flat against the kitchen tiles. Forrest poked at it with the bat, feeling the same singing rage he had felt earlier in the day. Ripped from the binding and scattered all over the kitchen and dining room were pages from *Little House on the Prairie*. He picked up the title page and read Marisa's inscription to Clare at Christmas. *Get Pa to do some of the reading!*

Anything of Cate's left in the house, anything that meant anything to her—the artwork of her friends, china from Marisa's mother, the vase that a friend in college had made for her, her favorite books—had been torn or smashed or defaced. Zitek and Lykaios had gone through the house in a frenzy of desecration. The children's dressers had been emptied and their contents strewn around with a malice he could not fathom. The smell came from the bedroom.

"Professor Forrest!" Jacob called sharply from the front porch. He heard another angry voice, and just as he looked out and saw Zitek's arm pointing toward him, the picture window shattered and a bullet slammed into the wall behind him. He ducked, ran to the switch, turned off the lights. Through the ruined window he saw Zitek pacing the front walk with a pistol. Shouting for Jacob to get off his porch. Hiding the bat behind him, Forrest opened the front door. Zitek laughed and waved the gun in his direction, stumbling a little. Drunk.

"I've got your ass," he shouted. "Breaking and entering. I can shoot both of you and get off scot-free."

Jacob had his hands up, scared, and now Zitek pointed the pistol at Forrest.

"Bullwinkle fired me!" Zitek yelled. "Because of you, asshole."

Porch lights were coming on in the neighborhood.

"Think again, Zitek," Forrest said. "I have a key, the title is in my name, I'm the one inside the house, and I'm unarmed."

Zitek took a step backward, trying to aim the gun at Forrest's chest, but Forrest stepped back inside and Zitek fired again through the window. More glass shattered onto the floor.

"Just to clarify your legal position," he called, "in stand-your-ground cases, the assailant is the one coming from *outside* the house with the gun and threatening the one *inside* the house who has a legal right to be there."

"Fuck you!" Zitek raged.

"And in this case, you have to ask about motive. How is killing the two of us going to help you? You're looking at a murder trial and a slam-dunk conviction and years of being raped in prison by big Aryans who love a pompadour on their bitch."

More neighbors were shouting now and it suddenly spooked Zitek. He furiously fired another shot that hit near the front door and turned to run to his car but tripped on the sidewalk and sprawled forward into the street. His pistol skittered away. Forrest was already out the door, down the sidewalk, and standing over him in the middle of the pavement as he got to his knees and started to stand up. With a high, singing rush of pure rage, he cocked the bat and started to swing it toward Zitek's head.

"*NO! NO!*"

A terrible, tearing cry.

He checked his swing, stumbling forward from the momentum. The boy stood nearby, both hands toward him. "DON'T!" he shouted. Forrest stared at him, still feeling the jagged pulse of murder strong in his head, the rage shaking his whole body. He looked down at Zitek terrified beneath him.

Sweet God, he had been that close.

Zitek got to his feet, holding out an elbow as if to ward off Forrest. Neighbors surrounded them at a distance. Someone picked up Zitek's pistol and passed it to a man who took out the clip and checked the barrel.

"Listen to me," Forrest said, leaning close to Zitek. "You'll never see your family again."

"Who gives a fuck?" Zitek said. "You roped me into that life."

"*I* roped you in?"

"You can't even see who you are."

"Before long," Forrest said, "you're going to remember who Cate is. You're going to realize you've thrown away the best thing you're ever going to get in your life. Now you have Melina Lykaios, and God help you with that bitch. Marisa and I loved you, Jason. What's left of your life is the hell you've chosen."

Zitek spat on the pavement. Sirens were approaching, and his head jerked toward the sound. The neighbors were closing in. A woman from next door was coming toward him from the sidewalk, her children behind her.

"Get some help, Jason," a man called from across the street, not unkindly.

"Fuck off," he muttered as he stumbled away from Forrest and wrenched open the door of the Camry that Forrest had given to Cate when she was in college. He started the car and eased forward. The sound of the sirens rose and rose, but then the flashing lights went past a block away. Some other emergency. Zitek gave Forrest and then the whole neighborhood the finger as he did a U-turn and drove away.

Under the streetlights winking on in the growing darkness, neighbors turned to stare at Forrest, stirring among themselves, watching, their faces obscure in the dusk, not calling out. They had all seen him almost kill Zitek. He had come that close. He stood for a moment and then walked back to Cate's house to close the front door, as though it were the most important thing he could do. Close the door. Coming back toward the car in full sight of the neighborhood, he stopped, suddenly dizzy, and closed his eyes. He tilted his head back, exhaled. His heart hammered wildly, dangerously, in his chest. An old man. When he opened his eyes, he was staring up into the big crepe myrtle.

A tricycle. Avila's tricycle. Sweet little Avila. Their gift from the Christmas before, dangling there, handlebars down, tassels hanging askew. The bat was still in his hand. Jacob had tried to take it from him, hadn't he? But now he used it to push up on the seat and dislodge the back wheels from the limbs. He caught the tricycle as it came free and fell. He set it down on the dead grass, set it down tenderly, and burning sorrow spiked upward through his nostrils like a pair of sixteen-penny nails.

15

SAVING MIRIAM

"COME ON, SHE WAS PLENTY OLD ENOUGH," CLOVER SAID.

"She was fourteen!" Hermia cried.

"Ninth grade? Did you not grow up in a small town? I had boys at that age. And this wasn't just some boy, this was *Duke*. This was for her soul. What you need to understand about Duke is it's an *honor*—but listen, I won't even try to explain it. You've already made up your mind."

Hermia's heart was pounding. Flashes came to her of her stepfather's nighttime visits when she was fourteen.

"Clover," Hermia said, "think what you're saying. From what you've told me already, you're an accomplice to statutory rape."

A harsh laugh broke from Clover. "Rape? That girl was more than willing. Besides, Duke says those who love God and neighbor are above the law. It's right there in St. Paul. What he did saving her was love of neighbor, and if it's love, it's not a crime."

"Have you *read* St. Paul?" Hermia asked.

Just then, thank God, Jordan tapped at the door and backed into the room with a tray that bore the French press, two mugs, and a sugar dish and cream pitcher. The sweetheart had added two large muffins from the Left Bank. Setting down the tray on Hermia's desk, she poured the coffee for them and served each of them a small plate before excusing herself and leaving the room.

Clover ate distractedly, swiping at her mouth with the napkin, not meeting Hermia's eyes. She drank the coffee in nervous sips, and as she set the mug down, she began to tremble. Hermia crossed the room and started the gas fire in the fireplace. She put a blanket around Clover's shoulders and guided her over to one of the armchairs where she often sat to have talks with the women.

"Help me understand what happened," she said softly.

"The thing is," Clover said, "he's gone."

"How long ago?" Hermia asked.

"Months. Four thousand people were there ready to hear him. That was the night he was going to talk about how he lost his eye. It was all about the passage, 'If thine eye offend thee, pluck it out.' We thought he was going to talk about—well, you know, about what he had been like before. We had a band down from Atlanta, and they got tuned up and played some hymns, and then our pastor came out and did a reading, but by this time there was a lot of stirring around. Somebody shouted, *Where's Duke?* and the pastor had to admit he didn't know. He told us to pray for him. Maybe he had been in an accident. The choir sang 'A Closer Walk with Thee,' but people started to leave. I think he left when Miriam wouldn't do what he said and help the baby to Jesus."

A chill came over Hermia's heart.

"What do you mean? You don't mean—"

"She wouldn't listen to him, but he kept after her. That's when Josiah took her over. Right then. Duke suggested she go somewhere in Atlanta, you know, to help the baby to Jesus, and here's Josiah, mean as Hell. Josiah knew who Duke was, and Duke was out of there. He knew nobody would understand him."

"Clover, my God—"

"No, listen!" she said fiercely. "I've been with lots of men, too many men, and he wasn't like them. Duke was holy."

"Tell me why you say that."

She talked for an hour. At the end, despairing, she looked up at Hermia.

"I brought her here. Now what should I do? What should I do?"

Hermia did not hesitate.

"We'll bring the baby here," Hermia said. "We can take care of her for now. Come and see her whenever you want. And then I think we should find someone generous and good to adopt her."

Clover wept without restraint. When she finally left, Hermia sat drained and exhausted. Her neck still hurt from sleeping in the armchair all night, and she rolled her head around, wondering who she could talk to. Jordan and Deirdre should know. She would need to tell Forrest and Marisa. But not right now. Right now she thought of Chick.

Why Chick? Because—well, what could she say to herself? Because he loved her? Maybe some residual feeling from so long ago, that almost accidental night. She saw that her attention flattered him. But wasn't it really that of anyone she knew, he was just.

Over the past few years, maybe because Alison always said something critical about their choices when she visited, Chick and Patricia had become particular about the kind of eggs they bought—brown ones, free range, that cost about twice as much as the eggs he had grown up on. Patricia would fry up sausage or bacon and make grits, but eggs were Chick's specialty. He usually scrambled five of them for a big omelet and put in various kinds of cheeses. Sometimes he would sauté onions and red peppers, but today, having received a text from Hermia as soon as he and Patricia got back from church, he could not wait for an omelet. He turned the heat high and melted some coconut oil in the pan, whisked the eggs briskly and poured them in, adding shredded cheddar and hovering over them, pushing gently from the sides to build up the middle.

"What's the hurry?" Patricia asked.

"Hermia called me about the girl who died in the hospital yesterday."

"Hermia Watson again."

"There's this beautiful little baby, her mother's dead, and apparently the girl's mother—I mean the mother of the one who died, the baby's grandmother—showed up this morning."

"Wanting the baby?"

"I guess so."

He sprinkled some Parmesan on top of the eggs, divided them neatly, and put half of them on the plate for Patricia. She served up the bacon and grits and sourdough toast. They sat down at the kitchen counter.

"Lord, make us truly thankful for these and all thy blessings," they said together. "We ask this in Jesus's name. Amen."

"Mmm," Patricia said, tasting the eggs. "Are you sure you need to be getting mixed up in this, Chick?"

"I feel like it's my duty."

"It sounds like it could get legal," Patricia said. She gazed at him seriously across the table. "I know you think I don't appreciate you, Chick, but I do." She took another bite of her eggs. "These are so good."

"You just appreciate my eggs."

"Stop it. I love you. I know you try to be a good man."

What had gotten into Patricia? Maybe it was Rev. Hawkins's sermon that morning about loving your enemies.

"Have we had this bacon before?" he said.

"I don't remember. Alison's got me so concerned about additives."

"All the stuff we thought was making food better, they charge you now for leaving out." She smiled, and he felt a pang of sympathy, almost of pity. She was looking her age, almost seventy, and something was changing in her, he thought. Some kind of new seriousness. They never talked about it, but maybe it was the same sadness that came over him when he thought about how much closer death was, how this life was ending—such as it was, not that he had done much with it—and their daughter had "married," so-called, another woman, and they would never have grandchildren. There was heaven to hope for, but he would not let himself imagine heaven much because then it would be a disappointment not to get there. Chick Lee in heaven. It sounded almost scandalous, especially when he thought about watching Hermia walk ahead of him. Somebody had once pointed out that a good-looking woman's bottom had the shape of the ovule of a flower. Forrest probably. Meanwhile, down here on earth, he and Patricia would soon sink back into the great crowd of the dead that people remembered for a little while and then another generation passed and they were forgotten altogether.

Suddenly, tears started to his eyes.

"I love you too, Patricia."

"Oh, Chick."

He thought about all their years together and what else she might have done, who else she might have married, what other children and grandchildren she might have had.

"Thank you for giving your life to me," he said. And then there they were, good Lord, standing up and blubbering and holding each other as if they were on the Titanic and all the lifeboats were gone.

"You go on over to Stonewall Hill," she said after a moment, patting him on the back to release him. "I know you'll be a big help."

He felt a shadow of concern as he climbed into the driver's seat of his Lincoln. He was going to see Hermia Watson *with Patricia's blessing*. Did she have cancer? Was there something else she had not told him about? He drove into town, around the courthouse square, and down Lee Street to the fork and then into the driveway to the back of Stonewall Hill. Nora Sharpe's Outback was already there, and he saw the two women talking at the back door. Hermia waved him in.

Two hours later, shaken to the core, he went back outside. The day was getting cooler. He fumbled at the remote to unlock the car. A few years ago, he would have opted for the bigger Nautilus, but what was the point? He had nothing left to prove. Nobody was keeping tabs. All is vanity.

As he started out the drive, he thought that maybe he and Patricia could go for a walk—get outside, get a little exercise. They could stroll pleasantly around the neighborhood, maybe revive the mood from brunch and it would clear his head of all this. Maybe he would ask her about whether she would be willing to help Hermia. It might be more likely if she saw what he and Nora Sharpe had just seen.

When he got back home, she met him at the back door.

"What was the problem?" she asked. "Is everything okay?"

"I want you to see something," he said.

They sat in the den, and he pulled up the webpage for Mount Zion Congregation of Praise on the big TV screen. They watched an aerial shot of the church's huge campus and then an interior of thousands of people— multi-racial, all ages—in a great semicircle facing a stage. The sermons were archived, and he clicked on the last date under the name Duke. July 5.

A big man with thick blond hair and a patch over one eye sat onstage on a stool behind a lectern, holding a microphone.

"Who's that?"

"Just watch," he said.

A set of drums, several guitars, and a keyboard cluttered the stage behind him. His image filled a screen on each side of the hall facing the congregation, and behind him on a much larger screen were the Grand Tetons, with citations from Scripture superimposed in white letters.

> If you keep my commandments, you will abide in my love, just as I have kept my Father's commandments and abide in his love. (John 15:10)

> These things I have spoken to you, that my joy may be in you, and that your joy may be full. (John 15:11)

> This is my commandment, that you love one another as I have loved you. (John 15:12)

Chick turned up the sound, and they listened to the deep, rich voice.

What does it mean to command, *brothers and sisters? My father was a Major General in the Marines, and when he gave a command, his word went down through the ranks from the highest colonel to the lowest private. Good order comes from clear command and immediate obedience. Let's go back to Moses. You remember what Moses said in Deuteronomy 18 when the Israelites begged, 'Let us not again hear the voice of the LORD, our God, nor see this great fire any more, lest we die.' Do you remember that? What are they saying? They're saying that they need insulation from the Lord, because He is too much for them. So the text goes on: "The Lord said to Moses, 'This was well said. I will raise up for them a prophet like you from among their kin, and will put my words into his mouth; he shall tell them all that I command him. Whoever will not listen to my words which he speaks in my name, I myself will make him answer for it.' Do you hear that? The prophet of God is like a general. If you do not listen, you will have to answer for it.*

Can I get an Amen?

Amen, said the congregation, swaying in place.

I say to you, I am God's prophet when I speak on behalf of Jesus Christ, and this is my commission: to command in the name of God. Your commission is to listen to the Lord Jesus Christ. He is not a prophet like Moses, but God Himself, the Word made flesh. And He says to abide in His love, brothers and sisters. When do you abide? . . . Are you hiding from something? . . . Not when you abide. Are you avoiding something? . . . No, and it's not because you're afraid of something OUT THERE that you abide but because you love something IN HERE more. THIS is where your beloved is. Right here. Right here in the neighbors to your right and your left, behind you and in front of you. Right in this assembly of faith. Right in front of you on this stage. I am your beloved.

And who is it you love when you love Duke? Who do you love when you love your neighbor? said Thomas. *You know the answer. What makes you want to* abide *in love more than you want anything else? . . . Am I right about this: You want to* remain *in the love of Jesus Christ. And how do you abide in His love? You keep his commandments. Do you keep his commandments?*

He waited.

I'm sorry, he said, tapping the microphone, and looking offstage to one side. *I think there must be something wrong with the equipment. I don't think they can hear me.*

He waited as a murmur of protests began to rise.

We hear you!

We hear you, Duke!

I said do you KEEP HIS COMMANDMENTS? Can you hear me?

YES, DUKE!

Then keep His commandments the same way He keeps His Father's commandments. Would I tell you to keep His commandments and abide with Him if I knew you couldn't do it?

NO! they called back.

Obeying is up to you! You, Kyle Bodkin. Can you do it? I see you nodding. Will you abide in His love? You, Clover McPhee. Yes. Yes you will, I KNOW you will. And you, Teresa Hamilton, way in the back. You Mattie Riggs. You, Hiram Cartwright. I see y'all saying Yes to Jesus and I know what you're asking is How do I do it, Lord? How do I abide in your love? And His answer is right there behind me, writ large, not written in condemnation like the writing on the wall in the Book of Daniel at the feast of Belshazzar. Does it say Mene, mene, tekel, upharsin? *No, but something else is writ large so we will see and pay attention and not be found wanting. Writ as large as life eternal, writ with the light of the world. What is the Word of God Himself? WHAT DOES IT SAY?*

Duke got down from his stool and turned slowly toward the screen behind him, first silently reading what was written there. Then he held the microphone close to his lips and read it aloud in a whispering, wondering tone. *"This is my commandment, that you love one another as I have loved you."* He glanced over his shoulder at the congregation and said into his microphone, *Will you read it with me, brothers and sisters?* and the whole congregation read it in unison, some of them weeping openly, as Duke faced the words and repeated them.

His commandment is to love one another. Can we love one another? he asked them, turning suddenly toward them and lifting his arms. There were cries of joy, arms lifted in response all across the mass of people. *Brothers and sisters,* Duke said, *let* us *love one another.*

He came down from the stage and let himself be taken by the crowd. All across the congregation people old and young, battered and beautiful, embraced and wept and called out. The camera zoomed in on a young woman, a little frowsy, her heavy makeup ruined by tears, hugging an elderly woman who patted her back distractedly; then it found a middle-aged man, overweight, still wearing his Walmart shirt from work, with his arms in the air, his face shining with forgiveness for everybody who had ever ignored him, belittled him, mocked him, stolen his lunch money, tripped him in the locker room. And when the fervor at last began to die down, Duke, freed from those who held him, made his way back up to the stage and sat again on his stool, facing the mass of people who swayed and crested like the surface of the sea.

Amen, amen, but have we really felt it even yet? He dropped the microphone to the level of his knee, looking weary beyond telling, but then, seeming electrified by some sudden infusion of power, he lifted it again and spoke into it with deep, thrilling force. *Are we burning yet with the love that burns down the Vaticans and state houses and mansions of the law? Do you know why I came here to Georgia? Why I chose this place on all the earth? Because my father taught me the battles of the Civil War, and long ago, a general rode in his power and gave commands and this whole land was burning, city and country, houses and barns and fields, and I come now to set this land on fire with the new command of exalted submission. Burn it all down and build it new. A new beginning in the spirit.*

Do you feel the love burning in you? Yes. Is it cleansing you of every impurity like gold in the refining fire? Yes, yes. Amen, amen. I come with the torch and I pile up kindling against self-reproach and self-condemnation, the idol of law. Burn it, Clover! Mattie! Hiram! Burn with me!

Like a city in flames, the congregation burned, swaying and leaping and loud with tongues. And when it all died down, when weariness overcame them and they sank back into their seats, exhausted and still, musicians were already coming onto the stage behind Duke and taking up their instruments when he lifted his microphone one last time.

There's a fine hymn written long ago by a man dying of tuberculosis, a lovely hymn, and I want it to speak to our hearts today. Would you lead us, Sister Janice?

A large black woman in a patterned African dress stepped up to a microphone. As a blues guitar laid down the first chords, her voice came low and powerful. *Abide with me; fast falls the eventide.*

Chick turned off the TV and let out a long breath.

"My goodness," Patricia said, her hand on her heart. "We should get that man for our next revival! Who in the world is he?"

"The man who got a fourteen-year-old pregnant," Chick said, "after getting her mother's consent. He 'saved' the mother first and then the girl."

"Saved them?"

"Slept with them. Duke. No last name. Thousands of people would come every Sunday to hear him. He tried to get the girl to have an abortion, but she wouldn't do it, and when she began to act possessed, he disappeared."

"What do you mean she began to act possessed?"

"She would speak in other voices. She knew more than anybody could know. I heard her, actually. When she was at Stonewall Hill the day she died."

Patricia sat silent for a long moment. He felt more recriminations coming. But she surprised him.

"And now Hermia has the baby to take care of? I wonder if there's something I could do to help."

"You might call and ask," he said.

The thought hung there for a moment.

"Tomorrow," she said.

"I think I'm going to build a fire in the fireplace and watch the Denver Broncos. Do you want to sit with me?"

"Thank you, but I want to call Alison and see if she's okay. We haven't talked in a month or so."

Chick sighed and nodded. When he got the fire going—maybe Duke had given him the idea—he turned on the game. John Bell Hudson was probably the most exciting player in the NFL—always a threat to run and the league leader in passing.

Hermia Watson's son.

Hermia Watson's son with Forrest, her own father.

And Forrest was coming.

· · · · · · · · · · · · · · · ·

He dozed off watching the game, and when he woke up—Denver had beaten Seattle by three touchdowns—Patricia had already gone to bed. She usually stayed up later than he did, but maybe there was bad news from Alison. One of them having in vitro fertilization from a sperm donor or some such horror. *Heather has two mommies.* Good God. Chick shucked off his jeans and kicked them toward the laundry basket in the corner of the room, then pulled open the top drawer of his dresser to fish out the old exercise shorts he wore to bed. It was just 9:15, too early, but he could read for a while on his Kindle or watch a show and use the headset.

Had he taken his pills? Nope. He went back to the kitchen and swallowed three magnesium capsules and the tiny amlodipine tablet—blood pressure—that looked like zolpidem. Should he take a zolpidem, too, or risk letting nature take care of his sleep? There wasn't anything he was anxious about other than Eula's House, just another week of boredom ahead at the dealership. Joe Ashburn would be there with another salesman or two, and so would Rufus and the mechanics in the shop. What was the point of even going in? Maybe to look at Tierney, the new girl in Parts, a shapely little thing from Macon he had hired for her looks. He liked to watch her tease Roof.

He checked himself in the mirror. Still a belly, but by God, it was diminishing fast on this diet he'd started, all meat and vegetables and fruit, no alcohol, no grains, no dairy, and for sure none of the usual carbs that he filled up on. Who would have thought he would ever eat so many eggs? Or so many dates? In a few weeks, he would be down to his high school weight when he was middle guard for the Blue Devils. At some point, you were supposed to experience a daylong buzz of super-health, but nothing like that had happened. On the other hand, not having beer or wine (or gin or vodka or bourbon) kept his head clearer at night. He had read a book or two.

Grisham's *Bleachers*. Most of the time he just streamed a series. *Breaking Bad.*
The Wire. Patricia would sometimes watch *Downton Abbey* with him.

She had already started snoring, not the light snorkeling of her half-sleep
but noisy, deepwater abandonment. Luckily, she did not react to the buzz and
jitter of the phone on the dresser top. As soon as he saw Hermia's name, his
stomach turned over. Something had gone wrong.

"Hello?"

—She's home! You have to come see her!

Miriam's baby. He took the phone out into the hallway.

"I was about to get in bed," he complained. "I'll see her in the morning."

—Well, listen, Fr. Silber says he can't have a funeral Mass if she wasn't
Catholic. Can you call your preacher about doing the funeral in the morning?

"It's almost ten at night, and you want me to ask him for tomorrow
morning?"

—I need you, Chick, she said.

So of course he called Rev. Hawkins, who was already in bed. *Why did
they need him?* Chick explained about Miriam's death and the Catholic issues.
Why did they have to do it the next day? Chick did not know, but he thought
it had to do with Forrest. *Who was handling the arrangements?* Marshall's
Funeral Home. *Well, it couldn't be in the church because they were replacing
some of the pews, so could they have the service at Stonewall Hill?* Chick thought
so, but he would check with Hermia Watson right away if Rev. Hawkins
could hold. Rev. Hawkins held, Hermia said yes, and Rev. Hawkins said he
would do it. *Thank you thank you thank you,* she said. Rev. Hawkins asked if
Chick *knew anything about the girl who had died?* Not much. Just a child, just
fourteen, a sad story. *Did he have an appropriate text in mind, perhaps?* A text?
He thought about his Bible on the table next to his armchair. A text for young
Miriam? Not off the top of his head. But yes, he would be there early. Yes, he
would help however he could.

As he got into bed at last, trying not to disturb Patricia, he listened to
her snoring helplessly, guilelessly. It was somehow endearing. He closed his
eyes, listening to her and thinking about texts. In a moment, he was opening
his Bible and looking down into it, as though through dark water, and then
he was standing at the edge of this sea of words, page upon page, and then
he was sinking through a tide of quick, moving letters whose purpose and

meaning eluded him. As he sank, monstrous fish with lanterns dangling in front of their faces moved slowly before him, solemn as elders. Far down, far, far down in the depths, he came to the floor of the sea and saw that others, too, had gathered around, and he stood and stared without understanding into the welling blood of a text he ought to know.

16

BURNING

FORREST HAD A HARD TIME SLEEPING, AND WHEN HE DID sleep, he dreamed about Zitek and woke up unable to stop thinking. What had he ever done to offend Zitek, except try to be generous? At six he got up and quietly made himself some coffee in the Keurig that he had moved onto the bathroom counter the night before. He took his cup to the chair next to the window and set it down on the sill and opened his laptop to check into flights for Jacob. He saw a note from Marisa. Cate had arrived the night before, and Marisa was struggling to get the children settled. Forrest had not told Jacob that the Guizacs were hosting Cate's whole family—not that it would make him reconsider. He had been very natural with the kids back in Dallas. But Marisa asked what had happened with Zitek.

How would he answer her? She might tell Teresa that Forrest had exposed her son to a gunman who could have killed him. And that Jacob had kept Forrest from killing Zitek.

He closed the laptop and set it down.

Warm light seeped around the edges of the opaque shade. He sat for a few minutes trying to pray—which meant not considering his soul a closed system, as somebody had advised him once. *Ask and you shall receive, seek and you shall find, knock and it shall be opened to you.* As if in reply, his phone was buzzing. He stood, looking on the dresser, the bed—where was the damn thing? It stopped before he could find it, but it woke Jacob, who sat up with a huge yawn and stretched and headed for the bathroom. Forrest pulled up the shade to get the morning light and look for his phone. A lovely column of smoke shot with early sunlight was rising from Midtown.

His phone buzzed again, and he found it on the floor next to his bed. *Cate Zitek.*

"Cate?"

—My friend Laurie just called me.

She sounded preternaturally calm.

"Nice woman. I met her last night."

—The house burned down. My house. All my books and paintings. Her voice broke. All my clothes, all the kids' things.

Forrest stared at the column of smoke again.

"I can see it from my hotel room."

—I got a text from Jason last night, she said, weeping now. He said you got him fired.

"He told me the same thing."

—Dad.

"I didn't kill him," Forrest said. "Did anybody see him at the house last night?"

—Laurie heard something in the middle of the night. She saw two hooded people going around the corner of the house, but she couldn't see their faces. The fire started a few minutes later, and then—oh, God, Dad. *Our house, all our things*—I mean, you hear about people's houses burning and you shake your head and don't really imagine what it *means.* Pretty soon, the whole neighborhood was awake and out on the street at two or three in the morning. Sirens, fire engines, huge hoses. Everybody was scared it would spread.

"Do the police know Zitek had been there waving a pistol around?"

—They're looking for him. I called and gave them the information on my car.

"Do they know about Lykaios?"

A great sob broke from her.

—Oh God, Dad, I don't know, I mean—it's humiliating enough just to—I started to say something about her, but.

"You didn't tell them? Come on, Cate. She's a prime suspect. Who else besides you could tell them about her?"

—*You!* She was sobbing again.

Right. He could tell the police, who might just be looking for him anyway after the episode at *Phoe*.

"She and Zitek probably took her car. Any idea where they might go? You know Zitek best."

—Do I? I have no idea. New York, maybe. Wherever that bitch came from. Dad, what are you going to do?

"Go over to the house and then down to Gallatin. One of Hermia's girls died in childbirth. I don't think there's anything else I can do here."

—One of the girls died? Oh, Dad, it's just—oh God.

Half an hour later, they checked out of the hotel and drove back to Cate's house. Two policemen were there, and a fireman was still hosing down the remains of the little three-bedroom on Greenwood Avenue—hot ashes, blackened beams, the shingled roof collapsed into the ruins. When Forrest identified himself as the owner of the house and the grandfather of the children who had lived there, the officers let him through the yellow tape.

"Please don't disturb any evidence, sir!" one of them called after him.

Looking at the ruins, Forrest remembered a woman who pleaded with Sherman to spare something for her children. Sherman had denied her, writing his wife later—almost wonderingly—at how he had hardened his heart. And here was Zitek, who wanted to destroy his *own family's* home and its memories and all their beloved things and force his wife and children into desolation and homelessness. Zitek had been funny and smart, moody, deep, somehow dangerous, always interesting. His intelligent commentary penetrated appearances. He had been an incisive movie critic and a good investigative journalist for *Phoe*, exposing corruption in the city council, suggesting reasonable alternatives to expensive neighborhood planning projects, proposing rerouting roads to help neighborhoods on the Jane Jacobs model. At home, he was a good chef with a sense of Italian cuisine he had picked up from his time in Rome. And yet he had turned on the Forrest family with such vengeance, Forrest had to wonder what they had done that he found so unbearable. Was it just the responsibility of being a father, the sense of open possibilities closing off? Was it ideological—this new woke religion—taken up in earnest or in imitation? Some kind of desperation?

The evidence of Zitek's turn had been the piece he wrote on Robert E. Lee when his statue was removed from a park in Atlanta, and then had come his subsequent championing of Sherman. Irritation about it had been part of Forrest's reason for suggesting Sherman to Jacob. Zitek had gloated about the removal of Lee, describing the man as a cruel master to his wife's inherited slaves. The article was aimed directly at Forrest. Zitek knew of Forrest's inherited Southern reverence for the paradigm of the magnanimous Christian gentleman. So Zitek attacked Lee and proposed a statue of Sherman and fed Lykaios the misinformation refiguring Forrest as a plantation owner, smugly conscious of his white privilege, proudly perpetuating the central symbol of slavery. It was richly ironic. Forrest had loved a black woman so intensely it had broken his life in two. He had loved her daughter and given his estate to Eula's House in a gesture of redemption. But Zitek saw only condescension, coercion, the use of cynical means to get to self-centered ends. Zitek saw, in fact, nothing but Zitek.

17

GLORY HALLELUJAH

SALT LAKE CITY, WORLD CAPITOL OF MORMONS. HERE HE was, whoever he was. Likeliest was Walter Peach. Son of terrorists, self-centered, enamored of being enamored, patchily brilliant, psychologically unstable. A sinkhole, someone once called him. Possibly also called Karl Guizac. But maybe they had moved the dial and tuned in this other soul, which meant he was now William Tecumseh Sherman about to enter his everlasting fame.

Four three two

SOCRATES: Whoa, buddy, you're lying there half-dead, being pumped up and down, and you're telling me you're General Sherman all set to turn a bunch of Yankees loose on Georgia?

SHERMAN: We're ready, and I tell you what. Orlando Poe—I love that guy. Did you see Atlanta burn? Perfectly engineered. And now we're going to cut a great goddamn swath through Georgia, amen amen, I say a mighty reaping of Rebs. Not to change the subject, but did you see that little widow back there beside the burning barn, running back and forth trying to protect her cow? Cute little spitfire. Bring me that one for dessert, waiter. Whip up some of her cow's cream to put on top.

SOCRATES: You're losing me a little there, buddy.

SHERMAN: So here's a question for you, Socrates. Big speech up at Gettysburg last year, Lincoln says this is a great civil war "testing whether this nation, or any nation so conceived and so dedicated, can long endure." Well, a nation needs laws to long endure, am I right?

SOCRATES: I bet you're right, but what are we talking about?

SHERMAN: I captured Atlanta and saved Lincoln's political hide, but not by proving all men are created equal. Everything in your experience says hell no to that. Anyway, it never crossed my mind I was dedicated to a proposition.

But I'm getting off track. I was asking about law. Now here's the issue: I'm going to set thousands of men loose on a defenseless civilian population. The question is, do I want them to obey the law? Hell no. What's law in a situation like that? The first thing is to let the abolitionists convince my boys that everybody in the South has already defied the Constitution and broken the laws of God *just by being there*, and then I let slip the dogs of war. These people need to be punished, if you see what I mean, because it will be good for them. Then the second thing is to encourage the men to believe that in circumstances like these, they ain't bound by the law, even though they represent the Union and stand for it, so to speak. Do you know how it feels to be free of the law when you come upon a house full of defenseless people who hate you? Best time you ever had! Treasures looted and animals shot and the screams of women and children and the stink of ashes—and all of it just glory hallelujah. Excuse me officer, could you pass me my terrible swift sword? I need to cut down that ham hanging in the smokehouse. And would you look at this fiery little belle?

SOCRATES: We're on the air, here, buddy, so let's try to keep it decent.

SHERMAN: I mean you pretend everything's proper is what I'm saying but you let them know to *have at it*. It's summer, boys, and school's out.

Walter Peach?

He was in his office at *Sage Grouse*, but the walls were gone. Dry snow covered the floor and drifted, white and cold.

Something was coming.

Indoors again. An office.

Mr. Peach, I'm Jerome. I want this to be a comfortable experience for you.

After a long, sincere moment eye to eye, Jerome touched the top paper on a stack before him. His face was smooth and tanned and textured as though some superb cream had rediscovered its perfection that very morning. His eyes were blue, his nose Roman, his chin firm, which Peach found amusing for some reason. Jerome's hair was an artifact, all fades and swoops, no strand out of place. He propped his elbows on his desk, joined his hands, and looked up at Peach. Each knuckle and finger could have been Adam's originals. Beneath the jacket of Jerome's tailored charcoal suit, his blue cotton shirt had a subtle gloss, and his necktie of apple red, buried-treasure gold, and winedark-sea-blue asserted itself with a perfect knot.

Thanks. I'm okay, Peach said, smiling and expecting a smile in return. Instead, the tissue beneath Jerome's left eye began to quiver.

You're okay? Jerome said. No sir. You wouldn't be here if you were okay. I was kidding about wanting this to be comfortable for you.

Peach looked down at his old jeans. A little grimy on the thighs. A lace on his walking shoes had broken and he had retied it with a fraying square knot. His shirt was passable—he had probably put it back on the hanger only two or three times since Teresa washed it. He took off his baseball cap. A little grease stain on the bill. Next to Jerome, he didn't look great, he had to admit.

You're judging my soul by my clothes, Peach said.

Pretty shabby.

Half the billionaires in Silicon Valley don't dress any better.

They wear clean clothes, Mr. Peach. Look, I'm trying to take you seriously. When you say you're okay, you mean what exactly? I believe you if you mean you find ways to deal with your underlying despair. If something's unpleasant to think about, you put it on hold.

What do you mean? I face things, Peach said. I don't have anything on hold.

Jerome lifted his Adamic hands.

Wow. What was I thinking? Of course you don't. Do you really want to do this?

Do what?

Jerome pushed his chair back. Behind him, the floor-to-ceiling windows showed skyscrapers in a gradual perspectival diminuendo. An expressway curved into the distance, blue mountains posed gorgeously against the sunset, white beaches resisted the incursive ocean. But underneath, too, the distances opened. The floor was glass. Gripping the arms of his chair, Peach gazed down, dizzy with vertigo, through the countless diminishing floors of the building. Thousands and thousands of people swarmed purposively through offices, hallways, cafeterias, gymnasiums, chapels, stairways, lobbies, bedrooms, bathrooms. Vastly busy, simultaneous, meaningless, smaller and smaller and farther away.

Beneath them all was a gaping darkness, an atmosphere of nothingness. Not just nothingness, but nothingness in decay, nothingness with a smell.

You know every single one of those people, Jerome said, and they all know you.

The way he said it filled Peach with dread.

Suppose they could *vote* on you, Jerome continued, gesturing down through the floor at the thousands below. A simple thumbs-up or thumbs-down.

As Peach watched, all the people below stopped what they were doing and looked up. He felt a bottomless terror.

Vote on what?

You. Your life, Jerome said.

My life? You mean whether I live or die?

Not at all. You don't get to die. Didn't we establish that earlier? You are immortal, like it or not. No, I mean whether your life has been a success or a failure.

What does that even mean, success or failure?

Exactly. You don't know. Let's say it means whether your life has been worth the expenditure of existence. Have you added something to the great whole, or have you basically been a drain?

He looked down through the glass, beginning to recognize faces and remember stories.

So these people. It's whether I helped them or hurt them? Used them or loved them? Something like that?

His high-school English teacher. She had singled him out early, she had helped him with his poetry, but he had always derided her self-importance and her affectations. He had done something to hurt her, some act of ingratitude, he could not remember what. Others were crowding up to be seen, and the more people he recognized, the more it felt like an abyss. There had always been a pinch of proud self-regard where the flow of his natural affection might have been.

He saw himself in a small room in winter—his foster father Judge Lawton's home office. He was looking out the window at the neighbor's house, where a self-pitying old woman lived with her sick husband. There were brownish spider eggs suspended in a web between the glass and the screen.

One of them, he realized, was his heart. As he looked, it began to break open with the thousand crawling legs of his tiny self-pleasures, his gluttonies and lusts and meannesses.

Stand up, Peach.

The demand terrified him.

Stand up, I said.

The floor was now solid, a pattern of carpet tile, and Peach stood, tentatively, shaken.

Let's talk about all the ways you're a failure, why don't we? I see why you're a drinker.

I'm not a drinker, Peach said. Grant is the drinker. He stuck with me when I was crazy, and I stuck with him when he was drunk.

Among the faces down there had been Dan McCook. Tom Sherman. His boy Willie.

Grant? Stay with me, Peach. You're Peach. Don't try to be somebody else. You're a drinker.

Peach focused on Jerome. Peach, Peach.

Wow, *a drinker.* Right, I used to drink too much. But I could always quit cold turkey. I didn't have withdrawal symptoms, which means I was never technically an alcoholic. I never went on binges. I never missed work. I drank too much at night and figured out how to keep from having hangovers.

Cut it out, Peach. You rely on alcohol. You use it to numb the misery of who you are.

I used to do that, Peach said.

You still do. You drink because you're a failure.

Peach looked at the man, whose looks were beginning to shimmer, as though he were being projected upon the air and the signal were getting faint.

A failure. A drinker. Good stuff, Jerome. Who's writing your script?

And at best you were supposed to be some kind of . . . *poet?* Jesus, whatever that even is. Jerome kept his finger on the page when he looked up. And you committed adultery?

I did. I have been forgiven by God and by my wife.

Seriously? And you killed your own child?

Peach met the man's gaze.

I backed the car over my infant son. I have spent my life regretting that day. That's when I stopped writing poetry and started drinking too much.

Out of self-pity?

Absolutely.

There's no coming back once you've forfeited your gifts like that.

I believe in God's mercy, Peach said.

Cut the bullshit. There's no second chance for a loser like you. You're a sinkhole, Cump. Everything you touch goes bad.

You called me Cump.

I meant—

Jerome disappeared in a small malodorous puff.

Do you need to catch your breath?

In Jerome's place was Martin Kilgore, Peach's favorite professor at the University of Georgia. From Shakespeare and Milton to Stevens, Wilbur, and Glück.

Kilgore seemed pleased to find himself with Peach.

Walter, he said. You look awful.

Hell, Martin, I'm dying of Covid.

Oh, that's right. That's what this is all about. Your exams.

I hope somebody's checking all these inquisitors for orthodoxy. Everything feels like it's all over the place. I don't feel like I'm getting a lot of moral support.

Kilgore smiled and lit a cigarette, and the smell of it brought back something in Peach. A black pinprick of dread appeared in his abdomen.

You probably shouldn't smoke.

What difference does it make? He looked down at the notes in front of him. I'm supposed to say you were my best student, Kilgore told him. That's more or less true. Best after Braxton Forrest, but not brightest in the usual sense. Your papers were self-indulgent. You never believed in the form of the student essay. Talk about papers, my god—you remember that dark-haired girl from Atlanta in your Shakespeare class? Her papers were so good they made me cry. I wanted to jump her bones whenever I read one. But you were the one with the soul for Shakespeare. The potential to be an important poet.

That's kind of you.

Potential is like a string of firecrackers you keep on the closet shelf. You have to bring it outside and light the damn thing, Walter. Do you plan to write something? I know you've had your troubles, but the way you handled them was about as bad as it could've been.

I had a rough spell.

Fifteen years? You call that a spell?

Is that how long it was? I've started over. Forrest came to the rescue.

Braxton Forrest? Kilgore acted surprised.

Cut it out, Martin. You already know everything about me.

You're right, I do. If Braxton Forrest is your savior, I'm worried. If there had been a Me Too movement in those days back in the English Department, he would have been the prize goat.

He's changed.

I doubt it. You either. You say you've started over, but it looks to me like Forrest came into money and bought your life.

What does that mean?

He gave you a job, he gave you a house, he set your agenda. If he weren't subsidizing *Sage Grouse*, what would you be doing? You're the only employee except for that Transfiguration boy who helps with the graphics. Well, you were until Forrest rebooted the whole thing in your absence. Whoops, off script. In any case, you don't take any responsibility for the business end of it.

What do you mean he rebooted the whole thing? Listen, the point is to preserve my gifts, not fritter away my time with details.

Preserve your gifts? Smiling, Kilgore stood up and rubbed his face with both hands. Whew. *Preserve your gifts.* You're a journalist, Walter, and that's only because Forrest made you one. Think about why he's doing it. He's hoping for something more from you than Socrates Johnson.

Sage Grouse is kind of famous. Subscriptions are way up. And listen, why didn't you ever write anything yourself? You were my best teacher. You opened up Shakespeare and Eliot and Stevens, you made me respect Frost, you showed me what language could do, but you never published a word, and then you just left teaching so you could be president of some foundation, whatever that was, and make a lot of money. I always loved you, Martin, but don't preach to me.

This isn't about me. I'm here to help you. Do you ever suffer for what you write?

Suffer for it?

You have to suffer for real art.

That's bullshit. I don't picture Shakespeare suffering. It just flowed out of him, play after play. Besides, what I do is just satire. It's just a website.

Exactly. Forrest won't say it, but he wants you to find your ambition. You've fallen into an easy smallness. You let yourself be little. Why is that? Because of your sins? Go to confession. What Forrest wants to see is the greatness of soul that's possible for you.

For me? Greatness of soul?

You have to risk something. Kilgore sat down and stubbed out his cigarette in an ashtray that materialized just in time. Otherwise, where's your salvation?

Salvation?

Martin Kilgore had never talked about salvation. A strange unease came over him.

My God, Walter, you need salvation if anybody ever did. That's the chronic ache you feel at the root of your soul. You don't like who you are. You've been running scared for most of your life. You don't think God has any real interest in you, so He's just letting you be damned by a shitpile of sins. You pray but without believing you're heard because you don't really believe in God and so you don't hope. On the other hand, you do believe in God, but you don't think you're worth His trouble, so you hide. His eye is on the sparrow, he knows the hairs on your head, but you don't believe for a second that God has any interest in you. You're the *pusilla anima*, the small soul. You don't have to be. You have to open up and accept your own agency and the real nature of hope.

Peach felt like a man attacked by a swarm of yellowjackets.

Come on. I am large, I contain multitudes. Where do you get off saying I have a small soul?

You used to scorn Walt Whitman before you realized that not a single poem of your own, not a single line, would be remembered tomorrow, much less when you're dead. Tell me this: what is it you hope for? Here you are with a great capacity of intellect, all this talent, and yet you content yourself with the little pleasures of the day and the little pleasures of the night.

Peach squirmed. You're just plagiarizing from Nietzsche. Is he working for Team Heaven now?

Kilgore did not reply.

So what do you want?

What do I want? For you to be who you are. You're scared of it, aren't you? Just scared. You're a coward. Scared to risk it. You don't want to fail at something you really try for, so you don't put yourself out there in a way big enough for actual joy or agony. That's what I'm looking for here, so let me ask you again, and this time I'll wait for an answer. What do you hope for?

Success, I guess. Recognition.

Do you mean recognition for your poetry? Maybe you should write some. Do you want prizes? Fame? You should probably do something to earn them.

I know all that stuff doesn't really mean anything. It's all vanity.

So what is it you hope for? The happiness of your children? Your wife would say she hopes for their salvation. You don't really know what you hope for from them—except maybe accolades for being their father. But what do you hope *for* them? What do you hope for your wife? What is it that you could really, actually help bring about for her? I'd love to see an achievable goal, Walter. For her, for your kids, for you.

Achievable goal. Jesus, Martin, you've turned into a management book. Next you're going to talk about the difference between goals and objectives and how to measure known results.

Kilgore put his face in his hands for a moment before he looked up at Peach.

Your irony lets you dodge the truth that's standing there in plain sight. You need to *do* something. Think about everything that Ellen has suffered while you blunder along with your series of failures.

Peach looked at him for a long time and then began to smile.

You said Ellen.

Kilgore shook his head and bitterly pinched in his lips.

Suddenly back in front of him were the three judges.

As before, the central one said, this tribunal will be speaking to you in your persona as General William Tecumseh Sherman.

It's my son who's writing about Sherman, not me.

There was a long silence. Finally, the one in the middle spoke again.

As before, the tribunal will be speaking to you in your persona as Gen. Sherman. You must answer as you understand Gen. Sherman would answer, though of course it will be your own soul on trial.

He flared with anger, but the three looked at him so dispassionately that the same terror as before came over him.

I understand.

Atlanta has fallen. You have forced the evacuation of the civilian population of the city. You have repeatedly emphasized the vulnerability of your lengthening supply lines down through Tennessee and northern Georgia, and Gen. Nathan Bedford Forrest in particular terrifies you because of his suddenness and brilliance. Some generals, even Grant, still think you should chase down the army of John Bell Hood in your rear and destroy it, but you insist that Gen. Thomas can handle Hood while you march to Savannah. You propose to move away from supply lines altogether. In your telegram to Grant on Oct. 9, you propose that you "break up the road from Chattanooga and strike out with wagons for Milledgeville, Millen, and Savannah." You tell Grant that the "utter destruction" of Georgia's "roads, houses, and people" will "cripple their military resources," whereas you would lose a thousand men a month trying to defend the roads. You say, "I can make the march and make Georgia howl." Even Lincoln is skeptical.

At this moment on the afternoon of Wednesday, Nov. 2, 1864, you have not begun, but you have just received your approval by telegram from Gen. Grant for the march. You have already consulted with Orlando Poe, your chief engineer, about his plans to destroy Atlanta's railroads, roundhouses, arsenals, and manufacturers, and at this moment, you are alone in your office upstairs in the splendid Atlanta home of John Neal, where you have set up your headquarters. Are you hopeful?

Sure, I guess so, Peach said.

You guess so?

Lots of things to consider.

There was a protracted silence. The three examiners did not look at each other. The middle one finally spoke.

Mr. Peach, our instructions are clear, are they not? You are to answer in your persona as Gen. Sherman.

Peach was about to complain that he did not know enough about the historical circumstances, but just then he glanced out the window at a carriage pulling up in front of the house in the shade of the live oak that shadowed the gate through the picket fence. A woman stepped down from it, dappled with sunlight, and he felt a surge of interest. By God, it was Nora O'Hearn, his wife's niece. One of the officers gestured her toward the front door and offered his arm, glancing up at the window where he stood and giving an informal nod to say that she was coming up to see him.

Mr. Peach, said the middle interrogator.

I don't know who you people are, he snapped in irritation. Did Stanton send you? You sound like those goddamn reporters always prying for news and running me down and ruining what I'm trying to do. What does it matter if I'm hopeful? What do you need to know for? Rebs can read, if you didn't know that. They've got spies all over the north, and if I find out you're sending things to the newspapers, I'll have all of *you* court-martialed as spies, like I did that Knox bastard for the *Herald*. They should have strung him up, and I blame Lincoln for getting him off.

Our only concern is with your hope.

So you just want a quotation. I hope we crush these old men and Rebel women into howling helplessness so we can all go home. I hope we break their spirit like a beaten horse.

We mean hope for yourself. What do you hope for?

That girl I just saw. The respect of good men.

Not power?

He was pacing the room with nervous energy.

I'm not one of those Yorks or Lancasters always jockeying to kill the next one in line. I'm not hunchbacked Richard. I don't care about power, except to be able to do what needs doing—to get it organized, to get the best men working, and to do it right. I hate politics. So what do I hope for? Fame that gives me the fear and respect of everyone I meet. The kind of fame that weakens the knees of women. Fame that eclipses my circumstances. I hope the only reason anybody remembers the name of Thomas Ewing or Ellen Ewing is because of me. I hope that what I do, people will remember forever, the way a woman remembers the man who first had her. History hardly remembers a gentleman.

What about Gen. Lee?

People will remember his rebellion. The brilliant gentleman traitor. I can beat Lee if Grant can't.

What difference does it make if you're remembered if you're dead and can't enjoy it?

I don't know. I just want it.

So you hope for glory?

Too fancy a word for what I want. I don't care about public honors. I want the respect of the best men, and I want pretty women in bed as my prizes, just like the kings in Homer.

There was a knock at the door, and one of his lieutenants opened it to let in the woman he had seen enter the house below. He stood to greet her.

Nora.

The three examiners did not react.

Do you hope for salvation? Do you hope in the resurrection and the rewards of everlasting life?

You sound like my wife, he said impatiently. Is that what this is about? Religion?

He was eager to be alone with Nora.

Please answer the question.

I hope in the salvation of fame and the consolation of sex. I do not expect to survive my death, nor do I want to. I hope for the extinction of misery and the erasure of memory.

And is that your answer, Mr. Peach?

My answer in my persona as Sherman.

And do you hope for the same things?

The door behind Nora opened, and three small daughters ran to her, hugging her legs and looking up shyly at Peach. Nora held them and met his gaze without sadness. She did not speak.

No, he said.

Gratitude burned in his heart. What was happening?

What then?

Not erasure but the grace of self-forgetfulness in perfect happiness. Happiness is perfect accord in action with the highest calling of my nature. I hope for a life that is the same as the one I have lived and am living but altogether new in my full-hearted presence to it.

Would you call it hope for the resurrection and the life?

Is that what those words mean? If those are the right words to use, yes.

Do you think such happiness is attainable without believing in the purpose and meaning of the passion and death of Our Lord Jesus Christ?

For most of my life, I have thought of Jesus as extraneous, a story from elsewhere, certainly not an inner truth.

Do you still think so in your heart of hearts, despite your outer conversion?

No.

You sound hesitant.

It is a terrible price. I do not think that I could make the same sacrifice if it were asked of me, God help me. I fear my own weakness when it comes to offering my life for others. I don't feel worthy of salvation.

But do you hope in Jesus Christ?

Yes.

There was a pause.

And what do you hope for Gen. William Tecumseh Sherman?

He thought for a long time.

What his wife and children hoped for. His change of heart. A liberation from the attempt to alleviate some deeply embedded anguish. His recognition of mystery. His peace.

Do you think he found it?

He opened his mouth, but words did not come. He felt the man's anger deep within him, a growing accusation: who was he to speak for William Tecumseh Sherman?

He shook his head.

The judges were silent for a long time. The one on the right sighed and spoke quietly.

Pass.

18

ARRIVALS AND DEPARTURES

TERESA HAD WAITED UNTIL CATE'S ARRIVAL ON SUNDAY night to make sure that she and the children were comfortable in the house. Introducing Little Marisa to Jimmy, Clare, and Avila had been a revelation. Two years younger than Clare, her daughter proved to be a born impresario as a hostess. Little M, five years old, had presented the distinguished kitchen, the amazing wood stove, Jacob's inviolable room, her father's equally inviolable office, the view of the neighboring sandstone cliffs, the stairway, the bedrooms, the toys, and anything else she could think of. Marisa kept meeting Teresa's eyes and biting her upper lip.

Leave-taking was hard, but Marisa had been around long enough for Little M not to be distressed at the idea of her mother being away for a week. Teresa actually had no idea how long it would be. It all depended on Walter's Covid. The uncertainty of it weighed on her heavily, and she hated to leave home. They had lived in many places, but nowhere like this. When they would gather at night to read stories to Little M or talk over the day in front of the wood stove or say the rosary, she felt the sense of home very deeply. Things inherited from her grandparents in Alabama had an ancestral bearing. She had many responsibilities in the house itself, many things to maintain that she never thought about until she was no longer there to do them. She had forgotten to tell Marisa about putting bags of salt into the water softening system. But how would Marisa wrestle forty-pound bags into the big container in the crawlspace? Walter or Jacob had always done it, and she herself did not know the procedure—if they even had any salt. She needed to call one of the Transfiguration boys to do those chores until Jacob got back.

Accepting a lodging would be hard, too. She hated to put herself at the mercy of people she hardly knew. She would be an imposition, and she wished there were some other way, but she could not afford more than a night or two at a hotel. It felt crucial to be in Salt Lake City if they brought Walter out of the coma. He would know that she was in the lobby of the hospital (if they would let her be) or in her car outside.

That morning, before daylight, when the children were all still asleep, she put her bags in the car and came back inside to get her coffee and say goodbye to Marisa. Her friend stood in the kitchen weeping. When Teresa approached, full of concern, she turned and whispered, "Jason Zitek burned down Cate's house in Atlanta."

"Oh God!" Teresa cried.

"All their things. All Cate's books, their artwork, her manuscripts."

"Thank God I haven't left yet. I'll call the Hellyers right now. You and Cate are going to be too upset to take care of these children."

"No, you go on. We have the day planned here, and there's not a thing you can do. You take care of Walter. I'll call you when they arrest Jason."

Praying for them, she reluctantly started out from De Smet and drove toward Farson past the signs to South Pass and the profiles of the Oregon Buttes to the east. The Red Desert—all that shifting and unstable ground, full of sand dunes, part of the Great Divide Basin that stretched most of the way across the state. After the junction at Farson were vast, bare spaces, scrubland with signs that warned her that antelope could run almost as fast as she was driving. Vast stretches of emptiness, mountains in the far distance, intermittent refineries, an occasional house in the distance, a small store as forgotten and unvisited as her mother's grave.

Why had she not remembered to download an audiobook on her phone? She had nothing but her own worried thoughts. Poor Cate, now consigned to perpetual exile. Everyone in her own family dispersed. She imagined Rose in France and wondered whether a French boyfriend (Walter's thesis) was a compelling explanation for her prolonged absence. Was Rose living in sin? Speaking of sin, what would prolonged exposure to Braxton Forrest do to Jacob? Why in the world had she let him go? The hope of getting Sherman out of his system? Or had she still been in a state of shock? Literate and sophisticated as he was, Forrest was a barbarian, as though recourse to the life of a pirate lord were never far from his mind. Sword in his teeth, maidens cowering becomingly. She smiled at the image. It was hard not to love the man, though it might be a little necessary to temper his influence on an impressionable mind.

The route bypassed Kemmerer and then joined US 189, which went south past an immense power plant, past quarries, past abandoned motels that must have been a dream of wealth before the interstates came. The road intersected I-80 a few miles east of Evanston. She stopped for a hamburger at one of the Evanston exits, and then drove on through the mountains until she came to the long downhill curves east of Salt Lake City, huge sandstone formations darker and taller than the ones behind her house outside De Smet. Big trucks downshifted loudly, using the engine to restrain themselves on the grade. Cars around her made sudden lane changes with reckless speed. Finally, the vista of Salt Lake City opened up below, and she thought of the Mormons first coming over these mountains with Brigham Young. Mormons far outnumbered Catholics, not just in Utah but in De Smet. She knew almost nothing of their history.

She had downloaded directions to a little town called Bountiful, and she followed her phone's guidance to I-15 and then north to her exit. The Hellyers were a lively couple in their fifties, very open and accommodating, very sympathetic about Walter. Their daughter worked for the outdoor program at Transfiguration.

Mrs. Hellyer gave Teresa a set of keys, one for the front door and another for the back entrance to the apartment. She showed her the kitchen, the coffee, the refrigerator with its generous supply of snacks and sparkling water, and the well-lighted bedroom.

"It's just lovely," Teresa told her. "I so much appreciate this, Mrs. Hellyer."

"Marjorie." She held out both hands to take Teresa's.

"And I'm Teresa. Please don't worry about me one bit. I need to spend my days down in Salt Lake City close to the hospital."

When Marjorie left her, she lay down on the bed and closed her eyes, picturing what her time would be like. On the map it was only fourteen miles from the house in Bountiful to the hospital, but what if it snowed? The driving worried her. The steep hills in Salt Lake City—at least she had the Subaru. She would find a coffee shop near the Cathedral where she could catch up on email and call home and talk to Marisa about how things were going. Or call Jacob to check on him. Then she'd go to Mass and head to the hospital. If it was warm enough, she might sit outside and draw. Faces, landscapes, clusters of buildings. It would be like prayer to practice the act of attention. There was a grace of seeing. She was drifting into a dream about Rose, who was carefully explaining to her why she had become a Mormon in France, when her phone began its little homage to Philip Glass. Startled, she sat up and looked at the screen. UoUH: the hospital. Billing again, maybe.

"Hello?"

—Is this Mrs. Karl Guizac?

"Yes, this is she."

—Just a moment, please.

What did that mean? The woman was getting somebody else to talk to her. Someone was going to tell her Walter was dead.

—Mrs. Guizac?

"Yes."

It was a male voice with an Indian accent.

—This is Dr. Dilal Ranasinghe. I'm calling about your husband.

Her soul seized.

—We're going to bring Mr. Guizac out of his coma briefly to do some tests and adjust some of his medications. There will be a window of opportunity for you to speak with him in about, let's see . . . in about an hour or an hour and a half. You will probably have about five minutes to talk, not much more than that. Will you be available to speak to him?

"Of course!" She was flooded with gratitude. "Is there any chance I can see him?"

—As you know, we are still under strict quarantine. In fact, you will not be able to enter the—

"But can you tell him that I'm here?" she interrupted. "As soon as he regains consciousness, please tell him that I'm here, I'm in Salt Lake City. I'll be at the hospital if there's any chance I can see him."

—Of course, Mrs. Guizac.

She got directions on her phone and grabbed her purse and jacket. It took her a little over half an hour to drive down from Bountiful. On the way, she called Jacob.

"How are you, sweetheart?"

—Hi, Mom. We're okay.

"Marisa told me what happened with Jason Zitek."

—Sure, but not right now. How's Dad?

"You're in the car with Braxton."

—Exactly.

"I'm calling because they're going to bring your father out of the coma for a few minutes. Can you talk to him?"

—Talk to Dad? Jacob said, sounding as incredulous as if he were being asked to speak to someone beyond the grave. When? I mean, what will I talk to him about?

"Just tell him what you're doing. Talk about Sherman."

The way they numbered streets in Salt Lake City—everything centered on the Temple—confused her at first, but she got to the hospital early. She walked directly to the entrance, intending to be somewhere inside when Walter called. But as soon as she walked through the sliding glass doors a uniformed guard intercepted her beneath a large sign that said NO VISITORS!

"My sympathies," he said unsympathetically when she told him why she was there. "Please wait outside."

She went back to the car. At least her phone was charged. Waiting was excruciating. Just sitting there. But where else could she carry on an intimate conversation? Not in a coffee shop. Not in a library or a church. She might as well stay where she was. Another half hour passed. She said the rosary. Another twenty minutes. She had begun to think they had forgotten about her when the phone sang, and she saw the name KARL appear on the screen.

"Walter? Thank God."

—Teresa. You've been. Gone. So long.

He sounded terribly weak.

"Oh it's so good to hear your voice. Thank God. Listen, I'm right outside the hospital. Right outside!" she repeated, as if it were urgent for him to know. "As close to you as they will let me be. Marisa is in our house with

Cate and Cate's children, and they're keeping Little Marisa. I'm here for you as soon as they let me see you."

—How. Are you?

"Getting by. We miss you so much. Rose is still in Europe. Jacob went on a long road trip with Braxton so he could finish his Sherman research."

—Sherman.

"They're in Georgia now. Please call him if you can. It's important to him. Right after you talk to me."

—I. Hope they. Let me.

"They're going to be in Gallatin by tonight. Back at Stonewall Hill. That all seems like a different lifetime. But I am just so glad"—she could not control her voice—"so grateful to be able to talk to you. When are they going to let you out?"

—They're. Putting me. Back under.

"Oh, no. Oh God, Walter."

—I have. Dreams. I thought. I divorced. You.

She shook her head. What in the world did he mean?

"Divorced me?"

—I married. Somebody else.

"Who would that be?" she said testily, thinking of Nora O'Hearn.

—Don't know. And married. You. Again.

"Well thank you for that."

The doctor came onto the phone.

—Time's up, Mrs. Guizac.

"Dr. Ranasinghe, could he please call our son just quickly? It would mean so much to me."

—It will have to be quick. He needs to be back on the ventilator.

The prospect of retracing Sherman's route out of Atlanta changed Jacob's mind about leaving. Already, he had saved Forrest twice from his own violence. In the car, as they left Atlanta, Jacob read aloud from Sherman's *Memoirs*:

"*About 7 a.m. of November 16th we rode out of Atlanta by the Decatur road, filled by the marching troops and wagons of the Fourteenth Corps; and reaching the hill, just outside of the old rebel works, we naturally paused to look back upon the scenes of our past battles. We stood upon the very ground whereon was fought the bloody battle of July 22nd, and could see the copse of wood where McPherson fell.*

"Behind us lay Atlanta, smouldering and in ruins, the black smoke rising high in air, and hanging like a pall over the ruined city. Away off in the distance, on the McDonough road, was the rear of Howard's column, the gun-barrels glistening in the sun, the white-topped wagons stretching away to the south; and right before us the Fourteenth Corps, marching steadily and rapidly, with a cheery look and swinging pace, that made light of the thousand miles that lay between us and Richmond. Some band, by accident, struck up the anthem of 'John Brown's soul goes marching on;' the men caught up the strain, and never before or since have I heard the chorus of 'Glory, glory, hallelujah!' done with more spirit, or in better harmony of time and place."

"That's enough," said Forrest.

"Just this little bit."

"Then we turned our horses' heads to the east; Atlanta was soon lost behind the screen of trees, and became a thing of the past. Around it clings many a thought of desperate battle, of hope and fear, that now seem like the memory of a dream; and I have never seen the place since. The day was extremely beautiful, clear sunlight, with bracing air, and an unusual feeling of exhilaration seemed to pervade all minds—a feeling of something to come, vague and undefined, still full of venture and intense interest.

"I'll skip some. *There was a 'devil-may-care' feeling pervading officers and men, that made me feel the full load of responsibility, for success would be accepted as a matter of course, whereas, should we fail, this 'march' would be adjudged the wild adventure of a crazy fool. I had no purpose to—"*

His phone buzzed in his pocket. Please let it be Emily.

Dad. His stomach clenched. He punched the green circle to accept the call. "Dad?"

—Son. His voice sounded very weak and hoarse. Can you. Hear me?

"I can hear you, Dad. I'm in the car with Professor Forrest. You must be doing better."

—I have to. Go back. Under. Put your. Phone. On speaker.

Puzzled, Jacob set the phone in the holder clamped into the air vent and pushed the speaker button.

"Walter, I've been praying for you," Forrest said.

—I'm. *Sherman*. Most of the time. In these. *Exams*.

Forrest looked at Jacob, puzzled.

—And I've got to. Find. Some way. To save. *Sherman*. Or I can't. Go to heaven.

He sounded deadly serious.

"You're not going to heaven! I mean—I mean, you're going to come through this, Dad. I know you will."

—Only. If I. Save Sherman. He's. He's—

"Dad . . ."

—Brushing. The dust. Of history. Off his. Shoulders—

His father succumbed to a fit of coughing.

It's time, Mr. Guizac, they heard a woman say.

"Dad, don't try to talk," Jacob said. What was he talking about, anyway? He sounded crazy.

—This starved. Bitter. People. Like Dresden.

His voice faltered and wheezed weakly.

"Seriously, Dad, don't try to—"

—His heart. Hangs like a stone. In its. Web of blood.

Another fit of coughing.

Somebody take that damn phone from him.

—Don't be fooled. Into. Sympathy.

Wheezing, exhausted.

Please put on the mask, Mr. Guizac.

—My soul. Is stitched. Onto his. Pray for me.

"Dad," Jacob said. "Seriously, Dad. You should—"

—Should

Five four three two

He had been lying still for many ages. The forest had grown upon the soil that had built up century after century upon the rock. Soon he would stand up and show who he was.

God of hosts, he would say, I shall bestir myself.

And the great rocks would shatter and flee from his rising forehead and the forests would slip from his torso and the ridges of his great back like a dropped robe and he would stand.

Gigantic, rising and rising.

Stand up, stand up for Jesus Ye soldiers of the cross.

A high, thrilling soprano. Mattie. Or Leah. Teresa had a fine alto voice but not—no, Teresa was Guizac's wife, stupid dying Goozac.

Be it known to all men by these presents, I am the great William Tecumseh Sherman. I will stand up, but not yet and not for Jesus. I will lie and wait until they do not expect it, and when I stand up, it will be for everlasting fame and the sign shall be that armies of little men will climb my greatness.

Whereupon I shall rise, filthy with the settled dirt and the rock of ages upon ages. I will glance to the north where tiny railroad cars come along on the threads of their steel. I will turn and shake away lost time and raise the forests to brush away the grime of all the ages since Cyrus the Persian and Scipio Africanus. I will look toward the south and the little town of Marietta and beyond it to the river that I will cross in my easy stride. Atlanta, the skyscrapers and interstates, the huge and unrelenting pressure as it spreads its traffic and its shopping malls and apartment complexes into the small towns and renames the forests and lakes and make subdivisions of the beaver ponds and blackberry thickets and subjects complacent and unsuspecting nature to the Union. I will be avenged. Something will come larger than to any mortal man. The whole land will be a burnt offering to—

To what, Walter?

I was speaking as Sherman.

A burnt offering to what? Not to God.

He thought about it.

Maybe to the Union?

To the *word*, perhaps? Not the impossible fact but the transcendental notion? This destruction and terror a holocaust to this word Union, emptied of its

of its

Beep beep beep

Chick's phone buzzed a little before noon. Tierney in Parts. She said Roof had her looking at some mouthwatering tailpipes.

"Any customers?"

—Mmm, a few. Nobody for a car, though. Some action out in the service department, and I've sold a couple of really sexy head gaskets. Made my knees a little weak.

"I should be in after lunch," Chick said.

—We'll see you when we see you, Boss Man. Just wanted to see if you're okay.

He loved the way she said it.

Since he was home for lunch, Patricia made some ham sandwiches and tomato soup and set out a bowl of chips. He told her the funeral was the next morning.

"Well, maybe I'll go," she said. "It's just awful what happened to that poor girl. You know, it could happen to any of us—any of us women."

Jacob was shaken. He was the one who had forced Sherman into his father's mind before this terrible half-life on the ventilator. *My soul is stitched onto his.* What could that even mean? Hadn't Sherman's soul already gone to judgment? Historically, how did Sherman even exist except in his words and others' words that summoned images of him? Maybe in the explanations of what he caused? And in what the events might mean? The reality of the past events penetrated the apparent solidity of the present—but what did you even mean by "the present" once you got past the first common-sense intuition of "now"—and why could he sense the eternal co-presence of times?

In his father's disjointed sentences, Jacob had glimpsed the great, looming angels of history, all these agencies and motions invisible to men, like the gods Aeneas had seen destroying Troy in that moment when the veil was pulled aside.

"I wish I had never mentioned Sherman to him."

"I'm the one who said you should do this paper."

"He said his soul was stitched onto Sherman's."

"Like yours?"

Jacob shook his head. "I don't know. I wonder what he meant by 'exams.' It didn't sound like medical tests, did it?"

"No idea."

After Lithonia, they took the access road onto I-20 and Forrest drove to Madison, where they turned off toward Milledgeville. Woods and rolling hills. For a moment on the way, he felt the thousands of men around him, the rollicking air of the foragers. A soldier with a scraggly beard ran into the yard of an unpainted house and snatched up a chicken and grinned as he wrung its neck in front of a distraught housewife. *Betty's my best layer!* she cried. *How'm I gone feed my chillun?* He tossed it to another man, *Here comes Betty*, who caught it and threw it, and so Betty flew all up and down the march, head limp, wings flapping out loosely. The woman stood stunned by the cruelty of it as her children came out of the house behind her. Finally, a soldier about Jacob's age caught the hen and took it to her and tipped his hat in apology. Some of the soldiers mocked him, but others looked down as they tramped on, shoes coated with the dust of the red clay.

"Jacob!"

Jacob looked up, puzzled.

"You want to see Flannery O'Connor's house? Third time I've asked. You checked out for a few minutes there," Forrest said.

"Did I? I guess so." Jacob made a face and shrugged. It had seemed realer than what was in front of him.

"Want to pay a visit?"

Jacob had seen Andalusia on a field trip from Gallatin years before, so he declined. A few minutes later they parked in town to walk the sidewalks for an hour. A noble town, modestly monumental, Milledgeville was full of the graces of the South, even with the tall elms stripped of leaves. Sherman had stayed during this exact season in the old governor's mansion, this very building, after Joseph Brown and his staff fled before the approaching Union army. But, looking at it, gazing around the city, walking the sidewalks, Jacob felt as he had at Vicksburg and then at Kennesaw. Nothing he saw ripped open the veil of the ordinary present. It was just somewhere something had happened, something that remained hidden from him and lost.

And so they came to Gallatin.

Jacob drove as they came out of the long stretch of woods and hills between the Ocmulgee River and Interstate 75. Just past the old Jenkins dairy farm, they turned north onto Highway 41. Through the tall elms and oaks along the road, the last light reddened the western clouds as they approached the courthouse square. He was surprised at how healthy the town looked, its old buildings refurbished and repurposed. Still anchoring the corner of the square, a tired soldier high up on a monument labeled CONFEDERATE, rifle propped on his shoulder, faced north and trudged toward defeat. Jacob turned onto South Lee Street. Except for one or two houses fallen into disrepair, the neighborhood looked pristine. Down where the roads split like a river around an island rose Stonewall Hill. Jacob paused at the gate as they looked up at its lordly aspect—the columns, the lights gleaming from within.

"Just go up around the drive," Forrest said. "We don't need to stop. We'll check in with Hermia tomorrow."

Two very pregnant girls sitting on the front steps waved at them, ducking their heads to see inside the BMW as they rolled slowly past.

That night in her prayer room, Hermia called Fr. Silber in Macon to tell him about the arrangements for the funeral the next morning.

"But I was going to ask you about exorcism."

—Exorcism? What are you talking about?

"I think Miriam was possessed."

—I'm not surprised after what this preacher did to her. Do you know if she was ever baptized?

"I don't know," she said impatiently. "What does that have to—"

—It's a matter of sacramental protection, an indelible spiritual mark of belonging to Christ. Frankly, I'm not sure what you want from me.

"I'm scared. I'm out of my depth. Can you just be here? And then would you baptize and christen Miriam's baby?"

He sighed again.

—What time is this funeral?

"Ten o'clock. I'll let you know where it is."

Fr. Silber did not answer for a long moment, and she felt her heart pounding.

—I'll be there, he said at last.

"Thank you! God bless you!"

19

MIRIAM'S FUNERAL

FORREST WAS GONE FROM THE ROOM WHEN JACOB WOKE. He used the bathroom and took a quick shower and dressed in his jeans, saving his good clothes for the funeral. Walking through the interior hallways of the Travelodge depressed him—dull carpets with stains, a disinfectant smell—so he went out an exit into the front parking lot and walked toward the lobby. The access roads along I-75 were crowded with fast food places—a Hardee's, a Subway, a McDonald's, a Waffle House, a Wendy's. Across the street was a Best Western and just around the curve to the north was a Holiday Inn Express. He could see signs across the Interstate—Days Inn, Burger King, KFC.

It was a cool, brisk day. He wished there were time for a run through the older town he remembered.

Forrest sat in the far corner of the breakfast room with his laptop and a coffee cup. At the table in the center of the room, two longhaired children of indeterminate sex slumped on their chairs; their teenage sister looked as though she had undergone shock therapy to erase the possibility of emotion, and he remembered Britknee with her donuts back in Dallas. Back to the room, the mother loomed like Godzilla over the breakfast counter, hands planted well apart, head lowered. Her immense bottom swayed at the room, pinched into random shapes by shiny-green exercise pants across the outline of her bikini underwear. She wore a red Georgia Bulldogs jersey (44).

Jacob wondered if simply seeing someone could be uncharitable.

"Waiting for her waffles," Forrest commented from across the room.

The woman turned around and glared at them both. A full moon of moles and pug nose and bad teeth. Her chin was powerfully undergirded with fat.

"I put in the batter," she complained. "I'm just waiting for the goddamn thing to beep."

"Listen, I'm good," Jacob said, holding up a placating palm and taking a seat across from Forrest, who sighed and widened his eyes and then spun his laptop around. The sound was turned very low, and Jacob had to lean forward to hear the handsome, charismatic, one-eyed preacher working a huge congregation, which responded with ecstatic calls and lifted hands.

"Did you hear that?" Forrest said after a minute or two.

"He's talking about Sherman?"

"Right. Turning the March into baptism by fire," Forrest said, "just like Zitek. I bet he read Zitek."

Jacob nodded, not surprised. Sherman took over everything.

"Who is that? How did you happen to find it?"

"Apparently he's the one who got the girl pregnant."

"The girl who died?"

"Sorry to drag you into this circus, Jacob. You came for Sherman, and he's the gift that keeps on giving. But as far as I'm concerned, you're done with that project—as I said back in De Smet before we left. A+. Above and beyond. You've looked so far into the soul of the man that it's changed your own and affected your father. I have questions about your interpretation, but I don't see how anybody could fault your effort."

Jacob breathed in sharply through his nose. "Well, I wrote another section."

BEEP! BEEP! BEEP! cried the waffle machine.

"Finally!" the woman muttered. Then a moment later, "Jesus effing hell! Look at these goddamn things!"

She turned and deposited something blackened and smoking on the table in front of the children.

"I don't want it, Mama," one of the children whined.

"After all that trouble? Eat the fucking thing." She raised her hand, and the child cowered, which made Jacob realize what she would have done if he and Forrest had not been present. He and Forrest examined the tabletop for a second or two. Jacob wondered if he should intervene. It seemed to be his role lately. Glancing over at the woman, he thought of Zitek and Cate. The responsibility, lifelong and unavoidable, of the children they had brought into the world. Jimmy and Clare and Avila, each one vivid and real. Zitek had simply turned his back on them, as though they had merely been an obstacle to his freedom. And look at these bullied children, their souls already stunted, stuck for life with this monster of a mother, no father in sight. His stomach tightened with dread at the utter vulnerability of children. Why did God allow it?

He went over to the counter, avoiding the waffle machine, toasted a bagel and made a bowl of Raisin Bran with lukewarm milk. As he turned to take them back to the table, the huge woman stood in front of him with an empty paper plate.

"Don't you judge me, boy," she said in a low voice. "You don't know the first goddamn thing about my life."

He met her eyes and saw an unfathomable hatred.

Shaken, he sat down to eat his breakfast.

"What did she say?"

"She said I didn't know anything about her."

Forrest shook his head as the woman herded her hostages out of the room. They both sighed.

"You said you wrote something else about Sherman. What did you write?"

"It's about Vinnie Ream. I'm not finished, but I have part of it done."

"We've got the funeral to get through. There's a real chance the state will shut Hermia down, which would put all her women out on the street with nowhere to go. According to Lykaios, who got it from Zitek, Sherman should have burned the place when he had the chance, because it's a living monument to patriarchal white oppression. *An obscenity built on the backs of slaves.*"

But Hermia Watson, he thought, had turned that cursed and haunted place into Eula's House. She had named it after the slave woman who died in childbirth, chained in the dark beneath the house because she had dared to say that a son of Farquhar McIntosh was the father. Could Stonewall Hill ever be redeemed? His family had fled it six years before. He dreaded going back.

That Tuesday morning, the women of Eula's House assembled in the chapel early. Hermia read a psalm and a passage from Ruth Burrows about accepting the ordinary. Some of them were sniffling, and she knew she needed to say something else. She sighed, bowing her head.

"They're going to bring Miriam back here for us to say goodbye."

"Here?" one of the girls said. "That scares me. What if—"

Murmurs.

"You're worried about Josiah, but Josiah's gone. We're honoring Miriam."

"Why can't we go to a church?" another said.

"We have Reverend Hawkins, but the Baptist Church isn't available. They've had repairs scheduled for a long time."

More murmurs.

"This morning we want to think about the soul of Miriam McPhee and what she suffered. This is going to be very hard," she said. "But when Miriam was clean of Josiah, when she was free on those mornings, don't you remember the way she found her voice that first time? How amazed she was? And how that sweet soprano would climb higher up the mountain than anybody's?"

Amen.

"You know why I think of you all as my sisters? Because all of us have had a life inside us that is not our own and somebody has threatened it. Maybe you yourself, like me. Every day, every single day, I pray for those three lives I aborted—not little clumps of inconvenient tissue like they told me, but whole lives. Whole lives, maybe a hundred years long, full of people and experience and love, some touch of love, under the sun and the moon on God's good earth. Oh Lord, to think what I cut off. I was Miriam's age the first time. Fourteen years old, pregnant by my stepfather. I thank God every morning that you women came to Eula's House. You know why? Because there is hope here. Because there's a way to support you and get your baby's life off to a good start. Miriam came here to have hope. Siobhan, you loved her, I know. Can we sing for our little sister?"

After a moment, Siobhan's voice rose above the sounds of weeping in the *Salve Regina.*

"You hop out," Forrest said. "They'll be coming with the hearse, so I should park in back."

Jacob went up the steps and into Stonewall Hill for the first time in six years. His heart was pounding as he gazed around him. Left and right, the foyer had a spacious grandeur, room enough for a splendid gathering. He walked to the center. When they had lived here years before, his family had owned very little furniture, and most of the house had been meaningless—large, dark, empty rooms. But now the place was big with life. New blue-gray paint showed the split-wood texture of the walls without darkening the interior. On the main stairway, women in various stages of pregnancy were going up and coming down, some of them pausing to look at him and comment to each other. Past Hermia Watson's office—DR. HERMIA WATSON, DIRECTOR—was the dining hall with handsome wooden tables on the hardwood floor. Light poured in through the big bow window at the far end of the room.

On the opposite side of the house as he turned, left of the foyer, were the solid wooden bookcases of a library with armchairs, tables, and lamps. Fluted wooden columns defined the spaces without interrupting the feel of openness. He could not remember what had been there before. Separating the library from the next room was a wall with three frosted glass windows, each with a Celtic cross inscribed in its center, and walking backwards fast, Hermia Watson came around the corner, calling "Y'all hurry up!" to the women behind her, who were carrying chairs. When she turned and saw him, she looked confused—and then gaped in recognition.

"Buford Peach!" she cried. "You gorgeous thing! So tall!"

"I'm Jacob now," he said, shy in the presence of the women, who walked past him carrying chairs and looking him over.

"Well, you're just in time, dreamboat! I need your help moving chairs from the chapel to the foyer to get it set up for the funeral. Where's Braxton?"

"Parking in back. Just show me what you need."

"I'll show him!" several girls said.

"No. *Unh-unh*. No, you won't." Hermia took his arm and walked him to the chapel door, which was inset with a stained-glass *Annunciation*, an angel kneeling to Mary. Directing him inside, Hermia genuflected toward the tabernacle and pointed out the folding chairs.

"I doubt if we'll need them all, but let's take them."

Near the entrance was a stack of foam kneeling pads. "These too?" he asked.

"I don't think we'll be kneeling for a Baptist preacher."

- - - - - - - - - - - - - -

As he made breakfast, frying up four pieces of bacon and making an omelet, Chick thought about shutting down the dealership. How many hours had he spent there yesterday? Three, maybe? For what? Partly just to joke around with Tierney. He would hate to lose that little perk. He should make a sign: **If she can't sell parts, parts can't be sold.**

Roof had been miffed when Chick hired her a few weeks back—how could the dealership afford another hire?—but now he kept showing her Parts magazines and pausing over his favorite tailpipes. And he had stopped spitting. Tierney murmured on cue and winked over Roof's shoulder at Chick. Chick almost felt sorry for the man. But in his office, he had gone through unpaid bills and then waited for customers like a spider in a house without insects. At five, he had told Hashbrown and Butler Kelly, his other salesman, to go home.

"Things'll turn," Butler had said. "People need cars."

"They used to," Chick said. "Maybe they're going the way of trains."

No point going in today. The funeral was at 10:00, and it was almost 9:00 now. He and Patricia would go. Hermia said they were not expecting anybody except the girls, and they needed to be there for that poor, scared child. Forrest was coming, she said. Besides them, he thought it would be Hermia, Bill and Nora Sharpe, Deirdre and Jordan, and the pregnant women. Twenty or so, at most.

"I feel old, Chick," Patricia sighed at breakfast.

"We're getting up there."

"No, there's a difference. You look fine. In some ways, better than you did as a younger man, Chick—more dignified, even a little more handsome. But I'm just—I'm turning into one of those old women you see. And I don't even have—I don't have—"

"I know," he said.

She dabbed at her tears, and Chick felt a pity for her that he could not remember feeling in their whole married life. What was going on? Patricia had always been critical of others to a fault, but now her judgmental nature seemed to collapse all at once, and she was once again the girl he had married long, long ago when they were young and in love and had their lives in front of them. Most of the problems came down to Alison. For years, she had been Patricia's project and prize, the gymnast, the prima ballerina, but their daughter had gone her own way so selfishly that it cut Patricia to the quick. Alison's "choices"—that sanctimonious word—filled him with rage. He loved her, but she had chosen self-indulgence over generosity, perpetual grievance over forgiveness. He pulled his chair around the table and put his arm around his wife. He had thought so much about souls, and he now felt intensely what her soul was, wounded, full of fear and regret.

"I love you more than ever," he said. "I mean it."

She straightened up, trembling a little, and sighed deeply.

"I love you too," she said, as though there were something lovably idiotic about him. "We should get ready."

When they arrived at Stonewall Hill twenty minutes later, Chick saw the hearse at the front steps and decided to park in back. Neither Hermia nor Thomas had said anything about a graveside ceremony, but he could get to the car and then to the cemetery easily enough. He pulled up the back driveway and parked between a BMW X3 and a new Toyota Tacoma, which gave him a little burn in his heart.

"Which way?" Patricia asked.

"Let's go through the back," Chick said.

"I forget you know the place so well," Patricia said. Not a trace of sarcasm.

When Hermia turned around outside the chapel, there he was.

"Hey, sweetheart," he said. "You're looking good."

He took her into his arms.

"Braxton," she said.

How did it feel to make a baby with your own daddy?

Her emotions overwhelmed her for a moment, tears sprang to her eyes, and she prayed the prayer always near her heart, *Lord Jesus Christ, Son of God, have mercy on me, a sinner.*

"Where in the world did you get Buford?" she managed to say, patting his back to get him to release her.

"Long story. A project on Sherman," Forrest said.

Lord Jesus Christ, Son of God, have mercy on me, a sinner.

"What's the plan?" he said.

Just as she started to answer, she heard Chick calling her. She led Forrest out into the foyer, where Doug Marshall, the burly funeral director, was directing Jacob and the women how to arrange the folding chairs with an aisle down the middle from the front door, leaving a kind of chancel in front of the fireplace on the inner wall. At the back near the main double doors onto the front porch, Chick stood with Rev. Milledge Hawkins, a thin, intense, white-haired man, who raised his hand when he saw Hermia. She walked up the aisle to greet him. He was dressed in a simple, dark-blue suit, a white shirt with a modestly patterned gold-and-blue tie, and black lace-up shoes.

"Thank you so much." she cried as she drew close.

"You're very welcome. I wish we could have accommodated you at the church."

"Oh, Chick told me. It's just wonderful you can help us."

When the two attendants from the funeral home appeared in the door, he walked back to give them directions. They unfolded a collapsible wheel bier and locked it into place at waist height just inside the front door. He helped them walk the coffin up the steps and onto the bier and then roll it to where he wanted it, five or six feet from the fireplace up front, perpendicular to the aisle, with the head to the left as the congregation faced the coffin. They lifted the coffin to spread a covering over the bier, then set it back down. Chick brought in a movable lectern and opened a Bible on it near the head of the coffin. When Rev. Hawkins was satisfied with the arrangements, he walked over to speak to Forrest.

"Mr. Forrest, thank you for what you make possible here. I'm Milledge Hawkins."

"Very pleased to meet you."

Looking over all the arrangements, he went over and slowly, reverently, opened the coffin lid to reveal Miriam's body. A visible shudder passed through him. He gazed down for a long moment before he walked slowly back up the aisle and out the front door. Hermia had not seen the girl since the moment she disappeared into the hospital, and her heart hurt seeing her now.

As the time approached, the women of Eula's House filed in and took their seats with a formality that surprised Hermia until she saw Nora Sharpe enter behind them. The women filled three rows, still standing, huffing a little, holding their stomachs, constantly adjusting themselves to get comfortable. Before she sat down in the front row on the other side of the Lees—Patricia was being awfully kind—from Rev. Hawkins, Hermia did her usual survey of her women, hushing the whisperers, reseating some of them. She put Jacob Guizac with Forrest and Nora Sharpe on the other side of the central aisle, and she was standing in front, talking to Chick and Rev. Hawkins about the order of the service, when she saw Clover McPhee come in and sit in the back row, followed a moment later by a big, red-haired man wearing khakis, a light blue Oxford shirt, and a blue sports jacket. The man glanced down the row at Clover, but Clover showed no sign of knowing him.

"About ready?" said Rev. Hawkins.

It was time. She nodded at Nora.

Chick felt absurdly responsible for everything, and he was relieved when, exactly at ten o'clock, Nora Sharpe stood up in front and hummed a note and the women broke into "Shall We Gather at the River?" Hermia gazed at Miriam's profile in the open casket and said the *Memorare* silently as the women sang. When the song ended, Rev. Hawkins stood and greeted everyone graciously, deploring the tragic occasion but expressing hope in the saving power of Jesus Christ and the promise of the resurrection. A draft of cold November air came suddenly into the foyer, and everyone turned to glance at the front door. Several men came in hurriedly. One of them gave a thumbs-up to the redhaired man, who nodded and gave a thumbs-up back as they ducked into seats in the back row. A few more people came in after them. Rev. Hawkins glanced at Chick, who subtly shrugged his own confusion. As arranged, he stood to read Psalm 23. All through the psalm, more strangers straggled inside, filling the chairs at the back of the room. When he finished, the women began to sing "The Old Rugged Cross."

Rev. Hawkins went to the lectern again. He read from Thessalonians and made a few remarks about the loss of one so young. "But I would like to call upon those who knew Miriam best to say a few words in remembrance." He glanced at Hermia Watson.

Instead, a powerful male voice came from the back of the room.

"I think I knew her best."

Every head turned. The big, redhaired man stood up from his seat in the back row and nodded to two of the latecomers, who stood up and went outside as he made his way down the aisle to the lectern.

"Yes sir, welcome," Rev. Hawkins said as he ceded his place. "Are you the young lady's father?"

"No sir." Chick had never seen him before, but something about the commanding way he stepped to the lectern and looked out at the people seemed familiar.

"Hiram!" the big man called.

Everyone turned to see what was happening. The front entrance opened and the two men reentered. One carried a pair of sawhorses while the other brought inside a door with its hinges and doorknob still attached. The redhaired man waited for them, took the sawhorses, and then laid the door carefully across them. Solemnly, he turned his back to the people, leaned down, and lifted the body of Miriam from the coffin. The room gasped. The girl had a radiance in death that Chick did not remember when Miriam was alive and Josiah reigned.

"What the hell?" Chick heard Forrest murmur.

The man turned back toward the gathered people and laid her on the door. He raised his arms and looked up for a long moment. When he looked down again, he moved to the body and leaned down and touched Miriam's hair. He kissed her cheek. Visibly trembling, he kissed the lips of the dead girl and then stood upright, lifting his palms, facing the gathering.

"Lord, remember Jairus's daughter. Lord, remember the faith of your servant and in this moment, among these witnesses, call out to her through me, *Talitha koum*. Little girl, arise!" Turning back, he extended his arms above the length of her body.

Rev. Watkins pushed back in his chair.

Everyone leaned forward, not breathing, waiting, watching. Dropping his arms, the man took the girl's face in his hands. "Beloved Miriam!" he said. *"Talitha koum!"*

She looked as placid in repose as though she were sleeping in her own bed and her eyes might open at any instant. Across the foyer near the library, Chick saw a Catholic priest caught, like Rev. Watkins, in evident dismay. The redhaired man bent close to the girl, listening, watching. Chick had never experienced a more intense silence. Was that a breath? The flicker of an eyelid?

At last, the man shook his head and let his hand drop lightly on the girl's brow. When a great sigh went through the expectant room, he stood and nodded. Tears came down his cheeks, and after another silence, he wiped them away roughly and turned to look out over the whole crowd.

"My God, it's Duke!" cried a woman in the back. "Duke! It's me, Clover."

He nodded and gazed at her with an unreadable expression.

"Clover."

"But your eye, what—"

Rev. Hawkins was standing now, trying to regain control of the service.

"I loved this girl. I saw her for the first time when Clover called her from her room to come and meet me, and she opened this door, this very door, and came out, and I loved her as soon as I saw her. Clover didn't like that, did you Clover? I questioned my love. I called it the lust of the eyes, I fought against it, I prayed about it night after night, but the thought of Miriam never left me in peace."

He stopped, head down, and in the silence, Rev. Hawkins said with dismissive authority, "Sir, please sit down. I don't know what you intend to confess here, but it seems to me that the law ought to know about it. Does anyone else—"

"Call the police if you want to," Duke said to him. "Call the law down on me, but *love*"—he opened his hands over Miriam's body, palms down, smoothing the air as though it were a sheet— "love *freed me* from the law, love for this girl who lies here like an angel slain. It would have been better for me if I had never seen her!" Duke shouted, and Rev. Hawkins backed away. "She would be alive now. But she would not be saved! When I saw Miriam again, she was in church beside her mother, and when I saw her eyes and I knew that she knew my love and welcomed it, a new conviction came on me. The great St. Augustine says there is only one commandment: *Love—and do what you will.* Love surpasses law. And Love was on me, power was on me, compulsion was on me. I went to Clover's house again. Like God's general, I commanded Clover, *Bring me Miriam.* My command freed her from her doubts and her responsibilities, didn't it, Clover? Miriam was like honey on the tongue, like dates in the mouth. But I did not knock on this door. I told her that if she wanted me, she should knock. And she knocked on this door from inside her room, and when she knocked, I opened. I opened her door joyfully, this door, and she was lovely, fresh from her bathing. I saw myself in her eyes, and she saw the fullness of love in mine. I said to her, I am the bridegroom. I closed the door behind me and came to her and she took me for her own and I saved her. I saved her, Clover! You know I saved her."

"Saved her, hell!" called a harsh male voice.

A chill went up Chick's back, and he saw Hermia shrink down. At first, he thought it was the dead girl speaking, but the terrified commotion among Hermia's women centered on a young Hispanic girl in the second row. The girl languidly stretched her arms over her head and yawned and looked around at the panic. "Bet you thought you got rid of me. All I ever wanted was to be left alone, but hell no. Cast out, belittled, my house taken and burned, my daughter raped and me mocked and now this goddamn mess." Duke edged away from the body, all his bluster gone, glancing up the aisle as Clover stood and rushed out through the front door. Rev. Hawkins stared at Chick, who saw on his face an outright terror, as though at last he had come into the presence of the people he had always read about with such calm assurance, the unruly crowds at Capernaum pressing forward toward Jesus, calling out, needing to be healed.

"I'm so sorry," he said, and to Chick's dismay, he walked up the aisle and out the front door behind Clover.

"Well, I guess I run off the preacher," said Josiah. "But hell, we still got Duke. Got that eye patch, like he plucked an eye out for offending him. Says his daddy's a general, which is also horseshit. Fact is, he's not Duke but Fr. Timothy Shearer—"

"God damn you," Duke snarled.

"You're way behind on that wish."

Forrest was standing now, walking toward Duke, so Chick also stood up. The girl held out a hand toward them.

"Y'all be still. Lemme tell you about this Duke, who used to be Fr. Tim, which sounds a little softer around the edges. He's on the run from a little case back in Troy, Michigan. Took an altar girl straight from the confessional on a Saturday afternoon. They found her pretty thoroughly used at a hotel in Detroit two days later. Fr. Tim, he was long gone. But I guess you couldn't give it up, could you?" he said to Duke. "I come to help when he said he wanted to send my little girl's baby to Jesus. And look at her. Look at my baby."

Duke strode up the aisle, fumbled open the front door, and fled down the front steps. The other strangers—followers, maybe, or friends of Clover—followed him out and closed the door behind them. After a moment, the girl straightened in her chair and stared confusedly around. She seemed to be coming out of it, to Chick's immense relief.

But then she saw Forrest standing next to Chick.

"Braxton Tecumseh Forrest, home at last. Do these folks know you got you a baby with your sister *and* your sister's daughter, who was—my goodness—*your* daughter, too. And here she is, Hermia Watson, right here with her Sugar Daddy. Why Hermia, honey, you could go on one of them talk shows." The girl pretended to hold a microphone and said in a whispery voice, "*Miss Watson, how did it feel to make a baby with your own daddy?* And Chick Lee here, too? Got to keep your men close by."

Chick felt himself flush scarlet as Patricia's face darkened. Oh Lord. It had been going so well.

Hermia desperately beckoned to the priest across the foyer.

Just that morning, Fr. Silber had found the Rites of Exorcism online—an unauthorized book, no Imprimatur. *The exorcist should be prepared to have the demon reveal the exorcist's sins, especially those which he has forgotten and not confessed and those for which he has not received absolution.* He felt no confidence that his soul was in good enough shape to confront the devil. Sometimes he woke in the middle of the night remembering some gratuitous meanness he had committed in his childhood or his teens. Other kinds of fantasies, never even to be hinted at among his parishioners, sometimes overcame him. He had not been to confession in weeks—and who knows how many sins he had forgotten?

This demon was broadcasting secret sins on a live feed, Hermia Watson was calling him to act, and Fr. Silber felt his own sins pressing forward to be revealed, his own weaknesses. Jesus felt like an abstraction.

Hermia gestured to him again. *Please please please* said her praying hands. He could not move.

He felt like a security officer paralyzed with fear during a school shooting. But exorcism was not so simple. Twice in his seventeen years as a priest, he had encountered people who might be possessed. There was a proper procedure, and he had followed it. He had notified the Bishop of Savannah, who had called in the trained exorcist of the diocese. Psychological and medical examinations had revealed that the first case, a boy from Dublin, was probably not suffering from possession, since therapy and medication helped him, but the second was more serious. The priest had carried out a full-scale exorcism on the woman, a widow in her fifties, all outside Fr. Silber's purview. Hermia had hinted at a possible possession the night before, but she should have told him weeks ago, and he could have taken the right steps. The evil thing had probably intimidated her. Even a rumor could undercut her good work. He had suspected something dark in her background, but nothing like what the demon had just revealed.

"Help us!" she called.

Fr. Silber suppressed his terror and started forward.

The girls around the possessed one were a tableau of fear. And then the thing's eyes fell directly on Fr. Silber.

"O sweet goodness!" he said with obvious relish. "Who have we—"

Someone brushed past Fr. Silber, and the voice stopped instantly. To Fr. Silber's surprise, it was the tall boy he had seen during Duke's performance and its aftermath. Pushing aside the chairs, the boy knelt down in front of the girl.

"That's not her talking," the boy said quietly.

There was a moment of choking laughter. The thing tried to mock him, but the words failed. What in the world? Fr. Silber wondered. The girl slid from her chair onto the floor, where she lay flat on her back, panting, back arching, her legs spread, knees up, as if she were about to give birth.

"Why don't you leave her alone," the boy asked reasonably, leaning over her.

With a long, rattling exhalation, the girl straightened her legs and went as still as Miriam, who lay dead on her bedroom door a few feet away.

"Come out of her!" the boy said, this time emphatically, in a voice that bore more command than any boy's could.

A shuddering wave went through the girl's body like something rolling under her, starting at her feet, lifting and dropping her limp legs, her pregnant belly, her torso and lifeless arms, and finally her head, thrown upward and falling back with a dull thump. A thin, terrible, inhuman flicker of tongue came out between her lips. And then to Fr. Silber's horror, the dull-brown, wedge-shaped head of a snake emerged from the girl's overstretched mouth; its scaled neck inched upward, wet with the sheen of her saliva. Above the girl's gaping mouth, it opened its own cottony-pink mouth with its dripping fangs.

The girl convulsed again, blue-faced, choking on the snake that wriggled free of her mouth like a live root pulling itself loose from tight soil. The snake's head and neck struggled upward—more of it—an arm's length of it now emerging from her throat and dropping onto the floor as it came, twisting up out of her body among the screaming witnesses, four feet long now, five, until at last the whole length came free from her and gathered on the floor as the girl's body fell back, gasping. They remained at the center of a circle whose wide circumference was comprised of the remaining spectators. The snake coiled, the head rising wide and thick as a man's hand, cold eyes fixed on the boy who still knelt calmly, his face and neck inches from it. It reared back to strike, white mouth open.

Fr. Silber thrust out the crucifix of his rosary.

"In the name of Jesus Christ, begone!" he cried.

He could not remember ever having said the word *begone* in his life. The serpent turned toward him. There was a long hiatus, or so it felt afterward, when nothing happened, as though many possibilities and fates were under consideration. And then the thing drew back, not far, still coiled, closing its mouth, tongue flickering out, holding him with the knowing malice of its eyes.

He had never felt such terror. Snakes had always terrified him—not the cold otherness of them but the familiarity, as though his own spinal cord had suborned the bottommost instinctual district of his brain and slipped free of the backbone and dropped hungrily, resentfully, into the dirt underfoot. And this was the loose, malevolent spine of some dark angel with no body at all.

But he spoke again.

"In the name of Jesus Christ, begone!" he said, commandingly, thrusting forward the crucifix.

It wavered and flowed back a little. It knew him, it knew him all too well, but he fought down his terror and raised the crucifix a third time.

"Begone from her, in the name of Jesus Christ," he commanded, astonished to feel the live power of his own words.

Again it wavered, as if considering whether to strike, but then dropped to the floor and uncoiled into a long S, flowing toward the inner wall of the house across the stone flagging of the fireplace. It could not have been more than a few seconds, but it seemed an eternity of fear and malice. When Forrest picked up a poker from the tools and struck at its back, it started to fling itself again into a coil to defend itself but then it seemed to panic at the limitations of its own body. It flowed fast toward the back corner of the fireplace and squeezed downward into a crevice, convulsing as it had when it came from the girl, cramming itself fatly in, spasming as Forrest struck it again, until the last lash of its tail jerked down into darkness.

Fr. Silber prayed, feeling less the exultation of victory than the certainty of what more must surely come. The boy still knelt on the floor, and Fr. Silber put his hand on the boy's shoulder gratefully.

Hermia stood trembling. She had not felt more completely alone since the time, all those years ago, when her stepfather had left her childhood bed that first time, that first time, when she was fourteen and bleeding into the sheets and could not tell her mother, because he had said it was their secret and put his finger over his lips. That commanding finger. That kingly silencing. Their secret, just their secret again and again until a child clouded the blue sky of her future and then her mother took her to that clinic and that killing and still more alone then, O Lord God O

Jacob came to himself on the floor of the foyer of Stonewall Hill. He was kneeling for some reason, and he looked up to see a priest standing over him, patting his shoulder. He was middle-aged, much shorter than Jacob, a little plump, with graying hair and a startled look as Jacob rose from the floor.

"Thank you, son. That was—well, it was magnificent. God bless you."

Sitting in front of Jacob, cross-legged and sobbing, was a young pregnant girl he did not know, clutching her throat and gagging disgustedly.

"Thank you," she croaked to Jacob. "Oh my God, thank you."

He felt empty and disoriented, though not as profoundly as he had six years ago at Stonewall Hill when he could not remember his own name. He knew who he was and where he was, but not what was going on. Folding chairs had been knocked askew in every direction from the neat rows he had helped arrange that morning. The women of Eula's House stood in a rough circle around him, one of them with a baby in her arms, all staring at him with expressions he could not understand. Near the chair where they had sat in front, Mr. Lee was talking to Forrest, who seemed to be trying to stop up a hole in the fireplace.

The body of Miriam McPhee still lay on the door across the sawhorses.

Hermia Watson had come up beside him.

"Aren't you something?" she said and touched his face. "Are you okay, honey?"

"I'm okay."

He stood up shakily. God, he wanted to talk to Emily. For days, they had done nothing but text. He wanted Wyoming—mountains and sagebrush and vast distances. Clear air. He even missed Sherman.

"So what's going on?" he asked Hermia Watson.

She was about to answer when the priest called for everyone's attention.

"Friends, we still have Miriam with us. Let's get her back into her coffin. Where are those men from the funeral home? Son, maybe you can help," he said to Jacob, touching his arm.

The two men from Marshall's Funeral Home rolled the bier with the coffin on it close to the door across the sawhorses.

"Can you get her feet, buddy?" one of them asked Jacob. "I'll get her head and shoulders and Jimmy can support the middle. You're going to need to swing back around this way, you see what I mean?"

"I guess," he said. Miriam's feet lay slightly splayed on the wood of her bedroom door. Strange that Duke had wanted her bedroom door. What had he said? *She* knocked and *he* opened? Not *he* knocked and *she* opened. Sherman had directed the battle of Atlanta with the body of McPherson laid on a door in the same room with him. His mother liked to quote Simone Weil's saying that the only people who really exist for you are the ones you love. But Sherman was used to dead bodies. Jacob had found his grandmother's body rotted into the bed out at Missy's Garden. When he hit his head and forgot his name. A different name.

He had never touched a dead body.

He took Miriam's cold heels in his hands. His stomach clenched, and he felt the leverage of her bones as they turned her body in the opposite direction and lowered her into the box. The two men arranged her and closed the coffin.

Everyone looked at the priest.

"I'm going to use my own authority to offer the Mass of the Dead. Ordinarily, you need to have been in the Church," he said, "but there's no time to clear it with the bishop. We're also going to baptize this baby during the Mass for her mother."

One of the women held a tiny infant.

"We need the permission of the parents for a baptism, but Miriam is dead and Duke—or Fr. Shearer—has vanished. I want Professor Forrest and Miss Watson to act as the parents. Are you willing?"

Hermia nodded uncertainly.

"Of course," said Forrest. "But you have to hear my confession first."

"Godparents," said Fr. Silber. "Mr.—?" He extended an interrogative hand toward Jacob. "What's your name, son?"

"Jacob Guizac."

"Godfather?"

"I mean, I guess."

"And Jordan?"

"Thank you, yes," she said.

"We'll gather in fifteen minutes in the chapel. Mr. Forrest, can you come this way, please?"

The two men from the funeral home were smoking cigarettes at the far end of the porch when Jacob excused himself and went outside, still a little unsteady. He nodded to them and walked down the front steps onto the circular drive. He could not rid himself of the feeling of Miriam's body as he helped lift her. The whole morning seemed unreal.

He needed to talk to Emily.

How long had it been? Today was Tuesday, November 17. They had left De Smet on Friday, November 13. Just four days.

He got out his phone—four bars—and checked his texts. Nothing from Emily since yesterday. He wrote a second reply to the last one she had sent. *Please call me. I love you and I need to talk to you.* He needed to hear her voice. Mobile phones were famously forbidden at Transfiguration. Emily could easily have used hers at her parents' house in town, but she hated cheating and wanted to obey the same rules as everyone else. Aware that it was futile, he called her number anyway, and of course it went directly to voicemail. *Hi, this is Emily, please leave me a message.* It did him good just hearing her voice, though, which sounded ironic saying the simplest things. *Hi, this is Jacob. Please leave me a message. Seriously, Emily, call me, please, please, please. On bended knee here. I need to talk to you.* She wouldn't hear it, but maybe she would intuit his desperation and make up some reason to ask for her phone. Except that she hated lying as much as she hated cheating.

Fr. Silber used a small room off the chapel to change into his vestments. He went in and turned on the lamp, closed the door, and sat down. Atrial fibrillation. He bent forward, breathing as calmly as he could, shuddering at what had happened, touched his chest, and waited for the fibrillation to pass. When it finally did, he took a deep breath and gazed down at the crucifix he had used to expel the demon—a three-inch bronze one blessed by St. John Paul II. The cross bar bent downward and the corpus of olive wood was patterned on the Giacometti-like figure of agony that JPII used. Fr. Cuddy had given it to him at St. Joseph's in Macon when he was just a seminarian many years before.

He heard the women preparing for the Mass. Using the number stored on his phone, he called the office of the Diocese of Savannah and asked for the bishop, but he was attending the General Assembly of American bishops and cardinals. Virtual this year, the woman told him. Was there anyone else who might be able to help him? Should he explain the situation to her? He thought not. He was on his own here. He needed to clear his head before he could say the Mass. He silently prayed a *Memorare*.

There was a knock at the door. Forrest. He took the chair across from Fr. Silber and made a long and harrowing confession that left Fr. Silber shaken. When he left, the atrial fibrillation started up again. There was another light tap at the door.

"Fr. Silber?"

He offered Hermia Watson the chair where Forrest had sat. He held his hand over his heart, head bowed.

"My women all know most of my story," she said. "It's part of my work with them—but not this. To be mocked like that. Right in front of him."

"Meaning Mr. Forrest," he sighed. "I know your benefactor, Hermia."

"More than that." When Hermia Watson met his eyes, he dropped his. He did not want to hear this.

"Braxton is my *father*, which I never knew until I was a grown woman living in this house. And he is also the father of my son. I knew that a long time before I knew that he was my own father."

His soul felt her wound. He did not speak at first.

"Are these," he said at last, very quietly, "the most important things about you?"

"It feels like they're so dark they can't be forgiven. I feel bound in my sin."

"Have you confessed what you did? What you consciously did?"

"Of course."

"Then you have received absolution. Listen to me, and I will say again what you heard: 'God, the Father of mercies, through the death and resurrection of His Son, has reconciled the world to Himself and sent the Holy Spirit among us for the forgiveness of sins; through the ministry of the Church may God give you pardon and peace, and I absolve you from your sins, In the Name of the Father, and of the Son, and of the Holy Spirit.' Your response is Amen. Say it, please."

"Amen."

"Believe that you have been forgiven. Your past is the story that the accuser can use to shake your faith. You're no different from any of us. We have repented, and Christ has forgiven our sins. Though your sins be as scarlet, they shall be as white as snow. We are assured of that over and over."

"But now you want me to stand there with a baby and say it's *ours*. Mine and Braxton's. It's just—it just seems—"

Fr. Silber nodded. "The girl's mother did the right thing in bringing the girl here to you. That was the right thing, Hermia. That was a blessing. This can be a blessing, too."

When she left, he slowly began putting on his vestments. What he was doing was irregular. He would have to answer to the bishop. He hoped that God would forgive him. He would say a funeral Mass and ask the eulogists to save their remarks until just before the final blessing. The baptism would immediately follow the homily.

They celebrated Mass in the small chapel—five rows of eight seats, divided four on a side by the center aisle. Miriam's coffin, closed now, was in the aisle near the front. Forrest, Hermia, and Mr. and Mrs. Lee sat on the gospel side in the front row, and Jacob sat on the other side with Nora Sharpe, Jordan, and Deirdre, who held the tiny, sleeping baby. Nora led the women in "Amazing Grace," the opening hymn. The Mass had a lovely sense of order and ritual after a morning of such wild disorientations. Braxton Forrest read from the Book of Wisdom. The women sang Psalm 27—"The Lord is my light and my salvation; / whom shall I fear?"—and Jacob Guizac read from Romans with such sincerity that Chick Lee's wife touched her eyes with her tissue. After Fr. Silber read the Beatitudes, he left a long silence before he spoke.

"I did not know Miriam. But Our Lord knows her, and He loves Miriam as He loves each of us. We need to give up our self-accusation, all of us, and believe in our forgiveness and discover who we are in the love of God. Let's remember Miriam in that love. Before the final blessing, I will ask those of you who have some words for Miriam to come forward and honor her life, but at this time, I would like to call forward the parents and godparents of Miriam's child."

Deirdre gave the baby to Jordan, who stood with the boy as Hermia and Forrest came forward. Jordan carefully gave the baby to Hermia, who took her up, smiling at the tiny fingers clutching at her thumb.

"In the Name of the Father and of the Son and of the Holy Spirit," Fr. Silber said. "What name do you give your child?"

Forrest looked at Hermia, obviously blank, and gave a small shrug.

"Madeleine Miriam Forrest," Hermia said loudly.

Forrest shrugged and nodded.

"What do you ask of God's Church for Madeline Miriam?"

"Baptism," said Hermia.

"Baptism," said Forrest.

"You have asked to have your child baptized. In doing so you are accepting the responsibility of training her in the practice of the faith. It will be your duty to bring her up to keep God's commandments as Christ taught us, by loving God and our neighbor. Do you clearly understand what you are undertaking?"

"We do."

"Praise Jesus!" cried one of the women of Eula's House. Many of them were weeping openly.

Fr. Silber turned to Jordan and Jacob.

"Are you ready to help the parents of this child in their duty as Christian parents?"

"We are."

And the baptism went on. Then came the Liturgy of the Eucharist. Before he gave the blessing, Fr. Silber asked who would like to say a few words about Miriam. Anybody but Duke, he said.

Chick was startled when the redheaded girl he had once seen in the dealership and again the day Miriam died started moving awkwardly up to the front.

"Tell it, Siobhan," one of the women said.

"You knew her, girl," another one added.

Siobhan stood at the pulpit, self-conscious, unused to speaking in public, but she lifted her head and wiped the tears from her eyes.

"Some of y'all knew Miriam, but I think maybe I did know her better than her mama. She would tell me things at night after everybody else went to sleep. I mean, I have a little sister her age and I kind of miss that little witch, you know. Miriam had her problems," she said, raising her eyebrows, and there was a murmur of laughter. "But she was a sweet girl, she was. Maybe too sweet, you know, the way she would give in if she saw you wanted something? She was funny, the way she saw things. But not about Duke. All that stuff he said. I mean, how would you be if your mama was to give you to somebody like that and it was just going to be one time? But y'all, she was so scared of him. He lied about all that. She was so scared."

She wiped her eyes again, and she was collecting herself to tell Miriam's stories, when they heard voices in the front of the house.

The intentions of Zitek and Lykaios could be reconstructed much later, at least in part, from their notes and texts. The plan was clear enough. They had left a bomb threat on Hermia's office phone, the same number where they had left the threat earlier that fall: Hermia would see the message light flashing as soon as she sat down at her desk. The women would once again evacuate the premises while the authorities came to investigate and once again find nothing, undercutting the credibility of any real threat to Stonewall Hill. Watching from nearby, Zitek and Lykaios would wait for the police to leave and take advantage of the half hour or so before the return of the women to set the house on fire. Burning the meager possessions of the residents would be justified by their liberation from Eula's House. It would be like accidentally burning the slave quarters in the act of destroying a slaveowner's plantation.

It might have worked. It was a regular workday, a Tuesday, but Hermia Watson did not go into her office at all because of the funeral. Zitek and Lykaios waited in the thick underbrush of the side yard (police later found the area) for any sign of evacuation. Several people arrived, but they saw no one leave, which incensed them. Why were they not taken seriously? No police came, either, which confused them. After an hour or two, one of them, probably Zitek, pulled out a pint of vodka (police found the empty bottle) and they began to drink, abandoning the relative sobriety that had made them more effective arsonists the Sunday night before. At one point in the morning, they saw several people leave hurriedly from the front door, apparently in a panic, which convinced them that their threat was being taken seriously. Residents must also be fleeing from the rear of the building, which they could not see. Allowing the evacuation a few more minutes, they then cautiously approached the front porch. A hearse sat in front of the steps, and they saw two men smoking, their backs turned, on the far side of the yard.

This scene must have puzzled them, but when they eased open the front door, they found the great foyer empty. A curious humming or murmuring came from deeper inside the house, but they did not consider it important. As Zitek sloshed out the gasoline from one of the two-gallon containers he had brought (he left them both behind), Lykaios gloated loudly that they were finishing what Sherman had started, and Zitek told her to be quiet. Everyone in the chapel heard them.

. . . .

"Find out where they buried the silver!" came a woman's rising voice, followed by her laughter.

"I said keep it down," they heard a man say.

Forrest stood up. "That's Zitek!" He beckoned to Jacob.

Siobhan paused in mid-sentence. Her eyes widened.

"I smell gasoline!" Forrest shouted.

Siobhan's water broke.

. . . .

Zitek had a very white shaved head. Lykaios was a spiky blonde. They kept trying to start the fire, but as Forrest and Jacob Guizac burst into the foyer, their resolve suddenly collapsed. They threw down everything they had brought and ran drunkenly out the front door and zigzagged down the drive as though someone were shooting at them. They crashed through a boxwood hedge and a line of cedars to the car they had left on the side of the road early that morning. The Gallatin police had left a ticket under the windshield wiper. Zitek began to curse, because now the police had the license plate number and could track the Rav4 back to Lykaios. Not only that, of course, but Forrest and the boy had seen them in the act of pouring gasoline. The boy had been making a video with his phone as Lykaios flicked match after match at the gasoline feeling its pungent way across the wood floor from the tipped-over can Zitek had dropped and pouring itself down through a floor vent. Not a single match would light. Worse, the house had not, in fact, been evacuated: it was full of more people than usual because of the funeral. Zitek and Lykaios could and probably would be charged with attempted murder as well as attempted arson, not to mention being caught for the actual arson in Atlanta.

Zitek's curses could be heard for blocks. He must actually have imagined that, because of his high purpose of rectifying history, he could burn this last bastion of the Confederacy with impunity and even be applauded by those few who recognized his hidden hand and understood his noble intention. This honor, however, depended entirely upon not being caught. Enlightenment must have struck him as he drove at sixty miles per hour up the four blocks of Lee Street toward the courthouse square, savagely pounding the steering wheel and screaming *we're fucked we're fucked we're fucked* (according to multiple sidewalk witnesses). Lykaios held one hand on the ceiling, one on the dashboard, as she screamed curses at Zitek. Their car skidded past the red light into the intersection at Main Street, just missing a Greyhound bus. A pickup truck edged forward, its driver cursing and giving them the finger, and then sped around him as Zitek backed up to get out of its lane.

They stared across the dead grass of the square at a historical marker about Gallatin County. It was a normal November morning in Middle Georgia, sunny and cool. A few people were coming down the courthouse steps. A block away, on the next corner, the statue of the Confederate soldier stood facing north, ignoring them. Zitek and Lykaios stared at it. Their ruined futures stretched out before them. What last gesture could they make?

Just at that moment, Forrest speculated, Zitek snapped.

20

EULA'S SHRINE

THIS TIME JACOB FOUND A CORNER OF THE LIBRARY. EMILY had still not called or texted or emailed, and his anxiety was beginning to build. She had forgotten him. She had found somebody older and more sophisticated. He watched the women as they went up and down the stairs, wondering if any of them knew how wrenching and terrible love could be. Would any of them understand what he felt for Emily? Or would all of them understand immediately? Would they mock him or sympathize?

Forrest had told him to call his mother. He had missed five calls from her that morning. No voicemails, but a text saying ANSWER YOUR PHONE! Maybe she had heard something about Emily. He touched the number.

—Jacob! Thank God! I've been trying to call you all morning. Why don't you answer your phone?

"There was a funeral here at Stonewall Hill. And Jason Zitek—I'll have to explain it later, Mom. Are you still in Salt Lake City? How's Dad?"

—That's why I was trying to call you. They're working hard with your Dad, but I don't know. He's still on the—he's been in this coma now for two weeks, and if they can keep him alive—oh honey, just saying it makes me cry—if they can keep him alive, he could be in the coma for several more weeks. I'm right here, but I can't see him. I don't know where he *is*, you know? He said something about dreaming all the time. He said such strange things to me the last time he was awake.

"Me too. About Sherman."

—Sherman! I know! Now he's in your dad's imagination. This damn Sherman. Excuse me.

Jacob smelled smoke, and he glanced around curiously. Probably something burning in the kitchen.

"Well, Sherman is a little like dad actually."

She was silent for a long beat.

—I have no idea what you mean by that.

"Disappointed for most of his life."

She was silent again.

—Okay, look, I've heard from Rose. She's still living with that family in France, and they don't seem quite as nuts about the Covid situation as people are here. Here, it's all Trump's fault or Fauci's fault, or it's the CDC, or it's a Chinese plot to kill off old people. Anyway, she's on a farm out in the countryside of France, and it sounds like the family loves having her. She might have a boyfriend. A French boy.

The smell of smoke seemed to be getting stronger. Deirdre came out from the dining room and asked some of the women to go up and check around to see if anything was on fire.

"Mom? Have you talked to Mrs. Forrest lately?"

—Several times a day. I want to make sure Cate and her kids are okay at the house. I talk to Little M.

"Does Cate know about Zitek?"

—She knows he burned their house down.

"He tried to burn down Stonewall Hill this morning. I thought I was coming for Sherman, but I mean."

—I tried to warn you!

"You were just worried I'd be too far away from Dad if something happened."

— I knew you were going with Braxton Forrest.

"There's a lot I don't have time to tell you. It's a lot more complicated." The smell of smoke was stronger. "Listen, Mom, let me call you back later. I need to help out."

—Oh my God, Jacob. Call me back!

Deirdre and Jordan had the women checking everywhere, upstairs and downstairs, to see where the fire could be. He walked through all the downstairs rooms, checking everything, and came into the kitchen just as they all saw smoke billowing up from a vent in the floor. They looked at each other.

"Eula's shrine is under there," one of them said.

"Oh my God," Jordan said. "Those candles."

By the time Forrest found the ER entrance, Siobhan was panting and wailing in the backseat of Marisa's BMW as Hermia held her. Under the overhang, a policeman and several big orderlies gestured irritably when Forrest pulled up. The policeman immediately came to speak to him.

"Sir, we've got an ambulance coming. I need you to move up."

"I've got a woman in labor in the backseat."

The policeman glanced through the window at Siobhan.

"Let's get some help here!"

The orderlies opened the back door and helped Siobhan inside the building as Hermia followed them. The policeman motioned Forrest forward. He found a spot in the parking lot, and he was almost back to the ER when an ambulance came barreling up, siren fading. The orderlies helped the paramedics roll out someone on a stretcher, an oxygen mask over the face. Another ambulance came up the driveway, less hurried, as the first one pulled forward out of the way. Forrest watched with a horrified conviction that it was Zitek and Lykaios. The second body on a stretcher had the sheet pulled up over the face.

"Mask!" barked a nurse as he came in through the sliding glass doors. He fumbled the thing from his pants pocket and pulled the elastic behind his ears. Hermia, wearing a blue paper mask, beckoned him closer.

"Can you do this?" she whispered, nodding to the receptionist. "I was just here with Miriam."

He sat down in the chair in front of the window. The receptionist looked considerably undernourished, but it was hard to see why. Ignoring Forrest, she worked a chocolate donut into her mouth without lowering her floral mask and sipped through a straw from a can of Coke beside her keyboard. She typed something, she raised her eyebrows at something on her screen, she clicked a few times with her mouse, she yawned, she rolled her head on her neck, she called back over her shoulder to someone he could not see. She did not look at Forrest. Finally, when she had allowed sufficient time for him to recognize her immense power, she called loudly, "Next!"

He said nothing.

"Next!" she said.

He did not speak.

Finally, she looked at him, irritated.

"Okay, what?" she finally said.

"We just brought in a girl who's having a baby."

"I saw her. From 'Eula's House'?" she said with undisguised sarcasm. "Name?"

"Siobhan."

"Funny name for a white girl. You want to spell that?"

"S-i-o-b-h-a-n," he said.

She looked at him to see if he was trying to fool her, then pursed her mouth and typed it in wrong, spelled it back, corrected it, corrected it again.

"Not that it makes a lick of difference, but last name?"

"Don't know."

"Don't know." Her mouth worked bitterly as she typed. "I hope somebody over there's keeping track of these women. That girl last weekend and now this one. Seems a little random. Sort of like an animal shelter."

Forrest tapped on the glass and leaned forward. "I'm coming in."

Startled, the woman jerked back to see him so large and so close.

"Cain't nobody come in here."

"I just want to get closer to you, sweetheart."

That flustered her a little.

"Somebody's gone need to fill out this form."

She retrieved several sheets of paper from the printer behind her and clamped them on a clipboard along with a Bic pen wearing a plastic sunflower that made it highly unwieldy. She passed it sunflower-first through the opening at the bottom of the window.

"I hope you ain't the daddy."

"May I?" Forrest said. He pulled the sunflower off and handed it back to her. "I have allergies."

"Take a seat, sir."

A TV in the top corner of the room babbled with some game show.

Down at the far end, Hermia raised her eyebrows at him. He walked past a thirty-something black woman and sat down across from a solid, red-faced man in his fifties, who was leaning forward, keenly alert and anxious, his heels bouncing from the balls of his feet.

As he studied the clipboard, Forrest thrust out his bottom lip and widened his eyes in case the receptionist had him under observation. He guessed at answers. Name? He did not want to ask Hermia for Siobhan's last name in front of the receptionist, so just Siobhan. The Duke principle. He had no idea what kind of insurance the women had, even though he was paying for it and he must have signed for it when Hermia asked him. He could not remember the street address of Stonewall Hill. Lee Street? He did not have the phone number—wait, he could find that. He had it on his phone. Nope. Hermia's mobile number, not a general office number for Eula's House. If there was one.

He sighed and walked over to surrender the clipboard to the receptionist.

"You're gonna need somebody with more information," he said. "I'm just helping out."

"So who's got it? That woman the other night runs the place and she didn't know diddly," the woman said, dropping the board on her desk with a clatter. "I can see her sitting there, by the way, but it ain't no use to ask her."

"Listen, I'm interested in the man they brought in earlier."

"Why's that? He the daddy?"

"Nothing to do with the baby."

"Say his name," the receptionist said. Forrest said it, and the woman sighed. "Spell it."

Forrest spelled the name Zitek.

"Where y'all come up with these?" she said. "His relation to you?"

"Son-in-law. Can you just tell me if he's the one they admitted."

"Looks like it."

"Can you tell me how he's doing?" After wanting to kill Zitek himself, the thought that the man might die filled him with dread for Cate.

"No sir. Can't share no information."

Forrest frowned and took his chair again.

"Here for a baby?" asked the man across from him.

"Partly. How about you?"

"My wife. She was making lunch and suddenly grabbed her head and said *Oh my Lord* and keeled over. When she came to, she didn't know me. Just like that. Just like that."

"That's terrible," Hermia murmured. "I'll be praying for her."

"Hugh Maddox."

Forrest shook hands as he and Hermia introduced themselves.

"I know who y'all are," Maddox nodded, his legs still bouncing nervously on the balls of his feet. "Y'all are kind of famous." After a moment, he looked up at Forrest again. "You hear what happened up at the courthouse?"

"No sir."

"That's what the ambulances were when you came in. That statue up on the square."

"The Confederate soldier. Oh Lord," Forrest said, filled with another premonition.

"These two swerved around in the intersection of Johnston and Lee, caused a couple of wrecks. I was stuck there trying to get my wife to the hospital."

"A car dodged them and ran right into me," the woman said.

"That was you?" said Maddox. "Everybody okay?"

"They're checking my boy for a concussion." She lifted a palm to them. "I'm Dottie Hodges. You went to school with my mama, Mr. Forrest. Patricia Redding. She remembers you."

"She was a brave girl. One of the first four black students at Sybil Forrest High School."

"Oh, I grew up hearing all that."

"So what happened to the statue?"

"These two parked in the middle of the intersection facing it and the woman got out with spray paint and started defacing it. Everybody was telling her to move the car," Maddox said, "including me. But then the driver got out, and I couldn't see what he was doing—"

"I could," said Hodges. "He was like a dog at a fire hydrant."

"Is that what it was?" Maddox asked. "People were laughing and holding up their phones, and the guy just lost it. Cussing, waving his arms. He got in the car and revved it up, and people scattered, except for the woman. She had more sense than he did. She had both hands out to get him to stop. Jumped right out in front of the statue, yelling, Stop! Stop! But he gunned it right into her."

"I'll never get that picture out of my head," said Hodges. "That poor woman."

"The base was built solid a century ago," said Maddox, "but he hit it hard enough to tip the statue over on top of the car. I heard them talking about life-flighting him to Macon. But that woman, Lord."

Forrest sat without speaking for a long time.

"He killed her?"

"Crushed her right into the base of the statue."

They all sat in silence for a long moment.

"That's my son-in-law," Forrest finally said.

The man stared across at him, and then as comprehension broke, his face changed. Mrs. Hodges had both hands over her mouth.

"Oh sweet Jesus. That was your daughter. I'm sorry, I didn't—"

"That was my son-in-law, but the woman wasn't my daughter."

Another silence.

Before they could speak again, a nurse came to the door and said quietly, "Mr. Maddox?"

Her demeanor foretold bad news.

In the back of the house, Jacob flung open the overlapping storm doors. Concrete steps led to a low, square, plywood door set into the foundation of the house. Smoke was leaking around its edges. He flipped up a hook-and-eye latch and pent-up smoke immediately blinded him. He bent over coughing and blinking, edging inside, waving his hands in front of his face to try to see where the flames were. He saw the little shrine in flames. Fire was licking up along the beams supporting the floor of the kitchen and spreading as he watched. Zitek's gasoline must have leaked down and run along the pipes and beams to the back of the house and dripped onto the burning candles and the offerings and remembrances the women had left for Eula. He backed out coughing, hitting his head twice. He ran to the back door and shouted inside, "Call the fire department! Where's a hose?"

Deirdre shouted back that the hoses were in the shed. She pointed and he ran. They were neatly coiled on hooks at the back. He looped the nearest one over his shoulder and ran back out and over to the back of the house, where he scrambled to screw the hose onto a faucet near the door to the crawlspace. Smoke was billowing up because he had stupidly left the door open and a strong draft was feeding the flames. He turned on the spigot, uncoiling the length of the hose behind him as he waded down into the smoke, water gushing from the nozzle in his right hand. He blindly ducked into the crawl space, immediately hitting his head again. He held the hose in front of him and thumb-sprayed the water into the interior, opening his eyes as much as he could stand to see where the flames were. Smoke seared his lungs. A wracking cough, more smoke. No air. He gasped, more smoke. Could not breathe had to get out.

He fought his panic. The door? Lost. Nothing but smoke. Crackling close by. He turned again, again, praying, trying to see, and finally saw light. But when he stumbled toward it, the fire opened its white mouth, fanged with flame, drawing back to strike, and he lifted the hose to spray, feeling the gush in his hand, but no more hose, the end, the end. His eyes closed on burning ash, and he could not breathe, and he pulled furiously, needing the hose, not wanting to die.

And just then realized the hose would lead him back.

He kept it taut, letting more of it drop behind him as he followed the live cool length, hand over hand, ducking low, a screaming need for air, trying not to breathe, keeping his eyes closed. He sipped a breath and smoke impaled his lungs. He hit his head hard, bumped along a pipe, hit it again, but felt the light increase. He stumbled toward the opening, hit his head on the frame, burst up the steps tripping out into daylight and onto the grass, the leaves and dirt and roots. Crawled forward. *Away away away.* Here was air, here was air. Facedown in wet leaves. Breathing. It hurt, but he was breathing. Thank God. Good wet cold air.

But the house was still burning. How would they hose down the flames? He puzzled over the question and tried to get to his feet and fill his lungs so he could go back down under the house but he could not get up. Someone helped him. Someone else shouted a name. His name? He had forgotten his name again. Someone grabbed him by the shoulders and turned him. His eyes felt like hot cinders.

Water gushed into his face. Yes! *Yes!*

But they were spraying him instead of the fire! He rubbed his eyes, beginning to see a little now. Another gush of water hit him and he flailed his arms.

"The fire!" he tried to shout.

"Here they come!" someone said.

Roar of a truck up the driveway, shouts of men.

The sense of urgency left him. He sagged, coughing and knuckling his pupils of ash.

Someone took his elbow.

"Come on with me, buddy. Jesus, let's—oh man, let's get somebody to look at you."

"I'm okay," Jacob said. But his head got very light and the day went dark.

Forrest and Hermia sat with Mrs. Hodges after Maddox left broken by the news about his wife. When she, too, left with her bandaged child (no concussion), Hermia sat with her hands folded, her eyes closed. Praying, Forrest supposed. As much as Cate or Bernadette, she was his daughter, not from his marriage, but from his passion for Marilyn Harkins, whose very name stirred his feelings after half a century. Had he somehow known Marilyn in her features when he first saw Hermia that weekend at Northwestern? How could he ever have suspected that she was his daughter? There had been no oracle. He had not presumed upon a familiarity, as Sherman had with Ellen Ewing—his foster sister, a girl who grew up in the same house. A kind of spiritual incest. Forrest was innocent by comparison. He could not have known that Marilyn was his half-sister or that he had a daughter with her. Or that he had a son with that very daughter.

And yet his very ignorance made his liaisons feel as fated as the crimes of Oedipus.

Now, thinking about Hermia, he bowed his head, pierced with remorse about what he had done to her life. Hermia at fourteen had not been like Cate or Bernadette at fourteen. More like Miriam McPhee. He had never done anything hurtful to her deliberately, though, unlike what he had done to Zitek. Eula's House was recompense, and now Zitek had come to ruin it because he hated Forrest. He had felt it bitterly, he realized, when Zitek wrote that column in *Phoe* about removing the statue of Robert E. Lee from a park in Atlanta—as though the man had researched Lee and anguished over the monument. It was never about Lee or Sherman. No, Zitek was privately planning his divorce and publicly flattering a constituency indifferent to the institution of marriage, much less its betrayals. He wanted to appear woke, anti-racist, *comme il faut*. The piece was all smugness and cant. It was Zitek being vain and servile, indulging some adolescent fantasy of being approved by an elite of his own imagining—rich, beautiful, casually contemptuous of anything traditionally held to mean something.

But did it help Cate and her children to ruin Zitek? No, it was just revenge. Revenge for what? For Zitek's ingratitude, for his rejection of his faith, for his repudiation of the beautiful life of loving each other and their children that they had imagined him building with Cate. It wasn't his public revelation of Zitek's adultery that got him fired. No one gave a shit about that. It was Forrest revealing that Zitek called his boss Bullwinkle—the implied contempt, especially after Ludwick had already lost face by having to retract the "You Lose Plantation" story. And then, after getting him fired, Forrest had confronted Zitek in a homicidal rage. He had spared him, thank God, but Zitek had burned down his own house in retribution. He had tried to burn Stonewall Hill, destroyed a public monument, and crushed to death the woman for whom he had rejected his whole previous life. In two days, Zitek had destroyed his future. But Forrest had expertly helped him. Not once had he intended anything charitable. He had been full of hatred and pride. He had felt the sense of injured merit of Milton's Satan in *Paradise Lost*.

Now, thinking about his son-in-law near death in the intensive care unit, he felt his own sin crushing him. He felt the Accuser.

He sighed. Hermia glanced up, sympathetic.

"What are you thinking about?"

"Zitek. Marisa and I loved him."

"You did a lot for him."

"Lately, I've done a lot *to* him. I got him fired from his job in Atlanta. I goaded him and provoked him. I don't think he would've done what he's done if he hadn't hated me. He thinks I scorn anybody who accepts my protection or favor. The more I helped him, the more he hated me."

Hermia nodded. "'So burdensome still paying, still to owe.' I've felt that a little toward my Sugar Daddy, as Josiah would say." When he glanced at her, she shook her head, and she touched his arm. "We knew not what we did." He held her gaze until she took a long breath and dropped her eyes. "I'm not sure where his life goes from here."

Her warmth and sincerity moved him. He was about to ask her to pray for her sister Cate when the electric doors opened and two men in uniform stepped into the lobby, one of them a local policeman, the other a State Patrolman as tall as Forrest. His uniform was immaculate, his pistol formidable. The receptionist went big-eyed and respectful when he leaned over to speak. Forrest saw her nod and then point eagerly at him. He could tell that she hoped she had gotten him in trouble.

"Major Rufus Adams, Georgia State Patrol," said Adams, offering his hand and not wincing at Forrest's handshake. "This is Officer Bill Smiley of the Gallatin Police Department. May we speak to you privately?"

"Sure."

Beneath the overhang outside, Major Adams led the questioning. "Sir, the receptionist told us that you know the man who was brought in this afternoon."

"He's my son-in-law. The woman with him was not my daughter."

Adams met his eyes. "I see. Your name?"

"Braxton Forrest."

Officer Bill Smiley's mouth pinched to the side and he winked at Forrest. What was that about?

"Could you spell your last name for me, sir?" asked Adams.

"F-O-R-R-E-S-T."

"You could have just said two r's," the major smiled.

Smiley winked again. A tic, Forrest realized. But something more, too. The man didn't like it that Adams, a black man, was in charge.

"Your son-in-law's name?"

"Jason Zitek."

"Could you spell that for me?"

"One T."

Adams laughed. "You got me. Seriously, though."

"Z-I-T-E-K."

"Thank you." Adams checked something on his phone and nodded. "Mr. Forrest, are you aware that Mr. Zitek is wanted by the Atlanta police?"

"I'm not surprised."

"Is there some reason that, as the part-owner of the house he burned down, you have not contacted the authorities?"

"Look at that. You already knew how to spell my name."

"Yes sir."

"I went by there yesterday. I had a more urgent matter in Gallatin."

"I see. Are you aware that the insurance policy on the house in Atlanta is voided by arson on the part of the owner?"

"I am. Zitek's not much of an owner. Five percent, to my recollection. Zitek did it to get back at me. He was separated from my daughter and having an affair with his editor at *Phoe* magazine, Melina Lykaios."

Smiley winked, winked.

"Get back at you for what?" asked Adams.

"It's a long story."

"Where is your daughter?"

"She and my grandchildren are staying at the home of a friend in Wyoming."

"Wyoming?" When his phone buzzed, Major Adams held up a forefinger and he took the call, wandering over to the edge of the overhang.

Officer Smiley took over. "The insurance company wants to press charges. They say there was some kind of collusion between you and your son-in-law."

His big stomach and wheezy voice reminded Forrest of Andy Devine, but he had a meanness in his eyes.

"I'll get in touch with my lawyers." That was a problem far down on his list.

"You hear what your boy did uptown? He killed that woman outright and like to killed several other people the way he was backing out into traffic. All because he was after that monument."

"And drunk."

Smiley winced and winked, winked.

"How you happen to know that?" Openly suspicious.

"Because he and his girlfriend were splashing gasoline all over Stonewall Hill and trying to set the place on fire. He was drunk when he left. I bet you he was still drunk two minutes later."

"How come you didn't call it in?" Smiley said accusingly. "I heard you was paying for them women down there," Smiley said, making it sound indecent. "Checking out the prospects, I reckon."

Forrest stepped closer to the man. "Sounds like that's what you've been doing, Officer Smiley."

Just then, Major Adams stepped between them and thanked Forrest. They exchanged phone numbers and Forrest started back inside. Smiley gave him a smirk and an upward jerk of his jowls when Forrest glanced at him.

Just as he sat down, a masked nurse came to the inner door and opened it slightly. "Miss Watson?"

Hermia started and stood up. The nurse pushed open the door just enough to display the newborn tucked into her arm.

"Oh praise God!" Hermia exclaimed, hurrying toward her, but the nurse drew back protectively, shaking her head.

"Got you a little boy." The nurse had a sugary, lingering voice.

"And how's Siobhan?" Hermia asked.

"Doing fine. She wants to see you, but of course we can't take you back there."

"Not even masked?"

"No ma'am," the nurse said. "It's hard."

The nurse held the baby long enough for Hermia to get a good look at him. She sat down next to Forrest with a sigh of relief.

"Thank God for some good news!" She reached over and put her hand on his and then withdrew it. "Thank you for being here." She shook her head and smiled ruefully and then she bent over to hide her face. His heart heaved strangely. "I'm sorry. I'd better get back to the house if—" She sat up wiping her eyes with a tissue from her purse. A lovely woman. "What a day." She gathered her purse and began to stand up when her phone vibrated on the end table next to her.

"Deirdre?" She sank back, her hand over her mouth. "Oh my God!"

As a boy of ten or eleven, he had been at the county fair on a hilltop outside Gallatin when news of a house fire spread through the crowd, and people left the lights and noise to find enough darkness in the parking lot or a little way down the hill to let them stare across the county's dark pastures and woods and creeks at the house many miles away. It was as distinct in the clear night as a burning city descried from the sea.

Stonewall Hill would be a conflagration far more unforgettable. He had always pictured it at night. When he had caught Josiah Simms trying to set fire to it years before, the consummation of burning had come closer and felt more inevitable. It had been fated ever since Sherman bypassed Gallatin and left intact old Farquhar McIntosh's elegant home. It was not spared, though, but merely fate delayed, decade after decade. Dread filled him now. They would go out into the parking lot and look to the east and see the smoke billowing up, huge and ominous like the end of days, the fulfillment of the little sunshot column of smoke above the house in Atlanta.

When Chick got to the office, Joe Ashburn greeted him with news: he had sold a new Explorer that morning. Not only that, but Butler Kelly had a friend of Bill Sharpe's coming back in the afternoon to look at one of the new F-150s. As he paused at the door of his office, Butler flashed him a thumbs-up from across the showroom.

"Told you," he called.

"One car!" Chick said.

"*Two.* Things are looking up," Ashburn said, and Chick felt a strange fondness for the man.

At his desk, he nudged the pile of bills. Taller every day. Selling a car or two might let him pay several of those, but not all of them. He needed a secretary to help get them in order, but how would he pay her? Suppose things did turn. Instead of thinking about closing the family business just short of its seventy-fifth anniversary, he could have a sale like the famous Moonlight and Madness back in the summer of 2009. Actually run a business instead of pretending to.

He turned on his computer, scrolled down through his business emails.

A couple of ominous-looking ones from Ford Headquarters in Dearborn. He snoozed them until after Thanksgiving.

He was rattled from the morning. This Duke character. Then Josiah turns up and Forrest's son-in-law tries to burn down the place. Quite a Tuesday. He was glad Patricia had been there or she would never have believed it. On the other hand, he dreaded having to answer for what Josiah had said about him and Hermia.

Speaking of Josiah, he had mentioned the name of a city. Athens? Cairo? Someplace in Michigan. He couldn't quite call it up. He stood up and started to turn off the computer when the name popped into his head.

Troy.

Might as well. He sat back down and typed "Troy Father Tim kidnapping" in the search bar.

And there was Duke, younger, smiling. A story about—

His phone buzzed. *Patricia!* She was already after him.

"Patricia. What's up?"

—Stonewall Hill is on fire!

He shot to his feet.

"I thought Forrest had run those people off!"

—Hurry!

"I'm coming."

He burst out the door of his office and shouted to Ashburn that he had to go back to Stonewall Hill. Ashburn flashed him a V.

"Trouble, Boss Man?" Tierney called from Parts.

Chick just waved at her and headed out the door for the Lincoln, keys in hand. He gunned it up College Street into town, where he saw emergency lights flashing in the intersection at the courthouse square. He slammed the brakes and stopped, open-mouthed. The Confederate soldier was gone, the sad-looking soldier marching north with his rifle on his right shoulder. The statue had been there his whole life.

He turned left a block before the square, paused at Main, and then accelerated through the back streets to the cemetery and out to Lee Street, where he turned left and saw Stonewall Hill rising from its majestic grounds a few blocks away. He did not see the billows he had expected. He gunned the Corsair down the hill and started left at the fork to use the back driveway but braked hard when he saw fire engines blocking it. Lights rotating, fat hoses snaking from the hydrant on the street across the yard over the stone walls and through the shrubbery toward the back of the house. He turned and started toward the front gate when a pickup truck blared at him as it passed on his right. City Plumbing. The driver gave him the finger as though he were in Atlanta and they would never see each other again.

The hearse still sat in front. He parked behind it and ran up the steps into the foyer, where smoke played eerily along the ceiling. Nobody there. Nobody in the library, nobody in the dining room. He ran to the chapel and looked inside. The coffin lay on the bier as before. He crossed the dining room to the far door into the butler's pantry and kitchen where smoke hung heavy. He snatched a dishtowel from the hook in the butler's pantry and wet it in the sink to cover his mouth and nose.

He had just crossed the doorjamb into the smoky kitchen when a fireman came through the back door and turned on a firehose. A taut torrent roared across the kitchen, and Chick leapt back just in time to keep from getting hit. It smashed everything fragile and movable against the wall, hurled the burner grates on the island stovetop into the window and sent glass dancing and shimmering above the scattering pots, the frying pans, toasters, blenders, vases of flowers, trays of growing herbs, blocks of knives. Cabinet doors burst open. Plates bowls mugs glasses danced in the gush and crashed down to shatter on the stone counters as soon as the stream passed on.

Abruptly, the water stopped.

"All good," the fireman called to somebody outside.

Water covered Chick's shoes and poured through the pantry and spread across the polished hardwood floors of the dining room, flowing down through any vents it found. Cautiously, he stepped into the devastated kitchen. Outside the back door, firemen stood talking and smoking. He heard the women in the yard singing "How Firm a Foundation," and it struck him as funny. Smiling, he dropped the towel in the butler's pantry and crossed the wet dining room, socks squishing, to the denuded chapel and the coffin. He felt along the lower edge of the coffin lid to see if it had been nailed shut. It had not. It rose smoothly on its hinges.

There she was. Miriam.

There she was. Her upper lip was a perfect cupid's bow over a plump lower lip. Her nose was a little thick at the nostrils, her complexion darker than her mother's, with a sprinkling of freckles across her nose and cheeks. Perfect eyelids, long eyelashes. She would have been a lovely woman. Already fully a woman in size and shape, but a child still in mind and soul.

Everything these days was about being a victim, and she was definitely a victim. And not a victim. Was Juliet a victim? He remembered Olivia Hussey playing Juliet in the movie that came out when he was still in high school. Full of passion but you wouldn't call her a victim, young as she was, which was Miriam's age. He remembered being fourteen, callow and yearning, all lust and hard-ons and leaping semen and shame and stupidity and self-doubt. He remembered dwelling on the images of girls. Plunging into sin and never thinking once that it was sin. Except that it made him feel unclean.

He prayed for her soul. He was weeping.

"Mr. Lee?" someone said behind him. "Are you okay?"

Startled, he turned. It was Jordan.

"Yes, sorry," he said.

Through the open chapel door, he saw firemen checking for smoke. The women of the house looked stunned as they came back into the house. And then Patricia appeared in the threshold.

"Chick! How long have you been here?"

"Just a few minutes," he said, carefully closing the lid above beautiful Miriam. "What's the plan?" he asked Jordan. "Will there be a procession? A graveside ceremony?"

"We're waiting for Miss Watson."

He and Patricia walked out into the empty foyer. He could still smell the gasoline.

"Look at me," Patricia said, stopping him. "Chick, look at me."

He met her eyes, his mouth twisting, expecting a bitter reproach.

"That boy saved this house."

He cocked his head.

"He took a hose down in the crawl space where the fire started and nearly died of smoke inhalation. But when he found out that the baby was still in the house—"

"What baby?"

"The one from—"

"They left Miriam's baby?" he exclaimed.

"Hush!" she said. "You can't make them feel any worse than they already do. One of the women put her in Hermia's room when they were getting that redheaded girl out to the hospital, and nobody thought of her in the panic about the fire."

"My God!" Chick cried.

"She's only been here a day, and she was sleeping so quietly. That girl who was going to help with her is off having her own baby."

"But my God!"

"Listen to me. As soon as that boy realized little Madeleine was still inside, he ran straight into the smoke and found her. *That boy*—" Patricia said, her composure dissolving, her eyes shining. "He just saw what needed doing and *did it*," she said. "He didn't think about himself. Not at all."

She took Chick's arm. They walked out the front and the two men from the funeral home emerged from the far side of the house.

"Were you guys just going to leave the coffin in there while the house burned down?" Chick shouted.

"Waiting for instructions," one of them said.

"Sweet Lord," Chick murmured.

Patricia was still smiling as they got in the car.

"Suppose Alison had met a boy like Buford Peach," she said wistfully.

Emily called him back, as always happened, when he didn't have his phone. He had left it in Jordan's car when she took him to Urgent Care and explained what had happened. The doctor shook his head. *That's why people die in fires.* He had inhaled burning particles and gases. Smoke inhalation was serious stuff. He wouldn't be able to run for a couple of weeks, but his lungs would recover—well, unless he got Covid on top of this, which would really be dangerous. He hadn't been exposed, had he? Jacob explained that his father was in the hospital in Salt Lake City with Covid. *So you were exposed? How long ago?* Jacob had to think. Election day. Two weeks ago. *And you haven't had any symptoms?* Nope. *You're probably okay. You might even be immune. Nobody knows much about this thing.*

So he got back to the car, picked up his phone, and the first thing he saw was the name Emily Turnbow. That beautiful name that had some secret connection to his heartbeat. Just listening to her voice on the message made him feel better. The mere sound of it could heal him. What had he been worried about, exactly? It was just that he loved her so much he could easily imagine other guys loving her for the same reason. Grown men. CEOs, statesmen, winners of the Nobel Prize for Literature. That little live twist of her mouth, the quickness of her response to what you were thinking or feeling, and her eyes, especially, the way they would meet yours, not all the time, but sometimes with this focus that tested for soundness or sincerity in whatever you were saying or feeling, as though she were taking it inside her into some mysterious, fertile depth that knew things. Her eyes would meet his—and *whoomp*—some kind of quick deep shock, and his heart would stand up like a watchdog hearing a new sound. It sounded stupid even when he tried to say it to himself.

He played the message again, holding the phone to his ear as Jordan left the hospital and headed toward town.

—*Jacob, I'm so sorry I haven't gotten back to you. It's been a strange time here. My dad has gotten Covid, too, probably from the students. His isn't too bad. It's going through Transfiguration big time. I haven't gotten sick yet, and I guess I'm just lucky, but there are people out at the reservation who have really been hit hard. Lots of deaths, at least ten so far. Several of us have been going to the hospital to sing and play for them, and I always think of your dad. We have to stand outside. Dr. Toner asked me if I would play some Mozart, and I saw all these faces in the windows smiling at me. I think Dr. Toner likes me. Anyway, it's been very busy going back and forth between school and home. Leave me a real message. Tell me when we can talk. I love you.*

"Emily," he said into his phone, which turned it into text. "I love. You. Too." He looked to make sure it had recorded without converting his words into something obscene or senseless, and then pressed Send. Who was Dr. Toner? He pictured one of the young professors, maybe in his early thirties, a brilliant theologian or poet who also played cello or violin and did things outdoors—rock-climbing, white-water kayaking—and had enough energy to organize extra charitable work and also bring up his eight or ten brilliant and pious kids, who were all in training as triathletes before they reached the age of reason. He couldn't remember exactly what Dr. Toner looked like, and it killed him. Crackles of jealousy arced through his blood. Of course, Dr. Toner liked Emily, why wouldn't he? Which meant she would like him—and then the image mercifully came: Dr. Toner was the tiny, white-haired woman who worked with the choir at Transfiguration. Dr. Turnbow had introduced Jacob to her one night that fall.

It was absurd how relieved he was. They were already almost to the courthouse square, where lights were flashing.

"Emily, huh?" Jordan said.

"Cut it. Out," Jacob rasped, smiling at her.

"Do you feel like walking over there?" Jordan asked.

He shrugged his consent, and she pulled into a parking place on the opposite side of the square from the monument. Several people glanced at him because of the bandages on his face and hands. Minor burns, considering. They skirted the crowd that had gathered. The area around the monument had been cordoned off with yellow crime tape. Jordan gasped as soon as she saw the damage to the base of the statue, which was stained a dull red, and the statue itself broken loose from its pediment. It had fallen forward onto the SUV that Zitek and Lykaios had been driving.

"Oh my God," Jordan said, both hands over her mouth. "I can't look at this."

Jacob nodded. "I'll be. Right back."

The police had closed off the block. He moved through the crowds milling around, taking pictures, speculating about who had done it and why. *Some fool*, a man said as he turned aside to spit tobacco juice into the brown lawn of the courthouse. Whenever he would go to the courthouse square as a boy during those years when his father had run the *Gallatin Tribune*, he would sit and stare at the monument. The pose was anything but dramatic—a common soldier marching with his rifle at rest on his shoulder. The graveyard in Gallatin had a hundred and fifty graves inscribed with the same word: CONFEDERATE. All of them anonymous. It struck him now for the first time that—*of course*—the statue represented those nameless men and boys in the cemetery. Maybe at the beginning of the Civil War there had been a stir of fiery rhetoric about states' rights and secession. But this statue was about melancholy duty—all those ordinary Southern men who went off and fought and died, not because they wanted to defend the institution of slavery and the pride of the planter class but because they were drafted or otherwise bullied by circumstance into fighting even when the war was obviously lost. Most of them were his age—or younger. All those boys killed at Griswoldville trying to stop Sherman's March. Many of the ones who didn't die lost an arm or a leg, and all of them who lived through the war came back half-starved and humiliated to a South ravaged by Sherman and his bummers, wondering *What now? What was that for?*

He walked back across the courthouse lawn, and he was opening the door of the car when his phone buzzed. *Emily.* He raised a just-a-minute finger to Jordan.

"Emily. Thank. God."

— You sound terrible! Are you okay? What did you mean about being in the doctor's office? Have you gotten Covid?

"Wow. Slow. Down."

— My dad's sick, and I'll probably get it, if I don't have it already. I'm at home. I've been having this headache all afternoon.

"I'll. Text you."

He could not figure out how to talk on the phone and text the same number at the same time, so he ended the call. He was not as dexterous a flicker-thumbed texter as some of his friends, but he managed to say that there was a fire at Stonewall Hill and that he got smoke in his lungs when he tried to help put it out. He also had a few burns. He could almost see her eyes, the full deep shock of her whole attention. She called him back.

—What's Stonewall Hill?

"Wait."

The house where I used to live in Gallatin.

—You're in Gallatin?

"Yes," he said out loud.

—Well, you sent me an email from Atlanta, but the last time we talked you were somewhere in Alabama. You said something about Gallatin and what's going on there now, but—I don't know—this headache is killing me and I can't concentrate right now. You want to try to talk tomorrow?

"There's a. Lot. To tell you."

—Tell me something right now.

"I'm thinking. It."

It was hard to say how, but he heard her smile.

—You haven't let your DNA nose around somewhere else, is that what you're telling me?

"My DNA. Has something. Urgent. To say. To you."

—Hush your mouth, Jacob Guizac.

"Say my. Name again."

—Jacob Guizac. Say mine.

"Emily. Turnbow."

—Say the poem you wrote me that first day.

"Can't. Breathe."

—I'm not sure I want to put Guizac at the end of my pretty name. It's like a burst of static. *Guizac.*

"How about. Peach?"

—Listen, I think I'm getting Covid, no joke. I'm getting chills. Come home. I miss you.

When Forrest opened their room at the Travelodge that night, the lamp between the two queen beds was already on. Either they had forgotten to turn it off, or the maid who cleaned the room had left it on for them. 10:03 said the red digits of the bedside clock. They were both dragging. The boy had bandages on his face and hands from burns, some of them second-degree, but not worse, thank God. His main problem was breathing: each breath brought an audible rasp as though he had asthma. The doctors at Urgent Care had given him an inhaler. *Better than burning niter paper, which is what Sherman did in San Francisco,* Jacob texted Forrest. Still thinking about Sherman. They had almost put him on oxygen, but apparently his oxygen was still in the high eighties even with the damage from the smoke. He was supposed to put an oximeter on his finger every hour or so to check his oxygen intake, and if it got below eighty-five, he should reconsider.

"Quite a day," Forrest said as he dropped his keys and wallet on the dresser.

"I keep. Thinking. About Zitek."

"Zitek?"

"Realizing. What he. Did."

Forrest shook his head, thinking of his brief conversation with Cate. Her tears. *Oh God! Oh God!* Marisa warned him not to say anything bad about Zitek.

"You go on and get ready for bed," Forrest said. "I still need to talk to Hermia and figure out what we're doing tomorrow morning. I'll walk outside while I make these calls. You need anything?"

"I'm. Pretty tired."

He had a strange look in his eye. The trauma of the day's heroism was working its way into him. Forrest remembered him as a boy—that clear-eyed, almost uncanny presence he had. Something of the same thing now.

Forrest took a room key and walked out into the parking lot and around the pool where he remembered sitting years before when he had first come to Gallatin. Thinking of Marilyn Harkins in her teens. All that passion. Another life. Now his concern was for the women at Eula's House. Hermia had given him the list of sixteen names. He patted his pockets and found it folded up in his shirt pocket. He unfolded it and glanced at the first few.

Siobhan Neely, 19. Fort Valley.

Siobhan *Neely.* That wasn't so hard. The hospital had discharged her a few hours after her delivery, worried that it wasn't healthy for a mother and her newborn to be around Covid cases. Or maybe because the insurance was questionable. But it wasn't healthy for her to be at Stonewall Hill, either, so Patricia Lee insisted that both Siobhan's baby and Miriam's newborn be brought to her house. Chick had brought two cribs from Stonewall Hill over to his place, and Siobhan and her friend Lashawnda were both set up in Alison's old bedroom.

Lashawnda Adams, 17. Atlanta.

Jo Linda Ashburn, 20. Roswell.

Bella Amorosa, 18. Marietta.

Couldn't picture Jo Linda or Bella.

Teresa Gomez, 16. Milledgeville.

The one Josiah had picked. He shook his head. It all seemed impossible. His phone buzzed.

—Can you talk now? Hermia said.

"Is everybody okay? I hope they got enough to eat."

The kitchen at Stonewall Hill would be unusable for days. Forrest had given Jordan and Deirdre credit cards, and the girls had bought hamburgers, tacos, fried chicken, and several large pizzas. After a call from Chick, Rev. Hawkins had let them use the church hall to camp out.

—We ended up having more than we needed.

"Are the women okay tonight?"

—Uncomfortable. But it's better than Eula's House. They're going to need to check it out to see if it's safe for all these girls. I didn't know smoke was so dangerous. They were pretty ferocious about getting us out of there.

"I'll call a cleaning service tomorrow."

—Wait until we hear from the inspectors. The fire department did a quick look, and they said it could have been a whole lot worse if Jacob hadn't gone under the house with the hose. He kept it from getting into the structure of the house, so we got the smell of smoke but not heavy smoke damage. I hope we can do it if it's not too bad—you know, if it's mostly cleaning the surfaces, laundering the curtains, washing our clothes. It will give us a good work to do.

"It can't be good for those girls."

—We'll see. What time do you want to get started tomorrow morning? We're going to keep it simple, right? Just meet at the cemetery?

"That's what I was thinking. I told Marshall to have the grave dug by early tomorrow. Why don't we say 9:00 a.m. for the graveside service? They'll bring the coffin and we can all meet there."

—I'll see if Fr. Silber can come down.

"That would be good. Let's just work with his schedule."

—I'll call him as soon as I hang up. I hope he's still awake. Listen, there's something else. The thing I've been dreading.

She fell silent for a moment.

—Somebody from the Department of Human Services is coming to Stonewall Hill tomorrow afternoon. There might also be somebody from the Department of Child Protective Services. I'm expecting to find them officially horrified, especially after the fire.

"It's my house," Forrest said. "I'll be there with you. I can be a pretty intimidating old man when I want to."

—*So* scary.

When he got back to the room, the light was still on beside the bed, and Jacob was not asleep. He was sitting up in the bed with his head propped on two pillows, gazing in front of him with a fixedness that instantly alarmed Forrest.

"You okay, buddy?"

No answer. Forrest could hear wheezing, but the boy did not seem to be in any physical distress. It was one of his flashes, one of the trances of his childhood that had emerged again in what he had seen and written about Sherman. It wasn't like the demon who had stolen the name Josiah, who could see your secrets and read your unconfessed evil, but some strange deep sympathy. Maybe a form of love.

"Jacob?" he said quietly.

The boy did not answer. He was elsewhere. Forrest could read on his face the subtle weather of his emotions. Who was it this time? Surely not Sherman again. But what did he know about a boy who would risk his life twice within a few minutes to save people he hardly knew?

He floored the accelerator and the hybrid leapt forward over the curb and ripped through the stiff shrubbery and he was screaming *Banzai!* when Melina leapt in front of him, her arms outstretched, her hands toward him, her mouth going NO NO NO her eyes meeting his for a fraction of a second before the car smashed into her and burst her body against the base of the statue and her organs exploded and her face slammed into the hood of the car and her head whipped back against the base of the statue where the word "Confederate" was spelled in raised letters they had spray-painted over. The airbags exploded and slammed his body back against the seat, the frames of his glasses ripping into his eyebrows and cheeks and then the roof crushed inward and

Rewind.

Again. Again.

Was there something he could change? Hit the brakes in time?

An odd thought occurred to him: he should not have done it at all. Not burned his house in Atlanta, not tried to burn Stonewall Hill, not tried to destroy the monument. Not left C—

But how could it be wrong?

But then why had Melina—

Oblivion.

Again. Tilting, toppling—shaken loose, not firmly embedded in the concrete, but tilting, crashing into the car her car the airbags exploding in his face.

Again the questions.

Who? he asked, coming once again out of the blackness. He looked around him. Hospital, IVs hooked to his arms. Nurses in masks, doctors in masks. One of them saw him and said something to the doctor, who turned.

Mr. Zitek?

He tried to nod. Nodding?

He passed out again. The scene replayed. Melina screaming for him to stop. That instant when she met his eyes. The horror as her pelvis was crushed against the concrete, her torso slammed down onto the hood of her own car, head whipped back into the stone

bursting face

smear

He knew what Hell was. Hell was to be conscious of himself and to be alone forever. Just to be himself. This was hell. This would be hell forever.

Again he woke up, opened his eyes, surrounded by faces. It was a mercy that there were others. Just others.

Mr. Zitek?

Doctors. Policemen.

Mr. Jason Zitek?

Policemen.

He tried to think. What had he done? He had burned his house. Couldn't he do what he wanted to with what he owned? He could smash his TV or burn his books or destroy whatever was his. He could burn his house. He could destroy smelly memories. Baby shit. Arguments. Stink of vomit. His wife's demands. Love me. Womansmell, habits, demands. Love the children. Pay more attention. Give them more time. Give me your life. Every bit of it. Be a slave to a Wife for Life, an awful lawful. Cate would not do this and would not do that but Melina would do anything. Melina would drink as much as he drank and never never never tell him to stop as long as he could give her what she wanted. He was a genius and her wildness set his genius free. She called him a legal slave when he talked about his marriage. She called

Cate Moo-Cate. She said the children looked stupid and smelled bad. She was the one who bought the gasoline.

So he could burn his own house. Shedding his doubt felt like a mouthful of liquor. Swallow. Let it come.

Destruction was his greatness. His liberation was destruction.

Policemen were fascists. Everybody knew that. Everybody said that. Defund the police. Law was just whiteness.

So.

The scene replayed. The death.

Jason Zitek had killed Melina.

Mr. Zitek?

He could not answer, but the men were still talking.

We'll need to talk to him when he comes around. Any idea when it might be?

Too soon to tell.

He saw Cate weeping. Moo-Cate. Where was she? Boohoo.

Weeping for *him*, and his children praying for him. *Jesus, please let Daddy live.* Stupid bullshit. But Clare prayed. And Jimmy. And the one he had been so angry about when Cate told him she was pregnant, the one who was going to cost so much money. What was her name, that little one? Avila. Falling asleep in her high chair, her little hand on a tangerine.

He had burned their house. Why had he hated them so?

Because Melina would do anything? Even right in her office. Right in her office.

But they were his children. Jimmy, Clare, Avila.

Pain was starting up, terrible pain. Whatever they had given him was wearing off. He saw himself in a mirror up on the ceiling. A broken body, a thing.

One thought kept tormenting him.

He had seen Melina in time. His felt his foot on the accelerator. He could have let up. He could have veered off.

There was a truth coming and he did not want it but he was helpless as it came rushing toward him.

He had wanted to kill Melina.

When he came back from the bathroom, the boy was asleep. A strange gratitude had come over Forrest, as though he had crawled onto a beach after a shipwreck. He crossed himself and said a prayer for Marisa and Cate and the children, for Hermia and all the women at Stonewall Hill, for Teresa and Walter and Little M. For the boy in the next bed. For Zitek. For the tender mercies of God.

21

GRAVESIDE

FORREST GOT UP EARLY, THIS TIME NOT DISTURBING JACOB, who had risen at least once during the night to use the inhaler. The boy would recover quickly, but he needed his sleep this morning. Picking up coffee and a sausage biscuit at McDonald's, where a cute cashier at the first window gave him a big smile and almost qualified for his waitress list, Forrest drove over to the cemetery in the half-light of dawn. Gallatin Cemetery. Miriam's mother had disappeared without making any suggestion about the disposition of her daughter's body. Why it fell to him to decide was one of those cosmic ironies best not examined too closely.

He rolled slowly down the paved central street of the cemetery, reading the headstones, the names he recognized from his childhood: Evans, Fletcher, Cox, Hill, Wright, Ivey, Honeycutt. Fitzpatrick, his beloved coach. Among the gravestones, whole complicated stories, every name interwoven, one way or another, with every other, like the root systems of aspens. A sensibility had vanished from the America of iPhones and Instagram. Social networks, but no deep past, no awareness of bodies and places and the reality of death, which pressed upon him now with a daily, melancholy insistence. What was that poet's name? Edgar Lee Masters. *Spoon River Anthology.* When he was little, his grandfather would sometimes bring him to the cemetery, cane in hand, and point out names and tell story after story, so many stories and names that his head would begin to ache.

He parked in front of the monument his grandfather had ordered for himself to ensure that his own story would have to be told—conspicuous in the middle of the cemetery, ten feet high, topped by a life-sized statue of a weeping angel. Under the name of Thomas Jefferson Forrest (1874–1964) was the inscription, "Give instruction to a wise man, and he will be still wiser; teach a righteous man, and he will increase in learning."— Proverbs 9:9. Below his name was Sybil Devereaux Forrest (1899–1971). "Charm is deceitful, and beauty is vain, but a woman who fears the LORD is to be praised."—Proverbs 31:30. Speaking of ironies. If someone could have given instructions to make his grandfather wise, he would have told him to marry someone besides Sybil Devereaux, whose charm was altogether deceitful and whose vanity was boundless.

Forrest wished he could remember one note of kindness from his grandmother, but he could not. She had vehemently insisted on disowning their son, Robert Forrest, whose grave was in the northeast corner of the plot, not acknowledged on the monument itself. Forrest's own mother had been buried back in Wisconsin, where he had visited only once since her death. Sybil Devereaux's niece, he suddenly remembered, had married Judge Lawton in Macon. *Lucinda*. Walter Peach's foster mother. He stood transfixed for a moment, feeling again the unreadable hint of a greater pattern.

Hermia had given Miriam McPhee's beautiful little daughter the name of Forrest, but it did not feel right to claim Miriam herself. Maybe they should bury her at Stonewall Hill. He remembered finding a graveyard once when he was exploring the property, a shrouded, mysterious memory: dense woods, the rotting remains of wooden markers scattered among tree trunks that had grown through the bones of the dead. When he mentioned it to his grandfather, old T. J. Forrest had not known of it, and when Forrest took him out to see it, his grandfather speculated that it was where the McIntosh family buried the slaves. The markers had probably been made by the slaves themselves. He had forgotten it until this moment. Hermia would want to find it and raise it from its dishonor and anonymity—if they could find it again. But why would they bury Miriam there?

He stood by his car, frustrated by having to decide something so quickly, when he saw the even more prominent monument that he remembered climbing in his childhood. The McIntosh plot was separated by a lane and a low stone wall from the section that contained the bodies of three hundred

Confederate dead, all but one of them "known but to God," men who had been brought south to the temporary hospitals in Gallatin from the battles with Sherman's army in the spring and summer of 1864. The bare word "Confederate" appeared on each stone, like the inscription on the statue Zitek had toppled.

Forrest walked over, stepping past the graves of people he had known. Bill Stewart, Ellis Newton, Robert Jenkins. Memories crowded him, wanting a taste of blood.

The McIntosh plot was large by Gallatin standards in this village of the dead—twenty feet of marble curb on each side. On the base of the marble monument, the name McIntosh was chiseled distinctly. Above it was an inscription:

> So stately his form, and so lovely her face,
> That never a hall such a galliard did grace;
> While her mother did fret, and her father did fume,
> And the bridegroom stood dangling his bonnet and plume.
> —Sir Walter Scott

Odd for a gravestone. Some irrecoverable story. Digging with his foot at indentations in the stubbornly rooted dead grass and fallen leaves, Forrest found stones embedded in the ground above four graves along the southern side of the monument, Farquhar (1804–1870) and Minerva (1820–1851), Lachlan (1836–1891), and Duncan (1840–1906). One of these sons had chained the pregnant Eula beneath the house. He had forgotten how Hermia substantiated the story. Letters? Diaries? On the western side of the plot were five small graves with names but no dates: Iona, Callum, Maisie, William, and Graham. He thought of the man in Jacob's story about Big Shanty. Probably one of the diseases that swept through and killed whole families—probably Minerva, too, mercifully, at the same time as her children. Cholera, maybe. Scarlet fever. Or typhoid, like Willie Sherman.

Farquhar McIntosh had built the original Stonewall Hill in 1830 when John C. Calhoun was Vice President and nullification was a hot issue—the year of the Webster-Hayne debates, when Daniel Webster anticipated civil war and waxed transcendental about the Union. "Liberty *and* Union, now and forever, one and inseparable." Sherman's principle, he supposed. That was the era when McIntosh had bought the land and built the plantation. Hermia had uncovered the story of Macintosh's octoroon daughter Zilpha and her "marriage" to Asa Graves in those years before the Civil War, before the whole system had begun to crumble into modernity. From Gettysburg on, but especially after Vicksburg, the Old South had been doomed. Perhaps it had been doomed as soon as it declared war, as Sherman had announced to his friends in Louisiana when that state seceded. Frederick Law Olmsted had prophesied in *The Cotton Kingdom* that it was doomed even before the war. By the beginning of 1864, every Belshazzar in the South had seen the handwriting on the wall. Starting from Chattanooga in the spring of that year, Sherman had defeated Joseph Johnston and then John Bell Hood and captured Atlanta and rested there like God on the seventh day: William Tecumseh Sherman, already victorious and celebrated, poised to begin his March into immortality and the obsession of Jacob Guizac.

He needed to call the boy. Was it still too early? 6:45. He tapped Jacob's number.

It went directly into voicemail. A moment later Jacob called back.

—Professor Forrest?

Cump no more.

"Should I run you out to the clinic? I heard you use the inhaler a couple of times during the night."

—Feeling better. So what's up?

"I'm at the McIntosh plot in Gallatin Cemetery. I've decided to bury Miriam here."

—Seriously? Is it okay with the family?

Forrest smiled.

"Your grandmother Alison Graves was the only known McIntosh descendent in her generation, albeit distaff, which means that your father and therefore his children are now the only known living descendants of Farquhar McIntosh. And since your father is in a coma and your sister is in France, I'll just ask you. May we bury Miriam McPhee in your gravesite?"

There was a long silence, then a harsh laugh that turned into a fit of coughing.

—Sir, Jacob finally gasped, you have my permission.

"Thank you! I'm going to call the funeral home and get them out here to dig the grave. I'll find out what time Fr. Silber can be here and let you know. You're okay spending a couple of hours reading or whatever?"

—I'm working on Vinnie Ream.

"Give it up, Jacob."

Half-awake, Chick Lee headed into the kitchen for his morning coffee. He usually set the coffee maker the night before so there would be coffee ready when he got up. Coffee gave the thumbs-up to daylight and time and God and family and responsibility, and then as the world came into focus, he would take his pills. But with a sinking recognition, he remembered that he had forgotten to get the coffee ready or set out his pills. Everything would usually be ready in his little green horsehead dish from Alison, but they wouldn't be there this morning, so he would have to remember all of them. Omeprazole, gemfibrozil, metformin, and then all the vitamins and minerals that help to get through the winter. Zinc. What else? Vitamin C, B-complex, ginseng, turmeric.

As he stopped in the bathroom, where he relieved himself noisily, he remembered the day before, even without coffee. The thing with Duke and then the Catholic funeral and the girl breaking her water and Forrest's son-in-law trying to set Stonewall Hill on fire and then the fire under the kitchen. Miriam's body. There was something important he was forgetting, he realized, as he left the bathroom and heard noise coming from the kitchen.

There was some reason he had forgotten to do what he usually did.

He walked into the kitchen.

"Good morning, Mr. Lee."

A young, pretty, redheaded woman was sitting at the kitchen counter with her breast bare, aiming her nipple into the mouth of a tiny baby, eyes shut, whose little fists batted at the air as he tried to get the—*got it!* The little guy went at it, redheaded as his mama. Score! All questions solved! *Sweet!*

"Hi," he said, heart leaping around strangely. "Good morning," he managed to say.

Siobhan met his eyes and smiled, making no effort to cover herself. He remembered first seeing her with her friend earlier in the fall when Hermia first came to the dealership to talk to him. Next to her was the friend herself, a black girl, whose name did not come.

"Oh, Chick." Patricia turned to smile at him from the stove, where she was frying what looked like a whole pound of bacon in the big cast-iron pan they rarely used. "I'm glad you got a little sleep. Coffee's made."

"Morning, Mr. Lee," added the black girl. "I'm Lashawnda."

Her bathrobe more or less covered her breasts but split open around the great, lustrous, naked pregnancy she was bearing toward term, and he got an unsought glimpse of underpants and bare legs, because she was less concerned about her modesty than about another baby, as tiny as Siobhan's, that she dandled in her strong arms. He would remember who that baby was, wouldn't he, after he had some coffee? He found his favorite mug and poured in a little cream before pouring the coffee and took a sip. Better than usual. Patricia must have ground fresh beans. Another sip. Yes.

The baby Lashawnda held was the one baptized the day before. *Something Forrest. Madeleine Miriam Forrest.* Yes! He wasn't supposed to believe in infant baptism, but he had loved seeing this child baptized. Washing away Duke. Casting out Josiah.

"Mmm-mmph, little sugar. Won't be long fore I can nurse you," Lashawnda said, teasing the baby's lips with the tip of her little finger. "But right now you got to take turns at Siobhan with her little redheaded mister man."

"Got to wait your turn, Miss Madeleine," said Siobhan.

What a morning. Besides the bacon and coffee, the room was full of good smells of milk and woman and motherhood. It was all intensely female. Chick felt like a eunuch in a harem. Except he wasn't a eunuch. He could feel the pulse in his temple, and, good Lord, his ancient groin. He eyed Patricia.

"Chick, honey, how about you make the eggs, you do such a good job. We need to get ready for the graveside service for Miriam."

Graveside service. Somebody had said something the night before. Could he afford to miss work for a second day? Maybe it was better when he didn't go in, because the dealership had ended up selling three cars the day before, and Joe Ashburn said somebody else had called just before closing time.

"When's the service?" he asked, trying to picture what they would need to do to get these young women there with tiny infants. "Is this out at the new cemetery?"

"Rest Haven's not new!" she said.

"It was when I was in high school."

"Back when you were new?" she said. "You were pretty cute."

"You're pretty cute now. You better watch out."

Patricia smiled at him over her shoulder.

"Whew, y'all!" said Lashawnda, fanning her face.

Just as he was finishing the eggs, Hermia called Patricia, something he never thought he would live to see, and Patricia answered cheerfully.

"Hermia? . . . The *old* cemetery . . . No, but let me put Chick on because he'll know where you mean."

She handed the phone to him as she served the eggs onto the plates and added bacon and toast.

"Good morning, Hermia."

—Good morning! Thank you for taking in the girls.

"Our pleasure," he said.

—They're okay?

Chick looked at Siobhan and Lashawnda. And the babies. And Patricia. "Just fine. Better than fine."

Siobhan and Lashawnda looked up at the same time and smiled at him.

—It's the McIntosh plot near that section of the old cemetery where all the Confederate graves are. I like the idea of Miriam there. It should be entertaining on Judgment Day.

"You sound pretty good for everything you went through yesterday."

—Maybe I'm just crazy. It's felt for a long time like something had to happen and now it happened. Fr. Silber says ten o'clock. The earlier the better, because I have to meet with some people from the Department of Human Services this afternoon. Listen, Chick, I can't thank you enough. I think you might be the best man I know.

He felt a little dizzy hearing it even though he told her to cut it out. When Siobhan finished nursing and her nipple came out and she remembered to cover it up, he went over and held her little boy and smelled his head and kissed his hair and gave him back. He did the same with Miriam's baby, laying her carefully back in Lashawnda's arms.

"What is it about the smell of babies' heads?" he asked Patricia. "Remember Alison's?"

He caught Patricia's eyes and saw her tears. Both of the young women smiled at him like good news.

And the girls loved his eggs. Good Lord, when had he been so happy?

They had been herded out of Stonewall Hill before they could get a change of clothes, so they dressed in what they had worn the day before. The facilities were not made for the task put to them that morning. Hermia's women commandeered every toilet and sink they could find in the bathrooms of the Gallatin First Baptist Church—the basement ones of the church hall, the ones upstairs near the church offices, even the ones for the Sunday school classrooms—and they paid no attention to the signs on the doors. Everybody needed a shower after spending the night on the floor and nobody got one, but an odd happiness pervaded them. Howls of laughter kept breaking out. When the time came, their rides to the cemetery were waiting behind the hearse from Marshall Funeral Home under the portico on the side of the church.

They climbed the stairs huffing and erupted into daylight wild-haired as a troop of Maenads. Loud, very pregnant Maenads. Cars out on Indian Springs Drive hit their brakes.

"Hush!" Hermia kept saying.

Deirdre and Jordan herded most of the women into the big used Transit 150 that Chick had donated to Eula's House earlier in the fall. Nora and Bill Sharpe took three in their Expedition, much to the delight of their little girls in their car seats. Hermia came up last. She wanted Bella Amorosa in the backseat of the Prius with Teresa Gomez, who had been very withdrawn since the experience with Josiah. One of the newer girls—Hermia could never remember her name, something plain—got into the passenger seat, and big Lolita Menendez squeezed into the back on the other side of Teresa. They all smelled like smoke: their hair, their skin, every fiber of what they wore.

Chick Lee pulled in behind Hermia. A moment later, the hearse rolled forward at a stately pace, and everyone followed, lights on, as they made the turn onto Indian Springs Drive toward the center of town.

"How you doing, baby?" Lolita asked Teresa Gomez sweetly.

"Not too good." Teresa burst into tears.

The girl next to Hermia—*Jane*, that was it (or was it June?)—turned around to look at her. "The whole thing was crazy. That man just took Miriam out of the coffin, I mean, and laid her out on that door and then talked about—I mean, can you believe that? I still can't believe it."

"She looked like Sleeping Beauty!" said Bella.

"Man doing his own I'm-Jesus show," Lolita said. "All about Duke. Josiah run *him* off anyway."

They fell silent, remembering, and then Teresa wailed, "That snake came out of me!"

Hermia shuddered.

"Girl," said Lolita, "I could say something funny, but."

"Hush your mouth!" Bella said sharply.

"I'm just saying. There's snakes and there's snakes."

It was only a mile from the First Baptist Church to the cemetery, so it only took a few minutes for their little procession to drive up Johnston Street and reach the barrier at Jackson Street that forced a right turn at the courthouse square. They could see the crane a block ahead at the corner of Johnston and Lee. The statue of the Confederate soldier hung from the cable, and several men on scaffolding around the base of the monument helped guide it back into position. Hermia did not know what she thought about restoring it. Was it glorifying the Confederate cause? No one could look at that poor, stoical soldier and think of glory. And yet, what *did* he symbolize? *God help us*, she prayed. How can we ever correct the past to our satisfaction? Wasn't that what Fr. Silber was telling her? We are here for a moment, just a moment. What can we do but love one another?

Spectators on the lawn of the square turned curiously to watch their small cortege. A minute or two later, turning onto South Lee on the other side of the courthouse, they solemnly processed down to McIntosh Memorial Drive, turned left, and entered the cemetery, where they pulled to a stop near a tent in the McIntosh plot. A low stone wall surrounded it, one corner in the cold shade of an old cedar tree, and on the other side, separated by a low hedge, were the ordered gravestones of the anonymous Confederate dead. She got out of the Prius, pulling her coat around her. It was a cold, fair day. In the distance, beyond the boundary of the cemetery, children cried out as they ran and dodged and swung on swings in the playground of the Gallatin County Elementary School. Beyond the playground rose the stands of the

Dan Fitzpatrick Football Stadium where Braxton Forrest had long ago led the Blue Devils to a state championship.

Seized by a sudden grief that had nothing to do with the day, she thought of John Bell Hudson and sank against the door of the car.

"Are you okay, Miss Watson?" Bella asked. "It's just so much at once."

Hermia nodded. "It's nothing. Just didn't sleep much."

In various stages of ungainliness and girth, the women stepped down from the van or stood up from the seats of the cars, all of them shivering in the cold.

Fr. Silber saw Hermia and left Braxton Forrest under the green canvas talking to the men handling the coffin. He walked over to greet her, beckoning Nora Sharpe to join them.

"How's everybody doing?" he asked.

"Fine," Hermia said. "They're in good spirits, considering."

They watched the women straggle toward the tent, hugging each other, singing snatches of hymns, some weeping, some smiling.

"What a day that was," sighed Fr. Silber. He gazed over at the coffin. "Now we haven't had time to talk about the service. It can be as simple as you like. Do we want music?"

"How about 'I Heard the Voice of Jesus Say' at the beginning?" Nora asked.

"Good. Maybe 'Amazing Grace.' And do the women know 'Abide with Me'?"

"We do."

"Here's what I have in mind," Fr. Silber said, and he showed them the short program he had drawn up. He had made copies to pass out. "The eulogy yesterday turned out to be—oh my Lord." He broke into a wonderful smile and opened his arms. "You're already up and about!"

Chick had parked behind Hermia. Coming toward them now was Siobhan herself, grinning hugely to the whole company, her new baby in her arms. Then came Lashawnda holding little Madeleine Miriam, followed by Chick Lee and his wife Patricia.

"Doctor said I was made for it, Father," Siobhan said, "which sounds like trouble. Maybe I should get a husband? Just look at this redheaded little Irishman."

"Another baptism!" said Fr. Silber. "Name the time." He traced a cross on the baby's forehead and then raised his voice to summon everyone under the tent, where the coffin was positioned over the open grave. He handed out the programs. Nora gathered the women near the stones of the McIntosh children, facing Fr. Silber—a brisk wind made them huddle together—and Forrest stood on the far side nearest the Confederate cemetery with Chick and Patricia Lee and the men from the funeral home. Jacob stood beside Fr. Silber holding a small silver bucket—what was it called? Converts like her either learned all the names of things immediately or never did. She never did.

The priest raised his hands for silence.

"In the Name of the Father, and of the Son, and of the Holy Spirit. We read in sacred Scripture: 'This is the will of my Father, says the Lord: that I should lose nothing of all that he has given me, and that I should raise it up on the last day.' O God, by whose mercy the faithful departed find rest, bless this grave, and send your holy Angel to watch over it. As we bury here the body of our sister Miriam, deliver her soul from every bond of sin, that she may rejoice in you with your Saints forever. Through Christ our Lord."

"Amen."

The women sang "I Heard the Voice of Jesus Say," with Lashawnda's thrilling soprano soaring above them all. When they finished three verses, Fr. Silber read, "Trusting in God, we have prayed together for Miriam and now we come to the last farewell. There is sadness in parting, but we take comfort in the hope that one day we shall see her again and enjoy her friendship. Although this congregation will disperse in sorrow, the mercy of God will gather us together again in the joy of his kingdom. Therefore, let us console one another in the faith of Jesus Christ as we pray in silence."

Now they bowed their heads. Hermia thought of the troubled life of Miriam McPhee and prayed for her and for her mother Clover, which made her remember her own mother and pray for her. She prayed for her enemies. For Duke. For Jason Zitek. For the soul of Melina Lykaios.

Now Jacob held the silver bucket as the priest dipped a spray of hyssop in the holy water and flung it over the coffin and the grave. Nora's voice lifted. *Amazing grace, how sweet the sound,* and the women joined her. Hermia's heart glowed. If the state shut her down, if everything failed and her work ended, there would always have been the moments when this chorus of women made their music whole.

Now Fr. Silber held up the prayer sheet with the responses of the congregation in bold lettering.

"You knew me, Lord, before I was born," he began as the congregation followed the words. "You shaped me into your image and likeness."

"*I breathe forth my spirit to you, my Creator.*"

"Merciful Lord, I tremble before you: I am ashamed of the things I have done; do not condemn me when you come in judgment."

"*I breathe forth my spirit to you, my Creator.*"

"You shattered the gates of bronze and preached to the spirits in prison."

"*Deliver me, Lord, from the streets of darkness.* Amen. The streets of darkness!"

"A light and a revelation to those confined in darkness."

"*Deliver me, Lord, from the streets of darkness.*"

"'Redeemer, you have come,' they cried, the prisoners of silence."

"*Deliver me, Lord, from the streets of darkness.*"

"Eternal rest, O Lord, and your perpetual light."

"*Deliver me, Lord, from the streets of darkness.*"

Now there was a long pause and then Fr. Silber stretched his arms above the coffin.

"Into your hands, Father of mercies, we commend our sister Miriam, in the sure and certain hope that, together with all who have died in Christ, she will rise with him on the last day. Merciful Lord, turn toward us and listen to our prayers: open the gates of paradise to your servant—"

"*The gates of paradise!*" cried one of the women.

"And help us who remain to comfort one another with assurances of faith, until we all meet in Christ and are with you and with our sister forever. Through Christ our Lord."

"*Amen.*"

Now, silently, Fr. Silber invited Hermia and the women forward, and each of them scooped up a little dirt to drop onto the coffin, followed by Forrest, Jacob, and the Lees. The men from the funeral home lowered it into the ground. They stood then silently, all the women weeping for Miriam and for themselves, until Fr. Silber, with hands outstretched, prayed over them.

"Merciful Lord, you know the anguish of the sorrowful, you are attentive to the prayers of the humble. Hear your people who cry out to you in their need and strengthen their hope in your lasting goodness. Through Christ our Lord."

"*Amen.*"

"Eternal rest grant unto her, O Lord."

"*And let perpetual light shine upon her.*"

"May she rest in peace."

"*Amen.*"

"May her soul and the souls of all the faithful departed, through the mercy of God, rest in peace."

"*Amen.*"

"May the peace of God, which is beyond all understanding, keep your hearts and minds in the knowledge and love of God and of his Son, our Lord Jesus Christ."

"*Amen.*"

"And may the blessing of almighty God, the Father, and the Son, and the Holy Spirit, come down on you and remain with you for ever."

"*Amen.*"

"Go in the peace of Christ."

"*Thanks be to God.*"

Now they stood in silence for a moment until the voice of Siobhan Neely broke clear and lovely above them.

Abide with me; fast falls the eventide. / The darkness deepens. Lord, with me abide.

22

TERESA ONLY

SHE SAW THE RIDERS FAR ACROSS THE VALLEY. THE DUST from their horses rose and drifted slowly as they rode hard toward her. She knew, now that it had come, that she had been expecting this day when she would feel more brutally than ever the loss of her husband and the absence of her son. Bitter contempt for these greedy soldiers and their intentions smote her the closer they came. Up the road, into the driveway. One of the first riders to dismount gave her a look and a downturn of his mouth as though he were saying, *Not too bad in a pinch.* He disappeared into the garage and came out moments later as the other riders thundered into the yard, crushing the Russian sage and the tulips she had planted. Her little vegetable garden they quickly stripped of tomatoes, beans, cucumbers, squash, everything. Meanwhile, the first soldier directed several other men into the garage, and they came out carrying all the boxes of canned goods and coffee and dried fruit she had ordered from Costco. They found Walter's cans of gasoline, and for a moment, she thought they would burn the house and leave her with nothing at all. She did not want to mention little Marisa, who was upstairs, hiding under her bed, because she did not know what they would do. Cate and Marisa and the Zitek children were hiding in the dense undergrowth down by the creek.

Already Teresa could hear men in the kitchen emptying her refrigerator and raking everything from her pantry into the bags they carried.

An officer came up to her, a short man with close-set eyes, a big nose, and scraggly sideburns. He had a slight limp and an impudent air.

No man around?

My husband recently died. My son is away at the war.

Whose side?

The one that defends widows and orphans.

He gave her an appraising smile. You're a pretty one.

She looked him in the eye. I trust that you will respect my grief.

Your little private grief in this republic of mourning? He smiled. We can't make exceptions.

Hey, Gen. Kilpatrick. You mind if I take this one?

It was one of the soldiers. He had Cate in his grip. Her dress was ripped and soiled, and her eyes glared fiercely from under her warpaint. The children, naked and smeared with mud, trailed behind her sullenly, herded forward by another soldier. What had happened to Marisa? What about Little M?

I wouldn't leave any witnesses, Kilpatrick said.

You got that one? Nice.

Nice one yourself.

Kilpatrick moved toward Teresa, his eyes hardening. Then came the flames, the children screaming, Cate's desperate *NO! NO!* and the cries suddenly

Philip Glass Philip Glass

She broke from the dream, felt for the phone, pushed the button, and gazed up into the half-darkness, shaking with terror. She let out a long sigh of relief.

Walter was already up, as usual.

No. Walter was gone. She was not at home, but where was she?

Where was she? What was this room? *Where was she?*

Mercifully, the world coalesced. The whole world, newly created, came into being with all its continuities—the connection of this day to the day before and her pinpoint of location on the continent and the globe in the expanding universe with its black holes and supernovae. Here she was. Here in a suburb called Bountiful just north of Salt Lake City. In the Hellyers' basement apartment. Walter was neither up early nor dead but in the hospital, and she was here for a reason that felt more and more meaningless: to be close to Walter.

She had indulged the fantasy of waving to him from outside the hospital so he would see her from inside his room, and his heart would lift and he would know that all would be well. But then she would remember that Walter was in a deep coma, kept on a ventilator day after day, week after week, pumped up and emptied, inflated, deflated. Mechanically kept alive. She had gotten a call yesterday from the doctor that they would need to bring him out of sedation again today after only twenty-four hours or so because they needed to adjust something—she could not get the details straight. He would be awake for a little while, maybe just a few minutes, but she would have another chance to talk to him, if she would like to take advantage of it. After that, if they got the medications adjusted properly, the next time he woke up could be weeks away, a month, so she had to take advantage of this opportunity. It would be at about 10:00 a.m.

She made sure her phone was fully charged but put the cord in her purse just in case. She dressed quietly and left the house by the back way and took the now-familiar route down into the city, where she pulled up at a little before 8:00 a.m. on the steep street beside the Cathedral of the Madeleine and went inside for Mass. She prayed for her husband, for her son, for Rose in Europe, for little Marisa. She prayed for Cate and her family, for Marisa and Braxton. She prayed for Jason Zitek.

At ten o'clock she was waiting at the hospital. It was a mild, clear day. She had parked in the highest and most scenic lot and the whole city spread out before her. Temple Square, the skyscrapers, the freeways, planes taking off westward at the airport, the strong mountains rimming the city. The Great Salt Lake shone to the north.

She had obsessively checked the charge on her phone and made sure it was on so she would hear it. As the minutes passed, her anxiety climbed. She checked her recent calls. Nothing. Perhaps something had been delayed—or perhaps Walter had died or—

Her phone rang and she answered immediately.

—Ellen? he said.

Ellen?

"Walter, thank God. I thought something had gone wrong. This isn't Ellen, sweetheart, this is Teresa. Your wife Teresa."

—You won't. Divorce me. It's all the. God damn. Catholic. Church.

Her heart froze. What was this? Who was Ellen?

"Walter, do you know who this is? Do you know who I am?"

—I'm a man, Ellen. Not a. *Eunuch.* Why don't. You just. Divorce me?

He was still in his dream. He had not fully awakened from his coma—probably the reason for the delay in the call. Her distress climbed. A few minutes, and then a month of silence? And what if he died? *What if he died?*

"Walter, we don't have long. I hope you'll remember something of what I say. Our son, our son Jacob is in Gallatin at Stonewall Hill, and they had a funeral there yesterday. Listen, Braxton's son-in-law, Jason Zitek, came in with his girlfriend and tried to burn the house but Jacob saved it. Our Jacob."

—I burn. Everything.

His laughter turned into terrible coughing, and she waited for it to subside.

"Oh, Walter. It feels like some great, momentous thing is happening. A shift in the ages, I don't know how to describe it, but it's like the world we knew has already begun to change into something else, like something shifted in the ground rules of reality. First this pandemic—and I wouldn't have believed in it if you weren't so sick—and now this election, Biden, my God, and Donald Trump. I feel so desolate without you."

—It all changed. When Willie. Died. In Memphis.

Willie? Who was Willie? Then it rushed upon her.

"Walter, *listen to me, listen!* You're not Sherman. You're Walter Peach. This may be the last time I talk to you—I mean for a long time—and I want you to hear me. I love you. I've always loved you. You hurt me deeply more than once, more than I thought I could stand, and I've had a hard time forgiving you, because it makes me doubt myself and wonder why I'm not enough for you. There's something that makes you unstable, maybe your childhood, but listen to me. There's nobody else like you, Walter. I will never love anyone else. You have to come through this, and when you do, I know you're going to do the great thing you were destined to do. I know you will. I believe in you."

He did not answer.

—Mrs. Guizac? said a stranger's voice, male and authoritative.

She sat back in shock. Had Walter even heard her?

"Yes?" she said, full of dismay.

—This is Dr. Ranasinghe. We've spoken before. I'm sorry, but we need to sedate Mr. Guizac again. I'm sure you have been receiving updates on the online portal.

"I—well, I never, I didn't—" She knew she was supposed to set up a username and password, but it was the kind of thing Walter or Jacob always did for her.

—We will be in touch about the next opportunity to speak with him. It could be some time, perhaps even a month. We will monitor him closely, you can be sure. Thank you for being available to him today. I'm sure it meant a lot to him.

"That wasn't him!" she cried.

—I understand. You should consider whether it's worth it for you to stay in Salt Lake City. Perhaps you should go back home.

And the call was over.

Go back home. After uprooting herself and making space for Cate Zitek and her family. An image from the dream came back to her. Cate with her savage children. Where was Marisa in the dream? Not there—and what did that mean? She sighed, gazing at the hospital hopelessly, sick with the futility of being there. If only she could have talked to Walter himself and not his dream. Whatever he was working out with Sherman.

Sherman. God, she was so sick of Sherman.

So what should she do?

Go back home, said the prophet Ranasinghe.

Why did it feel like such a defeat?

At least she could be home with Little M until Jacob got back from marching through Georgia. But then she thought of Cate and Marisa getting into a daily routine that her return—to her own home—would disrupt. A burn of resentment surprised her, much as she loved Marisa. She thought of the trouble the Hellyers had taken to make the apartment comfortable for her. But there was truly no point being in Salt Lake City.

She should call Marisa. Open her heart, say everything. And when she drove back to see the Hellyers, she would just let them know that things had changed. She could not help feeling that she was abandoning Walter— and wasn't abandonment the central wound of his life? She had been his stability, hadn't she, all these years? These other stupid amours had been ways to give his imagination some illusion of liberty, the way a storm of fresh heresy renews the wholesome air of orthodoxy. He never thought of how they hurt her because, to him, astoundingly, they had nothing to do with dissatisfaction with her—as though in this most intimate dimension of himself he did not feel the contradiction. And why was that? Because he knew that he could absolutely count on her. He loved her, no question. She was his firm foundation, like God, and it would take some threat of the absolute, irreversible withdrawal of her love for him to wake up. She would never, never turn from him, and not just because she knew that doing so would send him to Hell, but because she loved him. Him, Walter Peach, with all his flaws, in the mystery of the sacrament. Had she forgiven Nora O'Hearn? She thought so. Nothing could ever compare to that abyss when she discovered Walter's infidelity with Lydia Downs and confronted him and he backed up the car in a blind rage. The little body of their son curled under the tire. Even now, more than two decades later, the feeling of it came upon her like the black wing of Hell.

When she got back home, she and Marisa needed to talk over this straying of their husbands. Forrest had afflicted Marisa more than Walter had ever afflicted her—but it was more of an alpha-male, Old Testament robustness with him, whereas with Walter it was existentially disturbing, vaguely pathological, inscrutable in its intensity. His wounds became hers. It would be good to talk it out with Marisa. Maybe even with Walter himself someday, God willing.

A little farther up the slope of the foothills were trails where she could take a hike to clear her head. Why not? Maybe she could find a spot to sit down and call Marisa.

Fifteen minutes later, slightly winded, she sat on a large rock looking down over Salt Lake City from even higher than before. *This is the place*, Brigham Young had famously said. Walter had once read to her a dismissive obituary by an anti-Mormon contemporary. *His habit of mind was singularly illogical and his public addresses are the greatest farrago of nonsense that ever was put in print.* Someday she would give her mind to considering the Mormons. Not right now.

Marisa picked up right away.

—Teresa! How are you doing? Rissa honey, come here! It's your mommy!

Rissa? She already had a new nickname?

—Mommy! Guess what? Clare reads me stories about Babar. Jimmy is mad at me because I messed up his Lego car.

In the background, Jimmy complained that it would be okay if she hadn't hidden the pieces.

"So you're Rissa now?" Teresa said.

—That's what Avila calls me! I like it. Bye, Mommy!

"Marisa! You be good, I'll—"

—Too late, said the other Marisa. She's gone.

"How are you holding up?"

—We're doing fine. Don't worry about a thing. The kids are having a great time playing with each other, despite what you just heard. Cate and I love your house. These views are medicine for the soul.

"Yes they are. That's wonderful," Teresa said, but Marisa must have heard an undertone.

—What's the news with Walter?

"I just talked to him. Or tried to."

She felt herself tearing up. It wasn't just Walter's illness, but her own sense of being uprooted. Going to her own home felt like an intrusion. She felt shunted aside, both as a mother and as a wife, and the emotion felt selfish and ungrateful, because the Forrests had been boundlessly generous in pulling Walter from a dead-end job and giving their whole family a fresh start, even a new identity.

—But he's out of his coma?

"No, they just brought him around so they could adjust his medications. I don't understand exactly what they're doing or why they decide what they decide, but he had this little window of consciousness, and they let him call me. Or made him call me. O Marisa—

—What is it, sweetheart?

"He didn't even know who I was! He kept calling me Ellen."

—Who's Ellen?

"Gen. Sherman's wife."

—Oh no.

"What an honor for Sherman. Crazy people used to think they were Napoleon. I couldn't get through to him. And then they told me that they were putting Walter back under, probably for a month. You know what the doctor said to me?"

—To go home.

"Exactly. Go home. I don't know why it feels like such a . . . I don't know what to say."

—A defeat? Like everything you've done has been for nothing? Well, it hasn't.

"It feels like it." She needed to change the subject. "What have you heard from Braxton?"

The State of Georgia, Marisa told her, was investigating Eula's House for irregularities. Hermia Watson was afraid that her work in caring for unwed pregnant women was going to be shut down because of various violations: failure to abide by fire codes, inadequate documentation of the identities of the women, inadequate reporting of occupancy to state agencies, lack of proper insurance, and so on and so on. Forrest would be staying for several days to try to work through some of the issues. He had called Marisa the night before. Teresa listened with astonishment to the story of Miriam's funeral and the performance of the man who called himself Duke. Afterward, there had been a baptism at the funeral mass conducted by Fr. Silber from Macon, and Jacob was the godfather.

The story of Jason Zitek took longer, and Marisa had to go outside where Cate and the children would not overhear her. Forrest had told her about confronting Zitek in the offices of *Phoe* in Atlanta and then about Zitek with the pistol at the house in Midtown. Zitek had come back later that night to burn the house Forrest had bought for them.

"'The debt immense of endless gratitude,'" Teresa said. "Walter quotes that passage all the time." She immediately realized that Marisa might wonder *why* he quoted it, but Marisa took no notice.

They had stopped Zitek from burning Stonewall Hill, but then Zitek and Lykaios had attacked the Confederate monument in Gallatin. Lykaios was dead. Zitek had been life-flighted to Atlanta with major injuries, still unspecified. They did not know whether he would make it. If he did, he faced a host of criminal charges.

"I'm just—" Teresa said. "I mean, my troubles don't seem—how is Cate taking it?"

—Well, you can imagine. She's devastated. She still loves him. She thought there might still be some way to recover their marriage, and the impossibility of it is overwhelming her. Even if he lives, there will be trials, probably years in jail.

"The kids?"

—They don't understand, but they pick up the mood from her. It's good that Little M is here.

"Jacob told me yesterday about Zitek at Stonewall Hill but I hadn't heard about the monument." She paused, weakened by longing for her son. "When are they coming back?"

—Braxton thinks they can start driving back on Saturday and get here late Monday.

"I'll drive home today."

Marisa was silent for a few beats.

—You know what I'm thinking, Teresa? You should take a day or two to clear your head. You can't do anything for Walter that you haven't already done. You've been given this little respite, so take advantage of it. Just read and walk and pray.

"I want to be home."

Marisa sighed.

—It's Cate. She's an open wound right now and it might be good to take a day or two. I know I'm being presumptuous, asking you not to come to your own house after I ran you out of it.

"I can help her, Marisa. I've been through so much with Walter before now. Right now, Cate and I are in more or less the same situation."

—When you get home, let's say on Saturday, we can talk all night if we need to and go to Mass, all of us, on Sunday. And then next Thursday is Thanksgiving. We'll have everyone together again.

"Not Walter. Not Jason Zitek."

—But we have so much else to be thankful for.

Teresa tried to believe it.

PART III

HOMECOMING

I received yesterday afternoon your letter of the 22nd which I have read many, many times, and the burning words of which have sunk deep into my mind and heart. During the time that I have contemplated the grave step of which I spoke in my last letter, I have been suffering in anticipation the pain of your disappointment, and the grief of having wounded you; but I feel that grief and pain a hundred-fold more sharply now that I hear from your own lips as it were, how much you are hurt and chagrined, and how highly you disapprove of my choice of a profession.

Thomas E. Sherman to his father,
William Tecumseh Sherman, May 27, 1878

1

HOMEWARD

EARLY ON THURSDAY, FORREST AND HERMIA WATSON toured Stonewall Hill with firemen, policemen, state troopers, representatives of Georgia state agencies, and claims adjustors. On Friday, with Deirdre and Jordan in attendance to help find documents and call various women for interviews, they answered questions, provided testimonies, showed the sources of funding, and explained matters of safety. The officials wanted this form or that form. The claims adjustor sourly pointed out flaws and failures. Twice, when his temper flared, Forrest rose from the table with the intention of calling his lawyers in Atlanta; both times Hermia persuaded him to forebear.

By late Friday afternoon, matters had reached a state of truce. Impressed by the spirit of the place, the agencies agreed that Eula's House could continue with these concessions and those provisions, this guarantee and that intention. Insurance would be more difficult, of course. That afternoon, they allowed the women back in. All through the house, the women sang as they cleaned up. They laundered, wore masks and rubber gloves as they scrubbed the walls and floors, replenished supplies, and restored the kitchen, all the time calling to each other as joyfully as though nothing had been or could be the matter. That night, Forrest had dinner for Eula's House catered by the Left Bank.

The women loved it. They sat in the dining room. The Lees brought Siobhan and Lashawnda. The Sharpes picked up Jacob from the Travelodge and brought him with their girls, who loved little Madeleine and Fergus. A little smoky smell lingered in the rugs, but the whole house felt new.

On Thursday, Jacob finished reading a biography of Fr. Thomas Sherman and edited what he had written about Vinnie Ream. If he had been able to breathe, he would have taken a long run, starting at the Travelodge and encompassing the whole perimeter of Gallatin—down the access road along I-75 past the old women's college (now a training center for state police), past the farms at the edge of town, then up the road to the high school, looping the cemetery, out to Stonewall Hill, then through the old black section of town, past the hospital and out to the golf course and the armory, and back through the old mill village to the access road to the Travelodge. Instead, he sat in his room. He wrote, he edited what he wrote. Once he talked briefly to Emily, who had a mild case of Covid and had to join her classes online, which irritated her.

—It's not like it's serious, she told him. Oh, I mean—

"Right. Ask my. Dad. About that."

It was fun hearing her apologize. He talked to his mother, who said that she was still in Salt Lake City. She described how his father called her Ellen and wanted a divorce.

"She'll never. Give it to him," he said.

When the Sharpes picked him up at the motel, they arrived in their Expedition, and the size of it hinted that they were just getting started with the babies.

Bill Sharpe greeted him with a laugh.

He had seen his old teacher, Nora O'Hearn, at the funeral, but she had been so busy with the women of Eula's House they had not really spoken. She got out to greet him.

"Buford Peach. Aren't you something?" she said. "I am so proud of you." The long hug she gave him almost made up for his absence from Emily. She had small lines at her eyes now, and she radiated a new certainty and maturity, but she was as beautiful as he remembered. He wondered if he had fallen so instantly for Emily because she reminded him of something melting and golden about Nora.

After dinner, as they dropped him off, Bill Sharpe asked him if he'd like to drive out to Missy's Garden the next morning. Just to see the place. Just the two of them. Sharpe had been the one who found him there in the kudzu after he found his grandmother's body and hit his head. He took a long time to answer, but he agreed to do it. The next morning, Sharpe picked him up in his new F-150 and drove out past subdivisions that had replaced the farms Jacob remembered. Everything looked unfamiliar until they came to the house itself. Sharpe slowed and stopped at the near corner of the elegantly fenced property. They gazed over the grounds, now landscaped, with benches and signs where the statues were.

"What happened to Lydia Downs?" Jacob said. She was the artist, an old student of his father's, who had known Alison Graves and researched Miss Zilpha with Hermia Watson and helped recover the statues embedded in the trees during the property's century of neglect.

"Lydia got the garden museum started. Got some state recognition and funding. I think the Diocese of Savannah might have contributed toward restoring the statues. But the place didn't pull in people the way she imagined it would, and in the meantime, she married Hudson Bennett—you remember Hudson? Several years back they moved out to Yuma, Arizona. Hudson always wanted to be a cowboy, if you ask me."

Jacob said nothing, flooded with memories.

"Do you want to go in?"

Jacob shook his head. He remembered cutting through the dense kudzu with his father. The interior of the house with its scrabbling rats and detritus and smell. The locked door of his grandmother's room. And how he had gone back inside by himself and forced the door.

And Alison Graves. Alison Graves, who had wanted to be free, his father told him. The fugitive Alison Graves.

Decomposed into the bed, skull grinning from long gray hair.

He fought the image as he had often done.

"Do you remember that first morning?" Sharpe asked. "When I found you standing out in the middle of the kudzu?"

"I didn't know who I was," he said.

Sharpe began to smile.

"What?" Jacob asked.

"How's that going?"

- - - - - - - - - - - - - - - -

Forrest and Jacob started for home on Saturday. They took I-75 up through

Atlanta, past Kennesaw and Allatoona and Resaca to Chattanooga, talking about Sherman and Hood and Nathan Bedford Forrest, Grant's strategy, and Sherman's frustration with George Thomas in Tennessee. Northwest on I-24 took them past Andrew Lytle's Monteagle and up through Nashville. Forrest talked about the Fugitive-Agrarians at Vanderbilt, then Jacob reminded him about the Battle of Franklin in November of 1864 and the Battle of Nashville that ended the Confederate threat in the West. Near Clarksville and Guthrie, Forrest asked Jacob if he had read Allen Tate's poetry. They considered the Confederate dead, and Forrest wondered about the fruits of Tate's marriage to Caroline Gordon before reciting from memory Donald Davidson's poem of tribute to Tate and then talking about the ways Robert Penn Warren's friendship affected Gordon's novel, *The Strange Children,* which was set at the house Tate's brother bought for them near Clarksville.

When I-24 merged with I-57, Forrest pulled over for gas, and Jacob took over the driving. As he settled behind the wheel, he reached over the back of the seat for his laptop, pulled up a Word document, and handed it to Forrest.

"You said you'd read it."

"Seriously? Right now?"

"It's about Vinnie Ream. Did you know there's a town in Oklahoma named for her? Vinita, founded by the Cherokee journalist Elias Boudinot in the Cherokee nation in the 1870s. Why would a famous Cherokee name a Cherokee town for Vinnie Ream? Nobody ever named a town for Ellen Ewing Sherman. Speaking of Ellen, she wrote to her father in the 1870s that Sherman should have had a squaw as a wife rather than a civilized woman. I think she meant Vinnie Ream. She looks like she could be Apache or something."

Jacob glanced at Forrest to see his reaction.

"Meaning?"

"Meaning," Jacob said, "that Ellen knows he's sleeping with Vinnie Ream."

"You think she'd hint that to her father?"

"I do, actually, especially if rumors were circulating. I don't think it would surprise her father."

"Maybe she meant he would have preferred a wife who was used to being on the move."

Jacob shrugged as he pulled out of the lot, checking the mirrors, adjusting the seat a little.

"Home was always a problem for Sherman. He lived in somebody else's house in his childhood, and most of his marriage was spent away from Ellen. When he had the chance to be with her, she would always leave and go back to her father in Ohio. Then came the war, and he hardly saw her for four years, and when she did visit, his favorite son got typhoid and died. After the war, she never liked the social responsibilities that came with his fame. She hated being the old, frumpy wife with all these beautiful young women pressing themselves on her husband's attention. Burke Davis quotes somebody saying he never saw anything like the way women went after Sherman. He spent almost a year in Europe without her. Some biographers say he loved Ellen most, and I think he did in some way. But I also think he was sick of her, especially after Tom became a Jesuit, which nearly killed him."

"Are you going to show this project to your mom?"

Jacob smoothly accelerated onto the interstate.

"You keep saying things like that. You think Mom is Ellen?" he said.

"I'm not saying that," Forrest sighed. "But let's just put this damn thing to rest. We'll call it good after this, okay? This is it. No more Sherman."

"You and Emily. Okay," Jacob sighed. "But I still haven't done anything with McPherson. Or Tom. You know Tom went mad, don't you? I think he became a Jesuit because he wanted to punish his father for his infidelities, and I think he went mad because he sinned in the same way. Just a guess. But I bet he felt it as a damnable weakness whereas his father thought of it as sport."

Forrest did not reply. He sat holding the laptop.

"That's a lot of speculation."

"Somebody needs to write a new biography of Thomas Sherman. You talk about somebody whose life was dominated by his father. The only thing written about him was published in 1959 by a Jesuit whose aim was to—"

"Jacob! That's enough!" Forrest said. "I'll read this, and that's all."

2

VINNIE

SHERMAN WANTED TO BE THERE EARLY, AND HE WANTED IT
to be a Sunday. Ever since he left the Ewing household in Lancaster as a teenager, he had taken a special pleasure in violating the Sabbath. He had first
seen Vinnie Ream at a reception a week before. Her skin was olive, a little
Mediterranean. Or maybe somewhere in her background ran the wild blood
of Shawnee or Seminole. Her sculpture of Lincoln was an impressive achievement for any sculptor, but astonishing for a woman so young. He had always
admired women artists, he told her, and she met his eyes with a directness he
understood at once. She replied immediately to the note he sent her.

No one else would visit her on Sunday morning, she said.

He told her that the pieties of other people had always protected him.

He found the address, quietly climbed the stairs to the third landing, and
knocked lightly at the door. After a decent time, he knocked again, conscious
that the neighbors downstairs might hear him. A few moments later, the door
opened quietly, there she stood in her nightgown and robe, so small, with a
mass of curly hair around her face. Her big eyes, crusted with sleep, seemed
startled but full of wonder and welcome.

"Gen. Sherman! You're so early!"

"A habit from the field. I'm afraid I woke you," he said with a slight
courteous bow.

"I wonder if you might take a stroll through the neighborhood for a few
minutes?"

She smiled at him again, this time tilting her head.

When Sherman opened the door onto the street, he glanced right and left. Habitual caution. It would not do for word to get back to Ellen. Around the block, he passed an inn where a black boy about Willie's age was sweeping the previous night out onto the street. Cities were like armies, all about logistics—where to get supplies, what to do with refuse. At Maryland Avenue, a glimpse of the Capitol dome made his heart sink a little. He had always urged his brother not to go into politics, and his own distaste had long ago become a matter of public comment and humor. He was a military man, not a politician, and he hated every moment of his life that had been engaged with that kind of dirty business. He thought of Stanton, whom he hoped God would damn if there was a God, Stanton, that timeserving grub of a man who stood for all of those people in politics. Just at the height of Sherman's glory at the end of the march, the man had soiled his reputation. He thought less of Grant for being president, surrounded by such men.

Sherman was Coriolanus. He could quote the entire speech before the Senate, the scathing condemnation of democracies "where gentry, title, wisdom / Cannot conclude but by the yea and no / Of general ignorance." General ignorance had opposed Vinnie Ream's commissions for Lincoln and Farragut. He had seen it often with political generals during the Civil War. The odious McClernand. The worst things happened when the Army "must omit / Real necessities and give way the while / To unstable slightness." If he ever gave a speech in Congress, this is the one he would give:

> Purpose so barred, it follows
> Nothing is done to purpose. Therefore, beseech I you—
> You that will be less fearful than discreet,
> That love the fundamental part of state
> More than you doubt the change on 't, that prefer
> A noble life before a long, and wish
> To jump a body with a dangerous physic
> That's sure of death without it—at once pluck out
> The multitudinous tongue; let them not lick
> The sweet which is their poison. Your dishonor
> Mangles true judgment and bereaves the state
> Of that integrity which should become 't,

Not having the power to do the good it would
For th' ill which doth control 't.

How was it that Shakespeare, under a monarchy, could see so clearly into the dangers of democracy? His hands behind his back, he turned at the end of the next block and found himself colliding with a man coming the other way.

"Pardon me, sir," Sherman said, tipping his hat.

"Pardon, is it?" the man complained, standing back. He staggered, completely drunk at eight o'clock in the morning, and crossed himself. "Bless my soul if I don't know you!" A broad, florid, Irish face with huge sideburns thrust itself forward beneath a salute. "Uncle Billy! Patrick Logan, sir!"

Sherman reached in his pocket and found a few coins to give the man. Maybe he had been a good soldier once.

"I hope you weren't in the brigade with that damned Meagher."

"Never heard of the Irish bastard."

"Get yourself some breakfast, soldier. There's a war to be won."

The man took his money and attempted another salute. Sherman touched his shoulder and passed him, eager now to be inside Vinnie Ream's studio. Sculpted by those small, strong hands and made immortal.

"God bless you, Uncle Billy!" the man shouted after him. "We burned 'em good! All that good whiskey in Columbia!"

One of his, then.

He walked for another ten minutes to give Vinnie time to anticipate him.

"Gen. Sherman," she said at the door. "I am most honored."

She gave him a small, gracious curtsy that nevertheless conveyed her sense of irony about social conventions and about his earlier arrival that morning. A freshly washed face, a simple light dress that showed off the olive glow of her skin. Earrings—three pearls above a crescent of ivory—dangled from her ears. Out in the town, church bells were beginning to ring when she brought him inside. No artist could ask for a better space. Near the door, a lamp sat on an end table in the angle between an armchair and a white Queen Anne sofa with a tufted back and rolled arms. On an oval coffee table were two or three books, a folded newspaper—he would be interested to know which one she read—and an open letter on a calling card tray. He recognized his own handwriting.

The big windows were filling with the September light. Easels and drawings—hands, shoulders, knees, heads front and back, nudes male and female. A table was scattered with knives for sculpting and carving. To the left was a small, curtained area, probably for models. In the middle of the space, half-finished clay figures posed on stands. Toward the back wall, a half-open door revealed her bed, hurriedly made. She directed him now to her couch, where a fresh pot of coffee awaited him, with two cups and a small pitcher of cream.

"I admire your work, Miss Ream," he began, "which is to say that I very much admire you."

She sipped her coffee and gazed at him over the rim. "You must know how flattering it is. A small and unimportant person admired by a great and terrible man. I am overwhelmed."

Again, that shimmer of irony.

"Besides war, art is the only endeavor that has ever fully engaged my interest."

"The only one?" she smiled. "Gracious."

"I was first in my drawing class at West Point—not that my little talent compares to yours, of course."

"You draw?" she said. She met his eyes candidly. "Draw this tulip for me."

She picked up an envelope from the table—his own note—and turned it over to the blank side and gave him a pencil. She hovered near his shoulder as he drew. It took him a few minutes of concentration to render the delicate solidity in the cup of petals, the firm stalk, the slim vase. He could feel her breath on his neck and the light touch of her hand as she leaned forward. The perfume she wore.

"Well done," she said. "Now try me."

She drew back and sat still at the other end of the couch, occasionally meeting his eyes with that direct look as he sketched her. The distinctive mouth. It was impossible in a few minutes to do justice to her hair, but he captured something of her remarkable, soft, intelligent candor.

"Who would have thought it of Gen. Sherman? Did you ever do nudes in your art classes?"

"At West Point?" Sherman laughed. "Imagine bringing a naked woman in front of all those cadets."

"Oh, but you can't claim to draw until you try one. The body as aesthetic object, lifted from the straightforwardness of desire." That touch of irony again. "Would you like to try?"

By the third visit, he could tell Vinnie anything. She did not hate the Catholic Church, but she treated its moral constraints as though they were the strictures of the Muslims or the practices of the Sioux. They had nothing to do with her. He soon found himself confessing to her about Ellen. She leaned on his chest as she teased the stories of other women out of him.

"You'd have to know the Ewings. My infidelities kept me faithful."

"You are a mine of paradoxes," she said.

"I'm a bad man."

She was silent.

"Oh," she said, starting up. "I missed my cue! You're not a bad man, Gen. Sherman!"

"Good Lord. Call me something else. Call me Will."

"Will?"

"'Thou hast thy Will, / And Will to boot, and Will in overplus.'"

"Perhaps Will to boot, but I question the overplus. Though not clean past your youth, you have yet some relish of the saltness of time in you."

He played with her curls, lovely, lustrous, a blessing to the hand. The exact texture of her mockery.

"Father William, then," he said. "Or Cump. Cump was my nickname. From Tecumseh, my middle name."

"My first friends were Indians."

She wanted love stories. He told her about Lucette, the girl in Marietta so many years ago. Dona Augustias in Monterrey and the senoritas. Gloria, the housekeeper in San Francisco. The girl Miriam at Kennesaw. He mentioned a woman named Edna Calhoun in Atlanta, but did not elaborate.

"You *are* bad, Cump. Very, very bad. Put your head here." He lay back with his head in her lap.

"'The sweet recess of Eve,'" he said. "'Thus early, thus alone.'"

She kissed him lightly and closed her eyes, running her thumbs and fingers over his forehead and temples, shaping the immortal stone, as though he were lying in state and she were learning him. She adjusted herself subtly beneath him. "But you're not just a bad man. You're a great man. The greatest in the country. The greatest in the world."

"Millions of Southerners pray for my soul to go straight to Hell."

She told him that he could make his own history.

"Write your own story. Be the first."

"Flank the historians, you mean?"

"*Gallia est omnis divisa in partes tres.* You're our Caesar. And what you can't tell the world, you can tell to me," she said. "When I get old, I'll publish *The Secret History of General Sherman*. By Eponymous Anonymous."

He played with the ringlets falling around her ears, cupping the back of her small neck and drawing her mouth to his before speaking again.

"You need to burn my letters. Seriously, Vinnie. What we're doing can't get back to Ellen or my children. I'll tell you anything, but you can't put it in writing."

"Not for history's sake?"

"Especially not for history's sake."

"Suppose I can't keep a secret?"

He sat up. "Then you're as dangerous as a goddamn journalist."

"As dangerous as a woman scorned, like Ellen?"

He regarded soberly her teasing mouth, her small, ardent body. He looked around for a cigar but could not see one. He stood up, found his jacket, and fished one out from the inner pocket.

"Adam with a cigar," she said. "Yes, you may, Eve murmured, though he had not asked."

Sherman smiled down at her as she looked at him.

"Are you named for Lavinia in the *Aeneid?*"

"An aunt, actually. But why would you ask me that?"

"There's another one. The one in *Titus Andronicus.*"

Her brows came together. He saw the memory strike home. Tongue and hands cut off by the sons of Tamora.

She regarded him again with that direct candor. "You care about Ellen."

He toasted the end of the cigar and then lit it, a good Cuban one, and rounded the smoke in his mouth. If the talk was going this way, he needed a drink, too.

"She's the mother of my children."

"And your foster-sister," she said.

He let the smoke rise from his mouth as he appraised her. Who did she look like? Titian's *Venus* in the Uffizi? Slimmer, darker.

"But here you are with me," she said. She turned on her side and looked back over her shoulder. Ingres's *Grande Odalisque*.

He sat back down. "Here I am."

"Everybody will know about Ellen," she said, putting her head on the pillow. "And that's how it should be. But I have the secret history." She startled him by sitting up excitedly. "Tell me about Edna Calhoun."

"You need the context," he said.

From early September until the Army left Atlanta on November 16, Sherman had stayed in the huge Neal house squeezed between churches at the very center of Atlanta, the heart of the Confederacy. He gave the order to evacuate the citizens—fair warning of the destruction he intended— and Gen. John Bell Hood had complained with much posturing that such cruelty was unprecedented in the history of warfare. Mayor James Calhoun pleaded that many people had nowhere to go, that pregnant women near their confinement would be displaced, and of course the world had learned of his reply. He had told the citizens of Atlanta that they had to leave the city, which would be an armed Union camp. *War is cruelty, and you cannot refine it*. Didn't they see he wanted to protect them from harm?

They did not.

"Ungrateful things," Vinnie said, stroking his brow.

The first week or more before the order went into effect, he had been bedeviled by a long stream of Confederate women, young and old. All day long, between the dispatches he received from Halleck and Grant or messages that came from his subordinates, one after the other they came, all of them wanting some special favor, something he could do for them, and they expected it because they knew someone he knew at West Point or down in Charleston twenty years ago or out in California. The pretty ones displayed a coquettishness that he enjoyed indulging and then denying. Even when he was just out of West Point, posted in Charleston for a time, the boundless, teasing superficiality of Southern women would almost convince him that they were incapable of serious thought and intention, but he had learned that it was like a play of light on the sea surface over deadly riptides. Underneath were always calculation and self-interest so subtle in their principles that he longed for anything straightforward—lust or greed or anger.

But they reminded him of the exception in those early days in Charleston, twenty years before Atlanta. Mary Lamb. A painter. Her mother would let them sit out sometimes on the beach, and sitting beside her, Sherman would try his hand at the sea grasses or the landscapes nearby, which she could render so perfectly, the brush so delicate in her fingers, her face so intent, her tongue so pink at the corner of her mouth. Seeing her would enflame him. What did he ever paint in those days but Mary Lamb? Soft partings, the cries of gulls, withdrawing tides, intensities of storm and deliverance. In his letters to Ellen Ewing, he disguised his passion for Mary Lamb as a love for painting so intense that it might endanger his military career.

Other Southern women taught him nothing but guile. In Atlanta, he refused all of them with brusque politeness. He walked in an atmosphere of intractable hatred. He could feel it like a vibration, like a wave in the air. Everyone in Atlanta hated and resented the Union presence, and all their hatred came to focus on his person and his name. The women were bitterest of all. Serpents in every glance. If he made a single concession to a single one of them, they would use the precedent to undercut his whole developing plan to burn the city and march to the sea. He had to harden his heart. It would take utter desolation to bring these people to their senses. They could not be allowed to go their own way. McClellan might have been elected and when elected he might have let the whole Confederacy go, if he—William Tecumseh Sherman—had not delivered Atlanta to Lincoln as the great prize and assured him of victory in the election. *Atlanta is ours, and fairly won.*

"Edna Calhoun," said Vinnie.

"Wait."

Hood could no longer menace him. He had driven the Rebel army into Tennessee, where Hood was now the problem of the notoriously deliberate George Thomas. George had probably kept his bride waiting on their wedding night as he mulled over angles of attack—if not the very advisability of consummation. Leanness and speed were Sherman's forte. He saw the importance of what faced him and acted immediately.

Vinnie sighed.

What would have happened to Admiral Porter if Sherman had not driven his men to Porter's rescue in Deer Creek when the gunboats were entangled in a nightmare of willows? If he had arrived even half an hour later, the Confederate attack would have finished off Porter, captured the gunboats, and changed the war on the Mississippi, especially the attack on Vicksburg. He had arrived just in time at Chattanooga to divert the Rebs and give the success to George Thomas's attack at Missionary Ridge—though he had heard that the men themselves had advanced on their own without George's orders. He believed it.

Now, for almost two full months after the long campaign from Chattanooga to Atlanta, he had enjoyed good food and concerts by the Army band outside the Neal house at night. Fine beds. Once after an evening of drinking and smoking cigars and stories about Shiloh and Vicksburg, he had taken upstairs a beautiful creature dressed in a low-cut gown stolen from some belle's wardrobe. Her hand was light and yielding in his hand on the way up the stairs. A girl in her teens as young as Minnie. In the bedroom he used as his headquarters, he turned his back and began to unbutton his shirt, and he heard her close behind him.

"You don't remember me?" she said.

"Of course I do. You're Miriam."

There was such a long pause, he turned to look.

"I carrying your baby," she said.

"My baby. Really?"

She touched her belly. He put his hand to her cheek.

"He little yet," she said.

He did not believe it was his—if she was even pregnant—but he kept her with him. *You home*, she would say. A chambermaid by day. He would make provisions to take care of her when they left Atlanta. Send her north.

Despite the pleasures of momentary peace, though, he hungered now to bring the full horror of war to bear on this obstinate people. He stripped the army to its essentials, sent all sick or wounded men to the rear, and destroyed the railroads all the way to Chattanooga. He amassed cattle and rations. He would make dependency on supply lines—his obsession until now—entirely unnecessary. He would destroy Atlanta with the world watching him and cut loose from the railroad and disappear from sight in the great movement toward the sea. From the 1860 census, he knew all the counties of Georgia, with statistics of cattle, crops, and slaves. He sent out the order to "forage liberally."

Great. Yes, he was. He was great. He had become a very great man.

He knew from seeing Grant up close and from meeting Lincoln and other famous men that greatness was a story that they wore, a name they made by what they did, an aura that hung about them. But it was also greatness of soul. Moment to moment, they were just men, but something of fortune and genius and ambition had pulled from them a series of choices and actions that would become the story from then on. He, Sherman, was already a name. Newspapers across the North had derided his madness when he said they would need 200,000 soldiers to get the Confederates out of Kentucky. It made no difference at the time—even now it made no difference—that he had been right. It was simply the saying it, letting it into the air after those years of failure, all the anxiety with the Ewings, all the trickery of the press. But look at this great gamble of cutting off the supply lines—no more trains rumbling up behind them, no more rails for the Rebs to attack and destroy. All the same, he would have mule-drawn supply wagons rumbling along behind the Army, and meanwhile the men would be out foraging on the land, stripping the rebel homes of their goods.

He let it be known that the proud rebels deserved every desecration.

Hardness of heart, the absoluteness of war. There would be no mercy, no softening and kindness extended to families with their complacent, long-standing domesticity, their herds and barns and smokehouses, their art and furniture and silver. He would give that property to the fire, and the slaves would come milling shyly and cautiously and then jubilantly out of these houses, looking at him as their savior. But the Negroes were not his problem. They were Lincoln's.

Or Stanton's.

Destruction was his greatness. The looming angel of death, face hard for the photographers. The lines in his face and the bristle of his hair. The hawk who would tear the heart out of the trembling dove with its olive branch.

The men loved him now. They saw in him none of the pretensions of the professional military, and they knew he was the soldier that history would deify. Not his senator brother, not the good, ordinary, proper officers, but the brilliant, unconventional Sherman with his cigars and his asthma and his anxieties and his constant talk and his love of women. More than Lee, more than any but Lincoln and Grant, he would be the one they remembered. Lincoln, Grant, Sherman.

One afternoon at the end of October, there was a knock at the door.

"I don't know where this one came from, General." The orderly raised his eyebrows and closed the door.

A moment later, a lovely young woman came into the bedroom. Fair hair, an open, heart-shaped face, a fine figure. It was more than a month since the last evacuations had sent the citizens weeping out of Atlanta, north or south. He had not expected another Confederate woman making an appeal.

"Gen. Sherman?"

"Yes," he said, "how may I help you, Miss—"

"Calhoun. Edna Calhoun," she said.

"A relative of Mayor Calhoun?"

"You might say so."

"An in-law?"

"How well do you know James's family?"

"Not well."

She smiled, and Sherman was amused. Her eyes met his with startling frankness. She was brave to come at all. He bowed and stepped toward her to see if she would offer her hand, which she did, her left, ungloved. Hot, hot and moist. And it bore no burdensome weight of a wedding ring.

"How can I help you, Miss Calhoun? Please have a seat."

He gestured toward the facing red leather armchairs in front of the fire. She sat down with the fire to her right and crossed her legs, holding her purse in her lap. He took the chair across from her. She had the kind of posture that he found priggish in some women, but in her it accentuated a body kept under discipline like a spirited horse. He would love to draw her in that pose.

"Not Miss Calhoun, Mrs. My husband died on Missionary Ridge."

"I was there at Chattanooga. But you know that."

"I do." She tilted her head slightly. Sherman had neither apologized nor expressed his sympathy. "Perhaps you can help me. I think you should have special consideration for James, since he has been criticized for pro-Union sentiments—I won't say pilloried, because it might become literal. You can afford a little special treatment for him, perhaps? He has accommodated your requests."

Sherman studiously cut a cigar and lit it from a candle. She watched him without comment. He had not asked her permission.

A blue cloud of smoke rose as he sat back.

"You surprise me," he said. "I would think that receiving special treatment from me would compromise Mayor Calhoun more than anything else. The best thing I can do for him is to let him share the common fate."

"Perhaps you're right," she said, beautifully upright, a tulip on its stem. A finely laced boot showed from beneath the hem of her dress. She had an easy elegance in the surroundings, as though she had grown up in the house, accustomed to its luxuries. Perhaps she had. Perhaps she was one of the Neal family who had married a Calhoun. A widow who wore no ring.

Delicately, she leaned forward in her chair.

"Gen. Sherman, I did not come for James. I came to bring you an offer that will be of great interest to you." He watched with curiosity as she opened her beaded purse and reached into it, leaving her hand inside it as though she were still uncertain about revealing whatever it was.

She pulled out a small pistol.

"Oh, Mrs. Calhoun, I am disappointed in you. This is bad taste." Her hand was steady as she aimed the pistol at him. "I thought perhaps it would be a better cigar than this one," he said. "Or a flask of good whiskey."

"No, it's your death I've come to bring," she said. "You must have read about Charlotte Corday."

"Something in the Bible?" he said, turning down the corners of his mouth. "Can't remember."

"You do, too, remember. Judith is the one in the Bible, of course, and you understand the praise I will earn, since you are more Holofernes than Marat. Call out, if you wish, but I can kill you before your men can stop me."

Sherman raised his eyebrows as if he were impressed, but then yawned, to his own surprise. He did not doubt that she would shoot him, but he had no impulse to leap up and wrestle the little pistol from her. A Derringer. The men downstairs, grown complacent, had evidently not checked her purse. But he did not feel the slightest alarm. Over and over, he had written to Ellen and to Minnie that it was unlikely he would survive the war. He had thought he would be killed by a bullet in battle. Instead, this is how it would end. So be it.

He looked across at Edna Calhoun and smiled.

"If I had died at Vicksburg, my son Willie would still be alive. I caused his death. He was my great hope—a boy with all my promise and a shining good nature. There was nothing wrong with him, the way something has always been wrong with me. I'm grateful to you, Mrs. Calhoun."

"Call me Edna. There's an intimacy established, isn't there, in murdering someone?"

"Edna. My destined Edna."

"I had supposed you might fight for your life. A little passion—fear or rage—would make it more exciting."

"How can I resist your charm? I feel fate in your lovely arrival and your enchanting offer. Who else would kill me but a beautiful woman alone with me in my bedroom on the eve of my greatest triumph? A woman obviously not my wife, who has always loved her religion and her father more than she loves me."

"I'm so sorry. May I call you William before I kill you?"

"Cump, please."

"Cump." She smiled saying it.

"I was a banker in San Francisco, but Ellen hated the city so much that she left the children with me and went home to Ohio. Home to her father. I had a housekeeper who performed the duties of a wife, as Ellen would say. She always describes the bedroom aspect of marriage as a duty—except that it was never duty for Gloria Torres. She could be a bit unrestrained. Let's surmise that Ellen's God killed my favorite son, my beloved Willie, to punish my infidelity, which he might have overheard. Now He has sent you to kill me. But Edna, wouldn't it be more fitting to die in bed with you? You could shoot me in the very act."

"Oh Cump, how indecent."

She said it with an ironic twist of her mouth, and her fingers touched the laces of her bodice.

"My men would never interrupt me. They know the better part of valor."

When he laid aside his cigar and rose, holding a hand toward her, she calmly raised the gun and pulled the trigger. It clicked but did not fire. She pouted as though she had broken a nail or found a small stain on her dress. She let the gun drop from her hand onto the floor.

Sherman stopped talking.

Vinnie nudged him with the instep of her bare foot.

"What happened?"

He pursed his lips and shook his head and shrugged.

"Can't remember."

"Stop it!" she cried. "You're just teasing me."

"Let's see. Where was I? Yes, she opened her arms to me and said, 'Like my homeland, I have no one to defend me.'"

"She did not."

"She did. I remember it vividly."

"Oh, Cump, stop it. Let's put this onstage, like Othello and Desdemona. You do to me what you did to Edna." Vinnie lay back on the arm of the couch and spread her arms. "Like my homeland, I have no one to defend me."

"But what was it Sherman did?" He tapped his forehead with a fingertip. "Maybe he asked if he could draw her the way he drew you."

After a moment, she sat up again. "Seriously. What did you do, Cump?"

He said nothing.

"Was there even a bullet in the gun?"

"You could see the imprint of the firing pin. It was the same kind of weapon that Booth used later to kill Lincoln."

"And there she was with the man she had just tried to kill. She had no one to defend her. So what did you do?"

Sherman leaned forward and hardened his eyes and held the lighted tip of his cigar close to her cheek. She shrank back instinctively.

"You burned her face?"

He lay the cigar on the ashtray she kept on the coffee table and turned to Vinnie.

"I foraged liberally."

"What do you mean?"

She screamed with surprise as he showed her.

"If there was any resistance, I took everything."

"Oh Gen. Sherman!"

He enacted terrible scenes. Edna wept, of course, and just when his depredations were almost complete and she seemed most overcome, she pulled from her hair the long stiff pin that had been her recourse all along. He saw it, but he could do nothing, helpless as he was at that supreme moment. As he lifted his head, she drove the point up through his neck beneath the jaw, pinning his tongue to his palate and piercing his brain.

His torso reared upward, demonstrating his agony. Reared again.

"Oh my god!" cried Vinnie. "Oh my god!"

He fell dead upon her. Feeling no movement in him, Edna rolled his body away. Sherman dead. Unhousel'd, disappointed, unaneled—just as Ellen had always feared, just as Edna had hoped. When her heartbeat slowed and her breathing calmed, she rose on her elbow and looked at him, stroking his forehead. "Poor dead Cump," she sighed, smiling. "Covered in shame at the height of your glory. Poor, poor Cump."

Sherman sat up so suddenly that Vinnie screamed.

"I could a tale unfold," he whispered, "whose lightest word would harrow up thy soul, freeze thy young blood, make thy two eyes, like stars, start from their spheres."

He kissed her.

"What happened after you died?"

"Lincoln replaced me with George Thomas."

"George Thomas!"

"The war went on and on, like a fire that flares up afresh when you think it's extinguished. I believe it's still going on. It might never end."

Her hands rounded his head.

"Sculpt me," Sherman whispered. "Make me. Don't let anybody else do it."

"What would Ellen say?"

"Promise me, Vinnie. A simple posture, a real one. Standing or seated, not on horseback."

She smiled at him, stroking, testing.

"You have immortal longings on you," she said.

"Promise me."

Just then, someone knocked on the door.

"What in the world!" Vinnie cried, throwing a blanket lightly around her. "Nobody comes on Sunday."

"Tell them you're indisposed."

Sherman revived his cigar and sank back on the couch.

When Vinnie answered the door a moment later, he watched her peer around the edge.

"Yes?" she said.

"Good morning," Sherman heard someone say. "I'm Thomas Sherman. Is my father—" There was a pause while he took in Vinnie's deshabille, her disordered hair, her flushed face. "Is my—"

Sherman cursed and clamped the cigar in his teeth and sat up, snatching at his clothes.

"I'm sitting for a statue!" he called.

"Father?" Thomas called inside, his voice tragic and hollow. "I followed you here. I thought you might be going to a different church, I thought—"

3

THANKSGIVING

JACOB DID NOT WANT TO INVITE THE WHOLE TURNBOW
family to Thanksgiving, but his mother did it anyway. It was Sibelius he worried about. All that time away from *Call of Duty*. He went to pick up Emily
in the Honda, and the Turnbows followed him out Washakie Road in their
minivan.

He had hardly seen her, because the semester of classes at Transfiguration
had just ended on Tuesday and finals online would be the week after
Thanksgiving. All the way out, as the foothills of the Wind River Mountains
opened before them, she grilled him about the trip with Forrest. Had they
seriously talked about Sherman all that time? When he pulled into the
driveway, there was Forrest standing behind the very familiar BMW, waving
them in.

"The famous Emily," he said, taking her hand as she stepped from the car.
"Good to see you again."

"The infamous Professor Forrest," she said, giving him her quick smile
and her hand.

The Turnbows parked behind the Honda on the side of the driveway and
came up to join them. Jacob led them all down the walkway around the side
of the house toward the deck at the back, where the Turnbows murmured
their admiration for the view—the sandstone cliffs north and east, the creek
bottom, the vistas to the south along the foothills of the Winds. Mrs. Turnbow

had apparently thought they were the only guests, and she was perplexed by Forrest's presence. *Who is he?* he heard her whisper to Emily.

The house was not big enough for a large party, but it was intimate and warm inside. It smelled wonderful as they came in through the sliding glass door—aromas of turkey and dressing, rolls in the oven, vegetables warming on the stovetop. Beautiful pies cooled on the stone counters. The children came crowding up to Jacob, whom they considered their property, and he fended them off comically, making his way to the wood stove. He had built a strong fire before leaving to pick up Emily, and now he opened the side door to adjust the logs and add more while his mother and the Forrests talked to the Turnbows. Testing the political atmosphere, Dr. Turnbow asked what they thought about the allegations of voter fraud in Pennsylvania.

"Perfect storm," Forrest said. "Covid's the excuse for absentee ballots, then late returns get counted after they know the vote count elsewhere. I don't envy Mike Pence. He has to certify the election come January."

Dr. Turnbow nodded down at them. Forrest asked what they'd like to drink as Jacob's mother took coats to put on Jacob's bed. Jimmy had latched onto Sibelius to show him what he had made with his Legos.

"I once made a German Panzer with over a thousand parts," Sibelius said. "It had like a rotating turret and . . ."

"Whoa," said Jimmy. "Mom, he made a Panzer!"

Jacob watched Cate come down the stairs looking ten years older than she had in Dallas two weeks before. Avila hung on her hand.

"Cate!" said Jacob's mother. "Let me introduce you to the Turnbows."

Cate nodded politely and exchanged greetings, but then looked about uncertainly.

"Where's Clare?"

"With Little M in the bedroom. They're fine," said Mrs. Forrest, steering her daughter into the kitchen, where they stood above the steaming pots on the stovetop. "What is it? Are you okay?"

"Jason texted that he felt his toes this morning," she said in a low voice.

"That's good news, isn't it?"

Cate shrugged, her mouth twisting.

Jacob felt embarrassed to be overhearing them. He clanged the fire iron in the rack and stood up, dusting his hands, and started down the hallway to the garage to bring in a few more logs for the fire. The colder air felt good.

Whether feeling his toes was good news for Zitek in the long run, Jacob could not guess. He had been pinned by the airbag before the statue fell onto the car and bent his neck violently sideways. At first, he had had no feeling, and the doctors had feared total paralysis, but over the next few days, he had recovered the use of his hands and the feeling in his torso. If he could feel his toes, he might not be paralyzed at all. But if he escaped paralysis, he still faced prison from the charges amassed against him in the three days of his spree with Lykaios. The legal consequences would become clearer over the next few months.

When Zitek came out of his coma, he told Cate that in his darkest moment, when he had felt the full force of what hell would be like, he had seen her face, and it had saved him.

What did you say to him? Mrs. Forrest had asked when she and Cate sat leaning together in the living room and Jacob was doing the dinner dishes, not meaning to eavesdrop then either.

I asked him if the deal was to put me there instead.

Oh honey.

He said he had been blind. He said he couldn't see his own evil. He asked me for forgiveness.

What did you say?

Oh, Mom.

Did you forgive him?

After what he did to us? You want to know what I told him, really, Mom? I told him to—

"Jacob?"

He fumbled the top log of the stack he had piled onto his arms. It tipped off, he bumped it trying to catch it, and it crashed into the empty wine bottles next to the trash cans.

"Oh my gosh, I'm sorry," Emily said. "I was just checking on you."

She righted the bottles and picked up the log, placing it on top of the stack of five or six that he held in front of him.

"You okay?" she said. "You're not zoning out?"

"Thinking about Zitek."

"Nothing to do with Sherman, though?"

He shrugged and shook his head. Always a little Sherman, but he did not say it.

When they went back in, he carefully fumbled the logs into the bin beside the wood stove. Across the room, Dr. Turnbow was speculating from his Olympian elevation, gesturing with a glass of bourbon, that Trump would have to be removed from the White House by force, and Forrest was saying something under his breath. Everyone seemed distracted, so Jacob led Emily over to show her his room. She assessed it with one ironic glance.

"Nice shirt."

He had left it over the back of the desk chair after his run that morning.

"Okay, let me show you upstairs," he said, smoothing his hand into the small of her back, hoping to get her alone for a few minutes. They started up the stairway, and just then, his mother's voice rose.

"Jacob, can you slice the bread?"

They came back down the steps. He hated the feel of blushing.

At dinner, Jacob missed his father's rolls—a recipe from a Zen baking book he had bought in college. But, yes, he sliced the bread, a local sourdough loaf with a hard crust that Mrs. Forrest said was better than anything in New England. His father had ordered a special bread knife just for this sourdough, so he should feel privileged to use it. Everyone picked up a plate to be served the turkey that Forrest had expertly carved and the Italian sausage stuffing Mrs. Forrest made. His mother's casseroles steamed with Alabama goodness. She always said they were bona fide Methodist because she had learned her cheesy squash casserole from her grandmother and her marshmallowed sweet potato casserole from her Aunt Grace. There were good Southern beans with bacon and onions, real mashed potatoes, more vegetables, cranberry sauce—a huge feast, still with all those pies to come.

It was getting dark outside, and the big picture window reflected the gleam of good china and silverware and crystal on the dining room table as they took their seats. Forrest was at the interior end near the Japanese screen that divided the dining area from the living room, and Jacob sat nearest him with his back to the glass. Emily, sitting across from Jacob, could see the red rock cliffs behind him, but Mrs. Turnbow, nearest him on his left, faced into the kitchen across from Cate, and Mrs. Forrest beside her sat across from

Jacob's mother. Dr. Turnbow sat at the opposite end from Forrest. His mother could get up and bring things from the kitchen and Cate could tend Avila in her highchair. Emily offered to move over a seat, but Cate insisted it was fine. Little M, Claire, and Jimmy sat with Sibelius—much to Jimmy's delight—at a smaller table in the middle of the kitchen.

"Mom won't let us play video games," Jimmy said.

"Probably smart," said Sibelius.

Forrest led them in grace, and Jacob's mom added a prayer for her husband and for Jason Zitek.

"Any news about Walter?" Mrs. Forrest asked as they began to eat.

His mother shook her head.

"I haven't talked to him since last week. That day in Salt Lake City."

But news flowed constantly inside his father, Jacob knew, a man caught in an alternate world he could never have invented consciously, a world given to him as reality is given. A vast and intricate dreamscape. And the spiritual trials of Walter Peach were dominated, he saw in a coalescence of recognitions, by the question of the salvation of William Tecumseh Sherman.

Three examiners in long black robes, their faces indistinct from overwhelming brightness, faced Walter Peach, who was also William Tecumseh Sherman. In front of him, laid upon a door set up on two sawhorses, was the dead body of Gen. James McPherson.

"Jacob?" his mother was saying worriedly. Emily was staring at him, too. They were all staring at him, Forrest keenly, Cate with a glimmer of recognition, the Turnbows curiously, Mrs. Forrest kindly. The expression on Emily's face scared him most, because he remembered it from the Granite Gill.

"That *had* to be Sherman!" Emily said, failing to hit a tone that would dismiss everyone's concern. Her foot desperately nudged his under the table.

"I was thinking about Dad." After a moment of waiting for explanation, the eyes dropped and the forks, embarrassed for him, moved toward beans or dressing. "No, see, Dad's the one who's Sherman."

Dr. Turnbow asked Cate to pass him the butter.

"You were gone, buddy," Forrest said.

"Just being yourself," Emily said.

"No, what I mean is that my dad is dreaming the whole time he's in this coma. I think my Sherman project got into his imagination right about the time he got Covid and went under, and now there's something about Sherman that he's struggling with. He told us when we were in Georgia—that short conversation, mom?—that he had to save Sherman to be saved himself. It's like if he dies—sorry, sorry—but if he dies, he can't get into heaven unless Sherman does. It's all gotten twisted in his imagination."

The adults looked at him now with more sympathy and comprehension. Dr. Turnbow nodded.

"I don't know where he got Covid, but he caught Sherman from Jacob," Forrest said.

"And where did Jacob catch Sherman?" asked his mother. "But Jacob's right. Walter thinks he *is* Sherman. He called me Ellen the last time I talked to him, and he meant Ellen Ewing Sherman. He wanted to divorce me—meaning Ellen. At least I hope he meant Ellen. What was Ellen like?"

"Very respectable," said Jacob. "Very Catholic."

"Hmm," said his mother.

"We talked a lot about Ellen Ewing," Forrest said. "Jacob read me passages from her letters. Smart woman. She knew Sherman too well to suit him."

"Imagine that," said Mrs. Forrest.

"Beautiful young women adored him—"

"Vinnie Ream," said Jacob. "Mary Audenried."

No one else knew what they were talking about.

"But Ellen worried about his salvation," Forrest said. "Sounds like Walter's dreamworld taps into the Ewing family. All the Sherman children followed Ellen's lead, and Sherman hated it. Their son Thomas was a Jesuit priest."

"I didn't know that," said Mrs. Forrest.

"Edmund Wilson's good on Ellen," Jacob said, and Forrest nodded.

The mood of the table was solemn, both at the mention of divorce and at the idea that his father might in fact be dying.

"What is the prognosis for Mr. Guizac, if I may ask?" said Dr. Turnbow gently. He was so tall, it was like having someone standing at the other end of the table.

"Thank you," his mother said. "The doctors aren't giving me anything definite, but he's no worse. I just wish I could talk to him," she smiled, "and not Gen. Sherman."

Her humor softened the mood, and Jacob relaxed a little. Emily gave him a soft bump under the table, then a wink and a flicker of smile when he looked up. He concentrated on his plate—turkey breast and gravy, Mrs. Forrest's dressing, sweet potatoes, green beans without the "Yankee squeak" that his father hated, squash casserole with cheese, cranberry sauce, the good sourdough bread with butter.

A hum of happiness rose inside him. He wondered what had happened to Nelda back in Alabama.

"So you left things stable at Stonewall Hill?" his mother asked Forrest.

Forrest wagged his head noncommittally.

"Stonewall Hill?" Dr. Turnbow asked.

His mother looked at Jacob, then at Forrest.

"Well, Braxton, how would you explain Stonewall Hill," his mother asked, "to those not blessed with our Southern heritage?"

"The family home in Gallatin, Georgia," Cump said. "A monument to the Old South, according to some. My grandfather T. J. Forrest bought the place from the heirs of a man named Farquhar McIntosh, who built the original structure back in the 1830s on his plantation. There were additions before the Civil War, but my grandfather almost doubled its original size and added the Greek revival columns—the big porch, all that. But the terraced hill that gives it its name was part of the original McIntosh inheritance."

Dr. Turnbow nodded. "But Mrs. Guizac asked if you left it—"

"Call me Teresa, please," interrupted his mother.

"Teresa asked—"

"If we left it stable?" Forrest said. "She means the home for unwed mothers that Marisa and I fund. It's run by a woman named Hermia Watson—"

"You turned the old plantation into—what do your friends call those?" Dr. Turnbow asked his wife.

"Maternity homes," said Mrs. Turnbow.

"There was trouble there this past week," Mrs. Forrest said. "One of the girls died in childbirth. The child's father was a preacher in Griffin—"

Avila stood up in her highchair and Cate had to scramble up to keep her from falling out.

"Mommy," Clare said. "I miss Daddy's lasagna."

"Okay, honey." She sat back down with Avila in her lap, her face stony, fending off the child's sticky hands.

"They caught Duke, by the way," Forrest said after a moment. "Chick Lee called to tell me."

"Well," Mrs. Forrest said. "Lots to deal with this past week, so Braxton had to stay there a few days."

There was a brief silence.

"Hermia's handling it now," Forrest said.

There was a pause. What they were not saying grew. Jacob felt Mrs. Turnbow looking at both the Forrests. At his mother. At Cate. For a moment, he studied the dressing, the beans, the slices of squash embedded in the casserole, the bread, the diminishing butter on the inward curve of the edge of his plate.

"Teresa," said Mrs. Forrest brightly. "Tell us about your last days in Salt Lake City."

He let out his breath slowly. His mother explained how she had taken a day to tour Temple Square, fending off enthusiastic young women who wanted to talk to her about being Mormon. The next day she had gone up to Antelope Island and tried to understand the history of Great Salt Lake. Her hosts, the Hellyers, were very understanding about the situation at the hospital, and they had offered her the apartment whenever she needed to come back. Wonderful people. On the way back to De Smet, she had stopped at a rest area outside of Salt Lake City just to gather her thoughts, she said, and she thought maybe she understood now what people meant by a panic attack. It took her an hour to get over it. And then the emptiness when she got past Evanston and up into the country toward Kemmerer and then from Kemmerer to Farson—just the sagebrush and the Exxon refineries and the lonely pump-jacks working and the occasional antelope or mule deer. It was the landscape of kenosis.

"But I'm grateful for those hours," she said. Everyone was silent. She sighed and looked at Jacob. "You haven't said much about the trip back from Georgia with your lunatic mentor."

"We had a pact. If either of us mentioned the name of Sherman, we had to listen to an hour of Rachel Maddox."

"Not true," Forrest said, smiling. "Did you know Sherman used basically the same policies against the Indians as he did against the South? He once wrote to Gen. Philip Sheridan that he thought the solution in the West was to exterminate all the Indians. He said the same thing in a letter to Ellen. The extinction of the buffalo was his idea—take away the nomadic life, get all the Indians on reservations and dependent on the Union, make them into farmers. Control them, keep them from straying. He was out here a lot."

"In Wyoming?" Dr. Turnbow asked and took a sip of the Pinot Noir they had brought.

"Absolutely. Visiting forts. He brought his son Tom to Yellowstone."

"When was that?"

"I want to say . . . 1872," Forrest said, looking up at Jacob. "Before Tom became a Jesuit."

"The summer of 1877," Jacob explained. "Sherman wrote reports about that expedition. Tom published several descriptions of it later in a Jesuit magazine. The trip was right after he graduated from Yale, the summer of the Nez Perce uprising. Gen. Oliver Howard was chasing Chief Joseph, and Sherman wanted to stay out of the way. This was the same Gen. Howard who had been in charge of the attack at the Dead Angle in the Battle of Kennesaw Mountain. He was a very religious man with a big head, literally. Gen. Logan never forgave Sherman for picking Howard—a West Point man—instead of him to replace McPherson in Atlanta."

They all looked at him with curiosity. Or was it pity?

"By the way," he went on, unable to stop, "Orlando Poe was with Sherman's little group in Yellowstone. A general in his own right by now. This is the engineer Sherman relied on all the way through Georgia to get him across rivers. Also the one who organized the destruction of the major buildings in Atlanta just before they marched out on November 17, 1864. You might not realize that he designed most of the lighthouses on the Great Lakes."

"Hmm," said Dr. Turnbow.

"Aren't you just a *mine* of information?" Emily said.

Jacob filled his mouth with dressing, and there was a lull of murmurs and compliments on the food as the table recovered from his enthusiasm. Dr. Turnbow took up the topic of homeschooling with Jacob's mom, and Mrs. Turnbow turned her head to listen.

"Clare," Cate called. "If you and Rissa are finished, can you please come take Avila? We'll have dessert soon, okay?" The two girls came over, and Cate set the child on the floor to go with them. "You can sit in front of the wood stove and watch the fire, but don't get too close."

She turned back to the table. "Clare and Jimmy need to get back to school," she said to Forrest.

"We can find you a place in De Smet. Maybe you can teach up at the college in Riverton."

They were all keeping their voices down and their tones equable, but Mrs. Forrest leaned over and said she thought they belonged back in Atlanta where all their friends were.

"Mom," Cate said. "He burned down our house."

Feeling his attention, Cate looked up and met Jacob's eye, and he sat back, embarrassed. She leaned close to Forrest and whispered. Meanwhile, his mother was answering the compliments of Mrs. Turnbow, who recognized the private nature of the Forrests' conversation and said that the silverware was just exquisite. Wasn't it nice to have inherited things? It was such a connection to the past.

Everyone was talking to someone else. He had Emily all to himself.

"DNA is a funny thing," he said, softly kicking her foot and leaning toward her. She instantly reddened and made a face at him. But he was undeterred. "You know, it's this spiral, this double helix of adenine, cytosine, guanine, and thymine, coded with everything we talk about as our genetic makeup. We tend to think of it mechanically, as though it were just like Jimmy's Lego parts, unfeeling and unconscious—you know, this fits into this, this doesn't fit this."

Emily gave him an incredulous look.

"So we imagine it the way we'd imagine mere matter, and yet it's obviously *alive*, it's the very stuff of life, so I strongly suspect that in the general framework of being alive, you know, large to small, sort of like with fractals, there's a self-similarity between the fundamental character or inner feel of that spiral of DNA, this buzz of being, this pure *is-ness*, that lies at the heart of every cell of your body—so, I mean there's a self-similarity between *that* and your consciousness, the feeling of who you are, what you mean when you say *I am*, which is also the name of God. I'm not saying that DNA and

God are the same thing, don't misunderstand me, but there's a kind of divine *intentionality* you can feel because of where your DNA directs you. It's in the providence of God, so when it's saying *Here! Here! Hey! Here! This one! This one!* as emphatically as mine is right this minute, then—"

"Shut. Up," Emily mouthed.

"Are you interested in majoring in biology?"

Jacob looked up from Emily's face, puzzled, and then up again, and there, far above Mrs. Turnbow's forward-bent head, down at the end of the table loomed the attention of Dr. Turnbow, who must have overheard at least some of it.

Jacob opened his mouth with no idea what he was about to hear come out of it. His mother inadvertently saved him by dinging on her wine glass with her spoon.

"This is not a toast," she said raising her glass, "so much as a moment of thanks. I want to thank God that we are all able to be here. I want to thank Braxton and Marisa for their extraordinary generosity in coming across the country to help me during this crisis in our lives—*this* crisis, which is not to say that there haven't been other ones they've also helped save us from."

Her voice broke, and Jacob almost stood, but she gathered herself.

"When I think back over these past years and imagine what our lives would have been without your help, I am just speechless. God bless you. But I also want to thank Dr. and Mrs. Turnbow for coming to our little college here and adding your beautiful presence to this community and for bringing Emily."

Jacob blushed.

"I just want to say what a strange time this year has been. Partly, it's been beautiful, an awakening. But also terrible. This epidemic or pandemic or whatever it is. I had begun to make fun of it as much ado about nothing—when, well, it became a big deal with Walter's illness."

"I'm sorry, who's Walter?" asked Mrs. Turnbow.

"My husband. His family name. That's a long story. But listen, I realize there's a mystery in all these things. But what is it that's going on? Even this election—it's as though the baseline of sanity that we had taken for granted had disappeared."

"Amen," said Dr. Turnbow.

"I keep thinking 'whom the gods would destroy, they first make mad.' It feels like the world is going mad. God is slow to anger and abounding in kindness, and I just—I'm just very grateful to have friends like you, to be in this community of generous, wholehearted, *sane* people, and to trust in God that he will save our world from our own folly."

Everyone was silent.

"Well," his mother said, "I don't know what I can do after making a speech like that except offer you dessert! Apple pie, pecan pie, and pumpkin pie. Ice cream, whipped cream, brandy, coffee, tea, you name it. Oh, I wish Walter were here to see you all."

"Wait just a minute, Teresa," said Forrest. "I *do* have a toast to make. I am not a great father, but I remember when my daughters were the age of the girl we lost at Eula's House. They were defiant and contrary, but also very self-conscious and sentimental, weepy. Unsure of themselves and their new bodies."

"Come on, Dad," Cate murmured.

"No, listen. You and Bernadette wanted to move ahead into your own lives, but you also missed the simplicity and maybe the protection of childhood. So when I looked at Miriam during that funeral, I thought about you girls. Suppose one of you was a virgin given by her own mother to a much older lover with the permission to rape her."

"My God!" said Mrs. Turnbow.

"That's exactly what happened in Sicily in my family," Mrs. Forrest said. "I met both the mother and the daughter, God help them."

"This Duke—well, this priest, because that's what he was—preyed on the girl's mother and her credulity in the worst way."

Mrs. Turnbow shifted uneasily in her seat.

"But that's not what I want to talk about. I want to raise my glass to the young man who has been the companion of my travels. I can't quite say what it has meant, because I don't think I've taken it in fully. I knew him as a boy, and now I know him as a man. He has the stuff of heroes in him, and if I were ever to go into desperate battle, I would want him at my side. To Jacob Guizac."

They all stood and toasted Jacob, who could not look up. When he finally glanced up at Emily, her eyes were shining. After a moment, Jacob's mother recollected herself and stood.

"My goodness. Let's have dessert."

4

THE DIVORCE

PEACH CHECKED HIS BOARDING PASS AGAIN WHEN HE AR-
rived where Gate 777 was supposed to be. The actual gate sign said 774. It
felt late, but nobody was queuing up to board, so he looked around for a seat.
A fat man with a mass of long, curly, black hair and a little mustache took up
half a row, extending, from incongruous short pants, huge, columnar, hairless
legs that anyone passing had to step over.

Do you mind? Peach said.

The man did not look up. It irritated Peach—the sofa-size butt and
thighs, the skin as pale as a death-cap mushroom, the calves like prize hams.
The man's feet were squeezed into small black sneakers. But most irritating
was the imperviousness, the mouth hanging open a little as he played some
game on his mobile phone.

Sir, do you mind? Peach said again, more loudly and sharply. Other
people glanced at him and raised their eyebrows. No response from the fat
man. Peach bumped the calf, and, as though it were an independent creature
with feelers, the whole huge limb slowly retracted toward the seat, flexing at
the knee and straining fat calf against fat thigh. The other leg still blocked his
way, so Peach did the same thing again, the same thing happened, and a path
opened before him.

Many thanks, Peach said sardonically, stepping through, and now the
man looked at him, meeting his eyes.

Marks of weakness, he said in a low rumble. Marks of woe.

Trying to get past you? Peach said.

Welcome to the exam. Take a look around.

What exam?

Exactly, dude. You might have missed out. Good luck with that.

The man's eyes dropped back to his phone like—like what? Like Ugolino's open jaws dropping back to the skull of Ruggieri. *Inferno 33*. The bottom of Hell.

Is that where he was?

Peach glanced around the waiting area. Weakness and woe did not begin to describe this bunch. What showed were marks of corruption and debasement, marks of social cowardice, marks of absurd self-regard, marks of habitual belligerence. An emaciated girl with blue hair and multiple piercings (inflamed nostrils, eyebrows, ears) pulled up her T-shirt (pierced navel) and stuck out her tongue (pierced) to show a tattoo on her stomach to the graying motorcycle gang member across from her, a man with a ponytail, his heavily muscled arms bulging from his Black Sabbath T-shirt and inked to the fingernails with evil images. Nearby, a middle-aged woman in a hijab shrank down in shame and terror as her husband ranted about the goddamn stupid airline and the goddamn stupid counter staff. Mothers, fathers, children, teenagers, old people, all the races, all the sexes and genders selved shamelessly in front of each other. Everywhere crackled little surges of desperate impatience for more than an airplane, everywhere was a dull misery of more than circumstance, an underlying distress, a meanness by default.

My God, they weren't going to make it, were they?

And they knew it. They all knew it.

And he was with them in this sludge of souls.

Across the room, Peach saw a seat and made his way toward it, avoiding inadvertently straying feet and people who stood up heedlessly slinging on their backpacks. Near the empty seat, a man in a tailored suit glanced up at Peach, and Peach could see on his face an instantaneous spasm of contempt in the skin around his left eye.

He supposed he deserved it. It was hard to look good in a hospital gown, especially with a cannula taped into the back of his right hand and an IV drip bag hanging from the rolling stand that squeaked along beside him. He was self-conscious about his hairy legs and his paper hospital slippers.

People behind him could see his butt if the gown gapped open, which was why he kept grabbing the thin cloth behind him. The constant beeping of the heartbeat monitor did not help his ethos.

Just got out, he commented to the suit.

Without your clothes? the man said, his scorn growing by the syllable. No clue you were supposed to *check out?*

Peach regarded him curiously, somehow not offended.

What are you dressed for? Business trip?

You're a funny guy.

Peach frowned and went down the line of seats to an empty one and sat, arranging the IV stand in front of him. What was funny about that question?

What exam?

Walter was nodding off when a large black man in uniform appeared before him.

Mr. Guizac? Would you accompany me, please? He stepped back to allow Walter to stand up and roll his stand past him. He cleared the way before him with obvious authority.

Folks, move your feet, please, we've got a candidate coming through here.

He directed Walter toward a door in an otherwise featureless gray wall near the entrance to Gate 774, which appeared to be rusted shut and dim with cobwebs. The other people in the lobby looked up with mild boredom, wondering, he supposed, the same thing he did, where he was going and why. The black man looked back at Walter with a slight smile and a tilt of his head.

You ready for this?

This what?

The examination.

What examination are we talking about? Walter asked.

The man chuckled appreciatively and touched Walter on the elbow, then opened a door with a semicircular handle that dropped back into the recessed hardware. He let Walter enter the room, where three figures who looked vaguely familiar sat behind a table.

Mr. Guizac.

He could not tell who was speaking. The three faces were downturned and shadowed.

I've been going by Walter Peach lately.

And William Tecumseh Sherman?

Right, he said. Some kind of glitch in my psyche, I guess. I'm not sure why it keeps happening. My son was writing on Sherman—this was an assignment from a friend of mine—when I got sick with Covid and the doctors put me into this coma. I'm in a coma, right? Sherman got stuck in my imagination. Some kind of associative phenomenon, maybe. I'm speculating here, of course. In any case, I seem to be asked to answer for Sherman, even though I'm not Sherman, not the least bit, and I don't know as much about him as my son does. Or Braxton Forrest.

You understand, do you not, that your salvation depends upon the salvation of Gen. Sherman?

Walter shrugged and shook his head.

That's absurd, frankly. You can't ask that of me. What has my salvation got to do with the salvation of Gen. William Tecumseh Sherman? As far as I know, he resisted having any faith, especially the Catholic faith, for his whole life. I haven't.

Maybe Sherman was forthright and you're a hypocrite.

I've tried to be a good Catholic since I started taking it seriously sometime back.

A good Catholic. Meaning what?

I go to confession, I go to Mass. I say prayers.

Say prayers.

The rosary and what not. I'm not sure what the deal is here. Frankly, I think it's unfair. I don't see how you could attach even the salvation of my wife or my children to me. Remember what Henry V says to that man who wants to hold him responsible for all the men who lose their lives in battle? "Every subject's duty is the King's, but every subject's soul is his own." When it comes to salvation, you're on your own. I need an explanation. In fact, I think somebody owes me an apology. Who ARE you, anyway?

They did not answer.

So you consider yourself spiritually superior to Gen. Sherman?

Walter's exasperation was not serving him well.

I didn't say that! In fact, I've already been grilled on this point. It's just that I don't have any way to enter the soul of Gen. Sherman and judge whether or not it's in a state of grace. *It* meaning his soul—as though it were somehow detachable from what he was at any moment in the seventy-one years and six days of his life. I don't know him at all except through what he wrote or others wrote about him, including my son.

That's understandable. But perhaps you can just say what you feel as you look upon the body of your friend.

The three men gestured toward the body lying on the door. McPherson, of course. It always came back to McPherson.

Grief, Walter said, sighing. Well, more than a simple grief. Mac was pretty close to Willie in those days when we were camped along the Black River after Vicksburg. There was something about Mac's jocularity that Willie loved. The way he would tease him. In fact, when I think about it, I realize there was a real kinship of soul there. What they loved in each other was also what they loved in me, though I had less of it, and I think that kinship made Willie my favorite among my children and obviously Mac my favorite among the generals.

But it's not just that, because Mac was going to get married, and I didn't give him leave because of the job we faced, and now . . . Jesus, when I think about how much I love women, how much being in the arms of a woman makes all this worth it somehow, I don't know, I think about the letter I'm going to have to write to his fiancée. I mean, look at him lying there, not great like me but a good general, a man among men. He was denied that joy because of me and how much I needed him. I don't think she can ever forgive me. If I can't make her understand the necessities of war, how could I possibly make God understand the March to the Sea or Columbia or—

Are you suggesting that God cannot understand William Tecumseh Sherman?

Everywhere I go in the South, I feel the hatred. I'm Attila. I'm the devil incarnate. All those people are praying that I go straight to hell. And when I think about writing to Mac's fiancée—and by God, I'm sorry, Mac, I can't remember her name—I think about all that rancor and unforgiveness piling up and piling up. So what are my options? Endless hangdog guilt, endless atonement? Or straightforward defiance? I choose defiance. Fuck them. I feed on the energy of their hatred. I whisper to myself, *evil, be thou my good.* Just kidding, gentlemen, just rehearsing a little Milton. By the way, I'm assuming you examiners are male, but I don't know why I should, since it's the women who hate me most. In any case, I don't think what I've done is really evil. Harsh, absolutely. Cruel, definitely. *War is cruelty*, as I told Mayor Calhoun.

You don't think it's evil to strip people of their hard-earned crops in midwinter and slaughter their animals? You don't think it's evil to destroy their livelihoods and burn their homes for an abstraction?

What abstraction?

The Union of disparate states.

They started the war.

The people whose houses you burn?

You're right, they're all innocent as buttercups. Listen, if they would swear their loyalty to the Union, they would be perfectly safe. At least from me. I can't answer for my men.

They don't care about the Union. They love plunder and destruction.

A brief silence ensues.

You started this policy of destruction when you were in Memphis, did you not? If guerrillas fired on your men from near a town, you would burn the whole town, regardless of the particular guilt or innocence of any one person who lived there.

It was effective. So was shooting Confederate prisoners if civilians fired on my men.

Effectiveness is the standard?

Read your Machiavelli. The effectual truth is that terror works.

Do you believe that salvation works? For example, do you believe that someone else can offer himself for your sins?

Salvation. Sweet Jesus, why is it always about salvation? Offer himself how? What do you mean?

Burning the homes of innocent people instead of punishing the actual perpetrators of the action against your men is an effective substitution, you said. It's effective if someone else takes the punishment for the guilty party, which prevents the next crime. Do you believe that someone else could deliberately take the punishment for your crimes? We have Walter Peach here, for example. Suppose we punish him to keep you out of Hell?

You seriously want me to take Walter Peach as some kind of equivalent to me? To my great soul? What are my crimes? I have not committed crimes. Crimes imply the violation of a good articulated by law, but I am already in

Hell, where there is no good but evil, as you call it. I have done nothing not justified by the practices of Hell.

For example?

It is late in the day, just after sunset. Sherman rides his horse up the drive at Stonewall Hill. The men with him do not stop but force their mounts up the front steps of the house. They pause on the porch, horses nervous on the wooden floor, and when one of them backs against the railing and breaks it, her hoof lashes out and the horse screams and scrabbles at the porch as she almost falls. But steady now, gathered, they go inside with a clatter of hooves, ducking to pass under the high lintel. The men pass a bottle man to man, then the last one corks it and comes back to the door and calls *Uncle Billy* and lobs it softly down to Sherman. He catches it left-handed.

To General Grant, Sherman says, and he drinks from the bottle confiscated from another house in town. Good whiskey. He turns in the saddle to gaze back toward the middle of Gallatin at the smoke rising from the courthouse, the shops and houses, and farther away, the depot and the dormitories of the women's college used as hospitals for wounded Confederates before they fled before him.

Burn it all. Why not? Who would stop them?

General! calls a Corporal who sticks his head out the front door. You want to do the honors?

Sherman gets down and ties his horse to the railing on the steps and walks up into the grand foyer to a great pile of paintings, smashed chairs and tables, books and papers, clothes and bedding all pushed against the inside front wall of the house. A feather mattress walks down the stairs on a cautious pair of legs, leaking a puff of feathers with each step. Two white women scream curses from the railing of the second floor as the men grin up, holding themselves obscenely.

Gentlemen, please, Sherman says. These are ladies.

Ladies don't talk like that.

General, says one of the men, if it was me, I'd use this here to get things started, and he hands Sherman a Macon newspaper.

Sherman reads the first few words of the top story. Jefferson Davis says that the Union army, now cut off from its supply lines, will suffer the same fate as Napoleon in Russia. He smiles and thanks the soldier. He wads up the page, strikes a match to it, relights his cigar, then drops the blazing newspaper and kicks it into the base of the pile, where other papers instantly catch fire. Flames lick upward into the leather-bound tomes and ledgers, the Shakespeare and Dickens, Balzac and Walter Scott, the intimate years-long diaries. Bundles of letters come loose in the fire and float upward, burning. Fire melts the silks and finds the cotton clothes and climbs the curtains and works on the dense wood of the furniture and the paneled walls. It hungrily ascends to the crossbeams. Other men on foot crowd in. Amid their whoops come the screams of women and the sounds of shattering glass and splintering furniture.

The horses panic and bolt outside. After a few minutes, the heat and smoke drive out the last of the men, who gather at the foot of the front steps.

Men, Sherman says, this is a canvas best appreciated from a distance.

He mounts his mare and rides down the drive to the front gate before looking back. Flames have found the second floor, and even from this distance he can feel the heat against his face. He hears screams and curses, women wailing. He sees pregnant women and women with infants running from the house and huddling under the tall oaks at the edge of the property, still backing away as the wind carries the sparks high up, high, high up into the night sky.

Still too close to see the full form of the fire, he rides out the gate and up the street toward the center of the burning town. After a few hundred yards, he stops and looks back. A tree blocks the view, so he crosses the road. Here he can see all the way to Stonewall Hill, unobstructed. Porches on both sides of the street are filled with women who stand clutching at their blouses and robes, staring at the conflagration.

Now the whole house gives its shape to fire, transparent now, transcending itself, revealing a different, original form deep within the house. But outlined in flame on the upper floor is the man whom he has feared and hated since he saw the display of his reckless courage on the Rebel retreat from Shiloh. Not trapped there, but looking out directly at him, larger than life, apparently immolating himself. Cruciform, he burns and is not consumed, and now one great arm lowers to point at Sherman.

Sherman's men gallop past him, panicked, followed by a horde of men on foot. Sherman turns his mare in circles, hearing the high shouts and the shots.

May I speak? said Peach.

You are speaking.

May I speak as myself? I have this feeling that the overlay of Sherman is peeling loose from my soul.

You are speaking as yourself. You are William Tecumseh Sherman.

No, I am Walter Peach. Or Karl Guizac, suit yourself. It is unjust to condemn me for the sins of a man who died a long time ago.

Would you die on his soul's behalf? If you knew it would save your own soul too?

For a long time, Walter did not answer.

Is this it? Am I going to die?

The room went dark. Walter could hear himself breathing. The rattle in his chest was growing worse. He felt around for the rolling rack with its IVs but could not find it. Had they unplugged him? He had been off the ventilator for a long time now, and it was hard to get enough air in his lungs. He needed to lie down, he was getting weak, he needed to

The three inquisitors sat at their table.

Now he was the one lying before them, nothing above him but starry sky. They spoke.

You are unconscious on your deathbed, surrounded by your grown children, all of whom are pious Catholics, all of whom love you, and all of whom are aware that you have scorned and resented the Catholic faith for your whole life, never more intensely than when your son Thomas Ewing Sherman joined the Jesuit order in 1878. All your life, long before you wooed and married her, you resented the faith of Ellen Ewing, who was constantly urging it on you. If there has ever been anyone aware of the teachings of the Catholic faith and proselytized on its behalf, you were that person. It is impossible for you to plead ignorance. You knew what you were denying, and you rejected it with the steadfastness of conviction.

If I am unconscious, I should be unable to speak, Walter said reasonably.

You as Sherman are unable to speak.

A coma within a coma. Very nice.

But you as Walter Peach can answer on his behalf. How you answer will determine both his salvation and your own.

That doesn't make any sense. Nothing I do can affect his salvation. I can't answer for him.

Can you be saved, General? You always want to point to your accomplishments and gloss over the issue of unbelief, but what about its effect on others, especially your son Thomas, who suffered you as his judging and disapproving father his whole life? Perhaps Thomas died well—the Jesuits say so. But let me cite a passage from a letter that Thomas wrote to his superior in 1913 after years of mental illness. Listen, please: *No hope whatever of eternal salvation—continual effort to choke back blasphemies against God. Blind obedience has brought me no amelioration. I will have no instant of peace in time as in eternity.* He signs the letter with the words *In utter despair.* Do you think the rejection implicit in your failure to convert, not to mention your son's lifelong awareness of not being loved as Willie was loved, led to Thomas's overstraining himself and eventually falling into sin and despair?

This is just unbelievable. I'm a dying man, and you torment me with this—

General Sherman, your children had the last rites administered to you when you were unconscious on your deathbed by a priest of the religion you repudiated. Do you think it is possible for this sacrament to be effective without the conscious confession of your sins and your belief in Christ? Do you think the funeral Mass, which was conducted by the son whose faith you repudiated, had any merit in God's eyes?

Walter burst through the persona being imposed on him.

Listen, I can't speak for Sherman, I can't confess for him. What you're asking of me is impossible.

In wartime, men die to save other men. Men fall on a grenade or take a bullet for their friends. In ordinary circumstances, people sacrifice themselves for other people. Are you saying that you are unwilling to do that?

Me?

You, Walter Peach. Are you so invincibly selfish that you would not die for this great man? Are you simply afraid to die?

I'm not sure what you're asking of me. To die for Sherman? He's been dead since 1891. He didn't want to be saved.

Love. We're asking love of you. This is the examination in love.

Love for Sherman? A terrible laughter broke from his lungs. May I request a short recess?

There was a silence.

Granted.

As he walked out, rattled and terrified, the black man reappeared, smiling with a deprecating air.

They treat you all right?

No, it was rough.

You'll be all right. You want to go out to the lobby for a little while? You can catch up on the news, get something to eat, look around. We'll go back in when they call us.

Thanks, friend. Much appreciated.

He rolled the IV rack out through the rows of seats. Most of the people who had been there before were gone, and others, nondescript, too vague to come into focus, had taken their places. As he approached the place where he had been sitting, the well-dressed man was gone, but two women sat there. With a start, he realized that one of them was Ellen Sherman and the other one was Vinnie Ream.

Let's get this over with, Ellen said to him. Embarrassing as it is to have everybody talking about you and this woman, I have not asked for a divorce because my faith forbids it. We have spent our whole lives together, Cumpy. Over and over, especially since the War, I have asked you what it profits a man to gain the whole world if he loses his soul. I bore you eight children. I hoped you would come into communion with me instead of just into bed, but the time has come, hasn't it, Church or not? Maybe I'll get an annulment, eight kids in, what do you think?

Was this the real Ellen?

You never meant to be faithful to me. I see more clearly now than ever that you have hardened your heart.

She suddenly raised her voice.

May I have your attention please?

Every vague presence in the lobby fell silent and turned toward her.

William Tecumseh Sherman, she said loudly, *I divorce you, I divorce you, I divorce you.* I believe that's all that is necessary to do at this gate. Any objections? Any questions?

No one had any.

That's that, then. Stand up you little minx, she said to Vinnie Ream, who stood a little bug-eyed and uncertain, big earrings dangling from her ears, an Oriental shawl draped across her shoulders.

Ellen seized Vinnie's hand and gave it to Sherman.

Go on and marry her. She'll look good on your arm when you go around and give speeches to all your old soldiers, won't she? Better than this frumpy old war horse. You deserve her, don't you, for being such a hero, Cumpy?

He looked at Vinnie, who stuck out her tongue at him. Just a little. Those slightly scornful, mocking lips.

Go ahead, Ellen said. Don't be shy. Say it to her.

I marry you, he told Vinnie.

Her idea, not mine, Vinnie said. I'm an artist, not a housewife.

Say it three times, Ellen demanded.

I marry you, I marry you, I marry you.

Whoopee, said Vinnie.

With a whoosh like the door ripping off an airplane in flight, the airport windows shattered outward, people and rolling suitcases and overcoats and loose trash flew from the lobby, a dog whining in its carrying cage rose into the inexorable draft that whipped it away, a small child waving its arms blew past, an old woman, mouth wide open, stripped of her blankets in an instant, all sucked into the howling darkness.

Sherman was gone.

The lobby was empty now, vast and empty. Winds blew across the bare carpets.

Teresa sat in Ellen's place.

We missed you at Christmas.

Christmas?

New Year's was sad without you. Another year. 2021 already.

New Year's?

Something was beeping. Maybe the signal to resume his trial.

It was time, he realized. What was he holding onto? Some bitter quince of ego, some demand of the self to be gratified by someone else's recognition—a woman, say, to sin for him, bend the knee to who he was and do what he wanted, some poor woman smitten despite the peril to herself. What was he that he should want this of someone else? Was it because homage and recognition would give him the illusion of being something more than a contingent creature who would die and be forgotten?

But now some feeling outside logic came whispering in, some hope. He could give himself up. He really could. It was not that hard. The stream of being he had dammed up for himself could flow out into the world if only he let go of himself. He could do it, by God. Yes, he could give his life, he realized with sudden courage.

Holding onto his life was the problem. It had been given to him, and he could let it go where it would help most. Give it away with grace and generosity. Ask that it be fruitful.

Even for Sherman. For William Tecumseh Sherman. He saw the man lying on his deathbed surrounded by his grown and grieving children. The great General Sherman. Struggling to breathe, distinctly refusing Peach's offer, as he had refused a far greater one. Refused it proudly.

But Peach could still give up his life. For Teresa, then. For Jacob and Rose and the friends of his life, Braxton and Marisa. For his enemies, too. He sighed with a brief regret for all he had been and for all he had never been. May God forgive him. He nodded, accepted the need, and died.

Something was beeping. After a moment, he stood up, looking for the man who had been his guide before, and catching his eye far across the room, lifted his hand.

The man crossed the room.

Yes sir? his guide said.

I'm ready to go back in. Face the music.

No need, sir.

What do you mean?

I can take you to the gate, sir.

He followed the man across the room to Gate 777. The man punched in a code and the beeping stopped. When Peach stood there uncertainly, the man tilted his head.

Peach knocked, the door swung outward, and inside was a luminous jetway where Walter could see at the far end a perfect circle of light that exceeded his vision without blinding him. He heard the strains of music that exceeded his capacity for bliss without obliterating him. He was seized by terror and joy.

Just go on in?

Yes sir. It's been a pleasure.

Walter shook the man's hand and crossed himself and stepped onto the walk.

5

HIATUS

TERESA WOULD ALWAYS LOOK BACK ON THE WEEKS THAT followed Thanksgiving with a bitter fondness. The Forrests found a simple Airbnb a few miles closer to town, but Cate and her children stayed in the Peach home. Teresa was spiritually and generationally closer to Marisa Forrest, but she and Cate Zitek had parallel situations, and Teresa came to love the younger woman—her openness about her feelings, her gratitude, her imagination.

Cate suffered more than Teresa did. Unlike Walter, Zitek was conscious part of the time, and he wanted to talk. Endless self-serving apologies, a miserable recognition of what he had done. She knew that he wanted her to console him, but she could not, and if she refused his calls, she feared the suicidal depression descending upon him as he contemplated the ruin of his career and the criminal charges that could keep him in prison for life. Worst of all, he wanted to talk to the children.

To say what?

Just to hear their voices.

After what you did to them?

I have a right to talk to my own children.

She would not let him. She hated his self-pity. It wore her down. His whole predicament came directly from his monstrous betrayal, and she could never trust him again. Never, she told Teresa.

It's going to hurt you more if you can't forgive him, Teresa would say. Maybe not yet. It might take you a long time.

She shared it all with Teresa. For her part, Teresa called the hospital in Salt Lake City daily to ask if there had been any changes in Walter's condition, and the report was always the same: no change. But she did not believe it. Jacob had convinced her that Walter inhabited an alternative world, unfortunately dominated by the question of Sherman.

What *was* the question of Sherman? Why Sherman? What was it about this man? Jacob would try to explain the keen intelligence and competence combined with a burning ambition. He wanted an immortality that he constructed, which was the whole point of his *Memoirs*. Sherman had chosen against Christianity, and especially Catholicism. But did that decide the question, as modernity seemed to think? Was rejection of salvation an exemption from judgment? If you didn't believe in Jesus, did that mean you were free of the import of the Incarnation? Sherman seemed never to credit the idea of salvation. He was like Flannery O'Connor's Misfit, who said, "I don't want no hep. I'm doing all right by myself." Was the soul immortal on its own terms? Or not immortal at all—which would make Sherman an epicurean? But in that case he should not care about Fame, whereas slights to his reputation enraged Sherman almost to the point of insanity, especially, Jacob insisted, when somebody named Edwin Stanton publicly criticized him for the surrender terms he had made with Joseph Johnston—if she was keeping these things straight.

She would shake her head, not understanding the complexities of the situation and not caring to plunge herself into the world of Sherman. She and Marisa would tell the two of them that they were sick of Sherman. Why did Cate and the children have to hear all this? But Jacob and Forrest kept at it, even if they left and went into town and sat at a table at Dunx, where Emily Turnbow would tell them she was trying to study for her finals. On and on they went. Someone should do a comparison of Lincoln and Sherman, Forrest would say at dinner, arguing that the ambitions of the two men were not that different and that Lincoln saw a kindred soul in Sherman. Jacob would ask whether Sherman really believed that the very dark and very real evil he loosed upon the South was actually good because it helped end the war and restore the Union, or whether he was just cunning enough to appeal to something beyond his own rage and his own ambition. Neither of them could imagine Sherman praying. Forrest would tell Jacob that it came down to one simple thing: whether you sought Fame—it always seemed to be in capital letters—for your own sake, or whether you would accept Fame, despite the dangerous toxins it released into your ego, because you were using your talents as fully as possible and Fame better enabled you to do God's will.

Teresa did not offer to read the pieces that Jacob had written. She thought they would upset her. But it was good to have the boy back in the house. He took care of putting the heavy bags of salt into the water softening system, which required that he go down into the crawlspace. The first time he did it he came up a little shaken because it reminded him of the fire at Stonewall Hill. He tended the woodstove and kept the house warm, often going out very early in the morning to bring in a cart load of wood. What especially moved her, though, was his kindness to the Zitek children. He had first met them in Dallas when Cate fled from her home in Atlanta, and now they looked to Jacob for entertainment. He would make up stories and play Legos with Jimmy and take him down to the creek on warmer days. When he carried Avila on his shoulders, he would duck to avoid the cross beams of the house and make swoops at Clare and Little M until they were all screaming with laughter. Little M was not jealous. She always seemed proud of the attention her brother was giving her friends. He kept them all in a good humor. Unless the roads were icy from a recent snow, he would set out on a long daily run, and the children would all gather outside the garage to watch his comic antics until he disappeared over the hill.

In the second week of December, Teresa received the call from the hospital that she had been dreading. Walter's organs had begun to fail—heart, liver, kidneys. Now it was only a matter of time, and whether that would be a few days or a few weeks, Dr. Ranasinghe did not know. *Can we be with him?* No, the protocols were still in place. *So if he dies, he will have to die alone, without his family present?* His silence wrung her.

When she told Cate and Marisa, they both wept.

"Whatever you need from us," Marisa said.

And then Cate said what Teresa had already been thinking.

"Teresa, you should call Rose."

Forrest had hardly remembered *Sage Grouse* during the two weeks when he and Jacob traveled to Dallas and Georgia and back, but starting after Thanksgiving, he had visited the offices almost daily. Forrest had been concerned about the financial viability of the website in Walter's absence, but Sam Warner had handled matters very professionally, meaning that he had kept up subscriptions and actually increased sponsorships. Dub Cross, a scholarly-looking junior at Transfiguration, had done a series of shrewd cartoons depicting Joe Biden as an empty sock being worn by political feet of various sizes, and Joe Brown had kept up his Everette Polinski dialogues in a parody of *The View*. Bitford Carbury was the surprise. His online presence had quickly evolved from a few, serious Constitutional essays that no one read into a popular character named Bitcarb, a geeky neo-secessionist and ardent junk food advocate whose obsession was states' rights. On his imaginary call-in talk show, he held, for example, that Wyoming was a *state*, whereas Colorado was a *colony*.

Forrest was coming down the front steps of the Grove Building, planning to stop by Dunx and talk to Jacob about the latest and surely last piece of Sherman—this one on his 1877 trip to Yellowstone with Tom—when his phone buzzed in his hip pocket.

Marisa.

"What's up?"

—Walter's dying. His organs are shutting down. Teresa just got in touch with Rose to come back from France.

Walter was dying? Somehow, he realized, though it made no sense whatsoever, he had always thought that Walter was staging his whole illness and coma as some sort of complex, ironic joke, a commentary on the pandemic. The truth that Walter could really die—was really dying—pierced him on a level he had felt only when he found what he thought was evidence of Marilyn Harkins' death when he was eighteen or when he heard of Zitek's betrayal of Cate. Bitter sorrow. The *akhos* of the Homeric world.

—Do you know where Jacob is? Marisa said. You were going to talk to him this morning.

As Forrest came out of the building onto the sidewalk holding the phone to his ear, he saw the boy across the street in Dunx, talking to Emily Turnbow.

"I see him," he said.

He waited for the light to change, and then crossed the street and opened the door. He hated this mission. Jacob's back was to him, but Emily saw him coming and her smile of greeting died when she saw his expression. Jacob turned to follow her look and stood, already edging backward, bumping the table, spilling their coffee.

"Is it Dad?"

"His organs are failing."

"But he's still alive?"

Forrest nodded.

"Thank God."

"Your mom called Rose. You'd better go home, Jacob."

When he left them, Forrest did not go back to the Peach house. Instead, he drove south, following the long curves of the road out toward South Pass and the Oregon Buttes until he saw the overlook for Red Canyon. He pulled in and sat gazing out over the vast landscape. What Walter Peach had been to him he could hardly articulate. Back at the University of Georgia, when both were much younger, Forrest had recognized the genius of the man and witnessed firsthand the tragedy of his early marriage—the death of his first son, Walter's despairing plunge into drunkenness, Teresa's stoical endurance. He felt that God had been working through him when he found Walter down in Waycross and gave him the new line of work, editing the *Gallatin Tribune* and beginning to exercise again the range of those gifts that perhaps someday he could more fully recover. But now it would not happen. Everything tipped over into that subjunctive abyss of everything he might have been. Death by Covid, which Socrates Johnson had sarcastically pretended was worse than Ebola or the Black Plague, felt harsh and bitter.

Worse still was the recoil of recognition. What about Forrest himself? He knew, as everyone knew in theory, that he could die at any moment. A drunk driver or a heart attack or an aneurysm could end his life without warning. More intensely than he had ever felt it, he knew that for all his bluster, he was as unprepared as one of the foolish virgins of Jesus's parable. What had his own life been? Thinking about Sherman had raised the question for him already, but now the coming death of Walter Peach made it much more intense. What would God say when Braxton Tecumseh Forrest came before the bar of judgment?

Ah, you have drolly observed hotel employees and waitresses. Well done, my good and faithful servant.

He had buried his talent and wasted his life.

What was it that the women always prayed?

Lord Jesus Christ, son of God, have mercy on me, a sinner.

Braxton Forrest prayed it.

That night, they all gathered in the small living room of the Peach house. Marisa had printed out a Novena to Saint Jude, patron saint of desperate causes, and she passed it out and asked Teresa to read.

"*Most holy Apostle, St. Jude, faithful servant and friend of Jesus,*" Teresa read, "*the Church honors and invokes you universally, as the patron of difficult cases, of things almost despaired of. Pray for me, I am so helpless and alone.*" Her voice broke, but only momentarily, and she said, "I am not alone in this, thank God. *Intercede with God for me that He bring visible and speedy help where help is almost despaired of. Come to my assistance in this great need that I may receive the consolation and help of heaven in all my necessities, tribulations, and sufferings, particularly the full recovery of my husband, Walter Peach.*"

When they finished the prayer, Marisa told Teresa that Hermia Watson also had her women praying the novena for Walter.

To Forrest, it all seemed strange, as many things about Catholic piety still seemed strange to him as a very belated convert. There was something so formal and established about it that it felt almost impersonal. On the other hand, just saying the words, he felt a power in them, like the buzz of current in a heavy-duty extension cord. How was a novena going to reverse organ failure? He had no idea. Could it? Why not knock and seek and ask? What else could they do but pray?

· 538 ·

6

EPIPHANY

TERESA AND HER CHILDREN WAITED AT THE ENTRANCE TO
the hospital. It was still early. The sun was not fully up over the mountains
directly behind them, but the peaks on the western side of the valley were
already awash in light.

They had come down from De Smet the day before, and the Hellyers had
welcomed all four of them. Jacob tried to sleep upstairs on the couch in the
living room, but he was too tall and ended up on the floor. He came down
very early, well before daylight, to the apartment where Teresa had slept with
little Marisa and Rose. His sister, mature now, without the edges of self-regard
that had been evident before, had arrived from Europe just before Christmas,
thinking that she was coming home for her father's death and funeral. Cate
had urged Teresa to let her drive to Denver to pick up Rose, and Marisa had
sided with Cate, and so Teresa had agreed.

Two days before Christmas, Dr. Ranasinghe had called—that distinctive
singsong voice—to say that Walter's condition had begun to stabilize. On
New Year's Eve, a Thursday, the last day of their novena, Dr. Ranasinghe
called back, to tell her that Walter was going to survive. Then on Sunday
afternoon, January 3, the day the Church celebrated the Epiphany, he called
her again.

—Mrs. Guizac?

His tone was reserved, and her heart sank. Dread overwhelmed her.

—I have news that I never expected to share with you. Tomorrow morning, we are going to take Mr. Guizac off the ventilator and bring him out of the coma. His lungs have cleared. Professionally, I don't believe in miracles. There is no explanation, in my field, for what has just happened. Tomorrow and Tuesday, we are going to help Mr. Guizac get to his feet and take his first steps. Can you be here to meet him on Wednesday morning?

"What? You're going to release him?" she exclaimed. "Oh, thank God! Yes, we can be there."

—Don't get your hopes up too much, but if he does well tomorrow and Tuesday, we will release him on Wednesday morning. Obviously, it's going to take some time for him to recover his strength, including the ability to walk, so we will send him home with a walker and recommend physical therapy over the next few weeks. He should really be in rehab, but we have no more room. You should arrange for someone to come in when you get him home.

"I can't believe it!"

—It's not just the physical part that's going to be hard, Mrs. Guizac, as we know from the other patients who have survived this disease. He has been in a different reality, and it will not mesh with the world you have inhabited over the same period. A month ago, we had a patient who had seen his father die and he could not be convinced that it was in his dream until he saw his father alive in the flesh. It's difficult to explain how intensely real their experience has been. One of our psychologists thinks these patients might suffer from PTSD in the months following the coma. It's going to require patience on your part. We have people you can call for support if you need to.

"Thank you. Thank you. God bless you."

Now the hospital doors slid open. Masked attendants rolled Walter outside in a wheelchair. He was masked and frail, almost skeletal. His clothes were loose on him, the same clothes he had worn when he left the house on Election Day—the good Wranglers, the blue Oxford shirt, and the cable-knit sweater he liked. His old Clarks. His skin was pale, with something of old age in the pallor, but his eyes were shining. His hand lifted to them.

"Walter!" she cried, running to him. He lifted his arms to her and she embraced him as gently as she would a newborn. He murmured his love into her ear, softly, with a small wheeze. He held out a hand to each of his children.

"So glad," he said faintly. "Jacob. Rose. Little M. Can't believe it."

Jacob greeted his father with their usual edge of comic irony, but Rose bent over to hug him, weeping onto his shoulder, and then knelt before the wheelchair, holding his hand, kissing his knuckles. Little M stood back a bit and glanced up at Teresa, as though she weren't quite sure who he was.

Two stocky blond male attendants—they could have been Mormon boys just back from serving a mission—stood politely to the side during their greetings and just as politely rebuffed Jacob when he tried to take over the wheelchair.

"We need to get him to the vehicle, sir," one of them said.

Standing by was a middle-aged Asian nurse—round-faced and tiny—who now handed a clipboard to Teresa and pointed out where to sign the release form. As she took it back, she gave Teresa several pages stapled together.

"Instructions for the next few days," she said with a weary smile. "You're very lucky."

Walter reached for the nurse's hand, and Teresa saw tears come to the woman's eyes.

The sun was out now, the mountainside above them lay in sunlight, the Great Salt Lake shone in the distance to the north. She breathed in deeply as she and Jacob followed the attendants to the Subaru.

"This isn't my Subaru," Walter said.

"Honey," Teresa said. "You totaled it. This is the new one."

His bottom lip came out as he shook his head. "What color do you call this?"

"Cosmic Blue Pearl," she said in her best Lauren Bacall.

"Cut it out."

The two men helped Walter to his feet and into the passenger seat and reached over him to buckle his seatbelt.

"Good luck, sir," they said, not quite in sync. They turned and rolled the wheelchair back across the pavement to the electric doors and inside the hospital.

She went around the car and got into the driver's seat.

"Mom, I can drive," Jacob said.

"I don't want to talk to my husband I haven't seen in two months from the back seat."

"So how about we put Dad in the back with you."

"We'd be talking over Little M the whole way. And it's too cramped."

"Well, you've got *us* back here," Rose said. "I mean, speaking of cramped. Jacob's taller than anybody."

"Okay, I remember this family," Walter said.

"Oh, Walter," she said, laughing, then gasped, choking on her relief, and broke into sobbing as compulsive as nausea. She bent over the steering wheel, hugging the rim, unable to stop crying.

"Mom," Rose said softly. "It's okay."

Someone beeped. She sat up and glanced angrily into the rearview mirror. The man in the SUV behind her calmly turned his palm upward in a *what's-the-deal* gesture. She started the car and pulled up a few yards and flung them all forward when she hit the brakes too hard and put the transmission in park so she could collect herself.

"Mom, let me drive," Jacob said, opening his door.

"No!" she snapped. "I'm fine, okay? Shut the door. Once we get to Evanston, we'll stop and you can drive then."

She took a deep breath and let it out slowly. *Lord Jesus Christ, Son of God, have mercy on me, a sinner.*

"It's been hard, hasn't it?" Walter said.

"Yes, it has." Wiping her eyes, she snugged her iPhone into the phone holder in the vent and asked it for directions home as she pulled out of the drop-off zone. It directed her onto Mario Capecchi Drive. There was a little snow on the road, but thank God the weather had been decent for the trip down. Rose had shown her the forecast that morning on her phone: a major storm was coming in from the west that afternoon, but they should be able to get home ahead of it, God willing. She drove carefully through the university campus past the football stadium and then turned left to follow Foothill Drive down to I-80.

Little M fell asleep almost immediately. Walter chatted with Rose about her time in France and asked Jacob what he was studying now that he had finished with Forrest.

"Math with Dr. Johannson. Definitely not obsessed."

As they started up the long curves through the mountains, Walter described the day when he woke up and the doctor told him he could breathe on his own. What it felt like coming out of two months of dreams.

"Dad," Jason said, "do you remember calling me when I was in Georgia?"

"Let's wait to talk about all that, okay? Tell me what's been going on at home."

By the time they passed Park City, Teresa had described Cate's exodus from Atlanta to Wyoming, and Jacob had sketched in what happened in Georgia. Teresa explained that Jason Zitek would be a long time in rehab and then potentially the rest of his life in jail. Marisa and the other Forrest daughter, Bernadette, were in De Smet with her, helping get her into a new place with the kids.

"So how's Cump?" Walter asked. "How are his Broncos doing?"

"John Bell Hudson broke his arm and they missed the playoffs," Jacob said. "Cump's up in Yellowstone."

"In the middle of the winter?"

"Seriously. Trekking around in snowshoes," Jacob said. "He said to tell you it's a spirit quest—the year he turns seventy and Joe Biden becomes president."

Walter snorted.

"Marisa thinks he's demented," said Teresa.

"Probably channeling some Mountain Man. Thinks he's John Colter. What's he done with *Sage Grouse*?" Walter asked.

"He hired some Transfiguration folks to keep it going. Sam Warner, Bitford Carbury, several Transfiguration students. It's going pretty well, but everybody misses Socrates Johnson. Especially today, I bet."

"Why today? I've just seen a little news the last day or two."

"Congress meets to certify the election count," Jacob said. "Mike Pence is the one who has to do it. Trump's been claiming widespread voter fraud, and I bet he's pressuring Pence to declare the votes of several states invalid."

Walter nodded. "I don't have much Socrates on call at the moment."

"Emily and I have been doing some non-political things for the website these past few weeks," Jacob said.

Walter tried to turn to look at him.

"How is Emily?"

"Glorious!" Rose exclaimed. "The nonpareil, the queen of hearts. One is helpless in her presence. Her very name—"

"When are you going back to France?" Jacob interrupted. "I know you miss your francobumpkin. I can't get it straight. Is he a farmhand or a country doctor? What's his name, Charles Bovary?"

Much as she was enjoying it, Teresa intervened.

"Jacob and Emily do an advice column warning off teenagers who might be tempted to attend Transfiguration College. Applications are way up."

"Caliban Kingfisher and Miranda Crossfire," Jacob said, leaning forward. "We give other advice, too. For example, Hermia Watson has been recording the women at Eula's House—"

"Eula's Mamas," Rose interjected. "Seriously good."

"So we strongly advise people not to listen to them," Jacob said, "which is making them famous. Nora directs the choir."

The name made Teresa stiffen.

"Where did they move after Stonewall Hill?" Walter asked.

"What do you mean?"

"After the fire."

"Walter, honey, they caught it in time," Teresa said. "Thanks to your son here. Our family hero."

She glanced over at him. Walter seemed far away, staring straight ahead at the highway.

"I saw Sherman burn it."

She fought down her panic.

"Walter, honey," she said. "That didn't happen."

"I saw it. It was as vivid as what I'm experiencing right now in this car. As vivid as the back of that truck ahead of us. This Vehicle Makes Frequent Stops."

"Dr. Ranasinghe told us you might have undergone things that don't— what was his word?—*mesh* with the real world."

"Who's Dr. Ranasinghe?"

"The doctor who talked to me. Your doctor."

He turned to look at her.

"I don't remember a Dr. Ranasinghe."

They rode in silence across the border into Wyoming.

When they reached the exits for Evanston, she asked, timidly, "Do you feel like eating?"

"Sure."

"I'm starving," Jacob volunteered.

"Any preferences?"

"*Preferences*," Walter said. "What a concept. Anything not on the intravenous menu."

She let out a breath. At Jacob's suggestion—he was consulting his phone—she took the exit for Front Street and a cluster of restaurant signs.

"*Preferences*. How about Mexican?" Walter said.

Her mother parked in the handicapped spot next to the door of a small Mexican place in the strip mall off Front Street. When Rose nudged her, Little M said, "What?" and reluctantly pulled off her headset. Jacob had been intermittently eaveswatching Matilda's battles with Miss Trunchbull. "Lunch," Rose said, and Little M closed the Kindle, still not convinced that the man in the front seat was really her father.

Whoever he was, Jacob and Rose helped him stand up from the Subaru. Setting both feet flat on the pavement, he tried to lean forward and get up but did not make it and rocked backward into the seat. He did it several times before they caught his arms and stood him up outside the car, weak from the coma and now stiff from the drive. When he leaned on them, he felt as frail as a very old man. Jacob retrieved the walker from the trunk.

Inside, all the customers, several trailing black cloth napkins from their tables, stood huddled close together, looking up at the TV bolted to a high bracket in the corner behind the bar. On the abandoned tables were unfinished plates of enchiladas and quesadillas, broken tacos and tostadas, smears of guacamole and refried beans, baskets of chips, shallow dishes of salsa, half-full glasses of iced tea, a margarita, rim of salt still intact.

The waitress, chubby and middle-aged, stood behind the customers, balancing a tray of lunch plates above her left shoulder, eyebrows pinched together.

"*Pablo! Pablo!*" she called back into the kitchen. "*Mira esto!*"

On the screen, men scaled the walls and invaded the iconic building. It was as though, Jacob thought, the Confederate flank attack at Bull Run, where Sherman had first seen action, had pressed the panicking Union troops all the way back into Washington and the Rebels had stormed the Capitol itself. Alternative history.

A shouting match among the customers in the restaurant turned so violent that the owner called the police.

"I can't do this," his father said.

Back in the Subaru, Jacob took over the driving, and they went through a window at McDonald's and divvied up the hamburgers and fries. He drove due east on I-80 and took the exit for U.S. 189 north toward Kemmerer through the Great Divide Basin. Rose sat in front this time. She kept turning to insist that the attack on the Capitol never would have happened except for Covid. The pandemic had changed the whole political landscape, even in France—not the disease itself but the way people reacted to it. A dark, primitive, communal fear had started up, as though everyone secretly felt that disaster had been long overdue. The more rational you thought you were, the more you wanted to "follow the science," the more darkly the terror afflicted you. There were strange contradictions. When the framework of business as usual shattered for a few months, people felt freer and happier than they had since childhood. Politically, of course, it was a pure disaster. The mixed messages of the CDC, the massive disruption of school closings, the divinized and demonized Big Brother Fauci, vaccines, Ivermectin, the *New York Post* and Hunter Biden's laptop, government giveaways that encouraged fraud, on and on. Some people thought China and Russia were using misinformation about the origin and nature of the coronavirus to destabilize systems of information and affect elections worldwide.

Glancing in the rearview mirror, Jacob saw that Little M, finally convinced by the way he teased her—and bored by the conversation—had leaned against her father and fallen asleep.

"Rip Van Walter and his little girl," said his mother.

"I never thought I'd see this little girl again," he said. "Or any of you. I went through the gate."

Jacob passed a slow-moving pickup truck. There was no one else on the road for miles ahead.

"What gate? What do you mean, Dad?" Rose asked, twisting around to look at him.

"I'll tell you later. Maybe around the wood stove when we get home. All those miles from here still. You know what I want after two months in bed?" he said with sudden force. *"Air and space!"*

"Look around you, Walter," his mother said. "You're back among us."

Up ahead, on the outskirts of Kemmerer, a huge coal plant rose to their left across several miles of bare land, surrounded by strip mines. Fossil Butte somewhere to the west. The ancient body of the earth.

"I want the mountains. I want to see from New England to San Diego. And history all at once. All the wars, all the great movements and all the particulars. The Oregon Trail and the Mormons and the herds of buffalo thundering across the high plains and the time before us and the time after."

"You just want to be God," said Rose.

"But I don't want to see Sherman. I've had enough Sherman."

"No more Sherman," his mother said.

"So Jacob, speaking of Sherman . . ." His father sounded drowsy.

"Yes sir?"

"I don't think Uncle Billy made it. Not my call."

"What do you mean, Dad?"

"Sherman's where he chose to be."

"Let's talk about Sherman later, you said."

"But I went through the gate before I was sent back home. I have to tell you about it. Oh," his father said, rousing himself. "Miriam sends her greetings, Jacob."

The Subaru veered onto the warning strip and the tires roared.

"Miriam?"

"Listen, I hate to do this, I've been out for so long, but God help me, I'm—"

"Are you okay?" his mother asked, suddenly alarmed.

"I've been there such a long time, and it's all okay. It all comes right. We're good, we're very good, but I need to know if—"

"Dad, seriously, Miriam?" Jacob asked.

But his father was snoring peacefully.

Rose fell asleep a few miles north of Kemmerer; when he glanced in the rearview mirror, he saw that his mother had also dropped off.

It was beginning to snow, just a few flakes. It was the edge of the storm coming in from the west that was supposed to dump two feet on De Smet, maybe more, the most they had had all winter. They should be able to get home ahead of it, unload the car, help his father inside, start a fire in the wood stove. They would draw up their chairs, talking over everything that had happened, maybe even what he meant by mentioning Miriam.

His phone buzzed in the holder attached to the air vent. Emily. Carefully detaching it, he held the screen up and glanced at her text.

> Some senior emailed the whole college inviting everybody to a stop the steal rally in De Smet. Our way to join the attack on the Capitol.

A few seconds later came another text.

> Why would this bozo think we would want to do that? There's nobody here anyway. Everybody's home for vacation.

Then a third one.

> Dr. Weald said this was a tragic day in American history and there was nothing to celebrate. He was pretty furious. He shut down student access to school email until school reopens.

A fourth.

> How's your dad?

He pressed the microphone image in the reply box.

> He's okay I'm driving now everybody's asleep I'll catch up later.

Rose stirred but did not wake up.

He clamped the phone back in the holder. Emily responded with two emojis, a Shh! and a wink. He hated to think that anything about Emily Turnbow was available in a library of emojis.

He rolled his head on his neck. If he did not turn east toward Farson, he could go north toward the tiny town of Daniel and the site of Fr. De Smet's first Mass back in 1840. A couple of years ago, he had joined a group of Transfiguration students on a pilgrimage up to the little chapel on the commanding height overlooking Horse Creek and Green River and the vast landscape to the north toward Hoback and Jackson and the Grand Tetons. A visiting Nigerian priest had celebrated the Mass for the two dozen or so students. But two thousand people had been in that first congregation— trappers, traders, Native Americans, mostly Shoshone. How in the world did a Jesuit priest by himself in the unscripted wilderness gather so many?

Should he just drive up that way? Everyone was asleep and he could surprise them. Maybe go on to Jackson and past the Tetons to Moran Junction and the turn toward Yellowstone, where he had once received a revelation that he could never quite recall but that was rooted in his heart as firmly as the love of Emily Turnbow. He thought of Cump Forrest up in Yellowstone, hooded and huge, tramping through the snow beneath the enormous evergreens, his eyelashes and beard shaggy with ice. Cump, demented. Sleeping among the elk, reciting Homer in Greek to the gathering packs of wolves.

The snow was falling steadily now. Whorls and tracings on the pavement ahead. He slowed and made the turn eastward onto a narrow country road with no shoulders that went straight ahead, up and down the hills of a barren landscape. A mile along it, a vision came to him: He and Emily were bundled into heavy coats and blankets in the extreme cold, and he had something in his hands, something that came heavily over his shoulder, a rope or harness, and he was pulling a load behind them, a sled, a loaded sled containing all they had, pulling it with killing effort through the snow as they carefully made their way forward in their snowshoes, trying not to break through the crust because they would sink down to their waists or deeper and exhaust themselves and lose an hour trying to get back out. There was some disaster behind them. Emily was holding a bundle tight against her chest, and when she glanced over at him and pulled back the blanket, he saw the face of their little girl. She needed to stop and nurse her, but they could not stop because of whatever was behind them, whatever was coming. One moment, he almost fell through, the load almost pulled him backward off balance, but at last, straining and exhausted, they came to the edge of the woods at the top of the hill. Before them lay a green land, the promised valley. No snow had fallen. Herds of elk and bison grazed peacefully in the distance. Far to the west, a bank of fog shot with sunlight stretched for miles along the river, and beyond it, rising and rising, jagged and splendid in the full light, shone the white peaks of the mountains, impossibly tall.

There, he said, turning to look at Emily, his heart full of joy.

Just a little farther.

A little farther.

"Are you okay?" Rose asked him.

He startled and focused on the road before he glanced at her.

"I'm okay."

"You looked . . . you know, how you used to look."

His mother was stirring in the backseat. Little M said she needed to go to the bathroom. His father was still asleep.

"We'll stop in Farson," he said. The snow fell more heavily now, the clouds massing behind them, wind whipping the sagebrush in sudden gusts. He eased the Subaru up to eighty-five, ninety. There was no one on the road, which looked flat for miles ahead.

But it was not flat. He came over a slight unexpected rise and flew a little. Not a hundred yards ahead, close on the left side of the road, a pronghorn tensed, lifting his head.

"Oh Lord," Rose gasped, putting her hand on the dashboard.

He did not brake, but lifted his foot from the accelerator, and as the car slowed, the antelope turned and ran along the small strip of gravel at the edge of the pavement, racing them, not looking back, going full speed now, neck and neck with the Subaru. Jacob glanced at the speedometer: sixty miles an hour. With a sudden burst of acceleration the animal veered across the pavement a few feet ahead of him.

Rose cried out. He felt his mother grip the back of his seat. Again, he did not brake. He lifted his open palm toward the pronghorn as it left the road and kicked up a thin trace of dust and rock, disappearing southward into the empty land.

"Sorry," he said. "I'll slow down."

Patience, he told himself. Just another two hours now.

He could still outrun the storm.

ACKNOWLEDGMENTS

This novel, set in the strange year of Covid-19 and the starkly divisive Biden-Trump election, quickly fixates on a figure from America's earlier and more potent disruption: Gen. William Tecumseh Sherman. Sherman has haunted the Southern imagination since his passage of destruction through Georgia and South Carolina in 1864 and 1865. Lionized in the North (despite Secretary of War Edwin Stanton's attempt to discredit him at the very height of his fame), he had a reputation in the South that rivaled Moloch's. I was born in South Carolina and grew up in Georgia. Sherman had burned both states and, in those years, there was still an unhealing wound in the psyche of the South. Decades ago, I considered writing a long poem about this man who waged war on a civilian population—a prelude to the practices of the 20th century—but instead, I made him a presence in my three novels, feeling that he remains the necessary antagonist, not just for the Old South and the Confederacy, but for the self-understanding of our own times.

My Sherman is fictional, an interpreted and surmised consciousness filtered through the sensibilities of his narrator in the novel, young Jacob Guizac, but also inevitably through my own. Jacob's viewpoint owes to his own circumstances, through which he understands Sherman's diaries and letters (available online as the William T. Sherman Family papers in the University of Notre Dame Archives), the *Memoirs* of Sherman himself, and the accounts of Sherman by many biographers and historians. I read Earl Schenck Miers' *The General Who Marched to Hell* back in the 1970s, when I also first immersed myself in Shelby Foote's monumental *The Civil War*. Other books encountered at various times and eliciting various reactions include Alfred E. Castel, *Decision in the West;* Burke Davis, *Sherman's March;* E. L. Doctorow, *The March;* Joseph T. Durkin, S.J., *General Sherman's Son;* Michael Fellman, *Citizen Sherman;* John Marzalek, *Sherman: A Soldier's Passion for Order;* Victor Davis Hanson, *The Soul of Battle;* James L. McDonough,

William Tecumseh Sherman; Robert O'Connell, *Fierce Patriot: The Tangled Lives of William Tecumseh Sherman;* Charles Royster, *The Destructive War;* Noah Andre Trudeau, *Southern Storm: Sherman's March to the Sea* and Marc Wortman, *The Bonfire: The Siege and Burning of Atlanta.*

Other and different acknowledgments are also due. The dream experiences of Karl Guizac (also known as Walter Peach) owe to my remarkable conversations with Jason Shanks, now president of the National Eucharistic Congress, and to his account of his experience with Covid-19 during almost exactly the same time period that my novel covers. His stories over lunch at the Legatus Summit on Amelia Island in January 2022 led to two lengthy phone calls about the compelling dreamworld he entered over the weeks of an induced coma.

I could not have finished the novel without a sabbatical from Wyoming Catholic College after my years as president, nor would the book be at all what it is without the experience of grave and joyful responsibility for this unique college over those seven years. But for the novel as a novel, I owe most to the editors at Wiseblood Books, whose questions and promptings have helped its form to emerge: Katy Carl, Mary Finnegan, Kathy West, and Joshua Hren. My gratitude to each of them is profound.

My gratitude to my wife Virginia—for much more than this novel—goes to the depth of life itself.

ABOUT THE AUTHOR

Glenn Arbery is Professor of Humanities at Wyoming Catholic College, where he served as president from 2016 to 2023. He has taught literature for over forty years. His book *Why Literature Matters* (ISI Books) appeared in 2001, followed by his edited volumes *The Tragic Abyss* (Dallas Institute, 2005) and *The Southern Critics* (ISI Books, 2010). His novels *Bearings and Distances* (2015) and *Boundaries of Eden* (2020) were both published by Wiseblood Books. He and his wife Virginia have eight children and twenty-five grandchildren.

www.ingramcontent.com/pod-product-compliance
Lightning Source LLC
Chambersburg PA
CBHW071652070925
32132CB00006B/20